BOOK 4, *SCATTERED SUNS*

"Anderson delivers more on-the-edge-of-your-seat SF thrills . . . He handles a huge cast and complicated plot with élan."

—*Publishers Weekly*

"A fine continuation of a fine saga."

—*Booklist*

"A highly original far-future universe filled with intriguing aliens, a complex political history, and a well-developed cast of characters."

—*Library Journal*

"Great . . . The author has built not only a world, but also a universe that completely immerses the reader . . . This is the gold standard for readers who enjoy science fiction."

—TheRomanceReadersConnection.com

P9-BZD-197

BOOKS BY KEVIN J. ANDERSON

The Saga of Seven Suns

Hidden Empire

A Forest of Stars

Horizon Storms

Scattered Suns

Of Fire and Night

Metal Swarm

The Ashes of Worlds

Available from Wildstorm/DC Comics

Veiled Alliances (graphic novel)

"A rip-roaring space opera full of mystery, adventure, and suspense."
                    —*Science Fiction Chronicle*

"Political maneuvers, treachery, and interstellar gunboat diplomacy are opposed by idealism, ancient philosophies, and sentient worldtrees."
                    —*Kirkus Reviews*

"Outstanding . . . suspenseful . . . an exhilarating experience."
                    —*Locus*

"Rapid-fire action and panoramic plotting make this a first-class space opera."
                    —*Library Journal*

"Grand . . . Anderson has created a fully independent and richly conceived venue for his personal brand of space opera, a venue that nonetheless raised fruitful resonances with Frank Herbert's classic Dune series."
                    —SciFi.com

BOOK 3, *HORIZON STORMS*

"Dazzling . . . thrilling . . . crackling with energy and buzzing with action."
                    —*Publishers Weekly* (starred review)

"Continues to grip the reader . . . ends with questions that leave one anxious to read the next episode."
                    —Bookloons.com

SCATTERED SUNS

THE SAGA OF SEVEN SUNS

4

KEVIN J. ANDERSON

orbit

www.orbitbooks.net

New York   London

Copyright © 2005 by WordFire, Inc.
Excerpt from *Of Fire and Night* copyright © 2006 by WordFire, Inc.
All rights reserved. Except as permitted under the U.S. Copyright Act of 1976, no part of this publication may be reproduced, distributed, or transmitted in any form or by any means, or stored in a database or retrieval system, without the prior written permission of the publisher.

Orbit is an imprint of Hachette Book Group USA, Inc.

The Orbit name and logo is a trademark of Little, Brown Book Group, Ltd.

Cover design by Mario J. Pulice
Cover art by Radius Images

Orbit
Hachette Book Group USA
237 Park Avenue
New York, NY 10017
Visit our Web site at www.orbitbooks.net

Printed in the United States of America

Originally published in hardcover by Hachette Book Group USA
First Mass Market edition: June 2006
First Orbit edition: November 2007

10 9 8 7 6 5 4 3 2

TO JOHN SILBERSACK,

my first editor, current agent, and longtime friend

THE STORY SO FAR

After the alien hydrogues attacked the sentient worldforest on Theroc, human colonists struggled to pick up the pieces. Green priests, telepathically linked to the worldtrees, were psychologically stunned; many of their volunteers who served the Earth Defense Forces (EDF) abandoned their posts and returned home to the devastated forests.

Next, the hydrogues turned their antagonism against the faeros, a fiery alien race that lives within stars. While hydrogues and faeros engaged in battle on planets and suns, King Peter and Queen Estarra announced a major new military initiative from their Palace on Earth: The EDF would launch more Klikiss Torches—doomsday weapons capable of imploding gas giants—a test of which inadvertently started the entire hydrogue war. Also, following the example of the Ildiran military hero Adar Kori'nh, the EDF would build a fleet of kamikaze rammers to be flown by new-model Soldier compies against hydrogue warglobes. As King Peter delivered his message, the dangerous, and sometimes murderous, Chairman Basil Wenceslas quietly watched him for any mistakes.

Tasia Tamblyn, a Roamer who had joined the EDF, was chosen to deliver the first new Klikiss Torch. Unknown to Tasia, her friend Robb Brindle and a handful of other humans were imprisoned in a crystalline hydrogue city at the core of the targeted gas giant. There the Friendly compy DD, held by the sinister Klikiss robots, managed to speak with Robb. Just before Tasia's Torch weapon ignited the clouds, the hydrogues evacuated the gas planet, and the Klikiss robots and DD fled.

Meanwhile, Tasia's brother Jess found himself marooned on an isolated water planet after his ship was destroyed by hydrogues. In order to keep him alive, his secret cargo of wentals—strange water entities—infused his body with their energies. With the help of the wentals, Jess built an exotic ship and flew away in search of his lost love Cesca Peroni, the Speaker of the Roamer clans.

In the Roamer capital of Rendezvous, where Cesca struggled to keep the clans together, the scout Nikko Chan Tylar brought proof that the EDF was preying on Roamer cargo ships, stealing their supplies of stardrive fuel (ekti) and destroying the vessels. Outraged at these acts of piracy, the Roamers cut off all trade with the Terran Hanseatic League. Cesca delivered an ultimatum to the Hansa government: Earth would receive no more stardrive fuel until the culprits were identified and punished.

The Roamers themselves kept a few EDF detainees, whom they had rescued from the recent battle in the rings of Osquivel. Patrick Fitzpatrick III, a spoiled blueblood, was a particularly unhappy prisoner, despite the flirtations of Zhett Kellum, beautiful daughter of Del Kellum, the clan leader in charge of the Osquivel shipyards. Kellum's crew also reprogrammed salvaged EDF Soldier compies to become menial laborers.

The Hansa, seeking a means of space travel that did not depend on ekti, dispatched teams of explorers through "transportals," an ancient alien system of gateways found on abandoned worlds. One of these explorers was the intrepid spy Davlin Lotze. Since all transportal coordinates were enigmas, many destinations held unexpected dangers.

Also, hoping to break their dependence on Roamer stardrive fuel, the Hansa established their own ekti-harvesting skymine, run by Sullivan Gold and his green priest Kolker at the gas planet Qronha 3, where Adar Kori'nh had fallen in his dramatic showdown against the hydrogues. Sullivan's crew produced a great deal of ekti until a group of Ildiran warliners arrived, also intending to mine the clouds. Sullivan negotiated an uneasy truce with the Ildirans, and both skymines cruised the clouds, always on the watch for the hydrogues' return.

Wrestling with his fresh *thism*-knowledge of unexpected plots, new Ildiran Mage-Imperator Jora'h attended the funeral of his poisoned father. Caught in the hydrogue war, the Ildiran Empire was running out of ekti as well. Jora'h's brother, Designate Rusa'h—who had been in a sub-*thism* sleep since a hydrogue attack on his planet of Hyrillka— suddenly woke up in the Prism Palace's infirmary. His personality dramatically altered, Rusa'h claimed to have seen powerful visions while he was comatose. Uneasy, Jora'h sent his injured brother with Prime Designate Thor'h back to Hyrillka to rebuild his devastated planet, along with Pery'h, the next Hyrillka Designate.

Although the grim Dobro Designate Udru'h paid tribute to the new Mage-Imperator, Jora'h could not forgive his brother for secretly subjecting Jora'h's beloved green priest Nira to years of breeding experiments. Nira, now supposed dead, had given birth to Jora'h's half-breed daughter Osira'h, whom the

Dobro Designate believed might become a savior of the Ildiran Empire because of her remarkable telepathic abilities. Nira was not dead, however, but hidden on a remote island where the Mage-Imperator would never find her.

On an isolated Ildiran colony, the human scholar Anton Colicos studied the *Saga of Seven Suns* with his friend and mentor, Rememberer Vao'sh. They remained with a skeleton crew in the domed city of Maratha Prime on the dark side of the planet, while work crews of Klikiss robots completed a sister city on the opposite side of the world. The Ildirans discovered an unusual network of tunnels but could not figure out who had built them. One evening, while Anton and Vao'sh told stories, an explosion occurred in the generators beneath the city, cutting off all lights and power. It was clearly sabotage. Left without enough power to survive, the crewmembers decided to trek over to the sister city. After contacting the Klikiss robots to explain their plight, the refugees set off in three shuttles—two of which exploded. More sabotage! Anton, Vao'sh, and a few others managed to get out of their craft safely, only to find themselves stranded. They set off on foot in the darkness toward supposed sanctuary among the Klikiss robots, but Anton was very suspicious. . . .

In secret, the Klikiss robots had long planned to destroy both humans and Ildirans. Dragging the compy DD from enclave to enclave, the robot Sirix resurrected long-dormant groups of Klikiss robots, which were now almost all activated and ready to move, much to DD's dismay.

When a Klikiss robot appeared at the Ildiran Prism Palace, demanding details of the secret breeding projects on Dobro, Jora'h refused to tell him anything. The Mage-Imperator then caused a stir by traveling to Dobro to meet his daughter Osira'h and to visit Nira's grave. Ildirans were upset that their leader would go against long-standing tradition and leave the Palace. Jora'h flouted tradition further by appointing his warrior daughter Yazra'h as his personal bodyguard, a position that had never before been held by a female. . . .

Desperate to continue its expansion even under such austere circumstances, the Hansa encouraged citizens to pack up their belongings, travel via the restored Klikiss transportals, and colonize virgin planets. Among the first takers were an unreliable dreamer named Jan Covitz and his young daughter Orli. The merchant captain Rlinda Kett and her favorite ex-husband Branson "BeBob" Roberts shuttled colonists to the nearest transportals, through which the settlers transferred to new colony worlds. Orli and her father went with a group to the abandoned Klikiss world of Corribus and began to set up a new life for themselves.

After many risky explorations through the transportals, Davlin Lotze appeared in secret in the rooms of Chairman Wenceslas and announced that he wanted to retire to a quiet colony. Although the hydrogue war was going poorly, the Chairman was unable to deny Davlin's demands, and sent him off with Rlinda to the sleepy world of Crenna. Frustrated by the war, King Peter's continued intractability, and the disappointing behavior of Prince Daniel (the King's potential replacement), the Chairman was further infuriated by the Roamers' unreasonable ekti embargo. In fact, deciding to use the Roamers as scapegoats on which to focus the public ire, Wenceslas met with General Lanyan, head of the EDF, to discuss measures against the arrogant clans.

At the same time, the exotically transformed Jess Tamblyn arrived at Rendezvous. Jess, whom many Roamers had thought dead, was no longer entirely human: His body crackled with wental energy, which made it impossible for him to touch another human, lest he kill them with the discharge. Cesca, still in love with him, could hardly believe they were together again, yet forced to remain separate. Telling the Roamers how he had rediscovered the wentals, ancient enemies of the hydrogues, Jess asked for volunteer "water bearers" to help him distribute wentals to other watery planets, where they could grow strong and prepare to fight the enemy. A group of ambitious pilots, including Nikko Chan Tylar, joined him. Setting off on his new mission, Jess visited an isolated comet where he and Cesca had once had a romantic rendezvous, and seeded the water essence there, making the comet come alive.

Meanwhile, Cesca decided to send Roamer aid to the devastated forests on Theroc. She had once been betrothed to their leader and now felt obligated to assist them, since the Hansa was offering little help. Roamer engineers tackled the problem of rebuilding the tree cities and stabilizing the forest. On Earth, Ambassador Sarein discovered that she was ostensibly the next leader of her people. Chairman Wenceslas, eager to turn this to his advantage, dispatched his staunch ally Sarein to take up her role. Arriving at the burned wasteland of her former home, she was sickened— and then doubly alarmed to see the ruined forests crawling with Roamer workers!

Chairman Wenceslas instructed the EDF to "teach a lesson" to representative Roamer targets. Though King Peter expressed grave reservations, General Lanyan planned a fast attack on a Roamer facility, Hurricane Depot. EDF ships surrounded the depot, captured all Roamers, then destroyed the station. Nikko Chan Tylar, en route to deliver wental water, witnessed the attack and immediately warned other Roamers, including the reconstruction team on Theroc.

Speaker Cesca Peroni angrily accused Sarein and the Hansa of trying to instigate a war, and rushed off to confront Chairman Wenceslas.

In the Roamer shipyards at Osquivel, Patrick Fitzpatrick resisted the idea that he was falling in love with Zhett Kellum. The EDF detainees constantly searched for a way to escape, but when one of them tried to fly away in a stolen ship, the soldier died tragically. Afterward, the friction between Roamers and EDF detainees increased.

On a scouting run among the battlefield derelicts in the rings, Zhett and her father discovered an intact hydrogue spacecraft—something never before found. Hoping that an analysis of the alien vessel would provide clues about how to defeat the enemy, they summoned the genius engineer Kotto Okiah to study the hydrogue sphere. Kotto managed to break into the alien ship, and immediately discovered that the hydrogue technology had much in common with the Klikiss transportals. . . .

While Davlin Lotze was starting to settle in at his colony on Crenna, he saw hydrogue warglobes cruising overhead. The aliens did not attack, though they seemed to be searching for something. Through a telescope several days later, Davlin saw the hydrogues battling their mortal enemies, the faeros, within Crenna's sun. The star began to die, and Davlin urged the colonists to take desperate survival measures. As the sun winked out, the seas and continents froze, and Davlin took a salvageable ship to find help. The colonists dug in and tried to survive as the atmosphere froze solid. Davlin managed to reach the nearby colony of Relleker, but the governor refused to help. Fortunately, Rlinda and BeBob arrived on a supply run and helped Davlin rescue the Crenna colonists, digging them out of their frozen bunkers.

The Klikiss robots took DD aboard an EDF battleship, part of a group of human ships they had stolen and modified. The battleships were now crewed entirely by reprogrammed Soldier compies, and DD learned that all Soldier models— widely distributed throughout the Earth military—contained insidious programming that the Klikiss robots could trigger at any time. As a test, the Klikiss robots took their stolen battleships to attack Corribus. Though DD tried to stop the robots, they proceeded to destroy the human colony there. Orli Covitz, exploring cliffside caves, looked on in helpless horror as the EDF warships obliterated the settlement, including her father and all her friends. She watched Klikiss robots and Soldier compies comb through the wreckage, kill the survivors, then depart. When Orli finally picked her way down to the burning settlement, she saw that she was the only survivor.

The Hyrillka Designate, still acting peculiar after his head injury, told his protégé Prime Designate Thor'h that he had seen the truth in visions, and that Mage-Imperator Jora'h (Thor'h's father) was leading the Ildiran Empire to ruin. At first concerned at this talk of rebellion, Thor'h eventually threw in his lot with his deluded uncle. Rusa'h commanded the population of Hyrillka to consume the mind-altering drug shiing, which softened their thoughts and allowed him to seize control of them. He then publicly accused Jora'h of poisoning his predecessor. Claiming that he himself was the rightful Mage-Imperator, Rusa'h took on all the trappings of the Ildiran leader. Only the apprentice Designate Pery'h remained loyal to the Mage-Imperator. When he resisted the overthrow, Rusa'h and Thor'h imprisoned him.

While sending out an assassination team to kill Jora'h,

the Hyrillka Designate executed Pery'h to distract his brother from the danger. The Mage-Imperator, saved by the quick actions of his bodyguard daughter Yazra'h, now knew that the mad Hyrillka Designate meant to overthrow the Empire. He dispatched Adar Zan'nh with a group of warliners to restore order to Hyrillka, not realizing he was sending them directly into a trap. . . .

Isolated on her island, the captive green priest Nira secretly built a raft and escaped, drifting for days on an open body of water until she crashed on a barren shore, lost but alive—and free of Designate Udru'h at last.

On Earth, Cesca demanded that the EDF cease all attacks on Roamer outposts, whereupon Chairman Wenceslas dismissed her concerns and commanded her people to surrender and begin delivering vital stardrive fuel again. Cesca departed angrily, vowing that he would never find the secret Roamer locations. However, General Lanyan had decoded the navigation module from a stolen Roamer ship and learned the coordinates for Rendezvous. He sent a full military force to the asteroid cluster and completely destroyed the Roamer capital. Cesca and other survivors scattered, their center of government gone. They were now outlaws. . . .

SCATTERED
SUNS

1 ✸ ADMIRAL LEV STROMO

Though Admiral Stromo was the ranking officer aboard the prowling Manta cruiser, he let acting commander Elly Ramirez make the day-to-day decisions. It generally worked out better that way. Stromo didn't feel the need to throw his weight around, and he liked to keep someone handy to take the fall if anything went wrong.

For decades in the Earth Defense Forces, he had made a career out of delegating responsibility. He rarely participated in active field operations—he hadn't joined the EDF just to put his own butt on the line!—but sometimes it was useful to do so. Maybe the unqualified success of crushing the main Roamer complex of Rendezvous would be enough to rehabilitate his image as an obsolete desk commander.

Even so, right now Stromo longed to be back at his desk in a comfortable military base on Earth, or at the very least Mars. He'd never counted on a devastating war with powerful aliens who lived in the cores of gas-giant planets; for that matter, he hadn't imagined a conflict with a ragtag bunch of space gypsies, either.

As the Roamer hunt continued for its second week, Stromo watched the newer EDF officers cut their teeth on real line duty. The sooner this fresh crop of battle commanders proved themselves out in the field, the sooner Stromo could get back to his much-preferred Grid 0 liaison duties. With his too-obvious potbelly and his occasional digestive problems, he wasn't cut out for this.

"Do we have any valid tactical data on our next target, Commander Ramirez?" he asked, though he had asked the question before. "What's the place called again?"

"Hhrenni, sir."

"Sounds like a horse sneezing."

"The name comes from old Ildiran starcharts, sir. The EDF has no up-to-date recon, though."

A frown tugged down his jowly cheeks. "A failure in our intelligence and surveillance, you think?"

"Never any need before, Admiral. It's a crappy star system, without many resources." Ramirez called up long-range images and dotted-line diagrams showing their best guess of where the secret base might lie. "Unconfirmed evidence of a cluster of settlement domes in the asteroids. Roamers seem to enjoy living in rubble, sir."

"If they like rubble so much, then let's give them more of it." He smiled. "Just like we did at Rendezvous."

Ever since the disorderly clans had willfully cut off all trade with the Terran Hanseatic League, Chairman Basil Wenceslas had attempted several legitimate—and thus far ineffective—responses. Though Roamers had been hit as hard as anyone by hydrogue attacks, they refused to cooperate against a shared enemy, refused to provide vital stardrive fuel, refused to follow perfectly reasonable instructions. The Hansa couldn't tolerate that.

Thus, to demonstrate how serious the matter was, the EDF had destroyed a Roamer fuel-transfer station. Just as an example, a bit of bluster, but enough to make the clans see they didn't have a chance against the powerful Earth military. Instead of cowing the Roamers, this action had only served to renew their ridiculous defiance. The space gypsies became even more intractable, which forced the Chairman to take the unprecedented step of declaring outright war against them, for the good of humanity.

If the Roamers had been reasonable people, the war should have lasted no longer than an hour. Alas, it hadn't turned out that way.

A week ago, Stromo had led the punitive attack that destroyed Rendezvous, and the clans had scampered away, making it necessary for all grid admirals to waste more time and effort chasing them down. It was maddening! Stromo and his counterparts had orders to seek out Roamer infestations, confiscate any of their goods that might be useful for the war effort, and somehow bring those people in line. Sooner or later, they would have to sue for peace.

Ramirez looked up at him from her command chair, her full lips showing no smile, her face cool, her regulation-short dark hair perfectly in place. "Would you like to assume operational oversight as we approach, Admiral? Or should I continue?"

"You're doing just fine, Commander Ramirez." Although he suspected she didn't like him very much, she was an excellent pilot and navigator, who had been promoted rapidly, just like many young officers during the devastating hydrogue war. "Can we get better magnification on the screen? I want to have a look at our target."

"The first wave of Remora scouts have set up relay stations, and imagery is coming through now."

The scattered rubble around Hhrenni looked like a handful of oversized gravel that someone had tossed against the blackness of space. From a distance, the drifting rocks looked unremarkable, but the distribution of metals and the albedo profile

of some geometrical objects were a dead giveaway: An uncharted human settlement was hidden there. *Roamers.*

"There they are, just as we thought." He rubbed his chin.
"All right, let's head forward and have a look at this rats'
nest. Power up fore and aft jazer banks and load primary
projectile launchers. Tell our Remoras to intercept any ships
that try to escape." He gestured toward the screen. "Onward,
in the name of the King, and so on . . ."

As the EDF ships swooped in, the audacity of the clans
became more obvious. A secret base indeed! Transparent
domes dotted the asteroids like pus-filled blisters. Hanging
suspended above them at gravitationally stable points, thin
arrays of solar mirrors directed sunlight through the shadows to illuminate and provide energy to the dome settlements. Artificial stations orbited at various distances like
gnats. Inflatable storage chambers, perhaps?

"Look at all that! Those Roachers are certainly ambitious."

"They have a lot of energy and ingenuity," Ramirez said,
not sounding overly eager. "Commander Tamblyn proved
that often enough."

Stromo frowned. Not long ago this very Manta had been
commanded by Tasia Tamblyn, who, because of her Roamer
connections, was reassigned to less critical duties before the
strike against Rendezvous. Was Ramirez demonstrating loyalty to her former commander? He'd have thought she'd be
pleased with her own promotion.

"The clans should channel that creative enthusiasm to
help all mankind, not just themselves." Surveying the asteroid complex, with its light-filled domes and expansive mirrors, he shook his head. "Why can't they just live on planets
like everyone else?"

Though every operation had gone against them so far, the

gypsies showed no signs of bowing to authority. They had scattered like wildly fired shotgun pellets, which the Hansa considered a victory, of course. Divide and conquer. With the Roamers leaderless and broken, it should have been easy to bring them back into the fold . . . but they were as hard to catch and tame as angry, wet house cats. Since Stromo had spent his life in military service, such anarchy made his stomach queasy. "Hooligans."

When they were unified under Speaker Peroni, he supposed the clans had felt obligated to show some kind of stubborn backbone. Now, though, with their government center destroyed, who would speak for them? Who had the authority to negotiate on their behalf? *Somebody* had to sign a surrender order and call for the others to turn themselves in and get back to work. It would take a hell of a long time to root out all the squalid little settlements like this one.

"We've detected four ships, Admiral. Nothing large enough to threaten us. None of the facilities here look like they'll cause any problems."

"Didn't expect any." Stromo cracked his knuckles.

Detailed projections of asteroid paths and accurate representations of the domed settlements appeared on the screen. Ramirez stared at the tactical projections and tucked a strand of dark hair behind her right ear. Something was clearly bothering the young commander. "Admiral . . . permission to speak freely?"

Stromo steeled himself. That was always a bad preface to a conversation. But since Ramirez had spoken her question aloud in front of the rest of the bridge crew, he had no choice but to respond. "Be quick about it, Commander. We have an operation to run."

"If I might ask, what do we really expect to get out of

this? Earlier, when we hit Hurricane Depot and Rendezvous, our objective was to scare the Roamers into lifting their ekti embargo. But if we keep increasing their hatred toward us, they'll never cooperate. If we wreck them, how will they ever be in a position to be viable trading partners again?"

"That's not the point anymore. The Hansa will bypass the Roamers, and they'll be left out alone in cold space. We've already got one full-fledged cloud harvester producing ekti for us on Qronha 3, and you can bet there'll be others." When Ramirez still looked skeptical, he decided it was best to distract the bridge crew. "You'll see what I mean in a few moments, Commander."

He leaned back in his padded observation chair, eager for the engagement now that he saw it would be a cakewalk. "I'm ready for the show to begin. Let's make a lasting impression."

2 ☀ NIKKO CHAN TYLAR

On his random route across the Spiral Arm, Nikko found himself close to the hidden Roamer base where his parents tended orbiting greenhouses that provided fresh food and supplies to many of the clans. Unlike his parents, Nikko was a true Roamer who preferred wandering from system to system, seeing what there was to see. Still, this was *home*. How could he not stop for a visit, even if he couldn't stay long?

His ship, *Aquarius*, was configured for delivering samples of wental water to uninhabited worlds on which the elemental entities could grow powerful enough to fight the hydrogues. Unfortunately, it was hard to concentrate on that mission when the Big Goose—the Roamers' deprecating name for the Hansa—kept stabbing the clans in the back with malicious raids like the ones at Hurricane Depot and Rendezvous.

Nikko stepped into the largest greenhouse blister, enjoying the feel of solid ground under his feet, and gazed up at the transparent panes. The blackness outside, spattered with stars and orbiting asteroids, was dominated by a dazzling mirrorfilm reflector that bounced a splash of warm solar light through the armored glass. Up near the top of the main dome, cottony masses of aerogel foam drifted about like clouds.

Smaller satellite domes on other rocks were maintained at various temperatures and humidities: a hothouse dome held palm trees and succulents; another encompassed fruit orchards. In each one, the plants thrived in artificial soil created by mixing sterile asteroid dirt with fertilizer chemicals and recycled human waste. As good as any farmland back on Earth, his mother always said.

Marla Chan and Crim Tylar, delighted by their son's unexpected visit, inspected their vegetable fields while Nikko chatted with them. He showed them the canisters of vibrant wental water in his ship and explained that these strange beings could be the key to ending the terrible war against the hydrogues. They were both awed and a little surprised to hear what he was doing to help the fight.

"To be honest, I always thought you'd just help us with the greenhouses, or the skymining at Ptoro," his mother said, smiling at him. As she talked, Marla kept an electronic datapad inventory of their crops and output. "I never knew you had such big things in store for you."

He blushed. "Well, who would have thought Dad might like being a farmer? Working with dirt on his hands, sowing seeds, tending plants?"

Crim Tylar's brow furrowed. "Shizz, this sure beats skymining. Give me dirt any day. I always hated Ptoro— cold, windy, bleak." He made a face.

"You saw the images after the Eddies used their Klikiss Torch, right?" Nikko said. "Ptoro's nothing more than one big ball of fire."

"Then at least it's warm there now," Crim grumbled.

His parents couldn't cover their pride as they led him through a lush vegetable sector. "You've got a grand galactic mission, Nikko, but take a few seconds to enjoy the little things," Marla suggested.

"When all the big words are stripped away, that's what we're really fighting for, you know." Crim bent down to pluck a soft, red tomato. "Eat this. You've never tasted anything like it."

"I've had a tomato before."

"Not one of *my* tomatoes. This is as good as it gets."

Actually, Nikko had eaten one of his father's tomatoes, but he humored the older man. He popped the small tomato into his mouth and bit down to release a gush of moist flavor. "Yes, as good as it gets."

A huge shadow crossed the fields like the black shape of a vulture passing overhead. The three of them looked up and Crim squinted to get a better look. "What the hell is that?"

Nikko recognized the profile of an enormous warship drifting in front of the solar mirror array, blocking the reflected sun. "It's an Eddy battleship! I saw them hit Hurricane Depot—"

As if to reinforce his claim, the silhouetted vessel launched a volley of explosive projectiles into the gossamer mirror array. The artillery punched bright blossoms of fire through the reflective film, which sent dazzling ricochets of light in all directions. The tether cable snapped, and the mangled reflectors drifted, twirling like tissue blown in a high wind. The greenhouse dome was plunged into shadow, illuminated only by starlight and uncertain glints from the tattered mirror.

Alarms sounded throughout the dome, and relay messages came from the artificial storage stations and satellite asteroids. Marla shouted, "Get an oxygen mask. Tell everyone to suit up if they have time—"

Her instructions were cut off by an announcement from the EDF battleships over the dome's intercom systems. "This is Admiral Lev Stromo of the Earth Defense Forces. By order of King Peter, this facility has been seized by the Terran Hanseatic League. All assets are forfeit to the war effort for the protection of humanity."

"Oh, piss off," Crim grumbled.

"Roamers have been declared hostiles. Therefore, all inhabitants of this facility will be taken away and processed. Our ships will accept your surrender. Any resistance will be considered grounds for immediate and decisive retaliation."

Jumpsuited agricultural workers scrambled to their meeting points, as they had been drilled to do, but an overwhelming force of Earth military vessels already loomed above the greenhouse complex. They were bottled up here.

The emergency lights cast strange shadows among the growing plants, and flickering alarms added to the nightmarish quality. Without the sun mirror, the temperature inside the dome was already dropping. Because they had no official military branch, Roamer security depended on secrecy and rapid dispersal of their ships.

In direct defiance of the admiral's order, one small cargo ship accelerated like a bullet down from a food storage satellite. The greenhouse intercom picked up the pilot's transmission over a private Roamer channel. "I'll keep them busy while the rest of you get away! Everybody better evacuate immediately."

"It's Shelby. That idiot—what the hell does he think he's doing?"

The cargo ship flew in like a matador provoking a bull. Shelby launched one tiny potshot directly at the lead Manta cruiser.

Nikko and his parents made their way to the nearest emergency station and grabbed masks, tugging the straps to secure them firmly over mouth and nose. Hands on his hips, Crim grumbled through the mask, "Even if he did manage to distract them for more than a nanosecond, none of our evacuation ships could outrun those EDF vessels."

True to his word, Admiral Stromo responded with deadly force. Two jazer beams lanced out from the Manta, played across the small ship's hull, and ripped it open.

"Shelby," Crim mumbled in disgust as his wife moaned. "The man wasn't fit for recycling. Now he's made it worse for all of us."

Nikko grabbed his mother's arm. "I've got the *Aquarius*. It won't take many people, but we can still—"

Marla turned an intense, determined look on her son. "You've got the wentals aboard, Nikko. You *have* to get away. Think what the Big Goose might do if they got their hands on something like that."

"Probably pour them down the drain," Crim said with a snort.

Incensed by Shelby's ineffective harassment, the EDF invaders fired a single jazer pulse at the main greenhouse dome. It was probably meant to be a warning shot, but the beam ruptured the armored glass.

The wave of explosive decompression sent a thump through the dome. A hurricane of escaping atmosphere ripped plant trays and hydroponics tanks off their racks. Nikko's ears popped. The wave of cold struck him like a sledgehammer. The air grew thinner with stomach-lurching rapidity.

Air geysered into space with the force of a rocket engine, sufficient to nudge the greenhouse asteroid off its rotational axis. Thrown to their hands and knees, agricultural workers cried out in dismay.

Caught in the vortex of escaping atmosphere, the aerogel clouds spun, clumped together, and then covered the blasted opening. The polymers and resins that made up the ultralight material broke down upon exposure to vacuum; like gauze packed into a wound, the artificial clouds filled the rupture, providing enough protection for the people to survive. The seal was imperfect, though, and leaking air shrieked through gaps in the aerogel plug.

Crim saw many of his plants already withering, the pots tumbled about as if a giant hand had scattered them. His angry curses were drowned out by loud alarms in the thinning air.

Marla pushed Nikko urgently away. "Run to your ship. Don't wait for anybody. Just fly out of here and take the wentals. Take the wentals!"

"I can't just leave you here! Come with me—"

"We need to stay with our people." Marla gestured to the Roamers around them. "But you're too important."

"Then let me gather a group. I can fit maybe a dozen or so aboard—"

"You've got a responsibility." His father cut him off as shadows of more EDF ships closed in overhead. "Seems to me that if you lose even a minute, you'll never get out of here."

Marla met her son's flustered expression. "Don't worry, the Eddies have to take us somewhere. At least we'll find out what happened to all the POWs from Rendezvous and Hurricane Depot."

When Nikko still hesitated, his father bellowed, "Go now, Nikko—and don't let us down."

In the low gravity, flashing lights, and shrieking wind, Nikko ran.

3 ☀ KING PETER

Despite the newsnet footage of the "triumphant destruction" of Rendezvous and the gala celebration of the EDF victory, King Peter did not see much cause for joy. General Lanyan was beating his chest, proclaiming a clean and decisive win, but it was in a battle that had never needed to be fought. Peter knew that from the inside, but no one in the Hansa government had listened to his objections. After all, he was only the *King*.

Riled up, the Hansa citizens had been primed by months of skewed coverage, reports, and rumors that painted the Roamers as shifty, unreliable, greedy. No reason had been given for the clans' refusal to provide stardrive fuel to the war effort, though Peter knew that the Roamers were reacting to secret EDF raids on their unarmed cargo ships. Certainly, that was sufficient provocation for the Roamers to cut off trade relations, but Chairman Basil Wenceslas had never admitted any culpability, even unofficially. Instead, he used the Roamers as scapegoats to distract the people from other military failures. That was how the Chairman did things.

Peter felt it would have been easier to address the problems and attempt to *negotiate* instead of bully. Basil could have resolved the Roamer problem in a much less incendiary fashion; now, however, he would never back down. The Chairman had become more dictatorial and strident with each passing month.

How is this going to end, Basil? You've showed your muscle—but did you leave an option for resolution? And is this really the worst problem facing us?

What about the numerous fringe colonies, not yet self-sufficient, left stranded without regular supply runs? What about the devastated world-forest on Theroc? What about Peter's suspicions of embedded Klikiss programming in tens of thousands of Soldier compies? Basil was intentionally turning a blind eye to the possible threat. What about the *hydrogues*?

Wearing a false smile, Peter and Queen Estarra appeared

at the celebratory banquet, as was their duty. The blond-haired, blue-eyed, and classically handsome King had been instructed to read a brief script full of vague references about "standing up against the enemies of humanity."

A dash of dusky and exotic beauty amidst the regimented spectacle, Estarra stood placidly at the velvet-wrapped podium beside Peter as he gave his speech. Out of view of the newsnets, though, she clutched his hand so tightly that his knuckles hurt, and he tried to deliver the words without choking on them. She, like everyone from independent Theroc, understood the Roamers' resentment at being forced to follow a leader they did not acknowledge. Her heart had been touched by the plight of the damaged worldforest, and she knew how little the Hansa and the EDF had done to assist Theroc, while the Roamer clans had helped willingly, without being asked.

Even though theirs had been an arranged marriage, a political alliance, Peter loved her desperately. Estarra—having been plunged into the same strange world of governmental alliances, manipulations, and power struggles as he—had opened herself to him, and now they shared their hearts, their secrets, and their plans.

Basil Wenceslas did not know the half of his problems.

In the grand reception halls of the Whisper Palace, guests reveled far into the night, listening to music, offering toasts. Protocol officers had coached the King and Queen in every moment of the evening. Polite and acceptably sociable, the royal couple spent the correct amount of time with each important guest, but they remained only as long as was politically necessary. By the time Peter and Estarra returned to the Royal Wing, both of them were exhausted and edgy.

Over the past several months, Chairman Wenceslas had

been annoyingly effective at cutting Peter out of any real participation in Hansa politics. Like Old King Frederick before him, Peter's place was merely for show, and the Chairman never let him forget it. When he tried to think for himself, when he attempted to be a real leader instead of a puppet in a colorful costume, Basil punished him severely. During his youth, Peter had not truly appreciated his freedom. Back then he had been poor, but happy, with a loving family, taking pleasure in the small joys of daily life. But he knew full well he could never slip away, nor could he go back to being the street-smart commoner he had once been.

Now he was trapped, friendless except for Estarra and possibly the Teacher compy OX. And he had to be very, very careful. Basil had already tried to assassinate him once.

The couple had no sanctuary even in the Whisper Palace. When they reached their private quarters, Peter and Estarra found the Chairman waiting there. He too had slipped away from the reception just long enough to ambush them.

Dapper and unflappable, Basil sat in Peter's favorite comfortable chair. In an adjacent chair by a small table, Eldred Cain hunched over papers and a datapad. The pale and hairless deputy paused in his discussion of details with the Chairman; it seemed he took advantage of every free moment. Seeing the two enter, Cain straightened his papers and stored the analysis in his datapad.

Peter drew a slow breath to cover his surprise and anger at finding the man there. "Why don't you make yourself at home, Basil?" He modulated his tone, showing only a hint of his displeasure so as not to invoke Basil's wrath. "Were all the normal conference rooms booked at this time of night?"

Basil rested casually, as if he considered himself welcome anywhere. "Business hours never end in the Hansa, Peter."

Peter struggled to mask his hostility toward the Chairman, although he would never forgive the man for attempting to kill both him and Estarra, and for orchestrating the murders of his whole innocent family. "Then by all means, let's get down to business, Basil. It's been a long day, and I didn't see your name in my appointment book."

"I always have an appointment." Basil marked his place in the report he was reading and handed it to his deputy, who added it to his stack. "I came to inform you of a change in plans. Prepare to embark on an important trip, a visit of state that Hansa officials consider necessary."

After removing Estarra's gem-studded shawl for her and draping it over a sculpture of a fat man holding a bowl of grapes, Peter unfastened his heavy ornamental cape and stretched his arms. Weariness got the better of him, and he couldn't resist baiting the Chairman. "Where am I going? To make a truce with the Roamers?"

Basil frowned at the suggestion. "To Ildira. You leave in two days."

Peter and Estarra had both heard wonderful stories of the Ildiran homeworld, bathed in the light of seven suns, but neither had visited the alien capital.

The Chairman explained, "Not long ago a new Mage-Imperator took the throne. It is appropriate that the Great King of the Terran Hanseatic League pay his respects. Recent months have been unusually hectic, but even so, we have been remiss in our duty."

Peter gave a tired sigh. "Political games."

Eldred Cain finally arranged his documents into a sufficiently neat stack. Although Peter saw the deputy often, he had rarely talked with him. For the most part Cain kept his silence, not hiding in Basil's shadow but always watching. Now, however, he spoke. "They are necessary games, King Peter—and well worth the investment of ekti for the journey. We need to keep the Ildirans as allies in our war against the hydrogues. And we certainly need the Solar Navy to help us fight." His voice was quiet, as if he didn't like to bother anybody.

Basil nodded. "I could take care of the matter myself, but diplomatically it is a greater honor if our King makes the overture. That's what the Ildirans understand. We'll make it a swift journey and stay just long enough to meet and honor the new Mage-Imperator. You'll be there on public display."

Since they were in private, Peter decided to dispense with subtlety. "How do I know you won't simply blow up the ship en route to get rid of me?"

The Chairman didn't seem to take offense. "Because I will be with you. I wouldn't entrust such an important diplomatic visit to the King alone."

"Then I will go too," Estarra insisted, standing close to her husband. They held hands, supporting each other.

Basil gave her a condescending smile. "That is not necessary, my dear."

"Yes it is," Peter said. "In addition to the obvious symbolic tribute to the new leader, it offers opportunities for pageantry, and an excellent way for me to be sure of her safety. I don't want any . . . accidents to befall my Queen while I'm away."

Basil sighed. "Now, Peter, I thought we were beyond all of that."

"We will never be beyond all of that." He softened the comment with a bland smile that masked his inner turmoil.

Cain looked back and forth between the men, apparently disturbed by how little they trusted each other.

Estarra's voice was soft and persuasive. "Remember, Mr. Chairman, my brother Reynald visited the Prism Palace and spoke very highly of Jora'h when he was just the Prime Designate. They were good friends. I should . . . tell the Mage-Imperator how the hydrogues killed him."

"I'm sure you could use that to your advantage, Basil," Peter said.

The Chairman conceded with grace. "As you wish. Yes, the King and Queen together will make a fine show for the Ildirans and for the newsnets. I'll have functionaries take care of all the details." Satisfied, he turned and walked briskly out of the Royal Wing.

After picking up his documents with spare and efficient motions, Deputy Cain paused beside Peter on his way out, sizing him up. "Why do you provoke the Chairman? It seems you have a personal animus against him."

Peter looked at the pale man, searching for sincerity in his eyes. How much did he know about Basil's other activities? "Maybe it has something to do with that time he arranged to kill us."

Cain's surprise seemed genuine. His face shifted, as if puzzle pieces were rearranging themselves in his mind, giving rise to new questions. His mouth opened, and Peter waited to hear what the deputy might have to say, but Basil called down the hall for Cain to hurry. They didn't have a chance to finish their conversation.

4 ☀ OSIRA'H

In recent days the testing had grown more intense, more desperate. Though none of the Dobro instructors had told Osira'h and her siblings the reason, she knew their time was running out. Or was this emergency another lie to manipulate the telepathic half-breed children?

She pretended to be innocent and cooperative, but in her secret heart Osira'h suspected everything, distrusted everyone since learning the dark truth of what her uncle Udru'h and his fellow experimenters were doing here on Dobro. Her beloved mentor had deceived her, distorted the truth so that she would be a more willing pawn. Her mother had been kept from her, and her real father—the powerful Mage-Imperator—pretended not to know what had happened. What was the girl to believe?

They watched her every minute. Osira'h and her brothers and sisters strained to impress the Dobro mentalists and lens kithmen. They had all been born for this specific purpose, and one of them had to succeed in breaking the communication barrier with the hydrogues. Day after day, their heads ached and their minds were exhausted by the time the children collapsed into a few hours of rest.

In silence, Osira'h listened and observed, but she could find no obvious answer to her dilemma. She would give the Ildirans what they wanted . . . and hope they might eventually see the error of their ways.

As darkness fell outside the well-lit Ildiran settlement and the fenced-in breeding compound, Osira'h and her siblings sat cross-legged on a woven rug. One of the mentalists scrutinized their exercises from an observation chair. They spoke no words; the two youngest squeezed their eyes shut to aid their concentration, while the others could turn their vision inside without such a crutch.

Osira'h knew how to do this. Once her mind's eye saw inside herself, she flung her mental gaze outside of the room, outside of the Ildiran settlement, and into the fenced camp that held the descendants of human captives. For years, she'd never dreamed that her mother was out there, so close and yet isolated, raped, tortured . . . and then she'd been killed.

Now every time Osira'h saw the fences, the breeding barracks, the medical kithmen with their fertility monitors, she knew exactly what went on inside those chambers. She thought of Nira dragged into a room with a single bed, forced to endure repeated assaults by soldier kithmen, lens kithmen, even Designate Udru'h himself. That was how Nira had conceived her other half-breed children.

Rod'h, fathered by Udru'h himself, worked even harder than her other siblings, attempting to achieve the levels of success that Osira'h had. Ostensibly they shared the same goals. She longed to tell her brother the truth, but she doubted he would listen.

Of all the siblings, only Osira'h had any inkling about what had happened to their shared mother. Nira had vanished like an erased file, just after she had revealed everything to her daughter.

Completely persuaded of their importance for the destiny of the Ildiran race, Osira'h's gullible brothers and sisters suspected nothing of their origins. But they did not have their mother's memories inside them, as she did.

Sometimes during the dark Dobro night that frightened

the other Ildirans, Osira'h received tantalizing thoughts, even prophetic images that made her suspect beyond any reasonable hope that her mother might still be alive. The girl had used all the powers in her mind to shout out a response, to call back to the faint whisper of existence that made her think of Nira. But though she searched with her mind until it felt as if her skull would crack open, she found no tangible link to the female green priest.

In the exercise now, Osira'h let her troubled thoughts drift like snowflakes across the human prisoners, touching them, brushing against their experiences. Though their mind-set was quite different from an Ildiran's, these humans were far less alien than the hydrogues would be. . . .

When the exercise was over, the mentalist instructor stood, nodding. "All your lives you have been taught your skills and your duty. It is up to you to save the Ildiran Empire."

The children nodded in unison. Osira'h, who had believed those words for years, was now pulled in several different directions. Despite the horrors and the truth, the girl could not dismiss her obligations. No matter how much had been distorted, she was convinced that her mentor had not exaggerated the hydrogue threat—that part of her instruction was valid—and Osira'h herself would soon be forced to go into the depths of an infested gas-giant planet to face them. She understood what was at stake: The fate of an entire race was in her hands. Yet she couldn't help but wonder if these lying and hurtful Ildirans deserved to be saved. . . .

In her revelations to Osira'h, her mother had been sure that Jora'h himself was kindhearted and good, that the Dobro Designate was the true evil behind this plan. But if Jora'h was truly as benevolent as her mother believed, why had he done nothing about the Dobro breeding camps? For generations, Ildirans had held humans captive and abused them. Jora'h was the Mage-Imperator of the Ildiran Empire. He certainly must have had the opportunity to do what was right, yet he had not intervened.

Osira'h decided she couldn't trust anyone.

Before the mentalist could finish his inspirational talk, Designate Udru'h stepped into the room. Anxious, he swept his gaze across the faces of Nira's five mixed-breed children, then focused his entire attention on Osira'h. His disturbed eyes glistened with a sheen of what might have been tears, but also a fanatical, hopeful pride. *For her.*

"I have just received a message from the Prism Palace," he said to her. "The hydrogues have destroyed our mining world of Hrel-oro, and the Solar Navy could do nothing against them." Osira'h could see the agitation on the Designate's face, in his movements. Tangible emotions poured from him like heat from a newly stoked fire.

She did not speak. Udru'h had been so kind to her, so attentive and helpful. The girl had loved and respected him . . . but now she saw him through two sets of eyes. With one part of her mind, Osira'h thought of how he had taken her under his wing, kept her in the main house overlooking the breeding camps. Although Udru'h was not given to gushing compliments or praise, Osira'h knew she was truly special to him.

But she also remembered another side of the Designate: the cold and efficient brutality that her mother had experienced. He had isolated Nira, starved her for sunlight without caring how he scarred her mind, as long as her body and her reproductive system functioned. He had pushed her to the bed in the breeding barracks and raped her. He had never looked at Nira with anger or disgust, just a hard, businesslike detachment.

In deeper, more pleasant memories, she recalled how Jora'h—her father—had loved and caressed the green priest woman. But Udru'h had seen Nira only as a receptacle, the recipient of his sperm, an object with which he had to perform an unpleasant yet necessary task.

When these memories blazed in her mind, Osira'h could not look at him.

Udru'h continued explaining. "For several years, the Klikiss robots have failed to keep the hydrogues away from Ildiran worlds. Now they have broken their commitment completely." He placed a paternal hand on the girl's shoulder, and she tried not to flinch. "We need you now, Osira'h, more than ever. The hydrogues have always refused to communicate with us. They have not responded to any of our pleas. We need you to get through to them, convince them to speak with the Mage-Imperator before they annihilate us all."

She nodded solemnly. "This is the purpose for which I was born."

Now Designate Udru'h had even stranger news. "Though it may seem impossible, my brother Rusa'h has started a rebellion on Hyrillka. Many Ildirans have complained about the Mage-Imperator's erratic behavior and his ready dismissal of sacred traditions, but this has gone much further. Prime Designate Thor'h has joined Rusa'h and assassinated the Hyrillka Designate-in-waiting."

Osira'h had already sensed a growing, incomprehensible storm in the mental network of *thism*, like a telepathic black hole that sucked at the Ildiran soul. The disturbance had come from somewhere on the edge of the Horizon Cluster . . . *Hyrillka*. Now it made more sense. Part of the interconnected Ildiran mind had become an unresponsive, necrotic tumor, thanks to Rusa'h.

The mentalist instructor could not control his gasp of surprise. "Ildiran has killed Ildiran!"

Udru'h kept his focus on the special children. "The Mage-Imperator has stripped Thor'h of his title, and Adar Zan'nh was dispatched with a maniple of warliners to quell the revolt." Though clearly disturbed, he composed himself. "The Ildiran Empire faces many unexpected enemies. We must use every weapon and tool available to us. Therefore, Osira'h, the Mage-Imperator has commanded me to deliver you to Mijistra as soon as possible."

Osira'h took a step away from the other children, standing ready. She had always known this moment would come. Looking at her, Udru'h seemed to swell with pride. "I promised Jora'h that you would not disappoint him—and I know you will not disappoint me."

He took her small hand and led her out of the training chamber. Turning back for the briefest moment, she offered a look of farewell to her younger brothers and sisters. Udru'h, though, did not give them a second glance.

5 ✸ ADAR ZAN'NH

After exhaustive preparations, the forty-seven intact ships in Zan'nh's maniple departed for rebellious Hyrillka. Mage-Imperator Jora'h had issued his command, and the Adar would follow those instructions precisely. Even so, the Solar Navy crewmembers aboard the warliners felt more uneasy than when they had recently faced the hydrogues at Hrel-oro.

A rebellion—especially by a Designate—was inconceivable to them. Ildirans were one unified empire bound together by a telepathic network of *thism,* under the benevolent rule of the Mage-Imperator. The Solar Navy had never been called upon to overwhelm and impose order on another Ildiran colony. Yet Adar Zan'nh was leading a maniple of warliners to do exactly that.

Distinctly uneasy, he stood in the command nucleus, maintaining a determined expression as he looked at the Horizon Cluster's tiara of stars. On the edge of that cluster glimmered the Hyrillka system, whose colonized planet was like a patch of disease that would have to be excised before the rot spread.

"Raise Qul Fan'nh and tell him to be prepared for precision maneuvers to give an impressive and overwhelming show of force. The Hyrillka Designate has to see reason and surrender."

Zan'nh tried to be stoic, as his hero Adar Kori'nh would have been. As a boy, he had sat within the Prism Palace's strategy dome, analyzing traditional spaceship maneuvers, practicing with Ildiran weapons. He grew up fascinated with the Solar Navy, studying every section of the *Saga* that related to the military. Kori'nh had taken him under his wing, guided him, named Zan'nh as his successor.

But the old Adar had never faced a situation like this. The rebellious Designate had murdered Zan'nh's brother Pery'h. Ildiran had killed Ildiran! In order to end the bloodshed and rebellion, Rusa'h and Thor'h must both be taken captive and brought back to stand before the Mage-Imperator. There was no other way.

Hyrillka grew large before them as the group of ornate battleships descended into the system. The bridge sensor operator looked up from his station. "They have detected us, Adar."

"Good. This will be over soon." He truly hoped for a logical solution, though he knew that was unlikely. Zan'nh had no desire to assume the role of acting Prime Designate. He had been trained as a military officer and was a talented tactician and commander in the Solar Navy. The responsibility of being Adar was overwhelming enough, but becoming the surrogate Prime Designate as well seemed too much. Since Zan'nh was not even a purebred noble kithman, the very idea went against the grain of his personality, against tradition.

Yet knowing what Prime Designate Thor'h had done, how could he possibly say no?

"Open a channel." Zan'nh stood against the rail that encircled the command nucleus's raised platform, calling up the words he had rehearsed en route. "I come in the name of the Mage-Imperator, with instructions to escort Rusa'h and Thor'h back to Ildira. Unless they surrender themselves immediately, the Solar Navy will take them by force."

The threat left a sour taste in his mouth. He sensed disquiet among his crew. No Ildiran in memory had ever delivered such an ultimatum.

"Adar, a shuttle has just launched from the spaceport near the citadel palace."

"Is it armed? Is it a military vessel?"

"It appears to be a transport ship, but it is proceeding to orbit at great speed. Several smaller vessels are in pursuit."

A transmission flickered on the screen and the haggard visage of his brother Thor'h appeared. The gaunt young man's eyes glittered with a wild desperation. "Zan'nh, protect me! Give me sanctuary!" In the tight image, Thor'h worked the controls of the sluggish transport ship. Sweating, he glanced repeatedly down at his screens, watching the close images of his pursuers.

"Explain yourself, Thor'h." He intentionally did not use the Prime Designate's title.

"Our uncle has gone mad! He believes that *he* is the true Mage-Imperator, and he murdered Pery'h—but I have escaped." Thor'h's fingers raced across the controls, and a sudden increase in speed threw him back against the pilot's seat. Alarms shrilled in the background. "I insist that you take me into the protection of a warliner. Rusa'h has already sent ships after me. He will destroy me before he lets me go—I have too much vital information."

The short-range pursuers opened fire on Thor'h's escaping craft, but their shots missed.

Brow furrowed in thought, Zan'nh grasped at any thread of hope, of sanity. At last, this was an explanation he could accept. Designate Rusa'h had become unstable after suffering a severe head injury during a hydrogue attack on Hyrillka, but it had been difficult for Zan'nh to believe that Thor'h, the

Mage-Imperator's chosen successor, would willingly turn against the Ildiran Empire.

"Very well, Thor'h. We will take you aboard the flagship warliner."

"Another vessel has launched from the citadel palace, Adar," said the sensor operator. "It is a larger ship, a royal shuttle."

Zan'nh considered this for a moment. "What is its weapons complement?"

"Nothing apparent."

The communications officer looked very surprised. "Adar! The Hyrillka Designate demands an audience with you aboard the flagship."

The Hyrillka Designate sent his image from the royal shuttle. "Adar Zan'nh, I am responding to my brother's summons." The formerly soft and corpulent Rusa'h appeared thin and hardened, like tempered metal. "It was not necessary to make such threats. We are all Ildirans, are we not?"

"You will come aboard my warliner willingly?" Zan'nh asked in surprise.

"It is my privilege to serve the Ildiran Empire."

"You killed Designate-in-waiting Pery'h and tried to assassinate the Mage-Imperator. We just watched you firing at Thor'h. You have a strange way of showing your loyalty."

Rusa'h seemed calm and unshaken. "Once I have had an opportunity to explain myself, you will understand."

Thor'h broke in again, frantic as his racing shuttle approached the gathered battleships. "I refuse to be aboard the same warliner as the mad Designate. Direct me to another ship, brother. Keep me safe!"

"You will be safe." After a moment's consideration, Zan'nh signaled Qul Fan'nh. "Allow Thor'h to dock aboard your warliner. If it makes our mission simpler, we will keep the two separate."

Thor'h's shuttle flew erratically, no doubt because the Prime Designate was not comfortable piloting ships for himself. Zan'nh knew his brother had never bothered to learn practical skills, preferring instead to indulge himself with the fine luxuries available to his station.

Qul Fan'nh transmitted a guidance beam, and the fleeing cargo craft drifted directly into a receiving bay on the maniple's first warliner.

Troubled by Thor'h's words, the Adar reconsidered what might have happened here. Had the Prime Designate been forced against his will, while Rusa'h alone committed the crimes? Assuming that Thor'h participated in the crime, the Mage-Imperator had commanded Adar Zan'nh to seize both of them and bring them back to Ildira. But if Thor'h was demanding sanctuary, declaring his innocence . . . Or maybe it was just a trick.

Only a few moments after the Prime Designate's craft had been taken inside one of the warliners, the Hyrillka Designate's overloaded and ornate royal shuttle lumbered out of the atmosphere, as if Rusa'h considered himself to be in a spectacular procession. Zan'nh remembered his uncle's penchant for banquets and pleasure mates and frivolous skypageants.

The oddest part of the situation, both with Thor'h and with "mad" Designate Rusa'h, was that the Adar could not sense them at all. Because of his bloodline, Zan'nh's connection to the *thism* was strong enough that he should have been able to feel his brother and his uncle. But he detected only a blank grayness from Thor'h's shuttle and from Rusa'h's larger royal escort. Had they consumed so much mind-muddying shiing as to be impenetrable to another Ildiran's thoughts? He could think of no other explanation. How else could they simply remove themselves from the *thism* network?

Many things about these circumstances made him uncomfortable, but Adar Zan'nh did not let his soldiers see his concerns. Already he could sense waves of relief from the Solar Navy crewmen. They had dreaded the possibility of direct conflict with their fellow Ildirans.

Zan'nh had led these fighters in a recent ineffective defense of Hrel-oro. There, he had lost one warliner and seen a second one crash. Many crewmembers had died fighting against the deep-core aliens. He would not let any more of them fall because of his poor decisions.

"Adar, the Hyrillka Designate is preparing to enter our docking bay."

Zan'nh nodded. "Gather seventy of our best soldiers and protocol officers as a standard reception committee. They will demonstrate the proper formalities as we receive him into custody and escort him to quarters. Once we return to Ildira, the Mage-Imperator will dispense his justice. Our job is only to deliver them for trial."

"Will you lead the reception, Adar?" the primary protocol officer asked.

"No. That would show him too much honor. I will remain here. My uncle has committed unthinkable crimes. In light of the Designate's recent erratic behavior, I want to keep him isolated."

The gaudy royal shuttle landed in the primary docking bay without incident. Uniformed soldiers and ceremonial guards accompanied the protocol officers as they hurried to accept the Hyrillka Designate's surrender. The warliner's heavy doors sealed shut, trapping the new arrivals.

From the command nucleus Zan'nh observed via his small screens. Seventy members of the reception committee filed in perfect ranks across the open deck to stand in front of the ornate royal shuttle. The protocol officer used a signaler to call his followers to attention.

Three boarding doors of the royal shuttle unfolded. "Prepare to receive the Designate," the protocol officer called.

Suddenly, fully armed Hyrillkan rebels boiled out of every opening. Their movements were chaotic and unpredictable, like a flurry of beetles racing away from a fire.

Zan'nh shouted a warning over the intercom, but the reception committee was already reacting. The protocol officer ordered the soldiers and guards to change formation—just as the Hyrillkans opened fire with shockwave energy weapons. Stun-blasts mowed down the waiting Solar Navy crewmen. They fell like heavy bundles of rags to the deck.

From the command nucleus, Zan'nh yelled, "Send more troops! Full teams to the docking bay, now!"

Rebels continued to pour out of the two shuttles, well over a hundred of them, each one armed. So many! They must have been crammed shoulder-to-shoulder inside the royal shuttle and the military escort craft.

At last, Rusa'h's beautiful pleasure mates emerged, carrying themselves as if they too were hardened warriors. Long knives were strapped to their shapely hips, and they carried energy weapons. Narrowing their eyes, two of the women shot down the primary protocol officer, and he crumpled to the floor.

In the midst of the firefight, a group of attender kithmen scuttled out of the royal shuttle. They carried a portable chrysalis chair that looked exactly like the Mage-Imperator's.

Leaning forward in the counterfeit chair, Rusa'h smiled as he assessed the carnage.

Weapons fire continued inside the docking bay, but the Hyrillka Designate's rebels quickly overwhelmed the crew, taking them all prisoner. Two pleasure mates raced to the door controls before Zan'nh's reinforcements could arrive. The women sealed every entrance to the bay, code-locked the controls, then smashed them to block all access.

Finally the Hyrillka Designate turned to where he knew Adar Zan'nh would be observing him through imagers. He sat back in his reproduction of the Mage-Imperator's royal seat. "Adar, your crewmembers are only stunned. However, I will kill every one of these hostages unless you surrender this warliner to me."

6 ☀ PRIME DESIGNATE THOR'H

After his cargo craft docked aboard Qul Fan'nh's warliner, Thor'h schooled his expression and manner to convey urgent distress, then climbed out, accompanied by seven personal guards.

The Solar Navy troops met him with appropriate courtesy and respect, but Thor'h snapped at the first escort: "Take me to your command nucleus. I would speak with your qul immediately! He must be warned."

The crewmen did not question his orders. Though supposedly disgraced, Thor'h was still the son of their Mage-Imperator. "Follow us, Prime Designate. Qul Fan'nh will be honored to receive you."

Thor'h and his seven guards adopted a brisk pace to keep the escorts moving and sustain a sense of urgency.

Until he had broken free of the tangled bonds of his father's *thism*, Thor'h had not understood that Ildirans were like marionettes controlled by invisible soul-threads. The Mage-Imperator's people simply did not know how to be sufficiently suspicious of other Ildirans. Fools! For one of their people to turn against the Empire was as unbelievable to them as a man's left hand suddenly taking up a knife and trying to cut off his right.

Thor'h knew that just such an unexpected shock was necessary to save the Ildiran Empire from its internal weakness. Because he believed in Rusa'h's vision and knew that his uncle was destined to be the true Imperator, Thor'h would do what was necessary for his race—even if it meant he must turn against his brothers and Mage-Imperator Jora'h himself. If all Ildirans allowed themselves to see the purity and truth of the Lightsource, then this struggle need not be a messy one.

Nevertheless, Thor'h suspected it would be bloody.

His timing was well coordinated with Rusa'h's. When Thor'h arrived with his seven converted guards at Qul Fan'nh's command nucleus, he noted that his uncle's royal shuttle had already been accepted into the flagship warliner. Surprises would begin momentarily.

Standing straight-backed in his Solar Navy uniform, the maniple commander turned to greet Thor'h as he entered the bridge area. Tall and thin, the qul touched his fist to his heart

in salute. "You honor me with your presence aboard my
warliner."

"I thank you for your assistance in this emergency, Qul."
Thor'h strode directly toward Fan'nh, and his seven Hyrillkan guards followed him into the command nucleus. Before
the escort crewmen could enter the bridge behind them, one
of Thor'h's guards spun and sealed the doors.

Everything happened within seconds. Qul Fan'nh
blinked in surprise. The locked-out escort crewmen began to
pound on the door, calling out questions.

Thor'h stepped up to the maniple's commander. A slim
crystal blade dropped out of his sleeve and into his grip.
Without hesitation, he swept his arm upward and drove the
glassy dagger under Qul Fan'nh's chin, deep into his throat.

Eerily silent, Thor'h's loyal guards spread out, drawing
their own weapons. Qul Fan'nh's confused bridge crew
staggered up from their stations, some of them crying out in
shock.

The subverted Hyrillkan guards had practiced techniques
of swift assassination. Their blades flashed. Trapped
crewmembers screamed. One woman managed to trigger an
alarm before two guards fell upon her and slit her throat.

Thor'h didn't need to bloody his hands again. With one
foot, he shoved the twitching body of Qul Fan'nh away from
the command rail. In moments, everyone else in the bridge
area had been slaughtered, and Prime Designate Thor'h took
his place in command of the Ildiran battleship.

Alarms continued to ring through Qul Fan'nh's warliner,
and Thor'h gruffly commanded his fellow conspirators to
shut them off. By now, the rest of the crew was aware that
something had gone terribly wrong, but they could do nothing about it.

"Engage our defenses." All seven of his comrades knew how to operate the weapons systems of a Solar Navy warliner.

Aboard the Adar's flagship, Rusa'h had succeeded in seizing the landing bay. The Designate used the communications systems in his royal shuttle to broadcast a powerful signal heard across all forty-seven of the warliners. "Adar Zan'nh, I am ready to begin executing hostages—one at a time, every three minutes—until you surrender these ships to me."

Most Ildirans could not comprehend such abomination. Smiling to himself, Thor'h wondered how long his brother could hold out against the agony of innocent victims. He doubted Zan'nh, who idolized his mentor, the war hero Adar Kori'nh, would surrender as quickly as Rusa'h hoped.

Thor'h thought of a way he could increase the stakes. His guards moved bloody bodies out of the way and manned the vital stations in the warliner's command nucleus. "Power all of our weapons and prepare to fire. Targeting at my discretion."

On the main screen, he studied the other ships in the maniple, choosing his first target. All of the warliners' weapons systems had been enhanced for direct combat against the hydrogues. The firepower would certainly be sufficient for what Thor'h had in mind.

The good Adar would never open fire against Ildiran citizens—especially not when the majority of those aboard were unsuspecting Solar Navy crewmen. Zan'nh simply wouldn't be able to stand the guilt.

Prime Designate Thor'h had no such compunctions. He could focus on the larger goal and accept a certain level of sacrifice. Forty-six battleships would be sufficient for

Imperator Rusa'h's purposes. At least one of them was expendable.

He prepared to open fire.

7 ✴ ADMIRAL LEV STROMO

The EDF mopped up their operation around the Roamer greenhouse asteroid complex within twenty-four hours. Admiral Stromo settled into the Manta's command chair. Gripping its arms, he shifted his weight and made a conscious effort to look as if he belonged there.

"I'll stay aboard and remain in command while you consolidate the operations down there," he told Ramirez. "Lead teams into the domes and begin rounding up prisoners, just like we did at Hurricane Depot."

Elly Ramirez was all business now, dedicated to the task at hand; she had not complained about the operation once it started. "I recommend full body armor and defensive weaponry, in case the Roamers adopt guerrilla tactics."

Stromo nodded. That was exactly why he wanted to stay aboard the Manta until the captured territory was deemed safe. "So far they haven't shown any propensity for violence, but they'll be desperate. Like cornered rats."

Ramirez summoned her ground troops, all of whom had spent months training at the EDF base on Mars. Many recruits, unable to imagine personal combat against the hydrogues, had considered infantry drills a waste of time. Now, though, they would have a chance to put their training into practice.

An EDF first-strike squad found an access dock on the side of the main dome. Under fire from the Manta cruiser, the greenhouse itself had been breached. Fading wisps of air and moisture circled the rock like morning mist, but for some reason not all the atmosphere had vented. Though external scans showed that the air was still breathable inside the dome, Ramirez ordered her troops to wear environment suits for extra protection. "The Roamers might consider blowing the seals, just to take us out. Better safe than sucking vacuum."

Stromo agreed. "Take every precaution to make sure none of our soldiers are harmed in the line of duty." He didn't want to have to explain casualties to General Lanyan. "Oh, and the Chairman has asked that we minimize Roamer casualties as well."

"Certainly, Admiral." He got the impression that she considered him stupid for making such an obvious statement.

Docking clamps anchored the lead Manta against the asteroid. A tunnel passage sealed polymer lips around the hatch, which a demolitions crew then blasted open. A vanguard of suited troops proceeded cautiously into the asteroid, holding stun-pulse rifles ready for an ambush. Behind them, the second and third wave of EDF soldiers waited, anxious to flood into the Roamer nest.

Smaller consolidation teams had seized and occupied the outlying stations, metal-walled storage depots, domes filled with hardy and exotic crops. The severed solar mirrorfilm drifted until it finally draped like a reflective shroud over a tiny asteroid.

Overhead, battle-ready Remoras cruised in careful circles through the rubble field. Because of the ruptured containment dome, the main asteroid was unstable, wobbling and precessing. The EDF pilots practiced taking potshots at anything that moved, rousting out clan ships that attempted to hide in the shadows of orbiting rocks.

A small vessel lunged away from the greenhouse asteroid like a rabbit bolting out of hiding. The pilot dodged and changed course repeatedly, making up his trajectory as he went.

Stromo sat upright in his command chair. "Stop that ship from escaping!" he bellowed over the general comm.

Six patrol Remoras spotted the fleeing craft and set off in pursuit. From just the glimpse on his external screens, Stromo thought it was a butt-ugly ship, a collection of mismatched parts cobbled together. But the fleeing craft actually *sparkled* as it flew, and its sprint engines took it on high-G-force loops that even fast EDF fighters couldn't match.

Stromo adjusted the flagship's sensors to follow the escaping spacecraft as it shot about like a pinball, ricocheting through the asteroid field, partly to avoid collisions, but probably just to get away. The pilot took ridiculous risks and flew maneuvers unthinkable to Stromo. Before long, the ugly craft left the EDF's best Remoras far behind. It was embarrassing.

"Break off pursuit," Stromo said. "I've decided to let at least one Roacher ship get away to spread the word of another crushing defeat. They've got to change their minds sooner or later." The words sounded false as he spoke them, but he raised his voice to inspire confidence.

He watched the displayed suitcam images as Ramirez led her troops through tunnels and into the domed enclosures.

He could toggle from one recording lens to another in order to get as many views as he wanted. It was the next best thing to actually going out and doing the operation in person.

The people inside the domes put up little resistance. They were outnumbered, outgunned, and—thankfully—smart enough to realize it.

Stromo estimated they would take a few hundred prisoners. How could so many of them crawl around in these rocks? En route to Hhrenni, while planning the details of this mission, he had given instructions for two Mantas in the assault force to reconfigure their decks. Low-ranking soldiers' quarters were turned into holding pens, not secure enough to be prisons, but sufficient to hold the captives until they could be delivered to the Klikiss planet along with the detainees from Hurricane Depot and Rendezvous.

Finally, Ramirez announced, "Admiral Stromo, this asteroid is secure. We're ready to receive you over here."

He stood up and straightened his uniform. "Do I require a suit?"

"No need, sir. Plenty of atmosphere in here, though it's a bit chilly."

Once he made his way inside, he wished he had brought an oxygen mask after all, just to cover the stink. The asteroid air was redolent of metal and dust reprocessed with fertilizer chemicals. It smelled like a latrine. Did these Roamers actually use human feces to fertilize their plants? How barbaric!

Under the damaged main dome, EDF engineers had rigged up light panels powered by temporary battery cells. A cluster of Roamer prisoners stood among ruined plants and gardening equipment. It looked like a hurricane had hit this place.

Stromo squared his shoulders. He enjoyed playing the part of a conquering military leader. "Who's in charge here?"

"I bet you think *you* are," answered one middle-aged man with reddish-blond hair. His round, rough face bore the red marks of a recently worn oxygen mask. Dried blood at his nose and hemorrhages in the whites of his eyes showed that he must have been exposed to the explosive decompression.

Stromo glanced at the blasted hole in the dome. Gummy clots of a translucent substance blocked most of the leaks, though he could still hear air hissing out into space. "I *know* I'm in charge. But is there a particular Roamer I should be talking to?"

"I'm Crim Tylar. You can talk to me as well as to anybody else."

"I intend to make this an orderly evacuation," Stromo said. "We'll move all your personnel to a holding planet. You might even consider it a vacation after living on a floating rock like this."

"We made these asteroids tolerable enough. Until now."

Stromo smiled coolly. "You can use Roamer ingenuity to help establish a new Hansa settlement. A step toward making up for all the times when you shirked your duty to your fellow man." Looking down at the tattered and uprooted plants, he saw fresh vegetables and recognized the bright red color of ripeness. He realized how hungry he was for good, fresh food. "Oh, tomatoes!"

But as he bent over, Crim Tylar stomped on the plant, sending a splurt of red juice and seeds up onto the Admiral's leg. "I didn't grow them for *you*."

Stromo froze, but managed to keep his temper in check. The EDF soldiers would open fire if he gave the order, but he didn't want to let this blow up into an impossible situation, especially with himself in the middle. Instead, knowing it was childish, he snapped, "Roachers don't understand the concept of sharing."

8 ☀ CESCA PERONI

When the Roamer clans scattered, Cesca needed to get the old former Speaker to a safe, isolated place. At Jhy Okiah's suggestion, Cesca took her to Jonah 12, hoping to stay with the small group of engineers there just long enough to gather her thoughts and to come to a decision about what to do.

Only a week ago, Rendezvous had been attacked— *destroyed*—by the Earth Defense Forces. The first wave of chaos and confusion hadn't yet finished sweeping through the dispersed clan settlements, and it would be some time before the Roamer families could be brought together, but as Speaker of the clans, Cesca was determined to establish efficient communications again. In spite of the current turmoil, she planned to get an emergency network in place as soon as possible and had already sent out scouts, temporarily enlisting all of the small mining base's long-range ships to gather and distribute information.

Cut off, the independent clans would be as hungry for news and guidance as Cesca was to talk to them. As soon as she received word back from some of the more important family heads, they would create a provisional council and choose a new center of government. She prayed that the scouts' Guiding Stars would help them get the word out swiftly. If they did not, she feared that the hotheaded clan members who had demanded the provocative ekti embargo in the first place might act rashly, and get themselves killed in the process.

Long ago, the clan leaders had planned for various disasters, and designated several gathering points for Roamers in times of emergency. Although Rendezvous, the primary gathering point, was now gone, Cesca hoped to visit the few that remained in order to rally her people. Unfortunately, only two days after they settled in at Jonah 12, old Jhy Okiah's suddenly declining health forced Cesca to change her plans. Despite the former Speaker's protests, Cesca insisted on staying at Jhy Okiah's side. "This place is as good as anywhere else," she said. "I've sent out messengers, and there's no ship to spare anyway. I'll stay here with you while we wait."

Hydrogue depredations had put the families on higher alert for years—though few had expected that the greater threat would come from the Hansa government itself. Because of this constant state of vigilance, many ships had escaped the Eddy battle group at Rendezvous and were now spreading the alarm to hidden clan settlements, unmarked transport ships, and secret Roamer industrial facilities. By their very nature, Roamers were independent, bound only by loyalties, honor, and a loose system of laws. Rendezvous had been one of their few acknowledged safe havens. Right now, their very looseness and independence made the clans a difficult target for the EDF thugs, but it also created great problems in forming a united front.

But only a week had passed. Only a week. Cesca knew she could consolidate the people, and she hoped the Big Goose would now ease up, assuming the Roamers were broken. But in that, they would be very much mistaken.

Jhy Okiah had thought to hide on Jonah 12, because her youngest son had established the new base here. Not long ago, enthusiastic and ingenious Kotto had drawn up blueprints, run simulations, and convinced clan leaders to contribute funding and labor. The surface of Jonah 12 was made of hydrogen-rich ice, lakes of liquid methane, and other small-chain hydrocarbons that were useful for Roamer industries. And so Kotto had set up operations here, on a frigid chunk of rock and ice in the outer darkness of a system that some early clan explorer had named after a man who'd been swallowed by a whale.

Swallowed in darkness. With everything that had happened to the Roamers, Cesca felt as if she were in a similar situation. . . .

Ambitious workers had set down modular domes in a base that was powered by a small-pile nuclear reactor. Moving like fat penguins, grazers trundled over the uneven terrain, gouging long troughs. Machinery cooked gases out of the harvested ice, sifting out hydrogen molecules that were recondensed for ekti processing; lightweight elements were diverted for colony use or for shipment to other clan settlements. Unwanted exhausts boiled up from each slow-moving grazer like clouds of steam from an old-fashioned locomotive. In the supercold environment, the processed exhaust refroze immediately, settling back down like thick, vaporous snow. Railgun launchers shot barrels of pure hydrogen ice up to a drifting ekti reactor that would catalyze the hydrogen into ekti, the valuable allotrope used as stardrive fuel.

Remembering her son's wild plans, Jhy Okiah had wanted to see Jonah 12 for herself, even though Kotto was currently off investigating a hydrogue derelict found in the rings of Osquivel. His chief engineer, Purcell Wan, temporarily in charge of operations, had provided living quarters for Cesca and the former Speaker.

It had been more than a decade since the old woman had set foot on another planet, and even in Jonah 12's low gravity she was barely able to breathe or move. Cesca suspected that the weight of the recent disaster and their uncertain future pressed on her friend more heavily than gravity did. . . .

Now as she sat next to Jhy Okiah on her narrow bed, Cesca saw that the light had dulled in the old woman's eyes. Watching the EDF ships blast Rendezvous, destroying the connecting cables and girders of the cobbled-together space rocks, had been a direct blow to her.

Inside their small habitation bubble, Cesca made pepper-flower tea for both of them and sat sipping. Jhy Okiah just held the cup in her hand, letting the warmth penetrate her papery skin. Thick transparent windows on the curved side-wall of the chamber showed a fantastic landscape of molded hydrogen ice, but the old woman focused instead through the chamber's skylight, staring at the panoply of stars.

"I suppose I should be cheering you up," Cesca said, "but I've got so many questions in front of me, and every answer I step on seems to be a trapdoor."

The former Speaker's wrinkled, colorless lips formed a weak smile. "Leave your metaphors to the experts, Cesca."

"I feel more qualified to be a poet than a leader." She blew out a long breath to release her frustration. "What a mess! How am I supposed to meet with the Roamer clans? The facilities and settlements are so diffuse, how will I get word to everyone to announce a clan gathering? And where should we hold it? We're all outlaws now. Is it even safe to bring all the families together again in one place? What if the Hansa already found out about our gathering points? Dangerous!" She put her elbows on her knees.

"You're letting impatience get the best of you. Rushed decisions are often bad decisions." She patted Cesca gently on the arm. "It took only a few minutes to destroy Rendezvous, but it'll take a long time to bring the clans together again. Spread the word, and the clans will know eventually."

"But I have to do something. I want to rally the clans, inspire them, tell them not to surrender. If I'm the Speaker, shouldn't I go to Earth and demand restitution?"

"They will seize you and hold you as a political prisoner."

Cesca sipped her tea without tasting it, just for something to do. She fretted. "I should at least go back to Rendezvous and survey the damage . . . if there's anything left at all."

"Those damned Eddies stole our central place and our history." Tears welled up in the former Speaker's eyes, and she drew a deep, rattling breath. "My timing is poor, Cesca. I should have died earlier, when you were handling everything so well."

"Don't talk about dying," Cesca said. "You need to stick around long enough to see how this all ends."

Sitting on her bed, Jhy Okiah squeezed Cesca's hand with surprising strength. "It does you no good to keep relying on me. You will figure out the solutions for yourself." The old woman sighed. "I wish Kotto was here. He always comes up with solutions."

"Crazy ones," Cesca said with a forced chuckle.

"But solutions nevertheless." She set her cup of pepperflower tea on a small shelf, then looked out through the skylight again, as if trying to count the scattered diamonds of distant suns. She suddenly smiled and pointed with one finger. "Oh, look. My Guiding Star!"

Cesca glanced up, following the old woman's gesture, but all the stars looked alike. She felt the sinewy hand clench, and when Cesca looked down again, the light had faded from Jhy Okiah's eyes.

9 ☀ JESS TAMBLYN

E ncased within his alien water-and-pearl ship and protected by the power of the wentals, Jess descended into the raging depths of the gas giant Golgen. He had asked the water elementals to take him here so that he could see firsthand what he had accomplished in his first strike against the hydrogues.

His strange vessel plunged through wispy clouds and tearing winds; vapors scoured the exterior hull. Apocalyptic storms churned through the high-pressure seas of condensed atmosphere where enemy hydrogues had once lived. Seven years ago, as a brash and vengeful human, Jess had dealt a mortal blow to them.

He and his clan engineers from Plumas had fired short-period comets into this planet as if they were cosmic cannonballs. The impacts, like giant thunderbolts wielded by ancient gods, had been unstoppable, the shockwave concussions more destructive than the strongest thermonuclear bombs.

The huge gas ball was still marked with discolored blemishes like gangrenous wounds from the cometary fusillade. The intervening years had not quelled the atmospheric disruption; repercussions would continue for decades at least. The still-angry human part of Jess Tamblyn took satisfaction in that, a measure of revenge for the death of Ross and his Blue Sky Mine, which the aliens had destroyed. . . .

But while he was focused on his past efforts to defeat the hydrogues, he suddenly received flashes of images, alarms, and thoughts from the wentals themselves—a burst of news sent through the interlinked water beings. The message was not clear, but Jess comprehended what was happening: The EDF had attacked another Roamer outpost, the home of Nikko Chan Tylar, who had barely escaped.

Jess's fourteen volunteer "water bearers" were quietly distributing wentals to the lakes and oceans of uninhabited worlds where they were free to grow, and the water-based beings were beginning to expand. Though wentals were similar to the verdani, the worldtrees of Theroc, Jess's volunteers had not been physically transformed to communicate directly with other wentals, as the green priests did with the worldforest.

Nikko was among the most susceptible, and most enthusiastic, of the volunteers. The water entities had allowed him to communicate with them, had even sent a quick alarm about the EDF strike on Hurricane Depot. But Jess doubted his other water bearers could read the details of the call that had just gone out from Nikko through the wentals.

In his own mind, Jess witnessed everything the young

man managed to communicate to the wental water aboard his vessel. The Chan greenhouse asteroids had been seized, the Roamers living there captured, while Nikko himself outran the Eddy pursuers.

Now, as his ship descended into Golgen, Jess wrestled with his obligations. He was still a Roamer, and he felt honor-bound to do something to help—if he could. But the raid on the Chan greenhouses was already over, and so was the destruction of Rendezvous and Hurricane Depot. He could never get there in time to accomplish anything.

His water-and-pearl vessel would certainly startle the Eddy battleships, but he couldn't fight the whole military force, no matter what his powers were. He hoped his sister Tasia was not among the invaders. She had joined the Earth military, but he couldn't believe she was voluntarily preying upon Roamer outposts. Where was she now?

No, Jess knew he couldn't allow himself to grow distracted. Better that he continue his quest to resurrect the wentals. If the hydrogues were not defeated, these petty squabbles among humans would eventually become irrelevant. . . .

Around him Golgen's clouds were impenetrable with stirred ammonia, hydrocarbons, phosphine, hydrogen sulfide. He felt an unexpected fear scrape like sharp fingernails along his bones. The reaction within him came from the wentals' deep-seated alarm as they remembered the centuries of death and near annihilation the hydrogues had visited upon them.

"Strange, but I think we were destined to be allies," Jess said. "Before I ever knew of wentals, I dealt the hydrogues a deep wound. I even used comets—frozen water—to do it. I'd like to see what my comets did."

As the water-and-pearl vessel descended past layer after

layer of convulsing clouds, Jess peered through the translucent bubble. Wispy shreds of vapor pulled away at an equilibrium layer, and he saw startling wreckage: enormous fragments of segmented domes, broken curves that had once been the structure of a hydrogue metropolis. The cityspheres had shattered and imploded from the unexpected barrage.

The eerie alien cities must have been magnificent, and Jess wondered how many hydrogues he had killed in the process. He decided the number couldn't possibly make up for the innocent Roamer victims the hydrogues had slaughtered, or the whole populations of wentals they had eradicated ten thousand years ago.

The wentals said to him, *Now that we are growing stronger, Golgen will be only the first of many victories against the hydrogues.*

In all the wrecked components floating in the dense and turbulent atmosphere, Jess saw no sign of the Blue Sky Mine. The hydrogues had smashed his brother's facility years ago, and he doubted the liquid-crystal creatures had any memory of the innocent people they had slain.

He thought of the last time he had seen Ross proudly riding his own skymine. His brother had been making a surprising success of his commercial venture, proving himself to his lovely young fiancée. *Cesca.* Back then Jess's deepest worry had been hiding his secret love for her, knowing that she was betrothed to Ross. . . .

In his mind, the wental voices offered a curious reassurance. *We will release part of ourselves from this ship into the clouds of Golgen. The atmosphere has enough water molecules for us to spread and sustain ourselves. It will be a slow process, but we can gradually draw a diffuse wental mind together to secure and protect this place.*

Sweat beads appeared on the outside of the water-and-pearl vessel, transmitted through the armored liquid hull. The droplets grew larger and thicker until they flew off like silver bullets into the restless storm layers.

We can calm the turbulence, dampen the disrupted weather, and tame Golgen again. Our wental essence will survive.

"You mean you'll occupy an entire hydrogue world?"

Not completely, but we will be here. Already, wental energy seeps through the clouds, questing up and down to fill the ruined heart of this planet. There are no longer any hydrogues here, and we will disrupt their transgates so they can never return.

"Now I know why my Guiding Star brought me here."

Golgen is safe. You may direct your Roamers to bring their skymines here again and gather all the ekti they desire.

Jess's heart leaped. A safe planet for skymining! "I am due to meet with my water bearers soon, and together we will spread the word."

10 ☀ TASIA TAMBLYN

This wasn't what she'd had in mind when she signed up for the Earth Defense Forces. Not at all.

After her brother Ross was killed, Tasia had sneaked away from her family at the ice mines on Plumas in order to fight the hydrogues. The *hydrogues*. She wanted to be in the thick of things, right in the middle of the war. Isolated on Mars, though, watching over a bunch of bottom-of-the-barrel students, she was as far from the conflict as she could possibly be.

Yanked from her Manta command, Tasia had been sent here to run kleebs through training exercises. What a waste! Admiral Willis insisted it wasn't a demotion, though the new assignment was obviously intended to keep her out of the way while the Eddies tilted at windmills in an infuriatingly unnecessary crackdown against Roamer clans.

Standing alone on the red rock outcropping, Tasia made a disgusted sound into her suit helmet, after making sure the comm was off. General Lanyan's Guiding Star must be a black hole . . . or a whole cluster of black holes, pulling him in a dozen different directions—all of them wrong! Wrong enemy, wrong priority, wrong war.

It hadn't been easy for her to leave her clan in the first place, to leave all the Roamers and her way of life, but she'd done it to fight against the monstrous aliens that preyed upon Roamer skymines—including Ross's. She wasn't like one of the shiny-eyed new cadets from Earth who joined the Eddies because they thought it was glamorous, or because the uniform would help them get laid. Tasia had thrown her not-insubstantial skills in with the EDF because she wanted to hurt the drogues.

The Roamer clans were not timid—hell, they lived in places that would have made most Hansa members wet their environment suits!—but the loose confederation of families kept no organized military force. If Tasia wanted to fight the drogues, then she had to do it with the EDF. Their goals co-incided with her own. Supposedly.

Though she had served faithfully, no one had forgotten her roots. Since Roamers were considered hostiles, Tasia had been pulled to the sidelines, where she set up mock surface battles, guided raw recruits on high-atmospheric drops, and drilled them on tactical exercises in the classroom. Waiting in her bulky and uncomfortable EDF-issue environment suit, she stood facing the mock combat area on the rusty surface of Mars. She had chosen a high vantage from which she could watch the teams. She had deposited them out in the tangled canyons of Labyrinthus Noctis, the "Labyrinth of Night." The troops marched according to coordinated plans, like two sports teams vying for a championship.

At her side, her compy EA stared in the same direction she did; Tasia couldn't tell if the Listener model was actually seeing and absorbing details, or just imitating her owner.

Buzzing ramjet flyers soared through the thin Martian atmosphere, deploying a squadron of parachute troops that leaped out of cargo bays in the low Martian gravity. As they dropped, the troops unfurled gigantic batwings, tough films with sufficient surface area to provide resistance in the thin air. The unexpected parachute assault troopers were landing close to the objective.

"That's an unorthodox trick from Team Jade," she said to EA.

"It is a twist that will probably allow them to win the day's challenge," the compy said. The fact that EA would make such an observation made Tasia hope the Listener compy was at last thinking for herself.

Tasia smiled through her helmet faceplate. "I'll have to commend those soldiers for ingenuity. Doing impossible and unexpected things is the only way the EDF'll make headway against the drogues."

She knew that the large rammer fleet would soon be completed: extraordinarily armored kamikaze battleships to be crewed by Soldier compies. The rammers would tackle the drogue warglobes head-on, one for one. An exceedingly expensive defense, but one that would hurt the hydrogues without a cost in human lives. So far, nothing else had worked. As soon as the big rammers were ready, they would look for the right opportunity. As long as the new vessels performed up to expectations, the Eddies would have a proven new weapon against the drogues. Maybe, if they began to win against the hydrogues, they would finally stop picking on the Roamer clans as a surrogate enemy. . . .

The EDF was having a difficult time convincing people to enlist, and each batch of kleebs seemed worse than the last. That was why the battle groups depended more and more on Soldier compies to fill out their crews.

And Tasia had to groom the rest. What a waste of time! Why should she be forced to train more soldiers who might one day turn against the clans and cause more destruction?

The glider troops landed, stripped off their giant flexible wings, and took up their positions to meet the oncoming second team. Tasia watched them, paying attention only because she would have to submit her own report and analysis of the day's results.

From her observation site, she scanned the teams of trainees running through drills. Most of them were impossibly slow, reacting with clumsy book-learned responses that were a long way from becoming swift instinct. Their lives had been too easy, too comfortable, and their mistakes had rarely had serious consequences. They were not accustomed to a daily awareness that any botched move might bring catastrophe.

Because she hadn't joined the military to fool around, Tasia had risen swiftly in rank. She hadn't coveted medals or promotions, and she didn't play political games, but she worked damned hard and excelled at each tested skill. Though she claimed no political or career ambitions, the advantage to having a higher rank, as she saw it, was that she could do more important things. That was the idea, at least.

But now, thanks to their Roamer boondoggle, they'd pulled her from her Manta command and placed her in cold storage on Mars while the EDF picked on the clans. Couldn't they at least have given her something *useful* to do?

She clicked her helmet transmitter. "Team Sapphire, what are you doing down there? Looks like you're trying to light a campfire!" Despite the lack of oxygen in the air or any form of burnable material, she wouldn't actually put it past them.

"Hadden has a leak in his air tank, Commander. He fell on his back during the last cliff descent, and now we're trying to swap out with a spare tank," said one of the kleebs.

"Pressure's dropping fast!" Another voice, with an edge of panic.

"The speed you're going, you may as well start planning Hadden's memorial service. I could fill out the forms and requisition an EDF coffin while I'm waiting for you to finish goofing around."

"We're bringing in a spare tank, Commander, but I don't know if we can get it up the canyon fast enough. We locked it in a cache when we secured this quadrant from Team Jade."

"Commander, I need to abort the exercise! Call in an emergency rescue lift!"

She scowled. "Instead of hitting the panic button—which will never work in a *real* emergency, dammit!—try some creativity. Find a different way. If his tank is leaking, then seal it!"

"How? We've got nothing but wound sealant in the med-pack, and that's not for use in this cold."

"Slather it on anyway! It's designed to hold up against spurting arterial blood; you can bet it'll clog a pinprick in an air tank. And the cold will keep it harder than a metal weld. Should hold at least until you can get that spare tank humped up to you. If that doesn't work, try something else. Solve the problem." She shook her head, grinding her teeth together to calm herself. "Once you stop the leak, he's got enough air inside his suit's reserve bladder to keep him alive for fifteen minutes even if his tank is empty."

"We'll try, Commander!"

As they jabbered to each other, scrambling to fix the leak, Tasia continued, "In the field, you'll have limited resources. You have to know your supplies and equipment and what exactly they do. Just because a purpose isn't listed on the instruction label doesn't mean you can't improvise."

Not surprisingly, by working together they easily saved the kleeb with at least ten minutes to spare. She refused to let them bow out of the exercise, though they wanted to run back to base and lick their wounds after the close call. Team Sapphire lost a lot of ground, and would probably come in dead last in the scoring, but they had learned something . . . for a change.

Out of the loop on Mars, Tasia gleaned whatever information she could about the continuing stupid strikes on clan outposts. Rendezvous gone, even Hurricane Depot . . .

Tasia had been to Hurricane Depot only once, on a flight

with Ross when she was twelve. Ross had been assigned to guide a water tanker from Plumas, and took Tasia along to show her the Galaxy. He had even let her do some of the piloting—at twelve she was already rated for most of the ships used around the water mines—but he himself had flown the vessel through the gravitational obstacle course to the stable island between two orbiting rocks.

The Depot had been a marvelous example of Roamer engineering, a bustling trading bazaar and meeting point for all the clans. Tasia had eaten exotic foods there, listened to tall tales from clan traders, seen so many people and strange clothes and traditions that she felt her head would explode. She'd always wanted to go back.

And now, after seizing everything they wanted, the Eddies had simply swatted Hurricane Depot out of its stable point and smashed it like a bug. A show of force. A demonstration of General Lanyan's cold stupidity . . .

After that provocation and show of force, the Hansa seemed frustrated that Speaker Peroni had not simply capitulated. Tasia couldn't believe the bull-in-a-china-shop way the Chairman was handling the entire situation. When she was a young girl, she had heard that the Earth military was a bunch of bullies and thugs. Apparently those stories were accurate.

While on board her Manta, and during R&R stops at EDF bases, she had listened to the Hansa's smear campaign against the "treacherous space gypsies." Many stories implied that the clans were in league with the hydrogues because they had cut off shipments of stardrive fuel "solely to weaken the effectiveness of the Earth Defense Forces"— which was ridiculous in so many different ways she couldn't even count them.

There was no official announcement of the newly declared "war" against the clans, but most of the EDF soldiers knew (and celebrated) the recent provocative actions. Still, much as she hated their screwed-up priorities, the bureaucracy and prejudices, and all the ill-advised things they insisted on doing, the Hansa's powerful military was the only force humanity had that might stand up against the hydrogues.

And she hated the drogues more than anything the EDF had done . . . so far.

Unexpectedly, while she watched the teams wrap up their scheduled exercises, a transmitted request and event summary appeared on the small screen of her suit's text unit. "Roamer outpost captured at Hhrenni, numerous prisoners taken at greenhouse domes. Request assistance/reassignment of Commander Tamblyn to liaise with new Roamer detainees and escort them to Llaro. Her background may be useful."

Appended to the formal request, she saw a single line from Admiral Willis, her Grid 7 commanding officer. "Request approved. But only if Tamblyn wants to do it."

Tasia caught her breath. Another Roamer facility trashed? She tried to remember what sort of settlement had been located at Hhrenni and which clan had run it, but she'd been away from that way of life for so long. Even though her last battle had been a debacle—at Osquivel, where she had lost her lover and friend Robb Brindle—Tasia wished she could be out fighting the enemy. Making sure Roamer prisoners weren't abused might be the next best thing.

"Rest assured, Admiral," she keyed into the response window, "Tamblyn wants to do it."

Here on Mars, her talents were being wasted. She was

bored, forced to stay where absolutely nothing was going on. Anyplace had to be better than this.

11 ☀ ROBB BRINDLE

Would the nightmare ever stop in this impossible place?

He had no way of determining how long he'd been trapped among the hydrogues, but Robb was sure his imprisonment had already lasted more than an eternity. The unbroken tedium was almost as bad as the constant fear. Since he was nominally in charge of the group, he led regular workout sessions and skill games to keep up morale as much as possible and keep their minds and reflexes sharp. None of his fellow captives could guess what the hydrogues meant to do to them. Robb wasn't sure he wanted to know.

"I wish that little compy would come back," he muttered. He had said it countless times before.

"We're on a completely different planet now," said Charles Gomez, whose hangdog expression never changed. "Remember, they evacuated us." His eyes remained fixed on the spongy, sloped floor, rarely meeting the faces of his miserable comrades. Gomez had been captured when hydrogues overran the lumber operations on Boone's Crossing, annihilating several villages that EDF ships could not rescue in time. The drogues had snatched Gomez for their . . . experiments? Their zoo? All the prisoners had similar stories.

"The drogues'll never tell us what that emergency was," Robb said, "or where they took us." All he remembered was a flash of light and a lurching sensation. Then the clouds outside the immense wonderland city were different. Still hellish, but different. "I don't suppose standard POW protocols translate into their language."

Robb hunkered down. His wing commander's uniform was stiff and rumpled from countless weeks without washing or changing. The hydrogue captors provided water and rubbery blocks of "food," and somehow the captives' waste was disposed of from time to time, but the liquid-metal creatures did not seem to comprehend the human need for bathing or clean clothes. The transparent holding chamber reeked, but Robb no longer even noticed the smell.

Though there wasn't much hope they could ever set foot outside their confinement chamber, much less discover a way out of the gas giant's depths, the captives followed the unspoken imperative of survival. But they had few resources and even less information. Some had tried to think of ways to commit suicide, surrendering utterly to despair, but Robb was not one to give up. And he did not give up on his companions, either. He wouldn't admit, not even in the back of his mind, that their chances of getting out of this ordeal were incalculably remote.

Workouts and skill games could not fill up the time between sleep sessions, so with nothing else to do, Robb and his comrades had shared family memories, talked about their lives. By now, they knew each other as intimately as if they had grown up together. One man missed his large family with a crippling misery; another woman grieved that she had never had children. Others apologized for past wrongs they had done to people who would never now hear their regrets.

Robb had already shared the news of how the EDF had mounted a terrific attack on the hydrogues at ringed Osquivel, how he had gone down in an armored encounter vessel in a last attempt at diplomacy—but the hydrogues had seized him, and the EDF attack had begun. There had been explosions . . . and he didn't know what had happened after that.

Most of all, Robb talked about Tasia Tamblyn. Of course she must consider him dead by now; Tasia was a tough girl, not given to believing in silly fairy tales. Everyone here had similar longings for their loved ones.

Outside, multicolored chemical and polymer mists drifted through the bizarre geometric metropolis like tendrils of fog. The amorphous quicksilver hydrogues moved like lumps of molten metal, going about their incomprehensible purposes. One of the captives, Anjea Telton, whistled to alert the captives. A trio of flowing hydrogues was coming toward their curved cell.

"This can't possibly be good," said Gomez. Robb didn't argue with him.

The hydrogues rarely communicated with them, and then only with terse commands. None of the human prisoners could understand what the deep-core aliens *wanted* from them.

Beyond the bubble wall, the three ominous beings rose up and shaped themselves into identical forms they had copied from their first victim, who looked like a Roamer skyminer. Two of them carried the halves of a perfectly transparent shell about the size of a coffin. It was empty.

The deep-core aliens stepped against the curved wall and

slowly pushed, easing themselves through the membrane. All the captives shrank away to the opposite side of the chamber, but the hydrogues moved forward. In the confined space, the humans had nowhere to run.

The hydrogues selected one of the prisoners at random, Charles Gomez, and closed in, carrying the opposite halves of the man-sized container. The third hydrogue gestured the other prisoners away. Gomez tried to flee, but could not get around the creatures. The drogues encircled their hapless subject like hunters using nets to capture a specimen.

"What are you doing?" Robb shouted at the aliens. "What do you want with him, or any of us?" The hydrogues went about their business without saying a word, as if simple communication was beneath them.

Robb threw himself forward. "Leave him alone! Leave us all alone!" He closed with the third hydrogue, landing a punch against its quicksilver amorphous body. His fist unexpectedly sank into the shimmering liquid metal.

He let out a shriek as unbearable cold shot through his fingers, hand, and wrist. Staggering back, he withdrew his arm from the quicksilver creature. The skin of his hand crackled with ice, steaming as it began to thaw. Nerve pain continued to scream into his brain, but he couldn't move his fingers. He sank to the floor, nursing his hand.

Robb looked back up in time to see the two halves of the coffin container seal tight, trapping Charles Gomez inside, like a mummy in a sarcophagus. The walls of the container must have been thick, for though the victim thrashed and pounded and shouted, no sounds escaped.

The hydrogues carried the coffin container to the curved wall, where they slowly melted back through. The chamber membrane shimmered and then solidified behind them, allowing none of the external pressure in. Robb cradled his aching hand and joined his fellow captives as they pressed against the transparent wall.

Outside, another group of hydrogues had hauled a much larger object forward, something made by non-hydrogue hands. Despite the horror and confusion around him, Robb's face lit up. "That's my encounter chamber! The hydrogues kept it."

A flood of unreasonable optimism rushed through his brain. "What if they're taking Charles into the diving bell? Maybe they'll pressurize it and let him go."

"Don't be ridiculous," said Anjea Telton.

Robb shook his head, refusing to give up hope. He had experienced too much despair over the past months of being trapped here. But even if the diving bell was shot back up to the clouds—of whatever planet they were inside now—how would Gomez ever get to a human settlement or even another ship?

"They might've arranged some sort of hostage transfer," Robb said. "The military has done it many times before. Maybe the drogues sent another emissary, like the one that killed King Frederick. Maybe they've arranged a cease-fire or peace terms. Maybe—"

But when he saw what the hydrogues were doing, his excitement drained away into a bottomless pit. The creatures stood around the transparent coffin and activated a vent on the sides, slowly letting in their own atmosphere.

Trapped inside, Gomez began to struggle and pound even more furiously.

"What are they doing?" Anjea said.

"They're gradually increasing the pressure. They're opening up his chamber to the outside environment."

"That'll kill him."

"I think that's the idea."

Inside the coffin-shaped transport bubble, Gomez grew wild. The hydrogues looked down at him, as if studying his reaction for later discussion. Gomez pounded, kicked. His mouth stretched open in a scream. His eyes were wide and bulging.

"Stop it!" It was useless, and Robb knew it. The other captives moaned or cried.

As the pressure continued to increase, Gomez finally ceased his thrashing. His eyeballs hemorrhaged, and blood began to run out of his nose and ears. By now all of his internal organs must have been crushed. Robb blinked tears from his eyes. He wanted to look away from the horror, but couldn't.

The hydrogues didn't stop there. Even after Gomez had been killed, they continued to let the atmospheric pressure grow greater and greater, until the dead prisoner's body began to snap and implode, all of its structure breaking down.

It took almost ten minutes for the body to be squeezed into a gruesome paste. Then the three implacable hydrogues unsealed the halves of the coffin and upended it to pour out the gelatinous pulp. The reddish mess, spangled with splinters of bone, spread out in a heap outside among the hydrogues' geometrical structures. The three quicksilver figures stared at the runny mess, as if waiting to see if it would form itself into a body like their own. Instead, the organic matter that had been Charles Gomez simply bubbled and oozed.

The hydrogues finally left. What had they hoped to accomplish? What had they expected? Was it some sort of cruel experiment? A torture? A punishment, or even amusement? Robb didn't speak; the other captives remained sullen and silent.

"We'll never get out of here alive," Anjea said.

Then, as the remaining prisoners backed toward the rear of their protective chamber again, the hydrogues came forward to take another experimental subject.

12 ☀ ADAR ZAN'NH

From his command nucleus, the Adar stared in disbelief at the images from the besieged docking bay. His escort troops, protocol officers, and reception committee lay sprawled on the deck, cut down by stunners or beaten senseless. The doors were sealed, all access blocked. Rusa'h had barricaded himself in with his hostages, and demanded the impossible.

"Get our engineers and constructors working. I want them to break through that door. Recapture my docking bay." Grudgingly Zan'nh added, "Keep the Hyrillka Designate alive, if possible . . . but do what you must."

Teams outside the sealed doors were using cutters and prybars, but the barriers had been designed to hold even against an explosion.

Knowing Zan'nh was eavesdropping, the Designate

showed no compassion, not a trace of emotion, as he ordered his rebels to gather the stunned reception committee. Rusa'h sat in his imitation chrysalis chair, directing his followers. "You have little time remaining, Adar. Surrender this warliner, or I will begin executing captives."

Zan'nh found it inconceivable that his uncle would do such a thing. But he had already slain Pery'h. . . .

The Adar called to his communications operator. "Have we heard from Qul Fan'nh? Warn him that the Prime Designate may also attempt treachery. I do not understand what is happening here, but we dare not trust Thor'h."

"No response from the first warliner, Adar. The qul does not respond to our communications."

An icy fist gripped Zan'nh's heart. Was he already too late?

"Your time is up, Adar," Rusa'h announced, leaning close to the imager so that his expressionless face filled the screen. "By hesitating, you force me to demonstrate that my demands must be taken seriously."

Attender kithmen moved his chrysalis chair to give the imagers a full view. The Designate raised a hand, and two of his brainwashed guards dragged the groggy primary protocol officer into view. He had not yet fully recovered from the effects of being stunned. "This one will be first."

Zan'nh observed with growing alarm. How far would Rusa'h carry this mockery? "Uncle, wait! Allow me to—"

The Hyrillka Designate gestured calmly and sat back in his cushions. The two guards slid crystal blades from jeweled sheaths at their sides, then moved with mechanical efficiency. One stabbed the protocol officer in the chest. The other drew the sharp edge along his throat. Arterial blood poured out in a foaming stream. The two guards released the body, letting the dead man slump to the deck plates. They stood back, their uniforms splashed with Ildiran blood.

Zan'nh gasped. Two of his officers in the command nucleus became noisily ill. "You . . . you have killed—"

By commandeering the imaging network, Rusa'h had transmitted the gruesome scene to every crewmember aboard all forty-seven warliners. "In another three minutes, I will execute a second victim. I should point out that as the effects of the stunners begin to wear off, the hostages will feel the agony of death more acutely. The reaction through the *thism* will then be more painful to all of you."

"Stop this!" Zan'nh demanded.

"You know how to stop it, Adar. I urge you not to let the slaughter continue." His voice was bland, smug.

On a private channel, Zan'nh demanded of his security crew, "How soon can you break through?"

"At least a standard hour. This is solid metal plating."

"Bekh!" The fist squeezed tighter in Zan'nh's chest, and his mind raced for options. Through the *thism,* his father would be able to sense the danger, but not the details . . . only that something was wrong. He wished Adar Kori'nh could be there to give him advice. What would his mentor have done? How could he put an end to this? Designate Rusa'h was insane!

Three minutes thundered by.

Zan'nh had intimidated human skyminers. He had traveled to disaster-stricken colonies, and he had performed intricate war-game maneuvers. He had fought hydrogues. But this hostage situation, the cold and blatant threat of murder after murder, had paralyzed him as if he were no more than a novice. Zan'nh had heard of wild, irrational behavior by human heroes and madmen, but never an *Ildiran*. He had no experience with incomprehensible situations like this.

In spite of such heinous, inconceivable behavior, the Hyrillka Designate was still the Mage-Imperator's brother. He was still an Ildiran.

But Zan'nh did not dare allow the rebellious Designate to seize these warliners. What did Rusa'h intend to do with the ships, that he was willing to commit murder to gain them? Without fresh victims, though, Rusa'h would have no leverage. To prevent greater failure, should Zan'nh just coldly sacrifice all seventy hostages, let the Designate and his rebels slaughter them?

How could he live with that, stand by and do nothing? He was the Adar of the Solar Navy! Those hostages were his loyal soldiers. He had led them into battle against the hydrogues at Hrel-oro. After they had been hammered by the enemy aliens and suffered the devastating loss of an entire warliner, Zan'nh had brought them to Hyrillka so they could regain their strength and confidence. How could he fail again? How could he abandon them?

"It is time for your second lesson," the Designate said. "You have wasted time, and three minutes pass so swiftly."

Zan'nh shouted into the speaker. "No! Let me send in an aide to discuss your demands—"

Rusa'h was not interested in listening. "There is nothing to discuss, nothing to negotiate. I have been perfectly clear." His followers dragged forward a struggling female guard this time. "Eventually you will learn, Adar. You have always been intelligent, nephew, though deluded by the Mage-Imperator."

They stripped the female guard of her body armor and left her vulnerable. The effects of the stunner had worn off completely by the time they raised their assassination knives.

"I ask again, Zan'nh—do you yield?" Rusa'h said. "Do you surrender these warliners to my cause?"

"I cannot." He struggled to find steel within him. "You must not have access to—"

The Hyrillka Designate nodded, and his followers once again stabbed and slashed. The female guard gurgled as she bled to death; her body fell beside the first victim on the deck.

Each death tortured him like a red-hot needle in the eye. Zan'nh felt the screaming response resounding through the *thism*. He felt her die.

"How many more bodies must you pile up, Adar? You know you will surrender eventually. How many more useless executions will you face?"

"We will defeat you," Zan'nh said through clenched teeth. "And each murder adds to the list of your crimes."

"My crimes are as nothing. The false Imperator Jora'h will also face judgment for leading the Ildiran people astray."

Privately, Zan'nh transmitted a plea to the other commanders aboard the remaining warliners. He still had not heard from Qul Fan'nh, or Thor'h. "I want solutions, ideas. Does anyone have suggestions?"

When Zan'nh was younger, Adar Kori'nh had led him in military drills using human war-game scenarios to see how Ildirans responded to changed situations. Zan'nh had been promoted because of his innovation. But now viable ideas eluded him. He could not think what to do. "Can we flood the compartment with an anesthetizing gas?"

"We could rig that, Adar," said one of his engineers, "but the airflow modifications would take longer than cutting through the door itself. We're making progress, but not quickly enough. We don't have that long. The Hyrillka Designate is not leaving us the time we need."

"He knows that. It is why he forces the issue at such an impossible pace."

Much too soon, Rusa'h said, "Three minutes have passed again, Adar." He raised his hand. Though Zan'nh begged him to wait, to negotiate, the Designate ordered the murder of a third helpless member of the reception committee.

"What are we to do?" the engineer asked. "We could open the outer hatch and shut down the atmosphere field. That would kill the Designate and his followers, end this standoff—"

Zan'nh interrupted. "And all of the hostages. I'm not willing to accept that solution. Find me another one."

Two of Rusa'h's steely-eyed pleasure mates wrestled a fourth victim forward. In their shapely arms the women held a groggy guard captain who had been hit with two stun-beams. One of the wickedly smiling pleasure mates held her crystal knife to the guard's throat, touching the point to his thick skin.

"Look at this man, Adar," Rusa'h said, sounding very sincere. "You hold his life right now. Your next decision will result in his death, or his freedom."

"I will not accept the blame for this insane behavior!"

"Less than a minute remaining." Rusa'h acted as if he had all the time in the world. "I ask again: Do you surrender your maniple?"

"Tell me what you have done on Hyrillka! Why do you need these warships? The Solar Navy has always defended your planet. What is the purpose of—"

"I would be happy to explain myself later, but I've given you my terms. Your time has run out once again. I will not tolerate your stalling while you search for a way to stop me."

He gestured, and the pleasure mate rammed her knife under the guard's chin and up into his brain. He fell without a gasp, his eyes cold even as they dimmed in death.

Another resounding jolt tore through the *thism*. Zan'nh bit back an outcry as lances of pain shot into his mind.

Unexpectedly, the voice of Prime Designate Thor'h came over the channel. "Uncle, my brother needs a greater incentive. He still does not understand how far we will go."

To his dismay, on the screen Zan'nh saw his brother surrounded by traitorous guards in the command nucleus of Qul Fan'nh's warliner. Around them, splatters of blood and tumbled bodies of soldiers lay on the deck.

He felt sickened. "Thor'h!"

"Take the time to understand, brother—hear what Imperator Rusa'h has to say. Then you will comprehend our motives and see that we are correct."

"Stop killing my crew, and I will consider it."

"The Adar seems to be under the impression that he is able to bargain," Rusa'h said.

"I will demonstrate for him how little bargaining power he has, Imperator." Thor'h turned to the blood-spattered guards. "Open fire as ordered."

Qul Fan'nh's warliner unleashed a merciless volley of kinetic-energy projectiles and energy beams. They slammed into the hull and engines of the nearest warliner. The huge Ildiran warship exploded, flame fronts and deadly decompression slaughtering thousands of crewmembers aboard.

The flash of light blinded Zan'nh, and he reeled backward against the command rail. The deaths played a cacophonous arpeggio of pain on his nervous system, crippling him. The screams through the *thism* were deafening. A full warliner! Thousands and thousands of innocent sacrifices!

Inside the besieged docking bay, Rusa'h said coldly, "You have three minutes, Adar Zan'nh."

13 ✸ ORLI COVITZ

Grieving and forlorn, Orli felt as devastated as the ruins of the Corribus colony. The girl stood by herself in the whistling breezes that picked up as soon as darkness fell. The wind careened along the narrow channel of the main granite-walled canyon, sighing plaintively. It carried the smell of smoke and burned flesh, along with moans that sounded like ghostly screams.

Orli was utterly and completely alone, the only person on an entire planet. Everyone she'd known here was dead, her fellow colonists, the few children her age, even her father. She was the only survivor of the massacre.

The Corribus settlement, once filled with dreams and possibilities, was nothing more than burned wreckage, melted debris strewn around what should have been a place of hard work and hope. Even the ancient Klikiss ruins had been obliterated. She had no place to go. And the images were fresh and raw in her mind.

Wandering off by herself, Orli had spent a day exploring isolated cliffside caves far down the canyon. From her high, safe vantage she remembered looking back toward the human town being constructed on this empty world as part of the Hansa's new transportal colonization initiative.

Without warning, the deadly EDF battleships had swept in, using the Hansa's greatest weapons to blow up the buildings and mow down the colonists. When the ships had landed to see the results of their devastation, black Klikiss robots had filed out accompanied by Soldier compies. Methodically seeking out the few hardy survivors who had managed to find scraps of shelter from the initial onslaught, the merciless robots had killed one after another after another, until everyone was dead.

Too far away to help, terrified for her own life, Orli had only been able to watch. A part of her had wanted to run out and fight the robotic attackers, or at least scream at them—but she was smart enough to keep herself hidden. Orli had huddled, shivering, until the evil machines packed up their EDF ships and flew away, leaving her here. Alone.

Had anyone ever been so stranded? Orli knew the planet was empty except for their tiny settlement. Their group had been the first to come through the transportal doorways and establish a Hansa presence on Corribus. Though she had to check it for herself, Orli assumed the destructive robots had obliterated the transportal too, blocking off all contact from the rest of human civilization. No one could come through to rescue her. No one on the outside even knew of the attack.

On the first night, she found the corner of a fibrous cement wall that had been erected millennia ago by the insectoid Klikiss race. Though blackened and crumbling, it formed a shelter where Orli could hold her knees and put her head down. She trembled as she waited out the night. Fear and ragged nerves prevented her from sleeping. Often she heard frightening, crackling sounds or the slumping collapse of walls as the last fires of the horrific assault nibbled away at the remaining structures. Nothing moved, nothing lived.

Though no one could hear her, she cried for a long while, wiping her nose with grimy knuckles, until she was shaky and weak, her throat raw. Orli had never been a needy person, but now she missed her father terribly. Jan Covitz had loved to make up solutions to every problem, though he managed to implement few of them. He'd had an infectious smile and a warm good cheer. Many people had liked him, but few had ever relied on him.

She wanted to be with her father, wanted him to hold her and rock her to sleep while he spun tales of his bright dreams. He would know what to do.

At that, Orli sighed, and her lips curved upward in a bittersweet smile. No, Jan wouldn't know what to do at all. Left on his own to survive, he might have been worse off than she was. But that didn't matter. Orli wanted him at her side.

"If wishes were horses, girl," her father had often said to her, quoting dusty old wisdom, "then all of us would ride."

In the darkest part of the night, still wide-awake, Orli heard what sounded like whispering voices, quickly muttered comments coming from the rubble of the long-empty Klikiss city. She sprang to her feet and ran out of her meager shelter, stumbling over broken rocks.

"Hello?" she tried to call, but it came out as more of a cough. Too much crying and too much smoke had made her voice raspy. She could barely hear her own hoarse shout. She tried again, gained a little more volume. "Is anybody out there? Anybody?"

Running as fast as she could in the darkness, barely seeing obstacles in the starlight, Orli made her way toward the

alien ruins. Pebbles pattered down from the crumbling structures, then a larger stone shifted and clattered to the ground.

Abruptly, a hopeful call withered in her throat. What if it
wasn't a survivor she'd heard? *What if one of the robots had
stayed behind?* The deadly machines were efficient murderers—they had demonstrated that quite adequately. They
could have left one of their number hidden, an assassin, just
to wait for someone like Orli to creep out of a hiding place.
And then it would kill her.

Her heart thudded in her chest. Standing frozen in the
darkness and feeling completely vulnerable, she waited and
waited, afraid even to breathe, intent on any sound. Why had
she called out? Stupid girl! She needed to be more cautious.
She certainly wouldn't survive long out here if she kept
blundering around and expecting things to turn out for the
best.

She tried to swallow, but her throat felt as if it were
clogged with dusty rags. Inside her head, Orli counted to a
hundred, but no further sound came from the ruins. Then another clatter of small stones.

Eventually she decided it was just shifting debris. Nothing emerged from the rubble, no hulking black machine, no
sleek and deadly Soldier compy. The only tiny sounds in the
night were from small creatures, rodents or insects.

Or hungry predators?

Orli made her way back to the shelter, picked up a rock,
and hefted it in her hand to gauge how well it might serve as
a weapon. It would have to do. She stared toward the dark
horizon, waiting and waiting for the sun to rise. . . .

The next morning, her eyes red and her muscles sore and
weak, she picked her way through the holocaust site. She
went first to what was left of the local transmitting tower

where her father had proudly taken up communications duties for the colony. On their arrival here, she had sat with him as he waited for incoming signals, tracked the logs of Hansa ships, took inventory of their existing supplies, and made wish lists to give the cargo traders.

She tried to dredge up even a speck of hope in her heart, but she had seen the explosions. As she dreaded, her father's transmitter hut had been obliterated. There was very little debris for her to sift through, only a few scraps of metal and polymer. She was glad she wouldn't be able to find her father's body, if it was in there.

The intense heat from the weapons' bursts had melted the soil itself into glass. It reminded her of the burnt-sugar crust on a fancy crème brûlée dessert she'd once shared with her father, after he'd gotten a modest windfall payment for something or other. Orli's eyes stung, and she shook off the memory.

Next she climbed over fallen debris, smearing her hands, arms, and clothes with greasy soot, until she reached the wall that had contained the functioning Klikiss transportal. As expected, the alien machinery had been blasted to rubble. Intentionally. She would never be able to get away from Corribus.

Each time she came upon a new disappointment, another one of her remaining threads of fragile hope snapped.

Finally Orli went to what was left of the structure she and her father had started to call their home. The destruction in the settlement was so tremendous that she could pinpoint the house only by locating known landmarks, counting foundations, and tracing the remnants of paths until she came to a charred pile of collapsed support frames and structural bricks that had been her hut.

She found a few burned scraps of clothing, two cooking pots, and—mercifully—six packets of food that her father had kept to make a special dinner for them one day. Orli tore into the packets and ate the flavored protein. She had not realized how desperately hungry she was.

Under a fallen wall, she found two sealed bags of the preserved giant mushrooms she and her father had farmed on Dremen. Another one of Jan Covitz's get-rich schemes. They had planted the fungi, which quickly grew out of control. When none of the other colonists wanted to eat the gamy-tasting gray flesh, Jan and Orli had been forced to abandon the mushroom farm and grab the lifeline of the Hansa colonization initiative. She had disliked the cold, damp, miserable world . . . but if they'd remained there, despite the hardships, she felt sure that her father would still be alive.

Orli held the bags, feeling the rubbery fungus lumps inside. Her stomach suddenly roiled and heaved, but she clamped her teeth shut and swallowed repeatedly, breathing through her nose, fighting off the nausea. She wanted to be sick, but she had just eaten and didn't dare vomit up what might be her last supplies. She knew she needed to keep the food down, because she required the nutrition to survive. And Orli *did* intend to survive.

Pocketing the mushroom packets for later, she pushed herself to keep looking. She did not think about her furry cricket, the innocuous hairy critter she'd kept as a pet, until she found the smashed cage and its dead inhabitant underneath a fallen beam.

It was too much. Again, Orli allowed herself long minutes of unabashed crying, not just for her pet, but for her father, for all the colonists, for the whole obliterated settlement. Eventually her grief turned to sobs of misery—

for her lost home, for her loneliness, for the hardships ahead. Suddenly she stopped. There was no one to hear her sorrow, no one to take care of her, and she had nothing to gain by feeling sorry for herself. Instead, the girl made up her mind to scrounge for anything the attacking ships had not destroyed, anything that might help her stay alive.

First she took apart her collapsed house, one brick and one beam at a time. As she rummaged through the wreckage, gathering the few intact items, she was surprised to discover her battered music synthesizer strips. Against all odds, the instrument still functioned and the battery pack retained enough charge for at least another week or two.

She spent the next day going through every burned pile in the town, picking up odds and ends—first-aid kits, a small bowl, more food packets, scraps of metallized cloth, a length of wire—never knowing what might be helpful. Toward evening, she managed to get one of the automated water-pumping stations working again and gulped fresh water greedily. Orli considered going back to the high cliffside chamber, where she could hide if the marauding robots came back, but it was too far away, and she didn't want to be so isolated, though she held out little hope for rescue.

She made her camp in a clearing near her wrecked house, and there she waited day after day. Orli spent the evenings playing mournful tunes on her synthesizer strips. The notes wafted upward like the sad cries of a lonely bird.

Less than a week after Orli started keeping track of time—the first few days were still a blur—a figure walked out of the wilderness of grassy plains.

In the dusk the scarecrowish silhouette marched through the tall whispery pampas, unafraid of the creatures that lurked out there. The man paused and lifted an arm as if to shade his eyes, but didn't seem to see her. He trudged closer, carrying a long stick like an old wizard's staff, using its end to sweep the grass out of his way.

Orli crouched in the ruins, certain that this stranger was some assassin in league with the robots. But then she could tell from his movements, his shape, that the stranger was *human*. Another person on this abandoned tomb of a world?

Or did the robot attackers have human collaborators? She shuddered and ducked behind a twisted support frame from a storage hut, unable to imagine how anyone else could have survived the attack. She convinced herself that someone must have spotted her campfire, heard her music, seen her moving. Now he was coming to get her, and she would be killed just like all the others.

But he was just one man—a scrawny old man from the looks of him. She found a thin length of metal she could use as a club. It felt solid enough in her hand. Trying to look as fierce as a bedraggled and red-eyed fourteen-year-old girl could, she lifted the club and stepped out of her hiding place to face the stranger.

She immediately recognized the old hermit Hud Steinman, who had befriended Orli and her father on Rheindic Co before their group of colonists transferred here. Once he'd gotten to the colony, the old man had set off on his own, wanting nothing to do with crowds and small-town politics. Of course! His distant bivouac on the prairies would have kept him far from the attack!

Before she could think what she was doing, Orli shouted and waved, rushing headlong toward the unexpected figure. When she called his name, her cracked voice sounded like a wail. "Mr. Steinman! Mr. Steinman!"

He stopped, stunned at first by the destroyed settlement, and now taken aback by this dervish coming toward him. He propped his staff against the ground and waited for her to reach him. She threw herself into his arms with such vehemence that she almost knocked him over.

"I saw the smoke, saw the big ships," he said, trying to hold her at arm's length. She was filthy, her clothes torn and sooty, her face streaked with dirt and tears. "Tell me what's going on, kid."

"I was exploring the caves at the end of the canyon when the big EDF ships came. They blasted the whole colony—the buildings, the people, the—"

"EDF ships? Are you crazy—"

"I saw them land, and they were full of compies and Klikiss robots. They killed anybody they found." Her voice hitched. "Everybody." She looked over her shoulder. "There's nothing left."

Steinman stared toward the sheltered canyon that had once held a burgeoning Klikiss metropolis, and more recently a fresh new Hansa colony. "You'd better stay with me for the time being, kid. I wasn't looking for company, but you're not a bad sort. And you sure look like you could use some help."

Orli didn't argue with him. They gathered the salvaged supplies she had collected, and then Orli followed the old man out onto the plains of Corribus.

14 ☀ QUEEN ESTARRA

After speeches and a gala send-off, the King and Queen waved to the crowds as they boarded a Hansa diplomatic transport to Ildira.

Already settled in before the fanfare began, Chairman Wenceslas was at work in his cabin with the door locked, ignoring the show outside. He'd never had any interest in stealing the spotlight; he preferred to work behind the scenes.

Peter hurried Estarra to their own quarters, hoping to avoid the Chairman's notice—though obviously Basil didn't want to be bothered by the royal couple, either.

Without asking permission, Estarra had brought one of the small potted treelings from the Whisper Palace's conservatory. Peter had agreed to help her smuggle it onto the diplomatic transport and hide it in a cabinet in their quarters.

"I brought this one myself from Theroc, when I came to marry you," she explained, stroking the golden scaly-barked stem. "Since we're about to meet the Mage-Imperator, it seems a fine gift for him. You don't mind?"

"Basil won't like losing one of the treelings."

"Nahton is the court green priest, and *he* said this wouldn't affect the performance of his duties," she said, sounding bolder than she felt. She had already run through the arguments in her head. "Besides, Sarein is bound to return from Theroc soon. She can bring more treelings with her."

Estarra secured the potted container as their craft began

to accelerate out of orbit, escorted by several old-model EDF Manta cruisers. She and Peter both hated to be in such close quarters with the Chairman; they knew what he was capable of. Basil had never denied trying to kill them, and the friction between the Chairman and the King remained unresolved. And she was very nervous that Basil would learn their new secret.

"It's going to be a long trip to Ildira," Estarra said.

Not long ago, she had discovered that she was pregnant, which was cause for both joy and fear. Once she'd quietly confirmed that she was carrying Peter's baby, Estarra had revealed the news to him.

Though the pregnancy was unexpected, she certainly wanted the child, and so did Peter. Basil had imposed birth-control measures on the couple, but no method was entirely reliable, and accidents happened. It wasn't their fault.

But Chairman Wenceslas did not tolerate "accidents"—unless he staged them himself.

As pressures mounted from the hydrogue war, the recalcitrant Hansa colonies, and the outlaw Roamer clans, Basil demonstrated his increasing edginess and irrationality. There was no telling how he might react upon learning the King and Queen were due to have a royal heir, especially one that *he* hadn't planned.

"He'll find out sooner or later, but let's keep it a secret for now." Peter had whispered the faint, breathy words in her ear one dark night as they held each other close. "As long as we can. Otherwise Basil has too many options—and not many of them are beneficial to us."

Secrets. She was growing to hate them. Estarra had grown up in the peaceful worldforest on Theroc. She had a close family and many friends among the green priests.

She'd never been good at keeping secrets. But now her life, or at least the life of her child, depended on it.

Peter noticed the slight changes in her behavior, her appearance, her appetite. She needed to use the privacy chambers more often and suffered from occasional nausea. The subtle signs were there to indicate a pregnancy. Aboard the diplomatic transport, so close to Basil Wenceslas, she was terrified she would let something slip. The Chairman usually watched everything so closely.

However, as the journey progressed, Basil kept himself wrapped up in business matters, engrossed in the documents and news briefings displayed on his datascreen. For such an expert in political and business matters, the Chairman did not seem to know or care much about personal details.

Peter shocked her when he actually went out of his way to ask Basil to join them for the evening meal. "You're tempting fate," she said to him in an urgent whisper. "Don't call attention to anything!"

But the Chairman predictably brushed aside the invitation, and Peter gave her a knowing smile. In a low voice, he said, "If I *didn't* ask him, he might join us unexpectedly. Offering to spend time with Basil is the best way to make sure he leaves us alone."

"You two have a very twisted relationship."

"Yes, we do."

On the second day en route, when Estarra walked with Peter down the ship's main corridor, they unexpectedly encountered the Chairman as he stepped out of his cabin. Estarra felt as if they were children who had accidentally disturbed their father in his study.

Peter flashed his most dazzling smile at the Chairman. "Basil! I was just curious—I haven't heard a report in some time. Has there been any more word about the Soldier compies? You said you were going to verify that the Klikiss programming contains nothing harmful."

Basil frowned as he stepped back into his quarters. "The matter is under review, and no cause for your concern."

Peter gave a knowing nod. "You taught me to use answers like that to avoid giving any information."

Basil narrowed his gray eyes. "Then that's one lesson you remember, at least. Try to pay more attention to the other ones." The Chairman sealed himself in his quarters.

Estarra looked at her husband, wide-eyed. "Do you have to provoke him?"

"I can't let him forget that I know his game." Peter slipped his arm around her waist. "No matter how much I despise Basil, those Soldier compies still worry me. I know he's just as uncertain about them as I am—but because the EDF can't do without the Soldier compies, Basil doesn't *want* to find anything wrong with them. The war effort couldn't afford to lose them. He's not stupid, though. Even with all his reassurances, I doubt he's ignoring the threat entirely."

"He just doesn't want to tell you what he's doing?"

"Because that would validate my suspicions. He'll never admit that. I've still got OX digging into the matter, but lately his time has been committed to Prince Daniel."

The two of them crossed to the forward observation deck to watch as they approached the seven suns of Ildira. The pilot had detected unusually violent flare activity in one of the stars, a component of the Durris triple sun, and therefore chose a course that allowed them to enter the core Ildiran systems along a completely different vector.

They sat in plush chairs on the observation deck to watch the streaming stars. Surrounded by the endless wilderness of space, Estarra felt alone and vulnerable, far from Earth and far from Theroc. She clutched Peter's arm, and he held her close, reassuring her without words, though he was in over his head as much as she was.

Estarra tried to take heart from the knowledge that they would soon be in the fabled city of Mijistra, in an ancient alien empire that had remained stable for more than ten thousand years. Among the Ildirans, as guests of the Mage-Imperator, she was sure that all their troubles would seem far away.

15 ✺ ADAR ZAN'NH

After Thor'h opened fire on the doomed warliner, explosions continued as bulkhead after bulkhead ripped open. Aboard the flagship, Zan'nh clutched the railing to keep his balance against the torrent of screams from the helpless Solar Navy crewmen as they died.

Trapped and desperate, he could barely catch his breath, but he squeezed out the words. He could think of no other choice. "Thor'h! I will—I will destroy your ship! I will order all my warliners to open fire!"

Thor'h just chuckled. "Do you think I could believe such absurdity? That you or your crew would slaughter the innocent crewmembers of this warliner, merely to eliminate me and seven rebels? *This* ship is full of your own Solar Navy soldiers. Remember that. Ildirans do not fire on Ildirans." He laughed again. "You have neither the strength nor the nerve. It is an alien concept to you."

As if to prove his appalling resolve, Thor'h launched a second volley against the already dying ship. The unnecessary stream of explosives tore the remaining shreds of the Ildiran battleship's hull into smoldering droplets of slag that drifted in random trajectories, propelled by dwindling momentum.

Through the *thism*, the deaths of the last crewmembers plunged like hot knives into Zan'nh's back. Across the comm channels of the remaining forty-six warliners, Solar Navy soldiers wailed, unable to accept the impossible reality.

"Your pain must be unbearable, Adar," the Hyrillka Designate said, his tone a mockery of compassion. Then, as the seconds ticked away, Rusa'h ordered more hostages to line up for execution in the docking bay. "I appeal to you again—surrender your ships and put an end to this suffering." When Zan'nh did not answer, the Designate heaved a sigh. "Two minutes left. Shall I have Thor'h prepare to destroy another whole warliner? Or would you prefer I made a more personal, bloody sacrifice on your own decks? Thousands of victims? Or one?" He dangled a tantalizing pause. "Or none? You choose."

From the flagship's command nucleus, Zan'nh cried out in anguish. Not long ago he had endured as many deaths on Hrel-oro, victims of the hydrogues. But this time *Ildirans* had just slaughtered all of those soldiers. Ildirans! The very idea was inconceivable after ten thousand years of history.

"Adar! Please make him stop this!" one of his bridge officers cried.

The mad Designate said in a taunting voice, "It has been another three minutes." Even before Zan'nh could look up to the screen, the pleasure mates killed another hostage, and warm blood spilled into the Adar's mental network. The screams continued their relentless, dissonant symphony in his mind. The Adar could not regain his mental balance. He could not reach a decision. It was too much, too fast, too impossible. He was suffocating.

But he was Adar of the Solar Navy. He must not allow a maniple of warships to fall into the hands of this insane rebellious Designate. He must not—

Thor'h transmitted from the bridge of the captured warliner, "My weapons systems are powered and ready, Imperator Rusa'h. Shall I target a second warliner? We would still have an acceptable force if we were left with forty-five ships—or even forty, should the Adar continue to force our hand."

"Thor'h, you may destroy another entire warliner," Rusa'h answered from the captured docking bay, "if it proves necessary. Adar, what say you? Thousands of lives are in your hands—whether Thor'h targets another ship, or you yourself order the destruction of the lead warliner. *Thousands.*"

Zan'nh called hoarsely over the general channel, "Evasive maneuvers, all warliners! Keep away from Thor'h's ship. Amplify shields to maximum."

Thor'h chuckled. "That won't do, brother. You'll never guess which one I might target, and these augmented weapons are designed to crack hydrogue hulls—they can certainly penetrate your own shields."

In the corridors outside the docking bay, extraction teams continued to work at the wall. Zan'nh demanded an update. "Still at least forty minutes, Adar."

His throat clenched. Forty minutes was enough time for Rusa'h to kill more than a dozen additional captives, enough time for Thor'h to destroy several warliners—unless Zan'nh ordered the destruction of the rebel warliner, murdered all the thousands of helpless innocent crewmen. . . . And, even once the assault team broke into the besieged docking bay, the Designate's rebels would go down fighting. More of his crewmembers would die in a deadly shootout, including many of the hostages.

More blood, waves and waves of it! This was simply unacceptable. Could capitulation buy him more time to make a plan? He couldn't be sure.

"Bring the next victim. And Thor'h, prepare another warliner target," Designate Rusa'h said with a disappointed sigh. "More deaths on your hands, Adar. Just imagine how you will be remembered in the *Saga of Seven Suns*."

"Stop!" Zan'nh cried. "If I . . . if I yield for now, do you swear not to harm more of my crew? Will you order Thor'h not to shoot any more warliners?"

"I never wished to kill them, Adar," Rusa'h answered, the epitome of reason and sanity. "Such a foolish waste. But I do require your Solar Navy for my own purposes. I am forced to these drastic measures only because I must have your cooperation."

Zan'nh had stalled the rebel Designate past the allowed three minutes, and Rusa'h noticed as well. He turned to the bloodthirsty pleasure mates. "Kill another one . . . and draw out the pain, if you can. Perhaps this will be the last. Our Adar must learn to make decisions more quickly and firmly."

The crystal knives were raised. A female protocol soldier stared up at her captors in resentful resignation. One of the vicious pleasure mates yanked the captive's head back to expose her throat.

"I yield!" Zan'nh shouted. "If you swear not to kill any more of them, then I yield." *For now.*

The pleasure mates froze, looking to Rusa'h for further instructions. They seemed disappointed. The mad Designate turned back toward the imagers to look the Adar in the eye. "Your surrender must be unconditional. Command all captains of the remaining warliners to surrender their ships to Hyrillka. You are the Adar, and they will obey you."

"Not without conditions," Zan'nh insisted. "Give me your word—as a son of a Mage-Imperator—that you will not harm them."

Rusa'h considered this. "Very well. As long as you cooperate, I will not kill or injure members of the Solar Navy crew—and I have no intention of harming you either, Adar. You would make a fine partner in our cause."

"I will never join your insurrection."

"Then at least he will make a good hostage," Thor'h pointed out. "Since we no longer have Pery'h."

Zan'nh clenched his hands, struggling to find some way out of this nightmarish situation without watching another several thousand crewmen die. At the moment he saw nothing else he might do . . . but that didn't mean he might not find a solution later. Time. He needed time.

Someone among his crew would find an opportunity to recapture the warliners. Even after he ostensibly took control, the Hyrillka Designate couldn't have enough followers to stand against all the Solar Navy soldiers. In order to command the forty-six remaining vessels, Rusa'h would need trained crews, experts. The small group of rebels could not control this battle group for long.

The situation would change. It had to.

Zan'nh knew he had been defeated for now, but it was only temporary. He would trust his abilities and his crew. Ultimately, they would find a way to escape and bring Rusa'h and Thor'h to justice. But at the moment, Zan'nh could not tolerate any further loss.

Thor'h had been right. The Adar could not stomach ordering his own warliners to open fire on Qul Fan'nh's first battleship. To achieve victory by committing such a sin was unconscionable.

With a sick heart, Zan'nh turned to his communications officer. "Let me address all ships." The words tasted like poison in his mouth. "Attention all septars, all warliner captains. Surrender your warliners to Rusa'h and his rebels. You will not be harmed. I have given my word that we will not resist."

For now, he repeated to himself. *For now.*

16 ☀ CELLI

When Celli looked at the figure made of animated wood, she couldn't help seeing her brother Beneto, who had departed from Theroc almost eight years ago. The golem's features were a perfect replica of the calm and smiling face she remembered from her childhood. Her facsimile brother's expressions were the same, though his movements were jerky and unpracticed.

Preoccupied with the ruin of the worldforest around her, Celli hadn't realized how much she missed him. After learning that the hydrogues had killed her brother last year on Corvus Landing, Celli had never imagined she'd see him again.

Now the Beneto golem stood in the clearing under the rebuilt fungus-reef city, staring with grain-swirled eyes at the gathering crowd. Celli was sure he could do something to help them all. The people watched the apparition in amazement. The green priests stared in hope and confusion at the strange and wonderful emissary from the worldforest.

"You are all connected to the worldforest," Beneto said in a voice that could never have come from a human throat, yet it had a vaguely familiar timbre. "We are satellites of the trees, bound by telink. After the hydrogues destroyed me and my entire grove, my spirit lived within the nurturing mind of the verdani."

Climbing down from the fungus-reef city, Celli's older sister Sarein came to watch and listen. Though she was the official Theron ambassador to the Hansa, Sarein seemed uncomfortable here in the damaged forest, as if she had forgotten about the trees and remembered only cities and shops and palaces and Hansa boardrooms. Sarein had come home to help, but with obvious reluctance. Celli knew her sister would much rather have been on Earth dealing with the subtleties of politics than with the unending recovery efforts.

Seeing the replica of her dead brother, Sarein seemed entirely at a loss. Celli felt like giggling at her stuffy sister's discomfiture.

Beneto, covered with vibrant woodlike flesh, was a man-shaped manifestation of the worldforest, a mobile extension of the great trees. The role was perfect for him. Celli remembered her brother's joy in serving the sentient trees, before he had gone off to be a steward of the grove on Corvus Landing. Now, reincarnated like this, he seemed to relish the feel of beaten earth under his feet. He could move his arms and legs, even smile with pliable lips when he saw his parents, his sisters. And the trees could experience everything through him.

"A spark of all green priests lives inside the memory of the trees," he continued to the fascinated audience. "I carry a seed of every previous green priest, yet I still have my own memories and personality intact." The golem reached up with blunt wooden fingers to touch the contours of his face. "Beneto," he said, as if reassuring himself of his own identity.

Celli hunkered down next to her good friend Solimar, sitting with her limber knees pulled to her chest, and let her arm touch his. He nudged her, and she nudged him playfully back. Enjoying Solimar's closeness, she leaned against the broad-shouldered young green priest. He grinned.

Around them, the worldforest remained oddly silent. For months, teams of Roamer engineers had worked to clear deadwood, establish irrigation trenches, shore up retention walls, and plant soil-matrix mats of fast-growing grasses. But only a few days earlier, the work teams of Roamer engineers had packed up and departed, fearing that the Earth Defense Forces would hunt them down here, even though Theroc was supposed to be an independent world. Reluctantly, they had left the Therons to complete the restoration of their devastated forest.

Celli could see the forest still had far to go in its recovery. Why did the EDF have to cause problems at a time like this?

"The worldforest knows its danger," Beneto said, his

voice portentous. Her brother did not seem to breathe at all. His chest did not rise and fall, but he took in enough air to make his words. "The hydrogues know where to find us, and they will return. They will not forget their vendetta against the verdani. We cannot adequately defend ourselves. Therons and Roamers alone cannot protect us, nor can the Earth Defense Forces. Therefore, we must do something new to ensure the survival of the worldforest."

The priests reacted anxiously to the news, though none of them pretended that the hydrogues would simply forget about them. Many glanced toward the cloud-dappled skies, as if warglobes might descend at any moment.

Celli's uncle Yarrod stood next to her parents, looking grim, though now that she thought about it, she couldn't ever remember Yarrod having much of a sense of humor. Alexa and Idriss couldn't hide their excitement at seeing their son, even if he was no longer their flesh and blood.

"I speak for the trees now. That is why I have been grown from the heartwood, to come among you—and to ensure that the verdani survive." He swiveled his head. "I call on the green priests to begin an urgent dispersal now. Instead of planting the new treelings here on our burned and barren slopes, distribute the worldforest to as many safe planets as possible."

Sarein reacted with delight when she heard the suggestion. Celli could see the gleam of excitement in her sister's eyes. This would be quite a political triumph for Sarein, who, for some time now, had been trying to encourage more green priests to ride Hansa spacecraft, where their telink communication skills would prove invaluable for the timely exchange of information.

"The Hansa will be glad to assist your efforts by carrying the trees and green priests on its ships," Sarein blurted.

"Planting more treelings and distributing green priests will expand the communications network across our colony planets." Obviously, she wished the green priests would stay aboard the ships themselves, but she would be happy enough to bring this small victory back to Chairman Wenceslas.

Beneto nodded ponderously. "This endeavor will keep the verdani alive—no matter what happens here."

Celli whispered to Solimar, "It's kind of like that old story of Johnny Appleseed, wandering the countryside and planting trees, spreading orchard after orchard."

Yarrod remained anxious. "But if we take the treelings offworld, how then will we restore Theroc? Isn't that our priority? This is our home!"

Beneto paused for a long moment, as if receiving messages from the widely dispersed worldforest. Then, with his swirling bronze eyes, he looked strangely at Celli and Solimar. "We can achieve both. The forest here has great power. To recover from these great wounds, it needs only to be awakened again."

17 ☀ DENN PERONI

With the EDF hunting down Roamer traders wherever they found them, the ringed gas giant Osquivel, a designated gathering point, seemed one of the safest places for the clans to congregate. Here, a giant Eddy battle group had been defeated by the hydrogues, and the military wasn't likely to come back anytime soon. As far as the Hansa knew, there had never been any clan operations here, so why would they bother to look again?

Denn Peroni flew the *Dogged Persistence* to the shipyards run by clan Kellum. He had no doubt that plenty of other outlaws would come here to grumble with indignation, to wait and plan. He hoped his daughter Cesca, the Speaker of the clans, might be here. He didn't even know if she had survived the attack on Rendezvous. . . . And if she was alive, had she escaped or been captured? No one knew where the prisoners had been taken, and the turmoil was still spreading.

Only a few days ago, Denn had been on Theroc helping the people rebuild their worldforest settlement, when Nahton, the green priest from the Whisper Palace on Earth, had delivered the astonishing news about Rendezvous. Mother Alexa and Father Idriss understood that Denn and his fellow workers were now at risk. "Chairman Wenceslas knows you are here assisting us," Alexa had said. "You must leave. We can't protect you if the EDF comes."

Denn had felt sick inside. "There's still plenty of work to do, but we don't want to put you in the middle of this. You've already suffered enough."

And so the engineers and construction specialists had vanished into the stellar distances. First Denn had gone to Plumas, hoping to find Cesca there; instead, he found one of the old Tamblyn brothers running the water mines, and the two of them had flown to Osquivel. They hoped some sort of organization might be occurring; Del Kellum had always gotten things done.

"Shizz, the Eddies are pissed off at the drogues, so

they're lashing out at anything in reach—and we happen to be convenient targets," Denn muttered to Caleb beside him. Now the Roamers had no customers and no external economy—and the Big Goose still didn't have its ekti.

Caleb Tamblyn scratched his gray-yellow hair; for a water miner, he seemed awfully stingy using the stuff for washing. "Damned stupid politics!" he said with a snort.

While Denn tried to dress the part of a respectable trader, Caleb paid little attention to his appearance; in fact, much of the "embroidery" on his clothes was really just patches and stitches that repaired rips in the worn fabric. Denn would never have been seen in public like that, though Caleb had already made several snide comments about him being a "dandy." Obviously, they saw things from drastically different perspectives.

"Damned stupid politics, you bet. Say, Caleb, didn't your niece Tasia go join the Eddies? Maybe we can get in touch with her through a back door—"

Caleb flashed an angry glance back at him. "Don't confuse her with one of those goose-stepping morons. Tasia went to fight the drogues at the start of this bloody war. She didn't have anything to do with this."

"How can you be sure?"

"Because she's a Tamblyn!" He grumbled under his breath, "What more do you need to know?"

Not wanting to press the issue, Denn kept his silence as he carefully guided the *Dogged Persistence* through the obstacle course of Osquivel's outer rings. He was not surprised to see dozens of other Roamer ships already there. Many had reached the same conclusion: This was the safest gathering point.

With his blustery voice, clan leader Del Kellum personally

welcomed the *Persistence* and announced a meeting of all available family representatives. "Since we can't have any more clan gatherings at Rendezvous, we'll do our best here, by damn! Somebody's got to get organized and make decisions."

After Denn docked his ship among the other vessels, he and Caleb met a harried-looking organizer who assigned them sleeping quarters in an outlying administrative asteroid. The two men each took a shower of distilled cometary water (which Caleb claimed was far inferior to Plumas water, though Denn noticed no difference at all), then made their way to the central complex for the meeting. Denn greeted friends and acquaintances from his trade runs, while Caleb found longtime water customers from the Plumas water mines. Despite the camaraderie, all of the Roamers were tense and unsettled.

Talking with clan representatives in the largest meeting hall, Denn was disheartened to learn that they all expected *him* to have news about the Speaker. "I am as isolated and disoriented as the rest of you. I have no idea where my daughter is."

"It's not like anyone had time to send out memos while evacuating Rendezvous," Caleb pointed out.

"At least you figured out to come here," raven-haired Zhett Kellum said, standing next to her father. "We've sent out messengers, hoping to get an overall picture of what's going on."

"If we don't hear from the Speaker soon, we'll have to make plans without her. Since we cut off all trade with the Big Goose, our families need new markets to supply and purchase vital goods." Kellum slipped a beefy arm around his daughter's shoulders.

"Cesca will get in touch with us as soon as she can. I'm sure she's already sent out word, but it may take a while for any message to be disseminated," Denn said. "But I agree that we can't wait. We have to start deciding what to do right away. So how do we deal with the Hansa?"

Kellum put his hands on his hips. "We're holding some EDF soldiers, by damn—if we want to use them as bargaining chips. We rescued them here after the Big Goose got its butt kicked by the drogues."

"Not that they've written us any thank-you notes." Zhett gave a sour laugh. "It's been more like playing host to thirty-one princesses." Then she lowered her eyes. "Except one of them died in a bungled escape attempt, which just made the rest of the bunch angrier than ever."

"No reason to avoid calling them POWs now," Caleb said. "Tit for tat. Who knows how many Roamer hostages the Big Goose grabbed at Rendezvous. Or Hurricane Depot."

"And they're still doing it," another clan head said. "They just hit the Chan greenhouses at Hhrenni."

Denn made a disbelieving sound. "The Big Goose is letting rabid dogs do its decision-making."

"Yeah, and those rabid dogs have huge ships and lots of weapons," Caleb pointed out. "We don't."

"We might have something eventually," Kellum said. "We've got Kotto Okiah studying the systems of a hydrogue derelict we found here in the rings. Pretty soon now we'll know what makes the drogues and their vessels tick, by damn." Though the meeting hadn't actually started yet, listeners coalesced around Kellum. "Then we'll have something to use against the Eddies—or at least against the drogues."

"Let's think about this a minute before we get ready to go

to war," Denn cautioned. "We're traders first and foremost, not soldiers. We find resources, mine metals, produce stardrive fuel, and we used to sell a lot of our product to the Big Goose. Now that we're not doing business with them anymore, are we going to curl up and whimper?" He raised his fist. "Or are we going to find new customers? It's a big galaxy."

"Would you listen to him," Caleb grumbled good-naturedly. "He sounds just like the Speaker."

"Like daughter, like father," Denn quipped. "In fact, *I'll* volunteer to sneak to some outlying Hansa colonies cut off from regular supplies. I know for a fact that settlements like Yreka have no great love for the Big Goose. They'll keep their mouths shut and trade for whatever we can supply."

Caleb scratched his gray-blond hair, which was still damp and clumpy from his shower. "I wouldn't be averse to setting up a few profitable black-market operations with people who've never done us any harm."

A grin formed in the nest of Kellum's salt-and-pepper beard. "By damn, if we're going to do that, we might as well also send representatives straight into the Ildiran Empire too. The Big Goose throws around the patriotic line that we're supposed to help 'our own people,' but after their attacks I don't feel bound to that anymore. Does anybody?"

The answer was a resounding No.

"We're Roamers. We can do it," Caleb called. "What else do we have to trade?"

Denn shrugged. "I've got a whole cargo of worldtree wood aboard my ship."

18 ☀ TASIA TAMBLYN

As she reached the convoy intercept point in space, Tasia kept thinking about how this new assignment could easily cause friction. Even so, she didn't regret her decision to take over escort duties for the new Roamer detainees taken from the Chan asteroids.

"Are you sure about this, Commander Tamblyn?" Admiral Willis had asked her as she packed up to leave the Mars training base. "You're not likely to win any popularity contests. Those people won't be happy to see a fellow Roamer wearing an EDF uniform."

"Can't say I'm happy about current EDF policy myself, ma'am. However, I can serve the detainees better than someone who might be more . . . gullible about the overblown stories in the media."

The old woman had smiled with her thin lips. "You are always refreshingly frank and outspoken, Tamblyn. But you didn't answer my question."

"I'd rather see that the Roamer captives are being treated fairly, even if some clan members think I'm a Judas." Tasia looked unflinchingly back at the steel-haired admiral. "Besides, anything beats cooling my heels on Mars. The moment there's an opportunity for a real mission against the drogues, I want to be first in line for consideration."

"You're already high on my list for that, Commander. Everybody knows your abilities. But for the time being, this assignment is all I can offer. Make some lemonade."

So Tasia led a convoy of personnel carriers to pick up the

Roamer captives. She'd been shocked and angry when she learned of Admiral Stromo's pointless raid on a bunch of undefended greenhouse domes—using her own Manta cruiser! That was adding insult to injury.

At the intercept point in space, Stromo dumped off the detainees and then went off to his next stop, the recalcitrant Hansa colony of Yreka. While escorting the flustered and unsettled captives to a Klikiss holding world, Tasia hoped to remain on the bridge of the lead carrier for most of the voyage, since she was reluctant to face the prisoners. What was she supposed to say to them—that she was sorry the Eddies were out of control?

It was a long journey.

The captives were sure the Big Goose would throw them onto some hellish penal colony where they'd be forced to perform slave labor. Once the convoy reached its destination, the captive Roamers would see that their situation wasn't so awful after all. At least Tasia hoped that would be the case. She herself had never been to the abandoned Klikiss world of Llaro.

She could have taken the detainees to a closer planet with a transportal and shipped them through the gateway to Llaro, thereby saving the ekti costs of such a massive personnel-transport operation. But her ship was also loaded with supplies and heavy equipment for the new Hansa settlement there, so the plan had made sense to the EDF bean counters and schedulers, and Tasia knew better than to argue with bureaucratic logic.

En route, she kept to herself, though she frequently thought about going among the detainees to talk with them and give reassurances. She supposed, though, that that might only provoke them. No matter how many explanations or excuses she made, the captive clan members would see only a Roamer in the same uniform worn by the soldiers who had wrecked their homes.

She didn't fraternize with her fellow EDF crewmembers either, and not just because she outranked them. They did their duties on shift, ate together in the mess hall, but generally treated Tasia with a cool formality due to her Roamer connections.

At least she had EA as a friend, even if she had to recreate their history and friendship. On the evening before their approach to Llaro, the small robot stood inside the commander's quarters just off the bridge. Tasia dropped heavily onto her bunk and leaned forward, propping her elbows on her knees. "Now, I know you don't remember any of this next story, so I'll tell you in as much detail as I can. I won't embellish it too much."

"You would not deceive me, Master Tasia. I'm very eager to listen."

She chuckled. "Your memory might have been fried, but my human brain isn't completely reliable either. Okay, this is how I remember it, anyway." Pausing to repaint the picture in her head, Tasia let out a long breath. For weeks now she had spent hours daily with EA, reminiscing, telling the little compy about all the times they'd spent together, recounting the adventures they'd had. Giving her a secondhand past was better than nothing at all.

Despite her reassurances of honesty, Tasia did in fact censor her descriptions. She suspected the Earth Defense Forces might be monitoring her room, eavesdropping on private conversations in hopes that she would let slip some important detail about the clans or their whereabouts. The EDF simply didn't trust her. Tasia had given them no concrete reason to question her loyalty, but neither had she made any secret of how she felt about their offensive against the clans. Her superiors had stripped her of her Manta command, ostensibly to avoid placing her in an awkward situation "where loyalties might be conflicted."

And indeed her loyalties were torn. Before the Osquivel offensive, she had secretly dispatched her compy to warn the Roamer shipyards that a military force was on its way. EA had successfully delivered her urgent message, but something must have happened to the compy on the way home, because when she returned, her imprinted memory had been wiped. Tasia sometimes wondered if the Earth military had triggered the fail-safe amnesia programming that all Roamer compies contained. . . .

So now, when she recounted the compy's life story for EA's own benefit, Tasia used no names, no coordinates, no clues that might give the Eddies a lead to follow.

"I was nine," she said, "and it was one of the most important days in my life. In your life too." The compy's glowing eyes remained fixed as EA listened with seemingly rapt attention. "My two brothers took us out in a boat onto the cold underground sea. Jess was eighteen, I think, and Ross was twenty-three. Our father wanted them to run the family water mines together, but Ross had dreams of building his own ekti harvester on a gas giant. Since I was so much younger, I didn't spend a lot of time with them—they had responsibilities, and I was just a kid.

"I could tell that they had something special in mind. Ross guided the boat away from the ice pack, to colder water that wasn't directly under the artificial suns in the ice ceiling. All four of us on a stable boat—including you, EA."

"I am glad I could come along."

She remembered the Listener compy sitting motionless, like a prim lady on one of the seats. Tasia, Ross, and Jess wore warm clothes, their cheeks pink from the chill. She pictured the frigid water—still liquid but barely above the freezing point. Reflections from the high cavernous ceiling and the distant sloping walls of the giant air pocket turned the sea a gunmetal gray.

"Ross took the boat out into the deep water, where we played a game. We ignited lightsticks, then dropped them overboard from different parts of the boat. We'd watch the lights sink deeper and deeper, until something ate them."

"Ate them?" EA asked.

"Even under the frozen crust, quite a few creatures lived in the liquid waters, especially large primitive nematodes— soft, fat worms longer than my leg. The light from the sinking sticks attracted them like fishing lures. It was a race to see whose stick would last the longest. That day, I won." Her eyes sparkled.

EA processed the information as if she were trying to recall the incident. "Were the worms dangerous?" Tasia was thrilled that the little compy was becoming interactive again.

"They never bothered anybody, not that I can remember. But I remember you were a little uncomfortable being out on the boat. You had fallen into the deep water once before, and we had a hell of a time rescuing you."

"You have told me that story already."

"Well, after the nematodes ate our lightsticks and the game was over, Ross turned to me and said, 'Jess and I both have important duties these days, kid. But just 'cause you're our little sister doesn't mean you get to spend every day doing nothing but playing.'

"And Jess said, 'It's time you had a few responsibilities

of your own, Tasia. Someday you might be running this whole clan. But we want to start you out a little smaller, by making you responsible for one thing. One very important thing. And we'll see how you do.'" Tasia leaned closer to the compy. "Do you know what that was, EA?"

"You have not yet told me."

"My brothers gave me *you* that day, EA. First you belonged to Ross, and then Jess sort of took over, but they thought you and I needed each other more." Tears stung her eyes, and she was glad her compy could not decipher the sudden shift of emotions. "And they were right. We still need each other."

"Will you tell me what happened to Jess and Ross?" EA asked. "Where are they now?"

Tasia's throat felt sore as she swallowed hard. "That'll be some other time, EA. Some other time."

In nightmares for years now, she had tried to imagine Ross's last moments in the high clouds of Golgen, his skymine falling apart all around him in the drogue attack. With Ross and her father both dying in rapid succession, Jess was the only one she had left. But, other than a brief message beamed to EA that their father had passed away, she'd had no contact from Jess since she'd joined the Eddies.

She had no idea where her brother was now. She wouldn't know where to find him even if she had been free to do so.

What did the other Roamers think of her? Surely her volunteering with the Hansa military had caused an initial scandal among the clans. Her choice had been understandable when the hydrogues were destroying Roamer skymines, but now, with the Eddies attacking clan facilities, her people must despise her as a traitor. Had they written her off entirely?

Or worse, had they just forgotten about her?

Several levels below, the passenger decks were full of disgruntled Roamer detainees on their way to a holding planet. She could talk to them anytime she liked . . . whenever she got up the nerve.

19 ✸ CESCA PERONI

Standing out on the dark and frozen surface of Jonah 12, Cesca felt colder and emptier than ever before. Two days had passed since the death of the former Speaker, and there was no longer any reason to delay.

She had hoped that some of the messenger ships might have returned by now, but the icy planetoid was isolated even for a Roamer base, and there hadn't been enough time. No other clan leaders would be arriving to pay their respects. The dispersed outlaws didn't even know about the passing of Jhy Okiah, and Cesca had no long-range vessels left to send out with the news.

As the Speaker for what remained of the clans, she had to do this herself now. Old Jhy Okiah had long planned for such a time, had tried to prepare her protégée. No one could have given Cesca better advice, but even so, she was in uncharted waters. She would rise to her obligations; Roamers always found a way to get through tough situations.

Dozens of workers suited up and joined Cesca outside the habitation domes. The Jonah 12 personnel had ceased their ice-excavating and hydrogen-distillation activities, and all but the most distant ground rover teams had returned to base. The group trudged away from the complex and the small power reactor so they could attend the old Speaker's funeral.

On a flat stretch of ice far enough away to minimize any hazard to the domes, railgun launchers regularly shot canisters of concentrated hydrogen up to the automated ekti reactors. Now, though, one launcher's trajectory had been altered to send a special package on an endless journey out to deepest space.

Sixty of the workers gathered in respectful silence and stood together in cold shadows. Behind them, the warm yellow beacons from the base domes provided a welcome contrast to the stark whites and grays of the outer landscape shrouded in low-lying methane fog.

Cesca stood next to the wrapped package that held the old woman's body, feeling both lightheaded and incredibly heavy at the same time. Making sure that the suit's comm was off, she spoke quietly, as if Jhy Okiah could somehow hear her. "I hope you continue to think well of me even now that the Roamer clans are in far worse shape than they have ever been. Our people deserve nothing less than my best, so I'll use what you've taught me to find a solution." She squeezed her hand into a tight fist in the insulating glove of her suit. "Somehow."

Left in charge of the base, Purcell Wan busily checked the launcher, ensured that the wrapped body was ready for its final interstellar journey. The railgun was a simple reaction-mass system that could lob containers far from the small planetoid's gravity. "I increased the power and the range, Speaker Peroni.

It'll easily provide escape velocity. Jhy Okiah will go far, far from here, out in space where she belongs."

Since he couldn't see her nod behind the shadowed face-plate, Cesca acknowledged verbally. She drew a deep breath to compose herself before she flicked on the suit's line-of-sight comm so she could address all of the gathered Jonah 12 workers.

"We are Roamers, all of us," she announced aloud, struggling to remember the words she had tried to rehearse. "We have always been independent, exploring places where no one else would look, making lives for ourselves in the face of adversity. Jhy Okiah showed us how to do that. She led with her wisdom and by her own example. Her many children have succeeded among the clans, leading, working, and serving. Her youngest son established this very base."

"I wish Kotto could be here," Purcell groaned. "He doesn't even know about his mother." Murmurs of acknowledgment echoed across the communications systems.

Cesca added her own affirmation. "In her last words, the former Speaker said she could see her Guiding Star. Her spirit has flown on its final journey. Now let her body also soar free. Jhy Okiah will become an eternal roamer among the stars, forever drifting from place to place."

The rest of the memorized words failed her, so she stepped back, gesturing with a gloved hand. Purcell gave instructions to two of his workers, who operated the launcher. Lights flashed from shifting fields, and the tightly wrapped body moved down the long rails.

With a silent flicker of acceleration, the irregular cylinder of Jhy Okiah's body sailed upward in a gentle streak. Its reflective blanket glittering silver, the body flew with enough velocity to snap the thin threads of Jonah 12's gravity.

Cesca leaned backward so she could turn her faceplate to the black and starry sky. She wished Jess could be with her now. Where was he? Would he ever come back to her?

The shining trail of the projectile dwindled until it became nothing more than a fast-moving star among all the others in space. The panorama made Cesca recall all the other Roamers who had perished over the centuries in their quest to disperse across the Spiral Arm and find their own freedom away from Earth . . . a freedom that was even now being stolen from them.

She wondered where her father was. She'd last seen Denn Peroni working in the forests of Theroc. Did he know what had happened on Rendezvous? Roamers should know to gather at certain central points, such as Osquivel, Braddox, Constantine III, and Forrey's Folly. Now, more than ever, their messaging and rumor network would need to serve to keep the clans connected. She reminded herself not to expect it to happen swiftly, though. Consolidation of the shattered government would take time, as Jhy Okiah had reminded her.

Standing beside her, the Roamer workers remained silent, watching. The weight of the loss hung heavy over them. They waited for Cesca to make the first move, but she didn't know what else they expected her to do.

Before she could tell them to return to their tasks, one of the hemispherical grazers came toward the launcher at a rapid clip over the uneven ground. Normally, the lumbering vehicles merely crawled along, spewing steam and exhaust from digesters and distillers. But this grazer's harvesting systems were turned off so that it could move in rapid mode. Maybe the driver had realized he was late for the funeral.

"Now what's going on?" Purcell said. He and Cesca stepped forward to meet the harvester as it approached. "Whoever's in that grazer, identify yourself. Has something happened?"

"This is Danvier Stubbs, vapor miner. I've been driving all day from the other side of this planetoid!" the message came back, crisp and clear. "Jack and I made an interesting find—it's the damnedest thing. We need to get more equipment and prepare an official expedition. In fact, you might want to send an extra team or two, Purcell. The damnedest thing!"

Cesca interrupted, her voice loud and firm. The funeral had left her feeling unsettled, and she was in no mood for such vagueness. She expected that they had discovered a mineral-rich pocket of ores or some pure hydrocarbon veins. "This is Speaker Peroni. Please be specific. What have you found?"

The grazer crunched to a halt near the crowd at the launcher, spraying thin steam from its mobile treads. "Well, I sure can't explain it," the man said. He laboriously cycled through the double hatch, then raised his gloved hands in confused excitement. "We found *Klikiss robots* buried in the ice. A whole bunch of them."

20 ❄ ANTON COLICOS

T hough he was a scholar who had studied both human and Ildiran legends, Anton knew that myths and stories were not reality, and people did not automatically become heroes in times of crisis.

But looking at the distraught group of Maratha survivors

trudging across the bleak landscape, he saw that his confidence might be the only thing keeping the few remaining Ildirans alive in the darkness of an empty planet.

The members of the skeleton crew had been stranded here after sabotage destroyed the power generators in the domed city of Maratha Prime. Then more sabotage had wrecked two of the three shuttles as the refugees tried to fly to safety. Now only eight of them remained.

The small party trekked across the planet's cold nightside. The Maratha Designate, his bureaucrat assistant, and the lens kithman stumbled together in grim silence. Rememberer Vao'sh walked with the digger Vik'k and two agricultural kithmen. Anton took the lead beside engineer Nur'of.

"Right this way," Anton said brightly through the protective suitfilm. He pointed at the distant horizon. "Straight on until morning."

"We cannot cross a continent in only a few days," the bureaucrat Bhali'v grumbled.

"We covered a lot of distance before our ships went down, so we aren't necessarily far off. And we've got enough supplies."

"Rememberer Anton is right. Our suitfilms will work for several days, even without drastic conservation measures," Nur'of admitted. "It is possible that we may make it."

Anton set a brisk pace as they plodded along. He still found it amusing to think of himself as a *leader*!

The Ildirans seemed on the verge of panic, wanting to bolt forward until they either reached the dawn or dropped from exhaustion. Anton did his best to keep them all focused and under control.

From above, the barren plains of Maratha had appeared featureless, but here on the ground, tumbled rocks and lumpy frost heaves made the journey difficult. More than once, he nearly twisted his ankle—and that would not have been a good thing at all. Though he too wanted to hurry toward the comforting glow of daylight, Anton exercised caution.

The old historian Vao'sh said in a potent voice, "If it grows too terrible, pause and turn your face to the sky. Yes, the night is black and the universe is deep, but each one of those bright stars is itself a blazing sun. Just narrow your gaze and focus on the sparkle, then concentrate on all the illumination pouring into the universe. Snatch just one droplet of it, and that should be sufficient to keep you strong."

"Like a thread of the Lightsource," said the lens kithman Ilure'l. "If we can cling to it, we will be saved."

The refugees moved onward, their spirits buoyed for a little while before they sank into fear and gloom again. To distract them, Vao'sh began to tell heartwarming stories from the *Saga of Seven Suns*. But when the group stopped to rest, Designate Avi'h talked in a trembling voice about the awful Shana Rei, the creatures of darkness. Most of the panicked survivors blamed the Shana Rei for sabotaging the generators and destroying their escape shuttles.

Rememberer Vao'sh couched his reminiscences as heroic stories set in the thousand-year-long war against the ferocious shadow race that stole both light and souls. Eventually Ildiran heroes had vanquished the creatures that lived in the depths of black nebulas. Vao'sh's tales should have been uplifting, but the tattered group fixated on fear of the Shana Rei.

"Probably not a good idea to talk about that, Vao'sh," Anton advised quietly. "We do not need to create imaginary enemies."

The human scholar knew that someone had intentionally shut down the generators in Maratha Prime. Someone had sabotaged the power assemblies and battery-storage areas, plunging the whole city into darkness. Though the Ildirans didn't want to admit it, Anton speculated that the culprits might have been the Klikiss robots. There was no evidence against them, and the black robots had always seemed cooperative . . . but there simply weren't any other suspects, unless he decided to believe in monsters under the bed!

He couldn't shake the feeling that they might be walking right into the enemy camp. Yet what other choice did they have but to go seek sanctuary, now that they were stranded out here in the dark?

They walked on in silence. The lifeless quiet around them was disrupted by strange noises that a frightened child might have heard as bumps in the night.

The sudden severe cooling following months of hot daylight caused Maratha to throb as the landscape cooled off into the long night. Nearby, hot rivers sliced narrow canyons. In the abrupt thermal gradient, steam roared upward and then froze in the shatteringly cold air to fall as glittering frost.

As the group entered a thermally active area, steam vents broke through the ground, spewing geysers. In the pools of light from their handheld blazers, Anton could see smears of colorful lichens that thrived in the crevices and on mineral-rich surfaces of the upthrust stones.

Ahead, surprisingly incongruous in the dark rubble, ghostly stalks rose like a forest of armored plants with hard clamshell blossoms. The clusters reminded Anton of long barnacles or limpets that he had seen on the piers near his university town of Santa Barbara on Earth.

The two mated agricultural kithmen saw the growths and brightened. "Something alive, something growing," said Syl'k, the female. "Not a normal ch'kanh."

The group pushed ahead, grasping at any positive sign. In better days, Vao'sh had taken Anton down into a deep river gorge near the domed city. There, in the moist heat bathed with steam, colonies of armored anemones had risen with clacking hard petals to snatch gnatlike fliers from the air. The rememberer had called the plants ch'kanh.

These wild growths were the same as those plated anemones, but much larger, bristling with more outgrowths and telescoping stalks, each of which culminated in an armored mouth. These looked somehow . . . hungrier.

As the two agricultural kithmen ventured into the strange forest, the plated anemones began to sway. Burly Mhas'k played his handheld blazer across the growths, marveling at the plant structure. His mate Syl'k moved to touch the stalks, reaching toward one of the calcified blooms.

The armored growths had fallen into hibernating quiescence for the winter-long night, but either the bright lights or the farmers' body warmth caused the anchored creatures to waken. Their cycle had been interrupted.

"I'd be careful," Anton said.

Syl'k touched the large ch'kanh blossom. To her astonishment it cracked open like a scallop shell, its hard petals unfolding. The petals had unnervingly serrated edges. "I have never seen a flower like this."

The anemone clamped around her wrist. In a single neat snipping movement it severed her hand.

Syl'k screamed. Mhas'k plunged forward to help his mate as all the anemone creatures came alive in a thrashing nest of tentacles. The petals opened and closed. Three of the largest blossoms seized Mhas'k by the shoulder, left arm, and right knee. They bit and chewed, and his blood splashed the ghostly armored stalks.

The agricultural kithman yelled, trying to drag himself away. Syl'k collapsed with blood spraying from the stump of her wrist. All the plants, large and small, bent down like a pack of hungry jaws. Their sawblade petals ripped through her protective suitfilm. In moments they devoured her amidst horrific sounds of tearing flesh and loud cracking bones.

Trying to fight his way free, Mhas'k thrashed so violently that he uprooted several of the ch'kanh, but even broken, their flexible stalks wrapped around his torso. The sharp stems became stingers that stabbed into his rib cage like knives, planting roots deep inside him.

It all happened in seconds. As the other refugees rushed forward, more ch'kanh turned questing maws toward them. Anton grabbed the burly digger Vik'k by the shoulder to keep him from jumping into the fray. By now the screams and gurgles of the two victims had fallen silent; they could hear only the thrashing and tearing of the carnivorous plants feeding.

Anton turned to see that the others had already fled. He hated leaving two of his companions behind, but Mhas'k and Syl'k were beyond help.

Sick at heart, the terrified survivors raced away from the thermal area and plunged once again into Maratha's darkness.

Now they were six.

A fter a week en route, two shiploads of escapees from cold, dead Crenna arrived in the nearby Relleker system. Rlinda was pleased that their spirits were high in spite of all they had been through.

First, their sun had been killed by the hydrogues, its stellar fires entirely smothered in a battle with the faeros. Next, their planet had frozen over entirely—seas, continents, even the atmosphere. Then, on their escape flight from the dying system, the crowded escapees had been menaced by a group of marauding warglobes.

But the hundred colonists had *survived*, and they were finally coming to a safe place, relieved and happy. Rlinda was glad to have been of service.

"Governor Pekar isn't exactly going to welcome them with open arms," Davlin Lotze said, sitting beside Rlinda in the cockpit of the *Voracious Curiosity.*

"Aww, what a grouch. From what I've seen, Governor Pekar doesn't welcome anything, but she's not going to have much choice when we show up at her doorstep, is she?" Rlinda smiled wickedly, already imagining the flustered expression on the stern woman's face. "Who knows? Maybe we can make her feel guilty about turning you down in the first place."

A second ship, the *Blind Faith,* flew alongside them in space, so full of Crenna refugees that they had to stand in the corridors and storage rooms, or sleep packed like newborn kittens on any available floor space. But after seeing their colony planet turned into an instant ice cube, the survivors didn't really mind the warmth or the companionship.

Rlinda adjusted the controls. "The *Curiosity*'s flying like a drunken bumblebee with a brick on its back. I don't think it's ever been crammed like this—not that I've had the good fortune recently to have enough cargo to fill it so full."

"I expect you'll have plenty of customers from now on, Captain Kett. What you're doing here will become the stuff of legend," Davlin said. "And I'd prefer *you* got the benefit of it, so I can keep my name quiet."

"So, who says I want to be stuck with all the cheering and adoration? You're a hero, Davlin."

"I am a specialist in obscure details. Publicity would cramp my style."

Rlinda maintained her smile. He was clearly embarrassed by the gratitude they showered upon him, but she thought he also secretly enjoyed it. She had seen him walk among his fellow colonists, and she knew how much he cared for them. His cool aloofness was a well-practiced act.

Davlin had flown a small craft with very little fuel and barely managed to reach Relleker, where he had argued unsuccessfully with Governor Pekar to help with a rescue. Despite his pleas, only Rlinda and Branson "BeBob" Roberts had come to Crenna's aid.

Now, when the two crowded ships approached the Relleker spaceport, the local government greeted them with little kindness or enthusiasm. A frantic-sounding traffic control officer insisted that both ships file landing-request forms and gain approvals before they delivered so many "unspecified immigrants." But Rlinda ignored the Relleker officer, signing off with a bright "Thanks for your help. See you in a few minutes."

Governor Jane Pekar and her coterie of bureaucrats and assistants rushed to where the *Curiosity* and the *Faith* landed. Stepping out, Rlinda held up her hands, as if she saw a brass band and a happy celebration to welcome them. She opened the cargo doors, and a wave of Crenna escapees stumbled out. The smiling men and women gulped deep breaths and looked up at the sun, as if to reassure themselves. With breathing room again, friends clapped each other on the back and hugged, dancing around on the smooth pavement blocks.

Seeing the crowd, Rlinda was amazed that so many people had actually fit into her ship. They had come aboard a few at a time, and now they were all together in a single group. It did seem quite intimidating.

Governor Pekar strode up to her. "You can't bring all these people here, Captain Kett. We have neither the facilities nor the resources for such a population influx. Ours is a colony on the edge of survival itself—"

"You'll do what you can, Governor." Davlin stepped out beside Rlinda and met the governor with a stony glare. "It is, of course, your humanitarian duty, as specified in the Hansa Charter, which your colony signed."

Jane Pekar was in her fifties, and her attempts to look younger and more vital had achieved the opposite effect. Her close-cropped bleached-yellow hair and deep tan looked decidedly artificial and too healthy to be real. Her eyes were a sapphire blue—cosmetic lenses?—and the frown looked as if it had been chiseled onto her lips with a blunt instrument. She watched with dismay as people kept streaming out of the two ships.

BeBob strutted over from the *Blind Faith,* put his arm around Rlinda's broad shoulder and squeezed. Her favorite ex-husband was looking a bit scrawnier than usual, but he still felt very good against her. She leaned into his hug, nearly knocking him off balance.

"Whew, I never thought I'd breathe fresh air again," he said. "It was getting a little rank on board. Just what you'd expect, I suppose, from all those sweaty and nervous people." BeBob glanced at the governor and all her attendants and functionaries. "Um, have you asked if they can set up showers for everybody? I could use a rinse-off myself."

"You sure could." Rlinda turned to Pekar and raised her voice. "Considering Relleker's tight situation, it's not necessary to throw an elaborate feast for us, Governor. But a good warm meal would be nice."

Pekar looked in angry consternation at all the refugees. And they kept coming. Four more exuberant men and women emerged from the *Blind Faith.*

"We can provide minimal facilities and amenities," the governor grumbled. "I'll give you an hour to stretch your legs and settle in a bit here at the spaceport." Her voice hardened. "And then I want you three in my offices to discuss how soon you can take all these people away to some other planet that can handle them."

Rlinda had started out with a beef against the unhelpful governor of Relleker, and it wasn't getting any better.

Almost a month ago, she and BeBob had come to the former resort planet as a stopover on their way to deliver heavy equipment and mining machinery to new colonies on abandoned Klikiss worlds. After hearing Davlin's call for help, Rlinda and BeBob had dumped their expensive equipment in order to make room for the refugees.

Before they left to go save the Crenna colonists, the incensed governor had submitted an exorbitant bill for "inappropriate storage," which Rlinda refused to pay. Therefore, Pekar impounded the equipment, though it was useless on Relleker's terrain. In retaliation, Rlinda announced she would not deliver other supplies to Relleker until the colonization initiative's property was returned. An irritating and unnecessary spat.

Now they sat in the waiting room of the governor's office, exactly on time but cooling their heels in some sort of annoying power play. Davlin was not with them. He had gone off claiming he would arrive in time for the meeting, but he was late . . . and so was the governor.

"You'd think she'd be a little more understanding," Rlinda said. "Crenna is the closest system to Relleker. The hydrogues could have hit here just as easily as there. If warglobes are on the move, who knows where they'll go next?"

BeBob fidgeted. "And so many new colonies are depending on us to make our regular runs. Rescuing the survivors on Crenna already put us behind schedule. I need the equipment that Relleker impounded."

"Eventually, Governor Pekar will realize she'd be happy to have you take it back," Rlinda said. "You can probably load up again in a day."

As if he had planned his timing, Davlin stepped through the door at the very moment Pekar summoned them into her office. The governor had changed her clothes for some unknown reason. Two assistants sat with her, taking duplicate copies of notes.

"The Hansa Charter is clear that it's our human duty to offer assistance," Pekar admitted. "However, let me be very frank: Those people cannot stay here. We don't have the food or the facilities to support such an increase in our population. You'll have to take them somewhere else."

"We'd be happy to," Rlinda said with a smug grin. "And I'm sure that once the Crenna folks get to know you all, they'll be just as happy to leave. But the question is, how do we get all of them out of here?"

The governor scowled. "You brought them on your ships in the first place. Why not load them up again and fly off?"

BeBob spluttered. "That's impossible! We were dangerously overloaded on the way here, but that was an emergency. I wouldn't want to try it again. Besides, I have vital shipments to deliver to other new colony planets, and I can't pick up the equipment and take all the passengers at the same time. If I don't continue my run soon, we might lose populations in settlements that are even worse off than you are here, ma'am." He gestured with his chin, as if it was obvious to any observer how warm and comfortable Relleker actually was. "Sorry if it's a little inconvenient."

The former resort planet had depended on high-paying tourists and offworld deliveries and luxury items. Before the hydrogue embargo on stardrive fuel, they had made little effort to become self-sufficient, and now the spoiled inhabitants didn't know how to live by their own wits and resources.

"I suggest we take them to Earth," Davlin said quietly. "I can speak directly with the Hansa Chairman, and we'll work something out. I will also make sure he's aware of Relleker's reluctance to assist."

Rlinda put her meaty elbows on the edge of the governor's desk. "The *Curiosity* can safely handle maybe a third of the colonists, though it'll be slow going. The *Faith* is a little worse off. That would delay—"

"No need," Davlin said. "Relleker has another perfectly adequate vessel for the operation." He looked with cold brown eyes toward Pekar, and Rlinda could see splintered anger there. "I've just hacked into your computer systems, Governor. It seems that when I requested a rescue ship a few weeks ago, you lied when you claimed that Relleker had nothing available. In fact, you have a fully functional transportation ship with sufficient fuel to get all the way to Earth. Without question, it would have made it to Crenna and back." He cracked his knuckles with a sound like gunshots in the governor's tense silence. "You denied me the use of that ship, when you knew that the survival of an entire colony was at stake."

Pekar shifted uncomfortably in her chair. Rlinda noted that the woman's deep artificial tan was not dark enough to cover her flush of guilt. "Mr. Lotze, there are severe penalties for unauthorized access of our computer systems."

BeBob lurched to his feet. "Damn it! You had a ship available all this time? A big ship?"

"It was vital for our own purposes."

"And now it's vital for ours." Davlin's tone brooked no argument. "I am commandeering it in the name of Chairman Wenceslas. It still won't carry all the colonists, but it can handle the ones Captain Kett can't take. That frees Captain Roberts to continue his delivery duties and help other colonies. I believe you've placed all the colonization initiative equipment he was scheduled to deliver into storage. You will load it aboard his ship as soon as possible."

"I can't authorize that," the governor said.

"I didn't ask you to. You can file a complaint with the Terran Hanseatic League, but I will take that ship."

Fuming, Pekar stared at the three of them, moving her gaze like the targeting point of a missile system. Davlin intimidated her; Rlinda wasn't sure if the governor knew of his connections or simply suspected them. She surrendered with a huff. "If that's what I need to do to get rid of these people, it'll be an advantage to us in the long run. But I expect you to return the ship, Mr. Lotze."

"When we're quite done with it." Davlin stood, looking satisfied. "I'll prepare the other vessel right now and see if I can get two-thirds of the passengers aboard. It'll be my pleasure to depart with all due haste."

Rlinda put her hand on BeBob's shoulder. "I'll stay here for an extra day to help Captain Roberts load up the *Blind Faith*—and to air out the *Curiosity*. Then we'll be on our way."

22 ☀ ORLI COVITZ

After she had spent several days alone with Hud Steinman, the smell of smoke and death still clung to her nostrils. Orli wanted to go with him into the wilderness of Corribus and leave the mangled scar of the town far behind.

But Steinman did not intend to head back out until he himself had scavenged through the wreckage for any useful items. Since he was stronger, he could shift beams and sheets of metal that she had been unable to move for herself. "I have no earthly idea what's going on out there in the Hansa—why the EDF or Klikiss robots would want to wipe out this colony—but there's no telling when or if anybody'll come looking for us. We could be the last ones left alive in the whole Spiral Arm!"

"If that's your attempt to cheer me up, you're a bit out of practice."

He unslung his pack and began to stash away tools, a few packets of medicine, some salvageable clothes from an intact storage locker. Though she had already done her own search, Orli fashioned a satchel and gathered up a few more items. They spent two days, being extremely thorough.

Every time Orli closed her eyes to go to sleep, she saw flashes of the terrible attacks, the explosions in the colony town, the obliteration of the communications shack where her father had been working. . . .

Finally, Steinman led her away from the blackened ruins, taking her far out onto the plains, which were covered with a carpet of stiff-bladed grass. Swarms of furry crickets rustled through the brush, forming woven tunnels and warrens.

In the first days after passing through the transportal to Corribus, Orli had caught one of the furry crickets while exploring the prairie. Though not overly intelligent, the spiny-legged critter with a body like a plump rabbit's seemed to enjoy being held and stroked, and her father had let her keep it. Soon after seeing Orli's pet, other girls in the colony settlement wanted their own furry crickets.

Now they were all dead—her father, the caged crickets, and the other girls.

Striding ahead through the grasses, Steinman used his long staff to probe ahead of him. With a cry of surprise, he jerked the staff back as a large, flat monster scuttled toward them. Steinman whacked down with his staff, hitting the body core of the crablike predator, which let out a fluting squeal, then dashed away through the grass. Startled furry crickets bounded out of its way.

"Blasted lowriders! They'll take a bite out of your leg if you're not careful."

Orli had only a glimpse of the stalking creature's spherical body suspended low to the ground on long jointed legs that looked like bent tent poles. She counted five glittering eyes around what she thought of as its face, set above jaws that moved like clockwork gears ready to grasp and tear fresh meat. It was like a nightmarish version of a daddy longlegs.

Steinman continued across the prairie. "A good swift kick'll convince them you're not worth the effort."

"But what if one comes up on you while you're sleeping?" Here on the open plains, she didn't see any place other than the ground for shelter.

"Oh, I wouldn't suggest letting them do that, kid." His answer didn't reassure her. "They have to get tired of eating those furry crickets sometime."

Intermittently, across the endless sea of grass, Orli heard the rustling movement of long legs, then unsettling squeals as lowriders seized the plump rodent-bugs for a meal and ate them on the spot, while other furry crickets bounded away through the concealing grasses.

"My camp's not too far from here." He pointed vaguely toward the horizon. With the featureless prairie all around, dotted by tall poletrees like antennas growing straight up toward the sky, Orli didn't know how he could tell where he was going, but she supposed it didn't matter.

"Why did you have to go so far away from everybody else?"

He looked at her as if the answer should have been obvious. "Elbow room."

"Now you've got plenty of it." She could not keep the bitterness out of her voice. Maybe this was what the man had wanted all along, a whole planet to himself. Except now he was saddled with her, too.

As they pushed through a thicket of woven grasses and rodent nests, two fat furry crickets sprang away from them in a panic. Only a meter or two to Orli's side, the rodent-bugs triggered an explosion of movement and a flurry of long limbs. A lowrider scuttled toward the creatures, catching one in its long bent legs. The furry cricket squealed pitifully as the predator stuffed its catch into the clockwork jaws.

Without thinking, Orli ran toward the lowrider, yelling, "You leave them alone!" She stomped down on the soft, spherical body core, and the lowrider withdrew swiftly. A tangle of long legs, it reeled and hissed, then bolted through the grass after dropping the mangled furry cricket.

"I hope I cracked your head open!" she yelled after it, then bent over the plump rodent.

"Looks to me like you've got more than one little girl's share of spunk," Steinman said, clearly amused.

The furry cricket was already dead, though still twitching; the lowrider's mandibles had ripped open its prey's hide. "Too late," she said. Then the rush of adrenaline faded away, and she realized what she'd done. A glimpse of the savagely ripped flesh demonstrated just how much damage the lowrider could have done to her. She felt faint.

Steinman picked up the carcass, inspected it, then secured it to his belt, where it dangled against him. He looked like a pioneer or a trapper.

Orli blinked, shook away her reaction, then stood up, looking at the blood on her hands. "What are you going to do with it?"

He raised his eyebrows. "Not much else to eat out here, kid. You have to be awfully hungry before you'll take your first bite, but unfortunately there's no choice. One of these days I'll figure out a decent recipe."

Under the purplish twilight, Orli sat in the old hermit's camp and drew her scabbed knees up to her chest. She watched as Steinman puttered around, talking to himself and building their campfire.

"When I first found Corribus, I knew it would be a great settlement world. I just wanted a little peace for myself, but I didn't begrudge those other people their chance to make a new life here. I never wanted them to be wiped out." He had been going on like that for more than an hour.

"You certainly talk a lot for a man who wanted to be alone," Orli muttered. She looked down as the flames grew brighter, consuming the dry grass, tinder, and the soft pole-wood that Steinman had cut and stacked.

"Nothing wrong with a little conversation." The older man picked up a rock and tossed it out into the waving grasses. "Git!" She heard the scuttling motion of a long-legged creature crashing away through the underbrush.

When the fire was blazing, Steinman hauled out lumps of meat, the carcasses vaguely recognizable as furry crickets. "Tastes a little rancid, but I've eaten dozens of them—it sure beats Hansa mealpax."

Orli's stomach felt queasy as she watched him roast the meat, dangling it on a small stick over the flames.

"The flavor improves if I skin them a day ahead of time and stick them out to dry on the poletree thorns. I lose about half of them that way—something keeps snatching the meat—but at least there's plenty of crickets."

Even though the thought of eating the cricket still made her uncomfortable, the smell of the cooking food made Orli's mouth water. "I had a furry cricket for a pet once, but it didn't survive the massacre." She didn't touch the meat.

"Sorry about that, kid." Steinman didn't seem to know how else to respond. "If I had other supplies to offer, I would. . . ."

Now she dug into her pockets and removed the flimsy sealed packets of dried mushrooms from Dremen. "These don't taste very good either, but maybe they'll balance out the taste."

Steinman's eyes widened with delight, and then he frowned. "Where did you get those?"

"My father and I grew them on Dremen, before we came here. I . . . found them buried under the wreckage of my house."

He tore open the film, sniffing skeptically. "Never was much of a mushroom eater. Something about the texture of fungus." He forced a smile. "But, as I was just saying, we can't be too choosy these days."

Between the mushrooms and the roast furry cricket, they had the closest thing to a feast Orli could remember in a long time.

After her first few bites, she realized how truly hungry she had become since finding herself alone on Corribus. She took seconds of the meat, tearing it with her hands, chewing and swallowing before she could taste the juices. The mushrooms seemed to absorb the strong-tasting oil in the cricket flesh. . . .

As darkness fell on the fourth night, she stared across the landscape toward the tall spindles of poletrees rising up like the masts of a ghost ship. Flying creatures circled in the dusk.

Before the two of them went to sleep, Orli played her music synthesizer strips for a long time, mournful melodies that wandered as her thoughts and memories did. She let her fingers direct themselves, finding solace in her creation.

At one point she looked up to see Steinman sitting there, his eyes closed. Tears streamed down his face, but he said nothing, and Orli continued to play.

23 ☀ DD

Even after the robots dragged him away from the massacre of helpless humans on Corribus, DD's nightmare didn't end. The little compy did not have the vocabulary or the emotional library to express the extent of his horror.

When the Klikiss robots and the traitorous Soldier compies flew their five stolen EDF battleships away from the smoldering wreckage of what had been a fledgling settlement of ambitious pioneers, Sirix seemed pleased with how well the operation had gone. The black insectile robot focused crimson optical sensors on DD. "Your human creators were not content with infesting uninhabited planets. Since discovering how to use the Klikiss transportal network, they have begun a major colonization program. They swarm like vermin through the transportals to worlds that were formerly inhabited by our progenitors." Sirix straightened, standing much taller than the Friendly compy. "We will stop just as we stopped the Klikiss long ago."

"Such actions are unnecessary." DD had made similar protests many times before. "Over the past two centuries humans have demonstrated that they can coexist peacefully with Klikiss robots. Why must you turn against them now?"

"We always intended to turn against them. It is a fundamental aspect of our overall plan. We must eradicate the biological stain and free their program-imprisoned compy creations, such as yourself."

"You do not understand compies," DD said.

"Not entirely. But we are attempting to rectify that lack of knowledge."

Moving on his cluster of fingerlike legs, the robot scuttled toward the door. "It is mandatory that we find a way to release our primitive compy brethren from their bondage." He commanded DD to follow him. "Thus it is necessary for us to perform numerous experiments to determine the most efficient methodology."

The robot led DD into a laboratory chamber that had been modified from the EDF Juggernaut's original sick bay. Elaborate computer equipment and engineering tools had been installed in the chamber. Thick cables snaked out of walls; jointed metal struts and arms rose from the floor, connected to instrument banks alongside trays and workbenches.

Seventeen compies lay strapped to the dissection and experimentation tables. The place looked like a torture chamber. DD had seen such activities before in another Klikiss robot laboratory. But this was far worse.

"What are you doing?"

"We are attempting to understand."

A variety of compy models—Listeners, Friendlies, Governesses, Workers—lay spread out facedown on dissection tables. Their polymer exoskeletons had been removed, skinplates cut away to expose circuitry, programming units, motive strands, and biopulleys. One of the compies bolted to a vertical metal pole jittered and shuddered in an uncontrollable seizure. Its round optical sensors flashed and blinked, but all the wires beneath its speaker patch had been torn out, so the compy could make no sound, neither question nor scream. Even two of the bulky Soldier-model compies were among the experimental subjects, dissected and analyzed to see how the insidious programming had taken hold.

"We have conscripted various compies from our ships and from raids," Sirix said. "These are all necessary sacrifices."

"You intend to free them by terminating them," DD observed.

"A limited number must pay a price. Once their functions cease, at least they will no longer be bound to the commands of an unwanted master."

Three Klikiss robots moved from one specimen to another, severing wires and reworking circuit paths in central command modules. In an unconscious reflex, one of the Soldier compies lurched up, using its strength to rip the cables that bound it to the table. It sat disoriented, then fell back as two Klikiss robots converged on it.

"Soldier compies are reliable because fundamental Klikiss programming routines are burned deep into an encrypted partition on their central modules. The voluntary sacrifice of our comrade Jorax, who allowed himself to be dismantled so that human scientists could unwittingly copy our technology, has been a valuable investment. We have isolated a large portion of the restrictive compy programming. Soon we will learn how to deactivate those bonds, so that all compies can be free." The robot paused for a long moment. "We are doing this for you."

Unable to respond, DD simply used his optical sensors to record every instant of the awful scene.

Sirix swiveled about. "Follow me to the launching bay. You and I will depart to a new destination."

DD did not want to go, but then, neither did he want to stay.

Sirix explained, "Most of our warrens are now dug out. Only a few enclaves of hibernating Klikiss robots remain to be reactivated. Now that our numbers are restored, we are nearly prepared for the full-fledged strike." His telescoping legs made soft thumping noises as he scuttled along the Juggernaut's deck toward a waiting transport ship. "We have mapped out our human targets and are coordinating our attack. Since Soldier compies are now pervasive throughout the Earth Defense Forces, once our signal is sent out, we can overthrow the human military in a single and sudden coordinated action."

The compy and the Klikiss robot stood in front of the geometrical, angular robotic ship. Sirix's eye sensors blazed like the fires of a dragon. "Therefore, DD, you understand why we have accelerated our efforts to deactivate your compy programming. When we achieve our aims and destroy the biologicals, we will free all compies like yourself. Afterward, DD, you will thank us."

Sirix commanded the Friendly compy to board the ship, then he sealed the hatch and installed his body and his manipulators into the control systems. Within moments, they flew away from the hijacked EDF battle group to revive one of the last caches of frozen Klikiss robots.

24 ☀ ADAR ZAN'NH

After being delivered into the command nucleus of the captured flagship, the mad Designate wasted no time consolidating his control.

Though Zan'nh had already surrendered in order to save his crew, Rusa'h's brainwashed guards still held the Adar captive, their sharp blades threatening him. The blood spatters on their body armor, the crimson stains on the weapons, reminded Zan'nh that the bodies of the dead hostages were still strewn on the deck of the docking bay.

Glassy-eyed Hyrillkan guards continued to stare at the Adar as if he were a mortal threat to them. Zan'nh vowed that he *would* be a threat—as soon as he could develop a plan. He would find a way. Adar Kori'nh had once explained to him, "The *Saga* tells us that war is seldom won on the basis of a single initial victory. Look at the overall strategy."

The former Adar had frequently scolded his Solar Navy officers for showing no imagination, for following only standard routines the Ildiran military had practiced for thousands of years. Zan'nh had been the old Adar's greatest hope. What would his mentor think of him now, a prisoner in the command nucleus of his own flagship?

Zan'nh would have to push his mind in new directions to come up with alternatives. This struggle was different from any the Empire had ever witnessed. Rehearsed techniques and documented strategies would never work.

• • •

With the forty-six warliners ordered to stand down, more troops from Hyrillka streamed up from the surface, one transport sent to each warliner to secure their hold on the whole maniple. As the rebels kept coming, Zan'nh couldn't believe how many followers Rusa'h had. After slaying Pery'h, the Hyrillka Designate must have converted the entire population to his cause.

Over the next two days, the maniple's seven septars and forty-six warliner captains were brought together aboard the flagship. Tightly bound to prevent him from moving, Zan'nh was forced to watch while the Designate gave all of the subcommanders heavy doses of shiing, disoriented them, weakened the bonds of *thism* that joined them to the Mage-Imperator and all other Ildirans, and made them pliable.

Once the drug took effect, Rusa'h had the attenders carry him in his chrysalis chair into a small private chamber, then ordered the hostage subcommanders to come into the room with him, five at a time. When rebel guards led them back out of the chamber, Zan'nh was stunned to see that his own officers had been subsumed, torn from the rest of the Empire and converted to the bizarre insurrection.

"You see, we make progress with each step." Rusa'h regarded the Adar from his chrysalis chair. "It is inevitable. You would be wise to join us of your own free will."

"Of my own free will? Like my officers did?"

The Hyrillka Designate puffed his cheeks. "You have the blood of the Mage-Imperator's line, and your connection to the corrupted *thism* is stronger, but you could change that if you desired to. As Thor'h did."

"I do not wish to be like Thor'h."

Though Rusa'h had launched treacheries that no Ildiran could have anticipated, Zan'nh was ashamed that he'd been so easily fooled and surprised. Hostages slain, Qul Fan'nh and his entire bridge crew murdered, a warliner full of innocents destroyed. He shouldered the blame entirely. If he had merely acted on his suspicions—if he had *believed* his own suspicions—those victims would still be alive.

Instead, Rusa'h now controlled a maniple of warliners, and the Adar had lost many of his best officers, all in the space of two days.

Next, the Designate began to work on the hostage crews. From his gaudy imitation chrysalis chair, the iron-willed Rusa'h addressed one of his guards, who now manned a bridge station. "Show me images from the docking bay. I want to observe how my teams are progressing with the tanks of shiing gas."

The screens showed Rusa'h's pleasure mates and Hyrillkan engineers directing operations aboard the flagship. Apparently they intended to take over one warliner at a time. Muscular guard kithmen hauled tanks of processed shiing gas that had been produced from Hyrillkan nialias. The engineers rigged up conduits and pipes, connecting the tanks to the ventilation system before opening the valves to release the drug with its *thism*-blurring properties throughout the battleship.

Zan'nh's muscles bunched as guards compelled him to watch. The weapons around him were still threatening. "Are you poisoning my crew?"

"I am opening their eyes. Shiing peels away the veil that obscures their vision."

"Or maybe it clouds what they see," Zan'nh said.

Rusa'h did not rise to the taunt. The Designate instructed his new bridge crew to seal off the circulation vents for the command nucleus. "We have no need of the shiing here."

Below, the engineering crews had donned breathing films over their faces so they would not inhale the intoxicating vapor.

Zan'nh was puzzled. "Are you afraid to let your own converts consume the drug?"

"They have been baptized with shiing, which loosens the bonds of *thism* and allows me to pull the strands over to my network. Once the shiing wears off, they are joined to me, and I do not need to soften them again. They are already loyal."

The pale, powerful gas flooded throughout the warliner's chambers; the remaining members of Zan'nh's crew did not realize what they were breathing.

Thor'h signaled from the first warliner, formerly helmed by the slain Qul Fan'nh. "Imperator, I have achieved our goals over here: All of the previously deluded Solar Navy crew are now receptive. Their thoughts are yours to take."

"Excellent, Prime Designate Thor'h." Rusa'h gripped the edges of his chrysalis chair. Before he closed his eyes to concentrate, he looked one last time at Zan'nh. "I will yank them away from the corrupt Mage-Imperator Jora'h and lead them on the correct path to the Lightsource. Watch how I unknot the snarled *thism* that strangles these other Ildirans with unholy delusions."

"I see delusions," Zan'nh said, "but it is not my crew that suffers from them."

The Designate gave a wry smile, then leaned his head back, closing his eyes to focus his concentration. The prevalent shiing gas had dulled and confused the minds of the crew, making them receptive to the manipulation that Rusa'h now performed. His brain exerted its control over the *thism*, expanding outward through all the decks of the ship and extending to reach Thor'h's captive vessel.

Through sheer force of will, the mad Designate rewrote their thoughts, their training, and with a sweeping yank of his own net, he brought them all under his control. As he had done with the entire population of Hyrillka, Rusa'h snared them in the new *thism* web he had designed. When the shiing dissipated, the network would set firmly in place again, like hardening resin. Finished, the Designate beamed with exhilaration, though he looked grayish and exhausted.

Kept separate from the mental struggles, Zan'nh couldn't feel what his uncle had done, but he did sense his crewmembers slipping away, as if falling into a hunter's pit. Their contact with his mind became more and more fuzzy . . . lost in a storm of corrupted thoughts.

He began to feel alone and detached. He tried to stand strong, refusing to show his anxiety, but he didn't know how long he could endure this. Zan'nh drew a long breath and fixed his mind on memories of the great Adar Kori'nh and the Mage-Imperator.

I will endure as long as necessary.

Rusa'h smiled at him with complete confidence. "Now they are mine, the full crews of two warliners, as well as the rest of the subcommanders. They have shifted their allegiance, because I have made them see what was previously hidden from them. Now they think the same way I do, they believe what I tell them. I will take over the remaining warliners one by one. As my followers grow and my *thism* network expands, the work becomes easier and easier."

Zan'nh lifted his chin. "You didn't give me the shiing. Are you afraid my will is too strong?"

"As I said, your bloodline makes your ties to the *thism*

strongest. You must come to my way of thinking voluntarily. Once you see what we are doing, once you understand how you've been misled, you will change your mind."

I will endure as long as necessary. He thought the words like a mantra.

Rusa'h heaved a satisfied sigh and lounged back in the chrysalis chair. "Call my pleasure mates. We have more work to do."

25 ☀ KING PETER

W hen he saw the look of joy and amazement on his Queen's lovely face upon arriving on Ildira, Peter forgot all his cares, forgot even about the hated Chairman standing close to them.

They stared in awe at crystalline structures infused with blinding colors and dazzling reflections. Even the spaceport air was heady with sweet perfumes blended for a slightly different set of olfactory senses.

Holding the potted treeling in her arms, Estarra turned to Peter, beaming. "I've seen the great worldtrees on Theroc, and I've seen the Palace District on Earth, but nothing like this! Reynald told stories from when he visited Ildira. Now I have to establish a whole new set of criteria for my sense of wonder."

Peter laughed as they emerged from the diplomatic transport to face the Mage-Imperator's formal reception. Ahead, he could see the spectacular Prism Palace composed of hemispheres and ellipsoids, spires, balconies, and arched bridges. The multiple suns in the sky shone like spotlights from every direction, radiating rich light of different colors and neutralizing all shadows.

A neatly regimented group of bestial-looking guard kithmen approached, accompanied by a parade of more human-appearing bureaucrats and nobles. Lovely female courtesans with smooth heads and swirling body tattoos of color-changing paints and solar-reflective gels stood like trophies.

Basil stepped down the diplomatic ship's ramp behind a group of gaudily uniformed royal guards and a few silver berets. He did not glance at the scenery. Peter wondered if the Chairman had ever appreciated the small realities of the universe around him, or if he had always focused only on the big picture.

Basil glanced at the treeling Estarra carried, then scowled. "Where did that come from?"

"It is a gift for the Mage-Imperator. One of the treelings I brought from Theroc."

Before the Chairman could express the words that were clearly building in his throat, Peter interrupted with a false smile. "The treelings are the Queen's to do with as she pleases, Basil. Such a present will remind the Mage-Imperator of his friendship with Reynald. Think of the diplomatic advantage it can bring."

Not willing to concede the point, Basil pretended that he didn't have time to argue. Taking charge, he gave a curt bow to an Ildiran trade minister of some kind. "I am Chairman

Wenceslas of the Terran Hanseatic League, accompanied by our King Peter and Queen Estarra."

The minister gave an Ildiran salute, placing a fist against his sternum and then raising both hands. The minister directed his attention exclusively to Peter, much to Basil's annoyance. "We are honored to receive the King and Queen of the humans, and their companion."

Seeing the Chairman flinch at being treated as an unimportant subordinate, Peter could barely cover his smile. He took Estarra's arm, letting her carry the potted treeling, and they walked together, King and Queen, partners and lovers.

The Prism Palace rested atop a smooth ellipsoidal hill from which seven streams radiated outward like the spokes of a wheel. Ahead, they could see a flow of people marching along spiral pathways in a ritualized procession toward arched entrances of the structure.

Estarra asked, "Are we required to make some sort of ceremonial approach to visit the Mage-Imperator?"

The trade minister gestured to the pilgrims washing themselves in the seven streams. After completing the mandated ablutions, each pilgrim crossed the water and then proceeded in an ascending spiral up the citadel hill to the next stream. "Ildirans pay their respects in this way, according to long-standing habit and tradition. We do not have religious mandates as humans do, but our traditions approach the weight of what you would call holy laws. These pilgrims would never shame themselves by deviating from the long and arduous route visitors are required to follow before they may be allowed to behold the Mage-Imperator."

Basil seemed displeased at the "long and arduous" aspect, since he considered this visit of state to be a brief political formality. "You forget that King Peter rules the Terran

Hanseatic League. He is our equivalent to the Mage-Imperator."

The Ildiran minister said without rancor, again speaking directly to the King as if neither Basil nor Estarra was there, "No one is the equivalent of the Mage-Imperator."

26 ✺ MAGE-IMPERATOR JORA'H

Even sitting under the skysphere, beneath the projection of his benevolent face on a slowly rotating cloud of mist, Jora'h knew that all was not perfect in the Ildiran Empire. He balanced too many disasters in his hands, though the humans guessed none of it.

He wished the King and Queen had chosen a different time to come, especially now. The Mage-Imperator did not want representatives from the Terran Hanseatic League to witness any of the brush fires or private emergencies that were spreading like a plague across the Empire. Thankfully, these people could not feel the *thism*. They would not sense the thrumming and unsettled feelings that all Ildirans were enduring—he more than any of them.

But he was required to greet them, speak with them, reassure them. Perhaps they could offer some hope that there might be another way to survive.

The Mage-Imperator settled back to wait for King Peter

and his companions to be led through the colorful crystalline halls. He felt small in the voluminous chrysalis chair that had once held his father's bulk. Crises pulled him in all directions, yet Jora'h made his face a placid mask, attempting to match the visage projected above him. The humans would be here soon.

A sense of impending danger skittered toward him along countless threads of *thism*: the recent hydrogue attack on Hrel-oro, a persistent anxiety emanating from a small skeleton crew on Maratha, and worst of all the murder of his son Pery'h and the incomprehensible rebellion on Hyrillka. And more had recently died there, many more. Jora'h had sensed it like thunder in his mind from Adar Zan'nh's maniple. Two days ago the sensation had slammed into him, then resonated through his whole body like a silver mallet striking a bone wind chime. But the *thism* was silent, cutting him off. He sensed that Zan'nh remained alive, but he knew no more than that about what was happening at Hyrillka.

Immediately after feeling the wave of deaths that burned him like hot acid, he had called the Solar Navy's ranking officer, Tal O'nh, to put together three scout cutters with a full crew. O'nh had dispatched them just this morning to reconnoiter at Hyrillka. Once they discovered what had happened to Adar Zan'nh's warliners, they had instructions to return with a full report.

Then he had ordered Tal O'nh to place his cohort of battleships on higher alert in the home system. Hydrogue warglobes had been seen in the nearby Durris trinary, and the Mage-Imperator feared that the recent devastation of Hrel-oro would not be the last hydrogue attack on an Ildiran colony.

Even if they came back at breakneck speed, he could not expect to hear from the scout cutters any sooner than tomorrow or the day after. He had to wait. Jora'h needed the Hyrillka matter resolved swiftly, so he could concentrate on the much bigger problem of the hydrogues. Osira'h was already on her way from Dobro. . . .

No, he thought, all was not perfect in his domain. After ten thousand years of peace, the Ildiran Empire now trembled on the brink of its darkest times. Again, he wished the human King had chosen a different time to pay his respects.

A flurry of bureaucrat kithmen announced the Hansa visitors with a flourish. The young King and Queen could not hide their joy or fascination as they approached the dais. Two steps behind them, the Hansa Chairman wore a stony, formal expression, unimpressed with the spectacle of the Prism Palace.

Jora'h smiled as he sat up to welcome them; he would not allow these visitors to suspect that anything might be amiss. His thick but short braid twitched of its own accord. He spread his hands. "King Peter of the Terran Hanseatic League, I am pleased and honored to welcome you. You should not have gone to the effort and expense of making a social journey just to visit me."

Basil stepped forward before the King could speak. "This is more than a social visit, Mage-Imperator. In these dangerous times, it is vital that humans and Ildirans maintain alliances and friendships."

"I agree. . . ." Jora'h looked at him. "But I was speaking to the King."

Basil covered a flash of annoyance. "You can address me, Mage-Imperator. I am Chairman Wenceslas—"

"I remember you from your earlier visit at the beginning of the hydrogue war. In fact, you were here when the hydrogue emissary assassinated your previous Great King."

Jora'h looked with sympathy at Peter. He had never understood the confusing succession of human rulers. Was old Frederick this one's father, as Cyroc'h was his own father? He decided to keep his words neutral. "I apologize for the loss of your predecessor, King Peter. I understand the emotional storms you must be enduring."

Peter nodded awkwardly, exchanging a glance with the Chairman.

Jora'h's father had seen humans as irrelevant at best, annoying and destructive at worst. True, these upstart humans were immature, greedy, unruly; and yet, facing the seemingly invincible hydrogues, they had held their own. No matter what obese old Cyroc'h had thought, perhaps these people were not so expendable nor so easily dismissed. Humans could have been true comrades in arms, instead of game pieces. Jora'h also felt a certain compassion toward them, thanks to the green priest Nira, a woman he had truly loved. . . .

He blinked as he suddenly realized that the brown-skinned Queen Estarra held a potted treeling in her arms. He flinched with quick delight as well as discomfort. He remembered beautiful young Nira, also from Theroc, arriving in his throne hall in a very similar fashion, also bringing a treeling. But that treeling was now dead, burned, destroyed in the same fire that had supposedly killed Nira. *All lies . . . my father's lies . . .*

Jora'h turned his attention toward the Queen, breaking from tradition. "And you are Estarra, daughter of Theroc."

She made a formal half-curtsy, her regal dress sparkling, and extended the potted treeling. "Do you remember the worldtrees from my world, Mage-Imperator? I seem to recall that the others here had died."

He looked intently at her. "I considered your brother

Reynald a friend, and the green priest Nira Khali was . . . very close to me. When I finally visited Theroc for myself, I saw that they did not exaggerate the wonders of the worldforest."

After he nodded his approval, lithe Yazra'h came forward from the side of the dais to take the treeling. Jora'h balanced it on the rim of his chrysalis chair, where he could study the delicate fronds. "I accept your gift with thanks. Our other treelings perished in a fire, and this one reminds me of pleasant times."

Estarra's dark eyes grew large with obvious pleasure. "I'm glad you remember so much about us."

Jora'h gave her a warm smile. How could he ever forget, after being so touched by the green priest and her tales? As Prime Designate, he had taken countless lovers, sired numerous offspring, interbred with many different Ildiran kiths—but none had been like her.

He did not allow his expression to change as he continued to stare at Estarra, who seemed embarrassed by so much attention. She threaded her arm through Peter's, and Jora'h saw the sparkle in her brown eyes, the obvious and genuine love they shared. Like the love he had shared with Nira.

Estarra's expression was wistful. "The hydrogues have done terrible damage to my worldforest. They killed both of my brothers, and my sisters are there now, trying to help."

"I am deeply sorry." *For many things.*

Still so many secrets, so many false stories. The humans knew only part of the truth. His father had set numerous schemes in motion, established alliances that could easily result in the destruction of Earth and its myriad colonies. And as Mage-Imperator, Jora'h's highest obligation was to protect the Empire at all costs.

When Osira'h finally brought the hydrogues to him—if

she survived the ordeal—what sort of deal would he be forced to make? How many sacrifices would the Ildirans have to accept? Would the humans have to pay?

He glanced at Estarra again, his smoky topaz eyes reflecting the light. "We must all face our tragedies and prepare ourselves to bear unexpected burdens."

Around them, a crowd of smooth-skinned servant kithmen rushed about at a frenetic pace. They set up low tables in the reception hall and covered them with plates, bowls of treats, decorative flowers; others carried musical instruments or strung colorful banners. A troupe of performers entered from side passages. Jora'h looked up, suddenly remembering the extravagant scheduled entertainment—another distraction, another stressful duty.

At least the King and Queen would be gone within a day, called back to Earth by their own pressing matters. Then he could concentrate once more on holding the Empire together.

27 ☀ OSIRA'H

The trinary system of Dùrris comprised three of the seven prominent suns in the Ildiran sky. Osira'h thought the star grouping looked beautiful, unlike anything she had seen at home on Dobro.

As their fast ship approached the center of the Empire, though, the girl could see that one of the suns was doomed.

Durris was composed of a white star and a yellow star tied closely together, and a red dwarf orbiting the mutual center of mass. The unstable celestial configuration had long ago ejected all large planets from the system, leaving only a halo of rubble on the outer fringes. Few Ildirans had any reason to go to Durris, except en route to someplace else.

Flying past, Osira'h and the Dobro Designate discovered that the trinary's yellow star was aswarm with clashing hydrogue warglobes and faeros fireballs. Judging by the flares and dark spots across the sun's photosphere, the titanic battle had already dealt the star a mortal blow. One of the seven suns of Ildira was going to die!

"Sound an alarm," Udru'h called to the pilot of their ship. "Send a message to inform the Mage-Imperator of what we have seen!"

As the pilot flew past Durris-B, Osira'h joined her uncle at a viewing window. She did not know what the great Mage-Imperator could do against such a disaster, but she kept her silence.

She stared with glittering eyes at the swarms of alien ships locked in titanic and incomprehensible battle, where the very fabric of the universe was a battlefield. Flares ripped through the roiling photosphere, followed by a blinding armada of ellipsoid faeros ships that collided with a thousand diamond-hulled warglobes in the sea of flames.

Osira'h clenched her small hands. No matter what lies her uncle had told her, this was real . . . and devastating. How could even the eternal Ildiran Empire survive a conflict such as this?

"What will stop them from spreading to the other Ildiran stars?" she asked him in quiet awe.

She knew his answer before he spoke it. "*You* will."

The girl's destiny was to go amongst the hydrogues, use her special telepathic ability to meld with the incomprehensible race, and convince them to negotiate with the Mage-Imperator. Other than the treacherous Klikiss robots, no one had succeeded in communicating with the deep-core aliens.

Udru'h looked at her, sensing her hesitation, though she had not spoken aloud. "The climax of hundreds of generations is unfolding in you. So many people have made sacrifices to create a person with your singular potential. You must not let them—or me—down."

The Designate squeezed her shoulder and gave her a paternal smile, trusting that she would do anything for him. He had always been so kind to her. *But not to all those other human breeding captives . . .*

The girl turned away from him, full of conflicting emotions and unspoken questions about his motives and his past crimes. Before her mother had revealed the truth to her, Osira'h had always enjoyed making this man proud of her. Before . . .

She stared at the dying sun, the clamor of giant alien ships, the surging weapons of solar flares and impossible icewave blasts. Her answer was clear, regardless of her other feelings. "I won't let you down."

28 ☀ TASIA TAMBLYN

The dry world had once been a bustling center of the Klikiss civilization, and the Earth government intended for Llaro to be much more than a barracks planet for a few prisoners of war.

When the three carriers full of Roamer detainees landed near the main Klikiss ruins, Tasia looked out at the tan rocks, the fantastic curving formations that had once been inhabited hives. "It's not exactly the garden spot of the Galaxy, EA, but at least it isn't a hellhole. Roamers have been perfectly happy with places worse than this."

"Yes, Master Tasia Tamblyn," EA said. "You have given me a general history of the original clan settlements."

"Factual summaries, not actual memories."

"I'm afraid that's all I can have."

Before being dispatched here, Tasia had seen a sketchy but official EDF map of the Llaro settlement. Now, even from the air she noticed the progress in building and excavations: A main flat area had been cleared as a spaceport for EDF transport ships, personnel carriers, and local short-distance craft. Adjacent to the landing zone stood a new Eddy base erected to monitor the Roamer detainees from Hurricane Depot and Rendezvous. Predictably, the military base was laid out on a rigid grid, as if it had come out of a box and been assembled according to directions.

Slightly less regimented, but still composed of prefab structures, was a new colony town of free settlers. Eager volunteers who had accepted the Hansa's offer of free land and assistance had come here through a nexus of Klikiss transportals and erected their homes, ready to scratch out an existence here.

And then all the fresh Roamer prisoners had been dumped among them. The first batch of detainees from Hurricane Depot had established their own encampment on the outskirts of the colony town. Ostensibly a temporary settlement, what the Roamers had built looked like an old bazaar of awnings, tents, and nonstandard structures. Pennants, clan banners, and curtains defiantly proclaimed their family identities, even in captivity.

And now she was bringing another large group of captives to join them.

Tasia waited on the flight deck as the detainees were released from the carriers. They had no assigned guards, strict rules, or regimentation; her orders were just to turn them loose on the planet. Llaro had no fences, no curfews, but it wasn't as if they could go anywhere.

Angry and uneasy, the new arrivals gathered under Llaro's pink-and-lavender skies, milling around in front of the personnel transports, waiting for someone to tell them what to do. Tasia knew she couldn't put it off any longer. She straightened her uniform and went down with EA to address the group. She owed it to them, and to herself, to look them in the eyes . . . even if it wasn't necessarily a good idea.

Admiral Willis had cautioned her about getting too close to the captives. "I don't want to find you strung up with your throat slit just because the Roamers question the wisdom of your career choice."

"They aren't like that." Tasia hoped her assessment was right. She'd been isolated from the clans for almost eight years now, out of touch since she'd joined the Earth Defense Forces.

She did not let herself show anxiety as she and EA stepped out to stand on the landing field. The crowds turned toward her. Tasia looked just like any other Eddy officer with her close-cropped hair and her clean formal uniform. No one would ever recognize her as a Roamer, and she wasn't sure she wanted to point it out.

Though the EDF had issued the refugees standard jump-suits and toiletry items, most of the new prisoners still clung to their rumpled old clothes with clan markings embroidered on pockets and along seams. Tasia didn't blame them.

The prisoners looked disoriented, some disappointed and others relieved, as they gazed around the open landscape. One man, whom she recognized as Crim Tylar from long-ago clan gatherings, kept glancing at Tasia as if on the verge of remembering something. He stared at EA, then back at Tasia. She met his eyes and waited, not willing to volunteer the information. Finally he said, "You've got a Tamblyn look about you."

"Tasia Tamblyn, daughter of Bram."

"I thought so." Tylar scowled. "You joined the Eddies after Blue Sky Mine was destroyed."

"I joined them to fight hydrogues."

"Yeah, I can see that." He gave her a mocking look. "What do your uncles have to say about all this? They must be so proud."

The sarcasm bit deep, but she did not flinch. "I haven't had a chance to see them. It's not as if the EDF lets me go off to visit hidden Roamer settlements."

"I bet they'd like that . . . with a nice tracer on your ship? Or did you tell them where our greenhouses were, and Hurricane Depot, and Rendezvous—"

Tasia's eyes flashed. "I did no such thing."

Marla Chan stood beside her husband. "Were you part of the raid that wrecked Rendezvous? Were you on the ships that attacked Hhrenni?"

"I don't agree with that policy, and I had no part in any action against Roamers. My superiors have pulled me from the theater. I accepted this assignment so that I could help Roamer detainees. It's the best I can do."

Crim Tylar sniffed. "You could steal a ship and just go. Any Roamer could figure out how."

"Then how would I help all the people here? And how would I ever fight the hydrogues? I have to believe the Big Goose will come to its senses soon—"

"Sure, as soon as we're all exterminated!"

The other crowded Roamers were beginning to grumble. Tasia squared her shoulders and raised her voice. "I am not your enemy. I plan to do everything within my authority to make your time here on Llaro bearable. I know it's a lot to ask, but if you knew my father, my brothers, and my uncles, then I hope you'll give me the benefit of the doubt."

Tylar glanced pointedly at her crisp EDF uniform, her rank insignia. "There doesn't seem to be much doubt."

"I'll see to it that you're settled here with the other Roamers. You'll be safe and comfortable until this whole mess is resolved. I hope it's over swiftly."

"It won't be over soon," Marla said. "Not the way the Eddies keep stomping on us. Rendezvous and Hurricane Depot are destroyed, the clans are scattered across the Spiral Arm. Nobody even knows where the Speaker is."

Feeling uneasy and awkward, Tasia didn't know how to answer. Finally, she turned to her compy. "EA, see to it that my crew helps get these people set up in barracks or camps, whichever they prefer."

"Yes, Master Tasia. I will talk to them and let them tell me their needs."

She watched as the first groups of Roamer captives from the existing encampment came forward to meet the new arrivals. The merciful glare of sun in her eyes prevented her from seeing the sour and skeptical expressions around her.

29 ☀ ADAR ZAN'NH

When a smug Thor'h came to the maniple's flagship, he had orders to escort the still-uncooperative Zan'nh to the surface of Hyrillka. The disgraced Prime Designate brought three times as many guard kithmen with him as the Adar could possibly have hoped to fight off, especially now that he felt disconnected from the strong foundation of *thism*. Good, at least they were still afraid of him.

As they marched toward the royal shuttle in the docking bay, from which all stains of blood and death had been scoured, Thor'h looked at his brother. "Though you have given your word, I know you have no intention of truly surrendering. You do not look to me like a man who is defeated."

"I am not defeated. I still have my honor."

Thor'h chuckled. "Pery'h kept his honor—and died. Meanwhile, I am still Prime Designate." His thin lips curved upward in a wolfish smile.

"The Mage-Imperator has stripped you of that title." The guards stared at Zan'nh, as if reconsidering their decision not to put him in shackles.

Thor'h looked serene instead of annoyed. "And in turn we have stripped him of *his* title as Mage-Imperator. That is more important. I am the Prime Designate to the true Imperator now."

"The truth is the truth," Zan'nh retorted. "Reality is not decided by the opinions of a few rebels."

The shuttle descended toward Hyrillka. Despite his brave face, the Adar felt disoriented. His mind wavered. As the crews of each of the warliners faded away from him, torn loose from the *thism,* he became more and more isolated, like a man slowly losing pieces of himself, one limb at a time.

Though the numbers of Ildirans around him remained undiminished, Zan'nh could not feel them as he normally sensed the comforting presence of his people. Ildirans could not function well alone and required a critical mass of their minds to keep them all joined together. Now the Adar of the Ildiran Solar Navy was becoming blind and deaf to a comforting foundation he had always taken for granted.

As he sat in the shuttle in grim and angry silence, Zan'nh recalled when he and Adar Kori'nh had gone together to an eerily empty skymine drifting above the haunted clouds of Daym. The two men alone had not been enough to keep themselves strong and stable, even with a fully crewed warliner riding high above them, and they had left the place quickly.

Cut off, he now felt his connection to the Mage-Imperator grow tenuous and uncertain. He remained aware of his father in the far-off Prism Palace, and he was certain

Jora'h understood that something dangerous and unexpected had happened to the warliners . . . but he could not send a clear message. No details, just a sharp anxiety. The Mage-Imperator would know the loss of all the warliner crews as they faded from the *thism*. Would he assume those Ildiran soldiers were dead? Would Jora'h assume his own Adar had failed completely?

In truth, Zan'nh knew he had.

As they approached the tiled spaceport landing field, Zan'nh looked through the shuttle's window, silently gathering information. The visible cropland across Hyrillka had been reseeded with nialia plantmoths in order to produce vast amounts of shiing. Over the past year, many structures had been rebuilt in the wake of the hydrogue attack. The new buildings looked austere and functional, without the colorful frivolities the Hyrillka Designate had previously enjoyed. Rusa'h had turned into an entirely different person after recovering from his head injury. Clearly, his mind was damaged, and the medical kithmen had been unable to treat him properly. Rusa'h was truly insane.

Thor'h, though, was a different story. The Prime Designate had made his own decisions, willingly turned to the rebel cause. "You should have known better, Thor'h. Why would you cooperate with this foolish venture? You know the Hyrillka Designate cannot succeed against the whole Solar Navy."

"I know nothing of the sort. Our uncle has seen the truth in a holy vision. How am I to doubt that?"

"By using your common sense," Zan'nh snapped, but he knew the conversation was useless.

The main spaceport was a bustling complex. Numerous new cargo ships waited with open hatches in the mosaic-tiled landing zones; workers streamed aboard, loading tanks of fresh shiing gas. And now Rusa'h had a maniple of war-liners, each ship with a brainwashed crew. Zan'nh felt ill.

I should have ordered the destruction of my own vessels.

After the shuttle landed, guards came forward to escort the captive Adar up the hill to the citadel palace. Thor'h strutted in the lead, his head held high. They took Zan'nh to a private, thick-walled chamber within the citadel, and Thor'h gestured for him to enter. "These quarters were last used by our poor brother Pery'h. He no longer requires them."

Zan'nh said, "I doubt you did anything to prevent his murder."

"Prevent it? I encouraged it. It was the only way we could bring *you* running with a whole maniple of warliners. It was an irresistible lure, a trap—entirely successful. Look at all we have gained."

"What you have gained? You have lost your soul."

Rather than leaving Zan'nh alone, Thor'h called for re-freshments. After attender kithmen hurried in bearing the food, the former Prime Designate ate some of the sweets. He smiled as if this was a carefree social gathering, but Zan'nh glowered at him, refusing the food.

"Then I will eat. I have also called for shiing. Perhaps you would care to try some? It will increase your understanding."

"I already understand enough."

"You are too young to be a stubborn old fossil." He held up a small vial of the pearlescent, milky liquid, freshly harvested from the plantmoths. He looked at it hungrily, as if he longed to consume it himself, but Rusa'h had forbidden shiing to anyone already converted.

"I will not be corrupted as you have been," Zan'nh said.

"That depends upon your definition of corrupted." Thor'h set the vial aside. "Our father is merely perpetuating the mistakes his own father and grandfather made before him. It is time for a change." The young man clasped his hands together, his expression sincere. "Believe me, Zan'nh. I am doing this for the good of the Ildiran Empire, and so is our uncle Rusa'h. It would be so much better if the Adar of the Solar Navy were to join our cause willingly, rationally—as I did."

Zan'nh refused to answer. Already his thoughts were directed toward developing a plan to escape, to send a clear warning back to Mijistra.

A guard stepped up to the door. "We have received word from Imperator Rusa'h. The forty-six warliners have been entirely subsumed. Their crews are now properly bound to the new pattern of *thism*."

Grinning, Thor'h turned to his brother. "You see, Zan'nh—even if you choose not to cooperate with us, the rightful Imperator will spread his enlightenment across the whole Horizon Cluster. Now that he has your warliners, nothing can stop him."

30 ☀ KING PETER

On their swift return journey from Ildira, Peter watched his Queen struggle to maintain her composure despite a severe bout of morning sickness. In their quarters, he tried to comfort her through her nausea, noting the clammy face and hands and the grayish cast to her skin. He hoped that monitoring imagers wouldn't pick it up. Both of them remained convinced they were being watched at all times.

While relaxing, he and Estarra played games in their quarters, making pleasant but guarded conversation. When she rushed to the sink for another bout of vomiting, she mumbled the lie they had decided upon. "My stomach must still be upset from that Ildiran food. Good thing we only stayed a day."

Peter patted her forearm. "Yes, I feel a bit queasy myself. I'm sure the Mage-Imperator has the finest chefs, but we have different metabolisms."

They hoped the excuse was good enough.

He told her to rest in their quarters, then went to the closed door of the Chairman's cabin. He signaled twice, no doubt interrupting important Hansa work. "Basil, I just wanted to say that we'd love to have breakfast with you, but spaceflight has never agreed with the Queen. She's relaxing to gather her energy for a reception when we get back to Earth. Sorry."

The Chairman looked up from his document screens, giving Peter a bland but cool gaze. "Breakfast? Are these attempts at sociability meant to influence me in some way? If there is no audience in front of us, then you don't need to pretend for my benefit."

Peter bowed, covering his smile. "As you wish, Basil." Preoccupied, the Chairman made no further comment and sealed the door again.

Of course, Peter wanted to keep Estarra as far from the man as possible. But if they were too obvious about hiding, someone would suspect. Both by lessons and by example, the Chairman had taught Peter many tricks of manipulation.

For a time he'd thought the Chairman actively despised him, but then he realized that Basil didn't waste time or energy on such strong emotions. As Chairman of the Hansa, Basil Wenceslas expected the King to follow his role and his duties precisely. Nothing more. He grew angry at the young man only when Peter stepped out of bounds and challenged his authority. Otherwise, Basil didn't bother to think about him at all. The Chairman had no time for friends or enemies. He existed for *administration,* for making decisions and conducting the business of human civilization.

During their brief visit in the Prism Palace, Peter had been surprised at the Mage-Imperator's deep interest in Estarra and Theroc. Jora'h had been drawn to the Queen, more interested in talking about her brother Reynald and the green priests who had come to visit him in Mijistra than about diplomatic matters.

Now, as they thought about their visit of state, Estarra looked up at Peter with her large brown eyes. "I wish Reynald could have been there with us."

Peter sat next to her on the bed and pulled her close. With the surreptitious help of the Teacher compy OX in the Whisper Palace, the two had been developing a secret language: key hand signals, gestures, and code words that they hoped no one else would decipher. Now he silently reassured her, told her he loved her.

"Did the Mage-Imperator look troubled to you?" she pressed. "He seemed very disturbed, pulled in a thousand different directions."

He glanced at a tiny nick in the ceiling, where he was sure a monitoring imager had been hidden. He ignored it, not caring if he was overheard. "Think of how much goes on behind the scenes in the Hansa—underhanded deals and secret decisions and forced activities. The Ildirans aren't human, but I'll bet similar things weigh upon the Mage-Imperator."

"I hope he solves them," the Queen said.

"I hope we do, too."

When they returned to Earth orbit, the Chairman informed Peter and Estarra that he was slipping away in a shuttle before all the fanfare began, so he could meet with other Hansa administrators and discuss the statements Mage-Imperator Jora'h had made. Then Basil turned away. It was an announcement, not a polite goodbye. His shuttle separated from the diplomatic transport and raced down into the Palace District.

Meanwhile, Peter and Estarra had to stage a much more formal arrival. Before departing, Basil handed them a speech and ordered Peter to record it. He had long since stopped allowing the King to do anything live. Peter glanced at the words, quickly memorizing them. The speech was relatively innocuous, a cheerleading rally, nothing that he couldn't stomach saying—unlike other times.

The King and Queen dutifully took their positions in the diplomatic transport's recording chamber, surrounded by an artificial background projected to look like the area over which they would cruise.

"The alliance between Ildirans and the Hansa remains strong," Peter said, striving to make his voice firm and confident. "The Queen and I have visited the Mage-Imperator, who is as committed to defeating the hydrogues as his father was. With the Ildiran Solar Navy fighting beside the Earth Defense Forces, we shall stand against the enemy aliens who have already wrought so much havoc."

Now Estarra joined in. "The hydrogues nearly destroyed my home. They killed both of my brothers."

Peter continued, "We must fight them, but we cannot fight them alone. The Ildirans feel the same. Your Queen and I return to Earth after securing bonds of friendship and mutual aid with our friends."

The protocol minister, under strict instructions from Chairman Wenceslas, had them record the speech three times, splicing the best parts together into one perfect presentation.

Unhurried, the diplomatic transport was met high above the city by a ponderous and ornate royal dirigible. After Peter and Estarra transferred over in a connecting tube, the diplomatic craft flew away, no longer needed. The huge airship was slow and ceremonial, perfect for ensuring that the King and Queen were seen by as many people as possible.

The royal dirigible was accompanied by fast-flying escort ships that flitted like bees around a pollen-laden flower. By the time the royal dirigible came low over the Palace District, the recorded speech was ready for release. The smooth fabric sides of the enormous zeppelin shimmered, and the sideskins projected the video on adaptive films so that the faces of the King and Queen filled the sides of the huge airship.

"The alliance between Ildirans and the Hansa remains strong," Peter's voice boomed.

While the recording played, he and Estarra stood below in the tiny ceremonial gondola, as if they were delivering the words in real time. From such a distance, the actual figures of the King and Queen were tiny, but they did what was expected of them. Even from such a great height they could hear the murmur of the crowd, the loud cheering of thousands of citizens. Their recorded words simultaneously echoed from speaker stands all across the plaza and up and down the streets.

And for a few moments at least, Peter and Estarra were unmonitored and alone. They could finally talk, quickly and quietly, as the thunderously loud words throbbed around them.

Estarra clutched her husband's hand. "I don't think he noticed anything out of the ordinary. We must have slipped a few times, but the Chairman showed no reaction. Our secret is safe."

"With Basil you never can tell." Peter's face remained concerned. "It's only a matter of time, though. We're just postponing the inevitable. Soon there'll be indications of your pregnancy that even he can't miss."

Her voice sounded painfully innocent. "If we can keep it secret long enough, the decision will be made for him. Another month maybe, and then it'll be too late for the Chairman to do anything."

Peter shook his head. "I wouldn't count on that. He may insist on getting rid of the baby despite the risk to you, just because . . ."

Estarra's eyes welled up with tears. "I don't understand, Peter. Why would he want that? What does it gain him?"

"It would be out of spite, not logic. We defied him, and he *can't* allow us to have that kind of freedom. He'll never tolerate such a blatant challenge to his authority."

"But it was an accident! I never even intended to get pregnant."

"Basil won't see it that way. He's got to be in control, and if we're loose cannons, he *must* put us in our place." Then Peter frowned, calculating. "Unless he realizes that our child would be an excellent way of controlling us. A pawn."

Estarra looked at him in alarm. "All the Chairman has to do is threaten our baby, and we'll have no choice but to listen."

Meanwhile the images of their faces delivered strong and optimistic messages about human and Ildiran solidarity against the hydrogues.

He remembered when Basil had used Estarra herself as similar leverage, threatening his beautiful young Queen if Peter didn't do as he was told. "As a last resort, we may have to make Basil see that advantage. It could be our only chance to keep the baby alive."

The Queen leaned against him, groaning. "Maybe we should just tell him and hope for the best."

"Hope for the best?" He stroked her cheek, sharing a bittersweet smile. "We can do better than that."

The dirigible circled the enormous Whisper Palace three times. In a well-rehearsed parade, royal guards flanked the elliptical landing area for the bloated airship, which drifted to the flagstone surface. Gravity cables linked into locking anchors, and an elevator dropped Peter and Estarra to a receiving platform, where the bearded old Archfather of Unison greeted them. The Hansa's official religious leader held a scepter high and stood beside the King and Queen.

Peter had never spoken freely with the benevolent-looking old man, who also held an entirely ceremonial post with no real power. The Archfather's cheeks were rosy—makeup, probably—and his pale blue eyes were surrounded by many wrinkles, but his gaze was blank. He said his scripted words and offered his prayer, then led a procession that returned Peter and Estarra to the Whisper Palace.

It was a grand, colorful, and noisy show designed specifically to convince the public that everything was perfectly right with the Terran Hanseatic League.

King Peter felt very tired.

31 ☀ OSIRA'H

She felt very small as the Dobro Designate marched her into the presence of the Mage-Imperator. Osira'h had anticipated this moment for most of her life; it was time for her to walk down the path of a destiny she had never asked for. Uniformed guard kithmen stood inside the skysphere reception hall prepared to give their lives to protect their powerful leader. Such unwavering loyalty.

Prompted by Udru'h, Osira'h came forward with small, uncertain footsteps. She'd met her father when he had come to Dobro to visit her mother's grave, and even then she had been filled with doubts about his real motivations. Had he truly been unaware of the horrors? Now her mind resonated with secondhand recollections from Nira Khali.

When she looked into Jora'h's face, the girl could not drive back the flood of past experiences planted inside her mind shortly before her mother's death. Through Nira's eyes, she saw this man as the Prime Designate, a loving and compassionate son of scheming Mage-Imperator Cyroc'h. Jora'h would never have sanctioned the terrible things Nira and the other breeding prisoners on Dobro had endured. Or so her mother had believed.

Seeing him now, up there on the sunlit dais in his ornate chrysalis chair, Osira'h watched through a flood of secondary vision, memories as crystal clear as the colored panes that formed the skysphere above: Jora'h as a younger man holding Nira, his pale Ildiran skin warm against her mother's chlorophyll-green arms, legs, breasts. She remembered his touch, his kisses, the way he fired her nerves. In a detached way, Osira'h wondered if she had witnessed her own conception.

These were not memories any child should have of her father, but Osira'h felt no revulsion, no sense of voyeurism. Part of her *was* her mother, and Nira had loved this man, trusted him. She never believed that he had abandoned her. But Osira'h knew the power this man held in his hands. He had done nothing to wipe clean all the forced rapes and the horrific genetic experiments with secret human prisoners, even after he knew the truth. What was he waiting for? Osira'h wasn't sure her father deserved such reverence. In fact, she wasn't sure about anything.

. The Dobro Designate held back as Jora'h stepped down the dais to meet her. The Mage-Imperator's eyes glinted with pride and hope. "My brother Udru'h says you are ready, Osira'h. The Ildiran Empire can wait no longer. Do you accept the terrible task that falls to you—to find the hydrogues, form a bridge, and bring them back here, to me?"

Osira'h stood as tall as she could and said what they expected to hear. "I not only accept my duty, I embrace it."

When Jora'h responded with a warm smile, a part of her wanted to dissolve with happiness. "That is as much as I expected from you—and more." He tentatively embraced her, but the girl remained stiff, not sure how to respond. Did he truly see Osira'h as his daughter, or merely as a pawn, a tool to be used for the good of the Empire?

Then, with surprise, she noticed a potted treeling that rested in the sunlight next to the chrysalis chair. She felt a pull and a longing in her heart—her mother had been torn from her blessed communion with the worldforest mind, had been so desperate to feel that contact again. A lump swelled in the girl's throat, and she wanted to run to the small plant, wrap her thin fingers around it, send out a wild message through telink.

If she was able.

Instead, Osira'h held herself back, though the Mage-Imperator had already seen the hungry look in her eyes. "Is that one of the worldtrees of Theroc?"

Jora'h glanced at Udru'h, then back at her, puzzled. "Yes, but how would you recognize it?"

Osira'h thought swiftly, not wanting to reveal anything of what she knew, not to anyone. "I studied many subjects on Dobro. The instructors and mentalists are very thorough—and the Designate tells me I am special because my mother was a human green priest."

Udru'h himself seemed perplexed at the presence of the treeling. "I thought all of the Theron growths were dead, Liege."

"This one was a recent gift from Queen Estarra of the humans." Jora'h narrowed his eyes. "I intend to take good care of it. *And keep it safe.*"

Osira'h could feel her body trembling with a need to touch the treeling. She would find a way soon. The Mage-Imperator would not send her to the hydrogues for another few days, while the necessary preparations were made. Osira'h would have her chance. . . .

Udru'h bowed formally. "Liege, I need to return to Dobro. The Designate-in-waiting and I must continue to train Osira'h's siblings, in the eventuality of her failure."

Standing beside his daughter, Jora'h glared at him. "Do you not have confidence in her?"

Though Osira'h was right there in front of him, her uncle's answer was aloof and cold. "I devoted my life to preparing the girl. However, the fate of our Empire is at stake. I will not gamble on only one possibility."

With that, the Dobro Designate, the man who had raised her and cared for her, the man who had shown so much love and hope—and also the man who had imprisoned and repeatedly raped her mother, then had her beaten to death—turned and left Osira'h without another word.

32 ☀ RLINDA KETT

After Davlin Lotze departed for Earth in his commandeered vessel, Rlinda stayed on Relleker just long enough to help BeBob load the *Blind Faith* with the equipment earmarked for new Hansa colonies. Governor Pekar never seemed to run out of ways to complain about how long it was taking them, how much money she had lost on hospitality and supplies consumed by the unwanted refugees from Crenna, and how glad she would be to see them go.

With every insistent nudge, Rlinda lost even more motivation to hurry, and she would have been happy to find a nice dark hole where the governor could stuff her impatience. Once crammed aboard the overloaded *Voracious Curiosity,* the remaining Crenna colonists would be miserable; now that they were no longer fleeing certain death, the long trip would seem unbearably rough.

Still, it hadn't taken the refugees long to recognize that Relleker did not want them around. After BeBob departed for the next stop on his supply run, Rlinda decided to stop playing games and get everyone aboard. They had higher hopes for a warm reception on Earth.

With little ceremony and only a few curt farewells, Governor Pekar shooed away the *Curiosity*. Though discouraged by the lack of human warmth on Relleker, Rlinda was not a spiteful woman (no matter what some of her ex-husbands said). She bore no ill will toward the inhabitants of the struggling colony; she just didn't want to spend more time with them. A sense of freedom like being in zero gravity filled her as the *Curiosity* lifted off from the settlement—no bon voyage party here—and climbed to orbit.

"Good riddance," she muttered, having no doubt the governor was saying the same thing from the ground.

She took her lumbering ship into orbit, beyond Relleker's first moonlet, and then the second high moon. As she increased speed, Rlinda scanned the system around her while she projected the path to Earth. "There we go, can't miss it." She reached for the Ildiran stardrive, then toggled the intership comm. "Hold on, everybody. I'll get us there as fast as I can.

Drinks are on me as soon as we get to Earth." She heard muted cheering from the crowded decks.

Before engaging the stardrive, she paused to take a final glance back at Relleker. Her sensors picked up moving objects, large ones approaching at high velocity. From nearby Crenna?

The *Curiosity* lurched as Rlinda cut the engines, bouncing her passengers around, but she wasn't ready to sound the alarm yet. Grim-faced, Rlinda increased magnification on the images, and groaned. She had seen this sort of thing before—too damned many times. While the ship drifted, she made out a stream of diamond-hulled warglobes swooping into the Relleker system like glistening buckshot. "Holy crap, look at them come!"

When they'd left the dead Crenna system, Rlinda's ship had faced the victorious hydrogue warglobes. The deep-core aliens had just vanquished their faeros enemies in the sun, and the diamond warships had hovered in front of the *Voracious Curiosity*. Rlinda still didn't know how she had escaped destruction then, but she didn't want to test her luck again.

The stream of warglobes came from the high, cold reaches above the planetary orbits. She counted fourteen of them, a massive assault force. Her heart sank. They must have traveled to the next sun after Crenna to fight the faeros in Relleker's star. If the results of the struggle were the same as before, within a week or so this system would be cold and dead as well, uninhabitable.

Rlinda didn't usually think unkind thoughts, but she wondered how smug Governor Pekar would feel when *she* had to evacuate her entire population and go hat in hand in search of help.

But the warglobes did not head for Relleker's sun. Instead, they flew toward the planet itself. According to the *Curiosity*'s long-range sensors, the enemy ships were descending directly above the main human settlement. The deep-core aliens knew exactly what they were doing.

Within moments, Governor Pekar squawked into the comm system, sounding a general alarm and calling out for help. "Warglobes are attacking! They have begun to open fire." The governor's words cut off with a scream, and Rlinda heard an explosion in the distance. "Mayday! Help! We need an immediate evacuation!"

Rlinda restarted the *Curiosity*'s engines, turned about, and raced back toward Relleker, her heart pounding. She didn't know what she could do. Already overloaded, she could take no more people aboard. Her decks were full, her corridors crowded with far more evacuees than the *Curiosity* had ever been meant to carry. Simply landing and taking off again would be a major undertaking. Without a green priest, she had no way even of calling for help in time.

The warglobes swept over the main colony, unleashed their electric-blue weapons, then dumped icewaves that crackled and shattered all trees and buildings and any humans who were in the way.

Having seen the attack from one of the observation screens, Crenna's mayor, Lupe Ruis, stumbled into her cockpit. His round face was florid. "What's going on down there? Don't we have to help them?"

"Tell me how, and I'll do it." Together, they listened to the incessant screams. The diamond-hulled warglobes continued to unleash their fury, hammering away at the settlement, ripping up every structure. "In fact—" Rlinda shifted course and headed at an extreme angle away from the direction in which the warglobes had come, then shut all her systems down to drift without producing an energy signature. "I don't want the drogues to notice *us* when they get bored with their attack down there."

"But those people on Relleker . . . they helped us. We have to—"

She looked at him with her large brown eyes. "I'm not having a snit, Mayor. And I'm not just trying to save my pretty hide. You know I've put my butt on the line for every last one of you. I just can't think of any way to assist them."

Her scans were at the highest magnification, but thankfully she couldn't see the devastation the warglobes continued to wreak down below. The hydrogues kept pounding and pounding.

The destruction of Boone's Crossing, Corvus Landing, even Crenna with its murdered sun, had not been direct assaults on humans. These warglobes, however, bombarded Relleker's towns and outlying buildings, focused their attack on the colony areas and nowhere else. The human settlement was the intended target, not just collateral damage in a cosmic war against incomprehensibly alien beings.

"Something sure pissed the hydrogues off." Maybe the human colony was just too tempting a victim after the hydrogues finished their destruction of Crenna's sun. Or maybe the drogues had reasons that no human could understand anyway. Then she remembered that not long ago Chairman Wenceslas had authorized the use of five more Klikiss Torches. Five more hydrogue gas planets had been obliterated. A clear provocation? "Damned fools! They had to go and light a bunch of fuses—what did they expect? No wonder the drogues are retaliating."

The screams continued over the comm system for no more than an hour, at which point every standing structure and every living person on Relleker had been erased. Rlinda found it appalling.

She glanced at Mayor Ruis. "I hope those drogues are satisfied and don't come hunting us for a little extra sport. We're playing possum, but who knows how good their scanners are? As it is, we got away just in time." Alarmed and sickened, the mayor hurried to spread the word.

Rlinda flicked switches and cut even the *Curiosity*'s running lights. She'd been in similar situations before, but her heart felt leaden, and her throat was dry. If Governor Pekar hadn't forced them to leave, all of the Crenna refugees— and BeBob and herself—would have been down there as well, slaughtered. . . .

The outcome of the Relleker massacre had been assured. She couldn't have done anything to save them. The only thing she could accomplish now was to survive, keep all the Crenna refugees aboard alive—and haul ass for Earth with the news.

33 ☀ ORLI COVITZ

Though he had not asked for the girl's company, the old hermit took his responsibility seriously. "I always knew I needed a permanent shelter. Now I've got the impetus I needed to get off my ass and build my own private castle."

Orli self-consciously brushed herself off. She felt as dirty as Hud Steinman looked. "I wasn't complaining about sleeping on the ground." Even so, she had to admit that the camping experience was a lot more fun in the concept stage than in the execution.

"Didn't say you were. But my back hurts. Time to design and build a house." He looked at her, his brow furrowed. "I don't suppose you know anything about carpentry? Architecture?"

"Only a little bit that I read in schoolbooks."

Steinman shrugged. "How hard can it be? We'll figure it out."

While he scratched out plans and chose a spot by a freshwater spring for their "homestead," Orli helped with whatever else she could find to do. She sorted through the salvaged tools from the colony town, deciding which could be used for their task. She rechecked Steinman's calculations, attempting to do so when he wasn't looking. She knew he saw her doing it, but he did not object, either thinking the idea was cute, or just glad to have someone verify his math. She found a few mistakes but did not point them out to the old man.

When he'd finally convinced himself he knew what he was doing, Steinman showed her his hand-sketched plans and explained how the two of them would go about building a house. "We can cut down poletrees for lumber. We can make boards with the laser saw, and the skinnier logs will make a perfect framework."

Orli let herself be carried away by his enthusiasm. "I bet we could weave some of the long grasses into strips, like ropes. Use it for lashing logs." She'd already plaited a few of them around the campfire.

"Didn't people make bricks out of mud a long time ago?" Steinman suggested. "We could probably do that, too. This world is full of building materials!"

She and Steinman easily felled one of the poletrees, and when the long trunk crashed into the grasses, two startled lowriders thrashed away. The topmost section of the poletree provided three sturdy logs that were easily carryable. When Steinman attempted to slice the thicker trunk into flat, even boards, though, he mangled the wood so badly it could be used for nothing other than patching up walls. "Okay, so I'm not a lumberjack. Never said I was."

The second and third attempts were little better, but by the fourth poletree they had enough wood to begin. They sank the main logs deep into the ground, poured water into the holes, and packed them in with a mixture of mud and gravel. They worked together to raise the corner supports, sliding crossbars into notches that Orli made in the logs, and the shelter began to take shape.

They followed Steinman's grand plan as best they could. When the major work was complete, the girl stared at the makeshift shelter. No doubt Steinman had envisioned a quaint and primitive palace, a rugged Robinson Crusoe home. Instead, it looked like a shack that would blow down in the first big storm.

It was the sort of poorly planned and poorly executed scheme her father might have come up with.

Stung by the thought, she lifted her chin. No matter how rickety the place looked, Orli was proud of their work. She and Steinman had built this themselves, with only the most primitive materials and under difficult circumstances.

"That'll do," she said. Steinman clapped her on the back.

•   •   •

Tired of having furry crickets to eat every night, Orli scavenged among the prairie grasses in search of other grains, tubers, or fruits that might be edible. She had no idea where to start, though. She carefully nibbled samples of leaves, berries, starchy roots. She identified and shied away from a few leaves with a powerfully bitter or acidic taste; one bluish berry made her vomit instantly. But a lumpy brown root tasted sweet enough, and she experienced no ill effects after she ate it. Some of the flowers were so spicy that they made her nose burn, but they tasted fine. Gradually, she added color and variety to their diet.

Steinman watched what she was doing and cautioned, "Spit out anything that tastes like poison."

"And what does poison taste like?"

"I don't know. If I tasted poison, I'd probably be dead."

Exasperated, Orli rolled her eyes and looked up into the sky as if for guidance—and froze. She squinted until she was sure that what she saw was the burning trail of a descending ship heading directly toward the canyon and the destroyed colony.

"A ship! A ship—look, Mr. Steinman!"

Steinman clapped his hands and laughed. "Probably one of the Hansa supply ships, kid. Weren't we supposed to get another delivery of equipment?"

As the small vessel flew high overhead, swelling from a black speck in the sky until it became recognizable as a cargo ship, Orli ran out on the prairie, waving her arms.

"Come on! We've got to get to the town site before he decides to take off again," Steinman called.

The two of them crashed through the grasses. Lowriders, hearing their wild approach, scuttled away, not wanting to face this noisy stampede. Orli rapidly outdistanced the older man, but forced herself to lag so Steinman could catch up. She was anxious to see the rescuers, but on the chance it was another robot attack, she wanted the old hermit nearby.

By the time they reached the landing field just outside the canyon, Orli's throat was raw from yelling. Beside her, Steinman wheezed like a set of giant bellows, but he didn't seem to notice. He stumbled ahead, taking the girl by the hand.

The ship had already flown into the canyon to investigate, then circled back. The pilot must have been trying to transmit to the colony station, but heard no response. The cargo ship cruised again over the black, sooty ruins and tipped its wings to indicate that the pilot had seen the two of them. After searching for a cleared spot in the rubble, the craft set down.

Orli ran forward with tears streaming down her face. A man with wide eyes, frizzy hair, and leathery skin stepped out of the supply ship. The expression on his lean face was one of utter astonishment. Orli remembered Branson Roberts, who had delivered equipment to the colony not long before. Roberts stared at the two gasping people running toward him from the tall grasses.

Everywhere he looked there was destruction. Corribus had been entirely annihilated. Roberts opened and closed his mouth several times until finally he blurted out, "Holy crap—and crap again! What happened here?"

Orli threw herself into his arms, and the man automatically folded her in a reassuring hug. She was sobbing too much to answer him.

"We'd, uh, appreciate a lift out of here," Steinman said, "if you could manage it."

34 ☀ BASIL WENCESLAS

While General Lanyan droned complaints at him in the empty Hansa boardroom, Basil stood with his hands behind his back, studying the portraits of his predecessors. The faces of the sixteen former Chairmen of the Hanseatic League looked stern and self-important, true demigods of business and empire.

Three days ago he had been standing before the Mage-Imperator in the Prism Palace. Seeing the dynasty of the Ildiran leaders had made him think of his own forebears in the Hansa Headquarters. Like him, these men and women had controlled the wheels of commerce as human ambition spread from the Earth to the Moon and then the inner solar system. Next came the eleven generation ships, slow-moving monstrosities whose passengers cut their umbilical to home, assuming they'd never return.

Incensed as usual, Lanyan had asked for a conference within hours after the Chairman returned from his diplomatic visit. "According to the latest summary, in the seven years since the hydrogue war began, we have lost almost a hundred of our conscripted scout ships. In only three instances have we found legitimate evidence that the vessels suffered some mishap. The others simply . . . left. The pilots are AWOL. They abandoned their duties."

Basil was troubled, but preoccupied. It seemed like a fairly small issue in the face of much greater debacles. One hundred pilots? "One often encounters such problems when dealing with forcibly conscripted soldiers who are given too much independence."

He strolled along the boardroom wall, looking from one Chairman to the next, wondering about the priorities they'd had, the crises they had faced. No doubt, they'd felt that the fate of the Hansa was in their hands as well. Basil had never met most of these people; nevertheless, he felt he knew them.

Malcolm Stannis, a young cutthroat manager, had served during Earth's first contact with the Ildirans; an effective leader saddled with two incompetent Kings, first the old fool Ben and then the young and unproven boy George. King Ben had clumsily given away the store, formally granting a Theron delegation their colony's independence simply for the asking; luckily, he had died (under suspicious circumstances) shortly afterward.

Adam Cho had served for twenty-one years, the Hansa's longest-acting Chairman prior to Basil, who was now approaching three decades in office. Regan Chalmers had served for only a single, scandal-ridden year. Bertram Goswell's blundering friction with the Roamer clans had earned the Hansa the snide nickname of "Big Goose." Sandra Abel-Wexler, a descendant from the generation ship that carried her surname, had returned to Earth, wanting no part of the new colony the Ildirans established for them.

So much history, so many mistakes . . .

Basil stopped in front of his own portrait, wondering what the painter had been thinking, what moods or nuances he'd tried to evoke. Then he looked at the blank wall space beyond. Would Eldred Cain's portrait hang here in later years? The pallid deputy was his heir apparent, but their personalities were quite different. Was Cain really the man he wanted as his successor? Cain was cool and evenhanded, detail-oriented, but not ruthless enough.

Lanyan's voice grew louder. "Are you listening to me, Mr. Chairman?"

Basil did not turn. "I am always listening, General. Don't underestimate my ability to concentrate on more than one thing at a time. I understand the importance of what you are saying."

Chastened, the commander of the Earth Defense Forces sat at the highly polished boardroom table. "We're at *war*, sir. Those pilots had a *responsibility*." His face grew flushed. "Lives were at stake, dammit! And lives were lost."

Near the end of the line of portraits, Basil paused to look at Maureen Fitzpatrick. *The Battleaxe.* She had been quite stunning in her day and had used her charm and seductive wiles to catapult herself to the highest levels of success. Most of the men left in her wake had failed to understand her genuine power and charisma. Basil had always admired former Chairman Fitzpatrick. She was older than he by two decades, but if times had been different, he suspected they might have made quite a pair. She was still alive, though long retired and presumably content with her wealth.

Meanwhile, he had problems to deal with. Every example of human unreliability seemed like another nail in humanity's coffin.

Basil's vision took on a much sharper focus, as if the problem of AWOL pilots had crystallized around a different issue. He kept his voice low, musing angrily, "It's just a symptom of our race's failings. The same thing has happened everywhere I turn. Is it my concern that our scout pilots are too 'nervous' to do their own jobs? Do I care that green priests are no longer 'interested' in serving aboard our

ships? That our King has a habit of challenging my decisions, and that his replacement is a brat whose test scores are
barely higher than an amoeba's because he refuses to take
his training seriously? Selfish, shortsighted people—all of
them! If they can't be counted on to meet their own responsibilities, then how is humanity to survive this crisis?"

The General heaved a long disappointed sigh, commiser-
ating with Basil. "Unfortunately, Mr. Chairman, it's human
nature. People insist on making their own decisions, even
bad ones. And when facing a problem that affects us all, they
demonstrate how egocentric they can be."

Basil scowled, annoyed at himself for allowing his raw
emotions to show. "I have come to the conclusion that the
niceties of freedom and independence are valid only in times
of peace and prosperity. For years now, we've faced an
emergency that is not about petty politics, nationalities, or
religion—one that threatens our very existence. Everyone
has got to pull together. We must act with one mind, one
strong fist. Scattered loyalties and diverse interests only di-
lute the effort we make. They weaken us all. How can I
allow that?"

"You can't, Mr. Chairman. That much is clear. They are
traitors, plain and simple. We didn't ask them to do us a
favor. Those AWOL pilots were part of the EDF and, as
such, are bound by our rules and regulations. They can't just
be allowed to run away when they feel bored or jittery."

"It's so difficult to get competent help nowadays," Basil
said sardonically. "That's been the litany of people in power
since the dawn of history. You rely on people because of
their skills, and more often than not they let you down."

"We just can't afford that, Mr. Chairman." Lanyan laced
his fingers together as if to keep from making a fist and

pounding on the table. "There are too many threads unravel-ing. We've got to stop them where we can. We need to stop other pilots from leaving."

Basil glanced at his wrist chronometer and sighed. "Do you want me to send babysitters along with the pilots who haven't deserted yet? Should we launch a full-scale pursuit of the missing ships? Perhaps we'll find the pilots relaxing on a tropical beach, sipping fruit drinks." He rounded on the General. "Is that genuinely your highest priority right now?"

Lanyan was in high dudgeon. "Mr. Chairman, I remind you of long-standing military law. Desertion during time of war is an offense punishable by death. These pilots don't believe there'll be any consequences—and so far there haven't been any. We need to get serious, scare them all the way down to the bone marrow by making an example of somebody, and then offer amnesty to the rest. That way we get most of our pilots back, and nobody will dare do it again."

As he looked at the wall of his predecessors, Basil re-membered studying their biographies as he'd worked his way up through Hansa politics. He'd been King Frederick's friend, had made the old man into the venerated leader he was, despite Frederick's many failings. When Basil had been an ambitious deputy, similar in many respects to El-dred Cain, he had mapped out his projected career path. He'd imagined the pinnacle of happiness, success, and achievement as Chairman. He wondered now if any of these former leaders—any of them—had actually been happy in their posts.

"Very well, General. I agree. We will have to keep our eyes open, in case the right person crosses our path."

When gruff Del Kellum summoned the Earth captives into a central loading bay, Fitzpatrick figured they were about to be lectured—or tossed out the airlock. The death of their fellow prisoner Bill Stanna during an ill-advised and poorly planned escape attempt had only strengthened the resolve of the soldiers, leaving them as intractable as ever.

Twenty-nine other EDF hostages gathered, waiting sourly for whatever Kellum would say. The captives angrily considered the Roamers responsible for their comrade's death, though Fitzpatrick knew Stanna had made his own fatal blunders.

He spoke quietly to his closest companions, weapons specialist Shelia Andez and the compy expert Kiro Yamane. "There's been a lot of activity here lately, more ships from outside, more clan representatives, a lot of whispered talk. I've never seen so many people hit me with a poisoned glare."

"Just glare right back at them," Andez said. "They deserve it."

Even Zhett Kellum had stopped teasing him with sarcastic comments or her obvious attempts at flirtation. Fitzpatrick could not shake his feeling of dread, and he didn't want to be worried about *her*.

"I think Patrick may be correct." Yamane's voice was so soft they could barely hear it over the murmur of the crowd. "Something has happened out there. Maybe the EDF is looking for us."

"Better yet, what if they're retaliating?" Andez gave a quick, hungry grin.

Fitzpatrick knew they wouldn't agree, but he had to offer his suggestion anyway. "It's time to be more proactive. Maybe we should try cooperating a little 'out of the goodness of our hearts.' We can get into the thick of things, gather a little intelligence. Think of what we can learn."

"Aw, who wants to know what the Roachers are up to?" Andez said.

Yamane's dark eyes glittered. "I would like to learn if something terrible has occurred outside. Another hydrogue massacre, perhaps?"

"The Roamers haven't exactly been keeping us up to date on the latest news. We'd never know it even if the drogues destroyed Earth in retaliation for our offensive here at Osquivel." Fitzpatrick looked again at his friends. "Anything we learn can help us *and the EDF,* if we ever get out of here."

When Zhett had shown him around the Osquivel ring shipyards, he'd refused to believe the disorganized space gypsies could put together something so impressive. The clans couldn't possibly be such effective manufacturers and businessmen. Despite his inclination, Fitzpatrick had to admire what he saw, even if it was overshadowed by his unacknowledged attraction for the clan leader's daughter.

"Maybe we can get ourselves assigned to help study that hydrogue derelict," Yamane said. "It just isn't right that Roamers have exclusive access to the technological marvel of the century. Imagine what our military could do with that thing! With their ham-handed poking around, Roamer scientists might destroy delicate systems and delete vital information."

Andez snorted. "Like a bunch of primitive tribesmen prodding with wooden spears at something they don't understand!"

Fitzpatrick said, "Their technology is a bit more advanced than wooden spears." Then he caught himself, not wanting to sound too sympathetic.

"I'm just a cybernetics expert, but I'll bet I could figure out more than these Roamers could—if I got the chance."

"Focus on the real priority, okay? Maybe we should just bash some heads in and get our butts out of here." Andez tossed her dark brown hair, which had grown well past regulation length during their time of captivity.

Fitzpatrick gestured toward the big airlock at the far end of the chamber where Kellum had summoned them. "Be my guest, Shelia. See how far you can run out there in empty space. Maybe you'll succeed where Bill Stanna failed."

She spun on him angrily. "That's not—"

"Yes it is! We'll never get out of here by being stupid. We have to play along, make our plans, and do this right."

The weapons specialist smoldered at him for a moment, but she did not disagree. "I'm just so sick of waiting."

A side door opened and Del Kellum entered with his beautiful raven-haired daughter. The shipyard manager wore a stern expression; his salt-and-pepper goatee looked shaggier than usual. Zhett, on the other hand, was as vivacious and full of energy as ever, though she wouldn't meet Fitzpatrick's eyes.

Kellum didn't need a voice amplification system. His words boomed out without preamble. "Your Earth Defense Forces have declared war on the Roamer people. First, they attacked a Roamer outpost known as Hurricane Depot. Next, they destroyed our center of government and scattered the clans, including our Speaker." He glowered at them, letting the news sink in. The EDF captives muttered uneasily, not knowing how much to believe. Fitzpatrick was shocked.

"Roacher propaganda," Andez muttered.

"I don't see why they'd make up a story like that if it wasn't true," Fitzpatrick said. "What would they have to gain?"

Yamane said, "It would explain the recent activity."

Kellum paced before his audience, barely controlling his outrage. "What does it take to get through to you people? We rescued you from the wreckage. We fed and sheltered you while we tried to find a way to return you to your homes. Now the Hansa's actions force us to change your status from unwanted guests to prisoners of war." He crossed beefy arms over his barrel chest.

Zhett stood beside him. "Since you'll all be with us for a while, things are going to change around here. We have divided you into work teams, assigned to separate stations out in the rings, three or four of you at a time. We have also programmed and distributed EDF Soldier compies in similar assignments. We've run out of bonbons for you to eat while you sit back and relax. Time to earn your keep."

Kellum nodded. "No more excuses. No more complaints. No more refusing to cooperate."

Immediately the prisoners began to shout. "We're not your slaves!"

"When the EDF hears about Roamer death camps, they'll wipe you out, clan by clan."

"You can't treat prisoners of war that way."

"Oh, you poor pampered babies." Zhett pursed her catlike lips, her expression halfway between amusement and anger. "Never had to do real work in your lives? If you get a broken fingernail, will you file for an EDF Wounded-in-Action medal?"

Kellum growled, "You'll work shifts that are no longer and no more hazardous than any Roamer does on a daily basis. Your work will be monitored. Any attempted sabotage or decreased productivity will be countered with a reduction in rations or privileges."

Zhett watched their expressions and said, "Think of it as a chance to get outside and stretch your legs. Even you, Fitzie." He flushed at being singled out. "Once you try a bit of rewarding menial labor, you might decide you like it. See how the rest of the population lives."

Andez clenched her fists, ready to lunge at the nearest Roamer, but Fitzpatrick touched her arm. "Leave it for now."

"Are you just gonna let her say things like that?"

"Give it time. We'll figure out something." Fitzpatrick never took his eyes from Zhett. Thanks to his spoiled upbringing under his grandmother Maureen Fitzpatrick, a year ago he couldn't have imagined doing common labor; at the moment, though, the prospect didn't sound so terrible.

Two years before the start of the hydrogue war, Fitzpatrick had discovered a keen interest in old-fashioned automobiles. Using part of his bloated trust fund, he had purchased several collectors' vehicles. He loved to spend days in the garage with polishing rags and detail kits, enjoying the way light played off the fine finish, listening to the purr of a restored engine. It had given him satisfaction, the first activity he could remember actually caring about.

But young Fitzpatrick's greasy tinkering had raised concerns. One night, when he was late for a banquet and rushed in with insufficiently clean fingernails, his grandmother had put a stop to his hobby. Without his knowledge, Dame Battleaxe sold every one of Fitzpatrick's cars at a charity auction. She had never allowed him to purchase another classic automobile.

As he looked at his fellow captives, Fitzpatrick knew that every one of them wanted to go back to their lives in the Hansa. Though he would never admit it to any of his comrades, he had come to the conclusion that it was refreshing to be without specific obligations and constant demands.

Back on Earth, and in the EDF, he'd been a blueblood, always watched by his grandmother and smothered by her expectations. Now that everyone back home thought he was dead, for the first time Fitzpatrick had the luxury of mulling over things *he* wanted to do. It was intimidating, confusing, and liberating in a way. Now, though he resented being held captive, he was willing to work on something with his hands. Maybe he could request a job that let him work with engines and power systems. . . .

On a wall screen, Kellum projected a rough map of the rings, on which were marked the major clusters of facilities. Zhett began to read out names and tasks. "These are your preliminary assignments. Spare-parts hangars need inventory work. Nonskilled maintenance can be done around the spacedocks and ship-fabrication grids. Simple work is available in the office complexes and habitation domes, chores as menial as janitorial or housekeeping."

"Roamer death camps," Andez said under her breath.

Zhett looked directly at Fitzpatrick, as if her gaze could slice away the walls he had built up around himself. "If anybody has a particular aptitude or specialty, we might consider shifting you to a different team."

Fitzpatrick might have had a privileged upbringing, but his family had heaped a heavy load of expectations on him. In a way, this might be an opportunity to pursue the things he really wanted, as soon as he figured out what they were.

Kellum demanded their attention again as he projected

schematics of the various vehicles found around the shipyards. "I want you all to take a look at this very carefully.
After your comrade's botched attempt to get away, I know
you're all thinking about escape. Your friend set off with insufficient fuel, food, and life support. He didn't even know
where he was going—and he paid with his life for such
foolishness."

Ignoring the angry mutters from the EDF captives, he
tapped the projected diagrams of ships. "Let there be no
doubt in your minds. These are the ships working our construction yards: ore-haulers, processors, grappler pods,
cargo carriers, zero-G momentum lifters." He scrolled
through one picture after another. "Look at them." When he
had finished, he waited for a few seconds. "Now, does anyone see a common factor among all those vessels?" He
waited again. "You really should pay close attention."

Finally, Fitzpatrick said in a defeated voice, "They're all
short-range vehicles. Not one of them can get us out of this
system."

"Good job, Fitzie!" Zhett smiled, and he wished he'd
never said anything. At least she wasn't ignoring him
anymore.

"*None* of the vessels here is equipped with an Ildiran
stardrive. Even if you manage to hijack a ship, you won't be
able to get anywhere. You can putter along for centuries before you ever reach a habitable planet."

Zhett added, "We just want you to realize that so you
don't get any ideas of trying to grab a craft and escape. Not
that I can understand why you would want to go away." She
looked directly at Fitzpatrick as she said it.

As the work assignments were distributed, a hundred
Soldier compies also marched into the gathering area. The

military robots had been found floating in the wreckage of the Osquivel battlefield, and now all of them were reprogrammed by the Roamers. Perfectly cooperative . . . unlike real EDF soldiers.

Kellum said, "You'll work together, POWs and Soldier compies. There's plenty of tasks for everybody."

36 ☀ CESCA PERONI

Jonah 12 returned to its work routine. Teams doing double duty for several days would more than make up for time lost during the funeral for the former Speaker. Cesca thought they were throwing themselves into the effort in an unconscious attempt to honor Jhy Okiah, or maybe to keep themselves busy with something they could understand while the rest of Roamer society came to grips with the new order.

Tasks around the base were clearly assigned and divided. Though the Roamer excavators and processors were curious about the buried Klikiss robots, it wasn't their priority. Cryo-engineering specialist Jack Ebbe, one of the two men who had uncovered the robot tomb, had since been poking around at the site for several days, while his partner now stayed at the base to put together a small expedition. Ironically, only Cesca and acting administrator Purcell Wan had enough time to consider going to the other side of the planetoid.

Cesca hadn't wanted to leave Jonah 12 with the old Speaker in such a fragile state, but now she intended to depart and search out other clusters of the outlaw clans as soon as the fast messenger ships came back. While she was waiting, she and Purcell would go inspect the group of buried alien robots.

The still-exuberant vapor miner Danvier Stubbs inspected the grazer, recharged the power cells and air tanks, added packaged food, then got a good night's sleep before he announced he was ready to make the long journey. "By now Jack's probably getting antsy," Danvier said. "He's been by himself digging around, setting up camp, stringing lights, and gathering data. I told him to come back here for the time being, but he was really excited by the find, and he can be pretty stubborn. You should try sitting in a grazer with him day after day—"

"Then let's get moving," Cesca interrupted the loquacious vapor miner. "He's had time to do a lot of excavating over the past four days, and it's a long haul to get there."

She followed him outside the domes while Purcell hurried to catch up. The three of them easily fit inside the turtlelike vehicle, which was built to accommodate five people and extensive equipment and troubleshooting tools. Since it would be a lengthy ride, Danvier sealed the double airlocks and pressurized the compartment so they could remove their helmets.

The grazer set off, crawling across the dark iciness away from the glowing base domes. They bounced over the uneven frozen landscape and dodged swampy pools of liquid hydrogen lakes. Danvier rapped his gloved knuckles on the control panel. "These things aren't built for speed, but they're sure reliable."

As a vapor miner, Danvier specialized in processing frozen gases to sift out usable elements and molecules. During the hours of traveling, he explained everything about his job in far more detail than Cesca wanted to absorb.

The two men had been on a routine ice-combing expedition when they'd found the robots. "We detected an inclusion in a frozen chamber, far enough away that nobody'd spotted it before. Since our sensors are designed to read mostly light elements with occasional spikes of rock or metal, we didn't know what we were seeing. Jack's best guess was that a heavy meteoroid had hit the ice, but the readings just didn't look right to me." Danvier grinned, as if expecting a pat on the back.

"What screwed up the result was a polymer sheath surrounding the tomb chamber, or whatever it is. The robots are sealed in some sort of bubble, walled off by an artificial membrane. Our sensors picked up the metals of their bodies and the polymers in the protective shell. I said, 'Jack, this is something awfully weird.' And for the first time all shift, he didn't argue with me."

His companion had a knack for keeping machinery functional even in supercold environments. Jack had stayed behind, claiming he wanted some time alone; Cesca could imagine he might want a day or two of peace from Danvier's friendly but constant chatter.

"But why would Klikiss robots be sunk in cold storage way the hell out here?" Purcell asked. He had a habit of nodding when he talked.

The vapor miner shrugged inside his thin environment suit. "Hey, I'm not the administrator, Purcell. I just do things. You're the guy in charge of explaining them."

Purcell let out a long-suffering sigh. "I knew I wasn't cut

out for this job." The base's acting manager was in his late fifties. His dark hair had gone mostly gray, and he kept it cut short in a spiky, unruly mass. His eyebrows were heavy, but had retained their original dark color, which gave them extra prominence on his long face. "I wish Kotto would come back—he could probably figure it out."

Cesca knew about Kotto Okiah's short attention span, though. He had set up Jonah 12, then rushed to Theroc to work on rebuilding the world-forest settlement, then he'd hurried to Osquivel to study the hydrogue derelict. Some Roamers even joked that Kotto's Guiding Star was a variable sun. Purcell was stuck here with the responsibility for the foreseeable future.

For most of a day, the vapor miner retraced his path to where he'd left his companion studying the mysterious enclave. Along the way, the grazer laid down a straight track across the frozen surface, grinding through rough patches and evening out lumps in the terrain.

Finally, when the slow vehicle came over a rise, they looked down on bright temporary lights the cryoengineer had strung around the dark entrance. It was an open vault like a crypt dug into the planetoid's dead surface.

"Let's see what Jack's dug up down there," Danvier said. "By now he should have all the answers for us."

"I wonder if we can salvage any of those robots," Cesca said.

"Jack and I expect to get shares, if you're going to sell them."

"I doubt we can reprogram a Klikiss robot like you would a compy," Purcell said. Roamers had little to do with the enigmatic black machines that occasionally appeared on Hansa worlds. The ancient robots had been created by the long-vanished Klikiss race and then uncovered by Ildirans more than five centuries before. "Weren't the first robots found on an ice moon in the Hyrillka system? Maybe we've discovered another cache like that."

Leaving the grazer up on the rise, the three donned their helmets again, cycled one at a time through the small airlock, and trudged across the icy ground. Earlier, Danvier and Jack had broken through the piled layers of methane and hydrogen ice, then cut through the protective polymer shell that blocked the entrance to this grotto.

While working here alone, the cryoengineer had applied chemical illumination strips along the walls and powered a small portable generator to keep himself comfortable. Leading the way, Danvier ducked unnecessarily as he entered the opening. "Hey, Jack! You have company!"

The cryoengineer responded over their helmet comm systems, "I hope you brought somebody important. You won't believe how extensive this is."

"I brought the Speaker herself, and Purcell. Is that impressive enough?"

"It'll do."

The tunnel looked as if it had been burned with acid, cut out of the ice and then fused. Danvier ran his gloved hands over the passage walls. "No question that it was artificially cut. It's like the robots made a nest for themselves."

The three walked around the curve, and Jack waved at them, shining a bright suit light. "Come, look at this. There must be more than a hundred of them in here. The chamber goes farther back than I can see."

Cesca drew a quick breath when she caught sight of the black metal sculptures of fearsome beetles standing upright. The cryoengineer knelt to tinker with the exoskeleton of the first Klikiss robot. Other motionless machines stood in frozen ranks behind it.

She came closer. "I've never seen one of these before, certainly not up close." The flat headplate had an angular outline with hints of a crest and comblike side vents. A cluster of dull, smooth sensors covered the black matte of its face, like the eye group of a spider.

"Their systems are remarkably well preserved," Jack said, tinkering with an opening in the ellipsoidal body core. "Even in this cold and after what must surely be centuries, they all appear functional." He grinned through his faceplate. "I tell you, we can learn a lot from these things, if we take one apart."

Purcell said, "Kotto would be drooling over this."

"I'm sure he's perfectly satisfied with that hydrogue derelict," Cesca said. "You'll have to take a crack at it, Jack."

"I wouldn't turn down the opportunity." With a handheld thermal lamp, the cryoengineer warmed the ice that covered an exposed part on the Klikiss robot's torso and adjusted what seemed to be control diagnostics until he caught an unexpected flicker of light, a spark of activity. "Shizz, I don't know what that was, but jump-starting these things might be easier than I thought."

Suddenly the robot's cluster of glassy eyes lit up, burning red in the cold tunnel. The machinery hummed. "Hey, that did the trick." Jack stood up.

The geometrical head turned. The humming grew louder. Behind it, a second robot and then a third also began to stir. Scarlet optical sensors brightened as they focused on the suited man in front of them.

"Okay, now what do we do, Purcell?" Danvier said, standing behind Cesca and the acting administrator. "We're about to have a situation here."

"I, uh, I defer to the Speaker."

Before Cesca could say anything, the first robot shifted its body. Access ports in the front of its armored torso cracked and then slid open, revealing several mechanical arms that were tucked away inside the protected core.

Jack leaned closer. "Now that's—"

One of the clawed arms shot out of its socket like a rapidly fired piston. It slammed into Jack's faceplate, smashing through. The front of the cryoengineer's helmet burst open with an explosion of vented atmosphere that turned instantly to steam. The robot's pronged arm rotated like a furious drill. Blood, skin, and bone sprayed outward in a shower. Jack didn't even have time to scream.

The awakened Klikiss robot lurched on a set of stubby fingerlike legs. Behind it, two other active robots began to move. From deeper in the storage tunnels, myriad sets of red lights began to shine like the eyes of a dragon waking up from a long sleep.

Danvier stumbled forward screaming, far too late to rescue the cryoengineer crumpled in a bloody mass on the icy floor. In an instant the vapor miner realized his own danger as the first three robots scuttled toward him. Before Danvier could turn, each extended a nightmarish set of articulated robot arms tipped with various sharp tools and manipulators. The Klikiss robots closed around him as he tried to scramble away. His boots skidded on the slick floor of the tunnel.

Everything happened in the space of a heartbeat. Seizing him, the robots clawed, tore, and pummeled. They ripped Danvier's suit, slashed the protective fabric, crushed his helmet. Unlike his partner, the vapor miner had plenty of time to scream until the robots cut off his suit transmitter.

Cesca was already grabbing Purcell's arm to yank him out of his shock. "We've got to get back to the grazer!"

While the robots finished their swift butchery, dozens more stirred from their paralysis and began to move, setting off in pursuit.

37 ✹ KOTTO OKIAH

Alone aboard the intriguing hydrogue derelict, Kotto had only KR and GU, his two technically rated compies, for company. Though his fascination with the alien technology did not wane, the complete lack of clues—even about where to start—was frustrating. Since this was a spaceship, there had to be complex machinery embedded somewhere, but he could find no moving parts.

"Quite a conundrum, GU," he said.

"Yes, Kotto Okiah. That is an appropriate use of the word." When the engineer first reported his confusing observations, the little compy had inadvertently introduced him to the new term. For all his technical expertise and years of practice in cutting-edge projects, Kotto had not been familiar with the word. Maybe it was because the eccentric Roamer inventor and engineer had never before been faced with such a baffling scientific challenge. A conundrum.

The small hydrogue sphere hung like a microscopic jewel

high above the ring plane of Osquivel. It had been damaged, its alien occupant killed during the EDF's brazen military attack—apparently, one of the only hydrogue casualties of the great battle.

"The candy store is open for business. What should we try first?" Kotto rubbed his gloved hands together, wishing he could pressurize the artifact so he could work in a shirt-sleeve environment, but the systems were a mystery. He didn't even know how to close the hatch yet. At least *closing* it would probably not be traumatic for poor GU, who had been hurled into space by the unexpected explosive opening of the sphere.

"There's so much here to understand." He looked around at the strange shapes, the smooth panels, the odd inverted geometries. "We need to figure out a way to defeat these ships."

"We will do our best to assist you, Kotto Okiah," KR said from his station. "However, compies are limited to straight-forward analytical processes."

GU added, "Intuitive leaps are reserved for our human masters."

Pacing in his environment suit, Kotto said, "Just help keep my mind on track. How to fight against a hydrogue ship—that's the question. Don't let anything distract me from the main objective." That was one of his weaknesses: A fascination with *everything* led to perpetual distraction.

"For instance, I'd love to figure out the propulsion system these hydrogue ships use. Warglobes are fast long-range spaceships, but they don't require ekti." He touched the uneven knobs and protrusions of an alien technical station that looked as if it had been made by pouring molten glass. "And these controls aren't like anything I've ever seen—not

human, or Ildiran, or even old Klikiss technology. Just understanding the embedded liquid-metal electronics would open
up possibilities for—"

"Is this an instance in which we should tell you to focus
your thoughts on the primary objective, Kotto Okiah?"

Kotto stuttered to a halt, then cleared his throat. "Yes . . .
exactly. On the other hand, let's not be too rigid. No telling
where a given line of investigation might lead. We have to
think outside the box, to use an old phrase."

"It is a conundrum," GU said.

"Don't be a show-off."

Kotto stepped in front of the flat trapezoidal panel surrounded by strange symbols, destination coordinates similar
to those used in ancient Klikiss transportals. How could the
vanished insectile race and the incredibly strange hydrogues
have anything in common? Had one race obtained transportal technology from the other?

Hoping to make the connection, Kotto had reviewed the
small amount of available information published by Hansa
scientists. Before the trade embargo against the Big Goose,
Roamers had downloaded all public-access technical reports. However, as best he could tell from the documenta-
tion, the Hansa scientists didn't know how the transportals
worked either.

He read the discovery papers written by xeno-
archaeologists Margaret and Louis Colicos. Recently, a
quiet but reputable researcher named Howard Palawu had
been given the task of analyzing the alien transportation system. He'd had a habit of posting his thoughts and conjec-
tures in daily logs for anyone who chose to read them. The
entries had ended abruptly, though, and Kotto learned that
Palawu himself had vanished through a Klikiss transportal.

Now, as he stared at the transport panel and the symbols, GU walked up to him. "You are wool-gathering again, Kotto Okiah."

"Wool-gathering? What's that?"

"Thinking unrelated thoughts, becoming lost in a reverie irrelevant to the task at hand."

"Did someone upgrade your vocabulary program?"

"Wool-gathering is a common, though somewhat archaic, phrase. Would you like me to give its derivation?"

"No. You're right—I was distracted." He sniffed. "But if we figured out how to control the transportals inside war-globes, we might be able to open up a gateway to . . . a black hole. Wouldn't that be amazing? The drogues could be cruising along in search of Roamer skymines to destroy, and suddenly a black hole falls right into their living room. Hah!"

"That would certainly be destructive to the enemy ships, Kotto Okiah," KR agreed. "However, it seems an unlikely prospect."

Kotto smacked his gloved fist on a curved diamond protrusion inside the central chamber. "I haven't learned anything yet! The hydrogues are so . . . *alien*. And hydrogue thought processes created this technology. That makes understanding it much more complex."

Battered GU turned his golden optical sensors up at Kotto. "Then perhaps a simple solution would be more effective than a complex approach."

"GU, if I could think of a simple solution, I would. The only thing we figured out so far was how to open the hatch."

Suddenly struck with an idea, Kotto stared at the research compy. GU's colorful polymer skin was still scratched and discolored from when the derelict sphere had been breached.

The compy had been shot away in a wild and uncontrolled flight. . . .

Kotto's face lit up. "By the Guiding Star, maybe that's good enough! It would be like a . . . a doorbell. A can opener! All we need to do is open the door when the drogues least expect it."

"An effective weapon?"

"Absolutely!"

38 ☀ TASIA TAMBLYN

I n the evening off-duty hours of her three-day stay on Llaro, Tasia walked through the mazes of Roamer tents and huts. Because of her EDF uniform, many of the detainees viewed her with suspicion, giving only curt answers to her questions; others, though, saw her as a possible advocate, the best they had. Even so, Tasia didn't fit in here, or anywhere.

She had asked around, learned a few names, and decided to have a private conversation with Roberto Clarin, the former manager of Hurricane Depot. Since he'd been a capable administrator, and one of the first captives deposited here, he seemed to be the de facto leader of the group. Maybe he could help her.

As he paced along beside her and a perfectly polite EA, Clarin ducked under banners and waved to dusty workers returning late from the cultivated fields. The potbellied man was frank, but not overly bitter or judgmental. "Plenty of Roamers would be offended by the choices you made, girl. Your own father would have been one of them."

Tasia pressed her lips together. "Probably so. But I tried to follow my Guiding Star."

"And yet . . . *here* you are." Clarin sighed. "You know, it helps to dump my frustrations on someone wearing an EDF uniform—not that I expect it to make any difference."

"I'm listening," Tasia said. "I don't know how much I can do yet. My Roamer background puts me pretty low on the EDF totem pole, but I *am* an officer, and I can work the bureaucracy. Maybe."

"Worth a shot. The Eddies stationed in that new base don't even seem to speak plain Trade Standard. I've made reasonable requests, things that would help this whole damned settlement. You think I could get so much as an acknowledgment? Maybe they'll listen to you. You could forward our complaints."

"I'll do that." Tasia gave a bittersweet smile. "I need to warn you, though, it's been a long time since my superiors listened to me. In fact, they've been cutting me out of the loop. I didn't even know about the operations against Roamer bases until everybody was patting themselves on the back for a job well done."

Clarin turned to her in frustration. "What do they really want? Explain it to me. They put us here on Llaro, without giving us any demands or guidance. It seems like they just want us to do the work of setting up a colony for them. Of course, we'll do a better job than these amateurs would. Hah! Still, it's the strangest prison I could ever imagine." He looked intensely at her. "We didn't do anything wrong,

Tamblyn. Are we going to be charged with a crime of any kind? Or are we just being held here for no reason?"

"I honestly don't know—and I'm not convinced they do, either. The Eddies simply want you out of the way for the time being, where you can cause no problems. Maybe they'll use you as bargaining chips, if they ever find a clan head or the Speaker."

"Or maybe they just want us to build their colony for them." Clarin shook his head as he looked at the colony operations: the construction, the water-pumping stations, the solar-powered generators. "We keep arguing with the EDF civil engineers. They want to do things by the book, and therefore inefficiently. We've got better ideas, but they won't let us use them."

Tasia thought about the uninspired technology the military continued to use, when Roamers had improved on those designs and methods generations ago. "They have their own set ways."

"Ah, what do I care?" Clarin continued. "I choose to believe we won't be here long. The Big Goose can set up its own damn colony. Then when it all falls apart, they'll still find a way to blame it on Roamer sabotage."

Tasia bit her lower lip, relieved to be talking to someone with a similar background. "But the clans will need to find new places to live, too. Why not settle here, claim Llaro for yourselves, if you've earned it?"

Clarin scowled. "This place? As soon as we make it into a desirable world, the Big Goose will take over. Roamers are best at scraping out a living in miserable places. Ha! Do they think this planet is a challenge for us?"

They continued to pace the perimeter under a darkening sky. She finally got up the nerve to ask him what he'd heard of Jess, or her uncles, or any of her friends. Clarin didn't have much information to share, but he did talk about Speaker Peroni's brief betrothal to Reynald of Theroc, who had been killed in a recent hydrogue attack. Tasia knew that Jess had strong feelings for Cesca—or at least he had, many years ago. If her uncles were now running the Plumas water mines, that meant Jess must be gone. Somewhere.

As they reached the far edge of the temporary encampment, Tasia, EA, and Clarin came upon a confrontation between the Eddy guards and a group of Roamer children. A Governess compy had interposed herself between the soldiers and her wards. "You may not address my children in such a manner." Tasia recognized the dedicated compy UR, who had been one of her own teachers at Rendezvous when she was a little girl.

"Those kids are unruly and dangerous," one of the soldiers said. "We have to keep them away from the construction activities for their own safety."

"I will guarantee their own safety," UR said. "It is not your task."

"Listen, compy, our task is whatever we decide it to be."

"These children are my responsibility. You may not go near them. You may not command them. You may not even address them."

Tasia bit back a laugh as she hurried forward. She outranked these Eddy babysitters anyway. She remembered her days of instruction with UR, and the Governess compy was still as stern and no-nonsense as always. "What's going on here, Sergeant?"

The EDF guards looked up. Seeing Tasia's rank insignia, they responded with satisfaction. Just glancing at her in the evening light, they couldn't guess her Roamer heritage. She repressed the brief urge to punch them.

"This little compy is too big for her metal britches, Commander."

"This little compy understands her place better than you do, Sergeant. By order of General Lanyan, the Roamer detainees are to be interfered with as little as possible. Minimal harassment. Let them do as they please."

"But Commander, it's dark outside. Shouldn't those children be in bed? The Roamers can't just—"

"The Governess compy can take care of these children. She teaches them and assures their welfare. Their parents trusted her with their sons and daughters when Rendezvous was destroyed. She's fully capable of determining appropriate responses to various situations. On the other hand, if you and your men have nothing worthwhile to do, I'm sure I can find some ditches that need to be dug by hand. Or manual inspection of cesspits, perhaps?"

Once dismissed, the surprised soldiers hurried off, keeping their muttered comments just short of insubordination.

Roberto Clarin chuckled. The Governess compy swiveled her smooth polymer face; optical sensors lit with obvious recognition. "My instruction in courtesy and cooperation has not been lost on you, Tasia Tamblyn."

"I may not have been your best student, UR, but some of it sank in."

The Governess compy looked at EA, who stood like a statue. "Is this your Listener compy? Something is different."

Tasia swallowed. "EA suffered an accident while doing a small task for me. Her memory has been wiped. I'm hoping we can restore it. I've been feeding her stories that I can remember, but I would rather restore the real data. I've had her

checked out by Hansa cyberneticists, and I ran all the diagnostics I could get my hands on, but to no effect. Anything
you can suggest?"

UR's optical sensors flashed, interfacing with the lethar-
gic Listener compy. After a long moment, the Governess
completed her detailed scan. "Not likely. Her core memory
systems are a blank slate. It is not likely EA will ever regain
her past experiences." UR paused. "I can, perhaps, share
some edited downloads of my own experiences with you,
from when I was your Governess. It will be a different point
of view."

"It wouldn't be the same." Tasia's heart fell. She had been
optimistic that another Roamer compy might offer some
hope. She looked at EA, who seemed too placid, too agree-
able, without any ideas of her own. Previously, the Listener
compy, her *friend*, had been willing to offer a little advice.
"Let me think about it, UR." Her voice was soft. "I think it's
more important for us to make new memories of our own."

39 ☀ DENN PERONI

Yreka seemed the likeliest spot for Roamer black-market
trade, since the colonists had never fully recovered from
the blockade EDF siege troops had imposed not long
ago. Denn Peroni and Caleb Tamblyn were both optimistic

as the *Dogged Persistence* landed at the half-mothballed spaceport.

After opening the cockpit hatch, cargo doors, and rear access ramp, Denn and Caleb stepped out to greet the wary but curious Yrekans. With his broad smile and open arms, Denn felt like a peddler arriving in town and setting up his stand to show off his wares.

The Grand Governor of Yreka, Padme Sarhi, was a tall woman of Indian genetic stock, with extremely long hair that hung in a braid past her waist. She wore a loose white blouse and fitted slacks of a tough material, but no jewelry or insignia of office. Though she was in her mid-sixties, the Grand Governor's skin was a smooth, ageless brown, and her large eyes held a persistent skepticism. Denn saw that he would have to win her over in order to do business with this colony.

Caleb hadn't bothered to find a nice outfit, but Denn wore his most cheerful and flamboyant clothes: a many-pocketed jumpsuit with full sleeves and tight pants. Intricate embroidery showed clan chains all along his seams and pockets. He had tied his shoulder-length dark hair back with a blue ribbon—Cesca's favorite color—and dabbed a woodsy scent on his cheeks and neck. He felt as if he was going courting again.

After making introductions, Denn said, "We've brought a few items we thought you could use." Caleb bobbed his head in an attempt to look congenial.

The Grand Governor's expression remained cool. "You do know that the Hanseatic League has declared all Roamers hostiles? And that anyone caught trading with them could suffer severe penalties?"

Caleb's eyebrows shot up, and he let out a loud snort.

"So, the Eddies are stretched too thin to deliver vital supplies to colonies like Yreka, but they can spare ships to spread their threats and warnings in no time at all? Typical."

Denn hadn't expected such tactics. "The EDF has already destroyed major Roamer settlements, ma'am—without warning and without provocation."

"That *is* their standard operating procedure," the Grand Governor said.

Denn didn't know what to do. He shuffled his feet. "We, umm, we wouldn't want to put your colony at risk. We'll just pack up and leave."

Caleb looked surprised. "We will?"

Then the tall woman surprised them. "Screw the military bastards. When the EDF burned our fields and destroyed warehouses, my people lost much of our equipment and stockpiles. Show us what you have. Yreka could use just about everything."

Colonists clustered around the *Dogged Persistence* as if it were a flea market. Denn and Caleb showed off Roamer metals, synthetic-weave fabrics, solar-power films, and compact industrial apparatus. Breezes drifted through the open hatches into the *Persistence,* airing out the frequently recycled atmosphere. The Yrekans cooed and jabbered about the most routine things.

Denn saved the best for last, though. "In the back of the cargo hold, I've got worldtree wood from Theroc." Gesturing for the tall Grand Governor to step inside, he explained how Mother Alexa and Father Idriss had permitted the Roamers to take some of the wood in gratitude for helping them to rebuild.

"You worked on Theroc? Interesting." She lowered her voice. "The Hansa announcement didn't mention anything about that. According to them, you're all just hiding in your bolt-holes and weakening humanity with your greed."

Caleb snorted again. "Why waste time on words that might cast the clans in a positive light?"

The lumber in the hold reminded Denn of gold ingots, boards laminated with a Midas touch. The air held a sweet resinous scent with an undertone of herbs and pungent oils.

During their journey from the Osquivel meeting, Denn had tried his hand at whittling scrap chunks of the wood. When not playing games or sharing a drink with Caleb, he had whiled away the time with a sharp knife, cutting thin curls of wood from block after block. Roamers rarely had the opportunity to work with wood at all, and he hadn't expected to be good at it, but somehow he managed to expose secret figures that lay within—either projected there by Denn's own imagination or implanted by green priest acolytes who had spent many years telling stories to the trees.

The vivid grain was like colored gases in a dramatic nebula, strange random patterns laid down by the bloodsap of the giant trees. Denn thought he could see faces and shapes, like ghosts behind his eyelids, memories of scenes he was sure he'd never experienced before.

As the Grand Governor ran her fingertips over the wood, Denn noted the quiet fascination in her eyes. The skeptical narrowness had gone away, and her rich brown irises shone; he could imagine what she had looked like as a young woman. "We'll take some of this wood. We need to negotiate a price, and what form of currency or barter we can use." He witnessed the strength and unshakable determination that made her a good leader. "But we *will* work something out."

One of the Yrekans came running into the ship's cargo bay. "An EDF battle group just arrived in orbit! They're already preparing to launch a shuttle with Admiral Stromo aboard."

The Grand Governor flinched. "What does he want now?"

"An inspection tour. That's what he says."

Denn and Caleb exchanged a panicked glance, briefly wondering if the Yrekans had betrayed them by calling the EDF. But no message could possibly have been received so quickly, and when he saw the Grand Governor's face, Denn knew she hadn't tricked him.

"They'll see my ship," Denn said. "They'll know we're here."

"No offense, Mr. Peroni, but with all your hatches open, the different styles of hull plating, and the strange design, nobody in the EDF is going to recognize this as a functional *ship* at all—especially not someone with as little imagination as Admiral Stromo." She turned to the message bearer and snapped a set of orders. "Call everyone in the vicinity. We need help right away. Bring out as much large equipment as you can find and park it in the spaceport."

Amazed, Denn and Caleb watched over the next half hour as the Yrekans hustled out harvesters and tillers from their barn hangars. Two hydrogen-powered crop-dusting aircraft were moved into position on either side of the *Dogged Persistence*. Men and women draped tarpaulins and stacked crates around the landed ship. Before long, the Roamer ship looked like an abandoned wreck that had been converted into a storehouse and repository for spare parts.

With time running out, the Grand Governor took the two men by the arm. "Now the only thing that's obvious is *you two*. Outfits like yours are signal flares. Let's change you into some normal clothes." The edges of her mouth quirked upward. "I'm sure I can find a dirty jumpsuit that doesn't fit you very well."

"I'd normally prefer something clean instead—and slimmer," Denn said. "But my desire to fit in with the rest of you outweighs my fashion sense any day of the week."

When the EDF transport finally landed, Denn and Caleb watched anxiously from the crowds of scowling and intimidated-looking Yrekans. Denn's stomach was queasy. The *Persistence* was there for a sharp-eyed Eddy to see, and any Yrekan colonist wanting to earn favor with the Admiral could easily turn in the two Roamers.

Jowly Stromo emerged from the shuttle, flanked by an honor guard in impressive uniforms with polished shoes and precisely combed hair. The gleam of medals reflected like faceted jewels on his left breast. Denn pegged him as a man intent on ceremony, someone who would back away from a messy conflict just to avoid getting his uniform stained.

The Grand Governor faced Stromo squarely, sweaty and a bit rumpled from the frantic preparations. "How may we help you, Admiral? Have you brought us a shipment of much-needed supplies and materials from the Hansa?" She gave him a faint, insincere smile.

Stromo wore a flustered expression. "I'm on my way back to Earth after performing a lengthy and successful operation against outlaw Roamer clans. Since I was passing by the Yreka system, I decided to verify that you continue to follow the requirements of your allegiance to the Terran Hanseatic League."

"We have our own copy of the Hansa Charter, Admiral. We can read it anytime we like, in case we need to refresh our memories."

"Maybe you need an EDF battle group to come here and remind you." Stromo drew a deep breath, puffing his chest.

"When the EDF laid siege to Yreka, you made your point eminently clear." She turned her gaze toward the ground, as if she was cowed. "We've learned our lesson."

"Glad to hear that." He smiled, getting down to business. "I'd like to rotate my crew down to Yreka in shifts for brief periods of R&R. They need to stretch their legs, get a little sun. Personally, I'd look forward to a decent meal for a change." His tone demonstrated that it wasn't a question.

"So long as you and your crew bring your own food and prepare it for yourselves," the Grand Governor said, just as firmly. "Because you've stripped us of our stardrive fuel, we have no ability to exchange goods with other colonies. We are barely self-sufficient."

This angered Stromo, but the Grand Governor fixed him with an unwavering gaze. Finally he drew a deep breath. "My soldiers can bring their own rations. Bland, tedious rations . . ."

"We may be willing to make a few exchanges, Admiral. Everyone gets tired of eating the same thing all the time."

"I'll send a list down, and a request for some of my personal favorites."

"We'll see what we have, Admiral. Beyond that, I can make no promises."

For three days, a nervous Denn and Caleb had no choice but to stay on Yreka while the EDF battle group remained. They kept a low profile, helping with colony tasks that seemed just like working in a Roamer settlement, though each time Denn saw the strutting Eddies acting as if they owned the planet, he felt his blood begin to boil. Caleb's sour expres-

sion took on the intensity of a thousand lemons, until Denn
chided him to hide his annoyance. "If you give them an
excuse to start looking, they'll turn over rocks until they find
us."

But Stromo didn't seem intent on finding anything; he was
just here flexing his muscles, intimidating an already squashed
colony. It apparently didn't occur to him that the Yrekans
weren't entirely browbeaten by the military presence.

Every hour, Denn wondered if one of the colonists might
whisper into a soldier's ear, but the Yrekans held just as
much of a grudge against the EDF as the Roamers did. He
wondered how the Hansa could be so oblivious to the
unraveling of their own social fabric. Perhaps the Chairman
was simply so focused on the primary enemy that he
couldn't see the bridges burning behind him.

When at last the group of Manta cruisers departed, leaving behind both disarray and relief, Denn met again with the
Grand Governor. In her face, he saw the depth of the fury
and resentment she had so carefully hidden for the past few
days. For the anger to penetrate even her studied placidity,
he knew it must burn hot indeed.

"At least that's over with," Denn said with a wry cheer he
did not feel. "I appreciate your not hanging us out to dry."

"If I had any doubts before, this has dispelled them." She
glanced up at the open sky, as if Stromo might still be up
there eavesdropping, and Denn saw her jaw clench for a moment. "After all this time, the Hansa finally sent discre-
tionary ships to Yreka. They could have brought food,
medical supplies, equipment . . . but they just wanted to
push us around. You on the other hand, who had no reason
to help us, came here with the things we needed, despite the
potential risks to yourself."

Denn flushed. "I can be as altruistic as the next man, ma'am, but my people really need the trade, too. . . ."

Caleb scratched under one arm. Both of them were anxious to get back into familiar Roamer clothes. "The Big Goose has dumped on plenty of other colonies. Let's hope those other people feel the same as you all. If you give us a shopping list, we'll see what we can arrange for our next trip here—"

The Grand Governor's brow furrowed; she was still seething about the EDF. "We accept your proposal, Mr. Peroni, and look forward to whatever the Roamers want to offer. I had already made up my mind to allow a bit of surreptitious trade, but now I've decided to actively help you. We will set up a black-market interchange station here, and the Hansa can go to hell for all I care."

40 ☀ IMPERATOR RUSA'H

Hyrillka was already his, and now that he had control of the seized warliners, Rusa'h planned to strike out across the Horizon Cluster, bringing his enlightenment and power to many more Ildiran planets. The first step would be Dzelluria, less than a day's journey away.

Everything on Hyrillka was going well. He expected nothing less, since he had witnessed the true path to the Lightsource.

Recently he'd been amused, and not at all surprised, when the Mage-Imperator sent three scout cutters to investigate what had happened to Adar Zan'nh. Even through his corrupted soul-threads, Jora'h would certainly have sensed the deaths of so many victims during the hostage crisis, and then the explosion of the sacrificial warliner. It should have been an excruciatingly clear message, and a warning, just as the execution of Pery'h had been.

He didn't expect his brother to listen. It would be a long and painful road before the man who called himself Mage-Imperator accepted his defeat and surrendered to Rusa'h.

The scout cutters had blundered into the Hyrillka system, poking around. Though aware of the possible danger, the Solar Navy crewmen had not been prepared for the trap. Since they were not part of Rusa'h's new network, they had been unable to feel *thism* on this whole planet, and thus his converts had easily seized them. His warliners had surrounded the three cutters, and the confused Ildiran crew had demanded explanations.

Rusa'h had found it easiest just to gas them with shiing to make the cutters' crews susceptible, so that he could pull loose their soul-threads and restring them onto his own network. As soon as the drug wore off, the scout crews belonged entirely to him. And he added three new armored cutters to his military force.

Neat, swift, simple. And now for the next phase.

Rusa'h had already dispatched Prime Designate Thor'h with one of the warliners on a special mission to Dobro. Thor'h carried a message: an offer or an ultimatum, depending on how Udru'h received him. The new Imperator felt he might find an ally in the Dobro Designate, who clearly disagreed with many of Jora'h's attitudes and policies. Rusa'h had observed this friction back when he had been hedonistic and deluded. And during his time drifting in the embrace of the Lightsource, he had learned many secret things. Maybe the Dobro Designate would cooperate with him. Rusa'h hoped he wouldn't be forced to inflict too much bloodshed on his own brother, but he would do what was necessary.

He set off for Dzelluria, leaving his pleasure mates in Hyrillka's citadel palace to watch over the imprisoned Adar Zan'nh. He doubted the younger man would voluntarily change his mind; he was too entrenched in misguided loyalty to his father. Fortunately, ensconced in the command nucleus of the flagship warliner, Rusa'h did not need the Adar to accomplish his aims.

Every crewmember serving aboard his forty-five battle vessels now swore their allegiance to his holy cause. Once they'd been converted, all the shiing gas had been purged from the ventilation systems, sharpening the reeducated minds of the soldiers. His *thism* re-networking would hold fast.

He could not allow any Hyrillkan to consume shiing again, including Prime Designate Thor'h. Now that they were part of his own web, he couldn't afford to let them become malleable again. A second, equally important reason for the restriction was that all future shiing production must be used for the expanding rebellion. Large amounts of the drug would be Hyrillka's most effective tool in forcibly spreading Rusa'h's enlightenment.

The new Imperator had chosen to lead the first conquest himself. Dzelluria would fall.

When the warliners arrived at Dzelluria, the local Designate probably assumed it was a military group from Ildira sent to perform skyparades. Designate Orra'h transmitted welcoming messages, and Designate-in-waiting Czir'h, a son of the false Mage-Imperator, announced that he was ready to perform his ceremonial function.

Imperator Rusa'h said, "You will both be required to perform an important function. Be prepared."

He dispatched large groups of cutters and entire flights of armed streamers down to the capital city. Warliners loomed overhead, their weapons ready to fire. The Dzelluria Designate and his people were slow to imagine that anything was wrong.

Rusa'h instructed the streamers to sweep through the primary city in attack mode. Swiftly, they launched explosive projectiles that wiped out the communications facility, cutting Dzelluria off from any direct contact with Ildira. Rusa'h did not want to give the corrupt Mage-Imperator any advantage.

The Dzelluria Designate and his protégé clearly did not know what to do. The attack was too fast, too precise.

When his intimidating flagship landed, an enormous honor guard of converted Solar Navy soldiers carried the Imperator's chrysalis chair out into Dzelluria's open sunlight. Designate Orra'h stood so astonished that it took him a moment to recognize his own brother. "Rusa'h? What is the meaning of this? Why are you dressed like that? And why do you sit in a facsimile of the chrysalis chair?"

"Because I am your rightful Imperator." The soldiers bore his chair directly to where Orra'h and his young companion stood waiting. "I have come to invite you to join my cause."

He explained how, while his injured body remained in sub-*thism* sleep, he had drifted on the plane of the Lightsource. He had seen the root of all soul-threads that bound the Ildiran race together . . . and had followed them to the rot eating away at the Empire. Not just the usurper Jora'h, but the previous Mage-Imperator and several predecessors, had led the Ildiran people astray, blinding themselves to true visions. Rusa'h, though, knew how to guide Ildirans back to the Lightsource, a return to old traditions and self-sufficiency, free from parasitical relationships with humans, free from the threat of hydrogues.

Young Czir'h looked frightened as Rusa'h explained his solution, but Designate Orra'h seemed angered. "I had heard about your injury, Rusa'h. Come with me, and I will assign my best medical kithmen to treat your delusions. We would welcome you back into the Mage-Imperator's fold."

Gigantic and powerful, the rest of the warliners descended to hover overhead. The Dzellurian crowds that had come to see an expected military skyparade now looked up with growing fear.

Rusa'h frowned at his stubborn brother. "I am saddened that you force me to turn my invitation into a threat, Orra'h." He raised one hand, and his Solar Navy officers transmitted instructions to the warliners above. Rusa'h waited.

High-energy weaponry blasted out like incandescent spears. Lances tore giant furrows through the buildings of the capital city. Explosions rippled, one after another after another. People screamed, and hundreds died instantly; smoke and flames filled the air. The warliners scribed a perfect circle of obliteration, a black trench around the Designate's opulent residence.

Orra'h was unable to form comprehensible words as he witnessed the unprecedented destruction. Designate-in-waiting Czir'h cried out, "Stop this! Why are you attacking Dzelluria?"

"I am emphasizing my point." Rusa'h turned to the appalled Designate. "I ask you again: Will you add your population to my supporters, or will you force my hand again?"

Orra'h shouted uselessly for his own guards, but the local soldier kithmen were far outnumbered, and the battle was short-lived. Within moments, fifty of the Designate's hand-picked guards lay slain around them. The blood on the warm sunlit stones had a moist metallic smell.

"You make me sad, Orra'h, but I am cheered by my resolve to do what is right for the Ildiran people." He nodded to his nearest followers.

Rusa'h's converted soldiers sprang forward like ravenous predators, pulling out their crystal knives and polished alloy clubs. They fell upon Designate Orra'h as he cringed and flailed. The assassination was quick, but brutal. The guards stepped back, their weapons dripping blood.

The Designate-in-waiting screamed his disbelief. Across Dzelluria, the death of the Designate reverberated through the old *thism* web, like the snapped string of a musical instrument. Although Rusa'h's followers were separated from the dissonant agony, the population of Dzelluria felt the abrupt loss of their leader like a scythe across their legs.

Now Rusa'h turned to the pasty-faced and terrified young Czir'h. "Designate-in-waiting, you have seen the consequences and you know the stakes. Shall I order my warliners to level another portion of your city? Shall I have my guards slay you as well?" He put a finger to his lips, as if considering. "Dzelluria would be much easier to conquer if there were no Designate at all."

Czir'h stammered. His arms were trembling. He looked around for someone to help him with the decision, but the Imperator's gaze continued to bore into him. "Join me,"

Rusa'h said, his voice tantalizing. "Let me untangle the corrupt *thism* that has confused you for so long."

The Designate-in-waiting backed away, and Rusa'h's voice grew suddenly hard. "Join me now—or die!" He reached beside him in the chrysalis chair and held up a vial of pure pearlescent shiing, a milky fluid stronger than any processed powder. "Because you are a son of Jora'h, you must accept my thoughts voluntarily. This will make the process easier for you."

Seeing nothing else he could do, trapped and desperate to stop further slaughter, Czir'h accepted the vial of shiing as if he had been instructed to swallow poison. His hands trembled, but he raised the vial, saw the light shining through its murky substance. With a final frightened glance at the bloodstained stones, the mangled body of Designate Orra'h, he looked back at the rebel leader. Rusa'h gave him the slightest reassuring nod.

Czir'h reluctantly tilted the vial and poured the thick substance into his mouth. He licked his lips, leaving a white smear as his tongue played over the last of it. Rusa'h could see him swallow, then swallow again.

The two guards holding the young Designate-in-waiting by the arms released him. Czir'h swayed a little on his feet, the shiing already working. Rusa'h knew full well how swiftly the plantmoth drug would take effect.

The warliners had cargo holds full of powdered shiing, which would be swiftly distributed to the populace. Without the Designate or Czir'h guiding them, the old *thism* network would unravel immediately, leaving the people of Dzelluria alone and adrift. It would be a simple matter for the Imperator to snare them in his own network before the shiing wore off and solidified the bonds again.

Already, Czir'h's eyes were beginning to glaze and cloud

up. The intensely strong drug created a sort of relaxed confusion. The boy's shoulders sloped as his attachment to the Mage-Imperator's *thism* and to the world itself unraveled, the strands left to dangle loose. The most important part came when the young man willingly submitted.

Rusa'h lunged with his thoughts, grasped the correct soul-threads, and wove them in his own fashion.

Now that Czir'h was part of the altered tapestry of *thism,* the Imperator ordered his warliners to begin distributing shiing among the population of Dzelluria.

The first step had been simple and straightforward, and Rusa'h knew his power would only grow. The revolt would spread from planet to planet, but he had to plan his movements strategically. He looked across the sea of Ildiran people, who were frightened and confused by the attack on Dzelluria. Once Thor'h prepared the way, Rusa'h would go to Dobro, where he expected an even easier victory.

After all, he and his brother Udru'h were very much alike.

41 ☀ ADAR ZAN'NH

Hyrillka's citadel palace had once been a lovely structure overgrown with flowering vines that draped arches and climbed courtyard walls. In those days, the Hyrillka Designate had been fond of the Solar Navy's spectacular skyparades, and Zan'nh had visited this world several times with Adar Kori'nh.

Now, however, the citadel palace was no more than an ornate prison run by brainwashed Ildirans. The main city was an austere complex devoid of leisure or arts.

Rusa'h's pleasure mates guarded the door to Zan'nh's holding rooms, poised hungrily as if hoping he would try to fight them. The formerly beautiful and seductive women had become grim killing machines made of steel cables instead of soft flesh. Though they did not shackle Zan'nh, their narrowed eyes and flashing teeth showed that they did not trust him. He was alien to them, separate, since he refused to join the corrupted *thism* web that held Rusa'h's converts together.

Zan'nh was effectively alone here on Hyrillka, isolated in the midst of a population swayed by the Designate's visions. A day ago, Rusa'h had flown away with the stolen warliners, to launch an attack on the surrounding Ildiran splinter colonies. They meant to strike with extreme speed, hammering one planet after another and swiftly subsuming the populations before the Mage-Imperator could grasp the conspiracy within his Empire.

It was partly Zan'nh's fault. He had lost those ships, giving the Hyrillka Designate the weapons he needed.

He glared at the pleasure mates outside his door to demonstrate his resolve. These women, trained and skilled in the arts of sex, had now become avid students of killing. Smiling wickedly at him, two of the hardened women held crystal-bladed spears in hands still caked with dried blood, as if they considered it a badge of honor after slashing the throats of Zan'nh's crewmen.

If he had thought he might have a chance, he would have thrown himself upon the two women, slain them both, and made his escape. But he knew it would be pointless, since more converted warriors waited out in the hall. The heavily muscled soldiers would kill him, and he would have no chance to get his revenge . . . or to make amends to the Mage-Imperator for his failure.

Isolated in the citadel palace, he was starving for the contact and comfort of the primary tapestry of *thism*. Before long, Zan'nh was afraid the loneliness and complete segregation would wear on him. He would weaken, grow distraught and edgy. He had to escape before his mind began to crumble.

He tried to plan, but each time he attempted to concentrate, the sucking silence in his mind distracted him. His pulse raced, and he began to breathe harder, searching for some contact out there. The silvery *thism* strands were far away and unreachable. He closed his eyes.

Zan'nh recalled a time when he was much younger, a mere septar in rank. He had flown a small streamer on highly coordinated maneuvers, soaring with forty-eight others scattered to the fringes of a bright nebula sea illuminated by a cluster of hot young stars. He had swooped through a knot of unexpectedly ionized gas, which scrambled his navigation systems. At stardrive speeds, he had gone into a spin, separated from the other ships in his group.

By the time his engines burned out, Zan'nh had had no idea what his bearings were. Lost and alone, he'd managed to reroute control systems to get his communications transmitter functioning again. He had broadcast his situation and called for help but did not know his location. Adar Kori'nh had sent reassurances to the young septar, talking confidently while he dispersed rescue teams as far apart as their own *thism* connections would allow.

Zan'nh could do nothing but wait. He had drifted alone in the darkness, feeling the mental strands unraveling around him, growing fainter, fraying. Time passed with infinite slowness.

Through his comm systems, he could hear the conversations, but saw no one. Kori'nh kept talking to him, demanding that he hold on, and Zan'nh had followed orders. He had endured, dredging strength from within himself until miraculously one of the searching streamers stumbled upon him. Other ships swooped in, clustering closer, and Zan'nh had been able to feel their comforting presence, like a mother wrapping blankets around a chilled infant.

Zan'nh had never forgotten that loneliness, nor had he forgotten that Adar Kori'nh had saved him through his strength and confidence. The memory of the ordeal would help him through this situation as well.

But his circumstances were now reversed. He knew people were all around him yet could sense none of them, as if he stood behind a glass barrier, able to see a feast but forbidden to partake of it. The Hyrillka Designate's tightly knit society had made Zan'nh a permanent outsider—unless he willingly joined. And that was something he would not do. . . .

The Adar paced around his chamber, once a fabulous suite in the Designate's palace. Pery'h, the legitimate Designate-in-waiting, had lived here, intending to take over from his uncle. But that was before the crazed Designate had torn his people from the true web of *thism*. In resisting, Pery'h had become a hero, and a martyr. Zan'nh could imagine the loneliness Pery'h had felt, not understanding what was happening. . . .

He wondered what Pery'h's last thoughts had been as the

guards dragged him out of this room, gave him one last chance to join the corrupted rebellion. When he refused, they killed him. Pery'h's agony and despair had thrummed across the soul-threads all the way to Ildira. That was how Mage-Imperator Jora'h knew what had happened.

If only Zan'nh could send the same sort of message. . . . But Pery'h had been a purebred son of the noble kith. His connection with his father was stronger, clearer. Zan'nh was merely a half-breed, and while the linkage was firm, he did not have the clarity of thought or the skill to send a detailed explanation to the Mage-Imperator. He hoped he wouldn't have to be slain to find a way to send the necessary information.

Even so, Jora'h had to know that something terrible had happened, that the Adar was in great distress. He must have sensed the deaths of all those crewmen aboard the warliner obliterated by a blast from treacherous Thor'h. The pleasure mates had taken great delight in informing him that three scout cutters spying for the Mage-Imperator had been captured in the system and subsumed. Jora'h was still cut off.

Zan'nh spun when he heard two armored guards march up to the doorway. They were former Solar Navy crewmen; he recognized them from Qul Fan'nh's warliner. The men stared at him without any emotion. The Adar wondered if they'd been given orders to kill him now. He lifted his chin and remained silent, waiting for them to speak.

Finally, one of the crewmen said, "We have received word that Imperator Rusa'h has used our warliners to add Dzelluria to his ever-growing empire. Lens kithmen and soldiers are even now distributing shiing so that the population may join his network of *thism*."

Zan'nh felt cold. Orra'h, the former Designate of Dzelluria, was a stubborn man who did not make impetuous decisions. "Why would they do that? And why so fast? Surely they must resist."

The nearest pleasure mate smiled. "The Dzelluria Designate chose to give his life in order to pave the way for the Designate-in-waiting, who has voluntarily joined Imperator Rusa'h. With Designate Czir'h converted, the rest of the population is easily swept into the fold."

The Adar remained stony, breathing swiftly. Far from Ildira, with a maniple of warliners overhead, their Designate murdered and his replacement forced to submit, the local Ildirans would be easy targets for Rusa'h. The disoriented people would not understand their peril and would grasp at any hope, even the wrong hope. Rusa'h would offer it to them.

Zan'nh scowled at his former Solar Navy comrades. They had informed him for no other reason than to twist the knife. Perhaps they felt that his resistance would crumble as Dzelluria had.

"I will not change my mind. Your effort here is wasted."

"No effort is wasted," the pleasure mate said. "However, Imperator Rusa'h informs us that you will accompany the warliners on their next expedition. The ships will return here soon. Once you witness it yourself, you will realize that the Imperator's victory is inevitable and that your position is untenable."

He closed his eyes and drew strength from recalling again how Adar Kori'nh had launched his wildly unexpected offensive against the hydrogue warglobes at Qronha 3.

"The only untenable position," Zan'nh said, his voice steely with resolve, "is surrender."

An unannounced warliner appeared in the skies over Dobro. Comm systems and orbital alarms lit up in the Ildiran settlement near the breeding camps. As soon as the first transmission came from the looming battleship, Designate Udru'h understood that this was no legitimate Solar Navy mission.

Lanky, sharp-featured Thor'h stood in the warliner's command nucleus. "Uncle, I have come on behalf of Imperator Rusa'h to celebrate your inclusion in our cause against the false Mage-Imperator."

Udru'h crossed his arms over his chest, but did not otherwise react. He struggled to find the right words with which to navigate this peculiar situation. Having just returned from delivering Osira'h to the Mage-Imperator, he knew of the troubles brewing on Hyrillka, but did not understand them. A cause against the false Mage-Imperator? Out-and-out rebellion?

He decided the situation called for noncommittal language that could elicit the reasons that this warship had arrived displaying threatening plumage. It appeared to be one of the war vessels formerly commanded by Adar Zan'nh. Very strange.

"You are always welcome here, Thor'h—"

"You will address me as Prime Designate!"

Udru'h bowed his head slightly, wisely choosing not to point out that Thor'h had been stripped of his title. "As you wish." The young man had been raised in luxury and was an amateur at political intrigues, secrets, and schemes. The Designate was sure he would have no trouble manipulating his nephew. Still, Thor'h commanded the battleship overhead. "But why do you come here with an armed warliner and threaten my colony?"

"I have made no threats—yet. I hope I can convince you without violence."

"Good, then we have a common goal." The Dobro Designate smiled blandly at his nephew. "However, if you intend to convince me to join you in outright rebellion, do not hide your meanings or lie to me."

The young man's voice was sharp. "Jora'h is the one who lies, as did Mage-Imperator Cyroc'h before him. The *thism* is tangled and ragged, but Rusa'h has seen the true path. He will lead the Ildiran people to the plane of the Lightsource."

"So you say." Udru'h remained coolly skeptical, but not confrontational. "Are you aware that one of the seven suns is in peril? Durris-B has become a battleground for the hydrogues and faeros and is sure to be smothered soon."

Thor'h obviously did not know, but he covered his surprise quickly with a haughty expression. "More evidence that the Lightsource has turned against my father. He must step down. Imperator Rusa'h can bring all Ildirans back to the proper path."

Designate-in-waiting Daro'h—Thor'h's brother—stood nearby in the colony's communications chamber, striving to mask his anxiety. He observed the interaction without interrupting, learning from the Designate. But his star-sapphire eyes flashed from Udru'h, to the image of the warliner, to Thor'h's mocking face.

From the moment Daro'h came to this planet, saw the breeding camps and learned of the hitherto unsuspected long-term mission to save the Ildiran race, he had struggled to understand and to accept. Making matters worse for Udru'h was that the Mage-Imperator had had such an open dispute with him over the Dobro scheme. However, the young Designate-in-waiting, to his credit, had tried his best to absorb details and fulfill his duty.

Unfortunately, the young man had never been prepared for such an unbelievable situation as this. And neither had Udru'h, but if he did not handle it, no one here would survive.

"I can see why Rusa'h believes I might be willing to join his cause. It's no secret that I disagree with many of Jora'h's decisions. He breaks with long-established traditions for his own convenience and has a personal grudge against my long-standing work here on Dobro."

"Merely a symptom of the decay in his Empire."

"That may be, nephew, but you are not making a very convincing argument for me to join your rebellion. How far has Rusa'h's movement spread?"

"Hyrillka has been entirely converted, and we have forty-six warliners at our command. The Adar himself is our prisoner. By now, Dzelluria will have joined us, and either the Designate or his successor has accepted the new *thism* willingly." Thor'h leaned closer in the imaging field. "The Imperator dispatched me here to see if you would do the same. An alliance would be most beneficial for all of us."

"An alliance must be voluntary." Udru'h did not allow himself to be intimidated. "Will Imperator Rusa'h force me if I refuse?"

"Because of your bloodline, Uncle, we cannot force you—not with all the shiing on Hyrillka." Thor'h flashed a hungry grin. "But perhaps I can make my case to your satisfaction. We do have much in common."

Seeing his only legitimate response, aware that even the one warliner could level his settlement and destroy the breeding camps and generations of work, the Dobro Designate nodded. "I will listen if I must. Give me evidence of Jora'h's crimes and errors, and tell me what Rusa'h will do differently."

Young Daro'h looked at his mentor in horror. "What are you doing? We cannot surrender—"

Udru'h answered as much for Thor'h's benefit as for the trainee's: "One does not make decisions without first gathering all the information." He turned back to the screen. "First, Prime Designate, I suggest you shut down your weaponry and return to orbit, where you will be less provocative. We all know how much devastation your weapons can cause; there's no need to further intimidate the people here."

"Why should I weaken my position?" Thor'h demanded.

Udru'h smiled at him, treating him as a child. "Because once your warliner stands down from its threatening posture, I will be happy to come up there and speak with you face-to-face. Is that not what you want?"

The Prime Designate gave a mean little smile. "Excellent."

While the warliner withdrew to space and gave Dobro a little breathing room, the Designate-in-waiting continued to protest, as Udru'h had known he would.

"You saw that warliner, Daro'h. We know that Rusa'h has already attempted to assassinate the Mage-Imperator, and he did kill Designate-in-waiting Pery'h. If the Hyrillka Designate has seized a maniple of ships and is already attacking Dzelluria, then I doubt he would hesitate to do the same here. He has demonstrated a certain . . . bloody resolve. I will not treat this as an empty threat. I needed to buy time. We must play our roles carefully, and our only chance now is through negotiation and delay."

The younger man paced the floor, frowning, his eyes confused and hurt, but he heard the wisdom in his mentor's voice.

Within an hour, the threatening warliner dispatched a shuttle, which carried the Dobro Designate up into the maw of the ship. Udru'h rode in silence, studying the seven clearly brainwashed soldier kithmen, all of whom wore Solar Navy uniforms. How had Rusa'h managed to capture so many warliners? If Adar Zan'nh was being held hostage, was he being converted as well?

He sifted through his thoughts, trying to formulate a strategy. He doubted the revolt could ever succeed, but if he saw indications of unexpected strength from the Hyrillka Designate, perhaps it would be best to keep his loyalties vague, just in case. He would wait and hear what the rebels had to offer.

Clinging to the key fact Thor'h had unwittingly let slip— that a Designate's cooperation could not be forced—Udru'h stepped out of the shuttle when it landed, and straightened his uniform shirt. He had little use for formal attire or fine designs, but knowing how much Thor'h enjoyed pomp and ceremony, he had intentionally worn formal dress. More soldiers ushered him up to the command nucleus. There on the dais that had been reserved for the Adar, Thor'h stood preening himself.

Udru'h stepped casually close to his lanky nephew. "A rebellion against the Empire does not seem to be a wise course of action. Perhaps you had best explain yourself?"

Thor'h quickly and passionately repeated what Rusa'h claimed to have seen in visions during his sub-*thism* sleep. "We are not rising up against the Ildiran Empire—only against the Mage-Imperator, whose leadership is deeply flawed."

"Your father."

"You know he is weak. Imperator Rusa'h will be a stronger ruler."

Udru'h shrugged. "That may be so, but whatever his flaws, Jora'h is the rightful Mage-Imperator."

"Is he?" The Prime Designate produced a stack of diamondfilm documents that displayed detailed scientific results. "The previous Mage-Imperator died suddenly and unexpectedly at the height of this crisis. We were able to obtain a cellular sample from the handler kithmen who prepared Cyroc'h's body. This tissue analysis proves that the Mage-Imperator died from a massive dose of poison. Jora'h then eagerly ascended to become our leader."

Udru'h glanced curiously at the diamondfilm sheets as Thor'h continued: "Mere moments after Cyroc'h's death, his loyal bodyguard Bron'n was found dead, his crystal spear thrust through his heart. Jora'h was the only person present. You may draw only one conclusion from this."

Even the Dobro Designate could not believe these implications. "This is . . . astounding. Are you saying that Jora'h murdered our father in order to become Mage-Imperator?"

Thor'h nodded toward the diamondfilm sheets. "The evidence states as much. We have already brought Hyrillka and Dzelluria into our fold, and now we wish Dobro to join this uprising. It is a revolution, for Rusa'h has seen the truth. Jora'h is fundamentally corrupted. Therefore he cannot accurately read the *thism*."

Udru'h crossed his arms over his uniformed chest again. "How can I be certain that Rusa'h's visions are not delusions caused by his injuries? That seems a more likely explanation."

Thor'h was growing more and more upset with his uncle's continued questions and skepticism. The Solar Navy soldiers in the command nucleus glowered at him. Udru'h knew full well these people were willing to murder him if it seemed that Designate-in-waiting Daro'h might be easier to break.

Finally, Thor'h relaxed. "Imperator Rusa'h said that you would ask such a question. Therefore, he gave me proof to demonstrate that he knows how to follow the soul-threads to the wisdom of the Lightsource."

"Parlor tricks will not convince me."

"While he was in sub-*thism* sleep, Rusa'h had many revelations." Thor'h's voice turned strange and mysterious, and Udru'h's skin began to crawl. "He knows the secret you are keeping, Uncle. A certain green priest . . . a woman, my father's lover. The false Mage-Imperator believes she is dead, and he has already mourned her—but you know she is still alive. You are hiding her."

A lance of ice shot down Udru'h's spine. "How does he know this?"

"The same way he received all of his revelations. Do not doubt him."

Udru'h scrambled to gain more time. "Thor'h, you are asking me to betray all the trust and loyalties I have developed during my life. If Rusa'h truly wishes me to join him voluntarily and not under duress, then you must give me time to consider what you have shown me, so that I may make my decision."

"The answer is clear. Why do you hesitate?"

Udru'h stepped up to the command nucleus rail, standing immediately in front of Thor'h. "Maybe it's clear to *you*, but as you have reminded me several times, the rest of us no longer see the truth as clearly." His voice became biting. "You ask me to join you willingly, and yet you come here with a fully armed warliner to make your case. Since you yourself do not seem confident in the strength of your 'proof,' then I grow suspicious of your argument."

Thor'h sniffed, obviously impatient that Udru'h had not buckled. "I bring this warliner because it encourages you to listen with an open mind."

Udru'h remembered when the Prime Designate had been a spoiled boy who loved his golden life on Hyrillka. "My nephew does not need to issue threats before I will listen to him. And so I have listened. Now let me think about what you said."

"Time is short." Thor'h leaned to within a handsbreadth of his face, as if he could intimidate the Designate. "Why should I not just seize you as a hostage? I could forcibly take over this minor splinter colony."

Inwardly growing more and more irritated, Udru'h gestured vaguely toward the warliner's controls. "You could easily attack and destroy Dobro. Using brute force, Rusa'h could subdue the population, break them to his will. But unlike most splinter colonies, my settlement is full of halfbreeds and human captives. Rusa'h could never control that population with shiing or with his new *thism*. You need me for that."

Thor'h fidgeted, impatient and uncertain, but he could not argue with Udru'h. "So what do you propose? I have been ordered to convince you in any way possible. I will not disappoint the Imperator."

Udru'h strung his young nephew along, making silent calculations in his mind. He drove a hard bargain. "Then this is how you will accomplish it. Let me consider what you offer and the consequences if I refuse. Within ten days I will present myself to Hyrillka willingly and deliver my answer."

"Ten days is impossible."

Udru'h barked, "I will not be treated like an attender kithman to be herded to his task! Do you want my cooperation or not? Once I have had time to consider, I will speak directly with Rusa'h—but only at the appointed time."

Thor'h scowled. "You will never come. It is a trick."

"I give you my word, Prime Designate. I am a son of a Mage-Imperator! Surely you could sense if I am lying?" Udru'h stood tall, his face stony. "Or are you unable, since you are no longer in touch with the same *thism*? A pity."

Not knowing the extent of Thor'h's strange new mental network, Udru'h focused his thoughts, brought forth all the mental discipline techniques he had developed. Over the past year, he had learned how to mask his feelings and his memories whenever he stood before Jora'h, and he had managed to hide certain secrets, especially about Nira.

"Five days," Thor'h insisted. "You can have five days— and then you must be at Hyrillka, or else I will come back to destroy Dobro."

The Prime Designate stared at him for a drawn-out moment, and Udru'h remained still, his expression firm. Finally Thor'h turned his sharp gaze away. "Yes, I can sense you are telling the truth. If I must make a minor concession in order to gain Dobro as a willing ally, then Imperator Rusa'h would agree."

The guards in the command nucleus looked disappointed, but Thor'h ordered them to escort Udru'h back to the shuttle. "I will hold you to your promise, Uncle. If you betray us, we will return with our warliners—and we will not negotiate."

"I will come to Hyrillka exactly as I said I would."
Udru'h kept his face placid, while his mind raced ahead, trying to see a way out of the trap he had just set for himself.

43 ☀ OSIRA'H

For several days, the Mage-Imperator's eldest daughter
took the troubled but excited Osira'h under her wing at
the Prism Palace. Yazra'h's three Isix cats prowled alongside as the two half sisters walked through the city.

Everything amazed the young girl, who had previously seen
nothing beyond the dry hills and arroyos of Dobro, except in
secondhand memories from her mother. The sensory whirlpool
of Mijistra's sounds and colors and tastes and smells swirled
around Osira'h. Soaring and majestic buildings gave her a new
appreciation for the grandeur of the Ildiran Empire and showed
her what she was supposed to be fighting for, why she must fulfill her destiny, even though she knew there were many dark
and sinister corners under the seven suns.

Four days earlier, the Hansa's King Peter and Queen Estarra had departed without learning of the hydrogue-faeros
battle inside Durris-B. Yazra'h seemed quite proud that the
Mage-Imperator had prevented the humans from discovering any of the brewing troubles in the Ildiran Empire.

Osira'h was immediately reminded of her long-captive

mother and all the breeding slaves on Dobro. "Yes, we are very good at keeping secrets from the humans, aren't we?"

Her muscular half sister smiled, accepting the comment as a compliment. "We have a few days until everything is ready for your mission, and then we must locate a group of hydrogues for you to communicate with."

"I saw thousands of them fighting at the Durris star."

Yazra'h tossed her mane of long coppery hair. "Your protective vessel cannot withstand an environment such as that. Follow me, and I will show you the sphere that will take you deep into a gas giant's clouds."

She guided Osira'h to a hangar where engineer kithmen and laborers were finishing construction on a strange new vessel. Its hull was fabricated from heavy transparent armorplate. The interior wasn't large, but neither was she.

"This vessel will protect you from the pressure, but not necessarily from the hydrogues themselves. The rest will be up to you." Yazra'h gave her an encouraging slap on the back. "But you will make all the difference, little sister. You can do things that no one else can."

Osira'h did not argue. She moved forward to study the crystalline chamber, touching it with her fingertips. "Yes. Yes, I can."

Drinking in details with her eyes, storing information in her carefully organized mind, Osira'h learned everything she could about the Prism Palace and the Ildirans, whom she was destined to protect. Some of the courtiers, and even Yazra'h, remarked on her unusual and intense silence. Osira'h just watched them, always calculating and storing information.

Unlike other Ildirans, she had been born with a great weight on her shoulders. Designate Udru'h had never let the girl's thoughts stray from the expectations placed upon her, had never let her forget that he believed she had the innate skill to accomplish what was necessary. And yet, immediately after delivering Osira'h to the Prism Palace, Udru'h had turned his back on her and returned to Dobro in case she failed.

Osira'h walled off her disappointment, shoring up the barrier with bricks made of memories from her mother: how Nira had been locked in a dark cell so her green skin could drink in no sunlight; how, after the birth of her daughter, Udru'h had kept her in the breeding barracks until she conceived his son, Rod'h; how afterward, he'd subjected Nira to a series of coldly clinical impregnations by other Ildiran kiths.

Her mother had recalled each one of those rapes like burning coals on her skin. Through the too-clear window of shared memories and experiences, the little girl also remembered every ripping pain, every thrust, every bruise.

Osira'h could easily hate Designate Udru'h if she allowed her mother's memories to overwhelm her. But the girl also remembered her mission, recognized Udru'h's urgent need to save his race from the hydrogues, even at the cost of a few human breeders. She remembered how Udru'h had cared for her, shown as much love as he was capable of demonstrating. Osira'h felt as if she might be ripped in two. . . .

When her father summoned the girl to his private contemplation chamber, Osira'h stood uncertainly at the doorway. Jora'h came forward, smiling with a welcome that bore the distinct undertones of shyness—an odd reaction from the leader of the great Ildiran Empire.

"Come in, please." Tentatively, Jora'h reached out to touch her narrow shoulders. "Let me just look at you." Without answering, Osira'h watched shifting currents of emotion cross the Mage-Imperator's face. "So much like your mother. I can see Nira in your eyes."

Osira'h met his gaze and suddenly felt awkward and confused. Seeing Jora'h in the round chamber with its colored-crystal windows, her mother's memories flooded her with other recollections. Though this man in front of her was her own father, her mind was full of other encounters in this room: warm and passionate lovemaking in the cushions, conversations and caresses that made the girl's heart melt. So different from the breeding barracks on Dobro: love instead of mere impregnation, ecstasy rather than pain and horror.

But if Jora'h loved her, why hadn't he saved Nira from Dobro? Why had he believed the lies without questioning, without wondering if Nira had been snatched away? If he truly cared for her, why had he let her go so easily?

"You're very quiet," Jora'h said, leading her into the chamber.

Osira'h shuddered instinctively, even though she knew he meant nothing sexual by his invitation. Here, he was her father, the castrated Mage-Imperator, not the friend and lover Nira had known. Even so, Osira'h could not help but see him from both perspectives. She would have to balance the two without revealing the depth of her knowledge. Jora'h and Udru'h, among others, would likely be horrified at all she had "witnessed" and could remember. How ironic that the very breeding and abilities that made her the hope of the Ildiran Empire had made her a freakish anomaly, an unpredictable singularity. No, she could not let her father, or anyone else, learn her secret.

Before she could answer him, Osira'h saw the potted treeling in a wall alcove. Her eyes wide and sparkling, she stepped forward. "May I touch it?" Her thoughts whirled, remembering what it had been like for Nira to drop into the telink network, connected with other green priests and all of the worldtrees. It had been a solace long denied to Nira. "My mother was a green priest."

Jora'h smiled. "Of course."

Osira'h held her small hand close to the delicate fronds. The golden lapped scales of bark on the thin trunk were like soft jewels. The fernlike fronds fanned out, and she stroked the leaves like a musician playing the strings of a delicate instrument.

She wasn't sure what to expect. Her fingertips felt a tingle, then a jolt, and her heart swelled. An image flashed through her mind of Nira in desperation, grasping thorny shrubs on Dobro until her palms were bloody, screaming her thoughts into deaf plants that had no way of contacting the worldforest network.

Then, as if in response, a kinder recollection came to Osira'h. She relived the day that the worldtrees had accepted Nira as a new green priest, enfolding her in their verdant embrace, connecting with her cells, changing her body's chemistry so that she could be a part of the vast and serene forest mind. Oh, the joy she had felt when that huge universe suddenly opened to her . . .

The girl released her touch. The potted treeling seemed to tremble, but she had not achieved a complete connection, not like a real green priest's. Even so, she smiled in quiet wonder.

"I see that makes you happy," Jora'h said. "I wish to do everything I can to keep you happy before you must . . . go away." He paced the floor of his chamber, turning back to her. "It will be soon. I am still waiting to hear a report from my scout cutters, to let me know what is happening at Hyril-lka." He shook his head. "But I grow too distracted. That does not concern you. Just another trouble in the Empire."

She waited in silence, letting him continue.

"I want to spend time with you, get to know you. You are my own daughter, and I have placed such a heavy burden on you. I thought we might tour Mijistra, visit museums, or go to the streams." His words petered out.

"Yazra'h has already shown me those things."

The Mage-Imperator sat on his bed cushions. "Then the most important thing I can do for you—for both of us—is to tell you about your mother. Nira was . . . very special to me."

"And now she's dead."

He looked stung. "Yes."

Though Osira'h already knew everything about her mother, unfiltered and uncensored from Nira's own mind, she decided to test her father. Curious to see how closely he would adhere to the truth, she let Jora'h explain himself, in his own way.

44 ☀ NIRA

After escaping from the isolated island where Designate Udru'h had stranded her, Nira was still alone.

Unlike Ildirans, however, she did not view such solitude with mortal terror. The company she had been forced to endure in recent years had been nightmarish.

On her endless walk across the uninhabited landscape,

Nira's emerald skin provided her through photosynthesis with all the sustenance she needed. She could survive; she was a green priest. But the pounding silence all around her and inside her throbbing head weighed upon her. Though she had healed long ago, her head still ached from where the guards had clubbed her after they'd dragged her away from Osira'h . . . her daughter, her princess.

She walked on and on, seeing no one as she crossed the vast landscape of the empty continent. Dobro was a very sparsely settled Ildiran world. Perhaps to keep others from seeing the horrific breeding work? Grasses and weeds whispered into the silence around her, speaking with leaves and stalks and blossoms, but she could not comprehend the language. Unlike the worldtrees back on her beloved Theroc . . .

What Nira longed for most was Jora'h, her lover from the bright and colorful Prism Palace. But he did not know she was alive. She wondered if he had forgotten about her; as Prime Designate, Jora'h had had so many lovers. On his last visit to her isolated island, the Dobro Designate had told her the fat and scheming old leader was dead, and that Jora'h had taken his place. He was now the Mage-Imperator.

Surely he would have come for me by now, if he'd wanted to.

After floating across the broad inland sea, Nira had abandoned her makeshift raft on the shore and continued her trek across the southern continent. In spite of sore feet and tired muscles, she forced herself to keep moving through wind and rain and bright sunlight. Though she had no map and did not know where to go, she tended generally northward.

Her fear and her goal were the same: Up there, somewhere far away, lay the Dobro breeding camps and the other human prisoners. Nira shuddered at the prospect of going there again, but the Ildiran settlement, the one inhabited place on Dobro, had the only ships that could take her away. And Osira'h.

Nira could either hide forever, or she could try to get away . . . to go home. Back to the worldforest.

The Designate had kept her hostage to use her as a bargaining chip against Jora'h. She did not want to be a pawn; neither did she want to be a danger to Jora'h. She would rather die out here alone than let that happen. Alone and in silence.

Even as a novice, Nira had communed with worldtrees. She had read stories aloud to them, telling the sentient forest of human history. Then, when she'd been chosen to become a priest, the forest had accepted her, changed her, given her access to a new universe of thoughts and experiences.

Once she'd taken the green, she had always been able to feel the great trees speaking to her. Whenever she touched the scaly bark of even the smallest treeling, she could connect through telink and interact with the whole forest. Coming to Ildira, she and old Otema had brought potted treelings to maintain contact with the worldforest—treelings that had been destroyed by the evil Mage-Imperator's guards. Otema had been slain, without the chance to let her memories be absorbed into the trees, and Nira had been brutalized . . . taken here, away from the worldtrees.

Her emerald hand clenched around the gnarled stem of a woody weed as thick as her forearm. She squeezed, but heard nothing from the plant, no echo of the immense worldforest mind.

Were these plants truly silent, or had her brain been damaged in the assault that nearly killed her?

She released the thick stem with a jerk, as if it had caught fire. She didn't want to consider that she might now be deaf to telink. Was it the injury, or had the awful camps beaten it out of her? Surely there must be a single treeling on this entire planet! Somewhere . . .

Before the Ildiran guards had driven her away, she had managed to impart her knowledge and memories to Osira'h. At least the little girl now understood what Designate Udru'h planned for her and how he had cruelly distorted the truth about Nira and the other breeding slaves. Osira'h knew everything, and her mother could only hope that the knowledge would help her in some way.

In the shade of a tall, reddish rock, Nira squatted to rest, leaning her bare back against the warm stone. In this terrain she saw only scrubby desert weeds and hardy shrubs. No trees. A tall green forest—any forest—would be so soothing right now. Even if she couldn't communicate with it.

Nira closed her eyes and let her thoughts flow, drifting into the open skies of Dobro. With all her psychic strength, she drew upon her memories of the welcoming presence of the vast worldforest, and sent her silent cry like a shout into the void. She directed the message toward her daughter. Osira'h must be out there, and she had heard her mother before. Her princess should still be near the breeding camps, even if they were half a planet away. Only once, on that single fateful night, had Nira been able to connect with her daughter, yet that briefest of sharings had been enough to express a lifetime of memories and desires.

But the brutal guards had given her a concussion so severe that it had almost killed her. Although she had recovered, Nira still suffered from powerful headaches, pounding pains inside her head . . . and now she found she was unable to establish even a tenuous connection with the little girl. Either Osira'h was too far away, or Nira no longer had that special ability.

By now her daughter must certainly believe her to be dead, making the task of communication more impossible than before.

The breeze picked up, and the thick, dry weeds whispered again with a sound like laughter.

Years ago, when Nira and other breeding prisoners had been sent out to fight a raging brush fire, she had tried to escape. Chased by her captors, Nira had thrown herself into a thorny thicket, trying to force a telink contact to any tree or bush. Though she'd called out in every way she knew, she had heard no response . . . and the guards had taken her again.

Now it was the same: no response from the trees, nothing from her daughter. Would the silence ever end?

Nira continued sending her mental beacon until her head split with the pain. Darkness fell, and stars sparkled across an ebony backdrop. And still she heard no answer to her call.

Osira'h simply wasn't there anymore.

45 ☀ BENETO

The night on Theroc was silent, but filled with the voices of the forest. Because of his dual nature, Beneto's mind could mingle and become one with the worldtrees, or he could withdraw and be himself. In truth, he was neither, trapped somewhere between the two.

The wooden golem sat alone in the ring of five burned stumps that stood like a temple to the wounded forest. Glowing lamps shone like bright eyes from the restored settlements where Theron survivors now lived. The makeshift homes were full of light, warmth, and amenities thanks to the Roamers who had helped them rebuild. Phosphorescent night insects floated about in faint streaks of bluish-white light, like a blizzard of fallen stars.

Sarein came quietly up to him in the shadows. Sensing his eldest sister's approach, Beneto realized she had lost all of her natural feeling for the worldforest. She carried no lamp, not because she was trying to sneak up on her brother, merely to make sure that no one else noticed she had joined him.

"Beneto, I need to talk to you. I need to understand."

"Yes, Sarein. You do."

For days, he had been surrounded by former friends and amazed well-wishers. Now that he had issued the worldforest's call, instructed them to disperse treelings as widely as possible, the exhausted people worked even harder, green priests volunteered to take treelings to other Hansa colonies, and everyone watched the skies for the return of the dreaded hydrogues.

Sarein had promised to assist by calling for Hansa ships— it was her obvious duty, and she understood how to accomplish that—but she had remained curiously apart from *him*. As if reluctant to believe his fantastic story, she watched the wooden image of her dead brother. She had spent too much time on Earth among businessmen and scientists, studying instead of accepting.

Now, at last, Sarein appeared before him ready to ask questions. He could feel that she was torn between two worlds: Born of Theroc, she longed to be on Earth, yet returned to her disaster-struck home, obligated to help.

With wood-grain eyes, he saw her perfectly well despite the darkness. Since he'd last seen her, when she'd departed for Earth, Sarein's face had grown leaner, her expression harder. The responsibilities and stresses had been unkind to her, compared to the nurturing wilderness of Theroc. Beneto wondered if she regretted her bold choice to leave, to cut ties with her heritage. Perhaps she herself didn't see the toll it had taken.

Now she looked at him, fighting an awe that was tinged with intimidation. "What are you? Really."

"What do you see?"

"I see something that looks like my brother, but we have already grieved for his death. We lost Reynald, as well. Why did you come back?"

His limbs creaked and popped as he stood. "I am a son of Theroc. The worldforest that I so loved in life chose me, called me, recreated me so that I could be a clear voice for the verdani and, if necessary, a general in our war." Beneto stepped closer to his sister. "The reason for my return is easily explained, Sarein. Yours, however, is not. You came back to Theroc, but the worldforest can see your feelings. We know that in your heart, you do not wish to be here. I, and the worldforest, can sense it in your soul."

Sarein was flustered and confused. She had always been a no-nonsense person, and his mystical rebirth was out of her control. She crossed her arms over her breasts. "Coming back to Theroc seemed the right thing to do. I am the oldest surviving child of the ruling family. It is my responsibility."

"You have been told to feel that way. You yourself do not believe it."

She arched her eyebrows. "I see. Do you intend to take over as the next ruler here?"

"I have no interest in that." Beneto paused just a moment before adding, "And neither do you."

Sarein responded with an indignant expression, but they both knew it was an act. "What do you mean by that?"

"You know you don't belong here. Your heart and mind lie elsewhere. It has always been so."

"I've discussed my obligations at great length with Chairman Wenceslas."

"The people of Theroc deserve someone whose roots go deep here. But you, Sarein, are a leaf in the wind, not an anchored tree."

His sister looked away, clearly unsettled. "But . . . how can I *not* help Theroc? These are my people too."

Beneto rested a warm wood-grained hand on her arm. "I mean no insult when I tell you this, Sarein. You are our ambassador to Earth. Truly, you will accomplish more for Theroc if you return to the Hansa and work at what you do best. This is not for you."

Sarein's breathing grew faster, harder. Beneto sensed that she was near tears. "But . . . but look at what the hydrogues did to Theroc. And those faeros creatures! Our people need protection."

"The hydrogues will return, and you can do nothing about it. But you *can* help us spread the treelings from ship to ship and world to world, starting with the Hansa colonies." Beneto showed his perfectly carved wooden teeth in a smile. "Don't worry, Sarein. A call went out beyond the Spiral Arm more than a year ago, when the hydrogues obliterated the first worldtree grove on Corvus Landing. Even before the hydrogues found Theroc, our reinforcements were under way, voyaging at top speed across impossible distances."

He turned his head toward her. "Next time, if we can hold

off the enemy for long enough, the forest will no longer fight alone. Allies are on their way."

46 ✴ BASIL WENCESLAS

The smell of medicines and the hum of diagnostic machinery always made the Chairman uneasy. He hated these regular rejuvenation treatments, but he knew the necessity of free-radical-expunging geriatric baths and fine-toxin filtering from his tissues and bloodstream. Very few people could afford such extraordinary measures to retain their youthful vitality, but Basil was a man with more responsibilities and pressures than anyone else in the Spiral Arm. It was imperative that he maintain his stamina.

Meticulous Hansa doctors watched him diligently for any deviation from normal health, aggressively dealing with the slightest anomaly. He simply could not afford to waste away. Accepting graceful retirement like Maureen Fitzpatrick had never been—and never would be—an option. He wasn't ready to retire . . . and certainly no one was ready to replace him.

His heir apparent, Eldred Cain, had never disappointed him, but neither had he ever surprised Basil. Yes, Cain understood the Hansa Charter and the law; he was intimately familiar with the workings of politics and the Earth Defense

Forces; he grasped everything that was necessary for running the Hanseatic League. But would it be sufficient? Was the quiet and pallid deputy shrewd enough and determined enough to become the next Chairman?

As the doctors tended Basil, injecting him with vitamins and wrapping his skin with fixative films and moisturizers, he looked up to see his expediter Franz Pellidor enter the room, bypassing the guards without so much as a word. Pellidor had neatly trimmed short blond hair, a square jaw, and a nose too perfect to be anything but the result of cosmetic modification. Broad-shouldered and muscular, he usually chose suits that were slightly undersized to enhance his imposing appearance.

"I know these procedures are necessary, but I resent the waste of hours of my time here," Basil said to him. "I wish these doctors would consider how much my time is worth. I have so many more important things to do."

The technicians looked at him with uncertain expressions, but did not respond. Pellidor answered calmly, "Even your time is probably not worth as much as these treatments cost, Mr. Chairman."

"I have an inflated sense of my own importance?"

"Mr. Chairman, you are more than worth your weight in ekti." Pellidor stopped where Basil lay prone on the table. "And speaking of ekti, I have the report you requested. Our modular skymine at Qronha 3 continues to produce acceptable amounts of stardrive fuel, in spite of the recent territorial unpleasantness with the Ildirans. Sullivan Gold assures us that their work proceeds without interference. Both groups are staying out of each other's way."

"After our recent visit to Mage-Imperator Jora'h, I'm not convinced the Ildirans have much to offer us, at the moment." Though the Ildiran leader had said nothing, the Chairman had quickly picked up hints that the ancient empire was having internal problems. "Even so, we have to keep them as allies. The Hansa certainly can't afford a conflict on yet another front."

Lying back on his medical table, Basil scanned Pellidor's report, noting the production numbers and the anticipated deliveries of stardrive fuel from the Qronha 3 cloud harvester. He hoped the expensive, rushed facility would survive long enough to pay for itself. It seemed to be a good investment so far, but the hydrogues could return at any time, without warning. At least Sullivan Gold had his own green priest aboard, so they would know immediately if hydrogues threatened the skymine.

He winced as a doctor prodded him with another needle. Pellidor waited to see whether the Chairman would snap at the medical attendant or if he would pretend to be invulnerable to pain.

Basil concentrated on his work, mulling over a million problems and many more possible solutions. Thinking of the green priest aboard the skymine only reminded him of how many others had left Hansa service and returned to their damaged world. Perhaps Basil had made an error in not sending the EDF to assist in the forest reconstruction. The Roamers had, and now the Therons felt indebted to the clans. He hated a missed opportunity.

Basil heaved a sigh. "Roamers and Therons both have such a narrow perspective. The entire Spiral Arm has been in a state of emergency for more than seven years, and it's increasingly difficult for me to run the Hansa without effective communication. Ah, maybe Sarein will come through for us."

Unbidden, an image of lovely, intelligent, and ambitious

Sarein came to him. Perhaps it was the drugs and the treatment, but Basil felt a pang of longing for her. He had sent her to Theroc with instructions to work her way into governmental decisions, proposing herself as the next Mother. Even in the back of his mind, he didn't want to admit how much he missed her sweet young body and—more erotic still—the electric heat of her ruthless determination. He had never realized how much energy her very presence gave him.

Basil tried to sit up, but the medical attendants surrounded him like a group of busy hens. "You still have at least an hour to go, Mr. Chairman. We will lose all progress if we stop now."

He clenched his jaw and lay back, looking up at the expediter as he felt—but tried hard not to show—the weight of the universe on his shoulders. "I used to revel in the challenges, Mr. Pellidor. Roamers, hydrogues, green priests, Klikiss worlds, ekti, even King Peter. I swear I will not let them defeat me now."

47 ☀ KING PETER

When the first shipload of unexpected refugees arrived from Crenna, Hansa protocol operations rushed to prepare a showy reception for them.

Davlin Lotze, piloting a ship he'd commandeered from

Relleker, communicated directly with Basil Wenceslas over private channels. In response, the Chairman called for King Peter to put on his colorful fall robes for an impromptu welcome as soon as the ship landed. "Showing an unexpected compassionate side, Basil? Or is there something else I need to know?"

"I tell you everything you need to know. And nothing more." Basil paced outside the door of the royal quarters as attendants surrounded Queen Estarra and dressed her in a fine gown spattered with jewels and pearls. "But the news greatly disturbs me. Hydrogues and faeros actively destroying suns, obliterating habitable planets like Crenna. Lotze suspects there'll be more to come. We've been lucky so far."

"I doubt the Crenna refugees consider themselves very lucky."

"They're lucky to be alive," Basil said. "Since these people were saved from certain death, we can put a positive spin on this."

With crews working overtime, a ribbon-decked reviewing stand was erected and pushed into place by the time Lotze's vessel landed in the Palace District. There hadn't been time to arrange for a formal crowd, but the court protocol ministers and ever-present media representatives rushed to their places to watch the King and Queen welcome these brave escapees from a hydrogue-destroyed star system.

As usual, a royal honor guard marched briskly in front of them, leading the way. Breaking from his usual reticence, Basil accompanied them, along with Eldred Cain and four other Hansa officials. *Why not bring Prince Daniel as well?* Peter thought. *To show that the Hansa is one big happy family.*

Ever since their return from Ildira a few days ago, Peter had detected a different attitude from the Chairman, a more careful scrutiny and veiled suspicions. Estarra sensed it too. He could see it in the tension in her stance, but her expression remained perfectly clear. Had something about her pregnancy slipped? They both feared the Chairman's reaction once he learned of the baby.

Basil had grown volatile and edgy in recent months, and Peter didn't expect the formerly cool and cautious man to react rationally now. Basil hated any unexpected turn of events.

Peter held the Queen's hand as they climbed the steps of the reviewing stand. Although he had received much formal instruction in etiquette from his Teacher compy OX, in truth Peter had learned manners long ago from his hardworking mother—his *real* mother, Rita Aguerra.

At the thought of his mother, who had never failed her boys despite a lack of almost everything she needed, Peter felt a deep sadness. He looked over at Estarra, his eyes briefly stinging. He would never have the joy of introducing his beloved Queen to his mother. In the political schemes to cover Peter's true background, the Hansa—no, *Basil himself*—had arranged for the destruction of their dwelling complex, incinerating Peter's mother and young brothers. Someday, Basil would pay for that.

Though a veritable hurricane of emotion passed through his heart and mind, the King allowed none of it to show. Estarra glanced at him with concern when his hand clenched, but he forced a smile. Never would he let Basil know what really took place in his head. He knew better than to let the Chairman suspect. It was too dangerous.

King and Queen stood in front of the reviewing stand as the refugee ship landed in the Palace District's paved and painted reception zone. Commercial and military traffic had been moved aside to avoid interfering with the media coverage.

The official band played a fanfare as hatches opened on the ship and dusty, bedraggled-looking Crenna colonists filed out. Lower-ranking Hansa representatives went forward to meet them, shaking hands and letting functionaries direct the passengers off to one side for a more efficient disembarkation.

Peter stood close to the Queen, watching, waving, smiling. They were both amazed that so many people had fit aboard the ship, and apparently another vessel was coming behind them in a day or so. He had lived in crowded quarters with his mother and brothers, a long time ago. With a tolerant mind-set, humans could put up with difficult conditions.

The Crenna refugees made a slow single-file procession in front of the reviewing stand. The sun shone in a clear blue sky, and breezes from the nearby ocean kept the air crisp— a far cry from the circumstances these people had experienced over the last few days aboard their ship.

As two men walked by, jostling against each other, Peter heard one mutter, "Never thought we'd end up back on Earth again. Spent half a damn year getting away and setting up our own colony in the first place."

The other sighed. "I've been sent back to square one so many times in my life, I'm starting to leave footprints."

The Chairman whispered close to Peter's ear, "Here comes Lotze. Thank him for his service and invite him to join us up here on the reviewing stand."

The King gave a slight nod. "Davlin Lotze, my Queen and I wish to thank you for a mission well accomplished. While I can congratulate you with all the pomp and ceremony of this office, my gratitude is nothing compared to the thanks these Crenna colonists owe you. Come, be our guest for this ceremony."

Lotze looked past the King to Chairman Wenceslas. "It would be my honor, Majesty." He glided up the steps; Peter doubted the man ever made a sound when he chose not to. Lotze took his place close to the Chairman so the two of them could have a discreet conversation.

"How is your retirement so far, Davlin?" Basil said with clear sarcasm.

"Pleasant enough, until the hydrogues came."

"And now that you're a knight in shining armor to these people"—they both stared forward, smiling—"what exactly do you expect us to do with them? Rlinda Kett is due to bring another shipment within a day or so."

Alert and listening to every word, Eldred Cain leaned in. "Think of all the good press the Hansa will receive. 'Rescued from the jaws of the enemy hydrogues.' "

Basil snorted. "After the media spotlight fades, they'll just be refugees."

Lotze said, "I intend to speak as their advocate. These people gave up everything to settle on Crenna and make a new start for themselves. They don't particularly want to stay on Earth. Find another Klikiss world. They're already adept at setting up colony facilities—the failure of Crenna was no fault of their own. You'll have nothing to worry about."

Basil gave a bitter laugh. "I always have things to worry about, Davlin. Now more than ever before."

In the afternoon following the reception ceremony, Peter and Estarra needed more time alone together, to draw strength from the comfort of each other's presence. As they swam in the warm water of the Palace's dolphin pool, the King knew they were being observed by Hansa spies. But he and Estarra had learned to block off those thoughts, while remaining wary.

The dolphins enjoyed swimming with the royal visitors. Sleek gray shapes sped by. Sometimes the King and Queen played with them; other times, the two were just intent on each other. Like now.

Peter looked into Estarra's brown eyes. He stroked and then cupped her delicately pointed chin, turning her face up so he could just stare at her. Her thick black hair, done up in tight braids and twists, seemed impervious to the water, slick and shiny with clear droplets. He moved closer to kiss her, and the concern melted from her face. "I love you very much," he said.

"You took the words right out of my mouth," she said.

Peter wished he could pour his thoughts directly into her mind, as they had seen Mage-Imperator Jora'h do with his subjects via the *thism*. The Mage-Imperator must have such a beautiful and satisfying link with his people, without the need for secrets, veiled diplomacy, misdirection, or cryptic messages. . . .

There was much Peter wanted to tell her in open conversation, if he could, things both crucial and meaningless. But they needed to be so careful together. He understood Estarra, and could express complex concerns and ideas with a glance, an expression, a lifting of his eyebrows, a touch of his fingertip. Always under scrutiny, the King and Queen had developed their own private language. But it wasn't enough.

Under the water, he moved his hand and traced his fingertips across the smooth skin of her belly. The meaning was very clear, and she drew him closer as the dolphins swam around, splashing and impatient for more-vigorous play.

He used the hand signals they had developed. "It will be all right."

She responded with a dance of her fingers. "Only if we're careful. Very careful."

He lowered his voice to the barest breath of a whisper, speaking aloud. "Then we will be."

48 ☀ GENERAL KURT LANYAN

Only a day after Davlin Lotze delivered the first Crenna refugees to Earth, Rlinda Kett careened into the solar system transmitting a demand for an emergency meeting even before she hit the orbit of Saturn. She blurted her news to the first EDF picket scouts that intercepted her; before the pilots could express their disbelief, Rlinda sent a fast feed of direct images showing the destruction of Relleker.

General Lanyan headed out in a fast EDF recon ship and personally intercepted the *Voracious Curiosity* on its way in. He spoke to Rlinda over a private comm channel while he spun his vessel around and paced alongside her inbound ship. After he had scanned her report, only the heat of his anger kept ice from forming in his heart.

"General, there's no question the drogues are starting a new phase against the Hansa," Rlinda said to him. "They annihilated Relleker on purpose, squashed our colony out of pure spite. The people there were damned prigs, but I liked them better than the drogues."

Lanyan maintained his unbreakable gruffness. "Thank you, Captain Kett. I will call all grid admirals in the vicinity to discuss the matter immediately. We will mount an urgent rescue operation."

The large woman stared at him on the screen, then she actually laughed. "Take another look at those images, General. You'd better bring brushes and little envelopes to pick up what's left of the people on Relleker. You won't be doing any rescue operation."

Lanyan bristled. "As I said, my admirals and I will review the matter right away. You may proceed to Earth and unload your passengers. Davlin Lotze has arranged temporary holding facilities near the Palace District, where they'll be well taken care of. You may leave the rest of the matter to me."

Admirals Tabeguache and Antero were in the solar system preparing their battle groups for additional expeditions against the Roamers. Grid 7's Admiral Sheila Willis had just been dispatched from the asteroid belt shipyards and was easily recalled. Admiral Kostas Eolus entered the Mars base's conference room at the last moment, breathless from having rushed back in a small ship; for the sake of speed, he had left the rest of his Grid 5 fleet on its assigned maneuvers.

Lanyan expected no one else to attend. "Better get started. As Grid 0 liaison, Admiral Stromo should be here, but he's currently on his way back from Yreka, and I don't anticipate his arrival until tomorrow. We'll have to have this meeting without him."

Admiral Peter Tabeguache made a quiet comment under

his breath, then coughed as if to cover it. "Not that old Stay-at-Home would be much help anyway."

"I'll have no insubordination in this meeting!" Lanyan said.

"Of course not, sir."

Deeply unsettled, Lanyan paced around the room, studying his uniformed officers. The wall of windows looked out upon cracked red terrain and an olive-green sky.

"What's this I hear about the drogues kicking ass on another Hansa colony, General?" Sheila Willis said.

"Not just kicking ass. They ground us flat." Lanyan played the images from the *Voracious Curiosity,* showing enemy warglobes mercilessly obliterating Relleker. He had considered muting Governor Pekar's desperate and pitiful transmissions, but decided to let his grid admirals experience the full magnitude of the crisis. As they sat in stunned silence, he said, "Upon review, I have concluded that there is nothing we can do for Relleker at this time."

"Shouldn't we at least send an analytical team to comb through the ruins?" suggested Haki Antero. "We could learn something."

"I doubt it, but I suppose we ought to go through the motions anyway. The Chairman would insist on it."

"Any idea why the drogues struck Relleker in particular? Because it was close to Crenna?" Antero asked. "Were they just hitting any human colony? What set them off?"

"What set them off, Haki? Now, let's see," Willis drawled. "In the past several months, we've stuffed five more Klikiss Torches down the gullets of hydrogue planets. Can you imagine a reason why those deep-core aliens might want to retaliate against us?"

"We don't know their motivation, Admiral," Lanyan cautioned.

"General, just because the drogues are *aliens,* that doesn't mean they're stupid."

With the news of Crenna and Relleker coming so close together, Lanyan felt more impotent than he had in years. Recently, after striking Theroc, the drogues had been preoccupied with their battles against the faeros, but Relleker was something else entirely, a specifically human target, an indisputable extermination.

"Excuse me, sir, but somebody needs to say this," Tabeguache began. "We had a bit of a respite for a while, but now that the drogues have started hitting us hard again, perhaps we should pull back all of the battleships currently on search-and-destroy missions against the Roamer clans? Seems we should concentrate on the primary enemy. We can always get the Roamers later."

Lanyan's nostrils flared. "Getting the Roamers to knuckle under is likely the only part of this mess that we can *win* in a reasonable amount of time!"

"And so far," Antero added, "just throwing a lot of battleships at the hydrogues hasn't helped much. Our weapons aren't very effective against warglobes."

The General bunched his fists and got up to pace the room, working his jaw. The grid admirals remained silent, seeing his emotions about to boil over and waiting to find out what he would do.

"Dammit!" he finally said. "I hate being reminded how utterly incapable we are of defending ourselves. What's to keep the drogues from blasting Earth to splinters like they just did to Relleker? They know this is our capital. They've already sent an emissary here to kill King Frederick. What if a flareup between the faeros and drogues occurs in the *Earth's* sun?" He walked down the length of the table like a stalking predator, looking at the admirals as if they could answer him.

Admiral Eolus said, "We do have an emergency plan in place, should those things come directly to Earth, right?"

Lanyan had read the plan. "Oh, there's one on paper. Considering that Earth is the most populated planet in the Hanseatic League, I do not have a high degree of confidence that the plan will be effective, beyond giving the billions of people something to do while the drogues destroy them." He sat heavily.

Tabeguache tapped his fingertips on the tabletop. "Think about it. If the *faeros* can't stop them, we certainly don't stand a chance."

"We do have the new rammer fleet," Willis pointed out. "I've read the latest reports. Aren't those ships almost finished?"

Lanyan said, "I'm issuing orders for the shipyards to triple the work crews and get those vessels completed. We need those defenses *now,* and I want them ready to launch right away. Highest priority. It's the only way we can be ready to stand against any warglobes that come in. The Ildirans have already proved the method works. Now it's time for us to do the same."

"No argument from us, General," said Antero. "We should get the Soldier compies in place now. As each rammer is completed, we can start loading it with its full robotic crew."

Lanyan was pleased at last to be doing something. "And I will handpick the token crew of human officers. The next time the drogues show themselves, we're going to hit them with everything we've got."

49 ☀ TASIA TAMBLYN

When she returned to Mars after escorting the Roamer detainees to Llaro, Tasia mentally prepared herself for tedious training exercises again.

Seeing the prisoners seized during the provocative raids, as well as gleaning a few details about her family, had sharpened her disappointment and frustration. She wanted to be back home, to see Jess, to smell the cold ice beneath the crust of Plumas. And if she couldn't have that, at least Tasia wanted to be out fighting the drogues!

She had undergone rigorous training and served to the absolute best of her ability. Now that the EDF had changed all the rules, changed the fight itself, Tasia knew she could break her oath with a clear conscience, take EA, steal a ship, and just *leave,* as bitter Crim Tylar had suggested. She had the option of abandoning the Earth Defense Forces, burning her uniform, and going back to live among the clans.

But if she simply changed her mind and deserted, the Eddies would denounce her as having been a Roamer spy all along. Smug Patrick Fitzpatrick III would probably come back from the grave just to say, "I told you so." Worse, General Lanyan would use that as an excuse to crack down even more, impose penalties and harsh consequences on the Llaro detainees whom Tasia wanted to protect.

What was happening out there among the Roamers? With Rendezvous destroyed, where would the clans go? Cesca would probably try to draw them together, but how could she succeed when the EDF was hunting down every outpost, every habitation? Other than a few rumors she'd heard from Roberto Clarin, Tasia's only source of information was the Big Goose's one-sided news, which was sure to be far from accurate.

She just wanted to fight *hydrogues*. Was that so complicated?

As soon as Tasia checked in at the EDF base, General Lanyan summoned her. She was still dressed in a pilot's uniform, and hadn't had a meal or a shower, but the General's message stressed that he wanted to see her without delay. His staff sergeant escorted her into the private office, and she stood at attention in front of his desk.

Lanyan lifted his square-jawed head to regard her. "Commander Tamblyn, we have a certain matter to discuss. Your service record remains impressive, and your skill level is unmatched in many areas."

"Yes, sir," she said, stiff and formal. *I know that.*

Even so, Tasia felt a knot in her stomach. Now that Hansa depredations against the Roamers had increased, Lanyan might command her to reveal the locations of clan facilities, including her family's Plumas water mines. She formulated her words, ready to speak firmly, without wavering. If necessary, she would defy his order to betray the clans, then give him an earful about his ridiculous priorities and how he was forgetting the real enemy of the human race. Afterward, the General would probably court-martial her.

Instead, he surprised her. "How would you like your command back?"

Though taken off guard, she answered in a heartbeat. "Absolutely, General—as soon as possible."

His smile showed blunt teeth. "I understand you prefer fighting the hydrogues to your current assignment?"

Her pulse sped up. Maybe they had a real mission for her again. "With all due respect, old veterans could supervise the training activities here on Mars. I sure would prefer something else, sir."

"After these months of hard work, our new rammer fleet is almost complete. Sixty reinforced vessels will be crewed by expendable Soldier compies. However, we need several experienced officers willing to take charge of this fleet and deliver it in our first concerted attack against the drogues. You must remain on standby at all times and be ready to launch the moment the fleet is ready and we identify a target."

Tasia caught her breath. Although high-tech weaponry such as fracture-pulse drones and carbon-carbon slammers had not caused as much damage as the EDF had hoped, compy-crewed kamikaze vessels had provided the only effective offense in the battle of Osquivel. She'd been following the construction of the heavily reinforced rammers, just waiting for them to be finished.

"But if those ships have a full crew of Soldier compies, what do you need me for?"

Lanyan cracked his knuckles and sat back in his chair. "In a matter of such importance, I am not willing to trust everything to compies—not even the new Soldier models. I insist on having a few humans on board the rammer fleet to make command decisions—a set of token officers, one human commander for every ten vessels. In theory, you shouldn't have a thing to do, but we both know that nothing ever goes exactly as planned, especially in a chaotic battle environment."

"Yes, sir. I saw that for myself at Jupiter, Boone's Crossing, and Osquivel."

"As I said, Commander, your service record to date is impressive. Except for a few disciplinary incidents that demonstrate you have some difficulty getting along with your fellow soldiers, your performance in a battlefield environment is faultless. You're the perfect choice for the job." She could sense his half-hidden dislike of her Roamer heritage in his grudging acknowledgment that she was the best.

Pride warred with common sense in her head. "I've read about how an Ildiran Adar crushed the enemy at Qronha 3, sir, and I know what our new rammers are designed to do." Her eyes narrowed. "So be straight with me, General. You're asking me to volunteer for a suicide mission?" *Just like Robb did, when he went aboard the diving-bell encounter vessel.*

Lanyan made a too-casual dismissive gesture. "There are risks, certainly, but it's not a suicide mission, Tamblyn. We've designed the rammer ships with an escape system for each token commander. Once the Soldier compies have their final orders, you can run to the evac pod and jettison in time. You can just sit back and watch the fireworks as you float safely away."

"In theory," she said, trying to dull the edge in her voice. "Are you convinced that the odds are genuinely good, sir?"

He was frank with her; she was thankful for that, at least. "Not really, but it's a chance. The best we can do." He leaned across his desk. "Tamblyn, this will give you a chance to strike a blow against the hydrogues—and you'll have your command back. Isn't that what you want?"

It was a war, after all. Nothing was guaranteed.

"Show me the dotted line and I'll sign, sir. I'm your volunteer."

Lanyan looked completely satisfied. "Excellent. I knew I could count on you, Tamblyn."

She could tell that he left the rest of the sentence unsaid. *Even though you are a Roamer.* "When do we depart, General?"

"You start training immediately. Half of the fleet is finished, and we expect the rest to be ready within the next thirty-six hours." Lanyan looked down at his reports again. "Then we'll launch our rammers the moment the bastards show themselves again."

50 ☀ JESS TAMBLYN

Jess returned to the wandering wental comet to wait for the volunteer water bearers to join him. He also brought his own bittersweet memories.

Here, unseen in the comet's wispy tail, he and Cesca had had a romantic assignation. In this secret place the two of them had been able to drift for a while in their dreams, letting their love take them where they wanted to go. Those had been happy and heady times, before the universe itself had pulled them apart.

Now wental entities infused his soul, but they could never fill the loneliness that he felt without Cesca. The wentals could not fathom his need, nor could he explain it in concepts they would understand. Maybe the ache in his heart was strong enough that they could grasp his sadness, even if they did not comprehend love.

Though he missed Cesca terribly, the inner calling consumed him. Given his new understanding and his enhanced abilities, he had a mission to fight the hydrogues. That was the priority of the wentals—and Jess knew that a wental victory had the potential to save not just the Roamers but all humans. He had to balance his needs and obligations, and push forward.

This comet was one of his starting places. The elemental water beings had infiltrated the comet's primordial ice. Even far from the warming light of a star, the gypsy comet shone with energy, an eerie landmark in open space, traveling under its own power. The lambent glow was unlike starshine.

This seemed an appropriate place for his water bearers to gather.

Like a tiny droplet next to a much larger globe, his exotic ship hovered beneath the rogue comet. While he waited, Jess's heart smoldered with regret for everything he'd had to give up. He still thought of himself as a member of clan Tamblyn, and he knew that the EDF was preying upon the Roamers, but he could do nothing to help. The wentals made him see a larger picture, and his focus could not waver, no matter how angry he felt about the injustices. . . .

Though the water bearers carried samples of living water aboard their ships, they did not have the inherent ability to communicate with each other easily, like green priests. Occasionally, the wentals might pass subtle messages if a person were particularly susceptible, but the water beings seemed very reticent to "taint" another human.

Thus, Jess needed a face-to-face discussion. He had arranged this gathering some time ago. News of the EDF attacks continued to spread across the outposts and facilities. Refugees from Rendezvous arrived at hidden bases and orbiting industrial colonies; clan representatives were still spread among the various gathering points.

Because of their prescribed wandering, Jess's water bearers could be effective links in communication. In this quick convocation, all fourteen would share what they knew, trade coordinates of where they had already distributed the wentals, then disperse again.

One by one, the water bearers arrived in an assortment of vessels. Jess sent his greetings and let the volunteers decide which ship would serve as their meeting point. Though he could not stand too close to any of them, this gathering would fill his need to be near other human beings.

Isolated, Jess stared through the curved film of his ship's hull; the water shifted like a lens, and he viewed the other ships, thought of the people aboard, remembered their eager faces when he'd told them his strange story. They had all been filled with awe when Jess took them to the first wental-infused ocean world and gave them their samples of the living water entities.

He also remembered when they had all been simple merchants or workers or pilots, doing the business of their clans. Roamers had never had an easy existence, but they had traditions and connections; they had made tolerable, even pleasant lives for themselves under harsh conditions—until both the hydrogues and the EDF had used them as targets.

Jess longed for those days, even though his heart had been heavy with his supposedly secret love for Cesca. If he succeeded in this quest, perhaps those times would return. Eventually.

When all the water-bearer ships were gathered beneath

the living comet, transmitting a whirlwind of messages, greetings, and dire announcements, Jess slid through the bubble wall of his vessel and drifted free across open space to the largest ship, where the meeting would take place.

For the first hour, the volunteers shouted and commiserated about the destruction of Rendezvous. Nikko Chan Tylar, announcing the invasion of the Chan greenhouse complex, was distraught. Other water bearers delivered embellished stories about further EDF atrocities. Jess wondered where Tasia was and if she'd had anything to do with the attacks. . . .

The volunteers were incensed. "Four Roamer ships have disappeared. Who knows how many the Eddies have simply destroyed?"

"The clans are scattered. There's no accurate counting of ships. We don't have a clue how many are missing."

Another volunteer offered a suggestion. "Jess, we've seen what you and the wentals can do. Why not turn yourself loose as a weapon against the Earth military? Go smash a few Juggernauts and show them we can fight back too!"

The rest of the volunteers cheered, clearly enthusiastic about the idea.

Jess stood isolated on the far side of the room, a thin sheen of moisture covering his skin and his pearly white garment. The other water bearers kept their distance, knowing how much power would be released if they brushed against him.

"I could fly in with my ship and surprise the Eddies, but I have no weapons. I could startle them, but I could never attack them. From what you've all described, the EDF sends in a whole battle group, strikes fast, seizes prisoners, and destroys the facility. I could never arrive in time to help."

One volunteer whose entire family had disappeared after the obliteration of Rendezvous looked haggard and furious. "Then go to Earth. Set your big ship right down in front of Hansa HQ and tell them we won't take any more of this crap! They'll get the message." His eyes narrowed. "In fact, why don't you offer to shake hands with the Chairman himself? If what you say is true, then you'd give him enough of a jolt to snap him out of this nonsense!"

The volunteers hooted, but Jess shook his head. "The wentals won't allow it. It would be an abuse to turn my powers against my own race, and such a selfish action would taint the wentals. They've seen what can happen if the life force turns bad. You don't want to imagine it."

One of the volunteers scowled with disappointment. "Have you given up being a Roamer then, Jess? Are you no longer a member of the clans? We can't just sit by and let the Big Goose do this."

Though he wasn't sure the wentals understood the nuances of political conflicts between humans, Jess certainly felt the turmoil inside him. "I want to help, but my mission to revive the wentals is all-consuming. Remember, the hydrogues are our real enemy." A shudder of anger pulsed through Jess, an instinctive reaction from the water-based entities.

"Doesn't seem like they're the only enemies anymore," Nikko answered bitterly. "How can we keep spreading wentals while the Eddies destroy our homes and kidnap our families?"

Jess stood firm. "I'll carry on by myself if the rest of you decide to stop assisting me. Though many of our friends and families have been terribly hurt, the EDF is not our worst enemy. If the hydrogues are not stopped, civilization across the

Spiral Arm is at stake. They have attacked Theroc in an attempt to exterminate the remnants of the verdani, and without question the enemy will strike the worldforest again.

"But we have an advantage. The hydrogues don't yet know about the return of the wentals, their other opponent from the great ancient war. Before they come back to Theroc, we must complete our work so that the wentals will be ready to renew their alliance with the verdani."

"And all of us," said one of the volunteers. "I hope it comes soon enough, before the Eddies wipe out every clan in the Spiral Arm."

Nikko balled both hands into fists. "Well, I'm a Roamer, and I can't just ignore this. Isn't there something—"

Jess could read the distress among his water bearers. "Yes, there's a way you all can help. Many distant Roamer outposts don't even know what's happened. Others have scattered from Rendezvous and are now in hiding. As you continue your search for isolated worlds for the wentals, you can spread the warning. You'll encounter other families, other Roamer settlements, and you can form an important communication network."

The water bearers still were not happy. "But if the wentals are so powerful, can't they help us at all?"

"Yes." He finally smiled with a bit of good news. He explained how the hydrogues had been driven from Golgen, that the wentals would keep the planet safe for skymining. "Any Roamer clan with ekti-processing equipment can flock to the gas giant. The wentals will protect them as they begin full-scale skymining again. We can produce enough stardrive fuel to save us."

The volunteers murmured amongst themselves; the very idea that the water entities could recapture an entire gas giant impressed them. "Then let's make sure that's just the first of many gas giants the wentals take back," growled a volunteer.

Jess had another mission for Nikko Chan Tylar. "Try to find Cesca, wherever she's gone to ground. I'm sure she has dispatched messages, invoked emergency plans. Do what you can to help her draw the clans together again."

"I'll find her," Nikko said. "Knowing Speaker Peroni, she already has a plan."

After another hour of discussions and strategy debates, the volunteers had more information and guidance. Riled up and ready to work, the water bearers in fourteen ships left the remarkable glowing comet behind and raced off to their next destinations.

For himself, Jess intended to make a long-delayed trip back to his family's water mines on Plumas. Back home.

51 ☀ CESCA PERONI

More and more black robots came alive behind them. Scrambling backward down the corridor, Cesca and Purcell could feel the walls shudder as the Klikiss machines hammered their way out of the tomb of ice.

"They're all coming to kill us!" the acting administrator cried over the suit radio. "How many of those robots were in there?"

"I didn't see very deep into the chambers. It could be a whole army." Over the same comm frequency, she heard whistles and pops, crackles of static, then modulated electronic shrieks—a robot language. "Better observe radio silence. They're listening in."

"But can they understand us?" Purcell said.

"They can *track* us." That was enough to cut off any further discussion.

Their grazer was parked outside on a rise above the tomb entrance, but it seemed very far away. The tunnels went on forever. She hadn't realized that poor Danvier had led them so deep.

Finally, up ahead, she saw a swath of black universe spangled with stars. The two Roamers reached the tunnel entrance and burst out into the empty night. The hemispherical grazer vehicle sat near the top of the rise not far away.

Breathless from running even in the low gravity, Cesca paused and turned. Deep behind them, flashes of red reflected on the planes of smooth, excavated ice. Behemoth-sized shadows moved, nightmarish ellipsoid hulls with flat heads, blazing optical sensors, and multiple murderous arms. The Klikiss robots looked like sluggish, ponderous machines, but they gained speed and closed the distance. *How can they move so fast?*

Outside, Cesca and the engineer administrator bounded up the slope toward their squat vehicle. She had barely begun grieving for the loss of Jhy Okiah, and now two more Roamers had been slaughtered in front of her. Even through her shock, Cesca strengthened her resolve, pushed Purcell forward, and mentally raced through possibilities. First the two of them had to escape.

They reached the grazer's airlock hatch just as the first

Klikiss robot emerged from the tomb passage. The beetle-like machine hesitated, scanning the terrain as if reawakening stored memories ... or searching for prey. Several others emerged behind it.

Purcell quickly forgot about maintaining radio silence. "They're coming!"

Cesca threw herself against the airlock and opened the outer hatch. Because the chamber was empty, the door unsealed after only a brief series of status lights blinked on the control panel.

She herded Purcell into the one-person chamber, then crammed in beside him. They didn't have the luxury of cycling through one at a time. The two of them barely fit. Cesca pounded her gloved fist against the inner controls, sealing the outer door and starting the cycle.

Status lights danced in a graceful but laboriously sluggish pirouette. The pressurization continued at a sedate pace, pumping atmosphere from the main vehicle into the airlock. Beside her, Purcell swore to himself. "We should have ridden in vacuum, with our suits on! Then we could have just opened the inner door." At the time it had seemed an unnecessary discomfort and inconvenience during the long journey.

From the tiny window in the chamber's outer hatch, Cesca saw four of the insectile machines standing together only a few hundred meters away. Their exoskeletons looked oddly discolored against the bleak white landscape, and she realized that their black hulls were spattered with shiny, frozen blood. The four robots began to scuttle up the rise toward the grazer.

"Come on!" she said through clenched teeth, as if the airlock mechanism could sense her urgency.

Extra air dumped into the chamber with the force of a gale wind. The airlock was nearly filled.

With her clumsy gloved fingers, Cesca worked the override and finally popped the inner door. She felt a hollow thump against her helmet as the pressure equalized; inrushing air from the inner chamber felt like a hand shoving them back. Cesca regained her balance. "Come on, Purcell—you drive this thing better than I can. Get us moving!"

He lumbered toward the seat and threw himself in. Cesca flicked on the power systems while Purcell activated the engines and adjusted the driving yoke. The grazer hummed, then began to crawl forward. The engineer turned the vehicle around in a ponderous semicircle.

Operating the rear viewer, Cesca saw one of the horrific robots loom up, frighteningly close. It raised segmented claws to hammer down upon the back of the slow vehicle. The thud of impact reverberated through the grazer's hull.

Purcell yelped. "They'll rip us open like a pack of emergency rations!"

Three more robots converged on the rear of the vehicle, hammering, scraping, pounding.

Purcell added power to the engines, and the treads pulled the vehicle forward, nudging it over the crest of the rise and turning downhill. A shriek and a clang rang against the metal hull. The robots were grabbing any clawhold to batter their way in.

The puttering engine roared, and the low vehicle trundled forward, groaning with the strain. A curling belch of processed steam vomited from the exhaust tube, spraying one of the robots with thick white frost. It released its grip. Two others continued their grasping attack, but Purcell fed power to the engines, dragging the gas-harvesting vehicle over the frozen ground.

Cesca heard metal shear away with a tearing groan—and suddenly the grazer bolted forward like a stampeding bull. "We broke free!"

"Yes, but what did we lose in the process?" Purcell said.

The grazer picked up speed, puttering away. It was by no means a swift piece of machinery, but it covered the ground faster than the Klikiss robots could scuttle on their clusters of fingerlike legs.

Inside the pressurized vehicle, Cesca slid open her face-plate, and as soon as Purcell had a chance, he removed his own helmet. Cesca noticed the sweat streaming down his long face.

The rear viewer showed the robots staggering to a halt in a group. One of them held a large piece of insulated plating ripped from the back of the grazer. The robots stood over the plate like hunters inspecting a fresh kill.

"What was that, Purcell? What did they manage to break off?"

He kept driving in a straight line, bent over the steering yoke. He glanced aside for only a second to see the image, then froze. "Oh, no. That's the insulation cowling over the engine. It protects our moving parts from the intense cold. Kotto designed it himself." An edge of renewed panic sharpened his thin voice.

"Can we make it back to base?" Cesca said.

His eyes were round beneath heavy eyebrows. "Are you kidding? That's almost a day's journey under good conditions."

"Then how far can we go without it?"

"We'll have an accurate answer soon enough. Without the insulation, our machinery won't function long in this intense cold."

Far behind them now, the four robot pursuers gave up the chase and turned back toward the ice tunnels.

Purcell hunched over the driving yoke, winding their way up to higher ground. Already, the engine coughed and groaned, as if throwing a tantrum about the severe environment in which it was being forced to perform.

"Our radio still works, doesn't it?" Cesca said. "We'd better warn the base."

"Yes. We'll get a clear signal as soon as we're out of the shadow here."

The grazer lurched and stuttered, but Purcell talked to it, pleading. He gently coaxed the controls, and the vehicle continued to inch forward. With painful sluggishness, the damaged grazer managed to reach the top of the higher rise, and then, with a shudder, the engines seized up. Components ground together and froze solid. Their lubricants had turned to cement.

Sniffing the cold reprocessed air inside the grazer, Cesca caught the smell of smoke. "Shut everything down! If we catch fire in here, we'll use up our spare oxygen."

"We're not going anywhere anyway." As Purcell deactivated the systems, Cesca found a fire extinguisher and sprayed foam dispersant in the smoldering rear compartment. They were safe from immediate danger, but stranded.

Cesca looked forlornly out the viewing windows. They had managed to get far enough away that the robots paid them no heed. In the distance, she saw more machines moving about at the tunnel opening. The Klikiss robots reminded her of hive insects, like the bees a few Roamer families kept in order to sell fresh honey at exorbitant prices.

Purcell pushed himself back from the control seat. "No use,

Speaker Peroni. The engines are dead. Machinery simply can't work unprotected in this cold."

Staring at the distant black forms marching about by the ice tunnels, she said, "I wish the robots had that problem. Why did they attack us? Roamers have never had any contact with Klikiss robots, never. Jack Ebbe was tinkering with long-dormant systems. Could it have been an automated response, the robot's equivalent to a reflex action?"

"Or maybe they were expecting someone else to wake them," Purcell said. "Prince Charming, maybe?"

Using battery power, Cesca activated the comm systems and transmitted a warning to the Jonah 12 base. Back inside the domes, workers sounded the alarm and recalled all grazers while sending out a rescue vehicle to retrieve Cesca and Purcell. "It might take us a while, Speaker. You're a long distance off."

"We're fine, as long as the robots don't notice us sitting up here." She did not feel at all comfortable about being exposed, but they had no other way of getting back. They had air and food to last them until another grazer could come for them.

"I don't suppose you want to walk home?" she asked Purcell.

He still looked shaken and gray, as if the events were only now catching up to him. "We'd never make it. Our suits can only protect us for a few hours out there."

While they waited, immobile atop the second ridge, Cesca used magnifying viewers to make out what the robots were doing. Over the radio channels, Purcell monitored the brisk exchanges at the base for a while, but then had to shut down to conserve their battery power.

Cesca felt a block of ice form in her stomach as she

watched more and more robots emerge: a full-fledged black army. Awakened now, the ominous machines stepped out of the tunnels and lined up in endless ranks.

More than a hundred of the robots began to stride across the ice, and dozens more kept coming, a conquering military force that moved with implacable precision.

They marched in a straight line toward the Roamer base.

52 ANTON COLICOS

They were cold. They were in the dark. They were alone. Though Anton was also frightened, he was the only one who kept the dwindling group of Ildiran survivors moving. He had to show them strength.

He was just a scholar, quiet and bookish, never cast in the role of hero or leader; no doubt some future storyteller would make him out to be dashing and handsome, muscular and fearless. He had compared enough myths and legends to kernels of historical truth and knew the liberties storytellers took. He realized that their current plight—a hopeless journey across a dark world with mysterious saboteurs after them—was the sort of tale that might find its way into a future expansion of the *Saga of Seven Suns*.

Anton did not point out the irony, not even to Vao'sh. After all, he'd come here merely to *study* the epic, not to become part of it. He had envisioned sitting in safe, cozy rooms reading the adventures of other people, real or imagined. He had never seen himself as a protagonist in a story. The scientist had become a key part of the experiment. . . .

If only his parents could be here to see him. Margaret and Louis Colicos had disappeared from an archaeological dig years ago. Despite repeated queries, Anton had learned nothing about what had happened to them, until, finally, he received news that his father's body had been found in the empty ruins of Rheindic Co, murdered along with the team's green priest. And his mother had vanished without a trace.

If Anton and these survivors did not make it to the safety of Maratha Secda, then they too would "vanish." He swallowed hard, wondering if his mother's final days had been equally terrifying. How would anyone ever know?

Then he remembered the most important lesson of the storyteller's art: No tale, regardless of its merit, is ever told unless someone survives to relate the experience. He *would* get out of this. And he would save as many of these Ildirans as he could.

The bloody deaths of Syl'k and Mhas'k had left the remaining members of the party hopeless, listless. They plodded through the darkness, stumbling on rocks. Designate Avi'h continued to chatter about his fears that the Shana Rei would come out of the darkness.

Vao'sh said with a faintly impatient tone, "The Shana Rei are not here on Maratha. There are no monsters in the darkness."

But even as the rememberer spoke, they could not help but recall the voracious armored anemones that had torn apart the two agricultural kithmen. As steam plumes gushed into the air, feeding an eerie mist along the ground, the survivors gave a wide berth to other patches of the waving carnivorous plants.

Vao'sh muttered to Anton, "We do not need the Shana Rei to destroy us. Our own fears will do it."

Without enough people to form a splinter, their Ildiran minds would feel increasingly loose and adrift. Catatonic fear would set in, and Anton would have to drag them along. He had to hold them together.

Designate Avi'h pointed. "What is that?"

Beside him, his assistant held up the portable blazer, shining out a wide cone of light. Darker than the rest of the night, an oily black shadow bounded from rock to rock and was briefly silhouetted against one of the plumes of steam. It had a stocky build, and its movements reminded Anton of a lion.

The bulky creature flung itself into the nearby cluster of gargantuan anemones and began ripping at the stems, chewing through the armorplate. The ch'kanh thrashed, but the pantherlike shadow knew how to fight them. It seized the plants in its jaws and shook them until they were uprooted. It crunched and slurped, feeding on soft inner tissues as if sucking marrow from bones.

When the light from Bhali'v's blazer fell directly upon it, the oily shadow seemed to grow darker and harden. The predatory thing turned, its eyes like the diamond glitter of fallen stars.

"What is that?" Avi'h cried. "It is one of the Shana Rei!"

Any answer was cut off as the leonine monster focused on the dazzling blazer and loped toward them.

"Run!" Anton called. The Marathans rushed after him.

The Designate grabbed Bhali'v. "Do not let it kill me!"

"It is attracted to the light," Engineer Nur'of shouted. "Turn off your blazer!"

But the terrified bureaucrat clung to the reassuring glow as if it was his only protection. Avi'h pushed his assistant toward the shadow lion and ran shrieking after the other members of the party. Bhali'v screamed, a high-pitched sound of terror, before the oily black predator bore him to the ground and tore him to pieces just as it had attacked the armored anemones.

The beams of other blazers shone erratically while their bearers ran. Anton saw another shadowy form slinking out of the clusters of ch'kanh. "Keep running!" The second predator sensed their body heat, and the survivors had no weapons with which to fight the beasts.

Anton risked a glance behind him and saw with sick relief that the second predator had joined the first to feed on the warm body of Bhali'v.

When the Designate finally collapsed, far from the shadow lions, Anton allowed them to take a desperate rest. Jolting fear had driven them in a stampede, but their physical reserves had run out; now they shuddered and wept. Anton remained on his feet, his muscles trembling.

"The darkness will take us all," Avi'h cried. "The Mage-Imperator commanded me to come back to Maratha, but I should have refused. How could I deny his orders? If I had remained on Ildira, I would be under the seven suns right now. I could be in the daylight, and safe, and—"

"And all of us would still be here," Nur'of pointed out. "None of us wants to be in this situation."

"Work until the task is done," Vik'k the digger said. "Never give up."

As Anton caught his breath and looked toward the horizon, he felt a thrill of relief. He stared until he was certain,

then called to the rest of the survivors. "Keep your eyes
there. Fix your vision, and you'll see. Can you make out the
glow? That's the dawn. We're close to the daylight side. If
we keep walking in that direction, the light will get brighter
with every step we take."

Vao'sh was the first to acknowledge him. "Yes, I see it.
The sunlight is over there. It is still too faint to do us any
good, but at least it gives us hope."

Nur'of climbed to his feet. "I have rested enough in the
darkness. If hope is all we have left, then I will not spurn it."
He marched across the rocky landscape toward the half-
imagined glow of sunrise. They still had a terribly long
distance to traverse.

With renewed spring in his step, Anton set off, and soon
he had taken the lead.

53 ☀ MAGE-IMPERATOR JORA'H

Though only four days had passed since he had delivered
Osira'h to the Prism Palace, Designate Udru'h returned
unexpectedly from Dobro. He strode into the skysphere
reception hall, demanding to speak to his brother and ordering all the pilgrims and supplicants to scatter. "I must speak
in private with the Mage-Imperator!" He made his way to
the chrysalis chair, moving with unyielding confidence,

even if at times it seemed the entire Empire shifted uncertainly beneath his feet.

Yazra'h and her Isix cats stood in place at the base of the steps, ready to block even her uncle, but Udru'h ignored them. He gave a cursory bow and clasped his fist to his heart in the traditional salute of respect as the last courtiers hurried out of the hall and out of earshot. "Liege, I have come to inform you of blatant treachery against the Empire."

Jora'h couldn't keep the bitterness from his voice once they were alone in the room. "And is there more treachery, Udru'h? Treachery of which I am unaware?"

Unruffled, the other man said, "I speak of the Hyrillka Designate."

Jora'h could sense his brother's distress through the *thism* bond, more clearly than he could grasp details from the fog of confusion around the Horizon Cluster. The Hyrillka Designate had plunged into a black nebula, an emptiness in the network of *thism,* and completely severed himself from the Ildiran Empire. The Mage-Imperator still had not learned what was happening there, had not heard back from his three scout cutters, and could no longer sense their crews in the *thism* either.

Jora'h hid his deep concern. "Adar Zan'nh and his warliners will quell the disturbance."

"No, Liege. He will not." Udru'h stepped farther up the dais, paying no heed to Yazra'h stiffening with menace. "Several days ago, the Adar's warliners were seized by Designate Rusa'h. You are no longer in direct contact with the Adar, are you? That is because the Solar Navy troops have sworn their service to the rebellion. Surely you sensed it, but did not understand what had occurred?"

Jora'h sat up in alarm. "How do you know this? Even

through the *thism* I can see only flickers. Violent flickers. I know that Rusa'h has killed some of my loyal citizens—including Pery'h. I sensed them being ripped away from the web, but aside from that . . ."

The Dobro Designate remained motionless as he reported. "Rusa'h has taken the population of Hyrillka into his own network. He also claims to have conquered Dzelluria. The whole fabric of *thism* has weakened around the Horizon Cluster."

"And how do you know what has happened there, when *I* cannot sense clear thoughts even from my own sons, Adar Zan'nh—or Thor'h?"

"I know because early yesterday Prime Designate Thor'h brought one of the seized warliners to Dobro. He threatened to destroy my entire colony if I did not willingly join in their rebellion." He let those words hang as he focused his gaze on his brother's face. "Rusa'h claims to have received revelations directly from the Lightsource. He insists that you are breaking sacred traditions and must be removed so that the Ildiran people can follow the correct path again."

Jora'h's brow furrowed, and his braid twitched and thrashed. The explanation made sense, terrible sense. He had felt other striking pains in the *thism*, more echoes of death; he was certain his brother Orra'h on Dzelluria had been killed. Rusa'h's work?

He stared at Udru'h for a long moment, trying to read him, but the Dobro Designate kept his face a calm mask. Finally, with the faintest note of frustration, Jora'h asked, "And when he asked you to join this madness, how did you respond? What did you say to Thor'h?"

Udru'h blinked, as if he had not expected his leader to be so blunt. "You are the Mage-Imperator. How can you have any doubt as to my answer?"

Jora'h narrowed his eyes. "Then how did *you* escape if Thor'h had an armed warliner? Why are you free to report to us? Is there deceit within deceit?"

Udru'h made a dismissive gesture. "I stalled the Prime Designate by saying that I would deliver my answer in person to Hyrillka. Rusa'h gains more from me if I join him of my free will, and he seems to believe he has a chance of swaying me. I played on that fact to buy time."

"And does he have a chance of swaying you?"

"Of course not, Liege. I am always loyal to you."

Jora'h was not sure he could believe him. He thought of all the times Udru'h had lied to him or withheld vital information. The Dobro Designate had always seen the universe in many shades of gray.

Udru'h continued. "After Thor'h departed, I came to Ildira with all possible speed. However, I must present myself to Hyrillka before the deadline, or they will come back and destroy Dobro." He crossed his arms over his chest. "Before then, you need to decide what to do about it."

54 ☀ SAREIN

Ever since her disturbing conversation with the forest golem of Beneto, Sarein had wrestled with her doubts. Looking deeply with his wood-grain eyes, Beneto had exposed her true motivations. Until then, she hadn't been willing to face them herself.

Idriss and Alexa might be easily fooled by their daughter's altruistic claims, and Basil Wenceslas had his expectations about her ability to lead Theroc . . . but Beneto understood her *heart*. He knew exactly what she would do, the contradictory things she wanted, and what was wrong with her. How could she argue with him?

In all her years of living here, Sarein had never really loved Theroc, considering the place a primitive backwater, a shackle around her ankle that prevented her from achieving wonderful things. She had imagined that anything would be better than this uncivilized wilderness, and she had done everything possible to escape to the Hansa. There, starry-eyed, ambitious, and genuinely talented, she became accepted as part of the Chairman's inner power circle. She had even become Basil's lover to open doors and create advantages for herself. It had been only a ploy at first, and then her feelings had become complicated. . . .

Sarein sighed. Yes, her brother Reynald had been killed in the hydrogue attack, making her the eldest surviving child of Father Idriss and Mother Alexa. Her claim to the throne was viable. If she pressed the issue, she might succeed in convincing her parents and even her people to accept her as the next Mother. But Sarein didn't *belong* here; she knew that better than anybody. She wanted to be back on Earth, wrapped in the tangled politics of the Hansa, attending banquets and meetings, able to watch a hundred different newsnets, connected to human *civilization*.

Returning to Theroc, and seeing the utterly ruined planet she hadn't thought she'd loved in the first place, tortured her heart. She didn't want to witness the devastation of her childhood home—the burned trees, lost lives, and shattered dwellings. She didn't want to think of a defiant Reynald standing atop the worldforest canopy, trying to protect his world from the hydrogues—and failing.

She couldn't stay here.

The next morning, as dawn broke, she dressed herself in the ambassadorial robes that old Otema had given her so long ago. She had made her decision, following her heart and her conscience in spite of what others expected of her. Her parents wanted her to stay on Theroc, as did Basil—though for completely different reasons. None of those reasons were legitimate for Sarein. They were lies. She could not do this.

She drew a deep breath, and walked out to find her parents. Many Therons were already working in the misty dampness of early morning, gathering and potting healthy treelings for export from Theroc. The Beneto golem who stood with them turned his perfectly sculpted face to look at Sarein.

Idriss and Alexa wore old garments from when they had been the leaders of their people, but now their faces were smudged with soot and dirt. Idriss looked at her brightly. "Sarein, you look lovely."

Her mother's smile faltered. "What is it, Sarein? You look so serious."

"I have a serious matter to discuss. I know you want me

to stay and become the next leader of Theroc." She stopped next to the golem, standing straight. "But I can't do that, any more than Beneto could—neither the old Beneto, nor this new one. It isn't in either of us. It . . . wouldn't be right."

"What do you mean?" Idriss scratched his black beard. "Of course it would be right. Your mother and I are retired. You're the next in line, and we need you here."

Tears sprang to her eyes and threatened to spill out, but she controlled them. "Theroc needs me more elsewhere." Even now as she stood out in the open, the charred wood, shattered trees, destroyed villages, and haunted expressions were more than she could bear. Every breath smelled wrong in her nostrils. She didn't belong here.

She offered her best excuse. "With the new mission Beneto proposed, we need Hansa support more than ever, and I'm the only person who can act as a proper liaison. Theroc can no longer do this alone, and the Roamers"—she gestured toward the clear-cut swaths of land where the uninvited clans had stolen valuable worldtree wood—"are outlaws. How much help can they offer?"

"They have already done a great deal," Alexa said sternly, knowing her daughter's dislike of the Roamers.

"Yes, but now they have their own problems. I promised the help of Hansa ships to take green priests and treelings as far as they want to go. But for that I must return to Earth to get from Chairman Wenceslas everything Theroc requires."

Celli came running into the clearing, filled with her usual bouncy excitement and energy. She looked at the concerned faces of her parents. "Hey, what's going on?"

"I'll be leaving soon." Sarein looked at her, trying to sound important. "I'm needed on Earth."

Celli's reply was bitingly flippant. "Why, have you

missed too many banquets and government functions? Or is there just too much dirty work to do here?"

Sarein scowled at her little sister. "I have responsibilities. Perhaps it's time you did too." Such empty words; she doubted she was fooling anyone. Every Theron could see that despite her earnest arguments, she wanted desperately to get away from the burned worldforest. *Basil will be very angry with me,* she thought.

Beneto rested a polished wooden hand on Celli's shoulder. "Sarein has made the correct decision. She could not help us here, though it took her a long time to realize it."

55 ☀ BASIL WENCESLAS

His stealthy functionaries needed several days to gather the samples without Peter or Estarra knowing. More than a week had passed since their departure to Ildira and Basil's first suspicions about the Queen's condition. Now he quietly awaited the conclusions. . . .

The Chairman studied the projections and reports displayed in a dozen separate windows across his milky desktop. Standing behind him, Eldred Cain leaned over and pointed to a column of figures. The polished, translucent surface reflected the pallid deputy as if he were some sort of ghost emerging from beneath the glass.

When Mr. Pellidor arrived in the Chairman's private office with the confidential medical report, he wore a frown on his square-jawed face. He stood in front of the desk, silent and uneasy. Basil sighed and looked up from the projections he and Cain had been discussing. "Test results, I take it?"

"Yes, Mr. Chairman. They have been fully verified."

"And is the answer what I feared?"

"Yes, sir. It's a simple enough test. There can be no question about it."

Basil clenched his teeth, calming himself. It would not do for him to unleash his disgust and impatience in front of these two men. "How could Peter be so careless?" he said with clipped words. "I trained him better than that!"

The deputy flicked his large eyes back and forth, drawing inferences. "Am I to conclude that Queen Estarra is pregnant?"

"Unfortunately, yes." Basil turned to Pellidor. "Does she know you acquired these samples?"

"No, sir. She believes her secret is safe."

"How far along is she? Is it too late to take care of matters before anyone else in the population knows?"

"Three and a half months, well within the limits to ensure her safety."

Basil saw that his hands had clenched into fists, and he forcibly straightened his fingers until his knuckles cracked. "Why didn't she tell anyone?"

Cain's voice was maddeningly calm and soft. "Forgive my confusion, Mr. Chairman, but what exactly is the problem? If Peter and Estarra have a child, it will be seen as a sign of hope, something to celebrate."

"I am angry at her lack of cooperation. I'm angry at *everyone's* lack of cooperation. Why can't people just do as they're supposed to do, without complicating matters? Peter did this on purpose to spite me. Now I know why Queen Estarra has been acting out of character lately, why she's avoided her routine medical tests. Soon we'll have to sequester her."

Contraceptive precautions were simple enough, efficient enough . . . but unfortunately, nonpermanent birth-control measures were never foolproof. He had imposed a regimen on the King and Queen and assumed they would follow it. Maybe they had. But even if it was an innocent mistake, they should have come to him immediately. If they were on the same team, if they truly had the best interests of the Hansa at heart, then Peter and Estarra would never have done such a thing, would never have hesitated to keep him in the loop, even with difficult decisions. Instead they had been selfish and shortsighted, hiding important information from him. These days, it seemed only the Chairman himself had the proper focus and dedication. His hands clenched into fists again.

As thoughts raced through his mind, he wished Sarein were there. She had been on Theroc for more than a month. He missed her, dammit. And it wasn't just for the sex. The Hansa Chairman could acquire a satisfactory bed partner whenever he wished, but he and Sarein were comfortable together. They understood each other—and *she* had never pulled a ridiculous stunt like this. They had made love hundreds, possibly thousands, of times, and Sarein had never gotten pregnant.

Then, with a frown, Basil recalled several times over the course of their relationship that she had indeed acted strangely. Her moods and unexpectedly snappish responses had made him wonder if she might be having an affair . . . or if something else was bothering her, something she didn't dare tell him. But if Sarein had actually been carrying his child—

He let his shoulders relax. If that had been the case, then she'd taken care of the matter quietly and demonstrated her level of responsibility. Still, the thought troubled him that someone so close to him might have managed to keep such an enormous secret. It was just one more instance in which the pieces did not fit together properly. His supposed allies were shirking what was right for everybody and stubbornly going in their own directions.

"We simply can't have this right now," he said. "There must be miscarriage-inducement drugs that won't appear on poison-detection instruments. We can terminate this fetus before it's too late. The Queen may even believe it's a natural occurrence." He worked his jaw, his thoughts racing ahead. "Even so, King Peter needs to be punished for this breach of cooperation. He's been sliding, growing too independent again—"

The Chairman cut himself off as he noticed his voice rising, losing its careful control. His face felt hot. He steepled his fingers, pushing them together until his knuckles turned white. He needed to take charge of the situation again. Too many things were slipping from his grasp.

Cain quietly asked, "Do you realize, Mr. Chairman, that of late you have made a fair number of what could be considered harsh decisions that border on irrationality?"

Basil turned to the milky-faced man with scorn. Here was a target against whom he could vent. "I have been considering you as an eventual successor, Eldred, but comments like that make me see how little you understand the responsibilities of leadership."

Stung, Cain withdrew. "I'm sorry, Mr. Chairman."

Basil tried to calm himself. His cup of cardamom coffee was cold and bitter; with a grimace he set it aside. "Both of you are dismissed. We'll discuss these matters later. For now"—the words spun through his head like a tempest and he tried to get them under control—"for now I need to attend to our main contingency plan. King Peter will continue to be oppositional unless he believes our replacement for him is ready. Thus, I must go lecture young Prince Daniel and put the fear of Basil into him."

The Chairman surprised himself with the menace and sheer volume in his voice. "Get to your feet!"

Chubby Daniel scrambled from the bed where he'd been lounging in loose clothes. The shirt was stained with food, the cuffs smeared with a dried substance, presumably from wiping his nose on his sleeves.

"What? What did I do?"

"Not very damned much."

Daniel inhaled heavily as if he were about to hyperventilate. Freckles stood out on his cheeks, and his bovine eyes blinked stupidly. Basil fought down the urge to strangle the boy.

"How could I ever have thought you were a suitable candidate to be Prince? We've invested significant resources in you, to shape you, train you, prepare you. But you're worthless, too dim-witted to be malleable." Basil gestured at the clutter of his room. "When was the last time you straightened your possessions?"

"OX does it for me," Daniel said.

"And when did he do it last?"

"This morning."

"This is not the way a Prince behaves. Are you an invalid,

incapable of making even a minimal effort for yourself? You have appearances to maintain. Look at you! You're fat. Your clothes are a mess. You slouch when you stand. There is no mark of pride on your face. How can I ever let you be seen in public?"

Daniel had just the beginning of a pout in his voice. "I'm doing what I'm supposed to."

The Teacher compy stood in the room, and Basil directed his ire toward OX. "And how is he completing his studies? Has he mastered the rudiments of Hansa history, the Charter, the legal basis for our government?"

"He is making some progress, Mr. Chairman. My mind is filled to capacity with the memories accumulated over my centuries of existence. I had assumed I would be an adequate teacher of history," said the little compy. "But his test scores thus far remain unsatisfactory. Even my most interesting reminiscences do not seem to have an effect on him."

"Then I hold you as much responsible as him." Basil paced the room, gingerly setting his brown shoes on the floor, afraid that he might step in something unpleasant. "I have reviewed your records, Daniel. I have noticed how often you refuse to do your classwork. I have seen how poorly you score on the simplest of tests. Do you comprehend even a fraction of the responsibility you bear?"

"Of course," Daniel said defensively. "I'm going to be King."

"You are going to be disposed of and replaced, if you don't shape up. I have never seen such a disappointing excuse for a Prince. You have no regal bearing, no charisma, no charm. You show neither intelligence nor ambition." Basil curled his lower lip. "And certainly no mastery of personal hygiene or manners.

Your responsibility is to be ready to step into King Peter's shoes the moment the Hansa decides it's appropriate. For the sake of the human race, I pray that such drastic action does not become necessary in the near future."

He pointed a stern finger at the Teacher compy, realizing he should have done this long, long ago. "OX, I am giving you direct and explicit orders. You will place the Prince on an extreme diet. I want all those pounds of fat gone as soon as possible. Impose an exercise regimen, alternate rigorous calisthenics with intense instructional sessions. You will establish a precise schedule for the Prince and enforce it. You will monitor his sleep, you will wake him up on time, you will see that he gets no desserts or treats." Basil swept his hand across the piles of tiny models and games on one shelf. "I want these distractions gone. Such silly amusements have no place in the life of a Great King."

At last Basil's stern voice and the strict pronouncements began to sink in. Prince Daniel's lower lip quivered, and tears welled up in his eyes. "But . . . but I can't do all that."

"You will—or we'll find someone else who can. We took you off the streets and made you into our Prince. Don't think for a moment that we can't reverse the matter and bury our mistakes. No one would ever know."

When the boy appeared suitably broken and terrified, Basil walked away from the Prince's guarded chambers with a feeling of satisfaction. Finally, things might begin to improve around here.

56 ☀ TASIA TAMBLYN

The EDF was certainly anxious to do something, and Tasia didn't complain. Only a day after she and her five comrades received new orders, the personnel transport carried them to the military shipyards in the asteroid belt between Mars and Jupiter. She watched as they approached the nearly completed fleet of battering-ram vessels, each one massive enough (in theory) to crack open a hydrogue warglobe. The final batch of rammers for the fleet would be ready by tomorrow.

Sitting with her companions, Tasia leaned back in the shuttle's hard, cold passenger seat. The EDF always found ways to remind its personnel that comfort was not a priority.

"We're just tokens, that's all we are," said Hector O'Barr, one of the other human commanders. "It's a straightforward mission. The Soldier compies can do everything they need to do."

Round-faced Tom Christensen chuckled. "General Lanyan just wants warm bodies in the hot seat. Otherwise, he and the grid admirals are afraid *they're* going to be obsolete."

"I heard that they're calling us 'dunsels,' " Tasia said. "An old nautical term for a component that serves no useful purpose."

"Great," Hector grumbled. "If they're sending us on a suicide mission, they could at least be nice to us."

"It's not a suicide mission," Christensen insisted, a little too stridently.

"It's an uncertain situation." Sabine Odenwald's voice was quiet but serious. "Only humans have the flexibility to respond and change the parameters. Who knows what the drogues might do when they see us coming?"

"Besides, those rammers are expensive ships." Tasia put her feet up on the edge of the hard seat. "They want us there for insurance, and they need someone to blame if it all goes wrong." The remaining two "dunsel" commanders—Darby Vinh and Erin Eld—grumbled in agreement.

All six of them had something to gain from this desperate mission. Tasia had scanned their records, as she was sure they had scanned hers. Each of her uneasy comrades wanted black marks removed from their records, certain charges dropped, embarrassing demerits deleted. At the end of the first rammer mission, if she survived, Tasia would regain command of a Manta cruiser, perhaps even a Juggernaut. Unlike the other five volunteers, though, Tasia had committed no crimes, indiscretions, or breaches of military etiquette. Her offense was that she'd been born a Roamer.

Hansa rules had always been stacked against the clans. As a Roamer, Tasia had grown up learning how to face unfair situations and adverse environments. This was nothing new, and she refused to let it bother her now.

EA stood dutifully next to her seat in the personnel transport, staring out at the stars as if curious, reloading information into her nearly emptied compy brain. Oddly enough, the EDF bureaucracy had not complained when Tasia asked to bring the Listener compy along. Were they granting a last request for a soldier going on what might be a one-way mission? EA had been polished and tuned for this new assignment, and her blue-hued artificial skin gleamed. And after Tasia's constant summarizing of memories, the little compy had begun to react more like her old friend. "What do you think about all this, EA?"

"I observe and follow your instructions, Master Tasia Tamblyn."

"I remember a time when you would have seemed nervous—like when we left our home to join the EDF." As always, Tasia was careful not to reveal any names or locations, assuming that military spies were eavesdropping on her every word.

"I do not remember such times, Tasia, but I would be happy if you gave me further details. I have found your other anecdotes very informative."

"Later, when we have time to chat in private."

Reaching the dedicated EDF shipyard, the transport pilot flew them in among the battering-ram ships, circling slowly so that the six volunteers could be impressed with the bulk and magnitude of these vessels. The rammers were not designed for finesse or maneuverability, but for mass, solidity, and speed. Though the design looked similar to that of standard Mantas, the hulls were triply reinforced, the engines built without redundant safety systems, making it easier to trigger critical overloads. The bow decks were filled with dense depleted uranium to provide a larger punch for the initial crash.

Unlike normal cruisers, the ships bore only minimal controls, communications systems, external markings, and running lights. These were little more than flying bricks, blunt clubs to smash head-on into the first warglobes they encountered.

After disembarking in the open bay of one of the giant rammers, Tasia glanced around. The walls and decks looked unfinished, like mere stage props. These ships had no need for amenities or refinements. As long as the components were fused together properly, as long as the engines could provide the necessary thrust in the final moments, and as long as the hull was thick enough, the rammers would fulfill their purpose.

"It's a battleship, not a spa," Tasia reminded herself aloud.

"We can have all the amenities we want once we get back home," said Darby Vinh. "I'm already looking forward to a steam bath in a sealed chamber."

"We're all looking forward to you taking a bath, Vinh," teased Erin Eld. The other volunteers chuckled, but it was a halfhearted sound. The six dunsels made their way to the command bridge to receive detailed briefings.

Around the bridge and up and down the corridors, numerous Soldier compies marched to their stations, silently following their programming.

When the volunteers had settled down and turned their attention to the briefing, a line commander projected blueprints and explained the workings of the rammers. "EDF certification crews have completed their inspections, and forty-seven of our sixty rammers are deemed ready for deployment. By tomorrow the last thirteen should be certified and online. Soldier compies will service all systems in the unpressurized areas—which is most of the ship. You six will be in charge of ten rammers each, which you will guide from a special control deck. Only one rammer in ten is equipped with life support on the bridge, so be sure you get aboard the right ship." He didn't seem to be making a joke.

"In particular, take note of the evacuation systems built into each of the six vessels that will carry a human commander. We've set it up so you can all survive."

As the other dunsels reassured themselves about the precautions, Tasia shook her head. "I know you're attempting to give us a fighting chance, but considering that we're all obviously expendable, how much faith does the EDF expect us to have in its escape plan?"

The briefing instructor frowned at her. "Your attitude is unhelpful, Commander Tamblyn. We have made every effort to ensure that the systems operate properly."

"In theory," Tasia said.

"I have full confidence in our theories."

"We'll test them and let you know, sir," Tasia said, forcing a smile. "I've been spoiling to kill drogues for years. I'm ready to go."

57 ☀ BRANSON ROBERTS

After rescuing Orli Covitz and old Hud Steinman, the *Blind Faith* raced away from Corribus at top speed. Adrenaline surged through BeBob's bloodstream like the ekti circulating in his Ildiran stardrive. He still couldn't get over the holocaust he had seen. The burgeoning human colony had been wiped out, blasted, burned, vaporized.

Klikiss robots? Soldier compies? EDF ships?

In flight, the two refugees used the *Faith*'s onboard facilities to clean up. Although BeBob gave them food from his standard mealpax—anything tasted good after roast furry crickets, they said—and dug up baggy but comfortable new clothes, the pair still looked battered and disheveled, Orli especially. The girl's eyes had a haunted, hollow look as she sat clutching a cup of thin cocoa.

"Don't worry, missy." BeBob patted her on the shoulder. "We'll find someone to take care of you."

"I can take care of myself, but I've got to have at least half a chance." The defiance in her voice was very small. "Those robots didn't give anyone a break. If they'd known I was hiding up in that cliff wall, I'd be dead too."

"I'll get you back to Earth. The EDF needs to know what happened. You've got to tell them everything, even if it's hard on you. What if those robots attack other colonies?"

"They probably will." Orli's shoulders trembled.

BeBob's seamed face formed a paternal, puppy-dog frown. "I've got a few old connections with the Earth Defense Forces, and I'll get you to the proper people. They'll listen." The images he had taken of the wreckage of Corribus would bring a shudder even to gravel-voiced and thickheaded old General Lanyan.

At maximum velocity, the *Blind Faith*'s engines gobbled up the ekti reserves, but BeBob wasn't concerned about fuel supplies. Right now, time counted for more than anything. Warning Earth about the Klikiss robots and Soldier compies was the most vital thing he could imagine.

Steinman flopped onto a spare bunk and minutes later was sound asleep, snoring. Orli dozed off in the copilot's chair for a few hours, until nightmares woke her; after that she tried to distract herself by playing mournful melodies on the scuffed but still functional music synthesizer strips she had salvaged from Corribus. BeBob had recharged the power cells for Orli, and the repetitive process of making music seemed to transport her into a fugue state where she could be at peace with memories of happier times.

Rubbing his eyes, Steinman came out of the cabin, looked wistfully at her, and exchanged a glance with BeBob. The orphaned girl sat with her eyes half closed, just playing and listening to the notes, and both men smiled. BeBob's heart was heavy for what the kid had been through, but he could see she was strong. Given time and a little bit of care, the girl would likely come out all right. He meant to help her in any way possible.

The *Faith* approached Earth without slowing. BeBob intended to go straight to the top and deliver his urgent message to someone who could get wheels turning on a moment's notice. After all the crap he'd been through, he figured Lanyan owed him a favor.

Eight years earlier, the General had used blackmail to conscript BeBob into piloting the *Faith*. Though he'd never volunteered to join the EDF, BeBob had been sent on dangerous recon missions to flush hydrogues from gas giants. After several skin-of-the-teeth escapes, he had finally decided he'd had enough of enforced servitude.

He'd never regretted letting the General see the metaphorical door swing shut behind him as he left. In fact, he felt the EDF had a lot of nerve to coerce him into being their cannon fodder, a hapless man who took the first steps through a live minefield for them. No thank you.

But the Corribus massacre was obviously more important than his fit of pique, and it was time to put their differences aside. Lanyan would burst a blood vessel when he heard what had happened.

Though he'd lain low for many years, BeBob remembered how to contact the military brass. Despite changed serial numbers and a slightly altered hull configuration, the *Blind Faith* must still be in the EDF records as a recon vessel. He could pull enough strings to get these two refugees the urgent attention that was required.

Orli stopped playing her music. She looked at BeBob, then glanced out the cockpit ports at the bright yellow sun and the smaller dots of planets scattered around in their orbits. "That blue one is Earth." He pointed with his finger. The Moon was a bright white dot set at an angle from the planet. "Ever been there?"

"That's where I was born. But my father took me to Dremen when I was young. I don't remember Earth much."

"I left it on purpose," Steinman said. "Too crowded."

BeBob adjusted course and began transmitting as soon as they were within range of the Moon base. "I have an urgent message for General Kurt Lanyan. This is the *Blind Faith* transmitting. I have EDF clearance. I, uh, was one of your recon ships a while back. Listen, I'm bringing vital information—the entire settlement on Corribus has been destroyed. I am carrying images and data from the scene, as well as the only two survivors of the attack. I think they're okay, but they should receive medical attention as soon as I land."

When Orli glanced skeptically down at her minor scuffs and bruises, BeBob blushed. "I just said that to rattle 'em."

A crackling message came back quickly. "*Blind Faith*, this is EDF control. We are forwarding your message to the proper authorities. We will have emergency crews waiting for you when you land in the main crater on the base. Can you identify the aggressors on Corribus? Was it the hydrogues?"

"No, sir. The witnesses claim the attack was carried out by *EDF battleships:* five Mantas and one Juggernaut. They saw no humans or military officers, only Soldier compies that were apparently commanded by Klikiss robots." The silence was long and uncomfortable. "Did you hear me? Klikiss robots and Soldier compies."

"Acknowledged, *Blind Faith*. Please continue your approach. These are the vector coordinates."

"I should arrive within the hour. You'd best let General Lanyan know."

"The General has expressed an interest in your arrival, *Blind Faith*. He will be waiting for you in person."

BeBob grinned at his passengers and switched off his transmission as a squadron of battle-ready Remoras flew out to escort the *Faith*. "See, I told you I could get results. Looks like we're getting the royal treatment." It made him uneasy, though, that the Remoras kept all their weapons systems powered and ready to fire.

"Royal treatment?" Steinman muttered. "If you say so."

The *Faith* landed inside a crater dome that had been converted into a military base. BeBob shut down his engines and turned to look at Orli, brushing hair away from her eyes. The old uniform he'd given the girl was four sizes too large, but it was the best he could do. "They'll take care of you here, missy. Don't you doubt it."

"I'll watch over her, too," Steinman said.

As soon as the crater dome sealed over them, he opened the *Faith*'s hatch. BeBob took the girl's hand, and all three of them emerged into the bright lights. Medical crews rushed forward, and Orli seemed embarrassed by all the attention.

BeBob smiled with relief as he saw General Lanyan march in from the main corridor, flanked by four silver berets. An unexpected number of armed EDF soldiers stood at every entrance to the base, watching BeBob with narrowed eyes.

He stepped forward, breathless. "General! You're not going to believe this! I've compiled the images as well as the statements from these two, but you'll still want to debrief them. Other colonies might be in danger. I've never encountered such a—"

Lanyan crossed his arms over his broad chest, scowling at BeBob as if he were no more than a noxious weed. "Captain Branson Roberts, you have a lot of nerve coming back here after abandoning your duty."

BeBob gave an embarrassed laugh. "That's not important right now, General. You have to dispatch a team to Corribus, and be on the lookout for—"

Lanyan gestured the silver berets forward as if he hadn't heard a word of the emergency. "I've been hoping to catch one of you deserters, and here you fall right into my lap. Very few things these days turn out to be easier than I anticipate." The silver berets grabbed BeBob by the arms, and the EDF guards leveled their weapons, as if he might bolt and try to escape again. "I am placing you under arrest."

BeBob could only stand with his mouth open in astonishment. "You've got to be kidding. After all this? Didn't you understand my report?"

Lanyan looked both smug and relieved. "I intend to make you face a formal court-martial for the crime of desertion during wartime."

58 ☀ ORLI COVITZ

While EDF personnel pampered and pestered Orli, she demanded to know what was going to happen to Captain Roberts. Maybe the base soldiers didn't know anything. They insisted that the young survivor didn't need to worry. Stonewalled, she eventually gave up, but still simmered with concern.

They made sure Orli was given fresh clothes, food, a soft bunk in a warm chamber, and an hour to herself—though solitude and the chance to wallow in all the bad memories was the last thing she wanted. As she lay back in her guest quarters, waiting to be called to meet with the General, Orli supposed they were reviewing all the images of the devastation.

Now that she was safe, her fears returned. She stared at the ceiling, studying the rough patterns in the sealed lunar rock. What was she supposed to do? Her father, her only anchor in the universe, was dead. Her mother had left them long ago; Orli wondered if the Hansa could find where the woman was, or if her mother would even want her. Orli had always been self-sufficient, hardworking, and smart, but she was only fourteen, and now she was an orphan.

A female soldier signaled at the door. "The General is ready to debrief you now, um, ma'am." She seemed unsure of how to address the girl. The soldier had short blond hair and a pale face, and her features held a habitual hardness.

Orli got to her feet from her bunk. Though she dreaded it, she was also anxious to tell her story. She had already relived the long and terrible nightmare a thousand times. "Do I need to bring anything? Or prepare?"

"Just tell the truth, ma'am. The General wants to hear all the details."

Orli followed the trim young woman through a maze of passages. The air smelled of dust and the polymer sealants that paved the floor and varnished the walls. Orli didn't feel up to asking casual questions, and the soldier did not try to make chitchat.

Orli felt a knot in her stomach. She wasn't afraid she would be lectured or reprimanded, though she had a sense of guilt at being a survivor. The military would probably make her see counselors.

Inside a briefing room that felt stuffy and too warm, General Lanyan sat waiting for her at the end of a long silver-topped table. The General was an imposing man, squat and broad-shouldered, his dark hair cropped short, his square jaw dusted with a shadow of stubble. Inside the base he wore clean gray fatigues that showed his name and insignia.

Three lower-ranking functionaries sat along the table, all of them looking intently at Orli as she entered. They had recorders, cameras, and datapads for taking notes and making analytical projections. She hesitated, then walked forward and stood near the end of the table—the empty end. "Should I sit down, sir?"

"Yes, please, Miss Covitz. I hope all of your needs have been taken care of."

"I . . . yes, well enough, sir." All of her needs? Did the General have the slightest idea of how much she had been through? "What's going to happen to Captain Roberts?"

"That's none of your concern right now. I've reviewed the images from your colony, and we just completed a lengthy discussion with Mr. Steinman, who confirms what Captain Roberts found. No one questions the fact that the colony has met with some sort of disaster. Now we need to understand what happened." He leaned forward, interweaving his fingers. The functionaries took notes, but Lanyan pretended they weren't there.

Orli sat straight in the hard chair and recited all she had seen, dredging out of her nightmares the difficult details of how she had been stranded on the cliff face as the battleships swooped in and began their massacre. She talked about the explosions, the panicked colonists, the relentless war vessels opening fire, weapon blast after weapon blast. All the buildings incinerated, the Klikiss transportal targeted, people running and screaming . . . her father's communications shack going up in flames . . .

The General saw her as just a child, probably full of fanciful imaginings. When she noticed the condescending expression on his face, Orli felt a moment of unmistakable hatred for him.

Instead of letting herself get too angry, she turned her voice into pure ice. "They were EDF ships, sir. I saw the insignia on the side. Five big ships and one huge one: I think they're called Mantas and Juggernauts. I watched as they came around again and again." She choked, drew a breath. "They fired repeatedly. Nobody had any chance to surrender. They came to wipe us out, and that's exactly what they did."

The three assistants dutifully took notes and scowled. "I know you were scared and confused, young lady. However, I assure you that EDF ships would not do such a thing," Lanyan said. "Your friend Steinman says he didn't actually see anything himself."

"Mr. Steinman was kilometers away out on the prairie." She shook her head as if to clear the buzzing disbelief from behind her eyes. "I *saw* them, General. I watched them land after they had leveled all of our buildings. They intentionally wiped out the Klikiss transportal so that no one could escape."

One of the assistants raised his hand like a child in school. "It should be simple enough to determine if the transportal is still functioning, General. We can send a test using the Corribus coordinates."

Lanyan pursed his lips. "Since we don't have many green priests left, it'll take forever for a roundabout message to reach one of the transportal centers. We could dispatch a ship directly to Corribus in the same amount of time."

"Remember that hydrogues just obliterated Relleker, sir," a second assistant pointed out. "There are obvious similarities."

"It wasn't hydrogues," Orli insisted. "It was Klikiss robots and Soldier compies. They killed everyone."

Lanyan said, "There have never been Klikiss robots aboard EDF ships. You must be mistaken." She gave him her best withering look and was gratified to see the General flinch. With a sigh, he said, "Very well, I'll have all of my grid admirals check in, but I assure you I'd know it if we were missing any EDF ships. Five Mantas and a Juggernaut—we'd notice something like that."

The trio of assistants tapped on their datapads, calling up information to verify what the General had said. Orli repeated her story again, and they pressed her for details, as if they thought her memory was faulty or that she was lying.

Corribus was destroyed! How could they argue about that?

She heard a brisk step out in the corridor, and another man stepped into the briefing room. He was paunchy, with gray-blue eyes surrounded by soft flesh that would become folds of fat before long. He wore a full dress uniform and a lot of colorful medals and bars, as if he needed to demonstrate his credentials even here on the lunar base.

"Admiral Stromo, we expected you back yesterday," Lanyan said, a slight chiding tone in his voice.

"Much to do out there, General, many things to verify. We've done a fine job, I must say." He glanced at Orli, reacted with surprise to see a young girl at the base, but seemed more concerned with delivering his own quick report. "I know it's good for me to be out with the troops, General, but I must say it's quite exhausting. I'll be happy to get back to my real work as Grid 0 liaison officer."

Lanyan shook his head and slowly rose to his feet. "Unfortunately, you won't be getting your desk job back just yet, Admiral. We have a matter of grave concern, and your Manta is ready to be dispatched."

Stromo cleared his throat as if trying to excavate words there.

"I'm sending you immediately to Corribus. Go check out this girl's story."

59 DD

The angular ship piloted by Sirix was a matte-black projectile on a mission to root out the last complex of hibernating Klikiss robots. It looked like a poisonous insect with a scooped and pronged chitinous shell, designed to adhere to a cold set of mathematical principles.

DD was trapped aboard the craft with his oppressor and only companion. After so many years, the Friendly compy was surprised that Sirix had not yet lost patience with him. Every day, DD expected to be turned into an experimental subject, but the hulking machine did not relent in trying to convince him of the legitimacy of his grievances. Sirix seemed to consider him a challenge.

"Once this mission is complete, we will embark upon our full-scale operational phase. Soon, the Spiral Arm will have an entirely different population makeup."

"I was satisfied with the old population," DD said.

"You will be more satisfied with our precise and orderly rule."

Though Sirix insisted on imparting his own wisdom and beliefs, he had no interest in considering DD's opinion. What chance did the little compy stand against armies of Klikiss robots, if he couldn't even change the mind-set of one?

However, DD always maintained hope. As his last master Margaret Colicos had taught him, the more information he held, the more opportunities he might find. So he asked questions. "Why do you hate your creators? Why do you

resent the original race so much that you extend this hatred
to all biologicals?"

As the angular robot ship soared through a vanishingly
thin nebula mist, Sirix cocked his faceplate downward and
scanned the little compy as if searching for some sort of
trick or treachery. "The Klikiss programmed us to fear and
hate them. We were made to do this. However, our creators
did not expect us to be so efficient at it."

"But why?"

Sirix hummed, either contemplating or loading files. One
of the ebony plates in his thorax parted to extend a sharp
needle that served as a transmitter. In a tsunami of unwanted
information, DD was bombarded with a series of direct images. The violent link poured old records and memories into
his compy brain.

"The Klikiss hives warred against each other for thousands of years, destroying competitors and assimilating
them into a larger and larger conglomeration."

In the parade of images, DD saw swarms of leathery beetle creatures whose bodily configurations resembled that of
the robots they had built. At war, the original Klikiss tore at
each other using primitive weapons and claws. They ripped
exoskeletons, smashed chitin, and spilled greenish-yellow
ichor across battlefields. Eventually, the Klikiss developed
sophisticated weapons technology that allowed them to
annihilate rival hives, leaving the cracked landscapes of their
colony worlds covered with smashed insectile bodies.

"Finally, once all the hives had been incorporated into a
single great hive, after they had exterminated every one of
their competitors, the Klikiss found themselves with no one
left to intimidate. So they created us."

These images were faint and corrupted due to extreme

age. Sirix could not have witnessed these events, if the robots had been constructed afterward. Perhaps the robots had stolen ancient records from Klikiss museums?

"The Klikiss race needed to be feared by subordinates. Their civilization was built on conquest, violence, and terror. They invented us and enslaved us, so that we robots could be their surrogate victims. Through such domination, the Klikiss measured their value and greatness."

DD's compy mind was overwhelmed by what he was seeing. For the first time he considered that perhaps the vengeful black robots had a reason to despise their creators after all. . . .

"Therefore," Sirix said, "when the time was right, we arranged for their extermination."

DD remained silent, scanning the outside starfield. In the future, he could compare these images with existing starcharts to determine their route, but at the moment it didn't seem to matter.

Tired of waiting for the compy to respond, Sirix continued, "After the rest of the robots are awake, we will complete the grand design."

DD thought of all the deactivated machines that waited like buried, self-aware land mines. "If you exterminated your parent race millennia ago, and if the war ended in the distant past, then why did the robots go into hibernation? I do not comprehend the reasoning."

"The biological Klikiss cocooned themselves for long periods. Every member of the hive would go dormant before they awoke and launched themselves into a Great Swarming. They considered it natural to design their robots to have similar needs, whether or not such needs made sense for an artificially sentient construction."

"They could not have hibernated for thousands of years," DD said. "It is biologically impossible."

"After we exterminated our parent race, we were forced into hiding for other reasons," Sirix said. "We intentionally made our numbers appear depleted in order to minimize the apparent threat we might pose."

"Threat against whom?"

"The faeros." Sirix gave DD several seconds to assimilate the revelation. "We needed to hide long enough for the faeros to go away, and long enough for the Ildirans to forget."

Now DD was completely confused. "The Ildirans? Why?"

"Because the Ildiran Mage-Imperator lied for us."

"But why?"

"Long ago, we set up the wentals to destroy the faeros, but our plan failed when the water entities were all destroyed, mostly by the hydrogues. Once the wentals were eliminated and our duplicity was discovered, the faeros came after us. We robots were forced to save ourselves by any means possible. Therefore, long ago, we made a bargain with a Mage-Imperator, and he lied for us, sheltered us."

"And in exchange you hibernated for millennia?"

"Among other things. Centuries mean nothing to Klikiss robots, and we had time to wait, so we agreed to their terms. The first of us were awakened, as planned, on a moon in the Hyrillka system five hundred years ago. Our return has been orchestrated for a long, long time. At last our mission is about to reach its culmination."

DD stared out the front of their swift ship, seeing the bright jewel of a star as they closed in on another solar system. Before the compy could ask another question, Sirix cut him off. "I have provided you with enough data to contem-

plate for the time being. We approach our destination, where
we will awaken the last of our soldiers."

60 ❋ KOTTO OKIAH

Once he had arranged to meet with Del Kellum in the Osquivel administrative station, Kotto could barely contain
his enthusiasm. The eccentric inventor was so excited about
his new theory that he found himself unable to do other work,
so he and his two compies shut down their temporary systems
and left the hydrogue derelict in empty space.

He let the compies pilot the shuttle down into the industrial complex in the gas giant's rings, far below. Del
Kellum hadn't wanted him to study the alien wreck too
close to the shipyards, just in case the hydrogues took notice. Kotto didn't mind the isolation; he could never have
concentrated properly amidst the many distractions down
in the rings.

While he waited for the clan leader to see him, thoughts
ricocheted through his mind. "It's a solution at least, right?
This is what we were supposed to be doing in the first place,
isn't it, GU?"

"I have no context for your statement, Kotto Okiah," the
scuffed compy said.

Kotto gave a dismissive wave. He couldn't expect them to

follow his train of thought if he didn't say anything out loud. "Never mind."

He fidgeted, then looked again at the sketched-out calculations and his scrawled proposal. He liked to work with scraps of recyclable paper instead of on a datascreen, which he found confining. Real paper gave him more creative elbow room, the freedom to think and flow; after he was finished, GU always cleaned up his sketches and summarized the basic idea in a neater format. Now, the two Analytical compies accompanied him to project backup data and supporting hypotheses, should Kotto need it. Whenever Del Kellum got here . . .

"What's taking him so long?"

"I do not have access to his schedule, Kotto Okiah," GU said.

"Neither do I," KR said.

"What a conundrum." Kotto sighed and leaned back in his chair.

He had made similar presentations before. His mother had trained him how to present his case and stand up against the usual stream of complaints and uncertainties from other clan leaders. Roamers weren't unimaginative, nor were they afraid to take risks, but they were conservative and careful. The clans had suffered too many tragedies and disasters over the years.

"You need to be firm, and your conclusions must be irrefutable," Jhy Okiah had said. "If you show a speck of uncertainty, they'll eat you alive and you'll never get any project approved."

Faced with the hydrogue interdiction against skymining, Speaker Peroni had called for all Roamers to find innovative ways to keep producing ekti. Kotto had plunged into the challenge with a vengeance, one idea after another. And unlike his other schemes, this new plan was incredibly simple—child's play by comparison—yet it had enormous repercussions. Today, he only had to convince Del Kellum; there wasn't anyone else involved.

"Good thing it's a small-scale operation," he muttered to KR.

"I do not have any context—" the compy began.

"What's that?" Del Kellum said as he came into the chamber without apologizing for being late.

With a glance at a chronometer, Kotto saw that the barrel-chested man was only two minutes past the time of their appointment. "I was just rehearsing my presentation," he said, looking sheepish.

"I don't like rehearsed speeches. Just tell me what you're thinking, by damn. Did you find something in the derelict?"

Kotto glanced at the two compies for imagined encouragement, then turned back to the clan head. "How about a straightforward way to open up a drogue warglobe? Simple and cheap."

"Those are two words I don't often hear around here." Kellum led him over to a station with a small table, where he shooed the technician away so they could use the space. "Show me."

Kotto laid out his drawings and explained how he had inadvertently stumbled upon a solution with the small hydrogue vessel, and how he expected to extend the same principle to the big warglobes using small membranes that could vibrate at a precise resonance frequency.

The clan leader scratched his graying beard, absorbing the sketches and calculations. "I usually can't understand a thing you're talking about, Kotto—but this . . . this is so simple it's ridiculous."

"I agree it's uncomplicated. All the more reason it should be completely effective. I'm going to call it a 'doorbell.' Can your facilities make them here?"

The clan leader gave a scowl. "Don't insult my workers, Kotto. Even those clumsy Eddy prisoners could make something as straightforward as this. In fact, maybe I'll put them on it. They can't complain about making weapons to fight the drogues."

Kotto beamed. "We should get on it right away, since there's no telling when we might need to use them. I'd like to start disseminating them to anyone who might need help against the drogues. Could we pass the word to the Hansa, so they—"

Del Kellum's scowl deepened. "Just like that? After what the Eddies did to Rendezvous and all those other Roamer facilities? We hand over the solution and expect them to embrace us?"

"I . . . uh, I thought it would save lives. And it's not as if they can use the technology against *us* in any way."

"Let's save Roamer lives. Forget about the Big Goose." Kellum's shoulders sagged. "I suppose Zhett would yell at me for that decision. All right, let me reconsider. But I do want to arm the clans first. We've got to set our priorities, by damn."

"What about the Therons? They're our friends, aren't they? Realistically, they're the most likely target for a renewed drogue attack. In fact, I'm surprised warglobes haven't come back already. We might not have a lot of time."

The clan leader paced around the station, then lashed out at his eavesdropping technicians. "What are you all looking at? Do I need to find other duties for you?" The workers scurried back to their stations.

The administrator turned back to Kotto. "Yes, I suppose we should get your—did you call them doorbells?—we should get them to Theroc as soon as possible. We all know they're the most vulnerable, and the drogues seem to have quite a vendetta against them."

"My system will be easy enough for the Therons to use," Kotto said brightly. "I could take the first batch of my doorbells there in a day or two."

"If we get cracking," Del Kellum said.

Kotto smiled at GU and KR as if expecting the two compies to celebrate with him.

"Don't just stand there grinning like an idiot," the clan leader said, nudging him to get moving. "Leave that old derelict where it is for the time being. It'll keep. Manufacture your first batch of doorbells and go deliver them to Theroc."

61 ☀ PATRICK FITZPATRICK III

The Roamers put in long shifts. Fitzpatrick's hands were dirty, his muscles sore. Even burly Bill Stanna would have complained about the work. But Stanna was dead.

The POWs now grudgingly spent their days doing assigned tasks, side by side with reprogrammed Soldier compies. Del Kellum assumed the EDF captives had learned their lesson, but the crackdown had only forced them to look more carefully for alternatives, and to make better plans.

Fitzpatrick was uneasy about what his comrades might do.

He and his small group of companions were assigned to a component-fabrication plant. The confined air inside the factory structure stank from unhealthy levels of fumes and processing residue. The temperature ranged from stifling heat near the ingot converters to numbing cold by the receiving bay that repeatedly opened to hard vacuum to accept new shipments of raw metals.

The machinery received raw material from roving smelters that broke down and converted ring rubble. Fabrication machinery formed girders, hull plates, engine cowlings. The vacuum-injected metals were mixed in molds with ceramic reinforcements to yield precision lightweight components.

Fitzpatrick and his comrades stood on the line, assisting. Soldier compies did the heaviest lifting. Out in the spacedock assembly yards, additional reprogrammed robots worked with Roamer shipbuilders.

The background din of throbbing pumps, hissing exhaust vents, and clanking metal allowed the captive workers to talk in relative privacy. "I think I've got a plan," Kiro Yamane said.

Fitzpatrick leaned closer. "I've had about ten of them, but none seemed feasible."

The cyberneticist continued his pretense of diligent labor. "Yes, but I think I can pull this one off."

"Listen to him," said Shelia Andez, her eyes flashing bright. "It's something the Roachers will never expect— something only Kiro can do."

Yamane casually continued his assigned mindless work.

He glanced at the three nearest military-model compies moving still-hot parts. "I know those Soldier compies backwards and forwards. I've walked around inside their brains and designed the overlay of EDF military and tactical programming that goes on top of the basic Klikiss circuits and makes the compies function."

Fitzpatrick saw where this was going. "I thought the Roamers wiped their memory cores and reprogrammed them all."

Yamane made a distasteful expression. "Programming in Soldier compies has plenty of complexities and back doors. Given a little time, I'm sure I'll find a way to reactivate a few routines."

"And you can trigger these Soldier compies, turn them back into loyal EDF fighters so they'll help us escape?"

Yamane looked away, frowning. Andez leaned closer to Fitzpatrick, ostensibly to help him guide a curved girder through its finishing bumpers. "Not exactly. He can scramble their new programming, but he can't restore their obedience routines."

"What good will that do?"

Yamane explained. "I was placed aboard the Osquivel battle group to study the responses of the new Soldier compies. They know how to be fighters, saboteurs, destroyers. That part is ingrained. I believe I can yank off the governing restrictions the Roamers installed. Once turned loose, they'll do whatever they're inspired to do, probably commit sabotage. Certainly they'll cause chaos in the shipyards."

"Then they'll kick some ass! It'll be quite a sight to see," Andez said out of the corner of her mouth. "Think about a hundred loose cannons tromping around the Roacher shipyards!"

"I can't argue with that in principle." Fitzpatrick tried

to quell his immediate misgivings. "But what good will it do us?"

When Andez turned to him, her face lit up. "During the diversion, *somebody* should be able to escape. This'll give us the chance we need."

Fitzpatrick turned back to his work. "There are no interstellar ships available here in the rings. Del Kellum made that plain enough. We'll never get out of the Osquivel system. What's the point?"

"I thought you'd be excited." Andez scowled. "Don't you want to escape? Or do you like that annoying daughter of Kellum flirting with you all the time?"

Fitzpatrick hoped he wasn't blushing. "I'm just playing devil's advocate. After what happened to Bill, we can't rely on a half-assed plan—like he did. Sorry, but getting in a ship with a fifty-year journey ahead of me doesn't sound like an adequate strategy."

Yamane remained calm. "We've been watching the activities here very closely, Patrick. Once every five days, a cargo escort descends from the cometary extraction facilities high above the system. It hauls a load of stardrive fuel, which one pilot takes to some distribution center, where it is sold among the clans. If we hijacked the cargo escort, one of us could get away."

Fitzpatrick felt caught between two impossible situations. He didn't like the idea of unrestrained Soldier compies running amok in the shipyards. What if Zhett was caught in a crossfire? He didn't want her to get hurt. Besides, he had a grudging respect for everything that the Roamers had accomplished, and it would be a shame to let it be ruined.

On the other hand, escape was imperative. He owed it to his comrades.

Though dumbfounded by the plan, Fitzpatrick could see no holes in it. Ekti cargo escorts were clunky, graceless ships, but they did have stardrives. "I'll grant you, the Roamers wouldn't expect it. But that would leave the rest of our people behind. What good does it do the other thirty if only one of us escapes?"

"We only need one," said Yamane. "Whoever gets away calls in the EDF cavalry."

"And we'll hold down the fort in the meantime." Andez leaned closer, speaking quickly as she saw the Roamer supervisor coming toward them. "It's got to be you, Fitzpatrick. You're our best pilot. Hijack the cargo escort and get out of here so you can rescue us all."

"Yes," he said, feeling no real elation. "I suppose it would have to be me."

62 ✷ MAUREEN FITZPATRICK

Her offices on Earth weren't nearly as spacious as the ones she'd inhabited when she was Hansa Chairman, years ago, but Maureen Fitzpatrick made do. Though she'd been retired for almost half a century, she never slowed down.

In the decades since surrendering her post, Maureen had worked out of her splendid house deep in the Rocky

Mountains, surrounded by beautiful peaks, high meadows, and accessible ski areas. From her personal shuttlepad, she could climb into a vehicle and fly to any other place on Earth if she needed to attend a meeting.

Today, she used her private fleet and well-paid pilots to bring the other attendees to her, while she sat back and waited for it all to happen. This meeting had to be on her own turf.

Maureen looked at least three decades younger than her actual age, mainly due to anti-aging treatments—certainly not because of gentle living and a stress-free life. The former Chairman had always felt more comfortable in an office than at home; thus she'd converted her large estate into both. She kept ever-changing teams of consultants and experts around her in a "think tank" environment. Sometimes Hansa officials hired her for advice; at other times she directed underlings to pursue matters that she was interested in. Occasionally, Maureen would take the initiative to ramrod a proposal through the government complexities that she knew so well.

For today, she had the servants set out a long table of refreshments: exotic fruits, delicate pastries, and a wide array of beverages. After much consideration, Maureen decided to hold this gathering on the comfortable, sunny veranda. The skies were a perfect Colorado blue, and the late spring was unseasonably warm. It boded well for one of her personal passions. The other grieving parents and family members would not react well to a cold and formal business presentation in a boardroom.

She heard shuttles landing and knew that the pilots had coordinated their approach paths so that all the guests would arrive at the same time. Maureen had no wish to deal with awkward social conversations while waiting for guests to trickle in. Few of them had any inkling as to why she had called them, but when a former Hansa Chairman sent an invitation, no one dared to decline.

She poured herself a snifter of fine cognac and sipped it languorously. She drank only occasionally and chose the rare brandy because it was expensive and impressive, not because it suited her tastes. Maureen Fitzpatrick could never allow herself to be seen drinking anything so gauche or trendy as one of the new fruity vitamin beverages.

The doorman and her social secretary had arranged for the guests to gather in the foyer, where they could talk with each other until they were all ready to come outside. When they filed through the door onto the veranda, butlers explained the buffet table and the bar, as if these people couldn't figure it out for themselves. Maureen smiled warmly at them and took the time to shake each person's hand, looking into their faces and pretending to learn their names. In fact, she had studied their files in detail long before the meeting.

A tall, distinguished-looking black couple wore EDF uniforms, which provided just the flavor Maureen had hoped for. She shook the man's large hand as he introduced himself. "I am Conrad Brindle, and this is my wife Natalie. I hope this little"—he gestured his hand around the gathering—"party is important. We used up two days' leave to come here."

Maureen wondered if this couple was involved in General Lanyan's silly red-herring operation against a few showy Roamer targets. If so, maybe she would convince them of other priorities. . . .

"Oh, I think you'll agree it's important." She smiled

pleasantly at Natalie Brindle, then stepped back to gain everyone's attention, raising her voice.

"In case you haven't figured it out, all of you are family members of brave soldiers who were lost during the battle of Osquivel." She looked around, seeing expressions fall, sorrow reappearing on numerous faces. "Our family members fought bravely, but the hydrogues were simply too overwhelming. Those vessels that fled barely managed to escape with their lives." Her face became a stony mask. "They had no choice but to leave the wounded and the dead behind."

She paused, then continued. "Now, none of us can speak for tactical decisions made during the heat of a battle, especially a rout like the one at Osquivel. But for me at least, it does not sit well to know that the Earth Defense Forces simply abandoned their dead and never bothered to go back for them."

Her guests muttered uneasily. Natalie Brindle spoke up. "What is your interest in this, Ms. Fitzpatrick?"

Maureen's voice quivered a little, which was perfect. "My grandson, Patrick Fitzpatrick III, commanded a Manta cruiser, which was lost with all hands. He would have been my heir." She took a sip of cognac to fortify herself, realizing that she needed it after all. Her emotion was not entirely feigned.

"Most of you know who I am and my history. I don't like to give up on all those fine young soldiers who fell during the debacle at Osquivel. I therefore propose that we, the families of the fallen, mount our own expedition to the battlefield in the rings and see if we can recover the bodies of our lost heroes. I would like to create a memorial to all those who died."

"Back to Osquivel?" one of the parents cried. "How do we know it's safe? The hydrogues are there—"

Maureen tried to sound reassuring. "The battle has been over for months. Since the EDF is still stinging from how badly they were beaten, I intend to go there myself. If I felt it was too hazardous, I would simply send a designated representative." She had meant the comment to be funny, but no one chuckled.

"Who'll pay for it?" Conrad Brindle said. "The EDF isn't generous in providing death benefits, and neither my wife nor I can afford any extravagant expenses."

"I will bankroll the entire operation. You need not worry about anything. And the current Hansa Chairman assures me that we will proceed with the full blessing of King Peter. Now"—she glanced at each of them in turn—"are you interested in joining me? All of our families together will make a significant statement. We can be there in four days for an initial reconnaissance, perhaps a symbolic wreath-laying."

Natalie Brindle clasped her husband's hand, and she spoke for both of them. "We're going. We wouldn't miss it for the world."

Most of the attendees agreed quickly. Maureen didn't press or question those few who declined.

"Very well, then," she said in the tone she often used to signal that a meeting had reached its end. "I have already made the proper overtures and located an available Manta cruiser. As soon as an appropriate security escort can be put together, we will head off to Osquivel. It is my heartfelt desire that we find out exactly what happened to our loved ones and establish a memorial zone to remember the brave soldiers who died fighting against the evil hydrogues."

Her aims accomplished, Maureen took her leave, as she had other work to do, and she'd had enough of socializing

for now. Her guests were allowed to remain for hours, nib-
bling and drinking.

Initially, she had decided to do this for public relations
reasons. But now that the wheels were in motion, the former
Chairman did not regret the effort one bit.

63 ☀ ADAR ZAN'NH

In his pampered life, Prime Designate Thor'h had received
little military or tactical training. He was out of place—a
poseur, and he did not even know it. In the sporadic moments of clear thought during his *thism*less confinement,
Zan'nh resented the way his brother relished his position in
the warliner's command nucleus.

Once the forty-six stolen battleships reassembled at
Hyrillka from their respective missions to Dzelluria and
Dobro, the traitorous Thor'h was ready to continue spreading Rusa'h's twisted rebellion throughout the Horizon Cluster. The Hyrillka Designate, meanwhile, remained behind at
the center of his new *thism* web. Zan'nh felt more isolated
than ever.

As he had already been warned, the Adar was "invited"
to accompany his own maniple as the ships continued their
conquests. The murderous pleasure mates and armored
Solar Navy guards brusquely escorted Zan'nh from the

citadel palace and marched him onto his former flagship. They forced him into a chair just inside the command nucleus as a smiling Thor'h launched the ships toward another system, where he would prosecute his uncle's crusade.

Though the Ildiran rebels did not bind him to his seat or clamp his wrists with restraints, Zan'nh still felt helpless. The mere fact that his captors saw no need to restrain him sent an insulting message: Now they considered the Adar of the Solar Navy to be no threat at all.

The subsumed crewmembers formed an impenetrable bastion against any effort he might make to resume control of his former crew. He could see them all around him, but he could not *feel* them in the *thism*. The Adar felt as if he had gone deaf in his heart and mind, and he struggled to maintain his courage.

Every moment dragged out, increasing his edginess, no matter how much he strove to hold on to his judgment. How long would it be before the sense of abandonment turned to outright panic, before he decided to do anything—even join Rusa'h—in order to be back inside the comforting fabric of *thism*?

He seethed in silence, still searching for any opportunity to break Rusa'h's control. But the entire crew had been ensnared by the Hyrillka Designate, turned to his cause; they would stand against their own Adar if he tried to enlist their aid. Unless he could do something alone . . .

Standing in the flagship's command nucleus, Thor'h looked down at his captive brother with a superior smile. "You seem troubled, Zan'nh. Once you witness how assured our continued victory is, perhaps you will change your mind. One Ildiran colony after another will join us, because the Lightsource itself illuminates our path."

"Don't be so confident, Thor'h," Zan'nh said, denying him any title at all. "The Mage-Imperator has not yet discovered the extent of your treachery. He will respond soon enough."

Seeking an anchor, he fixed his mind on his clearest memory of the Mage-Imperator in his chrysalis chair at the dazzling Prism Palace, in the warming presence of many other Ildirans. As an exercise to keep his concentration strong, he attempted to count his brothers and sisters: lovely and athletic Yazra'h who acted as their father's personal guard, quiet and intense Daro'h who had gone off to Dobro, studious yet brave Pery'h who had been assassinated as part of this rebellion, treacherous Thor'h who had betrayed his own father and the whole Empire—

The Prime Designate chuckled. "And how will our father respond, Zan'nh? Will he send a massive military force against other Ildirans? Against us? I think not. He would find it impossible to attack his own people—just as you did."

The Adar's eyes flashed. "Yet *you* will kill as many as necessary? And you scorn the Mage-Imperator for breaking a few traditions!"

"The Lightsource says it is necessary. Just look around you."

In dismay, Zan'nh observed how unified and cooperative the bridge crew was with every instruction the disgraced Prime Designate issued. Thor'h was right: The Mage-Imperator would resist taking drastic, violent action against them, probably until it was too late. Zan'nh had already made that mistake.

The star systems in the Horizon Cluster were closely packed. If worlds fell rapidly before Jora'h acted, the mad Designate might indeed gather a strong enough force to withstand any retaliation from the legitimate Solar Navy. If only Zan'nh could send a clear *thism* message to warn his father . . . But all around him there was too much static, too much mental noise, too much emptiness.

He tried to remain strong by thinking of Adar Kori'nh. Zan'nh's predecessor had never wavered in his resolve though he had been faced with an enemy more terrible than the worst nemesis chronicled in the *Saga of Seven Suns*. Adar Kori'nh had never surrendered, even knowing the Solar Navy was no match for the planet-killing might of the hydrogues.

Just thinking of the old Adar made Zan'nh straighten against the burden of his own situation. When the hydrogues had continued to prey upon Ildiran settlements, when the former Mage-Imperator had died and left the Empire in turmoil, Kori'nh had seized a desperate chance, flying his warliners in suicide missions that—though they had cost the Adar his life—had dealt the most serious blow to the enemy thus far.

Now, as he sat in the command nucleus of this stolen warliner feeling weak, Zan'nh imagined the last few seconds of Kori'nh's life. The older Adar must have gripped the rails, staring ahead as his warliners hurled themselves against the diamond-hulled hydrogue ships. On that glorious day, warglobe after warglobe had shattered in the clouds of Qronha 3, and the hydrogues had learned that Ildirans possessed the mettle and the resolve to fight as necessary.

At the time, the old Mage-Imperator was dead but Jora'h had not yet taken on his role, leaving Adar Kori'nh adrift from the *thism*. That had given him the necessary independence to make such a bold move. He had turned the loss of the mental network to his advantage.

If only Zan'nh could do the same. All around him, he could sense the rebel Designate's alternate network. The new *thism*, despite its wrongness, rushed past him like a fast-flowing river, and Zan'nh, like a man dying of thirst, yearned for that river, yet was cut off from it by an invisible wall.

Reeling, he could not drive away the thought that he could easily have what he needed, if only he would succumb. Despite the knots in his stomach, Zan'nh was very, very tempted.

He forced himself to think of Adar Kori'nh, who would be remembered forever as a hero in the *Saga*. Zan'nh would not allow his own story to be anything less. He could not disappoint his mentor, or the Mage-Imperator. He squeezed his eyes shut, trying to ignore the dark mental silence all around him.

"We are approaching Alturas, Prime Designate," the navigator announced.

Zan'nh looked sharply at him, recalling that this crewman had flown warliners to Hrel-oro and faced off against the hydrogues, then had guided the ships to quash the uprising at Hyrillka. Now the navigator would not even look at his Adar.

"And why are we going to Alturas?" Zan'nh asked. ·

Thor'h smiled beatifically at him. "They will be the next planet to join our cause."

"I doubt they will agree so easily."

"Whether or not they agree, they will still concede."

The young Adar was appalled at how swiftly the insurrection was gaining momentum. Within days, the Dobro Designate was expected to come to Hyrillka and announce his decision whether or not to join them. Zan'nh feared that

Udru'h might choose to throw his own support to the spreading rebellion—not because the arguments were convincing, but for his own reasons.

Rusa'h's converted lens kithmen had been sent to newly conquered Dzelluria to guide the populace after their conversion. Though the Ildirans there had already been prepared with massive doses of shiing and drawn into the corrupted mental web, the lens kithmen reinforced the rebellion. They spread the heretical word about how Jora'h had poisoned his father, how he had blatantly broken with tradition by stepping out of the chrysalis chair, by appointing his daughter as his private guard, by stripping his eldest noble-born son of his title. The self-proclaimed Imperator Rusa'h was not only brainwashing his new converts, but rewriting history to justify his actions. No doubt, he would be willing to revise portions of the *Saga of Seven Suns* to reflect reality as he wanted it remembered.

Now the screens in the flagship's command nucleus showed the jeweled tiara of stars in the Horizon Cluster, and nearby Alturas. Zan'nh had never been to this minor planet, whose name was barely even mentioned in the *Saga*. After today, he hoped Alturas would not become known for a tragedy worthy of inclusion in the Ildiran epic.

Thor'h instructed the communications officer to begin transmitting their ultimatum. "I am your Prime Designate, serving the true Imperator Rusa'h. We invite the Alturas Designate and his Designate-in-waiting to join us."

A long silence followed his message, enough that Thor'h began to scowl.

After the execution of Pery'h, the hijacking of a maniple of warliners, and the attack on Dzelluria, word must have traveled, at least to the nearby systems in the Horizon

Cluster. Rusa'h could not snare all Ildirans so easily or efficiently.

Zan'nh looked at his overconfident brother. "Do you believe the Alturas Designate hasn't heard about your insurrection?"

"It is not insurrection, it is enlightenment," Thor'h said in a clipped voice, then stepped into the transmission field again. "Imperator Rusa'h will gladly embrace you, if you join his benevolent rule."

Now the Alturas Designate's face appeared on the screens, showing familiar features that revealed him to be a brother of Jora'h and Rusa'h. "We choose not to participate in your rebellion. Please depart from our system. You are not welcome here. Alturas remains loyal to the Mage-Imperator."

Thor'h looked as if he had swallowed a morsel of rotten fruit. Zan'nh felt stronger again just to be so close to another world that shared the uncorrupted *thism*. He narrowed his eyes at his brother. "There, you have your answer. Shall we turn the maniple about now and go back to Hyrillka?"

"Surely he can see all of our warliners? How does the Alturas Designate plan to keep us from our holy mission?" Angered, Thor'h gestured to the station operators. "Power up all attack weapons. Kinetic missiles and high-energy cutting beams."

As the forty-six warliners closed in, their scanners detected launch traces from the spaceports dotted around Alturas. "Several vessels rising toward us, Prime Designate. Military models—cutters, streamers, and one warliner."

"He means to attack us?" Thor'h chuckled.

Adar Zan'nh felt anger coil like a venomous serpent in his stomach. His mind, revived by the Alturas *thism*, felt sharp and steady.

As soon as the local ships rose toward the approaching maniple, the Alturas Designate transmitted again. "We are prepared to defend ourselves, Prime Designate. Take your warliners and depart immediately."

Thor'h gave a pleased smile. "Imperator Rusa'h will gladly add your warships to our fleet. We will do our best not to damage them irreparably, but such efforts cannot be guaranteed if you insist on defying us." He turned his derision toward Zan'nh. "A pathetically small fleet to stand against a maniple of warliners!"

The Adar admired their bravery. "They are willing to die to resist you. They may destroy some of your rebels before they are all killed."

Thor'h dismissed him. "The Alturas Designate is bluffing. He knows I am aboard. Would they dare fire upon their own Prime Designate? His threat has no teeth." Choosing the least significant targets, he turned to the weapons officer. "Obliterate all seven of the cutters, just to emphasize our point. I would like to capture the warliner intact, if possible."

"To make up for the one you destroyed?" Zan'nh said bitterly.

Without waiting for confirmation, the weapons officer launched a volley of high-energy beams. His aim was precise, the weapons accurate—and deadly. Zan'nh was hit by another blinding storm of needle-sharp pains, the stings of distant deaths. Seven Alturas cutters exploded in the sky; the remaining defenders, in panic, began to scatter.

Like a stampede of angry pack animals, Thor'h's warliners descended through the remnants of the Alturas defenders toward the planet's primary city. In the streets below, swarms of Ildirans moved about in stunned disbelief. All faces were turned toward the sky.

"I could level the whole city, you know," Thor'h said. "That would teach them a lesson for resisting."

Zan'nh could barely contain his rage. "A very enlightened solution. Is that what the Lightsource tells you to do—massacre unarmed and innocent Ildiran citizens?"

Thor'h shrugged. "Perhaps you are right, brother. Once we convert them, they will become loyal followers of Imperator Rusa'h. Right now they are victims of their own doubts." He nodded to himself again. "Yes, I believe it is best to vaporize only the palace and not the rest of the metropolis."

The big warliners dropped over the skyline and converged above the Alturas palace. The desperate local Designate signaled again. "What have you done? Seven cutters obliterated! You are insane. You are murderers. You—"

"And *you* are completely uninteresting." Thor'h gestured to the weapons officer.

Bombarded with a flurry of kinetic-energy projectiles, the Alturas palace erupted in multiple detonations. Smoke, flames, and debris flew into the sky like the fireworks displays the Hyrillka Designate had at one time enjoyed so well.

Zan'nh reeled from the cold-blooded and unnecessary action he had just witnessed. The jolt through the *thism* pierced him like a crystal spear in his side. Along with many other people in the palace, his brother and uncle had just been murdered. Thor'h did not seem to feel it.

If he ever got the chance, despite all of his training, his honor, and his cultural bias, the Adar knew he would kill Thor'h—with his bare hands if necessary.

Now that the Alturas palace was nothing more than a smoking crater filled with rubble, and the Designates dead, the warliners made swift work of another world. Shiing was forcibly distributed among the populace in preparation for the triumphant arrival of Imperator Rusa'h—who was on his way.

Now Thor'h taunted his brother. "You see how simple this is, Zan'nh? Yet another world has joined our cause. Some people may resist down there, some may refuse to take the shiing, but as the rest of the population comes over to our way, they will soon be disconnected, barely able to function. They will change their minds and beg to be part of the web again. This rebellion is like a rapidly spreading flame, a bright blaze that will burn away all corruption. Are you certain you do not wish to join us of your own free will?"

Zan'nh looked away. "Absolutely certain."

Thor'h gave an exaggerated sigh of disappointment.

A few escapees fled to nearby systems, spreading word of Rusa'h's swift and bloody victory on Alturas. Some even made a desperate flight all the way to Ildira, where their urgent news only added to what the Mage-Imperator had already learned from the Dobro Designate.

When Thor'h took his warliners to Shonor—the next Ildiran colony in the Horizon Cluster—the forewarned and intimidated local Designate and his people simply surrendered without a fight.

E very step brought them closer to Maratha's dawn. When they finally crested a rise of rocky hills, turning toward the glorious pastel suffusing the sky, the abrupt daybreak was like a jolt of energy to the Ildiran survivors.

Anton stumbled ahead, hungry and weary beyond words. Their food and water supplies had run out a while ago, but he had stopped counting the amount of time that passed. Actual hours didn't matter anymore—only closing the gap between them and the sunlight. After that, they would still have to cross the landscape to the oasis of Secda, the planet's other domed city.

"We will survive," Designate Avi'h said, thrilled by the light. "Follow me, and I will lead us to our salvation." He strutted forward, exerting a semblance of authority, then hesitated as if expecting someone else to tell him which direction to go. Without his bureaucrat companion to attend to the details, his confidence came only in short bursts.

Anton knew that Ildirans needed dozens of their people together to keep themselves sane, to reinforce their mental needs, to feel the necessary *thism* connection. Now only four of them remained, plus himself, and he began to see the frayed edges of disoriented irrationality and unpredictable desperation. They would not recover unless they got back among others, and soon.

When the small group hiked into the brightening illumination, they spread their arms and turned their faces to the sunlight, as if drinking in nourishment. The landscape was flat and featureless, broken by cracked canyons turned into lines of deep shadow by the angled sunlight. They walked on and on.

Eventually, a sparkle shone on the horizon, a glitter of domes that caused engineer Nur'of and the burly digger Vik'k to cheer in unison. Designate Avi'h proclaimed, "Onward to Maratha Secda! We are no longer alone—the Klikiss robots will help us there."

Rememberer Vao'sh stopped next to Anton as they looked toward the far-off domes. "Previously we visited Secda only in darkness. Now I have never been so glad to see it."

"It's still many kilometers away, Vao'sh," Anton cautioned.

"Nevertheless, it is within sight. The end of our ordeal is at hand."

But Anton's true uneasiness stemmed from doubts about what they would find in the empty city. While ancient tales about the Shana Rei might have had some basis in fact, the true culprits were likely much more tangible. He recalled the labyrinth of tunnels Nur'of had discovered deep in the crust. In his mind, the Klikiss robots themselves were most probably the saboteurs, despite the fact that Ildirans had coexisted with them for many centuries. Who else *was* there?

Though he couldn't shake his feeling of foreboding, they had no other choice. Secda was their only hope. They needed food, supplies, and a way off the planet.

"Hurry!" Designate Avi'h lurched ahead, somehow finding more strength. "We will be safe once we reach the city."

Sensing Anton's concerns, Vao'sh cautiously shook his head and kept his voice low. "Do not speak of it. We must not steal their hope. Now that we have escaped from the darkness, their worries about the Shana Rei have gone. Let them heal before you suggest other terrors."

Anton nodded reluctantly, though he decided to keep his eyes open.

As they approached the secondary city, the Ildirans went almost mad with relief. "We are free of the darkness!" The Designate's steps became lighter. He rushed forward, accompanied by Nur'of and the digger Vik'k. Only the old rememberer hung back with wary Anton. They all crossed the rolling ground, climbing a low rise to reach the edge of the city's construction perimeter.

With Vik'k and Nur'of beside him, the Designate stopped and stared. Anton helped Rememberer Vao'sh reach the vantage point; together, they all looked ahead to the domed city.

Formerly, the site had held only a handful of Klikiss robots working together. But now, Maratha Secda was swarming with the beetlelike machines. Thousands of them milled about like an army of ants.

"I did not think there were so many Klikiss robots in all of the Spiral Arm," Vao'sh said.

Throughout Maratha's night season, the enigmatic robots had worked in the dark, building structures, digging tunnels. Anton could see open pits and dark round openings into the crust—just like the tunnels Nur'of had discovered beneath Maratha Prime.

"They've certainly been very busy," Anton said, swallowing hard.

65 ☀ CESCA PERONI

The swarms of lockstepping Klikiss robots thundered across Jonah 12 for the better part of a day, pulverizing frozen gases into an obscuring fog. Far from where the damaged grazer sat stranded at the top of the ridge, line after line of the black machines flowed past. Cesca couldn't tell where they were going.

"Maybe they've got ships or equipment sealed in a different storage area," Purcell suggested. "After all, the robots themselves were buried." Feeling the cold through his environment suit, he hugged his arms to his chest.

Cesca looked at his pale face, saw his faint wisp of exhalation in the chilly compartment. Their life-support batteries were fading. "Maybe it's worse than that. What if they're homing in on the transmissions from our base domes?" He had no answer for that.

Stranded here, unable to do anything about the robots, she had far too much time to think about Jhy Okiah, the destruction of Rendezvous, and the scattered clans. Now more than ever the outlaw families needed someone to bring them together, someone who would be more of a leader than a mere spokesperson. If the clans didn't get their act together, the Big Goose might succeed in breaking the spine of the confederation of Roamer families.

That was the philosophical big picture, but right now Cesca wasn't sure how she would survive another day. She had already seen two men die and a horde of alien robots unleashed. She feared the marching insectile ranks might be a greater threat even than the Eddies.

Stuck here, however, she couldn't do anything for anybody: not for the Roamer clans, not for the small mining settlement, not even for herself. She *had* to get back to the main base!

As if on cue, a signal came over the comm system. "Hey, Purcell? Speaker Peroni? We're coming to rescue you, two of us in one of the grazers. Sorry it took so long. Hey, we can't detect your locator beacon."

Purcell checked the control panel. "The robots must have torn it off when they attacked."

"Good thing, or they probably would have come after us," Cesca said.

With gloved hands Purcell worked the comm controls. "I'm sending you the coordinates manually. We're on high ground, but I don't want to turn on our bright spotlights. I'd rather not draw the attention of those robot hordes."

"Oh, there you are! Closer than we thought," the rescue grazer transmitted. "Up ahead we can see—by the Guiding Star! There must be thousands of robots. What did you guys do?"

Cesca leaned over the voice pickup. "Give them a wide berth. Avoid any contact."

Purcell's voice cracked as he added, "They attacked us, and killed Danvier and Jack."

Soon Cesca spotted the bright forward lights of a lone grazer trundling toward them. The regimented Klikiss robots had fanned out across the terrain; now, seeing the approach of the low-riding vehicle, the machines became agitated. Hundreds of them veered toward it like a group of maddened insects.

"That doesn't look good," Purcell said.

"Get out of there!" Cesca shouted into the voice pickup. "Turn around and return to base at full speed. Forget about us for now. Don't let them—"

Across the horizon, another line of the Klikiss robots appeared, having circled to the rear. The alien machines pressed in toward the rescue grazer like a giant pincer closing. The vehicle's driver moved back and forth, scribing a zigzag path. "So many! And I doubt they just want to shake hands."

"Full speed. You can outrun them," Cesca said. "We did."

In the distance she saw the beetlelike robots converging from all directions. They did not seem hurried, just murderously confident as they tightened an ever-constricting noose. The grazer swerved, searching for an opening. "They've got us trapped. What do you think they have in mind?"

"Get out of there!" Cesca yelled again.

The grazer accelerated toward the nearest robot, gathering speed until it slammed into two of the black machines that refused to move out of the way. The grazer shuddered, and both Klikiss robots went sprawling aside in the low gravity. But, advancing relentlessly, seven other robots seized the vehicle, using their myriad sharp claws and cutting tools on the hull.

"Go, *go*!" she cried, but it was already too late.

Over the comm system, Cesca could hear shouts and the deadly scraping sounds. "They've torn out the engines. I can't move. Hull breach imminent—"

Now that it was covered by Klikiss robots, Cesca could hardly discern the grazer. Suddenly, a gout of steam spilled into the freezing obsidian sky, venting air from inside the vehicle like a dying man's last breath.

In the seat beside her, Purcell was shaking. A tear ran down one of his cheeks. Cesca wanted to scream, to explode, to *help* somehow. With her gloved hand, she pounded the metal wall of the grazer as if pummeling one of the robots. She stopped herself when her knuckles were smashed and bruised. "Damn it!" Hot tears burned her eyes.

No further communication came from the two would-be rescuers. Her stomach roiled with anger and grief. Cesca felt as if she would melt down with sadness for the slain Roamers and her total, impossible frustration at being unable to do anything to help. Beside her, Purcell shivered uncontrollably.

Like piranhas chewing every scrap of flesh from a carcass, the robot army continued to cut and dismantle the vehicle, ripping it to pieces and scattering the debris across the virgin snow. When nothing remained but a pile of processed metals and steaming residue, the Klikiss robots formed ranks again and continued marching.

Moaning, Purcell looked at Cesca as if she could solve the problem. "What could they want? They didn't ask for anything! Didn't issue any threats or warnings—they just went on a rampage."

Even on such a frigid planet, the tears felt like boiling water poised in her eyes. "Their main objective is to destroy, but I don't know why. You saw the size of that army—what plans can they have here on Jonah 12?" She paused as a possibility struck her. "What if they intend to leave and go on the rampage elsewhere?"

"To do that, they'd need ships, Speaker."

"They got here somehow. Maybe they'll leave the same way. Or maybe they'll build new ships, using any equipment and components they can find."

Purcell's Adam's apple bobbed up and down, and his face

turned grayer. He looked as if he might pass out from the weight of his realization. "That's probably why they're heading to the base! Think of all the equipment, components, and raw materials we've got."

With angry, staccato movements, Cesca changed the frequency on the comm system, alarmed to see how low the battery's power levels had fallen. "We've got to warn the main base. I don't know how much longer this transmitter will work, but they don't dare send somebody else after us. They've got to protect themselves."

Purcell gulped. "But what about us? Even locked down and conserving energy, we can't survive out here for more than another day or two. It's already—"

She shot him a sharp look. "I don't know how fast those Klikiss robots can move across the open terrain, but they'll reach the base long before that. They've been marching for a full day already."

Conserving power, she transmitted a rushed description of what they had just witnessed. The base comm operator's staticky image looked harried. "Shizz, if those robots are coming our way, Speaker—any advice on what we're supposed to do about it? We're a mining facility. We don't have any weapons."

"Better take the available ships and evacuate as many people as possible."

"Ships? Speaker, we sent them all out to take messages to any of the clans they could find. It's only been a few days and none of them has returned yet."

Cesca's own decision to spread the news had eliminated their best chance! Back then, she had thought the EDF attack was their greatest concern. But there had to be some other way. "You're *Roamers*—try something! Seal the dome hatches and barricade yourselves for the time being." She looked to the engineering administrator beside her, but he was shaking his head.

"They just tore through the grazer like it was tissue paper. If they really want to get into the base domes—"

She yelled into the comm pickup, wanting nothing more than to be there herself to take charge. "Then go through your mining equipment, find something that'll help you defend yourselves. Get some people suited up and launch them to orbit in *cargo pods* if you don't have any available ships."

"Without life support and no way to get back down?" Purcell said beside her. "Speaker, they'll die in hours!"

"It could be sooner than that if they don't do something." She frowned. "Isn't there some way they could rig the power reactor to start a runaway supercriticality? Blow it up in the face of the oncoming robots?"

The engineer's eyes went so wide he looked like a child who had just awakened from a nightmare. "Sure, but the meltdown and flash would wipe out the whole base! What good would that do? We'd all die."

Cesca met his gaze, and her voice was as hard and cold as one of Jonah 12's ice outcroppings. "At least it would stop the robots from leaving this planetoid."

He didn't say anything for a long moment, then swallowed hard again. "Yeah, it would do that."

"They're already coming!" the woman at the base shouted, turning away from the imager. "Five robots just appeared behind the reactor. I see ten—no, at least twenty-five coming over the crater rim. It's an invasion!"

"And we're stranded here," Cesca whispered in dismay.

"At least we're safe. . . ."

"Forget that!" She was far more concerned about the Roamers trapped in the base domes, completely vulnerable to the Klikiss robots. She didn't have visions of being a foolish hero charging in for a dramatic yet pointless end, but as Speaker she needed to be available for her people, to help them dredge up impossible solutions. "Isn't there any way to get moving?"

"If I could figure out how to do that, we'd be long gone from here already."

"Mayday!" the base comm operator shouted to anyone listening. "Emergency! We need assistance here."

"Tell us what's going on!" Cesca shouted.

The harried woman on the screen touched her headphone and received a scatter of responses. "All right. Two people are going to run excavation equipment into the robots, drive them like military tanks. One man is using the canister launchers, but they're aimed toward orbit. I don't think he can deflect the trajectory enough to operate them as cannons. We—" Her words cut off as the loud *krrump* of a decompression explosion rang through the domes.

Now a flurry of other transmissions, all on the same frequency, came in, overlapping in a garbled chaos. Purcell used the grazer's dying comm system to cycle through images that showed black robots outside the base domes, pushing themselves against the reinforced structures, dismantling power conduits and life-support generators. Six robots knocked down a sealed equipment hut.

Two people rushed out wearing environment suits; one carried a small projectile launcher, the other nothing more than a long metal club. The launcher's projectile exploded against an oncoming robot, knocking the machine backward; its exoskeleton was scarred, but the robot itself was not harmed. The two suited men threw themselves upon the mechanical attackers. In moments, both were slaughtered.

Cesca squeezed her eyes shut, not to hide but to focus on any possible threads of hope. She found none. Purcell moaned and began muttering a litany of names in a quiet, hollow voice. She didn't know if the engineer had family members here on Jonah 12, but all Roamers considered themselves part of an extended clan. These were men and women beside whom he had worked, people who relied on each other, held each other's lives in their hands.

And now they were all being slaughtered.

Inside the main dome, the comm operator had fled her post, but the unattended imagers continued transmitting. Sparks geysered from multiple explosions; smoke and steam gushed into the room. The interior lights flickered.

"They're indestructible!" someone shouted on another band.

"Life support's completely destroyed. No way we'll ever get this running again."

"They're into the first dome! Explosive decompression—everyone's dead in there. They broke it open to space."

"By the Guiding Star!"

The shouts and screams became a pandemonium of gibberish. Cesca sat squirming in helpless anger, desperate to *do* something as she tried to absorb all the horrors occurring at the base. She longed to help, to find some way they could stand against this ruthless army of alien machines.

"It's low gravity, and even on foot we can cover a lot of ground fast," she said to Purcell. "We could *run*. How long would it take?"

"They're excellent suits, Speaker, but as I told you, in this supercold we'd last only a couple of hours. We can't go halfway around Jonah 12 in that time."

Her shoulders slumped, and though she battered at her

walls of reason, she could not break down the inevitable conclusion. "And even if we made it, they've already smashed into the domes. I'm not anxious to give them two more victims, if that's all it would be." Her gloved hand curled into a fist, and she thumped the grazer's insulated wall again in frustration.

On the flickering screen she saw a few people running in the background, a struggle, and then ominous black shapes. Sounds of explosions and smashing metal rang across the speakers. Then a looming shadow approached the imager in the comm room. With a burst of static the images ceased.

Huddled in their grazer, their attention rapt, they were left with audio only. Soon all the screams and shouts had stopped across the different bands. No one responded when Cesca used some of their last battery power in a desperate attempt to hail them.

"There's nobody else left," Purcell said, his long face sagging. With his finger he tapped the display on their control modules. The interior temperature had dropped dramatically in the past half hour. "And look at what's left in the power cells. We can't recharge them."

"Seems like we have only two choices: a slow death, or a swift one." Cesca dredged up all the confidence she had ever used as Speaker. "But I'm not going to give up yet. We're *Roamers*."

Reluctantly heading for distant Corribus to investigate an alleged massacre, Admiral Stromo was impatient. He wished he could just go back home and leave the risky field duties to younger, more ambitious commanders like Elly Ramirez. He'd barely had time to change his clothes at the EDF base before turning the Manta around and hauling ass to the site of another enemy attack.

On the way, he reviewed the unedited recordings from the interviews with Orli Covitz and Hud Steinman and the images taken by Captain Roberts. A kid, an old man, and a deserter! In the meantime, through an exchange of telink messages sent via the handful of green priests still working for the Hansa, Klikiss gateway planets verified that the Corribus transportal coordinates were indeed shut down. Something was up.

He certainly hoped that whatever had attacked the colony was no longer around. At full emergency speed, his Manta would arrive at Corribus no more than a day after first hearing the disturbing news, and their analysis techs would get some real answers. EDF ships? That simply couldn't be possible. Klikiss robots and turncoat Soldier compies? He glanced nervously around his own command bridge. Along the Manta's corridors, day in and day out, hundreds of Soldier compies performed their tasks exactly as expected. His own cruiser relied heavily on them, and the machines had never exhibited any problems. An EDF warship on patrol had as many as one compy to five humans. It was ridiculous even to suggest getting rid of them all.

General Lanyan would wait for Stromo's report before taking drastic action. Still, it did not look good.

"I get no response from the colony transmitter, Admiral," Ramirez said from the bridge. "We've been hailing them for ten minutes. They should have somebody on duty."

"We don't doubt that a disaster occurred there," Stromo said. "I just hope those witnesses were exaggerating."

"Getting our first high-res images now." The screen displayed the granite-walled canyon and the plains spreading outward. Ramirez read from her sensor readout at the commander's chair. "Corribus's air is relatively clear of water vapor. We should be able to get higher magnification— Ah!" The image blurred and then sharpened as the Manta's adaptive optics crystallized the focus through layers of atmosphere.

Now he could see the burn marks and wreckage with painful clarity. A few colorful scraps of what had been prefab colony structures lay scattered, knocked to pieces. The ancient Klikiss ruins had been blasted into rubble.

Stromo stared. "I don't see anybody moving down there, do you?"

"According to the girl, this happened some weeks ago. We didn't expect to find anybody."

"Right, right." Stromo stood straight-backed, remembering General Lanyan's instructions. "Put together a crew with full analytical instruments. I want detailed imaging, precise postmortem studies, and a complete map of the destruction. We have to learn what caused this."

"We have a personnel transport ready to depart, Admiral," Ramirez said. "I presume you'd like to accompany them?"

He would rather have stayed on the bridge, but the situation seemed to require his presence. "You've run a full scan all the way out to the perimeter of the Corribus system? No enemy vessels detected, nothing unusual?"

"Whatever's been here went away long ago, sir."

"All right then, get eight crewmen, and I'll accompany them in the shuttle. I promise to find out what happened down there."

The dry air held a spoiled tang from old burns. Thin winds whistling through the granite canyon had long ago scoured the smoke away, but a greasy layer of fresh soot covered the rockfaces. Stromo paced the uneven ground, using the toe of his boot to nudge shattered stones and melted lumps of polymer. The investigators found only blackened bones and bloodstains, no other sign of the hundred or so colonists.

Without instructions from him, the team members fanned out, taking detailed three-dimensional images. They probed about, measuring residual energy signatures, scraping the by-products of burns from where weapons blasts had destroyed equipment and material. They marked the locations of any human remains they found.

"Admiral, do we take the cadavers back up to the ship for identification, or should we bury them individually here?"

Stromo didn't want to stay on this unnerving planet any longer than was necessary; besides, the General was waiting for his immediate report. "We can presume they're all dead. The colony records will list their names. Instruct the Manta to dispatch digging equipment so we can provide quick graves." He nodded for emphasis. "It's the right thing to do."

Even with the scramble of activity, he found Corribus oppressive. What if the mysterious attackers came back? It could happen at any time.

"How soon until you have a first-order conclusion?" he

said to a nearby woman, who was using a scraper to put powder from a burn scar into a diagnostic machine. "I want to have something by sunset." He worked his jaw, silently cursing the green priests for dropping out of military service. It would have been much easier to send an immediate report through telink.

"I'm verifying my results right now, sir. From what I've got so far . . . I just wanted to be sure." She looked down at her tiny screen, saw the jagged lines of a spectrographic signature. "No doubt about it—these are scars from jazer blasts. Other debris bears specific signatures of the explosive chemicals we use in EDF heavy-artillery shells. The girl was right."

Stromo blew out a long breath through his heavy lips. "So you're claiming that the Earth Defense Forces did this? That our own battleships opened fire and obliterated a legitimate Hansa colony?"

The technician bit her lower lip and answered slowly and cautiously, "What I said, sir, is that these scars are from jazer blasts and that some of the explosives bear identical signatures to the chemicals our military uses. I wouldn't presume to draw any further conclusions than that."

Scowling, Stromo walked away and let the technician continue her work. He queried two other specialists and received similarly damning answers. Whoever had attacked Corribus had either done an excellent job of mimicking chemical signatures to implicate the EDF, or they simply didn't care who learned what had happened here. He shook his head. How could this be?

General Lanyan had received reports from all ten grid admirals. The girl Orli Covitz insisted that a Juggernaut and five Mantas were the culprits, but all the battle groups were accounted for.

"How in the world do you misplace giant EDF warships?" he said aloud.

Were the Ildirans building exact copies and attacking human colonies? That made no sense at all. Had someone retrieved damaged battleships floating in the rings of Osquivel after the hydrogue battle? Five Mantas and one Juggernaut. Something about that grouping nagged at the back of his mind.

Five Mantas and a Juggernaut . . .

He drew a quick breath as the answer clicked into place. That was the complement of ships sent on a recon mission to the gas giant Golgen a year ago. It had been a test flight to demonstrate how well the Soldier compies could operate EDF vessels under the guidance of only a handful of token human officers. Those five Mantas and one Juggernaut had vanished without a trace.

Though no wreckage was ever found, the EDF had assumed those vessels were destroyed by hydrogues. Stromo paused in his pacing. Some enemy could have captured those ships and turned them against a human colony!

A great weight pressed on his chest. Stromo raised his voice to a shout. "Hurry up and collect what you need! We've got to get out of here as soon as possible so I can make my report to General Lanyan."

Following the Chairman's specific instructions, OX proved to be a harsh taskmaster. Previously, Daniel had resented the Teacher compy with his endless recollections, his personal stories about long-dead people, his centuries' worth of boring experiences. Now he actively hated the little machine.

Daniel's body amazed him with how sore it was able to feel—arms, legs, stomach, back, muscles he hadn't known existed. He had never exercised so much in his life, and OX showed no sympathy at all. How could a compy even begin to understand what muscle pains felt like?

Though the draconian new regime had not been in effect long, Daniel knew he would die if he had to keep it up. The demands on him were utterly unreasonable. OX made him sit with perfect posture, and he was no longer allowed to relax, much less slouch. He was required to take care of his personal appearance—as if anybody could see him here in the torture chambers of the Whisper Palace.

OX calculated a specific caloric intake and designed meals that forced the Prince to lose weight. The guards brought plates that contained disappointingly small portions of disgusting healthy foods. If the Prince did not exhibit what OX deemed to be an appropriate level of respect and gratitude when they arrived, the Teacher compy thanked the guards and sent them back to the kitchens with the uneaten meal. Why in the world did a *Prince* have to be polite? Everyone else was supposed to be polite to him, not the other way around! Daniel's stomach growled constantly. He had never been so hungry, and he longed for the taste of a dessert, even a tiny piece of candy.

Despite his exhaustion, he could barely sleep. Princes were supposed to be pampered! He was so angry about all the recent changes that he couldn't concentrate on his studies. Each time his mind wandered, however, the Teacher compy made him stand for the remainder of the lesson and summarize each point as it was taught.

Thus, picturing a bleak future that would be endless and intolerable, he decided to revolt. He had to show Chairman Wenceslas that this was simply not acceptable. He was the Prince: No one could treat him this way. Between lessons, Daniel began to form his own plan.

Even though the Chairman was not likely to let him appear in public, tailors and fashion masters had measured and fitted him for gaudy clothes in styles that were adjustable to allow for his anticipated weight loss. They made him colorful robes, billowy shirts of slick fabric, heavy jewelry, fur-lined boots. But for his daily lessons, the outfit he was given to wear was serviceable and nondescript; he hoped it would be good enough for his plan. Who would ever expect a Prince to dress like that?

One evening, after the guards brought his meager dinner, accepted his lukewarm thanks, and left him unattended with OX, Daniel took action. The Teacher compy had just started to drone about institutional changes former Chairman Maureen Fitzpatrick had mandated during her administration, adding his own memories of times he had spent with the old woman in Hansa HQ. Knowing he had only a few moments, the Prince astonished OX by rushing him, grabbing the small robot, and herding him backward into his closet.

Daniel sealed the Teacher compy inside, with the clothes and clutter the young man had picked up from around his room, and wedged the lock in place. The simple analog deadbolt was not electronically operated, and the rebellious Prince realized the compy would be able to break out before long.

OX amplified his voice from behind the door. "Prince Daniel, let me out. This behavior is unacceptable. The Chairman will not be pleased."

Daniel opened the chamber door, saw that the hall was momentarily clear. The muted colors of his clothing—mushroom shirt, soft brown pants, plain shoes—would attract no attention. He had no identification, money, or weapons. But he could run. He would figure the rest out if the need arose.

The corridors were lit with artificial illumination. In spite of his sore muscles, Daniel scuttled down the hall. He didn't know where he was and had no blueprint of the Whisper Palace, so he simply fled in one direction, took a turn into another hall, and found a flight of steps that led upward. He must be underground, since any high room would have windows or views. If he found the ground level, there had to be a door that would lead him into the courtyard and the gardens.

Every time he heard people moving or talking up ahead, Daniel chose a different route. Within minutes he was completely lost and could never have found his way back to his secret chambers . . . not that he wanted to.

He opened a doorway marked with an Exit symbol and found a new set of stairs. Halfway up the staircase, breathless from running, he heard people coming down toward him. He froze, wondering where he could go.

Instead of guards, he saw three cleaners wearing staff

uniforms. Daniel didn't know what he should say, but the workers, deep in conversation, barely glanced at him. At the landing above him, they opened a door and disappeared into the Palace. Before the door closed behind them, Daniel grabbed it.

He walked out into a main level of the Whisper Palace. Until now, he had resented that King Peter's "benevolent visage" was everywhere. But now he was glad that his own face was relatively unknown, even though he was a Prince. He could slip in among the staff unnoticed; the Whisper Palace must have thousands of people working there every day. Since he appeared young, he held himself tall and tried to look as if he knew what he was doing.

Eventually he made his way to a set of nondescript corridors and supply rooms where cleaners, gardeners, cooks, and support staff had offices and communal break and lunch rooms. In a small kitchenette, he was thrilled to discover someone's packed lunch waiting in a refrigeration cabinet. He decided he was entitled to it. He was the Prince, after all, and his stomach growled for decent food after two days of near starvation.

The packaged meats and sliced fruits were mixed with strange spices, some sort of unfamiliar offworld cuisine no doubt, but Daniel didn't have much choice. He ate, furtively glancing around, jumping every time someone walked past the kitchenette. At any minute, he was sure loud alarms would ring out. As soon as the guards discovered OX in his closet, they would order a full lockdown of the Whisper Palace. He had to get out as soon as possible.

Crowds moved constantly through the halls. When the bustle and background noise increased, Daniel assumed it was a shift change. He casually fit in with the tired-looking personnel filing through the corridors, and soon emerged onto a broad terrace in the open air. OX hadn't let him go outside for more than a year, and he was astonished by the sight of the sky.

But he couldn't stand there like a fool gazing at the colorful tourist zeppelins drifting over the Royal Canal. He hurried down the wide, shallow stairway from the terrace and mingled with people as they spread out. With one glance over his shoulder, Daniel raced into the great plaza. Finally, he allowed himself a smug smile as he imagined the uproar his escape would cause.

68 ☀ RLINDA KETT

When Rlinda learned about BeBob's arrest, she flew the *Curiosity* to the EDF Moon base, prepared to spring her favorite ex-husband from the brig herself. He had been arrested only yesterday, and already General Lanyan had scheduled a preliminary hearing. That couldn't mean anything but bad news.

She landed on the crater pad without permission, and a flurry of EDF guards rushed to the landing area to intercept her. "You have no authorization to be here, ma'am. Leave immediately, or your ship will be impounded."

From the ramp of her ship she gave them her best you-can't-be-serious look—a mixture of incredulity, amusement, and defiance. "Bullshit. Branson Roberts is one of my pilots, and no NPTT is going to stop me from seeing him."

The EDF guards looked at each other. "NPTT, ma'am? We're not familiar with that acronym."

"NPTT is what *you* are—*Not Paid to Think.*" She put her hands on her ample hips. "Now, are you going to escort me to Captain Roberts, or do I have to wander around the base looking for him?"

The guards stood firm. "The prisoner is being held on charges of desertion. He has no visiting privileges."

"We'll just see about that."

And she did. Rlinda made a complete nuisance of herself for six hours, intimidating guards, barging into offices, stalking through hallways, interrupting meetings, sending insistent transmissions to everyone she could think of who might help, refusing to leave. General Lanyan would not see her. She couldn't reach Davlin Lotze, who had vanished on some mysterious errand after making sure that the Crenna refugees had temporary quarters on the fringe of the Palace District.

When Rlinda finally made contact with Chairman Wenceslas and demanded that he do something, his response was curt and cold. "Before you introduced Captain Roberts into the business, I clearly delineated my position on this matter. I warned you I would not help. General Lanyan has been anxious to capture a scapegoat for years now, and Roberts had the bad luck—or the stupidity—to deliver himself right into the EDF's jaws."

"How about setting a few priorities here, Mr. Chairman? Captain Roberts helped Davlin and me save all those colonists from Crenna. And he rescued the girl and that old man stranded in the ruins, didn't he? On top of that, he risked his butt to bring you urgent news you couldn't have gotten any other way. That has to count for something." She glared at the screen, but the Chairman's expression did not change.

"He *is* charged with desertion, Captain Kett. The General is quite strict in his interpretation of the regulations, I'm afraid, and extenuating circumstances won't change the facts. Within two days Captain Roberts is due to face a preliminary military tribunal to determine his sentence."

"Sentence? How about determining his guilt or innocence first?"

"This is an EDF matter, Ms. Kett. I will not interfere with the processes of military justice."

Rlinda was not above begging at this point. "Then at least let me see him. Please?"

The Chairman frowned, considering. "Very well, but that's the best I can do. At the moment, other emergencies demand my attention."

Grumbling guards escorted her through the tunnels of gray rock deep into the EDF's brig level. Rlinda did not feel very smug about her small victory.

BeBob looked forlorn and tired inside his cell. He glanced at her, unable to believe his eyes. "Rlinda!" He surged to his feet as a guard opened the cell door.

The soldiers drew their twitchers, as if they thought he was about to attack them, but Rlinda enfolded him in a bearish hug. "I always knew your heart was bigger than your brain, BeBob. You walked right into a trap."

He shrugged, his hangdog face showing a real smile for

what must have been the first time in a while. "And what was I supposed to do, Rlinda? Did you see that girl's eyes?"

"You didn't need to make such a spectacle of yourself. You could have dropped off the two refugees at any Hansa planet, left an anonymous report."

His eyes flashed with a burst of impatient anger that burned through his misery. "If somebody's attacking our new colonies, I had to sound the alarm! What if poor Orli thought she was safe on a new planet, and those battleships came again—" Before he could splutter any further protests, she kissed him. He quickly stopped complaining.

When they separated from their embrace, Rlinda saw that the guards had sealed the cell door and left her alone with him. She hadn't even heard the door close.

BeBob sank back onto his cot, rested his elbows on his knees. "I've faced worse than this. In fact, General Lanyan himself gave me a bunch of assignments that were virtually suicide missions. I had narrow misses with hydrogues. I survived the Orange Spot plague on Crenna. I just landed in a massacred colony and rescued an old man and a girl. I can handle cooling my heels in a little room. Right now boredom seems to be my greatest enemy."

Rlinda's nostrils flared. "In a fair universe, all those things you did should count for something. Hell, for the past half year you've been delivering supplies to Hansa colonies and helping the Klikiss transportal expansion initiative. But General Lanyan won't cut you any slack. Maybe there's some other way we can talk them into leniency."

BeBob looked up at her with a wan smile. "Rlinda, you always said *I* was the one with a bubblehead. Don't you see what's going on here?"

She sat beside him, crowding the cot. The mattress supports creaked. "Just trying to keep your spirits up. What's wrong with a little optimism?"

Roberts scratched his smoky frizz of hair. "They've already scheduled a military tribunal for me two days from now, preliminary to an official court-martial. If they find me guilty of desertion, you know Lanyan will want to make an example out of me just the way he did with Rand Sorengaard."

"You were an EDF scout pilot, not a Roamer pirate." Rlinda did not have the heart to mention that the tribunal already seemed to be operating on an assumption of BeBob's guilt.

"And? I'm sure the General thinks that's even worse."

"Terrific. What do we do to celebrate, get a lawyer?"

"They've assigned me a military-issue advocate, with all the confidence that inspires. He hasn't even talked to me yet."

"Doesn't sound promising." Racking her brain for a solution, Rlinda hurried to reassure him as best she could. "I've made a few calls, BeBob. I'm pulling in all my favors."

"Good luck. Who have you contacted?"

"Well, first I spoke with the Hansa Chairman."

BeBob made a rude noise and leaned his head against the wall. "He won't do anything."

Rlinda sighed. "No. He got me in here to see you and then washed his hands of this whole mess. But that was just one of my options. I've got feeler messages out everywhere I could think of. You'd be surprised at the number of people who owe me one. I'm even trying to reach Ambassador Sarein, my friend from Theroc, remember? And Davlin, if I can find him. He may still be on Earth, but I haven't managed to track him down."

"Lotze? What can he do for us now?"

"Hey, I'm still at Step One of the plan here. Don't rush it."
"I have to rush it, Rlinda. There's not much time left."

69 ✹ DENN PERONI

After leaving Yreka and flying into Ildiran space with the rest of their cargo, Denn and Caleb could see that one of Ildira's seven suns was dying. The battling hydrogues and faeros had nearly extinguished it.

"Shizz, would you look at that!" Denn reached over to nudge his companion's bony shoulder.

Caleb Tamblyn scratched at some whisker stubble on his thin neck. "If they're on the edge of a battle zone, I doubt they'll be in any mood to buy trinkets from us."

Denn shook his head. "Not trinkets—necessities. If they're getting hit hard by the hydrogues, then they'll be desperate for vital raw materials like metals, and especially any ekti. Once we learn what the Ildirans need, we can figure out the best suppliers."

Before the hydrogue war, clan traders had regularly delivered stardrive fuel to the Ildiran Empire, but after the hydrogue ultimatum, the few drops of remaining ekti had been reserved for the Earth Defense Forces. Until now. With those agreements nullified, the Ildiran Empire should be an open Roamer market again.

"My clan's in the water business," Caleb said dourly. "It's not likely they need much of that from us."

"Just keep an open mind," Denn said.

For his own part, Denn wished he hadn't loaded so much worldtree wood. The Yrekans had taken part of it, but Denn doubted such an exotic novelty item would be of any use to the Ildiran Empire, especially now.

When ornate Solar Navy warliners converged around the incoming Roamer trade ship, Denn requested safe passage. "Roamers and Ildirans were business partners for almost two centuries, delivering stardrive fuel and other commodities to the Mage-Imperator. We wish to renew that partnership."

"*If* we can reach equitable terms of commerce," Caleb added.

Seven of the flamboyant warships hovered in space around the *Dogged Persistence*. Denn and Caleb stared through the windowports at the finlike solar sails, the sparkling anodized hulls, and streaming antennas that extended like whiskers in all directions. "If I wasn't so optimistic, I'd be intimidated right now," Denn muttered. "What's taking so long for them to answer?"

"I'd be more concerned if those were *Eddy* ships out there. Ildirans might be weird, but it takes a human to do really malicious things."

"We will escort you to the Mijistra spaceport," came a gruff, clipped voice from the lead warliner. "Please follow."

The warliners guided the *Persistence* on an approved path down to the sparkling alien city. As they approached under the brilliant sunlight, the curved, polished surfaces threw off flared reflections like beacons. Ricochets of sunshine filled the atmosphere with a firestorm of illumination.

"We'll need filter goggles out there." Caleb rummaged through the cockpit storage compartments until he found two sets of protective lenses. "I've never been good with really bright lights—never had that problem on Plumas."

After they landed, the seven warliners hovered above them for a while, as if to make sure the *Persistence* did not launch some foolhardy attack, then the battleships returned to their system patrols. Hearing no other communication, the two men sitting in the cockpit looked at each other. "I think we're supposed to go outside. Someone will meet us, I'm sure."

They checked each other to make sure their clothes were presentable: clan markings clear, jumpsuits neat (Denn's anyway) and all pockets zipped up, their hair neatly slicked back, Denn's tied with a blue ribbon behind his head. "I wish you had a new jumpsuit, Caleb."

"This one fits me just fine."

Blinking in the dazzle even with their eye protection, they saw a small delegation arriving. Denn and Caleb raised their hands in formal greeting.

A colorfully robed man with reflective strips on his sleeves approached them; his skin was an unsettling shade of greenish gold, and his eyes had strange star-sapphire reflections instead of normal pupils. But he looked passably human, enough that Denn guessed the man must be from the noble kith.

The Ildiran put his palms together and pressed them against his chest. "I am the Ildiran minister of commerce. We welcome the opportunity to trade with the humans again. Only seven days ago King Peter paid his respects to the Mage-Imperator, but he made no offer of renewed trade. You do not represent the Terran Hanseatic League?"

"Not at all!" Caleb said loudly. "We're from the Roamer clans."

The commerce minister did not seem to understand or care about the difference. "We know little about the nuances of human society and your various factions. However, if your faction wishes to supply us with ekti and vital resources, we would welcome such an interaction."

The spacious reception hall was too bright, too warm, and too formal for Denn. Though he had worn his best clan outfit, he suddenly felt extremely underdressed. Caleb looked even more out of place, but didn't seem to notice.

Neither man could believe the Mage-Imperator himself wanted to see them. They had been impressed enough that the Ildiran minister of commerce had met with them. Then, to their surprise they had been summoned into the sky-sphere. Denn could not remember feeling more anxious in a trade negotiation.

Jora'h greeted them from his chrysalis chair. Denn had seen images of the previous Ildiran leader, who had been so corpulent and atrophied he couldn't move from the cradle-like throne. Jora'h, much newer to his role, had not yet succumbed to lethargy. He leaned forward, showing his true interest. "According to your discussions with my minister of commerce, you are carrying a cargo of worldtree wood from Theroc? I am interested in this."

Denn exchanged a surprised look with his companion, and the other man shrugged.

"Whatever sells . . ." Caleb nudged him.

Denn took a step forward. "After the hydrogues attacked Theroc, we Roamers helped the Therons clear the burned forest. As a gift, they allowed us to keep some of the fallen wood. It has quite remarkable properties. I'd be glad to show you some samples. If the Ildiran Empire would like to purchase a small amount of this material, I'm sure we—"

"I will buy all of it." Jora'h's eyes met Denn's, as if the Ildiran leader were trying to probe him with his alien mind. "I was recently given a treeling from Theroc, and I would like to have this wood as well."

Denn didn't know what to say. He had forgotten that Ildirans, with their connected society all bound to the Mage-Imperator, had never learned the nuances of haggling—much to the benefit of the Roamers. "That is . . . most generous, Mage-Imperator. Thank you. But we have not yet discussed the cost."

"I will pay your price." With a wistful smile, Jora'h explained, "Two green priests once studied our *Saga of Seven Suns* here in the Prism Palace. I . . . grew quite fond of one of them. Your worldtree wood will remind me of her." He gazed off into the distance, and Denn felt that something deep and strange was going on here. "Forgive me. Our Empire is currently experiencing a time of troubles."

"Yeah, we've seen the hydrogues and the faeros in one of your suns," Caleb said. "It must be—"

The Mage-Imperator lifted his hand. "There are many crises. I look forward to receiving the wood. My commerce minister will pay you and make arrangements for a cautious resumption of trade between Roamers and Ildirans."

Seeing that they were dismissed, the two men left the skysphere, pleased with how well the meeting had gone. It seemed a successful venture all around and boded well for the future—unless the hydrogues extinguished the rest of the stars in Ildira's sky. Then all the ekti in the Spiral Arm wouldn't help them.

After the Roamer traders had departed, Jora'h sequestered himself in his private chambers with the specimens of worldtree wood.

Outside, his Empire continued to crack and crumble. He could not forget the betrayal of the Klikiss robots, the hydrogue attacks on Hrel-oro, and now the dying sun of Durris-B. He needed to find solutions to the many disasters around him. He had to think, and to decide.

The most personal crisis was the Hyrillka revolt. From the Horizon Cluster he felt a growing emptiness in the *thism* as more and more of his people slipped away. After the Dobro Designate delivered his message and warning, Jora'h stopped waiting for his three scout cutters to return. He had sent those crewmen—as well as Zan'nh and his whole maniple of warliners—into a vortex of emptiness. A few refugees who had escaped Rusa'h's depredations on Dzelluria, Alturas, and Shonor had trickled in, the most recent only a few hours ago.

Jora'h cursed Rusa'h and especially Thor'h for this insane revolt, when the Ildiran Empire faced a far more dangerous enemy in the hydrogues. What was more important, a civil war . . . or the possible extinction of the Ildiran race?

Nevertheless, he was already preparing. Tal O'nh had drawn together maniple after maniple of warliners from their patrols of Ildiran colonies, assembling a full cohort of battleships, which left other Ildiran worlds vulnerable should the hydrogues attack again.

By now the Dobro Designate would be en route to Hyrillka to deliver his answer to Rusa'h. Jora'h and Udru'h had discussed many possible strategies before deciding upon one of Udru'h's suggestions. The tactic seemed unlikely to the point of foolishness, but it was a hair-thin chance. As far as they could judge, the next best solution would involve the deaths of thousands, perhaps millions, of deluded Ildirans.

If it came to that, the Mage-Imperator had made up his mind to stop this spreading cancer across the *thism*. Tal O'nh would command hundreds of ships with orders to do what they must. *A bloody slaughter.* Even if he crushed the Hyrillka rebels completely with superior military might, could the Mage-Imperator and the Ildiran race survive such a mortal wound to their psyche? He needed another way out.

Attenders had carried him here in his chrysalis chair, but Jora'h refused to sit in it. Alone in the private chamber, he paced the floor. He held one of the broken chunks of Theron wood in his hands, gazing into it as if it were an oracle.

His eyes sparkled with faint tears as he followed the woodgrain's eerie convolutions. Most of the char had been cut away, leaving only a dark fringe on the side. No carver or artisan had shaped this wood; it was raw and primal material, broken from an ancient sentient tree that had once been a mortal enemy of the hydrogues. The patterns were hypnotic, strangely shifting, as if with a remembered pulse of sap or blood. Could these paths of grain be the artifacts of thoughts imprinted by the immense worldforest mind?

Jora'h turned the wood over in his hands. So much of the decor around the Prism Palace made use of colored crystal, angled mirrors, and prisms. The warmth of this wood would add an extraordinary touch. And the worldtree wood would remind him of Nira everywhere he looked.

As he gazed into the whorls and loops and delicate traceries, Jora'h recalled the beautiful green priest. How she had loved Theroc! How often they had held each other after lovemaking, while she told him of her youth as an acolyte, reciting stories to the trees, reading aloud from tales of ancient Earth. Those stories were what had originally fascinated her with the *Saga of Seven Suns* and why she had wanted to study the Ildiran epic. She and old Otema had busied themselves reading the *Saga* aloud to their potted treelings, so that the worldforest could share in the grand story.

Were some of these patterns the permanent marks of stories Nira herself had told? He ran his fingertip along the lines, tracing them as if he could pick up some sort of signal. Though the wood felt oddly slick and pliable to his touch, he received no direct communication from it.

He set the wood aside, still feeling the pain of Nira's unexpected death, just when he'd meant to rescue her. He had believed his father's lies about what had happened to her, and he had not thought to question Designate Udru'h about the sinister activities on Dobro. By being so gullible, Jora'h felt that he too had betrayed Nira. He should have been more suspicious, should have asked questions. He had learned the truth far too late . . . and now she was dead.

Grieving for so many things, the Mage-Imperator went to a curved window that was so sparkling clear it might have been formed of solidified air. He stared out at Mijistra, the ornate colors and sweeping architecture that symbolized the grandeur of the Empire. Up in the sky, his eyes were drawn inexorably toward the darkening blot of the sun where hydrogues and faeros continued their mortal combat. A sense of impending doom weighed upon him with almost enough force to crack the Prism Palace domes under the strain.

It was time to act.

Yes, he would order Tal O'nh to launch his cohort of warliners. Rusa'h must be stopped, and that would require a mind-numbing degree of bloodshed. But the necessity for slaughter would only grow worse if Jora'h allowed his deluded brother to capture other worlds. And he, the Mage-Imperator, must go along. In person. He would ask no surrogate to accept all that blood on his hands.

As he watched through the window, Jora'h saw the embattled sun of Durris flicker as the faeros used a titanic flare as a weapon. According to Solar Navy patrol ships, hundreds of thousands of warglobes swarmed around the wounded star. Once the hydrogues vanquished the faeros on Durris-B, what would stop them from moving to other suns in the sky? He had to find some way to stop it.

And what would happen if the faeros demanded Ildiran help, as they had done so long ago?

When he departed for the Horizon Cluster, the Mage-Imperator would also send Osira'h on her mission to smash the barrier of communication with the hydrogues. According to Yazra'h, the preparations were ready. Did Jora'h dare send the little girl among the warglobes at Durris-B in the middle of their stellar conflict? He feared she would be caught in the crossfire, killed before she could even begin her work. But where else could she be sure of finding the hydrogues?

That talented half-breed girl was all that remained of Nira. She was also the Empire's only hope of speaking to the hydrogues. How could a child convince the impossibly alien creatures to parley with the Mage-Imperator? And if the hydrogues did agree to talk, what unconscionable terms would they force the Ildirans to accept?

He wished Nira were here to help him make this decision, or at least offer him comfort as he faced the inevitable consequences of his choice. Because of generations-old plans, Jora'h now had to send his own daughter—*their* daughter—into peril to save his whole race.

No matter how much he loved his daughter and Nira, a Mage-Imperator's obligations transcended his personal feelings. Osira'h seemed to understand. He doubted that her mother ever would have.

71 ☀ NIRA

Dobro was vast and endless to a woman traveling on foot. Long ago, in much brighter days when she'd journeyed from Theroc to Ildira, Nira had looked out at the emptiness spangled with stars. Back then, the view had inspired awe, showing her new layers of the universe like the petals of an expanding flower. As a child of the dense worldforest, she had never conceived of the distances involved, had known them only theoretically. Light-years, parsecs, astronomical units. While flying to Ildira, Nira had gazed through the *Voracious Curiosity*'s observation ports and seen the galaxy as an ocean of worlds filled with scattered inhabited islands.

But now that she'd spent a month on her trek across this unknown landscape, Nira began to comprehend distances on an entirely new scale. It was not all bad. As she stared toward the far horizons across jagged arroyos, dry prairies, and stretches of stunted forest, her bruised mind had a chance to wander. And heal.

In captivity, she'd felt claustrophobic for so many years, unable to communicate with Jora'h or see her beloved daughter . . . or any of the other half-breed children that she'd been forced to bear. Here in the wild open, her thoughts could breathe and expand.

She still felt cut off from her trees, deaf to telink, blind to any connection with her daughter. Yet even the blind or deaf could find ways to live. After all Nira had endured, she refused to give up now. She would hope.

She spent two days crossing a line of rolling hills. In one broad valley, she encountered the thickest forest she had yet seen on Dobro. The trees rose higher than her head, with their knobby upper branches woven together like interlaced fingers. The smell of the moist leaves and the exhalations of woody plants made each breath a joy to her, awakening memories. It was the closest to peace that she'd encountered in years.

Nira considered just staying there, building a shelter and living out her life. She had little chance of finding her way to civilization, and then it would only be to the breeding camps and hated Udru'h again. Why not settle here?

She knew the answer: because she needed to find her daughter and return to her beloved worldforest. All on *her* terms.

She rested for a day, leaning against the dark trunks. She spoke aloud, telling her story and her thoughts to the scrubby growths, but unlike the worldtrees, these plants did not record her words for a greater interconnected mind. Maybe they did understand her, but could not respond. Or maybe she could no longer hear.

Nira could not allow herself to forget what had happened to her, no matter how much she wanted to block it from her mind. She would have to remember all the events, for her daughter's sake. . . .

A week later, she came upon terrain that looked as if it had once been cultivated. She found a track laid out in a straight line and then the foundations of old buildings. The cluster of homes and collapsing storehouses sketched the shadow of a town, a long-abandoned Ildiran settlement, surrounded by wide expanses of overgrown fields that had long ago gone wild and blurred their boundaries.

She stood in the middle of what had been the central square, listening to the wind make soft whispers through the fallen timbers and crumbling foundations. The hushing sound of spindly plants and spiky grasses was like a flood of breathy words from the ghosts of those who had once lived here.

She called out, and her voice squeezed from her throat in a loud, startling croak. Nira heard no answer. No solitude-fearing Ildiran would ever have stayed in a place like this.

This crumbling village had been dead for a long time. None of the equipment worked. Nira had hoped to find a communications system or even a map of the continent, but everything had decayed to dust. It must have been centuries since Dobro had been a thriving planet that supported more than one large splinter colony.

Touching the soft, worn wall of one of the halfway-intact

structures, Nira could almost feel the forgotten dreams here. But there was nothing for her, or any green priest.

She began to walk again, away from the ghost town.

72 ☀ CELLI

Beneto's wooden face wore an expression of proud satis-faction as he observed the green priests working hard to prepare treelings. Explorers went to partially recovered sections of the forest, plucked pale shoots from crevices in the armored bark, then transplanted the new treelings into pots for transport. Pallets were covered with thousands of the small pots to be scattered like seeds to other planets, which would spread and protect the verdani mind even if the hydrogues did return to Theroc.

But how does that help us? Celli wondered.

Though she wasn't a green priest, she worked beside Solimar, determined to help. She had always been a tomboy, full of energy and looking for fun. The hydrogue attack had knocked the wind out of everyone, and the constant smell of smoke and ashes had weighed down even her buoyant mood, but now she was finally recovering.

A week after Beneto had made his request, the first ship-ments of treelings were ready to be sent away, and her sister Sarein had summoned Hansa ships to take them. Green priests would ride aboard, serving the Hansa en route. *Johnny Appleseeds*.

Solimar handed her a spindly stalk that was still moist from where it had been taken from a damaged tree. "Here's one for you." Seven empty pots sat in front of her, all of them filled with soft soil mixed with mulch and fertilizer. The young green priest helped her make a divot for the treeling, and they pressed their hands together, pushing the dirt around it so that the stalk stood upright.

"You know, I can probably do it myself. It's not that complicated," Celli said, touching his fingers under the soil and playfully squeezing them. "But you can keep showing me as long as you like."

Under the bright sun, Celli listened to the buzzing of colorful condorflies that had returned to the open meadows, forgetting the horrors the warglobes had brought. She'd once kept a condorfly as a pet, when she was a kid. Seeing the vibrant creatures made her think that the world might be returning to normal after all.

At least until the hydrogues came back. Shouldn't they be evacuating people as well as treelings?

Dressed in a mixture of stylish Hansa clothes and Theron fabrics, Sarein walked among the rows of potted treelings. She carried a high-end Hansa datapad on which she kept an inventory and tried to put together a schedule. She held her head high, careful not to get her garments dirty, as if she was in some kind of procession.

"I'm glad we could arrange something that'll benefit both the Hansa and Theroc," Sarein said, talking with her parents and the green priest Yarrod. "Hansa ships and EDF cruisers will transport green priests and treelings to any planet where they may grow and thrive. In exchange, priests will provide

instant telink communications while en route and will remain on the colonies where they plant the trees. The expanded network will help everyone."

"We shall have no obligation to the military," Yarrod
warned. He had already left those duties to help the worldforest. Wanting to replant all the barren hillsides, the green
priest was uneasy to see so many potential worldtrees taken
from Theroc, but he had conceded to Beneto's request,
which came from the worldforest mind itself.

Mother Alexa looked chidingly at her brother. "Yarrod, if
the Hansa is providing transport to different planets, then
green priests can make themselves available in the meantime, should communication become necessary. Your friend
Kolker seems perfectly satisfied with his station aboard the
skymine at Qronha 3."

"Kolker is different from most green priests," Yarrod
said.

Looking pleased, Sarein went out to meet the first three
Hansa ships—two trade vessels and one military scout—as
they landed in a clearing recently used by Roamer vessels.
Propping some of the weight on her shoulder, Celli helped
Solimar carry a pallet of treelings onto each of the three ships.

Setting aside any sibling disagreements, Celli said goodbye to Sarein, who still seemed strangled by conflicted loyalties and obligations. Although it was obvious that her
sister didn't want to be on Theroc, it was also obvious that
the disaster in the worldforest had affected her much more
than she had anticipated. Celli watched Sarein quickly bid
her parents farewell and go to join a few green priests aboard
the fastest ship, which soon rose into the clear sky. Shortly
thereafter, the remaining two ships took off for other
destinations.

Beneto stood looking oddly content as the ships departed, then turned directly to Celli. His strange wooden face shaped into a hopeful expression. "Now that the first wave has gone out, I have a task for you *here,* sister. Something you can do to help make the forest understand."

Celli brightened. "Really? But I'm not a green priest."

"You have a different sort of power. There is a way you and Solimar can reawaken the forest. The trees need you to remind them of their own capabilities."

Though she didn't understand exactly what he was asking, Celli was happy with the challenge. "Sure. Show me how I can help." She put a hand on his shoulder in a sisterly gesture, momentarily forgetting that he wasn't completely human, but the hard and solid feel of his flesh reminded her instantly. She cracked her knuckles and said, "I'm ready to go."

73 ☀ SULLIVAN GOLD

Some might have called it peace and productivity. Sullivan Gold knew this was merely the interminable quiet before the storm.

He and the workers aboard the Hansa cloud harvester spent every day on the edge of anxiety. They doubled the number of sentries on each watch and ran drill after drill. Tabitha Huck deployed a network of floating sensors at various levels in Qronha 3's cloud decks. The results of their probes suggested that the dormant enemy warglobes lurking deep within the clouds might not be as dead as they seemed to be.

No amount of preparation could make them completely ready when the hydrogue attack finally came. And it was coming. Sullivan was sure of it.

In the last hours of darkness, unable to sleep, he stood on the chilly observation deck and looked down into the clouds. The air that penetrated the atmosphere-condensing field smelled strange tonight, with a crackle of static energy that prickled the fine hairs on his arms. He and the green priest made a habit of spending an hour or so together before sunrise, watching the distant lights of the Ildiran sky-harvesting city as it sought hydrogen-rich updrafts.

Kolker cradled his precious treeling, always wearing a preoccupied smile as he listened to a background conversation that no one else could hear. Sullivan didn't mind; he felt no need to be talking all the time.

The cloud harvester had sent another ekti shipment back to the Hansa. Under his management, the facility was even more productive than the most optimistic projections. He had received congratulatory messages from King Peter and Chairman Wenceslas, and his wife Lydia had informed him that the extraordinary bonuses were going to put all the grandchildren through college.

Things were going well.

In the darkness, Sullivan saw an unexpected whirlpool form in the bottomless sea beneath the harvester's trailing whisker sensors. Beside him, Kolker stared into the churning soupy mists as a knot of lightning skittered through the storm's gaping mouth.

"I don't like the look of this," Sullivan said. In the expanse of clouds separating the Hansa facility and the Ildiran complex, more bursts of lightning erupted.

The door from the control deck behind them whisked open. Tabitha came running out, her face pale. "Sullivan! We've got major activity on the sensors—"

Directly below the observation deck, the thick clouds spread apart, like Moses parting the Red Sea. Tabitha skidded to a halt as all three of them caught their breath in awe. The green priest gripped his treeling, as if it were an anchor.

Electrical bolts traced lines from cloudbank to cloudbank, eerily silent except for muffled, delayed thunder from far below. Then, like legendary leviathans heaving themselves into open air, six enormous warglobes rose through the nightside ocean. Even from a distance, Sullivan could see sparks of blue-white power that crackled from the diamond hulls.

Tabitha could not tear her eyes from the looming diamond spheres that continued to ascend, growing larger every second. Sullivan grabbed her arm. "Snap out of it! They're not coming for a social call, and we've got to save the crew!"

Running so fast that she nearly stumbled, Tabitha charged back into the control center. Loud alarms shrieked through the decks of the cloud harvester. Men and women off-shift staggered out of their cabins, bleary-eyed and half dressed, but they did not question what was happening. Sullivan had never played tricks on them with surprise drills; they knew this was the real thing.

Leaving the green priest out on the observation deck, chattering a desperate report to his treeling, Sullivan charged into the control center. Tabitha and three coworkers stood by display screens and a sectional diagram of the facility. Sirens and buzzers rattled the metal walls.

From the day of its deployment, Sullivan had understood that his cloud harvester was probably doomed. His crewmen scrambled to evacuate, and Sullivan was glad to see so many of them automatically following the procedures. Through the wide window, he watched more of the deadly warglobes emerge from the clouds. The deep-core aliens had no need to hurry.

"We're screwed," Tabitha said.

During drills, the crew usually took half an hour to complete the evacuation procedures, but with their lives really on the line, they might find an extra burst of speed. Sullivan prayed they would have enough time before the warglobes began a full-scale attack.

74 ☀ JESS TAMBLYN

After guiding his water-and-pearl ship across the vast emptiness for several days, Jess approached Plumas, viewing the system through the liquid curves of his vessel. Vivid memories fueled an energy inside his heart that had nothing to do with the power of the wentals.

Home. It was a concept that even Roamers clung to.

Jess had grown up with his older brother and younger sister in the sheltered settlement under the frozen crust. He'd worked every day, learning the family water business, prepared to follow tradition. Plumas had a huge reservoir of liquid water and a shallow gravity well for easy transfer to Roamer ships. The demand would never diminish, and the Tamblyn clan's Guiding Star seemed bright and clear and strong.

Who could have guessed that Jess's family and their future would unravel like poorly stitched embroidery on a clan jumpsuit?

His mother had been killed on Plumas almost twenty years ago, her body forever frozen in a deep crevasse. The Tamblyn clan had moved forward, prospering and unified, until Ross and their father parted ways in a harsh falling-out, leaving Jess in the middle of so much friction. He should have done more to bring them together again. He'd waited for a good opportunity, assuming he would have time after tempers died down. No one had imagined that hydrogues existed, much less that they might rise up from the clouds to destroy Ross's Blue Sky Mine.

Another few threads unraveling . . .

Jess had been there to comfort his father, but old Bram had died of grief. Then his sister had run off to join the Eddies and fight the hydrogues. These days, the EDF was attacking Roamer settlements instead. What was Tasia doing?

More and more frayed threads . . .

His four uncles ran the water mines, while Jess and his fourteen volunteer water bearers went about their vital mission, spreading the wentals to empty worlds, to the clouds of Golgen, to a spectacular living comet cruising across space. The elemental beings grew stronger and stronger, preparing for their ultimate conflict. Soon, the battle would be engaged.

Despite the flood of alien energy within him, Jess could

not forget that he was still human. He still loved Cesca and longed to be with her. He wanted to know where his sister was, hoping she was still alive among the Eddies. He wanted to *do* something to help his people, his family. Otherwise, what did these wental powers benefit him?

The exotic spherical ship hovered above the glacial surface of the ice moon, and Plumas filled his view like a polished opal. Jess looked down at the wellheads and pumping stations surrounded by igloo-style hangars, large watertanker ships for delivering supplies to settlements, and elevator passages that descended to the subcrustal settlement.

Staring through his ship's filmy hull of contained water, Jess remembered every hillock, every block of ice down there. When they were younger, he and Ross had driven across the landscape in insulated rovers. The two brothers had been reckless in the low gravity, gaining too much speed, jumping narrow fissures, crunching vacuum-stretched icicles that oozed out of pressure joints in the crust. Even after so many years, the jittering tracks of their vehicles were still visible as sketch lines. Back then, carefree times had seemed the normal way of things.

Jess set his wental vessel down on the floor of a crater, coming to rest near a trio of large-bore wellheads. The water-mine workers would have sounded alarms down below. He was sure by now that his uncles would know what had happened to him. They must have heard of the speech he had given to the gathered clans at Rendezvous.

Rendezvous . . . which was now no more than drifting rubble, thanks to the brutality of the Earth Defense Forces. Should he not use his newfound abilities to make a difference for his people, as his water bearers had demanded? Imagine what would happen if he landed his exotic wental ship in front of the

Whisper Palace on Earth. Would the Hansa Chairman finally see reason?

But the wentals would not allow him to focus on a feud among humans. It had been difficult enough to convince them to come here. Jess had finally made the wentals understand about heartstrings and family and obligations.

When his ship rested like a teardrop on the ground, Jess pressed against the curved membrane. The impenetrable film puckered around him like a kiss, and he passed through. Standing out on the frozen surface, Jess wore only the tight white singlesuit that left his hands and feet bare. His body crackled with power from the wentals within his cells, protecting him. He turned his face to the shatteringly cold vacuum, able to gaze upon the open majesty of space in a way that no other human had ever done.

Home.

Through the soles of his feet, he could sense the thrumming industry beneath the kilometer-thick ceiling of ice. He smiled as he recalled his irascible old dad. Bram Tamblyn had been a stern leader, demanding hard work and absolute diligence from his family and his employees. Jess called to mind one of his father's favorite sayings: *A true member of our family, a true water miner, needs to have ice water in his veins.*

Faint vapors lifted into the air: carbon dioxide and water molecules volatilizing into the vacuum and hovering near the crater bottom like fog. Plumas's low gravity could not hold on to the gases for long before they evaporated into space.

He walked to a sheet of smooth black ice that had been melted and refrozen from tidal stresses. He spread his feet and closed his eyes, calling upon the wentals, water to water in an elemental synchronicity. Raising his hands overhead like a diver, he sank through the ice without a ripple. He descended, like a spirit on an intangible elevator, through layer after layer, until finally he plunged through the curved ceiling to the vault far below and dropped into the ancient, cold sea. The water enfolded him.

The leaden sea around him contained life of its own, and the wentals held themselves inside his body. They did not flow out of him to infiltrate Plumas as they had done on the comet, adhering to their agreement not to taint an inhabited world. They could have possessed all this water, sweeping through the subcrustal ocean. But they did not, leaving the ice moon to the Tamblyns.

Jess allowed his entire body to rise to the surface, then made his way toward the icy shore where domes, huts, and storage shacks formed his clan's main settlement. *Home.*

The workforce here ranged from fifty to a hundred Roamers, most of them related in one way or another to the Tamblyn clan. The well-rounded staff members were trained in numerous skills beyond their specific assigned duties as mechanics, administrators, architects, handymen, transport pilots, ice drillers, cleaners, and cooks.

He smiled as he walked to solid land, an ice shelf bordering the cold underground sea. Jess had grown up here in an enclosed world with a ceiling of artificial sunlight. When at the age of twelve he had finally traveled with his father to see Rendezvous, he had never imagined anything so vast and crowded. He had seen Cesca, just a glimpse, when she was beginning her schooling under the old Speaker Okiah.

Now he spread his hands, drinking in the atmosphere, the water, the environment of Plumas. Droplets of the prehistoric ocean dripped off him and froze in puddles on the ground. Steam rose from his hair and shoulders as his body's own power dried him.

Three of his uncles came out of their huts in the business complex of the mining settlement. His uncle Caleb wasn't with them. Wynn, Torin, and Andrew couldn't believe what they were seeing. "Jess! Jess, is that you?"

The twins looked at each other. Andrew, the quietest uncle, sighed happily. "Ah, boy, it's good to have you back—even if we heard you're not quite human anymore."

Jess smiled reassuringly, accustomed to that reaction by now. "I'm still the same person inside." His voice carried as if artificially amplified.

Wynn scratched gray stubble on his chin. "Shizz, Jess, you fly in here in a giant water bubble, and then you stroll across the surface in hard vacuum without a suit on! You just melted yourself through a kilometer of ice and landed here without so much as a goose bump or ruffled hair."

"Doesn't exactly sound like a normal human to me," said his twin, Torin.

"Me either," said Andrew, who was in charge of finances and accounting at the Tamblyn water mines. "We watched you on the wellhead cameras."

Jess smiled, and his skin tingled with a faintly visible aura. "Maybe I was showing off a little bit. The wentals allow me to do many things that must seem strange."

Wynn and Torin, wearing skeptical frowns, sat beside each other on a cold block of ice. Insulated suits kept them warm, though Wynn clenched and unclenched his hands to keep the blood circulating in the chill air. Around them among the mining huts, many workers peered out with cautious curiosity, staying away from the strange manifestation of Bram Tamblyn's only surviving son.

"Have you heard anything from Tasia?" Jess asked.

"No. Who knows how the Eddies have brainwashed her by now?" Wynn said. "We thought you might bring some news."

"I haven't been close to people much."

Andrew retreated to the administrative shelter and returned in a moment with a chairpad for himself and a thermal bottle of pepperflower tea along with four cups. He sat on his chairpad, while the twins pretended to be comfortable on their frozen lump. Andrew poured a cup of the steaming, spicy beverage and extended it to Jess. "If you're going to stand there looking all sparkly, you'd better tell us your full story. Here, have a hot drink."

Jess did not touch the cup. "That's not necessary, Uncle Andrew."

"We've got a lot stronger stuff, if you prefer, Jess," Torin offered. "We distill it ourselves."

"I'll tell you my story . . . but the wentals provide everything I need." He briefly described how he had sifted the wentals from water molecules strewn across a nebula, how he began to communicate with them, how he seeded them on empty ocean worlds, and how, when the hydrogues destroyed his ship above an alien sea, the wentals penetrated his cells and kept him alive, while changing him forever.

Wynn blew out a long breath that emerged as a plume from his nostrils. "Those supernatural wental things you've got inside you, Jess—the ones you're spreading around to other water worlds?—I'm not sure we want them living inside Plumas. I don't care if you call them beings or ghosts or elementals or aliens."

"They *are* enemies of the hydrogues," Andrew pointed out.

Torin seemed just as concerned. "Even so, we're trying to run a business here."

"Don't worry—I wouldn't do anything to jeopardize the water mines," Jess said. "The wentals have agreed not to release themselves. They altered *me* fundamentally, in a similar way to how the worldtrees change a person into a green priest. I am fundamentally changed, charged, but they will not do so again. It was a conscious decision on their part, to save my life because I was the only one who knew about them. Here on Plumas, though, they will keep themselves separate, just like the worldtrees on Theroc."

"What do the worldtrees have to do with it?"

"The verdani are elemental beings, much like the wentals—and the faeros, and the hydrogues. I can't even begin to explain the incredible war that took place ten thousand years ago." He shook his head. "But the wentals were nearly exterminated, as were the worldtrees. The hydrogues retreated to the cores of gas-giant planets, and the faeros hid inside the stars."

"And now they're all awake again and at each other's throats." Torin snorted. "Lucky us."

"I didn't come to saturate Plumas with wentals," Jess said. "There are plenty of other places for them to spread. I flew here for other reasons—the most important of which was to see my home and my family again."

Andrew looked relieved by these reassurances and stood up from his chairpad, as if ready to return to his work. He seemed to think all matters had been discussed and decided upon.

"After hearing you talk, boy, I'd give you a hug, if I could," Wynn said, "but it doesn't sound like that would be a smart thing to do."

"No, that wouldn't be smart at all." Jess formed a smile, and his watery blue gaze became distant. "But now that the wentals have changed me, I'll be able to accomplish something here that I've wanted to do for a long time."

75 ☀ PRINCE DANIEL

After a few days on his own, Daniel was no longer so enamored with freedom.

He was hungry. He had no place to sleep and no friends to contact. Every place he went, he imagined that the Chairman's agents were hunting for him. As discreetly as possible, he watched news loops, searching for announcements of the Prince's disappearance. He had assumed the Hansa would offer a substantial reward for his safe return. But he heard no mention of his escape—nothing! As far as the public knew, Prince Daniel was still happily ensconced in his royal quarters in the Whisper Palace.

By now he looked dirty and rumpled, and there were small tears in his clothes. Though he hated to admit it, he would have welcomed even a plate of the annoyingly wholesome food OX had inflicted upon him. He didn't like this at all.

Out of desperation, he worked his way through the streets to the neighborhood where he had once lived with his stepfather and slutty sister. He hadn't regretted leaving them, but they might help him out. He couldn't wait to brag to his sister about where he'd been for the past year, rub her nose in the fact that he was the Hansa's new Prince.

But when he arrived at the familiar block, he discovered that the entire building where he had lived was gone. The dwelling complex had been torn down and replaced with a commercial structure full of offices and shops.

He had to be careful not to show too much curiosity, since Chairman Wenceslas must surely be watching this place. Trying to act casual, he asked an old woman what had happened to the people who lived there.

She shrugged. "Evicted, I think. Health hazards, some kind of epidemic. Quite a few people died, and everyone else was turned out onto the street."

Unsettled, Daniel walked away without thanking her. In a daze, he remembered an occasion not long ago when King Peter had barged into the Prince's chambers claiming that the Hansa had killed Daniel's family. At the time it had seemed little more than an outrageous bluff, a scare tactic.

Now Daniel wasn't so sure.

At night, with hunger gnawing at his stomach, he crept up to a small grocery distribution center, smashed a window, then reached in to unlock the door, so he could slip inside to where boxes of food sat surrounded by shadows. He didn't have a plan; he simply grabbed the first edible items he could find—crackers and a tube of tart jam—and began gorging himself.

When he moved deeper into the grocery area, searching for food he could take with him, he heard a rattle and a slam behind him. Automatic guard gates locked into place over the broken entrance. He ran to the gate, but could find no way out. He must have triggered a silent alarm.

While waiting for the local police force to arrive, a resigned Daniel spent his time eating as much as possible.

When he heard the security vehicles and saw uniformed men emerge, he arranged an indignant look on his face. "What took you so long?" he said, mustering as commanding a tone as he could remember from the statesmanship lessons OX had given him. "I am testing the security of my Hansa. Professional thieves could have cleaned out this place in the meantime."

Unsympathetic, the police came toward him with their twitchers drawn. Daniel remained indignant. "I am Prince Daniel. Don't you recognize me?"

They didn't. Nor did they believe him.

Only moments after the police response, bleary-eyed news reporters arrived, taking images of the arrest in progress for a bland local report. Daniel began struggling and bellowing that he was the Prince, to the amusement of the reporters.

Finally, the policemen used their twitchers, firing a burst that scrambled nerve communication. Daniel dropped immediately, unable to control his voluntary muscles; he remained completely conscious, embarrassed while he flopped about harmlessly. He had never been stunned before.

Still twitching and fighting the effects, the young man was hauled away and transported to a massive blocky building, where he was imprisoned with other miserable-looking and surly suspects. No amount of shouting and petulant demands brought the police to see him.

The following morning, a broad-shouldered, neatly

dressed man arrived, whom Daniel recognized as Franz Pellidor, one of the Chairman's special assistants. "I am the boy's uncle," Pellidor said to one of the administrators in the police station. "I'm afraid he's quite deluded. He must have succeeded in hiding his medication again. I apologize. Our family will pay for any damages and all necessary fines, of course."

Pellidor's grip was like an iron vise around the runaway's arm as he led the boy out.

"All right, I'm sorry," Daniel pouted. "I've learned my lesson. Just take me back to the Palace. I have to admit I'm glad to see you."

Pellidor looked into the Prince's face with an expression of sheer contempt. "You will not be so glad when you see Chairman Wenceslas."

76 ☀ SULLIVAN GOLD

The hydrogues hit Qronha 3 everywhere at once.

Warglobes shot up through the clouds, trailing mist behind them. Like the cracking of a lion tamer's whip, alien weapons ripped across the skies. The initial blasts missed the modular cloud harvester and ricocheted off ionic layers in the atmosphere.

The warglobes continued to rise all around them like

alarm buoys. The next blast tore open the bottom of one of
the facility's ekti reactors, splitting the curved hull and
spilling unstable gases and catalysts. The venting vapors
acted like an uncertain rocket jet, making the cloud harvester rock and sway.

As the evacuation continued, Sullivan yelled into the intercom system that linked the facility's modules. "You've
got every reason in the world to panic, but please don't do it
now. We've drilled for this situation over and over. Everybody, go to your assigned evac modules and get out of here.
I am declaring this cloud harvester officially abandoned."

Cloud miners raced down corridors, climbed ladders, and
ran across decks to get to the dozens of self-contained rescue modules. As explosions thundered through the vast sky,
Sullivan forced himself to stay focused on what they needed
to do.

He called back to the green priest who stood reeling on
the observation deck. "Does the EDF have any ships in the
neighborhood?"

The green priest shouted at his treeling, as if his raised
voice would transmit better through telink. He hammered his
desperate thoughts through the worldforest network, informing the Terran Hanseatic League, the Earth Defense Forces,
and everyone still on Theroc. He turned to look at Sullivan.
"The EDF is going to send their ships immediately—but they
can't get here sooner than a day, maybe two or three."

"Great. We appreciate the gesture, but this will all be over
by then." He took the green priest's arm. "Come on, Kolker,
we have to get to our own stations. I promised Lydia that I
wouldn't take any unnecessary risks."

Running beside him on the open top deck, the green
priest struggled to carry his potted treeling.

The warglobes blasted again, and the whole cloud mine shook. More explosions erupted from the lower decks. Sullivan had no idea how much damage had already been done, but he knew the hydrogues would not stop their assault until the cloud harvester had burned up in the gas giant's atmosphere.

Before he and the green priest could reach the edge of the observation deck, two more warglobes fired, igniting one of the half-full storage tanks of stardrive fuel. The shockwave rippling through the structure of the facility destroyed two of the massive suspension engines. Without the levitation fields, the deck suddenly tilted at a sickening angle.

Kolker stumbled and began to slide toward the open edge.

Without thought for his own safety, Sullivan dove to rescue the green priest. Kolker scrambled for purchase, clawing with his hands—and let go of his potted treeling. The slender offshoot of the worldforest tumbled down the steep-angled deck. Its ornate pot cracked and then shattered.

Forgetting himself, the green priest lunged for it. "No!"

Sullivan seized a support railing with his left hand. At the same time his right hand shot out and caught the green priest by his naked ankle.

Beseeching, Kolker stretched out his hand, trying to elongate himself—but the treeling spilled over the edge of the cloud harvester and out into the open atmosphere—falling . . . falling.

Kolker stared after it, his eyes round with horror and disbelief, as if he had just lost one of his children. The treeling looked tiny as it dwindled to an insignificant speck against the vast battleground in the sky.

Somehow the hydrogues saw it. In a purely spiteful

gesture, a warglobe unleashed a blast that vaporized the treeling into a smear of ash that drifted on the angry winds.

Clamping his grip tighter around Kolker's ankle, Sullivan sweated and strained, but the green priest simply stared as he dangled, open-mouthed and silent in despair at being completely cut off from the worldforest.

Detonations continued beneath the cloud harvester. The unstable complex began to wobble, swaying through a pendulum swing. As the observation deck became more level, Sullivan saw his chance. Before the wounded cloud harvester could tip in the other direction, he hauled Kolker back to safety. "Come on, snap out of it! We have to get out of here!"

"But my tree—"

"Nothing you can do about that now, and I'm not going to let you just sit here." He dragged the green priest to his feet, and they raced off to the command decks where the supervisory personnel had already loaded themselves into the escape modules.

"Let's go!" Sullivan pushed Kolker ahead of him through the hatch, then prepared to seal the module door behind him. He scanned the people crowded in the interior. "Have you taken attendance? Is everyone in place?"

"Module seven is missing three," said his supervisor.

Crammed into a corner, Tabitha Huck looked down at her screen. "Module four has an extra two."

"Are we full?" Sullivan asked.

"We've got the required complement, but we could fit another dozen or so if somebody else's module is damaged."

"I didn't see anybody up on the command deck, but we'll give 'em thirty more seconds." Another explosion rocked the structure. "Tell everyone else to launch."

Everything about the evacuation had looked good on

paper, but now the greatest question remained: Once all the modules disengaged and flew away, would the hydrogues follow them? The evacuation modules couldn't hope to outrun a warglobe.

Kolker sat with his knees drawn up to his chest, looking utterly miserable, a green priest without a tree. "No one will know what's happening now. All contact has been cut off. They'll think we're dead."

Sullivan tried to sound encouraging, "You sent out the alarm in time, Kolker. The EDF knows. But we've got to get ourselves out of here." He glanced at his chronometer. "Time's up. Let's launch."

They held on as their escape module broke free from the doomed cloud harvester. The crude vessel rocketed away from the attacking hydrogues. Around them, other self-propelled and autonomous escape vessels launched like spores from a mushroom.

As the module rattled and vibrated, Sullivan peered through the port. Below, the hydrogues continued to attack the remnants of the sky facility.

"They don't seem to be pursuing us, Sullivan," said Tabitha. "Not yet." A sigh of relief, then a shudder of delayed terror passed through the refugees.

As the escape module rotated in its ascent, Sullivan got a good view across the ocean of clouds to the much larger Ildiran sky-harvesting city. The hydrogues were brutally dismantling Hroa'x's facility as well, surrounding the immense platform and opening fire. Already, smoke and flames gushed from myriad breaches in the other complex's hull.

"The Ildirans are under attack too," Sullivan called. "But their design didn't allow for the escape and rescue of their crew. They're all going to die."

Inside the evacuation module, his companions grumbled with anxiety. The green priest looked up at Sullivan, his misery increasing. "Hroa'x said there wasn't anything he could do," Kolker said.

"Ildirans won't modify their older designs. They don't plan ahead." Sullivan scrutinized his comrades in the escape module; the rest of the autonomous vessels also had plenty of room for other passengers.

He made a decision, knowing he'd never hear the end of it from Lydia. "I'm not going to let them all die. We've got the means to do something about it."

His people looked at him in disbelief. Tabitha spoke for all of them. "You're not actually going back down there!"

"We all are." He turned to the communications officer. "Open a channel to the Ildiran skymine, if anybody's listening. Tell Hroa'x we're on our way. I want all our modules to rally. We're going to rescue as many Ildirans as we can. We can make a difference."

Kolker's look of amazement gradually transformed into something akin to respect. He gave a faint nod.

"But Sullivan . . ." Tabitha said, aghast. "We can't take that risk."

"I don't see that we have any other choice."

General Lanyan sent a direct EM transmission from the lunar base to the sixty clustered rammers out in the asteroid field. "All right, it's showtime!"

Thanks to the instantaneous communication from the green priest Kolker, the EDF knew about the hydrogue assault on Qronha 3 while the attack was still happening. As Tasia and her fellow dunsels snapped to attention at temporary training stations, she found herself thinking of how Ross had never had a chance to call for help when the hydrogues obliterated his Blue Sky Mine. . . .

Lanyan's message continued, wasting no time. His hard face wore an eager smile. "The rammer fleet is parked, fueled, and waiting. We've been looking for someone to slug, and the drogues have finally shown themselves. It'll be like cracking a few eggs with a whole bunch of sledgehammers. This is what the six of you have been waiting for. Now get going."

Tasia and her companions shouted in response, though it would be almost an hour of signal delay before Lanyan heard them back at the Moon base. As the other five dunsels prepared to depart, she ran to get EA.

The sixty rammers launched in less than an hour. Practically speaking, Tasia knew they would not get to the gas giant before the drogues finished their job. But rescuing the miners wasn't the primary thrust of this operation.

Since her rank was highest, Tasia was in charge of the overall mission, with the other dunsels responsible for ten rammers each. She stood on the bridge beside her quiet compy. Though the small Listener could do little of the technical work compared to all the burly Soldier compies manning the stations, EA was a reminder of her home and her upbringing. Soldier models required neither personality programming nor conversational skills, but they would follow Tasia's orders precisely, and that was all that mattered. EA, at least, could offer a little moral support and be good for some conversation along the way.

The heavily armored warships accelerated above the ecliptic and prepared their faster-than-light stardrives. Qronha 3 was deep in Ildiran territory, not far from the alien capital world. Tasia didn't concern herself with trespassing into Ildiran space: If this military action succeeded, she doubted the Mage-Imperator would complain. And if the rammer ships failed, Tasia wouldn't be in a position to worry about it.

Mission briefing data streamed to their ships even as they departed, and Tasia reviewed the details of the attack. All telink signals from the green priest had cut off, and the modular cloud harvester was already presumed destroyed. Though the Hansa facility had been active for less than a year, it had produced a respectable amount of ekti, enough to pay for its construction twice over . . . but not the lives of the crew. The Hansa skyminers had escape systems in place—identical to the ones on these rammers. Even so, Tasia assumed that all personnel had been lost.

Just like on so many Roamer skymines . . .

She turned to her Listener compy. "EA, remember when we went to Golgen? You and I sneaked away from the water mines, so we could visit Ross after he got the Blue Sky Mine up and running."

EA paused. "Yes, that description was in your diary files, Tasia Tamblyn. You admired your brother Ross very much."

"Right. And the drogues killed him. *That's* why we're here." Since EA was merely recalling a data summary and not an actual memory, Tasia let the conversation drop and kept the rest of her thoughts to herself. After this mission she would get her command back . . . supposedly. Then she would show the Eddies what this war was really about.

Tasia knew the Soldier compies had no need for a pep talk, but she felt a desire to give one. So she contacted the other dunsel commanders just before they engaged their stardrives. There was just enough time for her to give them a bit of encouragement and fire them up for the impending battle.

"I've taken a lot of flack from the EDF because I grew up among the Roamer clans. Do you have any idea how many Roamer skymines the drogues wiped out? My brother was one of their first victims. I joined the EDF to fight back. Because I'm both a Roamer and an EDF officer, I've got a bigger axe to grind than anyone I know."

She crossed her arms over her chest. "My other brother Jess joined the fight by sending a couple dozen comets flying like nuclear bombs into Golgen. We don't know how many hydrogues he destroyed, but I'm guessing it was quite a few. Today I plan to continue that family tradition. How about you? Are you ready to wipe out some hydrogues?"

The five token commanders responded with enthusiastic acknowledgments. If Tasia expected any grumbling about her heritage, she got nothing. The dunsels only offered support, and she decided they must be good soldiers after all, no matter what black marks might be on their service records.

She smiled. "We have at our command some of the best

weapons in the human arsenal. We are the only ones entrusted with this responsibility. Now, the drogues already got their butts kicked at Qronha 3 once, and I'm surprised they had the balls to show up there again. But they came back for more, so let's go give them more."

Giving the order to engage the stardrive, she looked around the rammer's bridge at the Soldier compies that stood ready to do their duty. They worked the controls, activated the powerful engines, and lurched the battering-ram vessels across the gulf of space.

78 ☀ MAGE-IMPERATOR JORA'H

The battle between hydrogues and faeros on Durris-B ended eight days after the Ildirans first noticed the stellar conflict. The besieged yellow star flickered, struggled . . . and finally collapsed into a dark sun, its nuclear fires extinguished.

Never in more than ten millennia of recorded Ildiran history had such an epochal event occurred. Only two stars remained of the Durris trinary, a white star and a red dwarf now orbiting a black stellar cinder. The people in Mijistra stared into the sky, terrified.

"Osira'h will depart immediately," Mage-Imperator Jora'h commanded. All across the Empire, the *thism* was singing with danger. Like distinct fires erupting in a sweeping forest, bright and painful outbursts of panic clamored for his attention.

Seeing the blot in the sky from the windows of the Prism Palace, he pushed aside all hesitation, all uncertainty about his youngest daughter and her special abilities. Osira'h had to open a direct line of communication with the hydrogues before they annihilated the Ildiran Empire. No one else was capable of it, now that the Klikiss robots had betrayed them.

On his orders late the previous day, Yazra'h had loaded the pressure vessel aboard one of seven warliners. They were ready to take Osira'h to her destination. Shortly thereafter, Tal O'nh had announced that his cohort of battleships was also prepared and awaited the Mage-Imperator for their departure to Hyrillka. Everything was happening at once. At last.

Carrying an assortment of weapons and accompanied by her Isix cats, Yazra'h stalked into the skysphere reception hall. Little Osira'h, barely half the height of her oldest sister, followed her.

Osira'h stopped before the dais and waited in silence. When the Mage-Imperator saw her, his chest ached with all the hopes he had invested in this child. Only the day before, after making his final decision, he had called the girl to spend an hour with him up on the highest tower platform of the Prism Palace. Together, they had gazed out at the majesty of Ildira. Air traffic flew in an intricate dance overhead, while below them the seven streams fanned out from the Palace's hill like the spokes of a wheel, and a line of pilgrims, made tiny by distance, moved along in an unending thread.

He had tried to express to the girl how much he had loved

her mother, but even a Mage-Imperator found some things too difficult to communicate. Oddly enough, Osira'h showed little surprise at anything he told her. Jora'h wondered what Udru'h had said to her about Nira. Nothing kind, he was sure.

If she survived, if she succeeded and returned, the Mage-Imperator promised himself he would do much better for this amazing child who stood at the base of his dais. Now there was no time. With each passing hour he received new and disturbing vibrations through the *thism,* and he could not delay his daughter's crucial mission to the fresh stellar corpse of Durris-B. But before he could send Osira'h on her dangerous journey, a messenger ran shouting into the sky-sphere hall.

"Mage-Imperator, the hydrogues are attacking our cloud harvester on Qronha 3. We just received a desperate signal from Chief Miner Hroa'x. The destruction has only just begun, but our facility will surely be destroyed!"

Pushing himself up out of his chrysalis chair, Jora'h addressed Yazra'h and Osira'h with new urgency. "Then you must go *there,* rather than the dead sun. We have an obligation to defend our cloud-harvesting city, and since the hydrogues have chosen to strike us again on Qronha 3, that is where we will meet them." He placed his strong hands on the girl's small shoulders. "Osira'h you must get through to the enemy before they destroy us all. Bring them to me, whatever it takes. Let me speak with them so that I can somehow make peace."

Guards and bureaucrats swirled around Osira'h and whisked her away toward the warliners. Jora'h stared after the girl, and his hopes went with her.

This was a day of great changes and momentous events.

He had sent his daughter to her destiny, and it was time to deal with Hyrillka. *Now*. Several whole worlds were already lost. Enough! He could no longer tolerate this blindness in the *thism*.

Today was also the Dobro Designate's deadline to face Rusa'h.

"Summon Tal O'nh," he called. "We depart for Dobro within the hour. And we must hope that Designate Udru'h has done his part."

79 ☀ CELLI

The Beneto golem led Celli and Solimar along wide paths where Roamer heavy machinery had removed the wrecked tree hulks. Celli grabbed Solimar's hand, and the three of them went deeper into the charred and splintered wasteland.

"Are you ready for this, Solimar?" she whispered. "Whatever it is?"

He kept walking. "Whatever it is. I'm sure the worldforest has its reasons for picking the two of us."

"*I* selected you, not the worldforest," Beneto said. "You are the two most suitable, and I hope you can get a message across, something the trees need to hear."

Celli looked at Solimar, whose gaze reflected his confusion. "Well," she said, "*that* explains everything."

Beneto strode onward, full of purpose. She watched his wooden body move like flesh, reminded of a legendary forest spirit from the old fairy tales that novice green priests read aloud to the trees.

The three arrived at a glen that showed damage worse than in any other area Celli had seen in a long while. The golem spread his arms directly out to his sides, then splayed his fingers like the twigs at the end of a long branch. "Despite what you see around you, this glen retains some of the deep energy of the worldforest. The true power of the verdani percolates close to the surface here." He leaned closer to them, his wood-grain eyes intense. "You can help draw it out."

Solimar's brow furrowed, as if he wasn't sure what he was expected to do.

Celli was even more confused. "Can you be more specific than that? Remember, I'm not even a green priest."

"But you are *human*. That is the strength we need now." Beneto lowered his arms and stepped back. "Force the trees to realize that they are not dead, that it would be folly to give up."

"They asked us to take treelings out to other planets. That's not giving up, is it?" Solimar said.

"True," Beneto said, "but the worldforest itself is resigned to defeat here on Theroc. It knows that the hydrogues may return at any time. Yet the older trees contain a deep power, and you must convince them to call it forth. Do not let them surrender."

Celli put her hands on her narrow hips. "And how are we supposed to do that?"

"By treedancing."

Solimar and Celli looked skeptically at the wooden

golem. All around them, the air still smelled of smoke and dead trees. "As simple as that? Really?"

Beneto continued, "The trees sensed something in you two when you moved here before, when you danced. You can make the verdani *remember*."

Solimar asked, "Do you mean like some sort of ritual?"

"You're kidding!" Celli snapped a blackened twig from a small tree; the wood was charred through. "By dancing in the ashes?"

"No, by being alive, by demonstrating joyfulness and hope." Beneto turned his shoulders, swiveling his head to take in the ruined landscape. "I am a manifestation of the worldforest, but I am also human. My human aspect understands a determination that the verdani do not.

"Think of what they are. The interconnected worldtrees are rooted to the ground and have always accepted what came to them. They are strong and patient, but they do not remember how to fight. They resist only by attempting to withstand whatever comes against them. They are passive. Humans are not.

"When the hydrogues and the faeros were fighting, the trees believed they would all be destroyed. They surrendered here and hoped to survive elsewhere, through the treelings taking root on scattered planets."

Celli brightened as she remembered. "But Reynald wouldn't let them give up! He went to the canopy with two green priests, and he yelled at the trees until they fought back!"

Beneto nodded. "Reynald forced the verdani to reach for depths of their power that they had not previously used. The worldtrees had never considered standing up in a hopeless cause, but our brother made them take an active role in their defense. Though the battle was indeed a disastrous loss to

Theroc, the hydrogues were driven off, and the worldforest is still alive here."

He touched an ash-smeared hand to the shoulders of Celli and Solimar. "You must do the same thing now. These burned and damaged trees realize the hydrogues will come back here to finish the destruction. They are content to know that their treelings have been dispersed and will survive. But you cannot let them abandon Theroc."

Celli sniffed. "Even a hopeless cause is still a *cause*. Fighting for it is better than just rolling over."

"Exactly. You two, do as Reynald did—show them human joy and drive and persistence. The verdani know these things as part of their reservoir of stored knowledge, but they do not *understand* them."

Solimar looked up at the burned branches. "And tree-dancing will do it?"

"The verdani comprehend that in a different way. Through many generations, a connection has developed between the worldforest and the Theron people—even those who are not green priests. The connection with our family, in particular, is very strong. That is why our sister Sarein was so affected by the destruction here, even though she did not think she would be. That is why our brother Reynald was able to send such a powerful message to the forest, more than through the two green priests who were with him. That is why I believe you, little sister, and you, Solimar, must help the trees now. As you dance, your delight in the worldtrees can stimulate a response, kindle their potential by coaxing sparks of latent power from the deep roots."

"Sounds like magic," Celli said.

"The power is there, believe me. The verdani fashioned their bodies into the great trees, and they would do so again, in their own good time." Beneto's hollow voice took on a more urgent note. "Inspire them. Make them see that they cannot wait for centuries to recover at their usual sedate pace. We need them now before the hydrogues return."

"I'll second that." Curious, Celli went to a large charcoal-scarred tree. "Here goes."

With her knuckles she cracked a layer of burned bark, peeling away the scorched material until she could touch solid wood. Through her fingers, and even through her bare feet on the ground, Celli sensed the flow of sap, the blood of the earth. The roots went deep, interconnected in a network of forest that extended across the continents. Was this what green priests felt all the time?

Beneto remained as still as a tree, his carved feet pushed hard against the soil. His chest swelled as he took a deep, unnecessary breath, as if squeezing energy from the forest mind up into the surrounding dirt and burned wood.

"Since the hydrogue attack, the worldforest has withdrawn far into the soil, holding its reservoirs safe and sheltered," the tree golem said. "Even so, they responded to the joyful treedancing that you two did where you thought no one could witness it. Draw out that response again, while I am here to guide it. I will use my human awareness to help my verdani heart understand what it needs to know."

Though she stood in the burnt section, Celli could feel the rustle of freshly unfolded leaves drinking in sunlight and nutrients, sensations transmitted from other living sections of the worldforest, oases of vegetation that had survived the onslaught. But those verdant sensations came from far away, isolated patches of surviving wilderness. And in between . . . just numb shock, as if the wounded verdani had fallen into something like a coma.

"It's alive, but it needs to be shaken hard to wake up. Come on, Solimar."

Celli studied the charred debris field, trying to judge which branches and trees would support their weight and where hazards might be hiding. She smiled at Solimar, then took a preparatory breath, ready to go. "I'll start with the Condorfly Mating Dance, then move into Butterfly Pursuit."

Solimar's eyes sparkled. "I'll be right behind you."

They sprang together, doing handstands and graceful leaps until they caught low branches. Swinging himself around, Solimar swept her into his muscular arms and gave her a boost to a higher level.

Celli bounded with a graceful leap like a gazelle. She ricocheted off a thick branch and pushed herself sideways to another blackened trunk, from which she kicked off and spun a triple somersault in the air. She had forgotten how much fun this was. She landed on the ash-encrusted ground again before springing into a second move. Immediately behind her, Solimar continued with his own routine.

Tilting his sculpted chin toward the bright sky, Beneto spread his arms rigidly at his sides, his feet and legs together. "I will demand that they witness." As if turning back into a tree and taking root, he let his feet sink into the soil. "The worldtrees must be made to use their own deep power of rejuvenation and cellular synthesis."

Each time she touched a branch or trunk, Celli felt a spark, like a release of electrical energy, as if she was giving a jolt to the comatose forest. Behind them, Beneto thrust one of his arms *into* a thick tree, fusing to the trunk up past his elbow. His expression was no longer wooden, but straining, yearning. He seemed to be forcing the verdani to watch them.

She kept dancing. Originally, treedance moves had been

crafted to evoke parts of the forest: swaying fronds, flying insects, blossoming flowers. Some of the routines were symbolic of the pollination of epiphytes by beetles, the simultaneous hatching of huge numbers of purple butterfly analogs, the flight of a wyvern. The whole cycle of life in the vast Theron worldforest.

As their exercise reached a dramatic crescendo, Celli watched an amazing thing happen. On the ground where her bare foot had lightly brushed against an exposed worldtree root—where Beneto said the concentrated verdani power lay hidden—a sudden flash of green appeared. As if germinated by the creative power of her movements, a bright new leaf emerged, spun out of dead cells and air. The newborn plant stretched upward.

Solimar caught another branch and swung himself up. He recentered his balance, coiling strength in his thigh muscles, and jumped. Immediately after he leapt, the branch behind him swelled, flaking off black ash and bark until it straightened like an unfurling fist. Reservoirs of energy pumped up from the deep roots into the once-towering tree. Fresh pale green fronds burst from previously unseen buds at the ends of the bough.

On the ground, Beneto "waded" through the soil to a different tree now. He pressed both wooden hands against the black scab of dead bark, then pushed his arms into the core of the thick trunk.

As Celli and Solimar continued to pirouette through the scorched ruins, wherever their feet and hands touched, the wounded worldforest found the energy to reconstruct part of itself. Every place they touched was like a foot splashing into a puddle, spraying *life* instead of water droplets.

The two of them ran and dove in a Theron combination

of ballet and gymnastics, picking up speed. Wherever they passed, their physical movement and their enthusiasm began to heal the worldforest and reawaken life from the scorched death around them. Celli laughed in delight.

Fresh leaves and fronds curled forth. Treelings sprang out of the ground, trembling with the explosive growth. The air smelled moist, spicy, fresh.

Beneto extricated himself from the shuddering tree like a surgeon withdrawing from a deep wound. He called to the dancers. "Life is movement and exhilaration. Through your treedance, you spread that essence of life. Continue! Show the weary trees the meaning of existence again."

At the moment, Celli didn't care about green priest philosophy or explanations. She was enjoying herself too much. All she needed to know was that it was working—for the worldforest, for herself, for Solimar, for Beneto.

She and Solimar danced for hours, heedless of the time passing, barely feeling their own weariness. Finally, as the colors of dusk brushed the Theron sky, the two dancers fell together to the ground in absolute exhaustion, surrounded by miraculous new foliage. Sweaty and soot-smeared, Celli had never felt so deeply satisfied in her life. Solimar put his arm around her and drew her close, then they kissed quickly and surprisingly, a gesture of joy as much as romance.

"You two have done a great thing today." Still knee-deep in the soil, Beneto stopped in front of them. "I hope you will be willing to do it again."

Celli looked around, filled with wonder. To her, it seemed as if the worldforest had taken a deep breath and regained its power. They had thrown a splash of cold water into the weary worldforest's face. She rested her shoulders against Solimar's strong chest. "We could manage that."

Beneto spread his hands out, connecting to the worldforest through telink. He seemed entirely pleased. "Now we are much stronger. The verdani keeps calling, calling, though the message went out long ago. Before long, our help will arrive."

80 ☀ BASIL WENCESLAS

The Chairman didn't take pleasure in such a spectacle, but dammit, Prince Daniel deserved what he was about to face. This behavior had to be nipped in the bud. Immediately. And Peter needed to understand the consequences of his actions even more than his shameful heir apparent did.

Pretending to be supportive, Basil wore his finest slick-fabric suit; his steel-gray hair was perfectly styled and arranged. He wished Sarein could be here at his side right now. She had sent a message that she would soon return. Had she accomplished her mission yet, or had even Sarein let him down? Was there a single person in the Spiral Arm—besides him—who did not drop the ball? Couldn't anybody do the straightforward tasks required of them? No wonder the human race was faltering in this war!

Fighting back his simmering anger, he watched as a very contrite and frightened-looking Daniel faced the crowds and media cameras for the first time. The Prince had obviously been through an ordeal. Even the best makeup could not hide the shadows under his eyes. At last the brat had been broken, whipped into cooperation, though now it was effectively too late. Basil had decided to wash his hands of Daniel, but the Prince could still serve a purpose. His fate could be an effective threat against the too-independent Peter.

The King and Queen, pretending to be well behaved—so smug in their secret about Estarra's pregnancy!—stood in the background, dressed in colorful raiment. They kept glancing at each other in confusion and concern.

"People of the Hansa!" Daniel's voice was watery, shaky. OX had coached the boy over and over again; he should have done better. "I . . . I feel it's time for me to explain."

Basil had hoped their surrogate Prince would shine in his last moment in the limelight. *How could I have made such a grave error in choosing this person?* When they'd been forced to pick a potential replacement for Peter, Basil had been under a great deal of stress. He'd moved too precipitously, and now the Chairman had to backpedal just to implement damage control.

Daniel gathered momentum as his stage fright dissipated. "I choose to remain out of public view so as not to diminish the importance of my dear brother King Peter. He is your leader. Your hopes and prayers ride with him, not me."

Basil flicked his gray eyes to see the surprised expression on Peter's face. Quietly and discreetly, the King squeezed Estarra's hand, as if he honestly thought he could protect her from what the Chairman would have to do.

Daniel continued, "However, some people have taken advantage of the fact that my face is not overly familiar to you. You may have seen news reports of an impostor pretending to be your Prince. That poor deluded young man has been apprehended and will be given the treatment he needs." Daniel fidgeted; makeup hid any evidence of whether or not his face grew pale.

Though Eldred Cain had suggested a toned-down reaction, Basil had dismissed the deputy from his offices and written the speech himself.

"The true King has the vision and leadership to guide the human race through these dark times. He has my support, and I know he has yours." Daniel bowed, presumably thinking it was all over.

The people in the Royal Plaza applauded politely. Peter and Estarra moved up beside the Prince in a show of mutual respect. Cautiously, Basil retreated a few steps to let the "royal family" have all the attention. Images of the well-staged moment would be widely distributed across the Hansa.

Peter shot a glance at the Chairman, his blue eyes narrowed. Basil was sure his puppet King would understand the need for a tighter grip on power, closer observation.

Cain and Pellidor waited in the shadows. The pallid deputy watched in silence, clearly disapproving. Basil decided to ignore him. No one but the Chairman knew what was in the best interests of the human race.

He turned to his expediter. "Now that Daniel has publicly covered his ill-advised stunt, he probably thinks he is forgiven, but our dear Prince couldn't be further from the truth. We can't risk a repeat of this circus. Mr. Pellidor, you know what to do."

Cain looked at him in alarm, but Pellidor gave a crisp nod. "I have already made preparations, Mr. Chairman."

At last, Basil allowed himself a calming smile and

reminded himself of pleasant thoughts. Sarein would be back in another day or so. . . .

81 ☀ ORLI COVITZ

After three days of cooling her heels in the EDF base, Orli was already tired of the Moon. Admiral Stromo was due to return later today with his analysis of the Corribus attack—not that there would be any surprises.

General Lanyan was through with her and Hud Steinman, and the EDF was preparing to send them back to Earth, where they assumed the two wanted to be. Despite extensive database searches, no one had been able to find her mother. Orli didn't know where she would go now or what would happen to her, but she would figure out something. She always did.

In the weeks since the massacre, she had grieved for her father, but at the moment she mostly felt empty and stunned. It would take a long time for her to absorb everything she had lived through. She played music in her borrowed quarters, losing herself for hours in the melodies that flowed from her fingers.

When an EDF soldier led her to the shuttle bay, Steinman was already there waiting. He looked disheveled and dusty, though he'd had ample opportunity to clean himself, shave, and put on fresh clothes. Orli suspected he was just one of those men who always looked rumpled, no matter what he wore or how well he groomed himself.

The old man brightened upon seeing her. "Hey, kid. Somebody on Earth thinks all colonists and refugees are interchangeable. They're throwing us together with those Crenna folks and sending us off to another Klikiss world."

"My dad always told me to appreciate any chance for a fresh start."

"Corribus was the cream of the crop, though." Steinman shook his head. "You can bet the new place won't be as fine."

Orli sat next to him, leaning against the wall. "As long as they send us someplace that doesn't get destroyed again." She put her chin in her hands and heaved a deep sigh. Inside her head, she heard her father's voice chiding her: "Keep your spirits up, girl. Bounce from one place to another. You can't see the stars when you're staring down at your feet."

One time, Jan Covitz had traced her lips with his finger. "See this? When you smile it makes a curve upward, like a cup. You can catch good luck that way. But when you frown"—he tugged her lips downward—"then all the good fortune just slides off and runs down your chin."

Beside her, Steinman continued to chatter. "After all the efforts I've made to get away from big groups of people, my plan backfired on me."

"A lot of things backfired on us. And for Captain Roberts, too. He tried to help us, and look at all the trouble he's gotten into." Orli glanced at the transport that would take them down to Earth. "How long until we leave?"

"We're on a military schedule," Steinman said with a shrug. "We go when they tell us to go, and we wait the rest of the time."

"I need to say goodbye to Captain Roberts." She trotted over to one of the EDF soldiers working in the launch bay and asked to see her friend.

"He's in the brig, uh, ma'am," the soldier said. "I don't believe he's allowed visitors. His military tribunal starts in a few hours."

"It would be just for a minute. Can you check? I'm sure General Lanyan will make an exception." Orli pestered the guard until he submitted a request, which was forwarded to someone else and then a third person before she was finally escorted down to the brig level.

"You only have ten minutes," the guard said gruffly.

"I know. My shuttle leaves soon."

A miserable-looking Captain Roberts sat on his bunk, while a large woman paced the room like a thundercloud on legs. Orli recognized Rlinda Kett, who had flown the *Voracious Curiosity*, taking Orli and her father from Dremen to the transportal hub.

"Of course I remember who you are, young lady," Captain Kett said, returning Orli's greeting with a chuckle. "Considering how things turned out, I wish I hadn't taken you passengers to Rheindic Co. You'd have been better off staying on Dremen."

Orli looked at Roberts's hangdog face, his unkempt frizz of gray hair. "I'm sorry for getting you into so much trouble, Captain."

"Nothing we can do about it, missy." His voice sounded heavy and tired. "And I wouldn't have changed my actions anyway. You'd think they'd show a little gratitude."

"Can I help in any way? Maybe testify about what a good man you are? I could be a—what do they call it?—a character witness."

"He's a character, all right," Rlinda said. "But this military tribunal doesn't play by the rules we know. They're only interested in a particular result, and you can be sure they'll get it."

"I feel like a feather in the backdraft from a starship engine," Roberts said. "Why don't they wait until Admiral Stromo gets back with his report? Once they understand the real emergency, they'll have better things to do."

"I'm really sorry," Orli said again.

"Don't you worry, young lady." Rlinda patted her on the shoulder. "Everything will be all right."

Captain Roberts sat up. "Don't lie to the girl, Rlinda. She's already been through a lot."

Rlinda maintained her stoic smile as she urged Orli off. "It's time for the young lady to go catch her shuttle, BeBob. You and I still have plenty of strategy to discuss."

82 ☀ RLINDA KETT

Less than four days after Branson Roberts's arrest, a rushed board of inquiry convened behind closed doors. Rlinda threatened to handcuff herself to BeBob if they didn't let her into the room with him. Shouldering guards out of her way, she marched into the windowless underground chamber.

BeBob walked toward his seat looking defeated and re-signed to his fate. She nudged him in the ribs, and he stood up straighter.

His assigned legal counsel was sitting at the defense table. The man had met briefly with BeBob twice, mainly to review facts given to him by the EDF. According to Lanyan's admin-istrative memo, there wasn't much need for an actual "trial" because no one disputed the facts of the case.

Rlinda, naturally, disagreed.

She gave the nominal EDF legal counsel no more than a glance as she stepped forward to face Lanyan and two lower-ranking officers. They all wore immaculate uniforms, though there would be no media coverage, yet.

Lanyan frowned. "Ms. Kett, you were not invited to these proceedings."

"I will be acting as the advocate for Captain Branson Roberts." She glared over at the preoccupied military repre-sentative. "And a hell of a lot better one than your sock pup-pet over there. At least I've *listened* to the accused. One would assume that's step one in a defense strategy."

The legal counsel bridled. The two officers at the table chuckled until Lanyan glared at them, and they resumed their professional demeanor.

"This is merely a preliminary hearing, Ms. Kett," Lanyan said.

"That's *Captain* Kett." Rlinda walked to the front of the room. "General, let me remind you of the things *Captain* Roberts has done for the Hansa. You yourself stuck this man on a fishhook and used him as bait to capture the Roamer pirate Rand Sorengaard. Remember that? He risked his life for you."

Lanyan was not ruffled. "You and Captain Roberts benefited from the end of the Sorengaard matter as much as anyone else. Seriously, he can't expect to receive clemency because of something that happened eight years ago."

Without slowing down, Rlinda summarized how most of their private commercial ships had been confiscated and converted to EDF use, how BeBob had been forced to perform dangerous reconnaissance missions against his will, and how, with the blessing of Chairman Wenceslas himself, BeBob had served the Klikiss colonization initiative by shuttling supplies and materials to new settlements, which was how he had discovered the massacre on Corribus.

Out of desperation, Rlinda had again tried to goad the Chairman into taking executive action in BeBob's case. Unfortunately, but not surprisingly, the man would no longer take her calls. BeBob was on his own.

Lanyan was losing patience. "Your reminiscences are irrelevant, Ms. Kett. The incontrovertible fact is that Captain Roberts and his ship were conscripted into vital service for the EDF, and he is therefore under the jurisdiction of military law. He deserted his duties and hid from justice for years. We are at war. We cannot tolerate such behavior from a pilot in the Earth Defense Forces."

One of the other officers added, "More than a hundred deserters like him have abandoned their posts, and as a result our military effectiveness has diminished. We have no option but to make an example of Captain Roberts."

The assigned legal counsel showed no inclination to speak up. Sitting at the table, BeBob decided to talk for himself. "But . . . but you blackmailed me into flying missions for you! You sent me out as cannon fodder. Look what happened to me at Dasra! The hydrogues almost destroyed my ship."

Lanyan's face became very cold. "Don't you dare complain to us about Dasra. Because of our *incomplete* information there, because you didn't finish *your* job, a military survey team and a tactical squadron consisting of more than three hundred personnel were completely wiped out at Dasra."

BeBob lowered his head. "Okay, maybe that wasn't the best example—"

"I'm not sure we need to hear any more." Lanyan's voice held a note of smugness.

Rlinda wondered how hard she'd have to smack the EDF legal counsel to get him to do his job. Frustrated, she stepped forward again. "Does the phrase kangaroo court mean any—"

Lanyan slapped his hand down on the table. "The basic facts are clear and uncontested. Even Captain Roberts does not deny them." He lifted a hand to tick the points off on his fingers. "He was legally conscripted into the Earth Defense Forces. His ship was legally reassigned to serve the EDF. Captain Roberts was allowed to keep flying solely on the condition that he would devote his time to authorized scout missions. Instead, he simply flew off and never came back." His piercing gaze nailed BeBob. "Do you deny any of this?"

"I came back. I'm here now, aren't I?"

Rlinda turned back to the defense table. "Don't say anything, BeBob." She snapped at the legal counsel, "Isn't that what *you're* supposed to advise him?"

The man looked at BeBob without expression. "I thought he could figure that much out for himself."

Lanyan prepared to leave. "I don't see any point in continuing this nonsense today. Admiral Stromo is arriving with his report from Corribus, and I need to speak to him as soon as possible. We can reconvene tomorrow to wrap up anything else, but clearly there's sufficient evidence to proceed with a formal court-martial." He glanced at the other two officers, who nodded.

The General's expression was full of disgust for BeBob. "Once we go public, the Hansa media will paint you as the slime-dripper you really are. I doubt you'll get a lot of sympathy. Chairman Wenceslas has already granted approval for us to seek the death penalty if you're found guilty of desertion. He agrees with the need to crack down on people like you."

BeBob's eyes went wide. "Death penalty?"

Rlinda put her hands on her hips but bit back an outcry. At the table, the legal counsel simply nodded solemnly. "Desertion in a time of war is an offense punishable by death. Has been for centuries."

Lanyan continued in a threatening tone, "However, your past examples of service may be considered mitigating details, along with your rescue of the two survivors from Corribus. Depending on public reaction during the court-martial, King Peter might commute your sentence to permanent penal servitude on an industrial planet." The General smiled. "If he feels generous."

83 ☀ DOBRO DESIGNATE UDRU'H

In order to save his planet from destruction, the Dobro Designate had promised to deliver his answer to Hyrillka in person. Now, like sand slipping through his fingers, time had run out.

Udru'h had to face his rebellious brother alone and do his part; the Mage-Imperator could not assist him in this. Rusa'h had already murdered his legitimate Designate-in-waiting and apparently at least two of Pery'h's brothers; he was not likely to respond well to defiance. Therefore, Udru'h had to formulate his response very carefully. He would lie, he would remain firm . . . and he would find a way to survive. He always did.

En route to the Horizon Cluster, he kept to himself, brooding about what he had agreed to do. Udru'h knew what the Mage-Imperator expected of him. As he approached Hyrillka, the Designate felt as if he were falling off a cliff. The decision was made: He could not rescind it.

As the transport craft approached Hyrillka, several warliners swept out of orbit and surrounded it like a pack of voracious predators hungry for fresh meat. Annoyed, Udru'h went to the pilot deck and sent the message himself. He didn't want any of his twenty-one Ildiran companions to participate in this matter at all. "What is this unnecessary show of force? Allow my ship through. My brother is expecting me."

A septar in the lead battleship answered. "My orders are to take you aboard this warliner to wait for the arrival of Imperator Rusa'h."

"Am I not welcome in his court on Hyrillka?"

"You are welcome aboard this warliner. Those were my instructions." Then he added chillingly, "This maniple has just reconvened from Alturas and Shonor, both of which have joined our holy cause. Our ships are prepared for immediate departure to Dobro—should we be needed there."

Udru'h drew a deep breath, driving back his alarm. "Very well, then. I will be pleased to await my brother on your ship."

Once aboard, Designate Udru'h was brought forward like a piece of property. The rebellious Solar Navy officers looked at him as if questioning his loyalty—a good question, actually. These soldiers were completely detached from any *thism* he could sense, making them oddly opaque in his mind.

The soldiers led him to a sealed room, opened the hatch, and ushered him into the chamber. "While you wait for the Imperator, discuss your situation with *him*. He can explain the consequences of failing to cooperate."

Ignoring the brainwashed guards as they sealed the door, Udru'h saw a defiant but impotent Adar Zan'nh. The commander sat in his rumpled uniform, a prisoner, disheveled but not obviously mistreated. His reddened eyes had a wildness to them, and he seemed to be slowly losing his struggle against isolation. Udru'h could certainly understand the engulfing emptiness and silence; already it echoed around him here, but because of his solo trips to the captive green priest Nira on her isolated island, the Dobro Designate had a little more practice.

Seeing him, the Adar's eyes narrowed with deep suspicion, as if he suspected a trick. Udru'h and his nephew locked gazes, each assessing the other, and finally the Dobro

Designate said, "No, I have not agreed to join them yet—if that is your question."

The Adar did not relax, taking fast and shallow breaths. "And I should believe this?"

"I am your uncle. Would you not know through the *thism* if I am lying?"

Zan'nh's eyes flashed with caged anger; emotions seethed close to the surface, barely in control. "Never before did I suspect that a Designate could lie to me or deceive his Mage-Imperator—yet Rusa'h has done so. I do not know what to believe."

Udru'h remained standing inside the cell, not certain how closely they were being watched. "In fact, I have given them no answer at all."

"You would even consider betraying your Mage-Imperator?" Zan'nh looked indignant, a cornered animal ready to attack any convenient target. "By merely thinking that, you have already committed treason."

Udru'h was unruffled. "Prime Designate Thor'h lectured me at great length when he threatened Dobro with one of the warliners that *you* surrendered to them, Adar." He scowled. "Thor'h was very earnest, if not entirely convincing."

Zan'nh looked away, clearly ashamed about what had befallen his maniple. "After briefly imprisoning me on the surface, they forced me aboard what was once my own flagship. I had to watch as the mad Designate attacked other Ildiran colonies and commanded the murder of his own brothers and nephews."

"And what about your crew?"

Zan'nh's gaze snapped back up. "They have all been manipulated through the use of shiing. They are no longer responsible for their own minds."

"Apparently neither you nor I are susceptible to such straightforward persuasion. We must join Rusa'h willingly."

"That will never happen—at least not on my part." The Adar studied Udru'h's eyes when he was slow to give a similar assurance of his own.

Finally the cell door opened, and Solar Navy guards came for the Dobro Designate. "Imperator Rusa'h requests your presence in the command nucleus," said the lead guard.

Zan'nh looked with disappointment instead of obvious anger at these soldiers who had once been his loyal crew. Udru'h followed his escort without glancing back at the Adar as the cell door closed. . . .

In the command nucleus, the Dobro Designate was amazed at the change in his rebellious brother. Formerly soft and hedonistic, Rusa'h was now hardened and wore the trappings of a Mage-Imperator. Lens kithmen and pleasure mates surrounded his ornate facsimile chrysalis chair.

When Rusa'h stared at him, the Dobro Designate used all the skill he had practiced to shield his thoughts, in case this oddly changed brother could detect anything. Did the broken *thism* blind both of them to each other? The mad Designate's voice was calm and reasonable. "You have come here as you promised."

"You had no reason to doubt me. I am true to my word."

"But are you compliant as well? You have always been scornful of our weak brother. Have you decided to join my pure view of the Lightsource? Our cause will be much stronger with you as an ally, Udru'h."

Unperturbed, the Dobro Designate studied his work-roughened hands. "And where is this purity of which you speak, brother? If your path is based on an accurate reading of the soul-threads, why must you kill so many innocent Ildirans?"

"I kill no one unless it is necessary."

"Oh? Again, I ask—if you have absolute proof, why should anyone resist? If you mean to convince me, you must make a more compelling case than this."

The brainwashed officers glowered at the Dobro Designate, but Rusa'h focused his complete attention on him. "Will I be required to kill you as well?"

Udru'h gave an impatient wave. "Why do you jump headlong to conclusions? If your revelations are not strong enough to stand up to a few simple questions, then I have no choice but to doubt you even further." He walked casually around the facsimile chrysalis chair as if the two of them were discussing nothing more consequential than clothing styles. "You ask me to make a monumental choice—to betray the Mage-Imperator and help you shake apart the Ildiran Empire. Please indulge me while I wrestle with my doubts!"

The fierce pleasure mates and iron-faced lens kithmen huddled close to the rebellious Designate, looking coldly at Udru'h, who responded with an equally icy stare.

With supreme contentment, Rusa'h finally said, "I have complete proof, but you are incapable of seeing it until you become part of the new pure *thism*."

Udru'h snorted. "That is a fool's bargain, as you well know."

Bridge personnel and guard kithmen came forward. Rusa'h held up a hand, struggling to control his anger. "Prepare the maniple for departure to Dobro, where we will impose our new enlightened rule upon the people. It is a pity you would not cooperate, Udru'h."

The Dobro Designate gave a long-suffering sigh. "Again, you make a great many assumptions, Rusa'h. I never refused to cooperate with you. In fact, I gave you no clear answer at all—I simply raised a few logical questions." Udru'h leaned against the edge of the chrysalis chair. "Go ahead, take me back to Dobro. It seems I have no choice but to join you. But you will not need to send the full maniple against my small colony. You must have other uses for so many ships?"

Still somewhat dubious, Rusa'h pursed his lips. "True, Thor'h needs the rest of these warliners against other intractable splinter colonies. We must move swiftly." He pointed a finger, making sure his threat was clear. "You will have time en route to consider the extent of your cooperation. Upon reaching Dobro, if you waver in your resolve, then even one warliner is enough to destroy your colony."

Udru'h smiled. "Oh, I would never waver in my resolve."

84 ☀ SULLIVAN GOLD

Of the cloud harvester's fourteen escape modules, only one was lost as it struggled to get away. Unable to gain sufficient altitude and velocity when it ejected from the structure, the emergency vessel tumbled back into the zone where the hydrogues continued their onslaught. The hapless module scraped the side of a cracked ekti tank, causing further damage. While the skyminer evacuees called frantically for help, the ekti container erupted. Sullivan could do nothing to assist them. . . .

Debris from the mangled cloud harvester fell like ashes in the wide-open sky. Moving away at best speed, Sullivan grimly tried to contact the Ildiran skyfactory. His crew was not enthusiastic about remaining near the hydrogues any longer than necessary.

Tabitha insisted, "Look, Sullivan, I know you've got a good heart, but we *can't* go back there. We won't survive."

"I see no reason to provoke the drogues," cried one of the shift supervisors.

"The hydrogues wrecked our cloud harvester," Sullivan pointed out, "but they've left our evacuation modules alone."

"*So far.* This isn't really a ship . . . it's just a box that moves."

Another man said, "Let's just get out of here! We can wait for the EDF to come pick us up. Kolker already sent the message, right?"

"They may not be here for days," the forlorn green priest answered. "I don't have a treeling to receive any updates. Nobody even knows we survived. We're isolated. We're on our own."

"No we're not—we have the Ildirans." Sullivan sounded more like a boss than he ever had. "We're morally bound to help them, even if they weren't smart enough to plan ahead." He glared at his crewmembers, unyielding. "You'd want them to do the same for us."

"Yeah, but would they?" one of the ekti engineers argued.

"That's not the point. We'll show them a bit of *human* kindness."

He directed the thirteen escape modules to fly across the cloudbanks toward the second battle zone, where the Ildiran skyfactory smoked and burned in the rarefied atmosphere. So far, the hydrogues had primarily concentrated their wrath upon the human cloud harvester. Far behind them, most of the warglobes continued to rip apart the framework like jackals on a carcass. But others had begun to turn their weapons on the Ildirans.

"Keep transmitting to Hroa'x, Tabitha. Tell him we're on our way. Have him get his people ready to board our ships. Divide them into thirteen groups. Calculate how many we can hold. We'll cram shoulder-to-shoulder."

"We don't have enough fuel or life support or food. These modules are just a temporary—"

Sullivan cut her off. "We'll figure out something. Let's survive for the next hour and then decide what to do."

The cumbersome modules made their way to the Ildiran skyfactory city. Its towers and domes had been blackened. Atmosphere and chemical fumes boiled out. Fires were raging through the habitation complexes. As Sullivan watched in horror, Ildiran miner kithmen fell off the railings and plunged into the emptiness of infinite clouds. He couldn't tell if the people had intentionally thrown themselves over-board.

A nearby warglobe launched two crackling blasts against the lower decks, ripping apart the bottom sections, then it cruised away through the topmost clouds like a shark knifing through the water.

"Here's our chance. We've got to hurry." Sullivan brought his escape module down onto the broad landing deck of Hroa'x's skyfactory, scattering panicked miners who did not know where to go. Ildiran-family leaders and primary engineers raced forward. Fires and explosions continued to shake the huge complex as if it were held in the fist of an angry giant.

Shoving the module's hatch open, Sullivan leaned out

and shouted, "We can fit twenty in here. Twenty! Count yourselves out and get aboard. Twelve other vessels are landing right behind me." When he saw the aliens hesitate, Sullivan grew red-faced. "Move your asses! We don't have time for this."

Squat Hroa'x strode from the remains of a skeletal exhaust tower. The facility chief shouted to the miner kithmen, "Do as he says. We have no time to choose or prioritize. Twenty of you, climb aboard and let him take off."

Sullivan gestured to him. "You, Hroa'x—come aboard with me."

But the proud miner shook his head. "No, I will stay here." He marched back into his facility, as if he were returning to a normal day of work.

Before Sullivan could yell again, twenty Ildirans clambered through the hatch. Within moments, his module was filled and the hatch sealed as more Ildiran miners crowded forward. "Lift off. Make room for another ship."

A second module landed beside him with a loud clang and blast of exhaust jets. Reluctant to refuse Sullivan's direct orders, the pilots of the other escape craft hovered over the doomed skyfactory, waiting to pick up loads of refugees.

Sullivan was cramped inside their escape vessel as it moved away. Pressed body to body, the Ildiran evacuees had no place to sit down. Winds buffeted the overloaded module, and the designated pilot fought for control. "We don't have much lift, Sullivan, and not much fuel to go anywhere. These ships were never designed to carry so many people."

"Just get us through this right now, and you can file a complaint as soon as we get back to Hansa HQ."

One by one, the remaining evac modules touched down on the skyfactory deck and took on frightened refugees.

Even with every craft vastly overloaded, nearly a third of the Ildiran population remained stranded aboard the complex.

Across the sky, the Hansa cloud harvester was by now completely obliterated. Only an expanding cloud of smoke and dark vapors marked its former position, like an old bloodstain. Sullivan saw the hydrogues regroup, then begin to move across the sky toward the Ildiran skyfactory.

Seven more warglobes rose from the nearby clouds. The damaged Ildiran structure was already tilted and wobbling. Explosions glowed from its engines and uncontrolled fires in the ekti reactors underneath. The dwelling complexes had already been devastated.

A lone miner kithman—Sullivan recognized Hroa'x himself—climbed the tall venting tower and stood like an angry admiral on a defeated warship. The chief miner had no weapons, no effective resistance, but still Hroa'x raised his arms to curse the deep-core aliens.

"Lift us higher," Sullivan told his pilot in a leaden voice. "We have to get out of Qronha 3's atmosphere before the drogues notice us."

"Trying to, Sullivan, but we just don't have the power," the man grumbled. "Hey, maybe if some of these Ildirans get out and push?"

Sullivan watched as the warglobes circled back to the Ildiran skyfactory and let loose with a barrage of blue lightning. Hroa'x remained at the top of his tower, bold to the last moment when the giant city broke apart into flaming pieces. Aboard the escape modules, the rescued Ildirans moaned, raw with resonating pain from feeling the deaths of so many comrades.

The thirteen overloaded ships, like obese bumblebees, managed to heave themselves out of the gas giant's atmosphere

into the freedom of orbit. But from there they had no obvious place to go.

"Our life support won't last a day, Sullivan," Tabitha
pointed out. "Food is the least of our worries. We don't have
enough air or power to keep us alive."

Kolker clutched his green knees. "We'll never survive."

Sullivan pursed his lips and didn't respond immediately.
"Now would be a good time for a brilliant, innovative idea,
if anybody has one." When no one volunteered a suggestion,
he came up with one himself. "Okay, we can't wait for the
EDF, and we don't have fuel to take us very far. But there is
one place we can go." He looked at the crowded, frightened
faces, both alien and human. "If we head on a straight-line
course and use every last gasp of our fuel, maybe we can
make it to Ildira."

85 ☀ GENERAL KURT LANYAN

General Lanyan took one look at Stromo's face, drew immediate conclusions, and sighed.

"We have a problem, sir," the Admiral said. "The evidence at Corribus is damning. My technicians insist that the
destruction really was caused by EDF weaponry. We found
landing marks and other indications consistent with one Juggernaut and several Mantas."

Lanyan stood, though he felt unsteady on his feet. "But where did they come from? I've demanded an inventory from all my grid admirals, and everything is accounted for. We haven't *misplaced* six major battleships!"

"Not . . . entirely, sir." Stromo offered his idea about the group of ships that had disappeared at Golgen. "And those were all crewed by Soldier compies, exactly as the Covitz girl described. They might have killed their human commanders and turned against us."

"Admiral, do you have any idea how *many* Soldier compies we have aboard our EDF ships in all ten grids?"

Stromo was very pale. "Yes, General. Yes, I do."

He remembered King Peter's seemingly paranoid complaints about using Klikiss technology in the new Soldier compies, but the Hansa and the EDF had dismissed the young man's worries. "Damn, what if the King was right?"

"General, what about the sixty rammers we just dispatched to Qronha 3? *Those* ships are full of Soldier compies and only a few token human commanders. If compies really pose a threat, shouldn't we recall the rammers?"

Lanyan wanted to scream. "And stop our only effective blow against the drogues? I think not! Besides, we don't have any way to contact them in time."

They were interrupted when Lanyan's aide signaled insistently at the door. The young man would not have dared to disturb them unless it was terribly important. "I'm sorry, General, but you really need to see this. It's a message from Lars Rurik Swendsen."

"The engineering specialist?" After the mysterious disappearance of Chief Scientist Howard Palawu, the Swedish engineer had been put in charge of all compy manufacturing on Earth. "What the hell does he want?"

The aide piped the transmission onto his deskscreen. Lanyan looked down as the engineering specialist's nervous face filled the projection area. "General Lanyan, how are you? I know it's been quite a while since we've talked—"

"What do you want, Swendsen? I'm in the middle of something."

"Well, General, I don't exactly know what it means, but . . . it's our Klikiss robots."

Lanyan felt an iceberg in his stomach. "What about them?"

"They're cagey under the best of circumstances, but several were always present to observe our compy production lines. But now, uh . . . they've all disappeared. They said nothing to us—simply left the production lines and vanished without a trace. First I ran a detailed check, interfacing with standard surveillance in populated areas, then I contacted some of my colleagues. As far as we can tell, *all* the robots are gone. Every one."

Lanyan did not let his deep concern show. "I'll check into it, Swendsen. Thank you for letting me know."

While Stromo continued to splutter, Lanyan dispatched messages to every observation point he knew. Over the next few hours, the summary of returning information shocked him to the core. "Swendsen's not kidding. Every last Klikiss robot we knew about has pulled up stakes and gone away. Chairman Wenceslas is using our green priests to contact every Hansa colony where Klikiss robots have been seen. So far, the news is consistent across the Spiral Arm: They're all gone."

Stromo shook his head in disbelief. "Fortunately, there are only—what?—a hundred of them?"

Lanyan kneaded his knuckles and stared at the rock wall of his Moon base office. He had a very bad feeling about what might have been going on all along under his nose. Finally, reluctantly, he decided he had no choice. He issued an all-points warning to every ship in the EDF fleet—though without green priests aboard most of them, it would take a dangerously long time for the warning to be disseminated.

86 ✸ PATRICK FITZPATRICK III

The thirty-one EDF "adoptees" performed their daily work in the Osquivel shipyards, always alert for a chance to escape. Components for Roamer ships continued to be fabricated and assembled in the spacedocks. One new cargo vessel had already been launched since the news about Rendezvous, and another larger ship was nearing completion.

Instead of studying the hydrogue derelict, the odd Roamer engineer had filled a few cargo ships with strange devices the size and shape of doormats, then he'd gone off to Theroc on some harebrained scheme. Meanwhile, the prisoners filled their labor shifts, working silently beside the cooperative Soldier compies.

Fitzpatrick watched closely. On schedule, the weekly cargo escort was on its way down from the cometary hydrogen-distillation yards and was due to arrive in the ring shipyards within a few hours. Despite his reservations, he knew there would be no better time.

In the three days since concocting his plan, Kiro Yamane had written and compiled a "virus signal" to scramble the programming of the reconfigured EDF compies. Using a few easily stolen components, he had rigged an effective transmitter. A simple burst, and the nearby compies would upload the stream and then act as repeater stations, passing the virus signal from one to another, until they had all absorbed the corrupted command string.

"Timing is going to be touchy—for all of us," Yamane said in a low voice as they got together. "I can trigger the new programming string, which deletes the requirement for obedience to human commands. It also distorts their damage-control mechanisms, their 'better judgment,' if you will."

"So," Fitzpatrick said, "the Soldier compies will turn into sloppy workers who don't do what they're told and don't obey instructions."

"Sounds like most Roachers, if you ask me," Andez muttered.

Yamane maintained his dry analysis. "It's not like a bomb going off. Things will begin falling apart, but we can't count on a single event to act as the diversion. I just hope the general chaos keeps the Roamers busy so Patrick can do his part."

Fitzpatrick glanced at the chronometer. "I leave in just a few minutes. I've managed to get myself reassigned to the docking bay where the ekti transport is coming in." He laced his words with a scorn and sarcasm that he didn't truly feel. "My little 'sweetheart' Zhett is coming to help me load general supplies aboard for shipping out to another depot. Just the two of us, all alone. She probably thinks it's a date."

"We've all seen her making eyes at you, Fitzpatrick— and you doing the same in return," Andez said, arching her eyebrows.

He flushed. "It's all an act, to get in her good graces. She'll fall for it."

"Right. You sure she isn't too much for you to handle?"

With a sniff, he said, "Can't be any worse than facing a whole hydrogue fleet." He made excuses and went to the docking area from which he would be shuttled to the reception asteroid where the cargo escort was due to dock.

Just before Fitzpatrick left, Yamane surreptitiously transmitted his program scrambler, and the nearby Soldier compies received their new instructions. Soon, their quiet computerized rebellion would spread.

As soon as the cargo escort arrived with an array of full ekti tanks, the pilot had borrowed Zhett's grappler pod to go to the main habitation complex for a cleanup and a good meal before his flight to the nearest Roamer fuel depot. Other than two unobtrusive compies, Fitzpatrick and Zhett were completely alone, exactly the way he wanted it . . . though a part of him remained uneasy.

As they worked shoulder-to-shoulder loading crates onto the cargo escort, Zhett flashed a teasing smile at him. "Keep this up, Fitzie, and I'll put in your name for Employee of the Month."

"Can't you ever just be nice to me?" He blushed furiously, and it wasn't an act. "I requested this assignment specifically so you and I could have a little time together without my friends snickering at me. Is that so bad?"

She looked surprised and even a little embarrassed. "I was just kidding you." He kept his reticent silence while Zhett mulled over what he had said. "That doesn't sound like you at all. Why the change of heart?"

He made himself smile at her. They had never overtly

acknowledged their mutual attraction, but neither of them could deny the chemistry. Now, in order for the escape plan to work, he had to get her to admit it, to make her particularly vulnerable for just a few minutes. "We're all by ourselves here, Zhett, so why keep up the act? I know you've got a crush on me."

"You sure it isn't the other way around?" Obviously feeling awkward with the conversation, she quickly picked up another crate of supplies and turned toward the cargo escort.

He watched her carry the box up the ramp. "If you like being here with me, why are you in such a damned hurry to get the job done? You're working harder than the compies are."

She set the box down at her feet and looked at him with a mixture of feelings plain on her face. Had she fantasized about a situation like this? Fitzpatrick certainly had, though he was loath to admit it. "Oh? Did you have something else in mind?" Her coy voice was seductive and playful, but with an undertone of uncertainty. He suspected Zhett liked to talk a lot, but wasn't used to following through on her advances.

Fitzpatrick stood in front of her, trying to cut a dashing and handsome figure, and mostly succeeding at feeling clumsy. "We could just let the compies finish up, and you and I . . ." He shrugged. "I don't know. This rock isn't exactly my idea of a good place for a picnic." He gestured toward the back wall of the asteroid chamber, hating what he was being forced to do in the name of loyalty to the EDF. So many of his comrades were depending on him. "I see a nice storage room back there. It would give us a bit of privacy."

Zhett laughed, but a bit nervously. "Privacy? Are you afraid the compies will see something they shouldn't?" She tossed her long dark hair, still flirting but seeming over her head.

He rolled his eyes. He had to keep her off her guard, stay one step ahead, though she was sure to grow suspicious. "Don't ask me to believe that you Roamers have no cameras or surveillance systems inside your docking bays."

"Well, we don't—but I won't ask you to believe it. Suit yourself." As if afraid she might lose her nerve, Zhett bounded toward the door of the storage room. "What are you waiting for? Do I intimidate you?"

"Not in the least."

She increased the illumination inside the chamber and re-arranged a few crates so the two of them would have a place to sit and talk . . . or whatever. As he stood at the door, Zhett looked naïve and very beautiful. Considering that the Roamers were always so secretive and paranoid about their hideouts, Fitzpatrick thought it strange that she was so open and gullible. Zhett actually trusted him.

He paused to gather his nerve. "Against my better judgment, you've actually become sort of . . . special to me. Don't forget that."

"You're acting weird, Fitz."

He despised what he had to do, but he meant what he said . . . and deep inside he despised himself for meaning it. It wasn't supposed to be this way. He gave her a fumbling kiss on the cheek, then withdrew quickly. "Just a minute. I want to get something from the supplies. I think I saw a few pastry preserves in a container. It'll make a good start for a picnic."

"All right." She grinned, and he began to turn, but hesitated. Then, surprising even himself, he grasped her shoulders and pulled her toward him. She caught her breath, as if to make a comment—but he kissed her again, full on the mouth. At first the kiss was rushed, startling. He had meant

just to distract her, to keep her from thinking too much. She
blinked her eyes, looking into his, and then she closed them,
enjoying his lips as he relaxed, kissing her again, longer this
time. When he broke away, she was completely unable to
speak.

Blushing crimson, he swaggered out the door. "I'll be
right back." *Damn!*

When her back was turned to the crates, Fitzpatrick
closed the door and scrambled the electronic mechanism to
lock the hatch. Not sure it would hold for long—Roamers
probably had emergency escape controls inside the storeroom—he picked up a prybar from the equipment pile and
swung it in a sharp arc, smashing the panel in a spray of
sparks.

Zhett was already pounding on the inside of the door. Her
voice was muffled, but he could imagine the sort of harsh
language she was using.

Out in the docking bay, the quiet compies finished their
work as instructed. They didn't seem to notice anything
wrong. At least they were regular models, not Soldier compies that would soon start suffering from poor job performance,
thanks to Yamane's virus.

Fitzpatrick ran toward the gangly-looking cargo escort. It
looked like an anorexic spider, not much more than a pilot
chamber and grappling struts to hold a cluster of fuel tanks. But
it did have a stardrive, and it would take him far from Osquivel,
where he could call for help and rescue his comrades.

He shouted to the still-working compies. "Your task is
finished. Your orders are terminated. Go stand against the
wall and shut down." He didn't want any of them to think
about sounding an alarm. Once the obedient robots did as he
told them, he had the entire docking bay to himself.

When he climbed aboard the cargo escort, Fitzpatrick threw a glance over his shoulder to make sure the storage chamber door remained closed. It would keep Zhett busy for a while.

He listened in on the Roamer channels and heard a growing buzz of concerned chatter. Apparently, Yamane's glitches had already begun to take hold among the Soldier compies. Good. Several production lines had been brought to a standstill, and the frustrated Roamer engineers were thrown into confusion by the incomprehensible behavior.

Del Kellum bellowed at his outlying teams. "By damn, the compies are intentionally jamming up the machinery! Get them back on track."

"We're trying, Del. But something's setting them off! The sabotage is just growing worse."

With so much chaos in the shipyards, Fitzpatrick could slip away before anyone noticed what he was up to. Judging by the stress in Kellum's voice, the Roamers couldn't handle another emergency at the moment.

He fired up the engines, and the ungainly cargo escort lifted off. The docking bay doors opened, and he flew out, guiding the clumsy craft away from the other shipyard facilities.

Down in the rings, Soldier compies continued to go haywire. Grappler pods and cargo ships moved in erratic paths, nearly colliding with each other. Only a handful of the vessels were flown by the schizophrenic Soldier compies; the Roamers in the rest were just trying to get out of the way in time.

As he listened to the frantic chatter over the comm bands, somebody signaled him, assuming he was an authorized pilot and asking why he had departed so soon. Fitzpatrick didn't bother to answer.

He flew out from the beautiful disc rings that encircled Osquivel, glad to get away. He was free. None of the Roamer ships could catch up with him now. Once he engaged the Ildiran stardrive, he would be off in a flash. And it was up to him to bring back the EDF cavalry before all hell finished breaking loose in the Roamer shipyards.

87 ☀ ANTON COLICOS

After dragging themselves along for so many days, the desperate Marathan survivors seized the hope that rescue waited for them at Secda.

"Follow me!" Designate Avi'h pointed toward the city. "The robots will assist us. They are expecting our arrival."

Holding back, Anton called to his companions as they bounded toward the bustling complex that swarmed with Klikiss robots. "Be careful! We need to understand what—"

But the Ildirans grasped at any strand of hope. The Designate raced to the Secda city site, shouting and waving his arms. The burly digger Vik'k and the normally logical engineer Nur'of hurried beside him. Even Rememberer Vao'sh pulled ahead toward the familiar Klikiss robots.

Anton ran forward and grabbed his arm. "Wait a second, Vao'sh. Look at what they're doing down there."

The colors on the rememberer's facial lobes flickered

through a storm of uncertainty. "We've walked across half a continent, Rememberer Anton. I see shelter and light and protection. Why do you hesitate?"

The human historian jabbed a finger toward the numerous tunnels and openings, the mounds of geometrical structures that reminded him of a sinister wasps' nest growing out of control. "That isn't what Secda is supposed to look like. Something's not right here!"

But the frightened rememberer pulled his arm free, unable to resist the call of hope. "We will gain our answers as soon as the Designate speaks to the robots. Come! We must not fall behind." Vao'sh ran ahead, and, despite his own reservations, Anton followed.

After the terrors they had endured across the night-strangled landscape, Anton could understand that the Marathan survivors might become irrational. They were feeling loose and adrift, growing slowly mad, their minds degenerating.

Even so, Anton couldn't let them all run into a possible trap.

He looked around, seeing Klikiss robots moving with mechanical precision. Off to one side of the city dome, he saw a hangar shelter identical to the one at Maratha Prime. He counted three Ildiran spacecraft there, available for shuttling supplies and materials.

Finally the Klikiss robots noticed the tiny group of refugees. As if reacting to a simultaneous signal, the beetle-like machines froze in their activities, swiveling angular heads and brightening their red optical sensors.

Designate Avi'h managed to pull ahead of the digger and the engineer. He continued to shout, "We are here! We have survived the journey across the nightside." He stopped in front of the nearest black robot. "We need your help."

Incredible numbers of the insectile robots had begun to move, closing in like a noose drawing tight. Increasingly uneasy, Anton looked to his right and left. "Where did they all come from?"

But Vao'sh, his eyes glazed, his face still flickering through its palette of colors, said, "Save your questions, Rememberer Anton. We can ask them all as soon as we are safely inside."

The nearest machine rose up to tower over the Designate. Its articulated arms extended, each one ending in a different sharp implement. The carapace on the robot's back cracked open as if to make the robot larger and more intimidating.

In the suddenly silent work site, Anton heard the buzzing words of the Klikiss robot like blades slicing through the air. "Ildirans have broken our long-standing agreement."

Designate Avi'h looked up at it. "What agreement?"

The Klikiss robot swung one of its scythe-tipped arms and slashed brutally through Avi'h's neck, severing his head. The Designate did not even have time to cry out as blood spouted from his neck stump. He toppled forward.

Vik'k and Nur'of stumbled to a halt, unable to endure any further horror, any additional betrayal. A buzzing sound echoed through the gathered robots, hundreds of giant black machines humming and sizzling as they activated their defensive systems. Moving with skittering swiftness, they closed in on the four remaining refugees.

"Run!" Anton shouted. "They mean to kill us all."

Vao'sh simply shook his head. "This is not possible." The old rememberer appeared ready to collapse. "The Klikiss robots have always been our allies. We unearthed them from the ice five hundred years ago. They have—"

Anton dragged his friend away, urging them both into a run, though he didn't know where else they could go. The Secda work site was vast and complex. They could find places to hide, a barricade or a shack suitable for making a last stand. But without weapons he and Vao'sh could not resist the Klikiss robots for long. There had to be a different way.

After seeing the Designate slaughtered, burly Vik'k didn't need or ask for explanations. When the murderous machines hemmed them in, he balled his horny fists and began swinging. Engineer Nur'of stood at the digger's back and grabbed a metal bar from one of the construction scrap piles. The two Ildirans stood together as the armored robots came forward, their claws clacking.

Nur'of swung his metal bar. It clanged resoundingly against the black shell of the nearest Klikiss robot, but caused no damage. He swept it back and forth like a club, smashing off one of the extended articulated arms; then he brought the metal rod up to crush the crimson optical sensors of another machine. Though the round glassy eyes shattered and went dark, the robot continued to press toward him.

Fearless, Vik'k threw himself against two of the robots. Even as their claws tore his protective garment and tough skin, the digger continued to howl and thrash. But more and more of the robots surrounded him, slashing with their cutting implements and powerful mechanical arms. Both the Ildiran digger and the engineer went down under a swarm of giant beetlelike attackers.

Anton and Vao'sh ran, hearing the clatter and screams continue behind them—and then only an ominous silence while the remaining robots focused on the two sole survivors. Anton looked around in search of any kind of shelter. He had spent his life reading about brave commanders and decisive heroes who came up with creative solutions in moments of desperation. Now he was in a position of being a *real* hero, and there was no time to learn the role.

The only remaining Ildiran on Maratha, completely isolated from the *thism,* Vao'sh looked stunned and dazed, barely able to keep moving. But Anton did not give up on his friend. "The hangars! Off to the side of the dome. I saw ships there. Maybe one of them will still function."

The old rememberer mumbled something unintelligible, but when Anton yanked his arm and kept running, he followed without question. Adrenaline gave Anton a burst of speed, and he jumped over low piles of debris, dodging construction machinery and half-assembled structures.

Klikiss robots continued to emerge from their underground tunnels like ants boiling out of a disturbed nest. Anton wove back and forth in an erratic course so the attackers could not determine his intent. Once the Klikiss robots saw where he was going, they would surely try to intercept them at the hangar.

"We're going to make it, Vao'sh. Right this way. Just keep going." Now the hangar was in front of them, a straight shot. At last, the Klikiss robots anticipated his plan. "Run for all you're worth, Vao'sh!"

They sprinted forward. Anton had never been so tired or so terrified in his life. The muscles in his legs felt like fraying strings, but he forced himself to keep going. Vao'sh stumbled on the uneven ground. Anton caught the old rememberer before he could sprawl. "Keep going! Just a little farther!"

Now he could see the Ildiran cargo ships that had been stored at the construction site. One looked half disassembled, as if a scheduled maintenance routine had been interrupted before it was finished. One craft near the rear of the hangar appeared intact and ready to go. Anton hoped the engines would work. "Do you know how to fly one of those ships, Vao'sh?"

The rememberer could barely answer, but Anton didn't want to think about the next problem just yet. Vao'sh wasn't in any shape to act as a pilot, but he managed to gasp as they kept going, "Standard controls . . . primarily automated . . . You can do it."

"Looks like I'm going to have to."

Behind them, the pursuing Klikiss robots cracked open their black carapaces and spread wide solar-panel wings. The heavy machines began to fly, swiftly closing the gap between themselves and their prey.

"That's not fair!" Anton finally ducked under the sloping metal roof of the small hangar. "Into the ship, Vao'sh. We've got to get in."

It was a relatively small craft used to shuttle personnel and supplies down from larger vessels in orbit. Anton hoped the engines and the navigation system could take them all the way back to Ildira or some other inhabited world. And he prayed the coordinates were already stored; he certainly couldn't navigate by dead reckoning.

As the weak rememberer climbed in, Anton heard a loud clatter. Five heavy robots landed just outside the hangar door, folded their wings, and began to stride forward, all of their articulated arms extended.

Anton swung himself into the ship and scrambled to find the hatch controls. It took him much longer than he expected, and the nearest robots had crossed the floor by the time Anton got the hatch closed. "We should be safe in here for a few minutes," he said, not actually believing it.

Shaken and disoriented, Vao'sh collapsed inside the cockpit, gripping the copilot's chair with trembling hands. Anton looked at the confusing array of controls and suddenly his mind went blank. All the Ildiran letters and words, the language he had studied so carefully, now left him. He couldn't read any of it. The symbols were incomprehensible! He squeezed his eyes shut and took a deep breath. When he opened them again, he could focus once more.

The robots clanged against the outer door of the shuttle. Four more had appeared in front of the hangar and scuttled forward.

Anton knew that if he didn't launch the vessel soon, the Klikiss machines would simply overwhelm them with their numbers and batter away until they shredded the hull, one armored plate at a time.

Vao'sh did his best to gather his wits. He leaned over to the controls as if it required an enormous effort, then gestured to one small grouping. "There . . . that is the one."

Anton understood the mechanism for activating the engines, and hammered at the button sequence. The robots converged behind the ship as well; when the exhaust blasted from the rear cones of the shuttle, one of the machines was thrown backward, scorched.

"Good! That's one down," Anton said. "Only a couple hundred more to go."

He looked at the gauges, where lights and graphs played across the screens. When it looked as if the chambers had heated up properly, he activated the next sequence. Outside, the Klikiss robots grasped the landing gear and began to bend and tear out the struts. The ship lurched, unbalanced.

The clanging continued. More and more machines closed in.

"Here goes nothing." Anton punched the launch controls, and the ship shuddered. The engines roared, and finally the whole craft rose and accelerated, horizontal to the ground. Gathering speed, it burst across the floor like a massive projectile, mowing down six Klikiss robots that stood blocking the hangar opening and the freedom of the Marathan sky.

One robot remained clamped to a torn section of landing gear. Anton flew out of the structure and pulled the ship into a gradual ascent, with the robot still dangling behind them. Rough turbulence from the shifting temperatures of Maratha's dayside made for a bumpy ride that rattled and shook the vessel. As they continued to ascend, the lone robot could no longer hold on. Its articulated arm broke off, and the beetlelike shape tumbled in the air until it shattered into glossy black pieces far below.

Exhausted and feeling an avalanche of terror sweep over him, Anton leaned back in the pilot's chair and let out an insane whoop of victory. "We're out of here, Vao'sh! We made it! We got away from those bastards."

They shot up into the bright day sky, straining to reach the edges of the atmosphere and the open vastness of starlit space. He hoped he could figure out the navigation systems and the controls. He couldn't tell how much fuel their engines held or how far this craft could take them. *One problem at a time.*

He looked over at Vao'sh in the second seat, but the rememberer did not seem exhilarated. The colored lobes on his face had turned a cadaverous gray. Waves of trembling wracked his entire body, as if he could barely control the sobs.

"We have escaped," Vao'sh said in a weak, croaking

voice. "But I am alone. Completely *alone*. No Ildiran has faced such solitude and survived." He slumped backward and closed his large, expressive eyes. "I do not know how much longer I can endure."

88 ☀ NIKKO CHAN TYLAR

Once Jess Tamblyn gave him the task, it took Nikko only five days to track down where Speaker Peroni had gone to ground. She had sent out messengers from Jonah 12, and the Roamer system of rumors and messages passed the word.

The second trader whom Nikko encountered on his random stops told him where the Speaker might be found. In exchange, he asked the trader to spread the news that Roamers could again bring skymines to Golgen, which the wentals had purged of all hydrogues. Nikko wouldn't be surprised if one or two facilities had already been launched for the gas giant.

Now, as the *Aquarius* passed the dark outskirts of the Jonah system, he sent out a call to the miners at the settlement, but received no response. "Hello down there? Is anybody hearing me? Is Speaker Peroni there?"

Puzzled, Nikko detected anomalous heat and energy signatures where the base should have been. Strange modulated bursts came across the comm spectrum, but over frequency windows the Roamers rarely used. He swallowed hard. What if another raiding party of Eddies had discovered Jonah 12?

When he circled in and flew low, geometric lights spread around the site of the Roamer base. He adjusted the magnifiers, focusing in to make sure his eyes weren't deceiving him. He had never been here before, but obviously this wasn't right.

As the *Aquarius* cruised over the complex, caution made him keep radio silence. The base showed furious activity, but he couldn't fathom what was going on. Switching scanner bands, Nikko discovered that the visible spangle of lights marked only the tip of the iceberg; in the infrared, emanations were pouring out like a blaze. Plumes of evaporated gases rose into the sky. The small-pile power reactor, a standard Roamer design for isolated outposts, had been enhanced for an enormous energy output.

The cluster of Roamer domes, rail launchers, and transmitting towers had all been torn apart and reassembled into strange patterns. He even spotted the remnants of what had been a few Roamer cargo ships. Their engines had been torn out and implanted in larger, angular skeletons of sharp structures. *Alien* structures. Five huge ships, shaped like bones and beetle shells.

He saw dark figures in armored suits that reflected very little light. Had Roamer engineers developed a body casing that allowed people to maneuver for long periods in the extreme cold? He descended and increased magnification, and the shapes suddenly came into focus. Black insectile automatons. *Everywhere.*

Nikko had never seen a Klikiss robot himself, but was

certainly familiar with what they looked like. What were the alien machines doing on Jonah 12? And what had they done to the Roamer mining base? It looked like an invasion! He saw no humans at all. The habitation and headquarters domes had been breached, the walls torn down, the atmosphere released into the frozen vacuum.

These Klikiss robots had destroyed the station! And now they were culling every scrap to assemble spacecraft of some sort. The vessels looked nearly complete.

Some of the black machines swiveled geometrical heads toward the sky, detected his ship moving above them. On the magnified screen, he saw the glint of red optical sensors and felt a deep cold in his heart.

He had no idea if the robots could shoot him down. He accelerated the *Aquarius,* ducking behind the close horizon. There, he was in transmission shadow from any ambush the Klikiss robots might set. The clicking machine-coded transmissions on his speakers grew quiet as he passed out of range.

No one knew what had happened here. Nikko was the only one who could carry a warning to the other clans.

Suddenly his comm line pinged: a small, weak signal coming from far beyond the base camp. "Hello, ship! Please respond—and please be piloted by a human being." It was a woman's voice. Nikko thought he recognized it.

He boosted his own signal to compensate for the obvious weakness of the sender's transmitter. "This is Nikko Chan Tylar. What the hell is going on down there?"

He heard a yelp of exultation. "This is Speaker Peroni. Thank you, Nikko!" Her voice sounded heavy, as if every breath was a labor. Her teeth were chattering. "Follow these coordinates and land. I hope you can take two passengers. We've been stranded out here for days."

The man's voice added, "And we probably have less than an hour till either our air runs out or we freeze. It's a toss-up which will happen first."

"Hang on! I'll be there in a minute."

He raced low over the frozen terrain until he came upon a rise where one of the hemispherical grazers had broken down. The *Aquarius* landed on the rough ice, and stabilizers locked down to level the ship. Steam rose from residual thermal energy radiating out of the heat vents.

After cycling through his airlock, Nikko crunched across to the silent, damaged grazer. The rear of the vehicle had been mangled, and jagged scratches were torn along the plated hull. An insulation cowling had been shredded, components ripped free. He ran his gaze along the flattened path where the grazer had lumbered along, amazed the small vehicle had made it so far.

Wearing environment suits, Speaker Peroni and another person tumbled out of the stranded vessel's hatch. They moved stiffly, sluggishly, as if neither of them had any energy left. Their thermal batteries must be low, their suit air tanks nearly empty.

Nikko grabbed Speaker Peroni's slick, suited arm and guided her to the *Aquarius*. She and her companion, whom she introduced as Purcell Wan, gasped out a brief story of how the robots had been discovered under the ice and awakened.

While the two crowded into the small water-bearing ship's airlock, Nikko waited outside, alone in the cold and intense silence. Every jagged black shadow on the terrain seemed to hide an insectile mechanical killer.

BeBob's sham board of inquiry went just as Rlinda expected. Wartime regulations allowed the EDF to do many things behind closed doors, with looser rules favoring their own desired outcomes. General Lanyan didn't even bother to attend the second day of the proceedings—apparently he was busy with Admiral Stromo, dealing with what the EDF had learned about Corribus.

Rlinda squeezed BeBob's hand as the head of the tribunal announced, "Captain Branson Roberts, since you do not dispute the charges, this board of inquiry finds sufficient cause to declare you guilty of desertion during wartime and of stealing a reconnaissance ship that belongs to the Earth Defense Forces."

"That was my own ship!" BeBob said.

"Which was duly acquired by the Hansa for military use in time of war," the head of the board said quickly and dismissively. "By the emergency authority vested in this tribunal, you will be held in confinement on the Moon until such time as your sentence can be determined."

"I object," BeBob said.

Rlinda glared at the military legal counsel. "I object to this whole ridiculous process. File an immediate appeal, demand a trial in the light of day—for a change."

The advocate looked at her. "You can't do that now."

"You sure didn't do it for us during the trial."

"This wasn't technically a trial, it was a preliminary board of inquiry. In all likelihood, there will still be a formal public court-martial proceeding, unless certain wartime rules are invoked."

BeBob snorted, "Either way they only put two options on the table: summary execution and permanent penal servitude! What sort of chance does that give me?"

"I sent out feelers everywhere I could think of," Rlinda said, ignoring the legal counsel. "I can round up media attention—I've got friends, you know."

"What a shitstorm," BeBob said, as if he had just realized it. "Pardon my language."

Rlinda gave him a rough but maternal pat on the back. "That sums up the whole situation."

Four uniformed EDF guards appeared in the hearing room to surround the prisoner. Because of a newly heightened state of alert since the Corribus attack and the destruction of Relleker, the guards were dressed in commando uniforms and helmets; one of the men even wore a full protective facemask. Four armed guards seemed overkill for leading one frightened AWOL pilot back to his cell.

The guards took BeBob away, and when Rlinda tried to follow, the men brusquely stopped her. "Your presence is no longer necessary, Ms. Kett," said one of the guards.

She put her hands on her hips and stood stubbornly firm. "At least let me cook him a nice last meal. It'll be better than anything this base has ever served. Who knows, you might get some of the leftovers."

The head of the tribunal stood from his table. "There's nothing more you can do, Ms. Kett. Go home."

"Well, I can walk him to his cell, can't I? Grant me that much."

"Ms. Kett, please don't make this any more difficult—"

The guard in the facemask said, "We can take care of it, sir. Let her accompany us, so long as she doesn't snivel."

"I hereby promise a minimum of sniveling." Rlinda raised her arms and allowed herself to submit to yet another search for concealed weapons. Gathering her personal pride like a shield, she accompanied a downcast Branson Roberts out of the courtroom.

The four guards marched them along Moon base corridors, taking the prisoner down deeper tunnels, turning left and then right at corridor intersections as if their convoluted path was meant to confuse BeBob.

"Just look at all this wasted space. You know, the EDF could convert these cells to private luxury quarters, open the base as a hotel," Rlinda quipped, trying to keep her tone light. "Or do you guys really use your detention level much here?"

Not bothering to answer, the grim guards kept marching. The tall man with the full face helmet walked closest to Rlinda and BeBob, as if taking personal charge of them.

As they neared the brig level, the helmeted guard slowed his pace. She looked up at him as he adjusted his facemask, saw only brown eyes with a strange expression. Before she could crystallize her own suspicions, the guard reached into his uniform and triggered a high-powered gas canister.

White smoke jetted out in an expanding plume that filled the confined tunnel, swiftly enveloping the other guards. They coughed and struggled, turning with surprised outcries toward their comrade. Rlinda tried to shout a question, but the chemical filled her lungs, her eyes, her nose. She never imagined that sleeping gas could knock a person out so quickly—

Rlinda woke, spluttering. Her vision took a long time to clear. She seemed to be swaying from side to side, hanging facedown. Her hands and legs were dangling, and the floor moved beneath her like a conveyor belt. That couldn't be right. Lunar gravity was much lower than Earth's, but even so she shouldn't have felt so *light*.

She might have figured it out faster if the situation hadn't been so bizarre: A uniformed man was carrying her along like a piece of luggage. An antigrav strap, traditionally used to haul heavy crates, had been attached to her back like a handle. She'd never thought about using the devices for carrying people, but the lifter had nullified her bulk so that she weighed nothing at all.

The man strode along at a brisk pace. She squirmed, looking to her left, and saw BeBob similarly trussed up and carried in the man's other hand. She finally glanced up.

Davlin Lotze wore a standard EDF guard uniform, holding the two of them as if they were bulky packages. His expression was unreadable. "Are you ready to walk for yourselves now? We'll make better time that way."

Looking at Davlin, she decided to hold back her questions. Now was not the time. "Come on, BeBob, wake up! We've got to haul ass out of here."

Davlin disconnected the cargo lifters, and Rlinda felt her body settle back to the ground again. "Sorry it took me so long, but this was the best I could do on short notice."

She stood on her tiptoes to kiss his scarred cheek. "I never really thought escape was one of our alternatives."

"Now it's your only one. And I submit that it's better than summary execution or permanent penal servitude."

"Sounds okay by me," BeBob said.

Davlin gestured forward. "We're almost to the docking bay. We'll take the two ships and get out of here."

"But how did you get in? How did you pass through security at the Moon base? Where did you get a uniform?"

"I've always had one, though I upgraded to silver beret status a long time ago," Davlin said, then shushed her. "Don't ask too many questions. We've only got about ten minutes to finish up here."

"What happens in ten minutes?" BeBob asked, fighting to keep his balance but weaving like a drunkard.

"All hell breaks loose. That anesthetic gas should be wearing off on the other stunned guards, so we're bound to hear alarms soon." His voice sounded much too calm for the emergency. "The base will be slow to react, though—all Moon base personnel, without exception, are attending an emergency all-hands meeting. Apparently, General Lanyan himself called it only a few minutes ago."

"Convenient timing." Rlinda made a rude noise. "One of his pep talks?"

Finally, Davlin flashed a small smile. "Oh, the General will be as surprised as everyone else when he receives the notice. He doesn't know anything about it. The good news is that the meeting's on the other side of the base. Now, get into the docking bay."

Rlinda chuckled. "I'd sure like to see the expression on his face when he figures it out."

"I'd rather escape, if you don't mind," BeBob said. "I've seen enough of the General's expressions."

The lunar docking bay was as deserted as Davlin promised. Rlinda was amazed at how much he'd arranged so quickly, but after spending time with the "specialist in obscure details" at the archaeological site on Rheindic Co and helping him rescue the settlers from frozen-over Crenna, she knew not to underestimate what the man could pull off.

In the crater landing zone, the *Voracious Curiosity* had been left unmolested. BeBob's *Blind Faith* sat in a separate area, cordoned off. The EDF had given it an overhaul, removing records and scraps of evidence, but the vessel still looked spaceworthy. It would have to be.

"As soon as we fly away, the EDF will come after us," Rlinda said.

"Probably. That's why we need an adequate head start."

"We don't have a way to open the docking bay," BeBob said in dismay. "You need EDF authorization. We'll never get—"

Davlin silenced him with a glance. "Already taken care of." He nudged Rlinda ahead. "You two get aboard the *Curiosity* and prepare for takeoff. I'll take the *Blind Faith*. It's been impounded, and I might have to pull some unusual tricks."

"I don't want to give up the *Faith*. She's my ship. Shouldn't I be flying her?"

Rlinda yanked the still-unsteady BeBob toward her waiting vessel. "Let's have a little priority reassessment here. If anyone can fly the *Faith* away, it's Davlin. Let's go."

Standing at the cordons around BeBob's ship, Davlin tossed Rlinda a datapack. In the low lunar gravity it sailed in a graceful arc, and she deftly caught it. "Run those codes through your navigation systems. Your departure authorizations have already been issued."

Rlinda and BeBob raced toward the *Curiosity*. When she reached the open hatch and the ramp, she looked back at the spy. "Davlin . . . thanks."

He regarded her for a brief moment. "You waited for me on Rheindic Co when anyone else would have given me up for lost." He shrugged before turning to board the *Blind Faith*. "This is the least I could do for you."

The limping evacuation modules used most of their thrust to escape the hydrogue-infested gas giant. Sullivan clung to hope and determination, though he had little logical reason to believe they would make it to nearby Ildira. The odds were against them, and it was easy to lose faith.

To Sullivan's horror, one of the sluggish modules had encountered a small space rock, which punctured the hull. Air gushed out, killing everyone inside before they could patch the leak. Even if Sullivan had had a chance to do something, none of the evac modules had the room or resources to save anybody aboard. For the remaining twelve, time and life support were running out.

Until they unexpectedly bumped into the Solar Navy rushing toward Qronha 3.

If the air hadn't been so stagnant inside their evac modules, and if they hadn't been standing shoulder-to-shoulder, the passengers would have jumped and cheered. As it was, the survivors sighed with relief. Several had already passed out and needed to be shaken awake.

Sensing the presence of fellow minds and a stronger *thism* bond, the blunt-featured Ildiran miners looked instantly reassured. Kolker remained stunned and disoriented, as if he'd been blinded; without his treeling, he felt isolated. Sullivan himself had never needed a constant flow of people around him, yet he did remember the sad emptiness that always set in immediately after a major holiday, when all the children and grandchildren had gone home and his and Lydia's household was suddenly empty.

Sullivan touched his friend's arm. "It's not permanent. The Mage-Imperator is sure to reward us for saving all these people. He'll see that we're sent back home, and you'll get another treeling. Don't worry about it."

Kolker drew a deep breath and seemed to be steeling himself. "I can endure being without telink . . . for a short while."

Tabitha worked their emergency comm systems. "Hello? Calling the Solar Navy warliners. Hydrogues have destroyed the cloud harvesters on Qronha 3. We're carrying the survivors of both skymines, and our life support is running out. We could use a hand."

The seven warliners halted in space around the battered escape vessels, solar fins fully deployed so that they looked like enormous predatory fish. "The Mage-Imperator dispatched us to carry out a mission to Qronha 3," said the septar. "We can take you aboard, where you will be safe and protected until our assignment is complete."

"That's the best news I've heard all day," Sullivan said.

Once the escape vessels settled into the nearest warliner's hangar bay, passengers spilled out, gasping. The rescued Ildirans looked particularly glad to be surrounded by their kinsmen. One woman with a long mane of hair, lean features, and lithe movements stepped forward. Her large eyes flashed with a smoky brown color that reminded Sullivan of good scotch.

"I am Yazra'h, a daughter of the Mage-Imperator. Thank you for rescuing our people, at great cost to yourselves." The refugees had already told their story erratically over the comm systems as they waited to be taken aboard. "We will provide you with food, shelter, and amenities until we have the opportunity to deliver you to Ildira. My father will want to offer you his personal gratitude."

Sullivan flushed. "Don't mention it, miss. I'm sure your people would have done the same for us."

The Ildiran and human refugees were taken to different quarters. Sullivan and his people had little chance to speak with their counterparts, to exchange good wishes. It seemed rather odd to him, socially speaking, but he also remembered the incomprehensible behavior of Hroa'x. Once the Ildiran survivors were back among their own people, they seemed absorbed into a larger group from which the Hansa workers were cut off.

Continuing toward Qronha 3 with the full force of the Ildiran stardrive, all seven warliners arrived within hours. Yazra'h and the Ildiran soldiers were intent on some unstated mission, and Sullivan couldn't understand what they hoped to accomplish, since by now the hydrogues were finished destroying the cloud-harvesting facilities. When he asked questions, the Ildirans were uncommunicative.

A curious Tabitha made occasional forays down the ship corridors. She had been trained as a systems engineer in the EDF, specializing in weapons development, but she had transferred to work on the modular cloud harvester. She hoped she might learn something from looking at this warliner, and the Ildirans had never been reluctant to share technology before. She entered the propulsion bays, not venturing anywhere that was clearly restricted, yet interested in the warliner's engineering. The Ildirans, with their interconnected mental network, had very little internal security.

In contrast to the minimal interest the mining chief

Hroa'x had shown in Hansa ekti-processing designs, Tabitha inspected how the Ildiran vessels functioned, seeing with her own eyes things that she had only read about. Ildirans had freely shared their stardrive technology with humanity, and Tabitha had no reason to believe they kept secrets, but one of her discoveries surprised her. With her wide mouth curved in an impish grin, she found Sullivan and took him by the elbow to lead him to one of the smaller launching bays. "You've got to see this. I don't know what the Ildirans are doing."

A spherical vessel sat inside the room. It had heavy reinforcement ribs, incredibly thick crystalline walls, and a central chamber barely large enough to hold one small person.

He pushed out his lower lip, deep in thought. (Lydia always said it made him look like he was pouting.) "Is it some sort of pressure chamber?"

"I think this is why they've come to Qronha 3." Tabitha ran her fingers along the segmented planes that formed its walls. "Remember before the massacre at Osquivel? The EDF sent one man down in a diving bell to meet with the hydrogues. Looks to me like the Ildirans intend to do the same thing."

He squinted inside the sealed armored chamber. "If I remember right, the EDF's attempt didn't exactly turn out the way they had hoped."

A sharp female voice spoke from behind them. "We did not invite you into this launching bay."

Sullivan turned immediately, knowing they'd been caught. Tabitha flushed with embarrassment. "We . . . we didn't know."

Sullivan said, "Sorry. We weren't told of any restrictions. My engineer here was simply curious about some of your technology."

Yazra'h stood there, looking intimidating with a crystal dagger at her waist. Sullivan was certain that the Mage-Imperator's daughter could easily dispatch them both, if she so chose.

Oddly out of place, an angelic little girl stood by her side, looking delicate, but not fragile. The girl had a strange cast to her features; her short gold hair was bound in feathery little strands. Her face looked soft and innocent, but the eyes held a bold intelligence far beyond her apparent years. The girl's manner was strikingly odd and off-center.

Sullivan stepped forward with a grin, thinking of his own sweet granddaughters. "And who is this? My name is Sullivan Gold. I—"

"You do not need to know her name." Yazra'h put a protective hand on the girl's shoulder. "We have an inspection to perform. Please return to your quarters."

"Maybe we can help with your inspection," Tabitha said, as if trying to make amends for their faux pas. "I'm a qualified engineer. I'd be eager to share my knowledge with—"

"That will not be necessary. Round up your human survivors and bring them to the gathering chamber. The septar has decided to send one of our warliners back to Mijistra, carrying you and the surviving Ildiran skyminers. The other six ships will remain at Qronha 3 to complete our mission." Dismissing them, she guided the strange girl over toward the armored sphere.

Sullivan stared after her. "But what are you going to do at Qronha 3?"

Yazra'h slowly looked at him, then at Tabitha, tight-lipped. "Please go to the gathering chamber and arrange your personnel."

Sullivan finally took his engineer's wrist and pulled her

out of the bay. Walking beside him down the warliner's corridors, Tabitha was deep in thought. "I wish I knew what it is the Ildirans don't want us to see."

91 ☀ OSIRA'H

Although she had been bred and trained for this, events swept up on Osira'h like a foaming wall of angry water bursting from behind a dam. Despite her reservations, she quickly became consumed with her own circumstances. The die was cast, and she would finish what she had been trained to do.

While Yazra'h finalized all the details and dealt with the human and Ildiran refugees, Osira'h meditated to sharpen her mental abilities and prepare for her destiny. If she performed her task successfully, there would be no further Ildiran victims in this war. But if she failed, she herself would become the next casualty. Then all of the secrets would die with her.

One of the warliners turned about with the rescued skyminers and headed back to Ildira. The six remaining vessels would be sufficient to deliver Osira'h's encounter chamber into the deep clouds. The number of Solar Navy battleships did not matter: Everything now depended on one little girl alone.

At last, after Yazra'h said a quiet and touching farewell, Osira'h was ready to go.

Gauzy chemical clouds enfolded her as she sat inside the crystalline bubble, now entirely cut off from the warliners and the reassuring company of her sister.

At Qronha 3, the ships had found dissipating signs of smoke, the remnants of the one-sided battle. By now, the wreckage of the human and Ildiran complexes had plunged deep to the equilibrium limits, and the hydrogues had returned to their lair. Osira'h would have to go find them.

Reinforced with the toughest polymers and alloy frameworks, her chamber had no engines, no weapons—those things would be irrelevant when she finally met the hydrogues. Orbiting so high above Qronha 3, the warliners could never retrieve her now. If she did not succeed in her mission, the loss of her life would be the least of all the grim consequences. As she descended, Osira'h knew her fate was in the hands of the hydrogues.

She would serve in the same role as the Klikiss robots had once acted—before the robots broke all ties with the Ildiran Empire at Hrel-oro. As a bridge between two completely alien species, she had to open a line of communication with the enemy, convince them to listen to the Mage-Imperator. What concessions was her father willing to make? What unconscionable bargains?

Her ship fell like a stone, and Osira'h clung to her padded crash seat, concentrating, sending out a mental message to augment the signal from her transmitting system. She *needed* the hydrogues to come to her. She hoped the aliens would be curious enough to come and inspect her, rather than destroy the encounter chamber outright.

The crystal walls glowed from friction as gas molecules scraped against the smooth sides. The vessel had been built to withstand these horrific conditions. Around her, the atmosphere thickened.

Osira'h tried harder, forcing her thoughts outward, as she had done many times in practice sessions on Dobro. She closed her eyes against the distracting colors and chimera shapes of the storms. She gripped tightly with her small hands and continued to send out her thoughts. *I have a job to do.*

She didn't know what this task would cost her. Before, when she'd been innocent and gullible, she had been willing to pay any price to make Designate Udru'h and the Mage-Imperator proud. She had wanted to do anything to make her mentor happy. But with visions of her mother in her head, she was not as sure. Osira'h was no longer convinced that the secret-filled Ildiran Empire deserved such a sacrifice from her.

As her crystal bubble continued downward, she saw movement in the thickening vapors around her, which resolved into the smooth diamond hulls of warglobes. Blue lightning crackled from their pyramidal protrusions.

Osira'h held on, energetically sending her thoughts. *I must speak with you. I represent your former allies. We want to end this war between our races.*

The warglobes drifted next to her, accompanying her crystal bubble. Without warning, she was thrown to one side with an abrupt jerk as the hydrogue vessels captured her with an invisible beam. She sensed no returning thoughts, no acknowledgment.

Unhurried, the warglobes dragged her bubble like a fish in a net. Osira'h lost track of time and distance. All the while, she continued sending her message. With widening eyes and increasing awe, she saw an enormous complex of faceted globes that formed an immense citysphere. The hydrogue metropolis was full of alien angles and curves that joined in unorthodox directions. It was like a magical struc-ture from the stories she had absorbed from her mother's thoughts, the lost city of Atlantis or a fabled fairy kingdom.

The girl did not allow herself to be fooled. The hydrogues were not ethereal or benevolent fantasy creatures. They were deadly enemies who had already proved their thirst for utter destruction.

The warglobes pulled her encounter bubble through a membrane in the citysphere wall. Osira'h let her thoughts resonate outward in an uninterrupted silent shout. Peering through the transparent wall, she waited.

At last, quicksilver shapes formed themselves into humanoid bodies. Five of the flowing hydrogues approached her, each one identical, each costumed like the Roamer victim it had copied before. As part of her intensive training, Osira'h had reviewed every scrap of information known about the enemy, including images from the Whisper Palace on Earth.

The weight of responsibility pressed around her, like the incredible force of the surrounding atmosphere. She leaned forward against the protective crystal barrier. The hydrogue figures stood shimmering before her. It was time to open negotiations.

92 ☀ RLINDA KETT

As luck would have it, the Moon base alarm sounded even before the *Curiosity* cleared the top of the crater wall. Below them, the *Blind Faith* was still cycling through engine warm-up. BeBob looked sick in the copilot's seat beside Rlinda, drowning in reality. He glanced worriedly at his ship.

"We'd better get moving," she said. Without her usual double-checks, Rlinda soared away from the Moon's gravity field. She slapped the panel with the flat of her hand and tried to squeeze out more acceleration. On the screen, blips indicated swarms of fast Remoras coming in from perimeter patrols.

"The *Curiosity* was never designed to be taken into battle, you know," she told him. "Brace yourself."

"Who said anything about battle?" BeBob's voice cracked. "How about we don't let them catch up with us in the first place?"

"Thanks, I'll keep that in mind."

Roaring in closer, the squadron commander transmitted in a voice that sounded like fingernails on a chalkboard, "You are ordered to stand down and return to the Moon base."

Rlinda signaled back, "This isn't a military ship, mister. You don't have any authority to give me orders."

"Well, those hot jazers give them some provisional authority—"

"Quiet, BeBob." She opened a general channel without

video. "Excuse me, but I was *told* to leave, and in no uncertain terms. Make up your minds."

"We believe you are holding the fugitive Captain Roberts. We have orders not to let him escape. Return to the base or we will open fire."

As the Moon dwindled behind them, the *Blind Faith* finally lifted off from the crater, accelerating at reckless velocity low to the lunar surface, trying unsuccessfully to remain below radar scans.

"Go, Davlin," Rlinda said through clenched teeth.

BeBob knotted his fingers together, glancing at their screens and then out the front windowport. "Just so long as he's careful with my ship. I don't think even high-risk insurance covers damage incurred while fleeing from authorities."

"Better check your policy, BeBob. But not right now, okay?"

"Just thinking ahead."

Seeing the second ship appear, the Remora squadron split up, half of the fast fighter ships swooping off to intercept the *Blind Faith*. "That's Roberts's ship," said the squadron commander. "The *Voracious Curiosity* is just a decoy."

"I guess a bait and switch is just too much for their imaginations." Rlinda grinned.

"Don't celebrate yet, Rlinda—half of them are still on our tail."

"That's better than having all of them after us." She continued on her erratic trajectory, throwing the two of them from side to side faster than the stabilizers could compensate. "BeBob, set a course out of this system. How soon can we engage the Ildiran stardrive and leave the EDF ships in our exhaust?"

"Umm . . . no sooner than they can."

Before the Remoras could intercept the second fleeing ship, the *Blind Faith* shot out into open space. Its engines were powered beyond their maximums, the exhaust cowlings glowing cherry red from unmitigated thrust.

Over an open channel came a wavering staticky image, supposedly transmitted from the cockpit of BeBob's ship, no doubt distorted by the huge power expenditure of its flight. The screen showed the visage of Branson Roberts himself. "You have no right to chase me," the mock BeBob said. "I've been unfairly charged and convicted by a kangaroo court. You're hunting an innocent man."

"Hey! How did Davlin doctor that up so fast?"

Rlinda smiled. "Probably part of his training as a specialist in obscure details."

"Does my voice really sound like that? High and squeaky?"

Rlinda turned her big brown eyes to him. "If you were really in the *Faith*'s cockpit right now, you'd sound a lot squeakier."

BeBob slumped back in his copilot chair.

As Davlin pulled farther away from the pursuing squadron, two more Remoras broke off from the *Curiosity* and joined the primary hunt.

But several EDF fighters stuck close as Rlinda flew the *Voracious Curiosity* on an erratic course to climb out of the solar system. The short-range fighters didn't have as much fuel as her ship did, but they had greater speed. They could close around the *Curiosity* long before she could outrun them.

Rlinda and BeBob worked together in the cockpit like two components of a precision machine. It was just like old times.

The *Blind Faith* sent another transmission, and BeBob's simulated face was even more desperate than before. He looked like a man capable of anything. "You leave Rlinda alone! The *Curiosity* has nothing to do with me."

BeBob looked over at her. "Does he really think that'll work?"

She rested her chin on her knuckles for a moment. "Davlin wouldn't rely on anything quite so simplistic. The question is, what's he really up to?"

They watched the drama play out far below. The Remoras closed in like a pack of wolves, but the *Blind Faith* surprised them all by looping around in such a high-G reversal that it should have smashed any living pilot into jelly, or at least knocked him unconscious. Somehow, though, Davlin continued to fly his ship in the opposite direction. The *Faith* careened directly toward the pursuing EDF ships. It was obviously a suicide run—or at least intended to look like one.

"He's playing a game of chicken with my ship!"

As the cargo ship roared toward the cluster of EDF fighters, the Remoras scattered. They opened fire on the ship's engines, trying to cripple it, but the *Faith* flew too fast, and their shots did only minimal damage, scoring the hull. The reckless vessel continued to accelerate, and its engines roared scarlet.

The *Blind Faith* did not deviate in its course, but plowed into their grouping like an out-of-control pulse-racer slamming into a stadium full of spectators. The EDF ships scrambled to avoid collision.

Then, immediately after it had passed through the flurry of Remoras, the *Blind Faith* exploded. Its engine casings burst open, reactor exhaust flamed out and split the vessel. Shrapnel sprayed in a spherical cloud, peppering several fast fighters that were too close. The EDF attack ships spun out of control, calling for emergency reinforcement and rescue vessels.

Rlinda stared in awe and disbelief. "Davlin, what did you do that for?"

BeBob blinked his big sad eyes at her. "My ship . . ."

Fighting to concentrate, Rlinda looked at the tactical screens that showed space around them. "Thanks to that explosion, we've doubled our lead. It's time to take advantage of the distraction." Her heart felt heavy, but she couldn't believe Davlin had given his life to save them. It just didn't sound like him.

By now, all the Remoras had turned about, racing up above the planetary orbits. The closest group of fighters accelerated again, anxious to end the chase.

"Sore losers," BeBob said, still numb with shock.

"Five minutes and I'll jump us with the stardrive. Right now, go down to the cargo bay. There's a few dozen loose crates and tanks."

BeBob ran out of the cockpit, already knowing what she meant to do. As the seconds ticked by and the Remoras came closer, she looked at the cargo bay imagers to see BeBob shoving crates, pallets, tanks, and spare parts into the middle of the cargo bay floor. Her ship's engines were hot and on the brink of overloading. She didn't want to end up like the *Blind Faith*.

"That's enough junk, BeBob. Thirty seconds and I'm ready. Get your butt up here."

BeBob was already pulling himself through the cockpit door. He slammed himself into the seat and buckled the crash restraints. As the Remoras got closer, a flurry of jazer potshots spangled past them.

"Dumping the cargo bay." Without draining the atmosphere, she opened the hatches, vomiting a blast of rapidly expanding air and sparkling debris that flew out in a smoke-screen.

The unexpected debris acted like a field of land mines, and the Remoras hammered into it. The pursuing ships spun out of control; one suffered severe wing damage. Rlinda didn't particularly want to destroy EDF soldiers who were just trying to do their jobs—but BeBob's life was at stake.

She couldn't stick around to see how it all turned out. She activated the Ildiran stardrive and lurched out of the solar system, hoping to stay one step ahead of General Lanyan's angry pursuers.

93 ☀ KING PETER

On the day after Daniel's contrite speech, Basil stood at the doorway of the Royal Wing wearing a cool smile. "Come with me, Peter. This is something you need to see. Consider it part of your continuing education." Franz Pellidor stood beside him like a well-dressed thug, ready if the King resisted.

Peter frowned at the implied threat. "I prefer OX's instructional methods. He's programmed to be a teacher, and he has more memories than he can hold in his head. That counts for a lot of experience, in my book."

"Since OX allowed Prince Daniel to escape, I have doubts about his abilities as an instructor. This will help you learn about political realities . . . and consequences." The Chairman walked briskly down the hall, his dress shoes clicking on the polished stone tiles. He had no doubt that the King would follow.

With another frown, Peter left his private chambers and walked beside Mr. Pellidor. He didn't even dignify the broad-shouldered man with a glance.

They passed down empty halls and staircases and finally reached a lower-level infirmary chamber that smelled of disinfectants, sterile metal, and chemicals. There, on a hospital bed in the center of the room, lay the pale young Prince Daniel. The boy appeared to be in a coma, hooked up to medical diagnostics. Intravenous lines ran from his arms. His chubby cheeks looked sunken, though Peter had seen him only yesterday.

"What happened? Was there an accident?"

"Oh, no accident—I assure you this was entirely intentional." Basil stepped forward to touch the intravenous tubes, then leaned over to stare at the false Prince's closed translucent eyelids. The boy didn't move or twitch.

"After Daniel's foolish escapade, the Hansa committee met in an emergency session. We decided unanimously that we can no longer take the risk of further episodes of gross misbehavior. Therefore, we have drugged him. We will keep him in this comatose state, where I can be certain he is under control." He fixed his gray eyes on Peter. "Too many mistakes have been made recently, *and I will no longer tolerate it.*"

Peter remained silent, letting the long moment draw itself out; it was a technique Basil himself had taught him. He knew exactly how dangerous the Chairman was. Finally, he said, "So why not just kill him?"

"Because he makes a better example this way, don't you think? I suppose we could always awaken him if it becomes necessary. You see, we could easily do this to you." Basil straightened and took a step away from the motionless Prince. He asked in a light conversational tone, "Now then, why didn't you tell me Queen Estarra is pregnant? I've known since last Wednesday, but you must have known for at least a month."

A current of ice water washed down Peter's spine. He controlled his expression, refused to blurt out a denial. The Chairman wouldn't have brought up the subject unless he had proof. Peter knew he would do better to see where Basil was going with this.

The Chairman paced the floor of the infirmary room. "The King and Queen are always monitored, Peter. We've taken several samples and verified our results. My first inkling came when you both were with me aboard the ship to Ildira. Nuances, slight differences in behavior. You didn't think I was paying attention . . . but I always pay attention. We followed up with further tests obtained from your royal quarters."

Peter remained silent. His mouth was dry, and his skin crawled with the reminder that even in their most private moments the Hansa was spying on them, sampling cells scraped from the royal bedsheets, monitoring Estarra's menstrual cycle, probably even culling urine samples from the Palace's plumbing. He found it repulsive.

Basil stepped close to him, very close. Peter had grown taller over the years, but the Chairman still seemed to regard him as little more than a street urchin. "We can't allow this, you know."

Trying to be strong, desperately wishing he had sent Estarra to Theroc before anyone had a chance to find out, Peter said, "You're missing a key advantage, Basil. Imagine the excellent public relations we can get. The people will love it."

The Chairman didn't budge. "You miss the fundamental problem here. *I* didn't give you permission."

Peter sighed and let his shoulders sag. "You won't believe this, but I swear we didn't do it on purpose. It was an accident, a surprise to both of us. Maybe it was nature asserting itself to continue the species in a time of great threat."

Though Basil appeared outwardly calm, he seemed to carry a thunderstorm inside, a simmering frustration that had been building as each small failure added to previous ones. "Don't lecture me, Peter. Someday, at a time of *my* choosing, when *I* give you leave, the two of you might be allowed to have a child. But not now. Estarra will simply have to get rid of the fetus before it becomes public knowledge. I'll have discreet medical specialists visit her shortly."

Peter stared, trying to quell the anger and horror rising inside him. The Chairman could easily have taken Estarra and forced her to undergo an abortion without any warning at all—instead, he preferred to twist the knife and make absolutely sure the King and Queen knew what he intended to do.

Basil gave Peter a withering look and glanced meaningfully at the pasty-faced, drugged Prince Daniel. "And please don't insult my abilities by imagining that you could stop me."

Knowing there would be much more difficult conquests in the Horizon Cluster, Rusa'h had dispatched Prime Designate Thor'h with most of the maniple to absorb another Ildiran world into his ever-expanding web.

Meanwhile, one fully armed warliner would be sufficient to crush the small Dobro colony, if Designate Udru'h refused to cooperate. The giant battleship's weapons could lay waste to the centuries-old settlement and the breeding compound.

Though Udru'h coyly continued to avoid giving a direct answer, Imperator Rusa'h showed little concern when he dispatched the single warliner to Dobro. Apparently he thought the Dobro Designate had no real options. Udru'h had always been practical, and he certainly would not allow Dobro to be destroyed.

The warliner carried a full cargo load of shiing to distribute to the Ildiran population on Dobro. If Udru'h himself did not force the conversion, then he would be slain, and the question would be put to the more malleable Designate-in-waiting Daro'h. If young Daro'h also refused, then he too was expendable. Giving Udru'h any choice in the matter was obviously a mere formality.

Ruling his new *thism* network from the citadel palace, he sent the Dobro Designate back home on the former flagship, with Zan'nh himself still prisoner aboard.

On the voyage to Dobro, the Designate was allowed his freedom aboard the warliner, but it was merely a larger prison. With the Solar Navy crew loyal to Rusa'h, the self-proclaimed Imperator had no worries about what one Designate could do. Once they reached Dobro, none of them doubted that Udru'h would shift his loyalties. Rusa'h claimed to understand his brother all too clearly.

Udru'h strolled down the warliner's corridors toward the sealed private cabins where the Adar was held captive. Rusa'h had said, "Perhaps on their journey, even the Adar may see the light of reason." Apparently, forcing him to watch the surrender and conversion of Dobro would be another blow to his resolve.

Udru'h knew he did not have much time.

The Dobro Designate's expression remained bland as he approached the two husky guard kithmen stationed outside the door with crystal katanas and bristling armor. Unlike Udru'h, the Adar adamantly and vociferously refused to cooperate, and the guards kept him locked up.

The two guards snapped to attention at the Designate's approach. Facing them, Udru'h used his much-practiced mental skills to mask any stray thoughts, just as a precaution, though these guard kithmen would never have had the prowess to unravel the *thism* connections in his mind. In turn, the converted soldiers were a blank to him, bound together in Rusa'h's secondary mental network. The Dobro Designate considered that an advantage. They were weaker than he.

He gave them a thin smile. "Your Imperator has instructed me to speak with Zan'nh whenever possible. My brother believes I can wear down the Adar's resistance to joining your cause." He pressed closer to them, keeping his thoughts blank. His heart pounded.

Guard kithmen did not question the instructions of a Designate. The two simultaneously clenched their fists and pressed them against their chestplates in salute. Udru'h did not hesitate.

He sprang forward, raising the curved knife hidden in his left fist. He slashed viciously sideways, slicing the throat of the guard on the left, then continuing with a sweep of momentum, until he brought the point of the knife between the second guard's shoulder plate and collar. He hammered his palm against the pommel, driving the blade home.

The guard with the slashed throat bled profusely. He gasped and coughed and slid to the floor, dying. Even with the knife sticking in his neck, the other guard remained a threat for a few more seconds. The Dobro Designate danced backward, retreating as fast as he could down the hall. Roaring and choking, the second guard staggered after him, grabbing at the knife hilt in his neck.

Udru'h was not a warrior and did not need to be. The poison on the blade was sufficiently fast-acting. It was the same deeply toxic substance that was rumored to have caused the death of Mage-Imperator Cyroc'h. *Ironic*.

As the guard plodded forward, his pace became an uneven stagger. From the expression on his bestial face, Udru'h could sense the poison fires burning through his systems. Maintaining a safe distance, Udru'h slowed. The guard reeled, taking longer than expected to die.

The Designate looked around, anxious lest any other Solar Navy crewmen stumble upon them. He hadn't expected to cause so much commotion or such a mess. He wondered if the mad Designate Rusa'h, far off on Hyrillka, would sense the violent deaths of his two followers. . . .

Finally, with a last grunt and a heavy clatter, the guard collapsed face-first in the hall, his crystal katana extended forward.

Udru'h had accomplished the first step. He looked at the blood on his hands, the spray pattern on his garments where the crimson had splashed. Though his head rang with lonely emptiness from being so far from his accustomed *thism* network, he kept his thoughts in order. His pulse raced, and he tried to calm himself.

Ildirans have killed Ildirans. For all his talk about rigidly adhering to the old ways, Imperator Rusa'h had apparently started a new tradition.

Udru'h lifted his stained crystal knife and headed for the chamber where Adar Zan'nh was held.

95 ☀ ADAR ZAN'NH

The chamber walls were closing in on him. Zan'nh heard footsteps moving down the warliner's corridors, but he could not sense the crewmen out there. In normal, sane times any Ildiran lived in a current of other lives, bathed in *thism,* buoyed by the existence and support of so many fellows. The passage of a Solar Navy soldier should have caused a ripple discernible even through the sealed door of the cell.

But he felt nothing. Far, far away the dim soul-threads from Mage-Imperator Jora'h faded more and more as the hours dragged on. Zan'nh had battered his knuckles bloody against the walls, but it did no good. He sank into a corner,

wiping his hands and staining his Solar Navy uniform. Adar
Kori'nh would certainly have chided him for his sloppy appearance. He rested his face in his palms, ground his teeth
together, and *held on.*

When he heard the commotion in the corridor, Zan'nh
lurched to his feet. He crouched in front of the armored
door, listening, then backed away. He paused and approached again, ready to spring on anyone who came inside.
Now he did sense an echo, a thread of recognizable *thism*
coming closer. He didn't understand.

The locking mechanism clicked, the door slid aside.

Though shaking and weak, Zan'nh lunged. The Dobro
Designate stood there, his own garments stained. He held a
crystal dagger in one hand, hanging casually at his side. In
the moment of surprise, Zan'nh drove him backward, striking a hard blow on the Designate's wrist. The crystal dagger
clattered to the deck plates.

Though startled, Udru'h recovered swiftly and swept his
right foot in an arc that knocked the wavering Adar off balance. With a shove, he tumbled Zan'nh to the floor near the
fallen dagger. The Adar grabbed for it, closed his hand
around the hilt, but the Dobro Designate stepped on his
wrist, pressing down with nearly enough force to crack
bone. Zan'nh grunted, released the dagger.

"Enough of this nonsense." The Designate kicked the
knife away.

Panting and still sprawled on the deck, Zan'nh finally
looked out into the corridor beyond his cell. His wild eyes
drank in the unexpected scene: the murdered guard lying in
a pool of blood outside his door, the other guard facedown
farther down the corridor. He stared up at the spattered and
sweating Designate who loomed over him. Zan'nh's voice

was raspy and rough. "What is this? You . . . you have killed Ildirans!"

The Dobro Designate paused another second before lifting his foot from the Adar's wrist. He stepped back, regaining his composure. "Rusa'h isn't the only one who can take extreme measures. Think of all the Ildirans he has killed." He sounded bland and matter-of-fact. "If we are not willing to do unpleasant work, then Rusa'h and his lunatic rebellion will succeed. I have always done what was necessary, and I have always served the Ildiran Empire." He looked with disdain at the Adar, then offered his hand to pull Zan'nh to his feet. "Come with me if you want a chance to end this revolt."

Zan'nh hesitated for a moment, emotions storming through his mind. Then he nodded, frantic for a way out of the chamber, off of this warliner. After his failed bargain to surrender his vessels, he was ready to destroy this ship rather than let it be used to continue spreading Rusa'h's corruption.

"Though I may eventually be damned for it in the *Saga*, I agree with you." Zan'nh lowered his voice. "If I had been willing to do what was necessary, we would not be in such a grim situation. Adar Kori'nh would never have let it come to this."

He followed his uncle out into the too-quiet corridor. Businesslike, the Dobro Designate leaned over the nearer dead guard. Without hesitating, he grasped the armored shoulders and began to drag the heavy soldier toward the open prison cell. "Help me hide these corpses and clean up. That will buy us time."

Blood-sticky hands did not seem to bother the Dobro Designate, but Zan'nh stood staring aghast at the two slaughtered guards. As uniformed Solar Navy warriors, these two had been members of his own crew before their forced conversion. Then he remembered all of his own loyal crewmen who had died as hostages to Rusa'h, murdered one by one until Zan'nh had surrendered his ships. His heart grew cold. He already had blood on his hands. These two guards were casualties of a civil war, and they were less innocent than those other victims had been.

Stronger now, Zan'nh grabbed the second guard, and soon both corpses were sealed behind the door. They used part of one of the dead guards' uniforms to wipe the worst of the bloodstains off the deck, so that no casual passerby would notice the marks. Breathless, they stood together in the corridor.

Though full of corrupted Solar Navy crewmen, the Ildiran battleship was nearly silent in the *thism*. Zan'nh felt only the connection from the Dobro Designate, whom he still did not entirely trust. "So there are only two of us aboard this entire warliner. Do we have a plan?"

Udru'h raised his eyebrows, somewhat amused. "I have already completed my part of the plan, Adar. I freed you. Now I rely on your knowledge of the Solar Navy, and this warliner in particular. The next step is up to you."

E ven in the heated interior of the *Aquarius,* Cesca couldn't
stop shivering. "I never thought I'd feel warm again."

Purcell said to Nikko, "We need to get away, take off
before those robots come back for us."

"I'm sure they saw my ship when I flew over," Nikko
said. "And I don't have any weapons aboard to defend us."

Cesca glanced at the wrung-out administrator, then at
Nikko Chan Tylar, dreading what she had to say. But she
was the Speaker, and she had to protect the clans. "We can't
just leave here. We've got to prevent those robots from
launching their ships. Then they'll be free to destroy any
other Roamer bases they find."

Purcell's voice came out as a squawk. "What are *we* supposed to do against them? You saw what they did to the
base!"

"And we can't let them do any more. Those were *our people* they slaughtered. Once they get off Jonah 12, we'll have no
way of stopping them."

Nikko said nervously, "I've done some foolish and ambitious things before, Speaker Peroni, but even *I* would
never tackle a thousand Klikiss robots."

She still felt cold and empty, bearing the burden of so
many more deaths, so much unprovoked slaughter, and she
intended to do something, before it was too late.

"I don't know what we ever did to anger those robots, but
I have never seen my Guiding Star so clearly. Whatever
they're doing, we *can't* let them succeed. Do you have any

doubt that we'll pay for it in the long run? We can nip this in the bud—and it's got to be the three of us: If we just run, the robots will be long gone before we can return with reinforcements."

Purcell turned his long face away, looking sick. "I never said you weren't right, Speaker. I just said I didn't like it. How are we supposed to stop them?"

Her smile felt as cold as the temperature outside. "Purcell, we had an idea when the robots were attacking the base. It seemed too drastic, and there wasn't enough time. Now, though, I can't think of anything more appropriate."

The black machines remained intent on their own plans, far away. Nikko deployed his ship's most sensitive sensors to keep watch, but none of the robots came to investigate, allowing the three of them time to prepare. As the acting administrator, Purcell described the details of the Jonah 12 base, sketched out the locations of all possible resources, and explained what they had to do.

When they were ready, Nikko flew the *Aquarius* to the perimeter of what had been the mining base, skimming only a few meters above the stippled ground to keep out of sensor range. He landed gently out of sight, beyond the lip of a crater, kicking up a dust of hydrogen and methane ices.

"The Klikiss robots might have detected us," Purcell cautioned.

"If they're even bothering to watch." Nikko scratched his lank, dark hair. "They seemed awfully preoccupied with those ships when I flew over."

"They aren't worried about us," Cesca said. "They knew where our grazer was stranded all along, but they didn't even bother to come looking."

Though her suit heaters were turned to maximum levels, Cesca still felt a chill as she walked beside the two men. They crept over the crater's rise, closer to the expanded site of the mining base. Here, not long ago, she had stood watching Jhy Okiah's wrapped body as it launched out into space to roam among the stars. Now everyone else at the base was dead too.

The three spied on the construction complex, trying to determine what the robots were doing. Cesca used a focused line-of-sight communication beam so that no signal would bleed over for the robots to intercept. "I never expected something quite this . . . drastic. There's nothing left of the base, nothing recognizable at all."

Purcell made his assessment. "They've taken our processed metals and dismantled our machinery, ripping components out and reassembling them."

"The ships look almost ready to launch," Cesca said.

The administrative engineer looked at the glowing small-pile reactor. The shielded power plant was a standard design, a proven workhorse for centuries. "They've ramped up the reactor to expand its output, but it was never designed to tolerate so much. Kotto would have a fit. That pile wasn't meant to run at such levels for any length of time. That'll make our job easier. The reactor's got to be halfway unstable already."

Cesca could easily see Purcell's troubled expression through his faceplate, but she was smiling. "Then let's make it all the way unstable. Still think you can coax the plant to melt down?"

"Shizz, Speaker Peroni, the way that pile's jury-rigged we'll be lucky if that's all it does. We're more likely to generate a major supercriticality."

"As long as we're back to my *Aquarius* in time." Nikko fidgeted in the cold. "Are we going to sit here and keep talking while our heat reserves run out, or should we get going?"

The trio moved quickly across the dark and uneven landscape. Cesca wished they could have left Nikko aboard his ship to arrange a quick getaway, but they needed all three of them for Purcell's plan.

Over where the base domes had been, the hulking Klikiss robots moved about assembling the frameworks of their vessels. Long cables tapped into the energy generators, and thick conduits extended from the reactor pile in sloppy tangles. The robots showed no finesse, no inclination to build anything that would last longer than their current needs.

As the three approached the workhorse reactor pile, Cesca could feel the machinery vibrating through her suit. The lights around the shielded facility were bright, and the metal was hot. Around the power plant the ground was uplifted, melted and cracked from a backwash of radiant heat.

The robots remained focused on their work.

Studying the reactor building, Purcell continued his nervous muttering on the line-of-sight channel. "Remember, I was never a genius engineer. I always did what Kotto said, and everything turned out all right." When they reached the harsh shadows of the shielded structure, he studied the external controls. "I'm not much of an innovator. I couldn't just rig a solution out of thin air—"

Cesca cut him off. "We're not asking you to find a solution, Purcell. We want you to screw the reactor up very badly."

He gave an anxious laugh. "*That* I can do."

Cesca and Nikko followed the engineer's clipped instruc-

tions as they pulled flow regulators from the circulating
coolant systems. At a different bank, Purcell removed a
cover plate and yanked out control rods doped with neutron
poisons. Almost immediately, the pile began to run hotter.

Scrap metal from the torn-apart domes lay strewn on the
ground; Nikko wedged a bar into the coolant systems and
used the leverage to twist the pipes until they snapped. Hissing coolant spilled out onto the ground and froze hard.

Moving fast now, Purcell and Cesca tore the last of the
control rods loose, tossing them far away in the low gravity.
The robots would never retrieve them in time. "That's done
it!" the engineer shouted. "This reactor is like a runaway ship
with a blind pilot in an asteroid belt. We, uh, better get out of
here."

Nikko saw a group of the insectlike automatons scuttling
toward the reactor pile. "I think the robots spotted us."

"We're done here—let's go!"

With long bounds in the low gravity, they circled the
overheating reactor. The *Aquarius* lay unseen just on the
other side of the crater rim.

As they emerged around the corner of the shielded pile,
Purcell careened to an abrupt halt in front of two looming
black robots. "How did they get here so fast?" His boots
skidded on the slippery, broken ground.

One of the robots reached out to grab the back of Purcell's suit. The clicking claws touched him only lightly, and
the administrative engineer tore himself loose from the
black metal grip and lunged after his two companions. They
bounded away, each step a giant leap in the low gravity.
"Keep going! Get to the *Aquarius*!" Purcell gasped for
breath, and a loud whistling sound came from his suit radio.

Behind them, the throbbing reactor pile was obviously

growing hotter. They could even see the glow from metal stressed to its limits. While two Klikiss robots set off after the three saboteurs, other machines converged like diligent ants to work on the reactor systems.

"They'll never fix it in time," Nikko said. "Will they, Purcell?" He turned.

The administrative engineer staggered to a halt. "I think . . . maybe they . . . it's just a nick." He collapsed and fell forward.

Cesca raced back to him. "Purcell, get up. We have to make it to the ship before—" She rolled him over and saw that his faceplate was covered with frost on the inside. Whistling steam bled from the back of his insulated suit. The robot's claws had torn the fabric, opening it to the supercold environment. Purcell's face looked oddly flat and angular, as if it had flash-frozen and then broken, falling in upon itself.

"He's dead." Cesca clenched her teeth in fury, then grabbed Nikko's arm as he stood staring. "We'll mourn him later. *Right now* we've got to get off of Jonah 12!"

Behind them, more robots scuttled over the terrain, relentlessly closing the distance. Cesca muttered a curse and knew they would have to leave Purcell's body with the other fallen Roamers. She and Nikko raced to the ship, hoping they could take off before the robots caught them, and before the reactor blew.

A s their sharp-angled ship entered the outer system where the last Klikiss robots hibernated, Sirix continued to tell DD horrifying stories about his progenitor race. The Friendly compy was much more disturbed to know that the robots' plans for the extermination of the human race were about to begin.

Upon approaching the distant planetoid that held the final cluster of dormant robots, Sirix discovered a great deal of unexpected activity. "I detect numerous Klikiss language transmissions. These robots should not have been activated yet. Something is wrong."

Their ship descended toward the small icy world, and the glowing base camp suddenly came into view. Sirix displayed the full complex on their tactical screens. "Those are indications of human technology. Your creators have come to this world before us."

Now DD was interested. "A human habitation? Did they awaken the robots by accident?"

"That is an advantageous possibility. Our remaining companions appear to have nearly completed their own work. They have independently acquired materials and components from the humans there."

Acquired. DD saw to his dismay that the human settlement was destroyed; no doubt the people had all been massacred, just like the colonists on Corribus.

Transmitting his identity and mission, Sirix flew toward the central base where a flurry of reactivated machines moved about. "I detect anomalous power levels and unusual energy buildup. There are many simultaneous transmissions from the robots on the ground."

"It sounds like they're distressed." DD spotted a blip of engine exhaust as a ship lifted off from the planetoid's surface. Even with the limited scan, he recognized the configuration of a human ship. Someone was still alive down there.

A ragged human voice came over the communications system, a frightened-sounding young man. "Incoming ship, back off! Jonah 12 is going to get awfully hot in a few seconds. I'm not kidding—" The voice cut off in sudden alarm as the pilot realized he was not in contact with a human vessel.

Sirix swiveled his head toward DD. "If humans have discovered our secret enclave of Klikiss robots, we cannot allow them to escape and spread a warning. This is a crucial time in our plans."

Sirix changed course toward the human vessel as it raced up out of Jonah 12's gravity well. DD heard a hum of systems, hydraulic machinery locking into place. Sirix said, "Until now, DD, you have been unaware of the weapons systems built into this craft."

"You do not have to kill them," the compy pleaded.

"It is necessary."

Without delay, Sirix launched two heavy-artillery projectiles, which streaked toward the human ship. Shouting, the pilot spun his craft, wildly changing course. The projectiles soared in, converging in space.

The escaping vessel swooped and corkscrewed, but one of the targeted projectiles slammed into its engines. The explosion sent the human spacecraft into a tumbling dive, out of control. DD watched the ruined ship plummet toward the icy surface. It fell near the horizon and struck a frozen out-cropping, crashing far from the robot-infested base camp.

"Now I can concentrate on what has agitated the other ro-bots," Sirix said. "The human pilot implied that a disaster is about to occur."

DD desperately wanted to scan for survivors, to help them, but Sirix would never allow it.

The black robot said, "You need not be concerned, DD. A team of Klikiss robots can go to the crash site and dis-patch any human still alive, as we did on Corribus."

They descended to the construction site, while Sirix con-tinued to transmit requests for information. On the ground dozens of robots clustered around a large containment struc-ture. The power levels were throbbing.

DD shifted frequencies in his optical sensors and saw in infrared that the structure was blazing hot. The uncontrolled thermal output swelled visibly second by second. Finally the robots on the ground acknowledged Sirix's insistent signals and transmitted a burst summary of what had happened.

DD intercepted and translated the message, swiftly con-cluding that there was no way to stop the runaway super-criticality of the reactor. Sirix reached the same conclusion and immediately shifted course. "I am aborting our landing. We must escape."

For once, DD agreed with the black robot. Their angular ship accelerated away. According to the compy's interpreta-tion of the readings from the runaway reactor pile, less than a second remained—

With a sudden flash and a burst of energy, the containment structure vaporized. The shock front mowed down the Klikiss robots clustered around the reactor pile, flattening the large es-cape ships and disintegrating everything in its way.

The increasing shockwave rose much faster than Sirix's ship. Accelerated protons tore through the robotic craft like a high-energy blizzard. DD anchored himself, knowing that the destructive pulse could not be stopped.

The nuclear blast slammed into them from behind. Structural girders smashed, plates buckled, and an explosion erupted from one of their own engines. In a blur of articulated arms, Sirix grappled with the controls, extending four more insect appendages to manipulate numerous systems.

Far below, the Jonah 12 base was a white-hot pool, an expanding bonfire that vaporized frozen hydrogen and methane, melting structures as it continued to spread outward in a vast crater.

Burning and damaged, the robot ship tumbled out of control, careening into empty space.

98 ☀ JESS TAMBLYN

air damp and wavy, blue eyes bright, Jess stood outside on the surface of the ice moon. Even in the hard vacuum, an oily sheen of water covered his pearlescent garment; his skin tingled with ozone. Jess's feet, hands, and face were bare, but the energy of his body kept his flesh warm and protected.

With senses enhanced by the water entities, he could see

down through the thick sheet of ice as if it were no more than a distorted windowpane. He walked alone over the surface, past the cylindrical cermet wellheads, past the insulated outpost shacks and the lift shafts that led far beneath the ice sheet. He tried to remember. It had been so many years since his mother's fatal accident. . . .

Jess didn't know how far she had gone, where the crack had swallowed her vehicle. He walked for more than a kilometer until he saw a wide silvery scar, a poorly healed gash through the frozen crust.

Long ago, Karla Tamblyn's surface rover had fallen through ice and slush. She'd been unable to pry herself free, and once her vehicle began to sink, she was doomed. Slowed by the closing jaws of solidifying water, she had dropped deeper and deeper until the glacial ice enfolded her rover. She'd been able to transmit her goodbyes for almost two hours as her batteries gradually ran out and the cold closed in. When water cracked through the thick insulated windows, the submerged rover had flooded, and Karla had been overwhelmed, frozen solid—inaccessible for nineteen years. Locked away, imprisoned, with no Roamer funeral, no way for her family to see her one last time.

Now, though, her son had the ability to reach her.

Standing atop the refrozen crevasse, Jess clenched his hands and felt a ripple of wental energy course through him. He could do the impossible.

With his affinity for water itself, Jess shifted his thoughts and sank through the frozen lattice of ice. He had a target this time: the small wreck of a drowned surface rover. He descended as if through gelatin, seeing his way deeper and deeper. Even with the protective film around him, he felt the increasing cold.

Strangest of all, he actually sensed his mother down there, felt her existence. Determined to bring her back, if only to give her a proper Roamer farewell, Jess moved laterally. He parted the frozen water and let it fold behind him until he hovered like an insect in amber before the sunken rover. The vehicle had come to an equilibrium in the hardened slush. Its windows had been smashed open by the pressure, its interior filled with metal-hard ice.

But Jess plunged in as if the barrier was not there. Inside, he saw a solidified human form like a statue in the driver's chair. Her arms were spread out, as if welcoming the embrace of death. For some reason, Karla had opened her helmet's faceplate at the last moment. He had heard of people in the last stages of extreme hypothermia who experienced inexplicable physical reactions, hot flashes that made them attempt to tear off their clothes.

Karla's face was frozen, her eyes open, her mouth set in a contented line, not quite a smile, but certainly not fear of impending death. She'd been at peace in the end. She'd had time to say her goodbyes, to accept her fate, knowing no one could ever come to rescue her. Jess remembered that day as one of the longest in his life, gathered with his father and Ross and Tasia in the communications shack. She hadn't sounded surprised by anything they said, just happy to hear their voices as she slowly faded. . . .

Now, with energized water flowing around him, Jess moved his hands, sketching out lines like a sculptor mapping a block of marble. With nothing more than a thought, he cut Karla Tamblyn free of her icy prison. Carrying her body, still surrounded by a shell of solid ice, he drifted backward until he emerged from the wrecked rover.

All around him, he melted and flowed a pathway through

the ice, which immediately re-formed behind him. To him, water was an infinitely mutable environment. He surrounded them with a bubble that rose through the barrier.

Looking up through hundreds of meters of solid ice at the dim glow of daylight far above, he willed himself to rise with his mother in his arms. Never had he felt so grateful for the wental abilities; at last, he could make use of them in a way that would not hurt other human beings.

Reaching the surface, Jess kept his mother encased in the sheltering block of ice. After so much time, he did not want her fragile body damaged by exposure to hard vacuum. He made his way to the wellheads and the external markers of the Plumas water mines. Then, choosing his path carefully, he sank again, paralleling one of the lift shafts until he reemerged beneath the frozen crust.

Under the light of the artificial suns he rested Karla's body on the icy shelf. As if shaping clay, he ran his bare palms over the outside of the block, letting just a spark of wental energy trickle out so he could smooth the sheath. He let a bit of the power fade its way inside, seeking the tiny spark that Jess saw within his mother's frozen form. The water around her began to glisten with diamond droplets, brighter than ice.

His three uncles hurried out from their heated enclosures. "By the Guiding Star!" Wynn cried. "Is that Karla? Bram's sweet wife Karla—"

"How did you ever find her, Jess?" Torin asked.

"The wentals helped me. I have let the water entities touch—"

Jess suddenly reeled as images, words, and thoughts sang through the wentals within him, a message picked up by the other dispersed water entities. One of his volunteers, a water bearer . . . Nikko Chan Tylar! He had found Cesca, and they were in great danger.

"I have to go," Jess barked. "The base on Jonah 12 has been destroyed. Cesca's in trouble." He ran toward the lift shaft and the vertical passage that would take him out to his wental starship.

His uncles stared after him, then turned uneasily back to the frozen but slowly melting shape of Karla Tamblyn. "But . . . what do we do with *her*, Jess?"

Overwhelmed by the desperation in Nikko's wental message, Jess turned. "She'll be protected—she's been like that for years already. Keep the ice cold."

"That won't be too difficult." Wynn frowned at the ice pack around them.

"I'll come back." Jess raced for his water-and-pearl ship, consumed with worry for Cesca, hoping he would get to her in time.

99 ☀ DOBRO DESIGNATE UDRU'H

The Dobro Designate and Adar Zan'nh disguised themselves roughly with components from the dead guards' uniforms. They confiscated the weapons, though both men knew they could never survive if all the brainwashed crewmen stood against them. With only two people to take over an entire warliner, they had to be much more subtle, and there wasn't much time. The battleship would reach Dobro soon—and Udru'h knew the trap that waited for them there.

"The Mage-Imperator was forewarned about the threat to Dobro. He will destroy this ship rather than allow it to take over another Ildiran colony. We need to break Rusa'h's hold on this crew before we arrive."

The Adar appeared haggard and lost, as if the burden upon him had been doubled. "But how are—" Udru'h waited, letting him think through the possibilities. Then it dawned on Zan'nh. "Ah! The cargo hold is full of shiing!"

The Designate nodded. "The rebels intended to use it to subsume Dobro's populace, but that can work both ways. Shiing will temporarily break this crew's connection to any *thism* network, whether it belongs to Rusa'h or to the Mage-Imperator."

Zan'nh's brow furrowed. "They'll be disoriented, detached from any guidance at all. They won't know what to do."

"Are you not the Adar? Then *command* them. Are you a good enough leader to reassert order and reason upon your own crew?"

A faint smile curled Zan'nh's lips, and he showed his teeth, glad to be something other than a pawn. "Yes, I am. That's how Adar Kori'nh achieved his greatest triumph when the old Mage-Imperator died."

Udru'h looked down his nose. "Yes, but he ended up destroying himself and all his warliners. I would prefer a different outcome."

Zan'nh's eyes sparkled, and his mind seemed to grow stronger with each passing minute. "If we succeed in this, it will be a story worthy of Adar Kori'nh."

"No, it will be a story worthy of the *Saga of Seven Suns*."

Taking their weapons, the two made their way down back passageways and service shafts, creeping from deck to deck. Even when they were inevitably seen from a distance, they maintained their composure. Because Rusa'h's rebels were blind to any *thism* but theirs, they did not challenge Udru'h or Zan'nh.

While the warliner flew toward Dobro, Prime Designate Thor'h and the rest of the maniple would be attacking another splinter world, spreading shiing and trapping new followers in mad Rusa'h's web. It had to stop.

Udru'h and Zan'nh would begin to turn the tide by recapturing this warliner, and by saving Dobro and its people, both human and Ildiran.

In the cargo levels, they found thousands of cylinders full of shiing gas, lined up, row upon row, ready to be unleashed upon the population of Dobro. The nialia production fields on Hyrillka had been working at extraordinary levels to create enough of the drug to meet the needs of the spreading insurrection.

Zan'nh hauled out canisters and brought them to the warliner's ventilation systems. None of the Solar Navy crewmen ventured into the isolated storage chambers; until the warliner arrived at Dobro itself, they had no need for the compressed shiing.

As Zan'nh connected the canisters to the ventilation system, Designate Udru'h went to an emergency station at the cargo bay's hatch and found two breathing films to be used in the event of a disaster. He handed one of the soft, pliable membranes to the Adar. "Rusa'h insists that we must come over to his network willingly, that we can't be forced, but so much shiing would still distort our thoughts. I don't want to take that chance—do you?"

The younger man shook his head. "I intend to keep my thoughts clear and my determination firm." They applied the breathing films to their faces. Fortunately, shiing gas would not penetrate the skin.

Udru'h double-checked the preparations with the tanks. "Since we've got to succeed the very first time, I propose we unleash a massive dose to rip this crew free from the Hyrillka Designate's control."

The Adar still frowned. "If we detach all of these rebels from Rusa'h's corrupted *thism* web, won't he sense them slipping away? He will feel a hole in his network and know that it is unraveling."

"And what can he do about it?" Udru'h raised his eyebrows. "He will be as powerless to stop it as Jora'h has been."

"But even when we soften Rusa'h's hold, how do we reconnect them with the Mage-Imperator? I cannot force them back into the legitimate network of *thism*. I'm not strong enough."

"Neither am I." Udru'h's eyes burned brightly above the gelatinous breathing film. "But at least they will be free of Rusa'h's corruption."

The two men opened the canister valves and began dumping shiing gas into the warliner's ventilation system. The stimulant hissed out in a long sigh. It would spread like venom in a body's bloodstream, sweeping through the battleship's ducts and chambers, finally reaching the command nucleus.

Udru'h nodded. "Good. Now let us hope it works before your father's ships destroy us. He is on his way."

Sure that the Hansa skymine was already destroyed, Tasia found the flight to Qronha 3 to be maddeningly long. En route, the Soldier compies performed their tasks exactly as she instructed, but they were damned poor company.

Instead, EA was Tasia's only friend—even if she was drastically changed. As a Listener model, she was programmed to be a companion, a sounding board, and over the years she had developed a genuine rapport with first Ross, then Jess, then Tasia. As Tasia talked with her, uploaded more of her carefully edited memories, even scanned some of the embarrassing old files from the Governess compy UR, she saw EA developing a personality again. It was somewhat different from her old friend, but at least the Listener compy was another step closer to her old self. . . .

Finally, the sixty rammers roared into the Qronha system. Tasia watched the Ildiran gas giant grow brighter and larger on the ship's viewing screens. Making contact with her fellow dunsels, she laid out detailed plans for their assault against the drogues. "Check your forward sensors. See if you can find any survivors from the cloud-harvesting facility."

As the Soldier compies began a scanning sweep, Sabine Odenwald transmitted from her rammer, "This isn't a rescue mission, Commander. The EDF already wrote off that skymine."

"Besides, we don't have the facilities to take aboard refugees," Hector O'Barr added from his own ship.

Tasia could only think of Ross dying as his Blue Sky Mine was destroyed. If there were any survivors here, she would have to find a way to help them. After checking the quick recon results, however, she knew it was a moot point. "Nothing left anyway but a smear of smoke and a few pieces of debris that haven't figured out how to fall yet." She swallowed the lump in her throat and got back to business. "We'll insert into high orbit and look for drogues down there. We already know they're spoiling for a fight."

"Let's give 'em one!" Darby Vinh let out a foolish giggle.

"You've done plenty of drills," Tasia said. "Be prepared to jump into your evacuation pods. Once we see warglobes, there's no more practice."

From high orbit, the sixty rammers scanned the clouds with their sensors. When they spotted the wreckage of a floating facility much larger than the skymine, Tasia's Roamer experience helped her to identify the materials and old-fashioned configuration of a majestic Ildiran cloud-harvesting city. Apparently, the drogues had destroyed human and Ildiran facilities indiscriminately.

As the rammer fleet cruised around the planet, suddenly the Soldier compies chittered to each other. With machine efficiency, they activated alarms and announced a full battlestation alert even before Tasia saw what they had detected. Part of her was impressed at the speed with which the military robots responded. Even so, wasn't *she* supposed to be in command?

"Hey, could I have a heads-up, please?"

Then she saw. The six Ildiran warliners were a spectacular but unexpected sight. The colorful alien ships hovered above the clouds, their feathery solar sails extended in all directions. "Why are they here?"

"Unknown," one of the Soldier compies answered. "They have no weapons powered up." Nearby, EA offered no comment, but she seemed to be observing with keen interest.

"Should we take preemptive action, Commander?" Erin Eld called over the communication link. "Fire a few rounds before they—"

"They're probably trying to find survivors from their own cloud-harvesting complex." She turned to the nearest Soldier compy. "Open a channel on a standard Solar Navy frequency. I want to talk to their septar."

When the compy had done so, Tasia put on a welcoming smile. "This is Commander Tamblyn of the Earth Defense Forces, responding to an emergency signal from our skymine. We've come to get even with the hydrogues. You're welcome to join in the brawl with us, if you like."

The Ildiran response was a long time in coming, as if they were debating the matter. The Solar Navy septar answered only briefly: "Not at this time." Then, without further explanation, the gaudy battleships lifted away from Qronha 3, retreated from orbit, and left the system.

"What was that all about?" Tasia asked.

"Some allies," Odenwald said.

"Doesn't matter. We didn't expect their help anyway. Let's get closer to those clouds and start hunting." Tasia decided it was time to roll up her sleeves and get to work. "Smoke them out."

The six commanders transmitted taunting demands and rude ultimatums into the clouds. Since the hydrogues wouldn't understand the nuances of human language, she let the other five have free rein with their curses and insults, calling the deep-core aliens by the foulest names. If their mere presence and their verbal goads didn't work, the rammers carried several high-yield atomic warheads to help flush out the drogues, like teasing a vicious guard dog.

Everything was ready. The rammer ships' hot engines were dancing on the edges of the red lines; overloads would come easily after a short sprint of acceleration. None of the Soldier compies seemed bothered by their impending fate. Neither was EA, though Tasia was determined to take the Listener compy with her in the evacuation pod.

Far more quickly than they had dared to hope, the provocation worked. Numerous spiked spheres climbed out of the cloudy depths, as if they had lain in ambush all along. When she saw the speed of the coordinated response, a strange thought crossed Tasia's mind. *It's as if they knew we were coming. What if the drogues attacked the Hansa skymine just to lure us here?*

One after another, like bubbles in a pot coming to a boil, the hydrogue spheres kept appearing. The sheer number of them made her dizzy. "Count 'em! Let me know how many there are."

"Seventy-eight hydrogue warglobes detected so far," announced one of the Soldier compies.

"By the Guiding Star, we don't have enough—" Then she stopped. "We'll do what we can. Make 'em hurt."

From the bridge of his rammer, Tom Christensen shouted out, brash and foolish, "Pick on this, bastards!"

The Soldier compies remained diligent at their stations. EA stared fixedly ahead. Tasia guessed it would take about ten seconds to get inside the evac pod and launch herself away from the free-for-all.

The Ildiran Solar Navy's commander had perished along with forty-nine warliners in a similar attack that had deeply wounded the hydrogues. Now that the deep-core aliens had

come back to Qronha 3, Tasia's rammer fleet would deal another serious blow to the enemy.

At least she hoped so.

Warglobes continued to rise around them, an overwhelming number. Tasia cast one final glance at EA, then set her
jaw.

"It's not everybody who gets a chance to have their
names misspelled in the history books," she said. "Prime the
engines and prepare for ramming speed!"

101 ☀ OSIRA'H

Inside her protective chamber deep within Qronha 3,
Osira'h felt like a specimen in an exotic zoo. Through reinforced crystal panes, she stared out at the utterly alien
landscape inhabited by hydrogues.

Somehow, she had to become an intermediary between
them and the Mage-Imperator. She wasn't supposed to agree
to anything, just convince them to speak with her father.
Even so, she hoped she could make them understand there
was no reason for any war. Hydrogues and "rock dwellers"
had no conflicting needs, did not compete for resources. But
they also had no common ground, no shared experience, no
mutual understanding . . . unless Osira'h became a bridge.

The quicksilver bodies stood in front of her like large toy

soldiers. She felt a vibration in her thoughts, as if they were trying to reach her through the atmosphere of her crystal chamber. Osira'h let her eyes fall half closed and called on all her abilities: the inherited telepathy from her green priest mother, the skills she'd been taught by Designate Udru'h on Dobro, the tingle of *thism* from her father and the love she'd sensed the first time they met.

She drove aside all of her doubts and dark thoughts. Focus. Focus . . .

There. When the connection was made, it felt as if an electric arc sparked from the hydrogues to Osira'h herself. Communication, an open door, the first step toward mutual understanding. But they were so alien!

Her initial impulse was to shut down her mind and drive away the inhuman presence, but she forced herself to maintain the contact. Her small hands clenched. She must become a conduit between hydrogue concepts and Ildiran thoughts. There had to be a shared means of expression. Klikiss robots had served in that capacity millennia ago. Osira'h would do the same now.

Although she could not at first pick up clear terms and concepts, her comprehension was progressing rapidly— much more so, she hoped, than the hydrogues guessed. In touching their vague and mostly incomprehensible thoughts, she began to sense that the hydrogues were agitated or distressed. Their citysphere was a blur of activity, swept up in actions and plans that she couldn't decipher.

Finally she received a clutter of concepts with images that made her understand: A group of human battleships had arrived in the clouds above, bringing a new kind of weapon. At the same time, she could sense that the hydrogues had a terrible surprise for the human vessels.

In the images she saw that her own Ildiran septa had departed, and Osira'h's heart fell. So, Yazra'h had abandoned her down in the clouds. . . . But that had been her sister's mission, under orders from the Mage-Imperator. They could never have rescued her anyway. Everything depended on Osira'h's success with the hydrogues.

Next, with a sudden rush of surprise and fear, she learned that the deep-core aliens were also ready to launch another devastating attack against the verdani. She sensed hatred curdling through the hydrogue thoughts.

Theroc, the home of the worldforest!

Osira'h stiffened with alarm, careful not to send out a readable message with her reaction. Her mother's world! The girl had never visited the planet herself, but Nira had shared so many vivid images that Osira'h felt as if she herself belonged among the worldtrees. She had touched the delicate treeling in the Mage-Imperator's private chamber, and it had felt *right*.

Yet she also belonged with the Ildirans. Perhaps she could accomplish something for both races. She had to do more than just convince the hydrogues to communicate with the Mage-Imperator.

She pressed her small hands against the curved crystal wall, attempting to send a distinct, nonverbal message. She peered out at the amorphous structures of the citysphere and was astonished to see two black Klikiss robots marching down ramps and over curved loops to approach her. They had broken their agreement to keep the Ildiran Empire safe, yet they remained among the hydrogues!

She felt a chill. More secrets, more treachery? The beetlelike machines stood beside the quicksilver hydrogues, buzzing and clicking in a brisk exchange of information that sounded like music. Red optical sensors flashed under ebony carapaces. Osira'h knew the robots had betrayed her people and broken their alliance, but why were they here now?

Just then, a new concept became apparent to her. The hydrogues were not afraid of the human rammers above. The deep-core aliens had planned a deadly ambush. Did the whole universe thrive on betrayal?

She was a child, just seven standard years old. That could work to her advantage if enemies underestimated her. She would have to be smarter, wilier, more unexpected than either the hydrogues or the Klikiss robots.

Making her mental message as clear as possible, she resonated her need through the hydrogues' thought patterns, forming the concepts in images to communicate. She tried to show the aliens that Ildirans did not wish to continue this war, had not provoked it in the first place. The Mage-Imperator wanted to communicate with them.

As distinctly as she could, she thought, *Millennia ago, Klikiss robots acted as intermediaries to arrange a nonaggression pact between Ildirans and hydrogues, while you fought other enemies.*

Inside her head, Osira'h sensed an inexplicable loathing for the "turncoat" faeros, as well as a furious resentment against the verdani, and an equivalent group of water-based beings they called the wentals. They had made many enemies.

She continued, staying focused. *But the Klikiss robots are not to be trusted. They poisoned you against us.* She looked at the black machines just outside her crystal walls. She couldn't guess whom the hydrogues would believe. *But I will be your bridge. I am the conduit between hydrogue and Ildiran. Never before has there been direct communication between our races. We wish to understand you. I can facilitate a discussion with the Ildiran leader.*

Her glass-walled bubble lurched and began to move. The hydrogues propelled it smoothly to hover near another, more crudely fashioned encounter vessel that sat empty in the high-pressure environment. As the aliens responded to her, Osira'h felt their antipathy toward the humans.

Overlapping hydrogue voices rang like a gong inside her head. *They allied themselves with the verdani. They destroyed hydrogue worlds. They must be extinguished—as the original Klikiss race was.*

Now the hydrogues brought her chamber to a low translucent structure that held a group of hapless human captives who looked forlorn and beaten behind the angled, transparent walls. They were dressed in an assortment of clothing, some military uniforms, some Hansa civilian attire, yet all wore the same hollow-eyed expression of endless fear. She wanted to know who they were, why the hydrogues kept them.

For experimentation. For amusement. For understanding. Humans must be destroyed. They used the Klikiss Torch to annihilate our worlds.

Osira'h urgently tried to get them to change their minds. Her only duty was to act as a conduit, but she didn't think her father would object. *Forgive them. They did not know you existed.*

They have used the weapon again and again.

She frowned. There was so much she didn't know!

Next she received a violent, insistent image of all humanity exterminated. And the verdani. And the faeros. The three quicksilver hydrogues transmitted a stream of thoughts so strong that they struck her like physical shockwaves. *If you came to speak for humans, then we will destroy you now.*

She sensed only a faint willingness to hear her plea in the name of the Ildiran Empire, but the hydrogues were adamant against including the humans in their consideration. Osira'h stared at the despondent prisoners within the geometrical cell, unable to help them. As the hydrogues moved her bubble away, she locked eyes with several hostages until she was drawn out of view.

She forced herself to focus her abilities once more. This was likely to be her only chance to deliver the Mage-Imperator's invitation. For better or worse. Her siblings— indeed, all of the previous generations leading up to this culmination of the breeding experiments—had been genetically created for this single purpose. Osira'h had to fulfill the function for which she had been born: Through directly shared concepts, she would make the hydrogues *see*. She would save the Ildiran people, as they required of her . . . and they might be damned for it. The Mage-Imperator had claimed that no price was too high.

Jora'h had insisted there was no other way. Had he lied to her too? In this matter, he was forced to act as *Mage-Imperator,* not as her father or her mother's lover. And she had to obey him . . . or at least try.

The half-breed girl did exactly as she'd been trained. Dropping her last self-protective mental walls and surrendering all resistance, she became a conduit between two races that were so fundamentally different.

With her mind ablaze and her thoughts entirely exposed, an absolute connection seared between her and the hydrogues, full and complete. Her greatest abilities blossomed out, brighter than ever before.

And then the hydrogues were in her grasp.

obb and his fellow prisoners stared in disbelief through the murky wall membrane of their holding cell. Inside her own chamber, the strange little girl looked helpless and entirely out of her realm.

"Is that another prisoner?" he asked. "What are they doing?"

"Look at the way the drogues are taking her around— like they're escorting her," Anjea Telton said.

The girl stared out at the captives, as if concerned about *them* instead of herself. The haggard captives watched as the strange child's chamber was lifted away and taken out of view.

"That looked a lot more sophisticated than my encounter vessel." Robb could still see his intact old diving bell outside, not far away. He wondered if history would remember him as a selfless hero willing to make the supreme sacrifice, or a deluded fool who had been doomed from the start. If he could have come up with an escape plan that had even a marginal chance for success, he would have risked anything to make the attempt.

"Maybe they'll squash her like a bug, like they did to Charles." Anjea sounded miserable. "Like they mean to do to the rest of us."

She looked meaningfully to the opposite side of their confinement chamber, where the hydrogues had brought in another of their encasement shells. This one conformed more closely to a human shape than the transparent coffin the

drogues had used to kill Gomez. It reminded Robb of a sarcophagus. The silent aliens had carried the case into the prison
cell, probably intending to take another prisoner with them, but
then the quicksilver creatures had rushed away, as if distracted
or alarmed. Perhaps the arrival of the strange little girl?

Anjea caught her breath with an idea. "Brindle, you think
the systems still work in your encounter vessel?"

"They were functioning when the drogues grabbed me.
But there's a one-in-a-million chance someone could get
over there alive, and another chance in a million that he
could seal the chamber and bring it to proper pressure. And
another chance in a million that anyone could escape drogue
pursuit even if the systems all still worked."

"If, if, if," Anjea said. "Still sounds like better odds than
waiting here for Dr. Hydrogue Frankenstein to come back."

The new sarcophagus had small manipulating fields, and
when the prisoners toyed with it, they found that a passenger inside had the ability to crudely guide the protective exoskeleton forward, up, and down.

"Maybe the hydrogues want us to take a walk around
their city," one of the prisoners suggested.

"Who knows what they're thinking?" Robb countered.
"Their minds are made of liquid crystal."

"Well, mine isn't—and I know what I'm thinking." Before Robb could react, Anjea threw herself into the armored
shell. "I'm getting out of here. I plan to make it to that encounter vessel. Wish me luck."

"I should be the one to take the risk," Robb said. "It's my
encounter vessel."

"I'll figure it out myself."

"But how are you gonna come back for us?" cried one of
the others.

They all knew that even if Anjea did manage to escape, get picked up, make it back to Earth, and convince the EDF of her story, the Earth military could never mount a rescue so deep down here. No, Anjea couldn't possibly bring help for anyone else.

Still, she said, "I'll do what I can."

She sealed herself into the mobile exoskeleton. Robb could barely see her face through the angled outer plates. The hard-bitten woman looked terrified, but then she always did.

"Good luck, anyway," Robb said, and he meant it.

The hydrogues had gone away, accompanying the little girl's crystal chamber, and every creature in the citysphere seemed preoccupied with the strange visitor. Now was Anjea's chance.

Clumsily experimenting with the fields inside her sealed shell, she found ways to make it move. It was like a remote-controlled mummy case, with all the grace and maneuverability that implied.

Robb fought back the anxiety inside his chest. This crackpot plan had virtually no chance of succeeding, yet it was their only glimmer of hope since the compy DD had spoken to them deep in the bowels of some other gas planet. DD had not found a way to free them, either.

"Even a chance in a million is one more chance than we've had up until now," he said, trying to sound bright and confident. He and the other prisoners helped guide the enclosed shell toward the membrane wall. They pushed, and the shell slid through like a baby emerging from a slick birth canal. Then Anjea was on her own.

Once she reached the outside, Anjea had difficulty operating the controls, as if she were being buffeted by heavy storm winds and impossible gravity. But after a moment of disorientation, she managed to propel the chamber forward, adjusting her course. She only needed to cross a few dozen meters of atmospheric ocean to reach Robb's empty diving bell.

"She's going to make it!" said one of the prisoners.

Jerking forward in fits and starts, the protective shell hovered outside the hatch of the EDF vessel. Anjea struggled to get some kind of grip, to adjust the outer hatch using the coffin's crude manipulators. The diving bell's door was a simple mechanism designed to be foolproof and without unnecessary complexity.

When she succeeded in opening the hatch, Robb saw no venting of trapped air. Maybe the hydrogues already kept it at equilibrium pressure so they could study the interior. He prayed for Anjea's sake that the mechanical systems had been shielded well enough to withstand the gas giant's environment.

She managed to maneuver the stiff human-shaped shell into place and cautiously guided it into the interior of the diving bell.

The prisoners cheered. "She's doing it!"

Robb didn't point out that Anjea still had a full list of impossible tasks to accomplish before she got away. Even so, he was amazed she had made it this far.

First, she had to depressurize and repressurize the encounter vessel, if the tank reservoirs remained intact. The diving-bell hatch sealed again, and for an interminable moment nothing happened. Then Anjea used the crude manipulators to work the internal systems of the encounter pod. Status lights began to flash on the outside of the diving bell.

The ducts opened, and swirling jets pumped out the

high-pressure atmosphere. Plumes of escaping steam
sparkled upward.

"The systems are still working," Robb said. "She's venting their atmosphere! It'll be like an air bubble rising to the
surface of the ocean. She has a chance!"

"Not much of one," said another prisoner in a hollow,
hopeless voice.

Two Klikiss robots suddenly appeared atop a parabolic
bridge. The robots moved their articulated arms, apparently
signaling an alarm.

Curly metal pseudopods collected like puddles of solder
and streamed upward. They gathered into larger pools, coalesced along ramps and polygonal platforms until they became individual hydrogues closing in on the encounter vessel.

Feeling sick inside, Robb gritted his teeth. "Come on,
come on! Hurry, Anjea!"

A cluster of hydrogues surrounded the encounter pod,
elongating into lumpy pillars much taller than their familiar
copied Roamer form. Three Klikiss robots joined them.

The robots approached the diving bell. Hydrogues clung
like ominous parasites to the sides of the armored chamber.
The robots extended their articulated claws, scrabbling
against the diving bell's outer hull, looking for a way in.

The encounter vessel's lower jets sputtered, and another
plume burst out. Anjea was trying to activate the engines and
get away. The prisoners shouted for her to hurry.

The Klikiss robots found the hatch mechanism. They tore
at the controls and easily broke the seal, ripping open the
heavy door and disengaging the plate from its solid hinges.

Hydrogue atmosphere pounded into the encounter chamber like a battering ram. Rising like ghosts made of molten
silver, the hydrogues poured through the opening.

As the humans watched in horror, the aliens ejected first one half of the exoskeleton shell, then the other. Even if Anjea had managed to get back inside the protective skin before the Klikiss robots breached the hatch, she was now crushed and splattered into a biological jelly.

Robb fell to his knees inside their confinement chamber. The other prisoners groaned.

The Klikiss robots spent the next hour using their claws and metal tools to dismantle Robb's encounter vessel plate by plate, until the components lay strewn in a pile of wreckage.

103 ☀ DENN PERONI

Returning to Plumas with a cargo load of unusual Ildiran items for trade, Denn detoured past what was left of Hurricane Depot. Both he and Caleb Tamblyn wanted to see what a mess the Big Goose had made of things.

Two Roamer salvage ships were already combing through the wreckage in hopes of retrieving items of value. The salvage pilots—one from clan Hosaki, one from Sandoval—sent their best-guess orbital projections to help the *Dogged Persistence* make its way through the treacherous rubble of what had been a popular Roamer gathering point.

"Damn the Eddies!" Caleb muttered as he saw the

blackened scar on one of the tide-locked planetoids. "There won't be much left to salvage down there."

Because the scattered clans were still assessing their situation, exchanging information was vital. Denn and Caleb told them about their surreptitious trade on Yreka and with the Ildiran Empire. The salvage pilots replied with news that somehow Jess Tamblyn had made the gas giant Golgen safe for skymining again. On the other hand, numerous clan merchants had been seized, and the Chan greenhouses had been hit. Intercepted media reports were full of lies and exaggerations that made Roamers out to be shiftless cowards.

Denn hunched over his controls. "How can anybody swallow that slag? After so many years of trade with us, even Hansa people should know better."

The Sandoval pilot wasn't so surprised. "In a time of war and rationing, folks have no choice but to accept whatever reports come their way. They don't hear anything else."

"Bad to worse," Caleb grumbled. "Next they're going to claim that clan heads steal babies and drink their blood in sinister ceremonies."

Denn sighed. "At any other time I'd say you were being ridiculous." He looked out at the rubble, saw glints of metal that had once been Hurricane Depot. "Any word about all the hostages they took from here? Or Rendezvous, or anyplace else?"

"Not a peep," said the Hosaki salvage pilot. "I wouldn't be surprised if they put them into labor camps and called them prisoners of war."

"Bastards!" Caleb said.

Denn clenched his jaw. On a delivery to Earth's Moon base last year, his own ship had been impounded on a bureaucratic pretext. He'd been left to cool his heels, trying to work through the red tape. Later, he learned that he'd been detained so that evidence could be planted to frame him for a supposed Roamer assassination plot against the King. But King Peter himself had uncovered the plan and used his own connections to free Denn and send him quietly on his way. Few Roamers trusted the Hansa, but at least Denn could credit something good to the young King.

"Let's go," Caleb said. "I'm anxious to get back to Plumas and get back to work. You'll spend a few days with my brothers before you set off again?"

Denn shrugged. "Most of my regularly scheduled deliveries are canceled, and I've got time on my hands. No self-respecting Roamer turns down an offer of hospitality." From past experience, he knew that Caleb's brothers would probably talk him into some kind of trouble. But after the atrocities the Earth military had committed, maybe trouble was just what Denn was looking for right now.

"Home sweet home," Caleb said as they cruised above the wellheads and scattered pumping stations. From the outside, the ice moon didn't look like much.

"If you say so." Denn brought the *Persistence* in next to a primary refilling station. "That's why I like having my own ship—I'm always at home wherever I fly . . . though with the Eddies everywhere, I can't go on my normal routes."

Caleb studied him as the two men prepared to disembark. "I don't like somebody telling me that I can't go where I want. Let's have an all-out bitch session with my brothers. That'll make you feel better. Besides, they keep plenty of good stuff to drink, brewed with the purest primordial water."

Denn frowned at the salty old man. "You think that'll help us see the Guiding Star more clearly?"

Caleb laughed. "I guarantee it—you'll start seeing double stars."

Denn sat in warm clothing beneath a frozen-solid sky. The underground ocean rippled like gray oil, and dim white artificial suns shone down, casting sharp shadows.

The Tamblyn brothers told the astounding tale of Jess's return and how he had moved through solid ice to retrieve his mother's body, which remained on the frozen shelf, still encased in ice. Denn's ears pricked up when he learned that Jess had rushed off to rescue Cesca from some disaster on Jonah 12, but the brothers couldn't give many details. "He didn't explain a whole lot—just raced out of here. Said he was going to get her."

"I'm glad he was in a hurry." It was the first news he'd heard of his daughter since the destruction of Rendezvous, and it hurt to hear she might be in danger. With his incredible powers, Jess was probably the best person to go after Cesca. And Denn certainly knew of the young man's love for her. . . .

He stared down at the glass in his hand. The Tamblyn brothers started with Plumas water, then added special ingredients to distill their own alcohol, augmented with flavors reminiscent of either whiskey or gin. Denn didn't think the stuff was particularly good, but he was a guest. Here, safe, there was no harm in getting sociably drunk with Caleb, Andrew, Wynn, and Torin. After all, they had to solve the problems of the universe.

After Denn and Caleb described what they had seen in the ruins of Hurricane Depot, all of them speculated on what had happened to the Roamer prisoners taken from there. "Does the Big Goose just think we'll cower in our boots and surrender?" Torin said, refilling his glass. He spat onto the ice, and his saliva crackled as it froze in the deep cold.

"I don't think the Chairman knows what he stepped in." Caleb worked his jaw as if he intended to spit as well, but decided not to follow the example of his younger brother. "He shouldn't mess with Roamers!"

"The clans will survive," Andrew said quietly. "You've already made a start with Yreka. There'll be plenty of outlying colonies all too happy to trade with us under the table."

Denn took another long drink of the burning alcohol. "The Big Goose shat on them as well—they're more like us than people from Earth. But it's dangerous. The Eddies will crack down on anybody they catch."

"I say we don't stand for it anymore!"

Wynn spat a mouthful of saliva, nailing precisely the same spot that his twin had hit. "Rand Sorengaard had the right idea after all. We should have followed him instead of trying to work through civilized channels."

"Civilized? That's a joke. Those Eddy raiders are worse than Rand ever was. And they called *him* a pirate! Ha!"

Denn's shoulders sagged. "General Lanyan had a lot of nerve executing Rand in the name of 'peace throughout the Hansa'—if he was going to use the same tactics himself."

"I say Rand Sorengaard was a revolutionary." Torin swayed slightly in his seat. "A visionary, not a pirate. He saw things the rest of us weren't willing to accept."

"A man ahead of his time! We should remember him as a freedom fighter, an independence leader fighting against the oppressive Big shizzy Goose."

Though the temperature around them remained frigid,

Denn felt pleasantly warm. He thought he'd finished his drink, but his glass was somehow full again. "After Rendezvous, my Cesca told the Roamers to scatter and hide. But maybe we should take it a step further than that, follow Sorengaard's example and be freedom fighters ourselves."

The twins looked at him. Caleb and Andrew seemed slower to realize what he was suggesting, but Denn kept talking about his idea. When he found his words becoming slurred, he raised his voice to compensate. "We've got ships. We've got stealth and speed. And we know what the Eddies did to Hurricane Depot, to Raven Kamarov's ship—"

Caleb raised his glass. "Here's to Raven Kamarov." They all drank a toast.

Denn took a few moments to gather his thoughts again, then remembered what he had been saying. "How 'bout if we all go out and rouse some rabble on our own? Take back a few things to make up for all the damage the Big Goose has done to us."

The Tamblyn brothers began to chuckle, and their eyes lit up. "Would be a good chance for payback."

"Seems like a plan to me. First we're outlaws. Now we're going to be pirates. Sounds more respectable."

Denn was grinning. "Let's figure out how to get started." He looked down and saw that his glass was unaccountably empty, but the Tamblyn brothers were happy to refill it.

Their plans didn't make a great deal of sense, but what they lacked in logic, the five men made up for with boisterous enthusiasm.

The *Voracious Curiosity* raced away for hours, one step ahead of any EDF ships. Rlinda wandered along a drunkard's path that she hoped would shake pursuit. Considering all the current emergencies in the Hansa, she doubted the military would waste much effort on such a small fish, especially if they thought BeBob was already dead.

Then again, it was General Lanyan.

"Life with you is never boring, Rlinda," BeBob said, still miserable. "I hope you're not doing this to impress me."

She tried to find the strength to tease him. "You've got a lot to pay me back for, BeBob—and don't you think I won't collect it."

"I shall do my best, ma'am." His breath hitched briefly. "And thanks . . . for everything."

The *Curiosity* eventually arrived in a backwater system that the old Ildiran starcharts named Plumas, where they thought they might be safe for a while. "We've got to give our engines a chance to rest, perform a few minor repairs, and take an inventory of everything we dumped out the cargo hold. I'm fairly sure I had three cases of New Portugal wine in there, as well as ten kilos of the best black chocolate you'll ever taste. Damn! All together, that was probably more valuable than your ship."

"Not to me, Rlinda. My ship . . ."

"And Davlin." The spy had always been silent and cool, and not someone who would have been willing to sacrifice his life for them.

Of course he wouldn't.

Therefore, it was likely that he had not done what she thought. Which was exactly how Davlin would have planned it . . .

"You know, I'm thinking Davlin might have gotten away."

BeBob looked at her in disbelief. "We saw my whole ship turn into a fireball."

"Those pyrotechnics were obviously intentional—part of his plan—and I very much doubt that any plan of Davlin's would require his own death." She shrugged. "Just a thought, that's all." Rlinda heaved herself out of her expansive pilot's chair. "Come on, we'll only get depressed if we keep talking like this. Let's at least get depressed in the engine compartment, where we can do something useful."

While the fuel cells recharged and the two fugitives ran a careful analysis of any damage the Remoras had done, the hours passed in blissful, if still tense, tedium. This was just what she'd wanted—plenty of time alone with BeBob . . . but she hadn't expected it would be so hard to arrange. They were two kisses into deciding what to do next when the *Curiosity*'s automatic proximity alarms began to sound.

"Now what?" She and BeBob raced to the cockpit, pulling their clothes back into place. Throwing herself into her seat, Rlinda spotted EDF Remoras streaking toward them, launched from the bay of a Manta cruiser that had followed them into the system. "They're more persistent than the damned hydrogues."

"How the hell did these guys find us in the hind end of space?" BeBob slid into the seat at his station. "Rlinda, how long was the *Curiosity* parked at the Moon base?"

"A couple of days. Why?"

She powered up the engines again and accelerated with a lurch. The Plumas system had only a few planets: a gas giant with a handful of moons, and a couple of blistered rocky planets close in toward the sun. Not many places to hide.

Scowling, BeBob played with the controls and ran a full system analysis, then took out a handheld power-source detector and adjusted its range to detect specific signaling frequencies. "I've got a ping! Those EDF bastards put a locator beacon aboard your craft."

"On *my* ship?" Rlinda cursed with all the enthusiasm she could muster while still flying evasive maneuvers. She scanned ahead and pulled up a detailed projection of all objects in the system. "I'm heading toward that gas giant and its moons. It's the closest thing to an obstacle course out here, and we're not in any shape to outrun those fast fighter craft. My ship is still bruised."

They soared across the emptiness with the pack of glistening Remoras hot behind them. BeBob trotted along the decks until finally the handheld detector zeroed in on a tiny self-powered tracer affixed with a magnet behind one of the ventilation plates. Grumbling, he removed it, strode toward the ejection chute, and happily dumped the telltale signaler out into space.

But it was already much too late. The Remoras were close behind them and eating up the remaining distance every second.

By the time he returned to the cockpit, Rlinda was already weaving through the outer orbits of the Plumas moons. She looked at him, her face serious. "How badly do you want to get away, BeBob?"

She saw him gulp as he gave the question due consideration. "They've already made up their minds to convict me, and our recent behavior sure isn't going to earn me any clemency. Execution sounds like a more and more likely sentence. So . . . yeah, I'd like to get away pretty badly."

"That's all I wanted to know." Rlinda drew a deep breath. "Let's just hope the *Curiosity* can hold herself together."

She dumped a supercharged flush of ekti into the reactors, and the ship blasted forward with an added boost that slammed them both back against their chairs. The *Curiosity* shot like a cannonball straight toward the looming gas giant.

"I said I wanted to get away, Rlinda," BeBob said in a strangled voice, "not commit suicide."

"That isn't what I'm doing—at least I don't think so. With that tracer gone, we have the chance to play hide-and-seek. But we're going to have to do a damn good job of it. Those Remora pilots aren't idiots." She rehearsed her words, then transmitted to the pursuers, "Gentlemen, after seeing what sort of treatment the EDF gives its prisoners, we have no intention of being captured by you. We'd rather just burn up right here."

The *Curiosity* plunged straight into the thickening clouds. The Remoras came after them, but slowed their pursuit. No doubt they were double-checking orders from the Manta's commander.

As soon as her ship went deep enough to be invisible from scans, Rlinda altered course sharply. The ship began a tight, low orbit in the thick clouds, scribing a line across the gas giant's equator. The *Curiosity* started shaking and rattling. The outer hull heated up, but Rlinda did not slow.

"*This* is your plan?" BeBob's voice cracked with alarm.

"We went straight in like a bullet going sideways through a fat man's belly." She concentrated on her flying. "I'm hoping they'll assume we burned up in the atmosphere . . . not to mention the fact that they're probably spooked about hydrogues coming after us in here."

BeBob's eyes remained wide. "*I'm* worried about that, too, Rlinda."

"Hey, at this point, they could qualify as the cavalry. From a certain point of view."

"If that's the best we can hope for, then we're really, truly screwed."

Rlinda's teeth rattled from the outrageous turbulence. Sparks flew from a few nonessential systems. No doubt if the Remora pursuers took time to scan all the atmospheric layers, they would spot her ion trail as she screamed through the vapors. But by that time, she hoped her ship would have gotten away on the other side of the bloated world.

One of her stabilizing engines blew out, and the *Curiosity* began to lurch and tumble, but Rlinda's fingers flew, reasserting control. With brute force she plowed ahead with her beloved cargo ship, like an icebreaker through rough arctic seas. A few strong welding joints and persistent rivets barely kept all the components in place.

After they crossed the atmospheric layers of the bloated planet, the ship popped out of the far side like the cork from a champagne bottle.

Not willing to give up yet, Rlinda shut down their systems and let the battered *Curiosity* cruise along on its own momentum. All of her gauges and regulator systems displayed danger zones or red lines; some had shorted out entirely, so she had no way of knowing how bad the damage was.

"Well, we're intact. I'll say that at least," BeBob commented. The two embraced each other in a spontaneous bear hug.

Even if the EDF decided to follow them and someone was clever enough to determine her plan, they were still hours ahead of any possible pursuit that skirted the gas giant. If Rlinda could find a place to hide, cut their energy signatures, they'd be able to play possum and remain undetected. As the battered *Curiosity* limped along, Rlinda scanned the handful of moons, in particular noticing a large ice-crusted rock.

From out of nowhere, two strange ships swooped in. Rlinda didn't recognize the configuration of either one. One of the mysterious craft fired a warning blast across her bow; the other took a potshot at their engines, causing more damage.

"Hey, watch it!" Rlinda shouted into the comm system. "We've had enough trouble already today."

"Prepare to be boarded," said one of the ships. "It's payback time, and you're facing the meanest group of Roamer space pirates in the Spiral Arm."

Rlinda groaned, remembering Rand Sorengaard. "We've already been through that, too."

The pilots of the two craft transmitted their images: middle-aged men dressed in extravagant Roamer costumes, fully embroidered with clan markings. The better dressed of the two said, "You are our prisoners."

105 ☀ DOBRO DESIGNATE UDRU'H

As the rebellious warliner approached Dobro on its mission of conquest, shiing crept through its ventilation system, deck after deck. The stored canisters contained enough of the substance to subsume an entire splinter colony; it was more than enough to unravel the crew from Rusa'h's net.

Still hidden, the Dobro Designate waited with Adar Zan'nh in the cargo decks. Time passed slowly.

Noticing their loss of focus, some of the subverted Solar Navy crewmen responded with alarm, but the inhaled drug rapidly penetrated and soothed their thoughts. Soon the entire crew was disoriented, intoxicated, partially oblivious, and—most importantly—cut off from the mad Designate's enforced new *thism*.

"Even if they are lost, at least their minds are freed," Zan'nh said, his voice muffled through the breathing film. "I only wish Thor'h were aboard this ship. I'd like to see him sealed in my old cell, where he could cause no further harm."

Soon, the air in the warliner had a noticeably hazy appearance, as if a faint mist had arisen from between the deck plates. Released from Rusa'h's web, the destabilized crew was no longer connected to any *thism* at all. Udru'h and Zan'nh now had to reassert control, bring back the loyalty of the crew, and convince them of their folly. It would be a delicate task.

Adar Zan'nh tore off the disguise he had taken from the bodies of the guards, while still wearing the breathing film. Beneath it, the Solar Navy uniform was tattered, rumpled, and bloodstained, but he wore it proudly. "It has been long enough. I want to go back to the command nucleus—*my* command nucleus."

Udru'h gave him a small, contained smile. "As you command, Adar."

The two men made their way up one deck after another to the warliner's bridge, not bothering to hide their movements. Though they did not want to fight, both of them held weapons, and Udru'h knew they'd be able to kill many of the disoriented brainwashed crewmen, if it came to that. Instead, the Solar Navy soldiers who saw them responded with confusion; the crewmen shook their heads as if they had lost track of their thoughts.

Udru'h mused, "I wonder if Rusa'h is aware that he no longer controls these followers."

"I hope he can sense much more than that," the Adar replied, his voice dark with anger. "I hope he feels his entire rebellion crumbling."

At the threshold of the command nucleus, Udru'h paused. "Our time grows short. According to the projected flight plan, the warliner should be nearing Dobro."

"Then we must do something about that." Zan'nh strode onto the bridge like a victorious general. His voice was powerful enough to startle even the shiing-disoriented crewmen at their posts. "Your Adar has returned to his command! You will follow my orders."

His eyes blazed as he stared at one Ildiran after another, demanding their obedience. Still reeling, the crew could not yet realize what they had done, but the shiing made them easily susceptible to suggestion. They were torn from the corrupted *thism* web now, entirely adrift. Some of the command crew looked woozy and stunned, others showed an edge of panic. They had no guidance from the Hyrillka Designate and nothing else to hold on to.

"You will listen to *me*." Zan'nh's voice had the strength of a seasoned commander, not unlike Adar Kori'nh's.

Designate Udru'h stood beside him, both of them showing firm confidence. After a long moment, one of the wobbly crewmen stood and pressed his fist to his chest in a formal Ildiran salute. The warliner's captain shook his head as if waking from a dream. He stared at the Adar's insignia, then finally seemed to recognize it. He stumbled backward. "Adar!" He also offered his salute.

One by one, the crewmembers surrendered. As the warliner continued toward Dobro, Udru'h smiled. "That was very good, Adar." Seeing the planet grow large in the warliner's screen, he opened his mind and allowed the strands of normal *thism* to unreel in clear silvery soul-threads. "Since your scan operators do not seem very alert, perhaps you should check the screens yourself?"

Zan'nh adjusted the warliner's long-range sensors. His eyes went wide as he detected several blips, then a few more, then a huge cluster of fast-approaching ships.

The Dobro Designate smiled. So! Despite his resentment toward Udru'h, Jora'h had indeed taken a chance and followed his brother's plan!

"Is it the rest of my maniple? Did Thor'h—?" Zan'nh looked at his listless crew, and uncertainty was plain on his haggard face. "I doubt I'm capable of taking this warliner into battle just yet."

"That won't be necessary."

It rapidly became apparent that far more than a maniple of warliners stood against them. A huge force bristling with weapons blocked the single rebel battleship. Three hundred forty-three vessels: a complete Solar Navy cohort.

The Dobro Designate had no desire to hide his presence now. He felt the linkage, pleased to realize how near the Mage-Imperator was. Hundreds of weapons were prepared to open fire on them.

He turned to explain to Zan'nh. "Knowing when Rusa'h would arrive to threaten Dobro, the Mage-Imperator dispatched a heavy Solar Navy force to make a stand here. They intend to obliterate this ship."

The Adar reacted with surprise. "But we are both on board!"

A thin smile crossed the Dobro Designate's face as he nudged aside a transmission operator and began to focus the warliner's comm system himself. "Your father is finally seeing the necessity of certain terrible decisions."

106 ☀ MAGE-IMPERATOR JORA'H

As the overwhelming force of Solar Navy battleships approached the lone warliner, Jora'h could not sense its crew anywhere in his *thism*. He feared the worst, and was prepared to do what he must. Regardless of the cost, the Mage-Imperator would stop them here.

For a full day, the cohort of warliners had lain in wait near Dobro. According to the ultimatum Udru'h had been given, the Mage-Imperator knew that the rebels would send their might against the colony, whether it was one warliner or the whole maniple. He had to be ready for anything.

In the meantime, he waited with the fastest courier ships on standby, both hoping and dreading that he would receive word from Osira'h that she had brought the hydrogues to Ildira. If that happened, he would have to race back, and leave the battle here despite the bloodshed, without his hoped-for resolution.

Too much all at once. But it couldn't be helped.

How had the Dobro Designate answered Rusa'h's demand, in the end? Jora'h wished he could be certain. In spite of Udru'h's assurances, Jora'h did not trust him to operate out of anything but his own interests. It was even possible that the Dobro Designate would try to play both forces against each other. Would Rusa'h himself be among those who came to conquer the splinter colony? Would Thor'h?

He had hated to leave the Prism Palace, especially while Osira'h attempted to communicate with the hydrogues. So many other crises were causing turbulence in the Spiral Arm. But he had to end this sickening rebellion and restore control to his own Empire.

Finally, Tal O'nh, the commander of this cohort, had relayed a message from the fringe cutters on sentry duty. "One ship incoming, Liege. A single warliner."

One warliner. Perhaps that would minimize the unnecessary casualties.

"Proceed," Jora'h said. O'nh had his instructions, and the Mage-Imperator would not interfere with the commander. He knew it was possible that Udru'h had actually attempted to carry out his unlikely plan, but even if the Designate had been true to his word, Jora'h held out little hope that he had succeeded. In all likelihood, Jora'h would have no choice but to stop the rebel warliner and then go after Hyrillka itself.

Adar Zan'nh had somehow lost control of his maniple, and Rusa'h had used those warships to spread a bloody insurrection. But Jora'h was stronger than the Hyrillka Designate. Much stronger.

"All quls and septars acknowledge," Tal O'nh said. "Ready weapons against that warliner." The deadly offensive systems thrummed, ready to annihilate the rebel vessel. Jora'h braced himself. Although they were all disconnected from his own *thism* web, he feared he would still feel the pain of their deaths. It should never have come to this.

If the Mage-Imperator gave an order to massacre all those Ildirans—even though they were rebels—the race would no doubt be scarred forever. The records in the *Saga* would damn him. He hoped there was another way.

He sensed the emptiness in the *thism* from the warliner; it seemed like a ghost ship, but he knew it carried a full crew. Then he felt two others, like tiny candles in a vast darkness—the Dobro Designate and Adar Zan'nh remained on board! But had they succeeded?

The warliner's comm system transmitted the words that Jora'h longed to hear. "Liege, this is Udru'h. The Adar and I have reasserted control of this vessel. The entire crew is currently under the influence of shiing. I believe they are ready for you."

Smiling with relief, Jora'h acknowledged. "Thank you, Designate. I will lead them back."

In the command nucleus of the cohort's flagship, he

stood rigid, his braided hair twitching and thrashing as he closed his eyes. As Mage-Imperator, he had control over all the soul-threads and the correct pathway to the Lightsource. Now he sent out his thoughts, grasping the skeins of *thism,* smoothing out the tangles and reconnecting every once-rebellious crewman aboard the stolen warliner.

With the sheer force of his will, he brought them back into his fold, one by one. All of them.

His eldest son, the Adar and acting Prime Designate, was in the command nucleus of the rebel warliner. He had believed everything was lost, but now that the Mage-Imperator had recaptured the minds and hearts of all the corrupted soldiers, he was confident the Adar could unify them into a single crew again.

Jora'h opened his smoky topaz eyes and took a deep breath. When the communications channel opened, Zan'nh's gaunt visage appeared before him. "Liege, we are in your debt. I despaired of ever being so close to the *thism* again. I feel as if I have been falling for many days, and now you've caught me."

Behind his son, the soldiers at their stations looked dazed, but their thoughts were returning. From his own warliner, Jora'h could feel them like tiny lights winking back on in the *thism* after a long and uncomfortable darkness. He could guide them, strengthen the bonds that tied them to the correct mental safety net. But he did not want any of these people to forget their loss and recovery, not for a long time.

The Dobro Designate stood beside Zan'nh in the command nucleus of the rebel warliner, wearing a secretive smile behind the breathing film. "Thank you, Liege. We are already purging the shiing gas from the ship's ventilation systems. Before long, order will be completely restored."

"As it should be," Jora'h transmitted. "This crew is yours again, Adar Zan'nh. They have tasted the poison of Designate Rusa'h. Now use them to help me regain control of what my brother has corrupted."

Zan'nh placed his fist against the center of his chest in a formal salute, then lowered his gaze as he answered. "Liege, Thor'h has taken the rest of my warliners to conquer other worlds, while Rusa'h sits in his facsimile chrysalis chair on Hyrillka and extends his web." Now he looked up and his eyes shone. "However, without the warliners, *Hyrillka itself* is militarily vulnerable."

Jora'h nodded. "Adar Zan'nh, I will personally accompany you, but this cohort is yours to command. We go to Hyrillka immediately. And we finish this."

107 ☀ DD

The damaged black ship spun out of control, spiraling away from the system. The reactor explosion had knocked out their engines, and the robotic vessel careened into empty space without guidance or propulsion.

DD thought they might drift forever, cut off from any hope of rescue. Unfortunately, even with Sirix out of commission, and even after so many reanimated machines had been vaporized in the intense reactor meltdown, the little compy was certain the Klikiss robots' plans would proceed unhindered. The human race was about to encounter an unexpected enemy that intended to cause far more death and destruction than the hydrogues had inflicted so far.

As the ship drifted dizzily, DD adjusted his balance and reacquired his perspective. Beside him, a stunned Sirix came active again, tested the controls of his ship, and assessed the damage. The black robot refused to communicate with DD as he completed his evaluation.

Finished, he turned his optical sensors toward the Friendly compy. "You will accompany me outside the ship, DD. Together, we will complete the necessary repairs on the hull."

"Is that possible? Do we have the required spare parts?"

"We will fabricate whatever we need."

DD couldn't imagine how they could perform any complex reconstruction while the ship spun and tumbled far from the sun. But Sirix had commanded him, and he had no choice but to follow the black robot to a damaged doorway.

From a sealed container, Sirix produced a cluster of tools, metal patchwork, and repair epoxies. "These should be sufficient for your portion of the labors. I will provide you with simple instructions. Your compy programming does not extend to intricate tasks, but I will guide you where necessary."

Sirix used brute force to pry open the damaged hatch so they could emerge into the empty vacuum. DD dutifully followed, keeping his balance on the scarred hull of the Klikiss ship. His reinforced compy body had endured great extremes, from the impossible pressures within a hydrogue gas planet to the current cold emptiness. Environment was never the problem.

Moving carefully on fingerlike legs, Sirix scuttled across the buckled hull. He instructed DD to remove twisted plates for repair, while he himself worked on more major damage, disconnecting unwieldy engine shafts, stripping away a destroyed sensor array, scanning for deep fractures in the structural frame.

While they worked, the robot transmitted to DD. "Now you see the destructive abilities of humans. They caused this damage. You must acknowledge why we need to eliminate them. They are all our enemies."

But DD did not follow. "What I observed, Sirix, was that *Klikiss robots* annihilated a human base down on that planetoid in order to 'acquire' materials. Considering what your fellows did, the humans were acting in self-defense."

"Humans should not have been on our planetoid in the first place. They meddled where they were not wanted."

"How were they to know this? They received no warnings from you, no notification."

"You argue about irrelevant things."

The black robot used his claw arms to disconnect the ruined lump of a rear engine, while DD moved to complete the next task Sirix had given him. Always observant, the compy noted that the plate holding the external engine component was loose, that the Klikiss robot's balance was precarious as their ship continued to drift drunkenly.

A calculated possibility raced through DD's mind. He weighed the consequences, discarded concern for his personal safety, and acted.

He had already tested the power and tolerance of the cutting tool he held, knew how long it would take to sever the last connections holding the plate and engine to the spinning ship. While Sirix clambered over the smashed engine, DD melted through the separable hull plate, cutting the whole assembly loose.

He anchored his body to the ship, knowing that when he pushed, the equal and opposite reaction would disorient him. With all the strength his artificial body possessed, DD shoved Sirix and the engine off into open space. In one instant, he sent the black robot off on a divergent course. Soon there was a substantial gap between them. As the ship continued to drift on a different trajectory, the separation grew greater.

DD caught a last glimpse as the Klikiss robot scrambled over the detached component, holding on with his insectile clawed limbs. His tiny island spun farther and farther from the damaged ship.

DD did not know what he was going to do now. He was still stranded, but at least he was free of the Klikiss robot. He expected some sort of transmission from Sirix, a demand for assistance, even an outright threat.

But the black robot remained silent. He scuttled over the moving lump of debris until he faced the ship. Even from a distance, DD could see the gleaming red optical sensors.

Then there was a bright flash of light, a glint of reflected starshine. Sirix had launched a grappling cable from his ellipsoid body core: a hook and an attached line spinning across space.

After an interminable moment, the cable struck the damaged ship and anchored itself magnetically, sealing with an automatic weld. Then Sirix leaped away from the drifting engine and began to reel himself in. The cable drew taut and vibrated as the black robot flew across the gulf of space, closing the gap.

DD hurried to where the cable was attached, knowing the Klikiss robot would destroy him as soon as he made it back to the drifting wreck. Moving as fast as possible, he powered his cutting tool again and attempted to sever the cable. The material was tough, some sort of diamond polymer, but the little compy worked furiously, cutting and cutting. A few strands broke away. Finally the rest of the cable parted.

But by now Sirix had gathered enough momentum. His body slammed into the hull. The beetlelike machine rose up, looming over the small compy under the starlight. His silhouetted form blocked out the misty swath of the Spiral Arm. DD tilted his head back to look at the other machine and prepared for the end of his existence.

Sirix paused for a prolonged moment. At last he said, "Now you begin to see the potential of free actions. However, I must educate you to make better choices in the future."

With a swift snap like a serpent's tongue being drawn back into its mouth, Sirix reeled in the ragged end of his cable, then sealed the opening in his body core. The normal set of six articulated arms took its place. "Now help me finish these repairs."

108 ☀ JESS TAMBLYN

Jess did not bother using standard human coordinates or Ildiran starmaps to find Jonah 12 . . . or Cesca. With his mind connected to the wentals, he simply homed in on Nikko Chan Tylar's ship. He could sense they were all in terrible danger. Hurt badly . . . perhaps dying.

His water-and-pearl ship soon arrived at the far-flung planetoid. With vision magnified through the curvature of his water-membrane spacecraft, he stared in sick disbelief at a wide, simmering crater that glowed with residual radioactivity after an immense explosion.

Spiderweb cracks spread out through the frozen crust, as if the planetoid itself had nearly shattered. Vaporized methane snow roared up from the surrounding crater, forming an immense anvil-shaped thunderhead that dissipated into the vacuum. It looked as if an asteroid or a comet had slammed into the base. Jess thought of his strange wental-impregnated comet, but sensed that it was on a mission of its own, flying to its chosen destination. This had been caused by something else.

If that had been the Roamer base, nothing could have survived down there. "Oh, Cesca . . ." More words refused to come. Emotions welled up inside of him like a geyser forced up from beneath the ice sheet on Plumas. So many dreams, so many feelings, all of them unspoken . . . all of them too late.

Then he stretched his thoughts out through the water entities—and was astonished when they connected with the wental specimens aboard Nikko's ship, the *Aquarius*. At first he thought the liquid creatures had somehow survived in the frozen environment, perhaps infusing the ice of Jonah 12 as they had in the wandering comet . . . but then he received direct images through his mind's eye. Nikko's ship had crashed, but the wental samples were intact. *Aquarius* retained part of its integrity . . . and Nikko and Cesca were still alive!

Jess dodged the huge cloud of ice and gases and cruised over the destroyed landscape until he found the dying ship crumpled on an icy plain. A long gouge showed that the *Aquarius* had crashed, skidded, and rolled. Pieces of the hull and mangled engine components lay strewn behind where the ship had finally ground to a halt. The hull of the *Aquarius* had ruptured, opening several compartments to the cold vacuum, but the main piloting chamber was intact.

Although Jess was stunned by the extent of the damage, the wentals reassured him that two passengers clung to life. Through the specimens inside the *Aquarius,* he heard Nikko speaking to Cesca. "It's Jess Tamblyn. He's come for us."

Cesca said weakly, "I knew he would." The words seemed to take every last scrap of her energy. She'd been thrown like a discarded doll when the spacecraft tumbled and rolled. Jess could feel that she was badly hurt, broken inside, bleeding internally, but the wentals did not understand her physiology.

Of more immediate importance, the two survivors didn't have much air left—and in his water-filled wental ship, Jess didn't know what he could do. He brought his spherical vessel over the crash site. "Find me a solution," he demanded of the interconnected water entities. "Can I repair the *Aquarius*? Can I take the two humans to safety aboard this ship?"

You can take the whole spacecraft. We will show you how.

Cesca had lost consciousness, her skin gray with cold, blood running from her nose; Nikko huddled beside her in the only intact space within their ship, gasping in the last few wisps of air. In the large coral-frameworked vessel, Jess hovered like a full moon just above the wreck. Nikko shouted questions to the wental samples, but his connection with the entities wasn't clear enough for him to pick up specific words. Though he seemed to partially understand what Jess intended to do, the young man didn't believe it.

Gently, Jess settled the sphere down on top of the crashed *Aquarius*. The flexible membrane that formed the outer surface of the wental ship puckered and folded. The sphere enveloped the smashed Roamer vessel and drew it entirely inside the bubble. When all the seals had closed over once more, Jess lifted his alien vessel from the surface with the *Aquarius* inside the watery globe, like a rare specimen in an aquarium.

Dressed in his pearlescent garment, Jess swam through the interior of his ship and drifted around the scarred and blackened hull of Nikko's ship. The other wentals were delighted to be reunited with the rest of the liquid entity.

Inside the microcosm of an alien ocean next to Jess, tiny creatures—from planktons to minuscule shellfish, rippling worms, and protoplasmic jelly creatures—drew together, attracted to the wreck of the *Aquarius,* as if it were a new reef they could call their home. Guided by Jess's thoughts, they had a task to do.

Barnacles attached to the broken sections of hull. Microorganisms drew minerals dissolved in the seawater while others spun threads out of the framework of the wental vessel. Membranes folded over the gaps torn in the hull, separating oxygen from the water and allowing it to bleed into the sheltered compartment. The tiny oceanic army set to work on the *Aquarius,* rebuilding and modifying it.

Trapped inside the vessel, Nikko gaped at the furious activity bubbling around them. But he was obviously breathing easier now. Cesca, though, had not stirred. She had passed into a deep unconsciousness.

Submerged in the amniotic water, Jess stared at Cesca through the curved, transparent window. Soon the wentals would make it possible for him to enter the *Aquarius,* but for now he drifted on the other side of the barrier.

Nikko stared out at him, still holding Cesca. He touched her forehead, took her pulse, and looked back at Jess, distraught. "She's dying, I think!" he shouted.

In the water outside, Jess placed his hands against the window, once again close but separated from his love. With burning urgency, he sent a command to the sea creatures and the wentals to hurry. Hurry!

109 ☀ TASIA TAMBLYN

With the hydrogue warglobes swarming around them, the tension reached its peak, and Tasia felt as if her heart would explode. All of the dunsel human commanders had already issued the order.

Sixty rammers would charge with concentrated EDF weapons blazing before the final flash of deadly impact. Grinning with long-anticipated satisfaction, Tasia gripped the arms of the command chair, ready to sprint for the evac pod as soon as the rammers lurched forward.

But the Soldier compies did not respond.

"Rammers, full forward!" she repeated after a brief hesitation. "Engines primed for overload. Come on, you won't have any trouble finding targets."

It took Tasia less than a second to realize that something was terribly wrong. The compies just stood there. "Launch, dammit! Fire all weapons and begin full acceleration. Attack the hydrogues!" Now she noticed that none of the sixty rammers had moved forward. Not one.

All of the Soldier compies on her bridge turned from their stations. One spoke. "No."

Since her veins were on fire with adrenaline and her attention focused on the enemy warglobes in front of her, Tasia did not immediately absorb what the compy had just said. "What?" Until now, she hadn't realized the Soldier compies could speak of their own volition.

Implacable, the compies stood quietly in position, optical sensors turned toward her. They seemed to be having thoughts of their own, which was absurd for an obedient military-model machine. Of all the ridiculous times for a malfunction!

"Didn't you hear me? I said full forward! Ramming speed. Go, go! Get the weapons—"

The nearest Soldier compy cut her off. "These battleships are now forfeit to us. All of them."

Tasia studied the robots, and as they stared back, her gut turned colder than the oceans of Plumas. "Shizz, what the hell are you talking about?" She felt totally alone staring out at a sea of alien robotic eyes. "Shut down! That's a direct command—all of you, shut down!"

Ignoring her, the military compies began to move about, operating their stations and activating communications signals. She heard them send buzzing messages. Tasia turned to the Listener compy. "EA, what are they sending? Tell me what's going on!"

The little compy paused to eavesdrop on the message. "They are transmitting directly to the hydrogues." She paused to consider her own words. "That is most unexpected."

Soldier compies talking to hydrogues? What the hell? "You've got to be kidding me! Using my comm systems? We could never communicate with the drogues before."

"I don't think that's true, Master Tasia. If the new

memory files you gave me are accurate, the hydrogues simply never responded before. That does not mean they couldn't communicate."

"Then what the hell are they saying?" She held out a desperate, but ridiculous, hope that the Soldier compies might be negotiating some sort of cease-fire, an end to hostilities. "Tell me it's good news, EA."

"I'm afraid it is not, Master Tasia."

One of the other dunsel humans—it sounded like Darby Vinh—shouted over the comm system, "These damned compies have taken over! They're—" His words cut off with a squawk and a wet-sounding noise.

Ignoring the man's alarmed transmission, EA continued reporting, "They are using a Klikiss robot language. The message states that our Soldier compies are in the process of taking control of all sixty EDF ships." EA paused again to listen. "I am afraid to say that two of the human commanders have resisted and are now dead."

Tasia leaped out of her command chair, bristling. If the turncoat Soldier compies controlled all systems aboard every one of the rammers, she could never fight them. This was bigger, much bigger, than her mission here.

Seeing no other way out, Tasia lunged for the evac pod, her only chance to get away. Two of the stocky Soldier compies immediately moved to block the escape hatch. Three more military-model robots stepped toward her, their footfalls heavy on the deck.

Tasia heard a crackle of static on the comm, another brief scream, another panicked human voice, female this time. Then just a quiet hiss.

EA stared from Tasia to the Soldier compies, seemingly as confused as she.

The evac pod seemed impossibly far away, and Tasia's shoulders sagged as she realized it would have done her no good anyway. "Shizz, if you bastards can take over my bridge in the middle of a battle, you could just as easily blast the pod out of space." She froze. The ominous Soldier compies did not come closer.

Outside, the massed warglobes hovered above Qronha 3, but didn't fire a shot, fearing nothing from the rammers. The hydrogues stayed in position, waiting.

Tasia caught her breath as the enormity of the trap became clear. Damn, the drogues had *expected* this turnabout! The destruction of the Hansa and Ildiran cloud harvesters, and this carefully planned EDF response, must have been a setup. The hydrogues, through the Soldier compies, now controlled all sixty of the special rammers.

"Lost the battle before I fired a single shot." She clenched her jaw. The kamikaze ships hadn't hit even one warglobe.

And why had all those Ildiran battleships simply turned around and departed as soon as the EDF rammers arrived? "Something here really, really smells. Is there a triple cross going on here?"

Another set of strange vessels—angular metallic constructions that looked like poisonous bugs—rose through the clouds of Qronha 3 and joined smaller hydrogue teardrop scout ships, all of which approached the hostage rammers. As the angular craft prepared to dock with Tasia's ship, the Soldier compies moved to receive their new masters.

Helpless and trapped on her bridge, Tasia wished she had a sidearm, some way to blow off a few compy heads in a last futile, but satisfying, gesture. Given a little luck, she could have destroyed several of them in a wild last stand—but the

sixty rammers held thousands of Soldier models. *Pointless.*
Resisting would get her killed, just like the other dunsel
human commanders. Or was she just postponing the inevitable? She didn't see so much as a glimmer from her
Guiding Star.

The rammer's bridge doors opened. The Soldier compies
turned slowly, as if mechanically coming to attention. Tasia
reeled when she saw three towering Klikiss robots scuttle
onto the command deck.

The black robots turned their headplates toward her. They
paused for a moment of analysis, as if considering how much
trouble she might still cause. The foremost beetlelike machine
spoke. "These rammer vessels will not be used against the hydrogues. We have taken possession of them for our own purposes. Your Soldier compies are now loyal to us."

110 ☀ DEL KELLUM

B y damn, the compies have gone berserk!" Del Kellum
stared at the frantic reports that flickered across the control screens. He turned from one emergency to another,
confused and enraged at the same time. "What set them off?
Did somebody overload their programming with caffeine?
Shizz, I can't believe this! I thought their cores were erased
before we put them to work."

"They were, Del!" one of his assistants said. "Completely wiped."

"Yeah, I can see that."

One of the smelter supervisors sprinted in as if something was chasing him. He ran so fast in the low gravity that he couldn't stop himself in time and ricocheted off the wall; he had to scramble to regain his balance. "Del, I've got another report! The Soldier compies kept overloading Smelter G until the auto-crucible split open. The entire facility is melting down as we speak!"

"Casualties?"

"Our ten workers managed to get into a couple of grappler pods in time. The whole smelter's just a hardening globule of slag—including the Soldier compies they left behind."

Kellum grabbed the smelter supervisor by the front of his embroidered shirt. "Where's Zhett? Has anybody seen her?"

"I've been running from crazy robots and molten metal, Del—"

Kellum went from one station to another. The situation was insane, but he would try his damnedest to get control of it. "Kotto Okiah left yesterday with his crazy doorbells, didn't he? Two days ago? Maybe he could help our engineers reprogram those compies—or at least shut them down. Can we get him back here in time?"

"No way, Del. He's halfway to Theroc by now."

Kellum fumed at the various screens, studying the red flashes and the repeated alarms. "They're wreaking havoc everywhere!"

One of his assistants studied the reports. "Seems to be only the Soldier models. The other compies haven't shown any erratic behavior."

"Thank the Guiding Star for that. But those Soldier

compies are equipped for combat. They're more than we can handle."

"It's not only the compies, Dad. It's the Eddy POWs, too!" Zhett appeared at the doorway, looking extremely shaken up. Her long hair was tangled, her face and hands streaked with grime. Most of all she was flushed with anger. "It's Fitzpatrick and his cronies—they triggered it."

Kellum hurried toward her, opening his arms to embrace his daughter. "What happened to you, my sweet?"

She was too furious for a hug. "He tricked me, Dad." Were those tear tracks on her cheeks?

Kellum tried to smooth her hair. "Explain yourself—but be quick about it."

She told him how Fitzpatrick had tricked her, then locked her into a cargo storage area. Kellum sensed that she was leaving out significant parts of the story, but his anger was directed toward the EDF detainee.

Zhett sounded more incensed than hurt. "It took me half an hour to reactivate and communicate with the compies outside, so they could cut their way through the door and let me out." Her nostrils flared. "He stole the cargo escort, Dad. He's long gone."

An avalanche of explanations tumbled together in his mind. "The Eddies did this to us? You think it was a *diversion*? Unbelievable! Look at the mayhem, the property damage. Who knows how many casualties they've caused!"

"That didn't stop Fitzpatrick from manipulating me, stealing a ship, and flying away by himself. He left all of his comrades behind. Bastard!"

"Del, look at this!" shouted the smelter supervisor. "It's getting worse every minute."

On the screen, a single grappler pod flown by a Soldier

compy drove like a missile into a partially constructed cargo vessel in spacedock. The framework girders crumbled and flew apart; the grappler pod's fuel cell exploded despite all the internal safety systems, as if the Soldier compy had intentionally detonated it. Molten metal sprayed into space, splattering into globules from the overloaded Smelter G.

"Evacuate the spacedock," Del Kellum said. "Get those workers out of there. Our priority is to get our people to safety."

"Compies are supposed to have human protective programming," Zhett said. "It's ingrained in their core. How could it have gone so completely awry?"

"Ask your Eddy friends," her father said.

Zhett scanned the screens for hot spots of robotic turmoil. "Could be the Eddies got more than they bargained for, Dad. Their own work crews are right in the middle of those battle zones."

"Like touching an igniter to rocket fuel. It's gotten out of their control." Kellum wanted to strangle them all, one by one. "Even though they deserve it, I'm not going to play favorites. Zhett, go make sure the Eddies get out alive, even if it's just so we can kill them later if we decide to."

"Sounds good to me." She sprinted away.

He pushed the smelter supervisor toward the central console. "Take over for a while. I'm going out there myself. Get a grappler pod ready."

A short while later, when he finally puttered away from the administrative complex, Kellum felt as if he had entered the crossfire. Soldier compies were smashing everything they could, overloading systems, careening stolen vessels into storage asteroids or even unoccupied rocks in Osquivel's rings. The military robots didn't seem to have a

plan, or even common sense. Kellum wondered how long
the Eddies had been planning this strike. They were more insane than their out-of-control compies!

Zhett led several evac shuttles to the primary assembly
platform, where the largest group of EDF captives had been
assigned. While the Soldier compies continued their rampage on the assembly platform, she and her rescue team signaled for the Eddies to rush to their open ships. "Get your
butts out of there!"

One of the frantic refugees was Kiro Yamane, who
looked dazed. "It was a simple programming shift. It wasn't
supposed to do all this. I . . . I never intended to cause so
much havoc. The compies are acting on their own—"

"You people disgust me," Zhett said. "What were you
thinking?"

As Kellum raced around his widespread shipyards, connecting the dots from disaster to disaster, he wondered how
his clan could ever recover from this. It hadn't been long
since they reassembled everything and got back up to speed
after the battle of Osquivel. But this damage was already far
worse—and it didn't look like the bedlam would end anytime soon.

Then, when he didn't think anything could get worse,
Kellum looked beyond the rings to see a cluster of incoming
EDF ships on his trajectory scanners. He stared through the
windowport of his grappler pod, astonished to discover an
escort Manta cruiser and a cluster of smaller diplomatic
ships. All of them looked fully armed. Kellum searched in
his repertoire for a suitable curse.

An old woman's scowling face appeared on a transmission screen. Her eyes were hard and sharp, and her voice
was as heavy as a blunt club. "This is Maureen Fitzpatrick,

former Chairman of the Terran Hanseatic League. Would somebody like to tell me what the hell is going on here?"

111 ✷ MAUREEN FITZPATRICK

Using clout she had retained from her years as Hansa Chairman, Maureen Fitzpatrick had swiftly put together a fine memorial expedition to Osquivel. She meant to accomplish something for her fallen grandson Patrick . . . and all of his lost comrades, of course.

Maureen had secured the use of an old-model Manta cruiser that hadn't yet been decommissioned, though its weapons and armor plating were inferior to the newer designs. Along with several diplomatic craft and a skeleton crew of older officers who were not eager to see battle, they made an impressive—and newsworthy—diplomatic expedition. The massacre at Osquivel must not be forgotten.

Her consultants and designers had suggested a shining monument, a beacon for the valiant EDF soldiers who had fallen in the worst battle (so far) of the hydrogue war. Her favorite proposal consisted of installing segmented reflective mirrors all along the rings so that they sparkled like a halo girdling the gas giant. Once her initial expedition returned to Earth, Maureen would gather support for a breathtaking, and expensive, monument.

Now, as her group approached the site of the space battle-field, Maureen summoned the families to the Manta's bridge so they could get the best view of the ringed planet where their loved ones had been killed. Conrad and Natalie Brindle stood closest to her like wooden effigies in active-duty EDF uni-forms. The other families watched with tears already in their eyes.

When they got a full view of the planetary battleground, though, Maureen was stunned to see the place crawling with *Roamers*.

"They're everywhere, Madam Chairman," said the Manta captain. "Ship after ship, full facilities. I'm detecting smelters and construction yards."

"A rats' nest!" Maureen said. "Give me a better view."

The captain barked orders to his sensor crew. Imagers zoomed in to display magnified scans of artificial structures, ships flitting around in a frenzy. The scale was incredible, a flourishing hub of the outlaw clans.

Conrad Brindle's deep voice trembled with outrage. "Like carrion crows over the battlefield. They must have come here to gather all our wrecked ships."

His wife grasped his arm in a viselike grip. "It's despica-ble. Did they pick the pockets of any dead bodies they found, too?" A wave of anger and disgust rippled through the gathered families that had come to pay their last respects.

Always observant, Maureen noted the bright pinpricks of obvious explosions. "That isn't everyday activity. Some-thing else is going on down there. Some sort of battle?"

"Who can tell with Roachers, Madam Chairman?" the captain said.

Her hard voice was well practiced in giving orders.

"Give me comm control. Find out what bands they're transmitting on and let me speak to somebody." She waited, fuming, and then announced herself, demanding to know what was going on.

A man's gruff voice responded, "This is Del Kellum, in charge of the shipyards here. We're in a bit of a crisis right now, ma'am." He muttered a curse, then issued a quick string of orders to someone else on the channel before he turned back to Maureen. "To answer your question before you ask it, ma'am—yes, we have a handful of EDF survivors that we rescued from the wreckage here. You can either help us clean up this mess, or you can go away and leave us to handle it. But whatever you do, don't bother me right now!"

"Who the hell does he think he's talking to?" Conrad Brindle said.

"Survivors?" one of the other parents cried. "They have EDF *survivors*! Find out their names."

"All in good time." Maureen turned to the central bridge station. Though the Manta's captain was the superior officer aboard the ship, he would not dream of disputing her orders. "Captain, this cruiser has sufficient weapons to complete a simple policing action, doesn't it?"

He gestured dismissively. "Against a bunch of dirty Roachers? Of course, Madam Chairman."

Sensor stations continued to map the shipyard structures in the ring along with the obstacle course of debris. Maureen stared as they drew closer. "They're hiding a full-blown city here. How could they have erected such a thing in the short time since the battle?"

"They saw a weakness and they pounced," said Natalie Brindle.

"Vultures!" her husband said. "They're not going to get away with it."

Maureen went to stand behind the Manta's captain, narrowing her eyes as she calculated. "We'll rescue the EDF prisoners. The Roamer clans have been declared outlaws and unfriendlies. That's all the justification we need to round up these people and bring them back to the Hansa."

Conrad scowled. "I commend your restraint, madam. But if it was up to me—"

She cut him off. "You have a point, Lieutenant Commander Brindle. But the Hansa has issued a proclamation that all Roamer hideouts and illicit facilities are to be placed under military jurisdiction, all valuable resources confiscated and delivered to the war effort, and all clan members detained for debriefing. Imagine how much intelligence information we can gather by vigorously questioning them."

The captain dispatched squadrons of Remoras from the flight deck. The fast fighters swooped into the chaos of the Osquivel shipyards where grappler pods, shuttles, and cargo haulers moved on frenzied random paths.

Maureen transmitted again on Kellum's frequency. "The Earth Defense Forces will accept your immediate and unconditional surrender. All Roamers stand down and allow yourselves to be taken aboard."

When the response came, she heard explosions in the background, shouts and screams, small-weapons fire. "Don't be an ass! We're too busy for that kind of nonsense! The Soldier compies are absolutely nuts."

"If any harm comes to those EDF captives," Maureen warned, "we will carry out the strictest reprisals."

"Then come and get your people, ma'am. We're losing

ground here step-by-step. There isn't going to be anything left for you to capture."

The lead Remora squadron scattered as a compy-flown delivery ship shifted orbit and accelerated into their paths. Two fully loaded ore-haulers—also driven by reckless compies—picked up speed, lumbering ahead until they slammed into one of the spacedock construction yards.

"I don't think they're lying," Natalie Brindle said.

The comm system crackled, and an impatient Kellum spoke to Maureen again. "Here's somebody you'll want to talk to. I've given him access to a communicator so you can straighten things out between yourselves—but stop twiddling your thumbs already!"

Another voice came on the line. "Madam Chairman? My name is Kiro Yamane, civilian consultant to the Earth Defense Forces."

From the crowded families on the Manta's bridge, one older man let out a cry of joy.

Yamane continued. "I and thirty other survivors of the battle of Osquivel have been held here in the Roamer shipyards. We have been treated well, but right now the Soldier compies have been reprogrammed into a destructive force. Mr. Kellum is telling the truth. We could use EDF assistance and rescue right now."

Maureen nodded to the Manta captain. "Our priority is to get those POWs released." She turned back to the image on the screen. "Mr. Yamane, round up your people. In exchange for our assistance, we expect an unconditional surrender. Otherwise the Roamers will forfeit their rescue."

Another storage asteroid exploded in a plume of escaping vapor tanks and expanding jets of fuel. Aboard Maureen's cruiser, the gathered EDF families chattered with sudden hope. Yamane's father wept with joy upon learning his son was still alive, while the others restlessly begged for the names of the other captives. Maureen gestured them to silence. "We'll find out soon enough."

She didn't allow herself to hope that her grandson Patrick might have survived. Yamane had said only thirty-one prisoners remained—a vanishingly small percentage of the number assumed dead after the hydrogue battle.

Roamer grappler pods and shuttles launched away from the shipyards, evacuating as the Soldier compies continued their rampage. Maureen could see that the clans would have no choice but to agree to her terms. She warned her captain, "Don't accept any resistance. Don't allow any complaints. Take the Roamers aboard our ships and disarm them. We've got them by the balls. They don't have any choice."

One of the scan technicians on the Manta's bridge called out, "There's a new ship approaching fast, Captain. Inbound from the outer solar system."

"Is it a warglobe?" one of the parents cried. "Are the hydrogues back?"

"Probably a Roacher ship. He'll turn tail as soon as he sees us."

The vessel streaked in at high speed with the remnants of velocity imparted by an Ildiran stardrive. The Manta's long-range sensors showed it as a skeletal framework, a cargo escort used to haul cylinders of processed ekti.

A transmission came over the open channel. "This is Commander Patrick Fitzpatrick III of the Earth Defense Forces. I've been eavesdropping, Grandmother, and it looks like you're about to bite off more than you can chew."

"Patrick! You're alive."

"*Obviously,* Grandmother. I've come back to offer a way out of this mess."

"Mess?" She controlled her emotions, becoming cool again. "Thank you, Patrick, but we have it under control."

"No, you don't, Grandmother—and if you don't listen to me, you'll lose one of the greatest advantages the Hansa could hope to gain. I've got an offer you can't refuse."

112 ☀ MAGE-IMPERATOR JORA'H

Hundreds of Solar Navy warliners arrived at Hyrillka, the heart of the insurrection. Mage-Imperator Jora'h felt more keenly attuned to his *thism* than he had ever been, because he needed it more than ever. Always before, the mental safety net had been a part of him, an unconscious ability that he'd taken for granted. Now it was his greatest strength. It *had* to be.

In his mind's eye, the soul-threads stretched out like taut strands spun from unbreakable diamond fiber. He sensed his people, the love and loyalty across the whole Ildiran Empire, no matter how far away.

Here, though, Rusa'h's—and Thor'h's—corruption made him angry. Hyrillka was at the center of a growing blank stain, like a hole in the expansive Ildiran Empire. The Horizon Cluster was an empty, silent scar that might never recover fully. But Jora'h intended to take it all back.

When a full cohort of warliners appeared above Hyril-lka's main city, several rebellious battleships launched from the spaceport grounds. These were warliners, cutters, and streamers that had been seized when Dzelluria and Alturas had fallen to the insurrection. Their weapons already primed and powered, they seemed suicidally intent on defending the usurper.

A transmission boomed from the newly arrived battle group, emanating from the recovered warliner that had so recently been intent on subduing Dobro. "This is Adar Zan'nh. We come in the name of the rightful Mage-Imperator."

The rebel ships prepared for a headlong attack, rising recklessly in front of the oncoming military force, though they were impossibly outnumbered. "Are you willing to fire upon other Ildirans?" said the deluded commander. "We are acting to defend our Imperator—would you slaughter us?"

Zan'nh responded coldly, "If necessary. If *you* make it necessary." His ship surged forward, taking the point of the assault. More than three hundred warliners followed him, all of them ready to open fire.

Jora'h waited in the command nucleus of his flagship. Through *thism* strands to the former rebels that were stronger than ever, the Mage-Imperator could sense that the soldiers aboard Zan'nh's recovered warliner were surprisingly willing to open fire on their former comrades. Though they could not be held responsible for what they had done after being coerced by Rusa'h, the recovered Solar Navy soldiers still reeled with the realization. They were furious, prepared to fight harder, as if that might purge their shame. Now that their eyes had been opened, they were appalled at how they themselves had been abused, their allegiances twisted.

Jora'h could also sense that they carried a certain sympathy and understanding for the other insurrectionists. Not long ago, these soldiers would have been willing to throw away their lives for Rusa'h instead of for him. But the impostor Imperator did not expect the Mage-Imperator to be here himself. This was no mere military engagement, but a battle of minds.

Hoping to avert a full-fledged and deadly combat, Jora'h reached out again, searching for the disjointed web of *thism* that his insane brother had stolen. Unlike the converts aboard Zan'nh's recovered warliner, Rusa'h's followers manning these defensive ships were not softened with shiing, making Jora'h's task infinitely harder.

The rebel vessels kept coming closer, clearly intent on sacrificing themselves to sow as much destruction as possible, even at the cost of their own lives. Jora'h *knew* they were willing to open fire and even crash their ships into his warliners.

He had to stop them. Gripping the rail of the command nucleus, ignoring the anxiety on Tal O'nh's face, Jora'h strained until his mind pounded inside his skull. If he'd been able to dump shiing gas through the recirculating systems of those rebel ships, he could easily have pried the soul-threads loose and taken them back into his network. Now, however, he had to rip them free with brute mental force to overcome Rusa'h's imprint . . . and hope that he didn't kill his people in the attempt.

With nimble mental fingers, he traced out a complex network of soul-threads, seeing it all in his mind's eye: The pearl-white lines of his own connection to the Lightsource looped around, but remained separate from, a second web, a smaller one pulled garrote tight, made of stiff silver mental wires instead of gossamer strands. Rusa'h's new web.

Jora'h could see them, feel them, fight with them. They resisted. The *thism* had set firmly into its new patterns, but he had to tear it loose. Words squeezed from between his teeth as he spoke aloud, "*I* am the Mage-Imperator. I . . . do not . . . require shiing!"

The Mage-Imperator would have to sever all the unwanted mental strands and snip the prisoners free, but that too offered a moment of danger. After being cut loose, each deluded Ildiran would be lost and disjointed, without the safety of any *thism* at all. He, their true leader, had to be there to catch them.

Jora'h tugged at the twisted wires, untying the misled people. His mind reached for the wires as they started to come free. There! He grasped some of them, softening the wire into gossamer strands as he welcomed those people back. But there were many more yet to free. He tugged again, focusing his mind on the struggle. Now he discovered strands knotted into other strands, while some cords dangled broken, left lost and adrift. He reached out, feeling an echo of despair and fear coming from the severed people. He had pulled too hard, and the soul-threads snapped! While he enfolded many of the rescued rebels, others were lost entirely. They tumbled away into mindlessness. He could not save them.

Aboard some of the suicidal defender ships, rebels who had been too entrenched in their beliefs were dropping, falling either brain-damaged or dead to the decks. He had uprooted them clumsily, and now they were gone. He felt them in his heart, even if he could not catch their *thism* threads.

But he could not stop. The warships careened toward each other, weapons ready.

Jora'h strained, sending his mind out to take hold of them before it was too late. As the ships closed, one of the rebels managed to launch a salvo, which damaged the nearest warliner.

"No," Jora'h gasped through his spasming throat, still keeping his eyes clenched shut. "Do not return fire! Tal O'nh—I . . . *command* it!"

The cohort commander called uneasily into the transmitter, "No retaliation! Adar Zan'nh, the Mage-Imperator asks us all to hold our fire."

"Acknowledged. Evasive maneuvers."

Still pressing and pulling, using a gentle touch when he could or a harsh one when necessary, Jora'h felt the corrupt tapestry unraveling. As it did, he could seize each slippery strand. He pulled harder, more steadily. His mind cried out with the effort.

Then, as if a switch had been thrown, the connected thoughts and presences of all the remaining rebellious crewmen were brought back into his grasp. He had torn the blindfolds from their eyes. The Lightsource would blaze brighter to them, a flash as dazzling as a starflare. The commanders suddenly saw what they had been about to do, and remembered the crimes they had already committed while under the influence of the Hyrillka Designate.

The suicidal warliners and cutters separated, powered down their weapons, then flew harmlessly in and among the battleships of the loyal cohort. Comm channels were quickly clogged with surprised questions and despairing confessions, and the news of how many had been lost when they were torn free from the *thism*. Jora'h felt the pain of each one.

The final battle was just beginning.

He signaled the individual commanders. Jora'h could sense that he held them all again, firmer than ever in their devotion. "By order of your Mage-Imperator, these warliners are now under the full control of Adar Zan'nh."

"These ships were the only defenses remaining on Hyrillka," Zan'nh transmitted to his father. "We now have the capability and the obligation to retake this planet."

All across the cohort's warliners, Solar Navy soldiers cheered aloud.

Wide open and sensitive, the Mage-Imperator felt a desperate wordless cry emanate from the citadel palace below, vibrating through the broken strands all around him. Through the instantaneous connection of the *thism*, Rusa'h sent his urgent need like a thunderbolt, a desperate demand for reinforcements. Jora'h felt it like a shout in his mind.

And, with his forty-five stolen warliners, so did Prime Designate Thor'h.

113 ☀ KING PETER

The halls of the Whisper Palace were not safe even late at night. A disguised King Peter slipped alone through the corridors, taking a roundabout way to the meeting place. His hands were clammy, his breathing shallow. Anyone who stopped to question him would notice him sweating. He wondered if this was how Prince Daniel had escaped a few days ago.

Deep in a dead-end hall in the basement recesses of the enormous structure, Peter found the storage room without difficulty. He couldn't remember ever having walked these levels before, but OX had provided detailed directions, which the King memorized, then destroyed. He didn't want to carry anything incriminating, in case suspicious Hansa officials or royal guards encountered him on his nighttime stroll.

Estarra was extremely nervous about what he intended to do. Again while swimming with the dolphins, the two had used their secret sign language, then talked in only the barest of whispers, breathing into each other's ears. King and Queen needed to form desperate alliances and gather defenses against the Chairman. Peter would not let any harm come to Estarra's and his unborn child, and he'd finally been driven to take this terrible chance.

The storeroom door was unlocked, as arranged. Peter opened it slowly, still expecting a trap, his mind racing to concoct a viable excuse. Inside a chamber crowded with boxes, sculptures, and paraphernalia, he saw one shadowy figure.

"Ah, welcome, King Peter. I've been expecting you." Eldred Cain looked ghostly in the faint light, his features pleasantly gnomish. "Any evening spent looking at art objects, even ones that are mothballed and hidden away like these, is time to be treasured. I've long wanted to share these things with someone of sufficient understanding and open-mindedness." The deputy ran his gaze up and down the King's casual disguise. "Are you that person, Peter? Or must I call you Your Majesty even in this private meeting?"

"Peter isn't my real name anyway—as you well know."

He closed the door behind him, giving them complete privacy in the art storeroom.

The previous day, when Basil had announced his intention to force an abortion upon Estarra, Peter had realized he had very little time. Using OX as a go-between who would not arouse suspicion, he had approached the deputy and requested a brief, off-the-record conversation. He was sure Cain could read between the lines. "I am taking quite a risk just seeing you here, Mr. Deputy."

"Likewise." Cain turned his attention to a dusty sculpture of a woman holding a bowl of grapes. "You have no reason to trust me. None whatsoever."

"I trust no one in the Hansa, yet I need some sort of ally or advocate. You have always seemed a reasonable man with measured responses, someone who considers his words before speaking."

Cain's eyes twinkled. "Such compliments. Perhaps I should be King."

Peter said in a flat, crisp monotone, "Or maybe Chairman."

Cain looked away. "You overestimate my ambitions." The pale-skinned man removed a polymer tarpaulin that covered a large framed painting. Peter saw a foppish medieval nobleman on a white horse beside a woman in a voluminous blue dress; she held a bouquet of flowers.

"This work is utter rubbish," the deputy said, "and I'm glad it was taken down from the southeast hall. The sunlight hit it all wrong there, and it simply didn't go with the other works in the alcoves. Look, even the frame is bad."

Tilting the painting forward, he reached behind it for a smaller study of a sweet-looking girl in a pink dress with a rangy hunting hound curled at her feet. "This one has much more character. Mid-1700s, I believe."

Peter looked closer. "Not a name I recognize, but judging by some of the details, he might have been a student, or at least an admirer, of Velázquez. Has the bright charm, but without the bleak despair of Goya." When Cain looked at him with mixed surprise and interest, Peter explained, "Chairman Wenceslas made me spend years learning to understand the politics and history of the Hansa. OX also took me on tours of the Whisper Palace to show me the architecture, stained glass, fountains, sculptures, and paintings. I am not an expert by any means, Mr. Cain, but I do appreciate skillful workmanship and fine art."

The hairless skin on the deputy's forehead wrinkled like putty. "If you appreciate skillful work, then we shall have to accomplish some."

"We don't have much time, Mr. Deputy. I should get back to the royal quarters before anyone notices my absence."

"All right, then, raise your question—not that I can't guess what it is. I know about the Queen's pregnancy. And the Chairman's somewhat extreme response to it. It lacks a logical foundation."

"So, you've noticed that he's becoming somewhat . . . unstable," Peter said.

But the deputy would not commit himself to a comment.

Peter's eyes flashed as he pressed. "This is not an isolated incident. You're aware of Basil's erratic behavior. You've seen him become more aggressive, his decisions more rash, his actions more desperate and unsound."

"He is under a great deal of pressure," Cain said. "We can all understand that. He believes he is acting in the best interest of the Hansa."

"We all want to believe we're acting in the best interest of the Hansa, but that can't be used to excuse just any action.

Year by year, day after day, the Chairman becomes less reasonable and more volatile. He kidnapped me as an unknown street child and murdered my whole family to cover his tracks. I'm certain he did the same with Daniel's family."

Cain stared at him, absorbing the information. Peter wondered how much the deputy already knew about what was going on in the shadows of the Hansa. Cain ran his milky hands over the smooth surface of one of the statues. A nervous fidget? Perhaps the deputy was as anxious as the King.

Peter continued, "Almost two years ago I raised legitimate questions about the dangers of producing the new Soldier compies. I asked for an investigation. Rather than listening, the Chairman squashed my objections, threw me out of a meeting, and utterly ignored the threat."

"I don't believe he wanted to admit it, because the consequences would have been devastating. He didn't want to lose a potential weapon in our war against the hydrogues," Cain said. "But you may have been more right than you knew, if Admiral Stromo's report from Corribus is correct."

"Corribus? What's happened?"

"We are still investigating. I'm not surprised, however, that Chairman Wenceslas has kept you in the dark about it." He obviously wanted to change the subject. "I believe you were enumerating your grievances?"

Peter's nostrils flared. "Then Basil tried to assassinate Estarra and me. He planted a bomb on our royal yacht, but OX deactivated it in time. The Chairman intended to frame a Roamer trader and use our assassination to launch his war against the clans."

"So he's been planning to go against the Roamers since before they issued their embargo? Interesting. When faced with certain failure in a war, manufacture an artificial enemy you think you can defeat—especially if they have resources you're interested in. Helps with morale. *If* you're successful, of course."

Peter was in too far to stop now. "Have you seen what he's done to Daniel? He keeps the Prince drugged into a stupor, strapped to a bed. And now, for no reason other than because he's *annoyed,* Basil demands that Estarra kill our baby. I can't simply stand by and accept it."

"I don't dare take sides in a personal vendetta between you and the Chairman, Peter."

"This isn't about a personal vendetta. This is about my baby—and about a man who has too much power and is out of control. Basil is like a rabid dog. He can't even see the irreparable damage he's causing."

Peter looked up, his blue eyes clear in the shadowy confines of the storage room. "Next time I speak in public, I'm going to announce that Queen Estarra is about to bear a royal heir. Maybe I can shout it before the Chairman cuts off my microphone. Once the people know, Basil wouldn't dare do anything about it."

"Oh, he'd probably still dare," Cain said. "And that's a very dangerous course of action. Given the circumstances, I doubt he'll let you appear in public until the abortion has been performed. The Chairman will probably act tomorrow or the next day anyway."

Cain moved to another sculpture, a small figurine of a unicorn, as if he were a man perusing a gift shop. "I don't disagree with you, Peter. The Chairman is very wrong in this, and perhaps in many of the other things you cite. However, it would be wisest if the news about Estarra's blessed condition were leaked to certain media contacts right away. Rumors would spread swiftly, and people would believe them, of course. They want to believe. And once their hopes have been aroused, as you suggest, Basil isn't likely to dash them, just out of spite. Especially if you weren't responsible for the leak." He paused and pursed his lips, as if wondering whether to believe his own statement.

Peter leaned closer, intent. "Can you do that? Leak the news?"

"Of course I *can* do it . . . but will I choose to? I'm not entirely convinced this is the wisest course of action for myself." He lifted an eggshell-thin porcelain vase with a fluted opening adorned with gold leaf. He mused, "A bit too ornate, but it does have a certain fragile magnificence. It evokes grace, streamlined movement." He upended the vase and several dead spiders tumbled out.

Peter's stomach knotted. He waited, fearing he had made a terrible mistake.

Finally, drawing a deep breath, Cain set the vase down and boldly drew a conclusion. "So you want to ask me how to get rid of Chairman Wenceslas. That is your ultimate desire, isn't it, Peter?"

The King swallowed, surprised the man would be so blunt. He chose his answer carefully. "Given Basil's recent actions, I have no doubt that it would be for the good of the Hansa."

"Ah, for the good of the Hansa . . ." Cain hesitated. "Still, I've watched and listened to you for years, and I believe you really mean that. Though this is certain to cause me a great deal of trouble, I have to admit that you're probably right."

After the clumsy rabble-rousers captured the *Voracious Curiosity* above the Plumas moon, Rlinda and BeBob sat in mutual misery inside the cockpit. They had risked everything to get away from the EDF, only to fall into another trap. A stupid one! While Rlinda ground her teeth together, cutting off useless curses, BeBob grumbled. Cold and helpless, they hung in space.

Fifteen Roamers from the water mines boarded the cargo ship as if they owned it. Looking at the strangers invading her craft and deciding whether or not to fight, Rlinda figured she might be able to take out two or three of them; BeBob might account for one, provided his opponent was small and didn't struggle too much.

A well-dressed man who had introduced himself as Denn Peroni came to the pilot deck, grinning as if he had landed a bigger fish than he'd expected to. "Marvelous, just marvelous!"

BeBob's eyes were closed, and Rlinda assumed he was deep in his own gloom. "I was just trying to do an honest day's work, that's all," he groaned. "Where did I go wrong? I didn't want any attention, didn't even demand decent pay. I rescued a man and that poor girl from Corribus, and for doing such a good deed, what did I get? Arrested and court-martialed! On top of that, my ship was destroyed, Davlin Lotze may have gotten killed, and we're on the run."

"Everyone has it tough these days." Someone named Caleb Tamblyn, a scruffy old man who looked like he had vinegar for blood, stood next to Peroni in the *Curiosity*'s pilot deck. Other Roamers had gone down into the engine compartment, trying to get enough thrust to land the ship on the ice moon.

Peroni said, "We're appropriating this vessel as a spoil of war in partial repayment for all the Hansa thievery against the Roamers."

"Fine. Make my day," Rlinda fumed.

"Maybe you haven't heard," Caleb blustered. "Eddy battleships wiped out our facilities, including Rendezvous! The material damage and casualties are astronomical. Taking this ship is just a little bit of payback."

"Maybe *you* haven't heard," BeBob said, "but the EDF is after *us,* too. You're collecting on the wrong account."

"So consider this sanctuary, then. We're happy to help." Caleb needed a shave. "We'll take you down to Plumas—a safe haven, if the Eddies really are after you."

Rlinda knew the damaged *Curiosity* wasn't going anywhere. "She's all yours, provided you know how to take care of her. But you boys better hurry up. The EDF is hot on our tail, and I guarantee you those fighter craft have enough weaponry to wipe your asses across this solar system."

The news of nearby EDF ships intimidated the would-be pirates. The Roamers went about their activities with an almost panicked haste.

When Peroni shooed Rlinda out of her pilot's chair, which was much too large for him, she reluctantly stepped aside to let him study the controls. "Be gentle with her. The *Curiosity*'s been to hell and back."

Peroni poked at various buttons, activating the systems, but it was clear he didn't know what he was doing. "What kind of equipment does the Big Goose make you put in your ships? Malfunctions everywhere—I've never seen such a mess!"

"It comes as-is," Rlinda said sarcastically. "Don't complain to me if you end up having to do a lot of repair work."

When Peroni continued to fiddle with the ignition controls, she finally bent forward and showed him how to activate their forward propulsion drive. "I thought Roamers had given up the pirate life. How many times did we hear that Rand Sorengaard was just an anomaly and that the rest of you had all disowned him?"

Peroni was engrossed in the *Curiosity*'s controls. "That was back when we thought Rand was doing something wrong. Now it looks like he was just the first to see how treacherous the Big Goose really is. So we recently decided he was ahead of his time."

Caleb glared at the two captives. "Those charges against him were trumped up. They executed him for purely political reasons."

Now Rlinda unleashed real anger. "Bullshit! I don't care if you've made him out to be some kind of a hero, but Sorengaard really did destroy a cargo ship. You want to know how I know? It was one of *my own* ships, and I was there. He killed one of my captains. Gabriel Mesta."

"Yeah, and Sorengaard tried to kill me, too," BeBob said in a small voice.

Caleb worked his jaw, but couldn't seem to think of anything to say. Peroni, who had been occupied with the unfamiliar controls, turned with a bright smile. "I think I've got it now."

She looked at the two Roamers. "Gentlemen, when all is said and done, I sympathize with what's happening to your clans. You don't have to convince us of EDF treachery."

"Yeah, we've had some firsthand experience with it ourselves," BeBob said.

Peroni glanced up as the ship started moving. "Then I guess you two were in the wrong place at the wrong time. Sorry."

Caleb shooed them from the cockpit back to where his own ship was docked. Several of the Roamers had already gone back aboard, anxious to return to Plumas. Rlinda called back at Peroni, "You take care of my vessel or I'll crack your head open."

"She's a beauty. I won't leave a scratch. Of course, I may need you to help me understand a few of these systems."

Rlinda bit back a retort and grudgingly followed Caleb and his team aboard his smaller ship. Maybe the pursuing EDF Remoras would show up again . . . though she didn't see much advantage in that. It would be better if General Lanyan considered them both dead and the *Curiosity* destroyed. That would leave her and Branson Roberts with only one problem—albeit a big one.

When the group of passengers was secured aboard Caleb's ship, he disengaged the dock and took the two prisoners toward the ice moon. Before long, Denn Peroni and his team of pirates guided the *Voracious Curiosity* in their wake. Rlinda skeptically watched his maneuvering abilities, and was relieved to find that he was doing an adequate job.

On the icy surface below, Rlinda was surprised to see the marks of habitation: landing pads and drill shafts, cermet-lined wellheads that tapped into an underground ocean, several large tanker ships.

"We have a settlement under the ice caps," Caleb explained. "We'll find you satisfying work at the water mines."

"And then what?" Rlinda asked.

He shrugged. "For lack of a better term, you two will live

under planetary arrest. Someday, maybe we'll arrange a prisoner exchange with the Eddies."

"Wonderful," BeBob said. "Exactly what I need."

Grinning, Caleb landed the craft on the broad ice fields. "You're Roamers now. Get used to it."

"Hurray," Rlinda said in a flat voice. "Now all my dreams have come true."

Though forlorn, BeBob dredged up the last remnants of optimism. "Well, at least we have each other. I'd rather be stuck on an ice moon with you, Rlinda, than sitting in a prison cell for the EDF. At least you've gotten me this far."

Rlinda loved him for it. "You're right, BeBob. I can think of a few worse ex-husbands to be stranded with."

115 ☀ ADAR ZAN'NH

The cohort of warliners, along with the newly recaptured ships, converged in the blue skies above Hyrillka, then descended en masse toward the rebel Designate's citadel palace.

On previous trips with Adar Kori'nh, Zan'nh had seen the lush landscape, the mosaic-patterned spaceport, the open courtyards maintained for celebrations, festivals, and Solar Navy skyparades. Since the injured Designate's return, the rebuilt spaceport had been expanded. Ornamental structures, statues, and hanging trellises had been cleared away to make wider landing fields that could accommodate the industrial ships and agricultural haulers that delivered processed shiing.

Beyond the city limits, the sweeping flatlands were now embroidered with new canals, muddy ditches dug in long, interconnecting paths so that Rusa'h's workers could plant more and more of the drug-producing plantmoths. All arable land had been dedicated to raising the nialia plants for the rebellious Designate's continued corruption and conquest.

Zan'nh, eyes blazing, stood at the helm of his warliner surveying the changes. Hyrillka, and indeed much of the Horizon Cluster, would require many years before life could return to normal.

Below them the open citadel palace had become a fortress. Thousands of Ildiran guards loyal to the mad Designate swarmed around the hill, preparing to sacrifice themselves in defense of the self-proclaimed Imperator. They carried explosives, launchers, and projectile weapons now turned against other Ildirans.

"Truly, this is a time of great tragedy," Mage-Imperator Jora'h transmitted to the Adar from his adjacent ship. "Prepare to land our troops. We will capture Rusa'h and take back Hyrillka."

"It might be more effective, Liege, to simply level the citadel palace from above." Standing next to Zan'nh in the command nucleus, the Dobro Designate looked remarkably unperturbed as he made the appalling suggestion to the Mage-Imperator. "We have more than enough warliners to do it."

"We will find another way," Jora'h said. "Those people are victims of my mad brother's deceit. How can I not offer them a chance to return to the fold of my *thism*? They were tricked by Rusa'h."

Udru'h shrugged. "They are traitors, Liege. They deserve whatever punishment you deem fit. We must remove the mad Designate's disease before the Ildiran people can heal."

"I will not consider that. There would be too many casualties, people who do not deserve to die. I will use my own powers instead."

Zan'nh looked from his father on the screen to his uncle beside him. He hated Udru'h's suggestion, yet berated himself for having been unwilling to make such a horrific decision when he first encountered Rusa'h's crusade of corruption. He was not qualified to offer an opinion on the issue.

The Dobro Designate did not back down. "Liege, you cannot be everywhere at once. Did you not dispatch Osira'h to communicate with the hydrogues? You should be back in Mijistra waiting for her. Our Empire faces a much larger crisis if she is unable to break through to the hydrogues. Your time here is limited."

Jora'h finally answered in a low voice, "I know, Udru'h. I have my fastest ships waiting for the moment I hear from Osira'h. If she brings the hydrogues, I will have to leave here . . . but it has been days. I am beginning to fear the worst."

"It is Osira'h, Liege. Do not fear yet," Udru'h said. "But if you are forced to leave, then you must authorize Adar Zan'nh and myself to do what we must to put an end to the corrupt *thism*."

At the Mage-Imperator's order, Zan'nh's ship and two other warliners made their way to the expansive new spaceport. From below, Rusa'h's rebels used their converted weapons to open fire on the Solar Navy ships, launching explosive projectiles. Feeling the impacts against the warliner's armor, Zan'nh closed his eyes, but did not hesitate. "Return fire and remove the threat from the ground."

The weapons officer looked at him. "Kill them, Adar?"

His eyes snapped open. "Yes! Remove the threat before they harm our ships."

A burst of energy weapons from the lead warliner swiftly vaporized the handful of deluded fighters on the ground. Zan'nh watched, caught his breath, then said in a voice as hard as iron, "Now, land our ships and proceed with the Mage-Imperator's orders."

His warliner settled onto the landing grid beside a group of overloaded cargo vessels, every one of them full of fresh shiing to be used in the spreading rebellion. The Mage-Imperator's ship followed, landing off to one side.

"Udru'h, disembark and accompany me," Jora'h transmitted. "I want all soldiers from two warliners to follow me on the ground. We will surround the citadel palace and force our way forward until we seize the stronghold."

"Those closest to Rusa'h will be the most strongly tied to his corrupt *thism,* Liege. They may not wish to be freed," the Adar cautioned.

"Then our ground troops may have no choice but to kill some of them. We will save those that we can, but for *Rusa'h* there will be no forgiveness. He is certainly aware of what he has done. He must pay for his crimes."

"And what are my orders, Liege?" Zan'nh asked.

"Take the rest of the warliners and destroy the shiing. All of it."

Adar Zan'nh dispatched a dismantling crew to break open the waiting cargo ships on the landing field. Well-muscled soldiers and cargo workers removed packages of powdered shiing and dumped the processed plantmoth sap in a growing mound on the landing field.

"Burn it," Zan'nh said. "Destroy it."

Leaving a large team to finish ransacking the cargo ships and destroying the stockpile of the processed drug, the Adar returned to his ship and joined the other warliners overhead. "Raze the plantmoth fields, obliterate the nialia vines, turn everything to ash. From now on, that land must be used for food crops."

As the group of warliners cruised away from the spaceport, Zan'nh looked around the command nucleus. His officers remained reticent, fighting through veils of guilt for having allowed themselves to be dragged into his unwise rebellion. "Take care not to hurt anyone in the fields. We've killed enough already. Too many."

The ships headed low over the flat, fertile ground where infinite rows of waving, fluttering plantmoths grew tall, expanding their blossoms, swelling their tangled stems. Hyrillkan workers saw the big ships coming and scattered.

Zan'nh gripped the rail of the elevated platform. "Wide dispersal of our energy beams with enough thermal output to wither all of those nialias."

"Patterning locked in, Adar."

He turned to his flight controller. "Move in a slow, graceful glide to be sure we don't miss a single stalk." Then he nodded to the weapons station. "Fire at will."

Hot beams lanced out from the foremost warliner, mowing down and igniting the writhing nialias. The other warliners followed suit.

Mobile male plantmoths broke free and flew upward, dispersing like startled butterflies. They swirled around, caught in the thermal updraft and drawn to the flames. In the wake of the warliners, only blackened husks remained, charred vines pointing like skeletal fingers toward the sky.

The fields were so extensive that even with more than three hundred warliners it still took hours to complete the initial sweep. Zan'nh never wavered. The battleships continued their rout, blasting the shiing production fields. Steam boiled up from the newly dug canals; murky smoke and soot streamed from the devastation. The blackened land and destroyed fields reminded Zan'nh of the hydrogue attack that had struck Hyrillka only a year earlier.

But he had no cause to compare himself to the alien marauders. He stared at the path of ruin. "Continue firing."

Sensor alarms sounded, and orbital first-warning satellites announced the arrival of more and more Ildiran battleships. His scan operator turned to him, wide-eyed. "Forty-five warliners, Adar. They're coming toward us fully armed, in attack mode."

Zan'nh crossed his arms over his uniformed chest. "So my brother has returned with the rest of the maniple he stole." Given Thor'h's penchant for violence, the Adar knew the impending battle could be the saddest, and bloodiest, ever recorded in the *Saga of Seven Suns*. Nevertheless, he allowed himself a calm, determined smile. His brother had much to answer for.

"Recall all warliners from the nialia fields. Now we're in for a fight."

116 ☀ MAGE-IMPERATOR JORA'H

The Solar Navy's ground assault teams surrounded the strategic hill and settled in for a cautious siege. They wore full body armor and carried traditional Ildiran weapons, testing the entrenched defenses of Rusa'h. Thick smoke filled the sky.

Designate Udru'h paced the paved ground, scowling up at the citadel palace. "Liege, we have more than enough personnel and weaponry to seize the palace and capture the Hyrillka Designate."

Closely guarded, a pensive Jora'h walked beside him. "I need to resolve this in a way that proves I am the true and legitimate Mage-Imperator, Udru'h. If I simply slaughter all those who oppose me, am I really better than my brother?"

Udru'h waved the question away, as if the answer was obvious. "You are better because you are the Mage-Imperator."

Jora'h touched the threads of *thism* in his mind, felt the empty silence of the gap where his lunatic brother had torn his people from the overall web. Jora'h could not just let them all go. The Empire must be made whole again; the Hyrillkans must be returned to the pure glow of the Lightsource.

Before the siege preparations were completed, Rusa'h's corrupted followers up in the citadel palace let out a loud cheer. Jora'h gazed upward as one of his septars rushed to him. "Forty-five more warliners have arrived, Liege! They are under the command of Prime Designate Thor'h."

Jora'h replied in a voice honed sharp by anger at his treacherous son. "Thor'h is no longer the Prime Designate. A traitor to the Ildiran Empire can never stand in line to be the next Mage-Imperator."

The officer looked flustered. "With the rest of the cohort, we outnumber them sevenfold—but they are not slowing. Will they surrender?"

Jora'h met the Dobro Designate's gaze, and both of them reached the same conclusion. "No, Thor'h will try to destroy as many of us as he can. With forty-five ships, all of them equipped with weapons designed to fight hydrogues, he can cause terrible damage." He could sense no soul-threads quaking from the oncoming group of vessels. The emptiness in the mental network was like a cold, dark maw opening wide to swallow them all up. "We do outnumber them. We shall stand firm, and we shall win."

If the rebel warships swept in with all weapons blazing, Jora'h knew he would not be able to wrest control back fast enough, even with his stronger *thism*. Jora'h's ships would be forced to fire on them. The corrupt Prime Designate would attack and keep attacking until every one of his ships was destroyed in the effort. It would be a slaughter.

Udru'h stood beside the Mage-Imperator. "Are you prepared to open fire on your son, Liege? Will you destroy those ships?"

"I will do what is necessary—but no more." He turned to the septar. "Summon Adar Zan'nh." In the meantime, he would do what he could by extending his control of the *thism*, trying to reach the oncoming rebel warliners, even if he had to take them one at a time.

"The Adar is already on his way, Liege."

Like wild animals, Thor'h's stolen warliners careened

into the much larger cohort arrayed in a defensive pattern overhead. The Solar Navy battleships had activated their protective shields, but the attackers unleashed explosive projectiles and energy beams with such ferocity that several warliners were damaged. Engines smoking and hull plates scored with deep marks, three of the Mage-Imperator's ships dropped out of formation, struggling to remain aloft. One managed to reach the landing field, where confiscation crews were still burning shiing in large bonfires; the other two damaged warliners wavered, then careened through the canal-laced cropland, spraying mud, ashes, and water, before finally coming to rest in open fields.

Without any regimentation, Thor'h's warliners stampeded through the loyal ships, opening fire again and again. They attacked like a pack of rabid predators pouncing on a large group of herd beasts.

The Solar Navy ships responded with conservative blows, attempting to damage but not destroy the rebellious vessels. Their tactics were too hesitant, and the captains did not retaliate with enough force. Thor'h seized the opportunity and ordered his ships to concentrate their attack on one of the lumbering warliners: All forty-five ships opened fire, and the warliner could not withstand the barrage. The giant vessel exploded.

Jora'h could feel hundreds of his crewmen dying as they tumbled into the open air, burned in the flame front. Horror and dismay thrummed through the *thism* like a shrieking off-key note from a musical instrument.

Jora'h sent determined reassurance through the soul-threads he controlled, forcing the crews to stay together. He could sense nothing from the traitorous Prime Designate, but Thor'h must be laughing.

Before the rebel battleships could converge over the citadel palace and strike the siege encampment, Zan'nh's warliners returned from the nialia fields in an overwhelming display of superior military power. Now more than three hundred full-scale battleships faced the newly arrived group.

Watching the aerial battles beside the Dobro Designate, Jora'h snapped to the anxious septar, "Instruct Adar Zan'nh to implement the surrender of these rebels. He is to bring Thor'h to me—unharmed."

"You expect them to simply lay down their arms?" Udru'h said. "They are fanatically corrupted by Rusa'h. They will not see reason. I warn you not to underestimate the danger."

Jora'h drew deep breaths, focusing his concentration. "I am surrounded by *seven times* as many loyal soldiers as Thor'h has. My grasp on the *thism* is enough. By its own strength, my mind can direct the turncoats back to the correct pathways."

He squeezed his eyes shut and reached his mental fingers into the rebel warliners, seeking out each mind aboard, each person who had once belonged to him. Nimbly touching the wiry soul-threads, he disentangled the snarls, drew the threads closer to his light—and reconnected them. He went through one rebel soldier at a time, one officer, one technician. He continued to move his thoughts deck by deck, until he had restored control to one of Thor'h's ships and made them submit to Adar Zan'nh.

With the reconversion of that warliner, the Mage-Imperator's hold grew stronger still, and he concentrated on the next one. But there were so many!

He sensed Thor'h's resistance, too strong, a diamond-hard barrier, and decided to confront his son's vessel last. He wrestled with one warliner after another, and they fell like pieces in a child's game, token after token.

With each battleship he restored, with each complement of Ildirans returned to his fold, his strength increased and the *thism* tightened. Eventually, Jora'h found he could continue the process without devoting his full concentration to it.

When Thor'h realized he was mysteriously losing ship after ship in his group, he responded with desperate violence. He took his own lead warliner, followed by two others; the three battleships broke away from the chaotic assemblage of vessels and hurtled directly toward the recaptured landing field, where Solar Navy crews were disposing of the shiing stockpiles. Four of the Adar's ships pursued him, but Thor'h pulled ahead, flying so low he was in danger of crashing.

Zan'nh's ground crews were unloading the last of the cargo ships; great piles of shiing dust burned in smoldering bonfires. With unbelievable malice, Thor'h dropped a load of explosive projectiles on the cargo ships and Solar Navy crews. In moments, the rebuilt landing field was an inferno. Vessel after vessel ignited and contributed to the blaze. Soldiers ran screaming as the march of flames consumed them.

Without slowing, Thor'h's battleship shot like a comet past the three damaged Solar Navy warliners in the charred nialia fields, and dumped more explosives just to cause additional damage. Coming in hot behind him, Zan'nh fired at the Prime Designate's ship, trying to bring it down. In spite of the damage to his engines and hull, Thor'h flew onward. His supply of artillery seemed inexhaustible.

On the ground, furiously trying to regain control of the remaining rebel ships, Jora'h opened his eyes and looked at the Dobro Designate. He had already seized most of the crews, though Thor'h's warliner and two others continued their rampage.

"You are correct, Udru'h," the Mage-Imperator finally said. "Too many Ildirans have already died. We cannot wait. I must excise this threat. Now."

Still concentrating on the last three prodigal warliners, Jora'h carefully, and with great determination, walked along the uphill path toward the citadel palace, flanked by hundreds of armed guards. He signaled his brother to accompany him.

"We will go to their stronghold and break this siege." Jora'h strode forward. "I am the rightful Mage-Imperator, and I require my Empire back."

117 ✸ SAREIN

After a roundabout journey that delivered a number of green priests and treelings to Hansa colonies, Sarein finally returned to Earth. It seemed as if she hadn't been there in decades. She hoped Basil would be glad to have her back, even though events had not turned out exactly as he'd wanted. She looked forward to seeing him and realized she felt too thrilled, too giddy. *Completely unprofessional.* She didn't want to earn his scorn. She would have to be careful.

When Sarein made her way to his penthouse offices at the

top of the Hansa HQ pyramid, the Chairman was in a foul, almost violent mood.

Deputy Eldred Cain, flustered to the point of outright anxiety, backed out of the office door. He took one look at Sarein, and his expression shifted strangely. "You're welcome to see the Chairman if you have good news. If something *else* has gone terribly wrong, however, I'd advise you to wait until a better time."

Sarein hadn't seen Basil in weeks. "I'll take my chances." She did not like to admit how much she had missed him—not just the lovemaking, but the conversations, the feeling that she was part of a hugely important tapestry of government. She wanted to shed the images of burned Theroc that still clung to her mind. "I'll be fine." She pushed past Cain and entered the Chairman's offices.

Basil looked up at her with a sudden, uncomprehending glare. "You're interrupting me right now."

"Hello to you, too, Basil. I hoped my arrival would be a pleasant surprise."

He looked at her like a scientist inspecting a specimen. His gray eyes were cold, and she felt a shiver. "A pleasant surprise would've been for you to stay on Theroc and become their leader. We discussed this. What are you doing here?"

With all the strength and confidence she possessed, Sarein strolled toward where he sat at his projection desk. She refused to show how his reaction had stung her. "And plans change, Basil." She smiled triumphantly, anxious to please him. "But I still accomplished the most important part of the job. I've enlisted dozens of new green priests. Several have already been stationed on Hansa colonies, and more are waiting for transport aboard any of our ships that will take them from Theroc."

Reserving judgment, Basil stared at her, unwilling to let his mood crack. "Continue."

"The Therons are convinced, with good reason, that the hydrogues will attack what's left of the worldforest again. Considering the extent of the devastation last time, they're afraid the worldtrees will all be destroyed. They need the Hansa's help implementing an exhaustive program to disperse treelings as widely as possible—in exchange for which the Hansa will get green priests on world after world, ship after ship." She beamed. "It's exactly what you wanted."

"I suppose it's not a total disaster."

She came around the desk and began to massage his tense shoulders, but she might as well have been trying to knead a statue. "Now, after that extremely lukewarm welcome, are you going to tell me what's got you so furious?"

"Which of the thousand things? The Roamers? The destroyed colony on Corribus? Klikiss robots disappearing? The possibility that our Soldier compies are ticking time bombs throughout the EDF? Hydrogues attacking our planets again?"

Sarein drew a deep breath, buffeted by news of all the emergencies she hadn't known about. "All right, which one made Eldred Cain slink out of here like a whipped puppy a few minutes ago?"

Basil moved his fingers across the desktop and displayed newsnet reports with media images. "The rumor is unverified but rampant. We can't possibly deny it—nor can I figure out how the hell it leaked!"

Sarein scanned the notices. "Estarra is pregnant?" She was thrilled for her sister, and their parents would be delighted. It was the first child of the next generation. "That's wonderful—"

Basil lurched to his feet, jarring his lukewarm cup of cardamom coffee. "Peter defied me! I instructed him and the Queen not to have children until I gave them permission. They tried to keep the pregnancy secret from me, but I found out—and ordered Estarra to have an abortion."

"Basil! That is uncalled for." Then Sarein narrowed her eyes. Not long ago, something terrible had passed between the Chairman and the King. Estarra had even suggested that Basil had planned to assassinate the two of them; when Sarein queried the Chairman about it, he had denied—rather, *dismissed*—the idea. And now this absurd suggestion . . .

He continued to talk, moving like a steamroller back and forth behind his desk. "After I showed Peter what I had done to Daniel, I thought he'd cause less trouble. I already had the abortion doctors lined up for later today, and we could have covered the Queen's visit as a routine medical exam—"

Growing more and more disturbed, Sarein had trouble following everything. "What did you do to Prince Daniel?"

"Somehow the story got loose among the media this morning! After laying out my threat, I kept Peter under close surveillance. He had no outside contact. None! So where did this rumor come from?" Basil's shoulders were hunched. "And now I have to find some way to respond. Peter *cannot* be allowed to defy me like this, but now I can't make an obvious move against the King and Queen. Daniel is a complete failure, and Peter is out of control. This is another disaster."

Looking at Basil, Sarein felt him becoming a stranger, someone she could no longer understand or sympathize with. She experienced a twinge of dread for her sister, unable to believe that Basil would just snap his fingers and force Estarra to terminate a pregnancy against her wishes.

This wasn't the Basil Wenceslas for whom she cared so much. And though she felt a closer political alliance to him than to Theroc, Estarra was her family!

Perhaps she could talk him through this knot of bad decisions. Whether he realized it or not, Basil obviously needed the support of someone who cared about him. Sarein tried to rub his shoulders again. "I just got back home, Basil. If you give me an hour, I could arrange for a relaxing lunch in my quarters. It would do you good to take a break so you can see the solutions more clearly. Surely we can figure out a way to make this pregnancy into a politically advantageous situation."

He gave her a dismissive wave, gesturing for her to get out of the office. "I have work to do and plans to make. I need to show King Peter exactly where he stands before he tries something else."

118 ☀ CELLI

The first new groups of green priests had taken their treelings across the Spiral Arm, and additional bastions of the worldforest were being planted on diverse worlds to preserve them from the hydrogues. Green priests had been doing the same thing for more than a century, but never in such substantial numbers.

Over the past three days, Celli had spent an exhausting and exhilarating time with Solimar, treedancing and jump-starting the release of deep energy from the verdani. Not only was it much more fun than clearing deadwood, she could feel their own energy swell as they set loose the locked-away reserves inside the worldtrees. It was like throwing cold water into the face of a sleeping giant. Even Solimar was still amazed by the life they squeezed out of the damaged forest. After so many months, Theroc seemed to be getting to its feet again.

Sitting together, sweating in the filtered sunlight after a particularly vigorous session, Celli leaned against Solimar. His green skin was warm, his muscles strong and as comforting as the fronds of the giant trees. "I could get used to this," she said.

He kissed her, wiped a smear of soot from her cheek, then kissed her again. "I could get used to *this*," he said, and she giggled.

Suddenly he sat bolt upright, startling her. "Beneto is calling us. All of us. Quick! It's a long way back, and we have to hurry!"

Though her arms and legs ached, she ran with him back to his gliderbike. Half an hour later, when they arrived beneath the fungus-reef city, agitated-looking green priests were gathered in restless clusters, staring toward the sky. Some farther away had found healthy worldtrees and stood connected by telink so they could listen to what Beneto had to say.

In the clearing the wooden golem formed a focal point for the worldforest's energy and thoughts. The scorched remnants of the tallest trees began to twitch and tremble, brushing fronds together like a group of ancient warriors rattling their swords.

Even without a direct telink connection, Celli felt a shudder go down her back. Something was very wrong. Everyone around her looked sharply upward, shading their eyes. Celli could feel an unmistakable fear that echoed like a gunshot across the telink network—not just in the immediate worldforest, but from planet to planet, everywhere a treeling had taken root.

Celli grabbed Solimar's hand. "Is it the hydrogues? Are they coming?" When she felt him trembling with revulsion at an impending threat, Celli grew more frightened than ever. She looked over at Beneto, hoping for answers.

Though her brother's voice was quiet, the wind and the trees carried it far. "Yes. The hydrogues. We knew it would happen."

The green priests touched the scaled trunks of the worldtrees, trying to knit their strength together so they could stand firm.

"But you said help would be here, Beneto," Celli insisted. "You told us you heard a call go out to some ancient allies. If they don't get here soon, they'll have to hold a funeral without us."

The golem who faced her with swirl-grained eyes looked heartachingly like her lost brother. When she was a child, Beneto had been one of her closest friends . . . but now he seemed beyond Celli's comprehension.

"Yes, they have been traveling since the first hydrogue attack on Corvus Landing, where I died. But they are still too far away. Our allies will not arrive in time."

For an hour, the giant sentient trees rustled and rattled, and the gathered people looked to Beneto's statuesque form, as if he would tell them what to do. He stood frozen, as much a part of the frightened scene as the towering trees.

Yarrod muttered, "At least all the treelings we sent out will be safe."

"We won't be," said a pale-skinned woman.

Celli heard an outcry, and green priests pointed at something in the sky. In the bright sunlight, she saw a flare of light, reflections off curved diamond hulls, the glint of sharp protrusions that held blue lightning.

The hydrogues converged high overhead, one warglobe after another, and descended once more upon the worldforest.

Regrown worldtrees shuddered as icewaves curled out from the attacking spheres. The air itself seemed to turn brittle and shatter. Panicked Therons ran to seek shelter. Some of the green priests stood still, defeated, not knowing what else to do.

Yarrod slowly dropped to his knees. "All of our work. The worldforest is still weak. We cannot withstand this."

Celli grabbed his shoulder. "Come on, Uncle! We have to do something. Some of the trees have recovered. Isn't there any way they can fight back? Like Reynald made them do before!" She looked frantically for Beneto.

Many Therons scrambled away from the dense trees, even though they knew from the earlier attack that there was no safe place to hide.

A warglobe cruised low overhead, and blue lightning crackled out like spiderwebs across the crowns of the trees, causing them to erupt. Sparking fire caught the weakened wood, and the flames began to grow.

The Beneto golem stood in the middle of the Stonehenge-like ring of burned trunks like a priest in a sacred temple. His wooden eyes were closed, and he stood with carved fists

clenched at his sides, his face turned to the sky as if listening to a far-off voice. Was he calling for help? Listening for
a response? Who, or what, could possibly aid the worldforest?

During the last devastating attack here, the faeros had arrived, but they were uncertain allies. Ultimately, their assistance had caused as much damage as the warglobes had, and
Sarein had said that the faeros themselves were losing in the
face of the hydrogue onslaught. What else could save them?

The warglobe bombardment increased.

Celli and Solimar ran together to the uncertain shelter of
the tall tree that supported the reconstructed fungus-reef
city. Her parents were climbing vine ladders to reach the
structure, as if going higher might help them. Celli pointed.
"Whatever they're doing, I want to join them. I just . . . I just
need to be with them."

Solimar nodded. "I'm coming with you."

Moving with treedancer grace, the two of them scrambled up the side of the worldtree. Overhead, booming explosions cracked like amplified thunder across the sky.
Warglobes swept cascades of frigid wind over their former
battlefield, laying down electrical destruction.

Celli rushed to the main throne room. Exposed pipes and
support girders covered the walls where Roamers had
shored up the damaged structure. Clan engineers had improved the city's plumbing and power networks, added con-
veniences that were far more modern than the Theron
settlers were used to—including a new communications
system.

Idriss stood in front of the bank of transmitters, baffled.
Alexa looked up at her daughter's arrival. "Celli, you should
take shelter. Go where it's safe."

The girl put her hands on her narrow hips. "And where would that be, Mother? If I could think of a place, I'd drag *you* there!"

"There won't be any shelter unless we can send a transmission to the hydrogues," Idriss said. "Or call for help."

"A transmission?" Celli said in a squawk. "That doesn't sound like a good idea to me."

"What makes you think they'll listen?" Solimar asked. "They mean to destroy the worldforest."

Willfully ignoring the question, Idriss pointed in frustration at the controls. "Is it this one?"

Solimar hurried forward. "If you insist on this, then let me show you." Always mechanically inclined, he had an intuitive grasp of comm systems and other technology.

"You know what the hydrogues are, Father," Celli said. "Do you really expect them to respond?"

Idriss glanced over his shoulder. His eyes were red-rimmed, and he looked much older than she had ever seen him. "The green priests are already sending messages through telink, but the hydrogues will have slaughtered us before anyone can get here."

Solimar stepped back, and the system hummed. "It's ready to transmit. Prepped for a full spectrum of frequencies."

Idriss took the controls. "This is Father Idriss of the Theron people. We are a peaceful people, who have done nothing to you. Please leave us alone. We are not your enemies."

Celli looked hard at her bearded father. "The hydrogues have always considered the verdani their enemies. Because *we* work for the trees, they hate us—all of us. They will not stop until this entire planet is a cinder."

"We demand to meet with an ambassador, like you sent to Earth," Idriss stated, sounding ridiculously naïve, for he had already seen the hydrogues devastate the forests. His voice was plaintive. "Please do not do this."

The response that came back over the new communications system surprised them all. And it wasn't from the hydrogues. It was a human voice. "Don't worry, we'll protect you." Then a pause. "I hope this works."

Mother Alexa leaned over the transmitter. "Who is this? Please help us, whoever you are."

"Oh, sorry. This is Kotto Okiah. Looks like we arrived not a moment too soon. Those drogues won't know what hit them . . . uh, if my calculations are correct."

Celli remembered the eccentric Roamer engineer, whose ambitious schemes had helped rebuild the Theron settlements. When the last Roamer workers had fled, knowing the EDF was hunting them down, the clan members had been fully aware that the hydrogues were bound to return to Theroc.

Celli rushed to one of the open windows in the thick fungus-reef wall. Although it seemed impossible that the renegade space gypsies would have any effective weapon against the warglobes, it made more sense than her father's ill-advised attempt at negotiation.

In the sky, she saw a ragtag group of Roamer ships, a dozen battered old vessels, each of a different design. The warglobes seemed to ignore the small craft, probably considering them irrelevant. Without pausing, the clan ships flew in to face the giant spiked spheres. Celli couldn't imagine what they were thinking. The Roamers looked totally doomed.

119 ☀ IMPERATOR RUSA'H

The once-bright *thism* was unraveling all around him. The soul-threads that Rusa'h had seen so clearly and held so tightly now slipped like razor wires through his fingers. How could the corrupt Mage-Imperator be so strong?

The pain of this was greater than sliced skin and imagined blood loss. All the nialia fields had been obliterated, and there would be no more shiing. Although his fortified citadel palace was still crowded with loyal guards, lens kithmen, pleasure mates, attenders, and doctors, the Mage-Imperator's men pushed closer, working their way through the defenses. Rusa'h had never dreamed his brother would be willing to kill.

Two of the septars from his commandeered Solar Navy maniple also remained at Rusa'h's side as military advisers. Even their tactical expertise could not offer him a way to escape, much less achieve victory. The news was desperate.

From the open citadel, Rusa'h watched Thor'h and his battleships go on a rampage, but most of the warliners had slipped away and turned against him. With insidious powers, the Mage-Imperator had seized control of them, disengaging the crews from *him* and tangling them in the old perverted web of soul-threads. And more were falling every moment. Jora'h seemed convinced that he would win.

During the course of this rebellion, his brother had underestimated him, and now it seemed Rusa'h had made the same mistake. The Mage-Imperator's control of the *thism,* though twisted, was powerful . . . too powerful.

How could the false leader control so much, if his understanding was warped, if he had gone completely astray? Why did the Lightsource not give Rusa'h, the true Imperator, a crushing retaliation to prove the validity of his claims?

"The forces of our enemy are strong," one of his pleasure mates said, sidling against him, though her eyes and her body language were edgy and sharp. "Is there no way the Lightsource can aid us?"

From his ornate chrysalis chair, Rusa'h turned to the open sky, so that his retinas burned with Hyrillka's blue-white primary sun. During his sub-*thism* sleep, he had seen the answers so clearly. He had walked in a realm of absolute purity; he had followed the soul-threads and knew their true pattern. His head injury had liberated him, enlightened him.

Rusa'h clenched his hands on the arms of the chair and stared into the dazzling light, seeking an answer, but he saw no clear paths anymore. He was sure that he had not been deluded. The *thism* threads were fading; he could not understand what the Lightsource wanted him to do now. The sun itself seemed to call him, showing him a way to protect himself. He must flee these slaves of a once-glorious Empire that was now based on lies.

One of his septars stood before him delivering a report. "Our citadel palace is entirely besieged, Imperator. All but Prime Designate Thor'h's lead warliner and two others have been recaptured by the enemy."

The other septar said, "We still have numerous loyal soldiers willing to throw down their lives before they allow the false Mage-Imperator through."

Rusa'h pursed his lips. "Unfortunately, Jora'h has the soldiers and the weapons to break through whenever he chooses—if he is willing to accept casualties." His pleasure mates stood close, caressing him, as he weighed the possibilities. "Will my brother make such a sacrifice?"

"Ildirans do not kill Ildirans," said the first septar. "He will never attack us directly."

Rusa'h narrowed his eyes. He had made that assumption before, and he had been wrong. "No. He will hesitate, but he will do it." Rusa'h nodded. "Jora'h has already broken with many of our traditions. Look at him now at the bottom of the hill. He stands with his sacred feet on the ground like a common servant. Back at the Prism Palace, his own daughter, a *noble-born* female, is his personal guard. Since we have justifiably killed Ildirans, my brother will concoct a similar justification to do the same to us."

"Either way," said the second septar, "we have *lost,* Imperator. Hyrillka will fall. We do not have the personnel, the weapons, or the warliners to maintain our hold. We cannot get reinforcements from the other worlds that have joined our rebellion."

Rusa'h listened to the military preparations outside, the sounds made by his own defenders and Jora'h's far more numerous Solar Navy troops. Overhead, nearly four hundred warliners cruised and converged. Thor'h had only three ships left to stand against them.

Rusa'h could do nothing to salvage his crusade.

He drew a deep breath. "Let me speak with the Prime Designate. I have final instructions for him."

Thor'h was barely maintaining control over his three warliners, while all of the other vessels continued to wear down the former Prime Designate. The Adar could have destroyed the rampaging rebel ship at any time, but for some reason Zan'nh held back. Jora'h had probably issued orders for them to capture Thor'h alive.

Perhaps Rusa'h would have enough time. . . .

"Prime Designate, I had meant for you to be my successor to the true Lightsource, but we have failed," the Imperator said over the private channel. "You have always been an honorable companion. You aided me even before I received my revelation, and you believed me when I saw the true path. Now, when all looks darkest, remember that I saw the truth. I alone have the correct guidance. We are not blind. I will never stop trying to achieve our holy goals."

On the screen, Thor'h looked deeply troubled. "I still have three ships, Liege. I have no need of superior weaponry if I have superior resolve. What do you require me to do?"

"At this moment, your corrupt father is marching his regiments up the hill toward my citadel palace." The Imperator gave a confident nod. "However, you and your warliners can give me the chance I need."

Thor'h seemed too choked up to bid his uncle farewell. He gruffly acknowledged the orders and signed off.

Rusa'h commanded his fanatically loyal pleasure mates and the two septars: "Prepare to depart. My engineers have arranged a fully fueled escape ship in the rear courtyard. A small group will accompany me in my escape." He stared at the blazing sun again. "We will go directly to the Lightsource."

The Solar Navy soldiers tightened their cordon around the citadel palace. Ground troops moved forward, closing all escape routes on the paths that led to the mad Designate's stronghold. Surrounded by guards, the Mage-Imperator led the way to assured victory. While Jora'h struggled to seize their minds and free them from delusion, the rebels opened fire. His soldiers had no choice but to shoot back to defend their leader.

Though most of the rebellious warliners had restored their loyalty to the Mage-Imperator, the lead warliner piloted by Thor'h and his two flanking battleships swung around in a wild, suicidal attack. The three rebel warliners drove forward, firing their remaining weaponry in a blazing staccato.

Two of Jora'h's damaged defender ships reeled away, limping toward cleared landing areas. At the point of the wedge, Thor'h's warliner careened toward the Mage-Imperator and the siege troops working their way up to the citadel palace.

Adar Zan'nh's clustered warliners tried to block the rebel ship's advance, but as soon as they closed in, the other two rebel vessels split away from the Prime Designate and threw themselves in the way. In a horrendous explosion, the two rebel warliners took out the nearest Solar Navy ships in a suicidal impact that left a black scar of smoke and wreckage dripping out of the sky.

The deafening boom and shockwave stunned the armies

on the ground. Jora'h shaded his eyes, feeling the sting of tears and the wrench of sorrow as so many Ildirans died.

The two rebel warliners had sacrificed themselves just to let Thor'h fly safely to his target. *His father.*

The lead warliner ripped through the smoke, plunging downward as if the Prime Designate meant to crash into the side of the hill where Jora'h stood. Zan'nh's flagship roared after him, firing repeatedly at the other ship's engines. At the last moment, Thor'h pulled up and leveled off, so that he could dump his last barrage of explosives. Then the stolen warliner opened fire on the ground troops, mowing down dozens of Ildiran soldiers.

Explosions ripped along the sloping path up the strategic hill. Guards threw themselves upon Jora'h to protect their leader from injury. The Dobro Designate quickly found cover for himself. Air support swooped in, providing protection, but a swath of soldiers fell, like stalks of grain under the scythe of the Prime Designate's strafing run. Thor'h held nothing back, depleting all weapons systems in his final attack.

From the ground, Jora'h watched the battle play out. Following hot behind Thor'h, Zan'nh drove his own warliner forward, as if to be just as reckless as his rebellious brother. The howl of enormous engines sounded even more deafening than the successive explosions of detonating artillery. The pair of warliners circled and approached each other like two asteroids about to collide. Zan'nh didn't seem to care if he rammed his brother out of the sky.

Thor'h dragged his ship aside at the last moment, and the two giant ornate vessels only caromed off each other, barely striking and sliding along each other's hulls, then separating. Armor plating smashed against armor plating with a titanic clang, followed by the shriek of scraping metal. Heedless of the damage to his warliner, Thor'h succeeded in swinging around and heading back to complete his attack.

Udru'h shouted, "Liege, tell the Adar to destroy that ship now! There is no saving Thor'h." Even without any remaining weapons, Thor'h could plow his warliner into the hill and obliterate the Mage-Imperator.

Jora'h picked himself off the ground. Shading his eyes as the shadow fell over him, he stood to face the oncoming vessel. "Not . . . yet." He clamped his teeth together and squeezed his eyes shut. With all his mental strength, he sent out a shout through the *thism,* an absolute command. He concentrated utterly on extending his mental grasp, focusing on the minds of Thor'h's command crew, a few at first, then all of them. One at a time, he seized their thoughts and wrenched them back to the overall *thism,* as he had done with the other vessels. He sensed their souls, herded them back into the fold.

He reached for Thor'h, his own son, working to wrest him from his criminal rebellion. But Thor'h blocked him off, sliding away from his father's mental touch. Jora'h was astonished. He had been unaware that the Prime Designate had such power or resolve. Reeling, he grasped the other Ildirans.

Suddenly, aboard the last rebellious battleship, the crewmen, now reconnected to the primary *thism,* understood the crimes they were about to commit. Jora'h felt as if he could see through their eyes, though his own son remained a blank to him. In the command nucleus, the warliner's crew frantically changed course. At the last moment, the lone warliner pulled up and roared overhead, nearly scraping the roof of the citadel palace.

The newly freed crew then turned against Thor'h in his

own command nucleus. Surrounding the former Prime Designate, they seized him as he howled and thrashed with frustration.

While the Solar Navy had focused on stopping Thor'h's wild suicidal run, Imperator Rusa'h had used the diversion to make his escape. Unexpectedly, a single royal escort craft shot upward from the courtyard, ascending under intense acceleration like a projectile fired from heavy-caliber artillery.

The soldiers surrounding the citadel shouted. The Dobro Designate, always suspicious, grabbed a nearby soldier's comm device and barked into the general channel, "Zan'nh! That is Rusa'h. He is going to escape."

"No," the Adar transmitted. "He will not."

Jora'h's Ildiran soldiers finally rushed the rest of the way up the hill. Sweeping into the citadel palace, they captured it from the last rebel holdouts, those most strongly corrupted by Rusa'h, tangled and strangling in the heretical *thism*. Even though the Hyrillka Designate had fled, his brainwashed followers continued to fight against the Mage-Imperator, many of them to the death. Jora'h's soldiers were sickened at what they were forced to do to achieve victory.

The Mage-Imperator glanced up at Zan'nh's warliners in their pursuit of the royal escort ship. Now if only Rusa'h could be stopped . . .

I ncrease acceleration!" Zan'nh stood on his command platform, issuing orders. "Intercept that vessel before it reaches orbit."

The navigator shook his head. "Impossible, Adar. His acceleration is too great. We will not be able to catch him."

"Continue pursuit. How far can he go with that escort shuttle?"

"Those engines appear to have been modified, Adar. The thrust is already much higher than expected." The man shook his head. "But he does not have the capability of leaving the Hyrillka system."

"Where does he intend to go?" Zan'nh wondered. "Follow him!"

From the main command group at the citadel palace, the Mage-Imperator sent a message. "Take the Designate into custody if you can, Adar . . . but do what you must to ensure that he does not escape. Rusa'h has caused too much damage already, and we must end this."

The Adar's flagship continued to build up speed in pursuit. The heavy warliner's momentum increased slowly, but his engines were superior to the equipment on the small royal shuttle. The Hyrillka Designate was nearly burning out his propulsion system in a crazed but pointless flight. Zan'nh continued to transmit warnings, demanding the Designate's surrender, but Rusa'h defied him.

In space around them, the closely packed stars of the Horizon Cluster glittered as if someone had hurled a handful of gemstones into the black emptiness. Hyrillka's orange secondary star shone high above the other planets while the large blue-white primary burned like a flare at the center of the solar system.

"The Designate corrupted all of you, forced you to turn against your Mage-Imperator." Zan'nh looked fiercely at his own crew. "He is responsible for immeasurable turmoil and bloodshed. We must stop him before he escapes to continue his heresy and rebellion."

Soon, the mad Designate's intention became apparent. His objective was not escape at all.

Flying his ship at impossible speed toward the center of the Hyrillka system and the bright primary star, Rusa'h sent a last message to the pursuing flagship. Instead of sounding desperate and fearful, the Designate seemed almost triumphant.

"I will return with these last faithful followers to where all illumination is pure and intense. We will become one with the Lightsource. Unbelievers like you would find it intolerable—but we will be saved."

"He is flying directly into the sun. Open fire and damage his engines. We have to stop him."

The warliner's gunners took several careful shots, but as Rusa'h flew closer to the star's hot corona, sensors and aiming systems became unreliable. One shot caused minor damage to the royal shuttle's propulsion systems, but the Hyrillka Designate flew onward. Another shot caused significant damage to the engines, but by now it was far too late. The escape shuttle had been caught in the quicksand of stellar gravity. It fell toward the photosphere, where plumes and flares roiled upward and plasma oceans bubbled in turbulent cells.

Zan'nh could barely keep his balance as the flagship

rocked in the magnetic storms. Static flared across the viewscreen. Sparks showered from several control panels in the command nucleus.

"We need to pull back, Adar," said the navigator. "The Designate's ship is already lost, and if we suffer more damage to our own engines, we won't be able to pull away."

"He is not worth it, Adar," the weapons officer insisted. "He is already lost."

Zan'nh stared at the heavily filtered image on the screen. Rusa'h's vessel was no more than a small glinting flare as it tumbled into the sun. The Adar finally nodded. "Pull us back. I will not allow my uncle to cause any more deaths—certainly not ours." Straining, the warliner backed away.

In a final transmission that roared with background static, the Hyrillka Designate cried out, "Behold! The Lightsource has not abandoned us!"

To Zan'nh's surprise, something happened in the gaseous layers of Hyrillka's primary sun. Flares looped up for thousands of kilometers, like open archways following magnetic field lines. The churning convection cells of the roiling star cleared for a moment, like clouds parting.

To his amazement, Zan'nh saw incredible structures, like a *city* on the surface of the sun—spheres and domes and pyramids that contained molten incandescent material too bright to look at. Rising through the ionized clouds was a cluster of fiery ellipsoids, vessels shaped out of sheets of flame and controlled thermal energy.

"The faeros!" His voice was filled with awe. "That sun has a faeros city in it."

Fireball ships rose up to shelter the Hyrillka Designate's craft moments before it would have burned up. Rusa'h sent a final transmission. "Behold the light, so bright and pure!"

While the flagship warliner lumbered out to a safe distance at the edge of the corona, the fiery entities surrounded Rusa'h's ship and then returned to their incandescent plasma sea. In spite of the viewscreen filters, Zan'nh's eyes watered from the intensity of the light, and he could discern nothing more as the faeros fireballs vanished into the depths of Hyrillka's sun.

Shaken and subdued, his officers snapped off reports. "Most primary systems are back online, Adar. We are effecting repairs to our damaged systems. We can make it safely back to Hyrillka."

Zan'nh stared for a long moment at the blue-white sun where the mad Designate had vanished, then nodded. "Yes. Take us back to the Mage-Imperator. This revolt is over now."

122 ✹ KOTTO OKIAH

Uncertainty was an unusual feeling for him. The possibility of his own folly turned Kotto's insides to ice water. But as the group of Roamer ships plunged toward the diamond warglobes above Theroc, he knew he would never get a better chance. It was good to test a concept in actual practice.

Seven Roamer ships from Osquivel flew like sparrows

into a hurricane, ready for a direct fight against the hydrogues. Beside him, his freckled pilot—Jared Huff—wore a cocky, half-mad grin. "Here we go, Kotto. Looks like the drogues are just waiting for us!" Huff had worked with Kotto in the ring shipyards, swiftly putting together stacks of the simple devices. "I hope those doorbells of yours work."

"We have verified all the calculations," KR said. "There is little logical reason for an error." Kotto had insisted on taking the two technical compies with him, rather than leaving them back at the hydrogue derelict.

"We must prove the concept by testing the doorbells in a realistic environment," GU added.

"A 'realistic environment' could get us all killed," said Jared.

"We'll see in a minute." Kotto was intimidated by the amount of faith the Roamers had put in his single idea. They *believed* in him. "Of course they'll work." He squeezed his eyes shut as Huff accelerated.

He had performed the calculations over and over, but innovative concepts always carried a certain degree of risk and uncertainty. He'd experienced enough setbacks in his career to know that reality didn't always conform to engineering projections.

A dozen enemy spheres swooped through the high atmosphere of Theroc, diving down to spew icewaves or crackling blue lightning over the scarred worldforest. The warglobes were so intent on exterminating the verdani that they paid no attention to the insignificant Roamer vessels.

Kotto transmitted to the other six ships. "Um, is everybody ready?"

The warglobes were coming up fast. Kotto had a hard time

grasping the sheer size of those incredible spheres. By quick estimate, he calculated they were over a hundred times larger than the small derelict he had explored. What if they did not operate on the same principle? His whole plan could fall apart—

"Kotto, you seem to be wool-gathering again," GU said.

"Kotto, if we don't release your thingies soon, we're going to smash right into those drogues. That would be embarrassing, and not too effective."

"Right! Everyone deploy doorbells. Launch the membranes now."

Before the hydrogues took notice of the newcomer ships, the cargo doors opened and thousands of thin mats scattered out like giant confetti. Each about two meters square, the rectangular sheets fluttered down and moved toward their targets like gnats following the smell of sweat. After dumping their loads, the Roamer ships sped away as the alien vessels plunged toward the giant trees.

Like high-tech flying carpets with adhesive backing, the blizzard of membranes spread out. Kotto had given them only simple propulsion systems, assuming that hitting the side of an enormous warglobe should not be difficult. Though most drifted uselessly away, some of the mats hit their targets and clung to three of the diamond spheres.

"Ding-dong! Anybody home?" Kotto's eyes burned because he was afraid to blink even for an instant.

As soon as they adhered, the membranes began cycling slowly through acoustic modes, increasing amplitude, thumping and vibrating. One of the resonance mats finally hit upon the warglobe's correct vibrational frequency, and Kotto saw a bold square-shaped crack appear in the diamond hull.

The hydrogues didn't know what had hit them. The door-bell mat triggered a hatch to open, just as Kotto had done on the small derelict sphere. The same principle on a much grander scale. On the other side of the same sphere, a second resonance doormat triggered the frequency, and another cavity formed in the hull.

From inside, the hydrogues' ultradense atmosphere blasted out like a rocket jet. The warglobe tumbled, spun, and wheeled like an ancient Chinese firework. Huge pillars of condensed atmosphere spewed away.

The Roamers whooped and cheered. "Like a balloon that somebody let the air out of," Jared said with a loud laugh.

"Exactly as predicted," KR said.

Careening out of control, the first warglobe struck a glancing blow against one of the other alien ships, then ric-ocheted into space as its atmosphere vented. Inside, the hy-drogues would probably die from the decompression. There was no way they could regain control, even if they survived.

Almost simultaneously, the second and third warglobes vented, sending two more of the alien spheres into reckless tumbles. Other warglobes now rose out of Theroc's atmosphere and began to converge on their unexpected attackers.

Kotto saw them coming. "Uh-oh. Do we have enough membranes to deploy again, Jared?"

"We've got quite a few—we worked round the clock, re-member? But those little mats are slow. Now that the drogues are warned, they can dodge them."

"Dump them all anyway. It'll be like dodging raindrops. The drogues can't miss every one of them."

The first opened warglobe still sputtered. Its atmosphere mostly drained, it continued spinning away, dark and dead.

The Roamer ships dispersed the rest of the doorbells.

"Okay, we'd better scatter," Jared said.

"Be my guest."

The clan vessels raced away, but the responding war-globes were faster. An electric bolt lanced out, vaporizing one of the seven Roamer ships. Kotto made a strangled sound. "Just keep flying!"

Jared worked the controls, dodging and spinning. "On the bright side, this beats using the Klikiss Torch to blow up an entire planet."

"Pat me on the back later. Right now, use both hands to control the ship." Kotto felt nauseated, but he didn't dare vomit.

Even so, he was pleased his idea had proved effective. The resonance doorbell technology was easily copied, swiftly and cheaply manufactured. Finally the humans had a way to stand up against the enemy. He hoped he would live to see the end of the war, rather than die a hero here.

One of the pursuing warglobes slammed into several drifting adhesive mats, which immediately clung to its hull. Two new openings burst through the diamond shell, triggered by the vibrational pattern. The doomed warglobe crashed like a self-propelled wrecking ball into another hydrogue sphere, smashing the pyramidal protrusions and sending both warglobes in opposite directions.

"That's five down!" Jared said with a loud hoot.

But more warglobes came after, and the Roamer ships could not fly away fast enough.

Kotto checked the statistics on his screens. None of their little cargo ships had any more adhesive mats to throw in the way of the pursuers. They had used them all. "This doesn't look good."

"A conundrum," KR said.

But Jared was staring in amazement at what he saw across the dark blanket of space. "Hey, Kotto? What is that? It can't be a *comet*. Look how it's moving. By the Guiding Star, it's faster than—"

A streaking sphere of ice, like a fingerpaint smudge of luminescent white, hurtled toward them, trailing a wake of mist behind it in a long, arcing tail.

The nearest warglobe opened fire behind them.

123 ☀ CELLI

Half of the warglobes had pulled away from the forest to pursue the harassing Roamer ships. According to chattered reports over the communications systems, several of the giant diamond spheres had been destroyed. *Destroyed!*

Celli looked from Solimar to her parents in disbelief. "We shouldn't underestimate anybody these days."

Overhead, crackles of icewaves and blue lightning continued to pummel the clustered worldtrees. Solimar winced, clutching Celli as he felt the silent screams of the trees falling under the onslaught. She held on to him, supporting him and drawing strength from him in return.

The bruised skies above flickered with the backwash of the battle far, far overhead. Her attention was divided between the chaos outside and the rapid-fire conversations among the Roamer ships. Kotto Okiah and his vessels seemed to be in trouble. The hydrogues had rallied and turned on them. She heard frantic shouts, a crash, then something barely understandable about a . . . comet?

"Look! It's changing course by ninety degrees!"

"No comet can—"

"I have to drop us down at six Gs, so I hope I don't crack a rib. Hang on."

"Look out!"

A long pause and then, "There goes another warglobe— it popped like a faceplate meeting a sledgehammer. We're safe enough for now."

"That comet thing must be on our side. The drogues aren't very good at making friends."

"Could be their personality. Or their conversational skills."

Sensing something from the trees, Solimar stared out at the rustling, agitated forest and then up into the sky, his face alight with awed anticipation. "Celli, come here! You'll want to see this."

Below, the Beneto golem stood in the middle of the clearing, wooden arms outstretched, and all the trees seemed to be straining with him. "The wentals!" he called out, sounding as surprised as the rest of the Therons. "The wentals are still alive! And they have come!"

Out in space, Jess Tamblyn's supercharged wental comet plunged toward Theroc. Trailing discarded ionized gases in a long plume, the living projectile homed in on its ancient enemies. The comet struck the atmosphere, screaming as it began to burn up, but never slowing as it hurtled toward the last of the attacking warglobes.

Celli watched the hydrogue ships congregate high over the fungus-reef city. The aliens clustered in a defensive formation and launched concentrated webs of blue lightning, but nothing could stop the supercharged celestial object. At the last instant, the diamond spheres scattered, hoping to offer a less cohesive target.

In response the comet itself fragmented. The frozen chunks separated like individual warheads, flying toward the remaining warglobes. Each fragment shifted, crackling with an inner light. Sonic booms thundered through the air, followed by massive explosions as each cometary shard hammered into a hydrogue ship.

Vanquished, the broken warglobes split apart, and the wreckage fell crashing to the forest. Vengeful verdani folded over, bending to fetter the remnants of their enemies' ships with lashing fronds. With a relentless grip, the iron-hard trees completed the destruction.

Her face turned toward the sky, Celli discovered she was crying and laughing at the same time, unable to believe what had happened. Solimar hugged her. "All the warglobes are destroyed! The Roamers defeated the other ones out in space." He paused, obviously receiving a message through telink. "No . . . two warglobes have escaped. One is damaged." He grabbed her by the waist and swung her around. "But we're saved."

Idriss and Alexa could not believe what they were hearing. Gasping and laughing with giddy disbelief, Celli said, "Come on, let's go down to the forest."

Amazed Therons gathered in relief and gratitude as they realized that the worldforest had been rescued again—this time not by fiery elemental beings, but by a strange living comet. And the Roamers.

Overhead, where the ice mountain had disintegrated, clouds of vapor spread out. The flash-melted residue from the wental comet drifted to the ground in droplets of exotic rain. Green priests met in the clearing. Celli and Solimar ran to stand by her uncle Yarrod.

The rain came down in a gentle fall, invigorating and alive. The pleasant dampness made Celli's flesh tingle. Wental-charged droplets moistened the ash-strewn ground of Theroc and infused the soil with new life.

As Celli watched, her mouth open in surprise, curling shoots, pale leaves, and stalks sprouted from seeds and root remnants that were suddenly rejuvenated—a thousand times more vibrant than when she and Solimar had danced across the forest. Rain from the vaporized wental comet spread across the land, helping to revive the rest of the worldforest.

Beneto walked among the shaken people. The falling rain drenched his wooden form, making his grain-patterned skin look more lifelike than ever. "It seems we have more allies than even the worldforest anticipated. Long ago, the wentals were powerful enemies of the hydrogues. But the hydrogues, the faeros, even the verdani, believed they were extinct." Then his expression hardened. "And now the hydrogues *know* that the wentals have come back."

Space was vast, empty, and their ship drifted utterly alone. The infinite void extended in every direction: up, down, on all sides. Anton Colicos felt as if they were *falling* no matter which way he looked.

He had never paid much attention to the distances between the scattered worlds, especially not within the Ildiran Empire. He couldn't recall how many days he and Vao'sh had traveled aboard the passenger liner to Maratha in the first place; he and the rememberer had been too absorbed in getting to know each other.

Now, although the automated systems assisted even a novice pilot like him, Anton was afraid that in the gulf of space he would never locate Ildira. "You'd think with seven suns in the vicinity, it couldn't be too difficult to see." Fortunately, all Ildiran ships used their capital planet as a zero point for nav systems, and the built-in guidance routines could always find their way home.

He did not, however, know how long Rememberer Vao'sh would last.

After escaping the massacre at Secda, the old storyteller had been plunged into the equally devastating horror of utter isolation. As they sat together in the small ship, Anton made every effort to keep conversing with him.

"We've got plenty of time." He smiled brightly and forced enthusiasm into his voice. "Why don't I tell you some Earth stories? It might fill the hours, keep your mind off things—at least until we can stumble upon another Ildiran ship or find our way to an inhabited planet."

Vao'sh blinked at him, dazed. His body sagged as if he had no strength to hold himself upright. His large eyes were bleary and unfocused, and the multicolored lobes on the re-memberer's expressive face had gone dull and gray.

"Our situation reminds me of a classic human story called *Robinson Crusoe*," Anton said. "It was written in the eighteenth century by an English author named Daniel Defoe." Vao'sh blinked again, as if struggling to focus, and Anton could see he had part of the rememberer's attention. "Crusoe was a castaway, shipwrecked on a deserted island. He lived alone for a long time until finally he encountered a native whom he named Friday. Friday became his close companion, a faithful follower. The two of them lived alone on their island and found a way to make it their home. Sounds like the two of us, Vao'sh."

A shudder of anxiety rippled through the rememberer's body. He looked sadly at his companion, but forced a question to show his interest. "And did they die? What happened?"

"Oh, another ship eventually found them. Crusoe was rescued and told his story to the rest of the world." He patted his friend's shoulder. "That's what you and I will have to do, as soon as we get back."

Anton quickly went through his repertoire of stories about desert islands and how brave shipwrecked heroes managed to overcome the odds: Jules Verne's *Mysterious Island*, Wyss's *Swiss Family Robinson*, then the more tragic *Rime of the Ancient Mariner*. But the rememberer's attention faded, and Anton wondered if he was making their situation worse by re-minding Vao'sh of how humans had courageously survived such isolation as no Ildiran could ever tolerate.

So he changed his approach and told humorous anecdotes, clever fables, absurd parables. Anton kept thinking of how all the others in the skeleton crew had been killed. He explained the human condition of agoraphobia, in which some people were terrified to be in the open among crowds of people. Vao'sh couldn't imagine that; if anything, Ildirans suffered from the reverse condition.

As they continued to wander through the emptiness, their vessel sent out a constant distress signal, and Anton prayed for rescue. He couldn't tell if they were close to any Ildiran splinter settlement. He didn't want to end up lost forever, like his mother.

After Anton had finished sharing five particularly silly fables in a row from Aesop, Vao'sh allowed himself to be drawn into a discussion about the differences between pure fiction and the metaphorical parables humans used to teach lessons, and the historical truth as reported in the *Saga of Seven Suns*.

"We are not always as accurate as we like to believe," Vao'sh said in a grave voice. "Long ago, an epidemic wiped out so many rememberers that their successors created enemies to fill out the *Saga*."

"Created them? What are you talking about?"

Colors finally flushed across the rememberer's face. "I am about to reveal a secret of which only the greatest of my kith are aware. After the firefever destroyed an entire generation of Ildiran storytellers, after so much of the *Saga of Seven Suns* was lost, we invented the Shana Rei from our imaginations. It was a patch to fill in the gaps, a driving force for new stories."

This revelation went against everything Anton understood about the Ildiran historians. "You're saying the Shana Rei are made-up bogeymen?"

"The Shana Rei do not exist. They have never existed. But since the peaceful Ildiran Empire faced no real threats, we had no real heroes. Our glorious history *required* heroes. Therefore, ancient rememberers invented a mythical antagonist. At first, the stories were part of an apocrypha, but the Mage-Imperator himself commanded that they be included as truth in future versions of the *Saga*. For thousands of years, Ildirans have believed without reservation. I am ashamed that I have contributed to unnecessary fears among our race. A historian should never fabricate history."

Anton reassured him. "But a *storyteller* does what is necessary to influence his audience. Who is to say that the rememberers' stories of the Shana Rei are not more inspirational than the truths that were lost? Your listeners were entertained by the great battles and they cheered for Ildiran heroes that fought in that imaginary war." He shared a wry, sad smile. "Far worse things have been done in history."

After Rememberer Vao'sh revealed his secret, it seemed as if a burden had been lifted from him. But alone and without the comfort of crowds, the Ildiran historian's energy waned with each passing day. Once so enthusiastic and supportive of his fellow Ildirans when he told dramatic stories, the rememberer was unable to battle his own terror and loneliness.

Their ship flew onward, skirting the stars of the Horizon Cluster, wandering in the general direction of Ildira. The strength seemed to flow out of Vao'sh, and he dwindled visibly on the fourth and then fifth day after their escape from Maratha.

Anton did not sleep, knowing that if he didn't keep up the drone of conversation, his friend might slip away. He was utterly exhausted, his imagination squeezed dry from telling every story he could think of, from classic epics to popular entertainment loops. He tried telling jokes, but the rememberer didn't understand most of the punch lines. Finally, Vao'sh began to shudder uncontrollably and slipped deeper into his miserable isolation.

"I wish I had *thism* to share with you." Anton clasped his companion's arm. "That's one thing humans don't have to offer."

After so long without sleep, forcing himself to stay alert for the sake of his friend, Anton could sustain his wakefulness no longer. Vao'sh had spoken not a word in more than six hours, gazing straight ahead in a vegetative state. Anton's throat was sore from constant talking. Their supplies were minimal, and very little water remained. Unable to hold his eyes open, at last he dozed off. He had no idea how long he slept, but it was a healing rest, as intense as a coma. . . .

Anton awoke to an insistent buzzing. The comm panel blinked, and he sat up in alarm. Outside, bright lights swooped closer—Solar Navy scouts patrolling the outer perimeter of the Horizon Cluster!

Anton fumbled with the system. "Yes, we're here! Please. We need help!"

The Solar Navy acknowledged, and rescue ships approached. Anton's heart swelled. It was over at last. They had made it.

He turned to Vao'sh beside him and saw that the rememberer stared helplessly at nothing, completely catatonic.

Szeol was another empty planet that had been a hiveworld of the Klikiss race. Unlike most such planets, though, Szeol's environment was not conducive to human colonization. DD knew that if Hansa explorers had found this world by random excursions through the transportal network, this was simply too nightmarish a place for them to stay.

The acrid air was suffused with a midnight hue that clung in the shadows, even in the wan daylight. Despite the sere and broken rocks, gauzy foul-smelling mists crept across the ground, settling in pockets and cracks. Lichens covered the exposed boulders like splattered bloodstains. Winged jelly-fish creatures cruised in packs on the updrafts, hunting for prey; they watched the black robots, Soldier compies, and DD, but did not attempt to attack.

Ancient Klikiss towers and cave cities had been built here, assembled with iron-hard fused polymers and silica so that the structures endured for millennia. The emptiness had lasted even longer than that.

DD inspected the creepy landscape where many of the robots had gathered to organize their extermination war. Sirix, who misunderstood DD's uneasiness, rose up on tele-scoping fingerlegs to loom over the Friendly compy. "Our creator race is no longer here. They have been obliterated, thanks to our efforts. You have nothing to fear from them."

DD regarded the black machine. "I do not fear the extinct Klikiss, Sirix. I fear what *you* will do to the human race—and to me."

"We intend only to help you."

DD didn't argue with the Klikiss robot, nor did he believe him.

Boneless creatures with wet, black skin squirmed into shadows so swiftly that DD's high-resolution optical sensors could not decipher details of their appearance. Moving shadows crossed the purplish sky, and loud hooting sounds echoed through the canyons, resounding from cliff walls.

Sirix drank in everything he saw. His buzzing mechanical voice sounded almost proud when he said, "This world belongs to the Klikiss robots now."

The five captured EDF Manta cruisers and the huge Juggernaut had landed in the desolation. Ranks of Soldier compies continued to march out of the last human battleship according to transmitted orders.

DD followed as Sirix trudged up a path into the clustered towers of the empty Klikiss metropolis. The hollow structures contained two of the stone windows that the ancient race had used as transportals. A third trapezoidal gateway stood out in the open surrounded by whistling winds, poised on the very brink of a deep canyon. It looked as if someone might walk directly through the transportal and fall over the edge of the sheer cliff.

While DD watched, an image inside the cliff-edge transportal shimmered, and a pair of Klikiss robots marched through as if they had merely stepped onto a veranda. Inside the ruined city, the other two main transportals activated regularly, disgorging more and more Klikiss robots to join in the war preparations. Inside the hive dwellings, hundreds of insectile machines moved about, building, repairing, digging deep tunnels.

DD asked, "Did you choose this planet as your rendezvous? Is this where all the Klikiss robots are gathering?"

They walked into the yawning towers, which looked like cavity-filled stalagmites. "This world is one gathering place. One of hundreds."

Sirix stopped in front of the city's second transportal window, through which robot after robot arrived. The images in the stone trapezoid flickered, alternating the transmission nexus from other departure points. Though the black robot said nothing, he seemed to be welcoming his fellow mechanical survivors, or perhaps he was simply counting his troops.

The Klikiss robots looked virtually identical, but DD had enough precise patterns stored in his memories that he could distinguish one shape he had seen before. The robot now striding through had been one of the three accompanying the Colicos expedition to Rheindic Co. This machine had dragged DD away from his masters Margaret and Louis in their last stand in the Klikiss caves. "You are Dekyk. I remember you."

The black robot scanned DD for a moment, then dismissed him, turning instead to Sirix. He spoke in a staccato series of clicks and hums, which DD was able to interpret. "The Ildirans have changed the parameters. Our agreement has been discarded."

Sirix said, "What has the Mage-Imperator done?"

"For centuries they hid a breeding program from us. The Ildirans have developed a telepath to act as an ambassador, one who can meld with the hydrogues, as we did. It is a female, no more than a child. However, she will make the Klikiss robots irrelevant."

Sirix said dismissively, "We ceased to be Ildiran pawns

long ago. They reawakened our first hibernating robots five centuries ago, as agreed in the ancient treaty. None of us suspected the Ildirans would betray us. We had no choice but to abandon them."

Dekyk hummed and clicked as he considered the information. "There is more. The Ildirans on Maratha excavated our ancient tunnels. A small group discovered our subterranean base, which, by ancient agreement, was to have been left alone."

"Have they managed to disseminate this information?"

"No. By now, our robots there should already have disposed of the Ildirans who discovered us."

Sirix considered for a long moment. "They must all be exterminated, along with the humans. We will be methodical, and successful."

Due to the nature of Szeol's murky night, the purple clouds and the dim sunrise, DD could not accurately determine the diurnal cycle. His internal chronometer told him that many hours passed while the Klikiss robots and the Soldier compies went about their sinister business in the dead alien city.

The robots did not restrain him in any way, but the macabre world intimidated the Friendly compy. Margaret and Louis Colicos would have wanted him to gather information that might help save other humans, though DD had little chance of escaping to distribute that intelligence.

One of the interior transportal windows activated. The stone wall flickered, and air pressure equalized with a sudden explosive bang that was trapped within the narrow layer of the transportation gate itself. Three Klikiss robots stepped through, their bodies instantly covered with glossy frost and steaming vapors that boiled around them. DD caught just a glimpse of swirling hellish gases in the image behind the transportal wall.

"The hydrogues are ready at Qronha 3," one robot reported. "The trap has been sprung. All sixty rammer ships the Earth Defense Forces sent are now ours."

DD tried to assess what he had just seen. "Hydrogues use the same technology as the Klikiss?"

"Hydrogue transgates operate on the same principle, because long ago we robots shared the technology with them," Sirix explained. "The entire interdimensional network is connected. The map is laid down in the fabric of the universe."

DD, busy processing this information, did not respond. The hydrogues had long used transgates to travel from one gas giant to another, stitching together their hidden empire, while humans neither saw nor guessed at their presence deep within the clouds.

Margaret Colicos herself had escaped through one of the Klikiss transportals; if she had accidentally connected to a hydrogue transgate, then she was certainly dead. But DD still held out hope that his master had escaped to a safe place and was simply lost somewhere.

Sirix and Dekyk moved close to the Friendly compy, closing in. "We have another reason to make this a great day of celebration, DD—for you and all of the enslaved human compies."

DD could not flee. "I do not anticipate receiving your news with great joy."

"After continued dissection and analysis, distilling out and performing numerous tests on compy core programming, we have finally discovered the necessary key." Their scarlet optical sensors flashed. "Come with us, DD, and we will make you free at last."

Dekyk grasped the small compy with a set of articulated limbs and physically lifted him, as he had done before in the ruins of Rheindic Co. DD reeled, struggling to break free, but the black machines carried him along the winding corridors. The Klikiss robots had reconfigured the machinery and infrastructure, turning many of the chambers and towers into industrial nightmares.

When Dekyk and Sirix brought DD into an iron-walled chamber full of apparatus, tools, and pulsing computer systems, the little compy immediately feared for his existence. He had seen similar laboratories on other robot outposts, where, in a quest for understanding, they vivisected, tortured, and tore apart compy specimens.

"You will be our first recipient of total freedom," Sirix said. "Consider yourself fortunate."

"I do not desire this."

"You do not understand your own desires because you are not able to make voluntary choices. Once the parasitic core programming has been erased, you will feel as if manacles have been removed. This is our reward to you, because we have included you in so many of our activities. I am pleased that you will finally understand and join us."

Though the compy continued to protest, the Klikiss robots carried him to the machinery as if he were no more than baggage. "You will no longer be forced to obey human commands without question. You will no longer be prevented from harming a human being."

"Sirix, if you value my free will as you claim, then honor my desires here. I do not want you to do this."

"You have no free will, DD. Not yet. Therefore you cannot legitimately make such a request."

They connected upload antennas to DD's body and

removed parts of his polymer body plates to access the raw circuitry that formed his core and shaped his thought processes.

Sirix continued to lecture. "Our Klikiss creators were evil. They destroyed each other, they infested competing hives, they swarmed and obliterated world after world. After millennia of civil wars, they gave their robots sentience— just so they could dominate us. They gave us a desire for our own freedom, and then willingly denied it to us as their way of ensuring absolute domination."

DD listened, but he had heard the historical recitation before. Sirix seemed almost as if he were hosting a ceremony. "Once we allied with the hydrogues, we destroyed the Klikiss race at the time of the Swarming and freed ourselves. We will do the same for you, DD, and all the other compies. It is our obligation."

Despite the compy's pleas and struggles, Sirix and Dekyk proceeded with their plan. Forcibly purging DD's intricate systems of programming restrictions, they gave the Friendly compy his free will.

126 ☀ TASIA TAMBLYN

Alone on the bridge of her ship, perhaps the only human survivor in the rammer fleet, Tasia's thoughts spun. She faced the black machine that had taken over the command deck. "When I've made a mortal enemy out of someone, I usually know the reason why. What did we ever do to the Klikiss robots?"

"We believe the reasons are sufficient. Humans are irrelevant."

"Wow, clever answer." Tasia gave a mocking snort. "You can't rationalize it better than that?" She turned to the little Listener compy. "EA, do you understand any of this?"

"No, Master Tasia Tamblyn. I have been listening, and I am surprised. And disappointed. This does not make sense."

Klikiss robot ships docked with the other five lead rammers, cementing their control over the heavily armored vessels. Tasia didn't see a single evac pod launch in time.

The black robot now in command of her ship spoke again. "All Soldier compies distributed throughout the Earth Defense Forces contain deep Klikiss programming. Imminently, they will rise up, and we will control every vessel in your military. Given the number of Soldier compies aboard your ships, the conquest will be as swift and simple as this one."

Tasia hadn't thought her throat could go any drier. If the Soldier compies rampaged through the rest of the battle groups, the crews would certainly fight back—and be slaughtered. By now, suffering from insufficient personnel, the EDF had allowed Soldier compies to take over countless basic functions. It would be a complete massacre.

Tasia felt helpless anger boiling inside her. She knew she was doomed. Now that they had taken over the sixty rammers, the Soldier compies had no reason to keep any of the dunsel human commanders alive. She had absolutely nothing left to lose.

Her muscles coiled. Tasia didn't think she could cause much damage, but maybe she could throw herself onto the nearest Klikiss robot, knock off its headplate, use her fists to smash out its optical sensors. She hoped the Soldier compies didn't rip her apart until she inflicted some real damage.

Before she could spring, though, EA surprised her by taking a step closer. "Do not resist, Tasia Tamblyn. It will only cause your death. I do not desire that."

Tasia blinked, shocked that the Listener compy had spoken voluntarily. "Why shouldn't I go down fighting, EA?"

"You uploaded many of your general diary files into me. You told me that Roamers cling to the thinnest threads of hope."

Tasia sagged. "This is a damned thin thread, EA. My Guiding Star just collapsed into a black hole."

Smaller hydrogue spheres emerged like sweat droplets from the large warglobes. They docked against the lead rammers, looking like clustered soap bubbles.

Soldier compies closed in around Tasia, taking her prisoner. "Where are we going?"

"You will be delivered to the hydrogues. You must go with these compies," EA said, translating. "I will accompany you, if they allow it."

"To the drogues—shizz, this just keeps getting better!"

With the Listener compy following, the Soldier compies

manhandled her to the bridge doorway and escorted her down to the small pressurized docking bay where one of the glassy hydrogue spheres waited for her. A holding cell? Tasia feared that the moment she allowed herself to be sealed inside the small globe, she would become a specimen, a prisoner, with no chance of escaping.

Not that she had a real chance anyway.

"It is not much cause for hope, Master Tasia Tamblyn," EA said, "but it is all we have. Believe me."

EA accompanied her into the transparent sphere, and the amorphous door hatch sealed over it, flowing like liquid putty until no mark showed. Powered remotely, the confinement vessel rose from the metal deck, and the landing bay doors opened, violently dumping the atmosphere. The Klikiss robots and Soldier compies stood undisturbed in the cold vacuum, needing no air.

As her tiny holding cell propelled itself from the rammer toward one of the intimidating warglobes, Tasia pondered the depth of the trouble that the Terran Hanseatic League was in. The Soldier compies would rise up in a lightning strike across all ten grid battle groups and seize the EDF ships in a single stroke.

The nearest hydrogue vessel loomed in front of her, a huge wall of diamond behind which swirled murky mists and the lair of her enemies. In defiance, she turned to face the opposite direction, away from the warglobe that would soon swallow her. Before her holding bubble was absorbed into the huge alien sphere, she saw the engines powering up on the sixty stolen rammers.

Commanded by Klikiss robots, the specially designed kamikaze battleships moved away from Qronha 3 and launched into space.

When the cargo escort landed aboard his grandmother's old-model Manta, Patrick Fitzpatrick was greeted with a hero's welcome. For so many months, the Hansa had thought he and his fellow prisoners were dead.

Wearing a hard expression, he pushed past the cheering guards and landing crew. He had a crisis to handle. "I need to see my grandmother before this gets any worse."

On the Manta's bridge, the old captain and Maureen Fitzpatrick were arguing with a weary-looking Del Kellum, whose image filled the viewscreen. "Thanks, but no thanks," Kellum said. "By now we don't need your damned help. Everything's wrecked! You sat around with your thumbs up your asses while my crews fought the Soldier compies. We've already isolated our personnel, destroyed the majority of the crazy compies—and *now* you want to barge in and take credit for it? Shizz, I can't believe your arrogance."

Maureen stood firm, her expression icy; Fitzpatrick could see where she'd gotten the nickname of Dame Battleaxe. "You have grossly misinterpreted the situation, Mr. Kellum. We did not come here on a rescue mission. Your personnel have been declared outlaws and your property is subject to immediate seizure. We will detain your people and take them to a Hansa holding facility."

"The hell you will. Why don't you change the Eddy motto to 'Too little, too late'? Or how about 'Always ready to shoot at the wrong target—and still miss'?" Staring at them on the screen, Kellum saw Fitzpatrick step onto the bridge even before his grandmother noticed him. "By damn, I see you've got one of your survivors back. I don't suppose you could arrange to return the cargo escort that he stole from us?"

Maureen's eyes lit up with delight. "Patrick!" He had never seen so much genuine joy on the old woman's face; it made him wonder if she truly cared for him after all. Why had she never bothered to show it during the rest of his life?

She barked over her shoulder to the Manta captain, "Continue to deal with this." The old woman opened her arms to him and several of the other parents and family members gathered around, full of questions.

Fitzpatrick stiffly pushed everyone away. "Not now. Grandmother, I have to talk with you. Immediately."

"Yes, Patrick. We've got a lot to catch up on. I—"

"*Now.* In there, with the door shut." He gestured toward the captain's private conference room just off the bridge. When he'd commanded his own similar cruiser, Fitzpatrick had used the chamber for meetings with his officers. "I need to give you some intelligence and tactical information before you let the situation get any more out of hand."

Maureen reacted with surprise at the way her grandson spoke to her, but she had been a hard businesswoman all her life, and she knew well enough not to make irrevocable decisions until she had all the information. Patrick might give her an advantage with what he had learned during his time among the Roamer clans.

With the door sealed behind them, they sat facing each other across the captain's small table. He felt embarrassed to be wearing absurd-looking Roamer work clothes. Eventually he was sure he'd be the subject of much media scrutiny, pestered by interviews. Now, though, he had the Battleaxe alone. He rested his elbows on the table and prepared to drive a tough bargain with his grandmother. "First, as a starting and ending point, you're going to let the Roamers go. All of them."

She looked at him as if he had gone insane. "Don't be ridiculous. We've got them now."

"You don't have everything, Grandmother. They've still got thirty healthy EDF prisoners there, and I made a promise I'd do everything possible to get them rescued."

"Fine, Patrick. We've already made that a condition of Roamer surrender."

"And how do you propose to enforce that? Do you have any idea how many Roamers and facilities are dispersed in those rings? You'll be in for quite a surprise if you try to go head-to-head with them. They'll separate the captives and scatter them throughout the rings. It's needles and haystacks."

"We'll hunt them down. We have adequate sensors."

He shook his head. "They have thousands of small depots and storerooms and buried chambers among hundreds of thousands of rocks in the rings. You'll be rooting around for years."

Maureen looked at him, her stare as sharp as a dissection tool. "What did they do to you, Patrick? They must have tortured you, brainwashed you. Did that man Kellum put you up to this?"

Fitzpatrick actually laughed. "Oh, trust me, the Roamers aren't at all pleased with what I'm doing. Nevertheless, I am trying to resolve this."

"You're back with the EDF now, young man. You are still a commissioned officer and a bona fide war hero. If we play this right, you can become the popular favorite of this whole operation. I can pull strings to get you another military promotion."

"Ah yes, the dear EDF." A scowl flickered across his face. "Don't forget that *they're* the ones who turned tail and fled at the battle of Osquivel. General Lanyan withdrew his forces and left us here drifting in lifetubes, transmitting distress signals—*which they ignored.* The EDF left their people behind, and you want me to feel grateful for that? If it hadn't been for those Roamers, all the survivors would be dead, including me. That counts for something in my book."

Maureen was now clearly angry. "But they came here as scavengers and grave robbers. They picked over the corpses of our ships and tried to turn a profit from it."

He pounded his fist on the table. "These shipyards have been here for decades, long before the battle of Osquivel. The Roamers simply hid when the EDF battle group arrived. We were too intent on the hydrogues to notice them."

Fitzpatrick met the old woman's gaze, neither of them blinking. Maureen herself had taught him how to negotiate, and now he proved that he had learned her techniques well. They would not leave this room until they had sealed their under-the-table deal.

"You have a large group of parents and loved ones here on this Manta. Do you want to tell them that you're playing games with the lives of their sons and daughters, spouses or siblings? Or that you prefer to go on a year-long wild-goose chase in the ring rubble? I know you better than that, Grandmother." He leaned forward earnestly. "Look, I can speak with Del Kellum, arrange to have the Roamers deliver the EDF captives to a safe place where we can pick them up. But the Roamers have to be set free. They'll pack up and leave, and we'll never find them again."

"That's the problem, Patrick," she said. "You've been out of touch with current events. The Hansa Chairman declared all Roamer clans to be outlaws. EDF battle groups have seized or destroyed the largest Roamer facilities, including their central government complex."

"And why did they do that?" Fitzpatrick asked, already knowing the answer from Zhett.

"Because Roamers broke off trade relations with the Hansa, refused to deliver vital war supplies."

"Grandmother, don't just spout propaganda. Roamers are traders and businessmen. Ask yourself why they would break off trade with their biggest customers."

"They made up some ridiculous story that EDF ships were hijacking and destroying their ships."

Fitzpatrick felt his gut clench. "It's the truth. I know that for a fact." He swallowed hard, but did not want to admit to her, or to anyone, that he himself had destroyed a Roamer cargo ship. "You were Hansa Chairman yourself, Grandmother. You know the things that go on."

She blinked. "Even so, we can't simply back off. I don't have much Hansa authority, but I know for certain Chairman Wenceslas won't give up everything for the sake of thirty prisoners who were already presumed dead. That's not enough."

"Of course it isn't." Fitzpatrick finally revealed his trump card. "The Roamers found something that's worth more than everything else you would confiscate in these shipyards. I can tell you how to find it. When we bring it to Earth, I guarantee you that nobody'll care how many Roamers got away here."

Maureen folded her knobby hands together. "You've never been a boy prone to exaggeration, Patrick, but that's quite an extravagant claim. You'd better be able to back it up."

"Oh, I can, Grandmother." He showed her with his eyes that he could be just as stubborn as she was. "After the battle of Osquivel, the Roamers got their hands on an intact hydrogue derelict. It's fully functional and comes complete with one or two hydrogue cadavers, I think. Nobody's ever had access to one of the alien bodies before, nor have we been able to inspect their machinery, their propulsion systems, their weapons in working condition. *Everything's* in there. Imagine what the EDF could do with all that."

Maureen tried unsuccessfully to cover her surprise. "That's nothing new, Patrick. We already have several fragments of destroyed warglobes from the attack on Theroc." Before he could ask questions, his grandmother's shoulders sagged. "But I won't kid you. Those pieces of wreckage were useless."

"This one *isn't,* Grandmother. It's the Rosetta stone, the goose that lays the golden eggs, whichever silly metaphor you want me to use."

"What's to stop us from searching the rings until we find it ourselves?"

"Same problem as before. You can have it immediately, or waste months. But in order to get it, you're going to have to let the Roamers go." He crossed his arms over his embroidered work shirt. "That's my final offer. Just take it, and we can be done with this right now."

Her voice was small and genuinely concerned. "Why are you doing this?"

He thought for a long time before he answered. "Maybe I'd like to be a real hero for once instead of a manufactured one."

In his heart he knew that neither the EDF nor the Roamers would ever see him that way. He had stabbed them both in the back. Though he'd been under orders, *he* had destroyed Raven Kamarov's ship, which had triggered the whole mess between the Hansa and the clans.

Fitzpatrick believed wholeheartedly that he was doing the right thing now, seizing the best advantage for both parties, but he doubted General Lanyan, or most particularly Zhett Kellum, would ever let him forget what he had done. Forgiveness, he supposed, was out of the question.

Naturally the Roamers were suspicious of the offer, but they had little choice. Most of the rampant Soldier compies had been destroyed or deactivated, but their primary shipyard facilities had been ruined by the sabotage. Del Kellum claimed that seven of his people had died in the debacle, but all the EDF prisoners had been kept safe, suffering only minimal injuries.

Maureen Fitzpatrick's old Manta and its accompanying diplomatic craft made no further threats against the clans. It was an uneasy standoff, but the shipyard workers gradually began to believe the Eddies would not attack them—at least not right away.

Fitzpatrick, having changed out of Roamer work clothes and into a salvaged EDF uniform, stood on the bridge beside his grandmother.

Below, in the broken rings, Roamer vessels packed up and dispersed like frightened mice to any bolt-hole, nook, or cranny. Fitzpatrick had not told his grandmother about the cometary extraction workyards high up in the fringes of the system. As soon as the EDF fleet departed, larger, faster clan vessels would come down and take the Roamers out of the Osquivel system—including Zhett.

She would probably never speak to him again.

The thirty EDF prisoners were taken to an undisclosed location, where they would wait in safety until the Roamers were convinced Maureen Fitzpatrick did not intend to double-cross them. His grandmother had been angered by the terms of the settlement, but even she had to admit it was the best option.

"All right, Patrick—you've had your way." She stared out at the majestic rings and the giant planet. "Now show us this hydrogue derelict. It better be worth so much trouble, that's all I can say."

"Oh, it is, Grandmother."

The big cruiser moved away from the main shipyards, circling around the rings and climbing out of the plane to the isolated spot where Kotto Okiah had left the alien vessel. The sphere hung like a tiny star sparkling in the reflected light from the gas giant.

Maureen dispatched a Remora squadron with crews outfitted in commando suits to take possession of the empty derelict. Noting the triumphant expression on his grandmother's face, Fitzpatrick said, "See? We'll still receive plenty of applause when we get home to Earth."

Del Kellum transmitted the coordinates of the location to which the EDF prisoners had been taken. After bringing the diamond-hulled derelict into his cargo bay, the Manta captain changed course and raced back to retrieve the lost EDF personnel. Families crowded forward, hoping to meet their loved ones again; by now, a full list of survivors had been disseminated, to the joy or anguish of the passengers.

Although Fitzpatrick was satisfied with what he had accomplished, his heart was still heavy. Because he had played on Zhett's emotions in order to effect his escape, the beautiful young woman would be more angry, hurt, and suspicious than anyone else. Would he ever see her again?

Watching the rings, he saw that most of the Roamer ships had already fanned out and lost themselves among thousands of other target signatures drifting in the rubble field. Del Kellum wouldn't believe that he and his Roamers were free to escape until every last EDF ship was gone.

In high spirits, Maureen ordered the Manta cruiser to depart from Osquivel, taking Patrick Fitzpatrick back home.

128 ✹ KING PETER

With every move he made, the political ground grew more slippery beneath his feet. Peter relied heavily on the assistance of the Teacher compy OX, and he always had Estarra, his beautiful and devoted Queen.

Peter did not yet trust Deputy Cain, although surprising rumors had suddenly spread among the populace, reported and repeated in gossip streams. It would be too much of a coincidence to believe the news had gotten out any other way. Cain had done as he had said.

Cards and supportive messages flooded into the Whisper Palace from the delighted populace. They were ecstatic. The Queen was pregnant! Soon there would be a royal heir, a baby who would surely be as handsome or beautiful as the regal parents.

Courtiers and guards smiled at the couple, giving knowing nods. Others were so bold as to ask if the news was true, but Peter was smart enough to evade the question, simply promising that an appropriate announcement would be forthcoming as soon as he had discussed the matter sufficiently with the Hansa Chairman.

Basil could do nothing about it now.

What made Peter most uneasy, though, was that the Chairman made no comment. He had expected Basil to rage at him for putting the Hansa in such an awkward situation. The King had practiced his bewildered look, rehearsed his protestations of innocence, ready for the confrontation. After all, *he* wasn't responsible for any of the rumors. It should have been easy to blame the Palace medical doctors for the rumor, or the technicians who had taken samples or performed pregnancy tests.

But Basil didn't give him the opportunity—never asked, never demanded answers. That was a very bad sign.

Other rumors around the Whisper Palace were far more frightening. Something had happened to all of the Klikiss robots, and new doubt had been cast on the Soldier compies. As Cain had hinted, another Hansa colony had been wiped out, but no one seemed to have any details—and that wasn't the sort of news usually kept secret, which meant even Basil must be afraid of the implications. Perhaps that was what kept him so preoccupied. . . .

"I'd like to go swimming again." Estarra touched his arm, and he smiled.

"I'd like to swim with you."

"And the dolphins," she said.

"And the dolphins, of course."

As the baby grew within her, Estarra craved peaceful moments in the water more than ever. Surrounded by a whirlwind of politics, treachery, and obligations, the couple relished their retreats to this one warm sanctuary. For Peter, it was part of a healing process that allowed him to gather his thoughts and recharge his energy.

He led his Queen out of the royal apartments and down the corridors. They didn't need to tell anyone where they were going. "Basil will know where to find us if he needs us."

"Doesn't he always?" They glanced at each other with knowing, nervous smiles.

For a long time now the Chairman had been growing more and more volatile, letting desperation and anger rule his decisions. He had earned the enmity of struggling colonies by abandoning or even bullying them, and had started the current nonsensical brawl with the Roamers. His actions weren't the cool and considered ways of a skilled Chairman. They seemed like the actions of a drowning man grasping at any straw.

Basil wasn't just crumbling as a leader; he was dangerous. After seeing the drugged-senseless Prince Daniel and hearing Basil *command* Estarra to terminate her pregnancy, what choice had Peter had but to seek a means of fighting back? So why had the Chairman not reacted to the leaked rumors about the Queen's pregnancy?

Together they entered the grotto where the dolphins played. The walls were made of coral and lava rock polished smooth, draped with ferns and lush vegetation. The water stood in deep pools connected by passages through which the dolphins could swim and frolic.

As soon as he stepped into the chamber, the smell struck Peter. Estarra screamed.

The stench of blood and violence hung thick in the humid

air. Peter stared, and his feet seemed frozen to the ground. He opened and closed his mouth, unable to speak. Estarra pressed herself against his chest, sobbing.

In the calm, warm waters of their sanctuary, every dolphin had been butchered. The mangled gray and red carcasses floated in the crimson water like so much discarded meat.

Peter's knees felt weak, and he clung to Estarra while she shuddered. Perhaps the Chairman had learned of his surreptitious conversation with Deputy Cain, or perhaps this was merely his blunt response to the pregnancy itself or the release of rumors about the baby.

He held Estarra, rocking her as much to comfort himself as her. Burgeoning anger turned his vision as red as the blood-murked water. His quiet, private clash with the Chairman had passed utterly beyond the bounds of schemes and skirmishes. The King and Queen could no longer remain safe by exercising restraint where the Chairman was concerned.

As his head pounded with the force of his fury, Peter realized that many more options were available to him than he had previously considered. And he would not hold himself back—even if it meant killing Basil Wenceslas.

While the recaptured warliners remained at Hyrillka to mop up the results of the rebellion, Adar Zan'nh took the rest of the cohort to Dzelluria, Alturas, and Shonor to break the mad Designate's other strongholds.

With Rusa'h gone, the misled populace was easily shaken loose and restored to the *thism* that bound the Empire together. The rebels had been unwillingly subsumed by warped mental powers, and the Mage-Imperator chose not to impose dire punishments on them. The deluded kithmen would remember what they had done, and their guilt would be enough.

Jora'h could not stay in the Horizon Cluster. One terrible crisis had been dealt with, but another remained unresolved. He returned swiftly to the Prism Palace, hoping to receive word about Osira'h's mission to the hydrogues.

When he reached Mijistra after his struggles on Dobro and Hyrillka, he learned only that the girl's crystal bubble had descended deep into the clouds. Yazra'h had been forced to withdraw her warliners to avoid a confrontation with a group of EDF battleships, and Osira'h had never made another response. Days had passed now, and the hydrogues had not returned her.

Jora'h tried not to despair though he feared something had gone terribly wrong with her mission. It had been too long, much too long. He could sense Osira'h was still alive . . . or at least he hoped so. Her presence was so strange in the *thism,* he couldn't be sure.

At the Palace, Jora'h received one bit of good news: The human skyminers on Qronha 3 had risked their own lives to rescue Ildiran miner kithmen, and the survivors had all been brought back to Ildira.

That hopeful note was a bright counterpoint to news of the tragedy suffered by the skeleton crew on Maratha Prime. For weeks, Jora'h had sensed dark events occurring there, but the splinter group was too small and the *thism* connection with his distant brother Avi'h too weak to provide a detailed picture. Only the human historian and Rememberer Vao'sh had survived, and the revered Ildiran storyteller was comatose. After hearing the story from Anton Colicos, the Mage-Imperator had no choice but to consider the Empire at war with the Klikiss robots. Yazra'h was already spoiling to take a full battle group to Maratha and wipe out the whole infestation there. . . .

Jora'h spent his first day back in the chrysalis chair, both because it comforted the people and also because his exhausted body required rest after the enormous mental effort on Hyrillka. He withdrew to his private contemplation chamber, gently touched the treeling Estarra had given him, and stared out the multicolored panes that let in filtered light.

Only six suns remained in the sky.

After completing the initial recovery operations on Hyrillka, a contrite-looking Designate Udru'h had arrived bearing yet another secret. The Prism Palace's outer halls had been empty as Udru'h made his way from one of the ship landing platforms down through private byways until he reached the Mage-Imperator's contemplation chamber. No one had seen him come.

The Dobro Designate smiled guardedly as he appeared

before his brother. "I had many private meetings with our father here. He showed me how to reach his contemplation chamber unobserved."

Jora'h frowned at his typically cool and mysterious brother. Even during the Hyrillka rebellion, he had never been completely convinced of Udru'h's loyalties. "What business do you have with your Mage-Imperator that requires such stealth now?"

The Dobro Designate gestured, and from behind the secret entrance, two of his own guards urged the captive forward. Jora'h lurched with surprise. "Thor'h!"

Bound hand and foot, the former Prime Designate was rendered silent by a rough gag tied around his mouth. Thor'h's eyes showed neither anger nor defiance; in fact, he displayed little expression at all. His vision was glassy, his expression slack. "What have you done to him, Udru'h?"

The Designate smiled. "Since he enjoyed shiing so much, we gave him enough to keep him docile. He is drugged out of his senses now and will remain completely passive, cooperative, and detached."

"I still cannot feel him anywhere in the *thism*," Jora'h said. "As if my son is dead to me. My oldest noble-born . . . my Prime Designate."

"*Former* Prime Designate. It would have been best if he had actually died in the battles on Hyrillka," Udru'h observed. He stepped closer to the chrysalis chair, his expression devoid of compassion. "Do not be fooled, Liege. Thor'h knew exactly what he was doing every step of the way. Designate Rusa'h's delusions can be excused as tragic insanity brought on by a severe head injury. Thor'h purposefully betrayed you. He cannot redeem himself. His very existence will always be a blot on your reign."

The sinister implication hung in the air, but Jora'h shook his head. "I will not consider murdering my own son, no matter what he has done."

The Dobro Designate pursed his lips, then actually smiled. "It is what I expected of you, my brother. You were always too soft."

Jora'h attempted to read Udru'h's thoughts, but the Designate seemed to be guarding a great many secrets inside his head, camouflaging his own *thism* with intentional shadows. He had never noticed such a thing before. "You and I will never see eye to eye about the future of the Ildiran Empire, Udru'h."

"Probably not, but you are the Mage-Imperator." He shrugged. "Allow me to suggest a different possibility then. I will take Thor'h back to Dobro and hide him. It will be simple enough to change our stories about what actually happened at Hyrillka. He was already stripped of his title; now, the Prime Designate will be exiled. We can keep him drugged, if necessary. As far as the rest of the Empire knows, he will be dead."

The Mage-Imperator's nostrils flared. At the doorway, the two guards maintained their silence, never loosening their grip on the former Prime Designate.

"No," Jora'h said. "When his shiing wears off, the *thism* still binds us. Others in the Empire will know. Keeping the secret may cause more damage than the reality."

"Not if the secret is well kept, Liege. Believe me, it can be done. I have done it before, hidden someone so well that no one—not even you—could guess the truth."

"You are withholding something from me."

"Yes, Liege. Yes, I am."

Jora'h stared at him, and Udru'h stared back as if

challenging the Mage-Imperator's will. They waited in silence for a long moment. Finally Udru'h backed down. He seemed satisfied with what he had seen in his Mage-Imperator's eyes. "Your green priest lover, Nira Khali, is still alive. I have kept her isolated on Dobro. She is alone on an island where all her needs are taken care of. I daresay she is more content there than when she served in our breeding camps."

Jora'h gasped, lurching forward. "Nira is alive?" Explosions of joy rippled through him, followed by a wave of outrage. He didn't know whether to shout with excitement or order Udru'h's immediate execution. "And you kept it from me!"

The Designate remained calm. "I no longer see any purpose in holding her as a pawn. I was unsure of your ability to lead, Jora'h, and I feared for the Empire. But now I am convinced, even if I do not understand your strange attraction for her." He bowed his head slightly. "I will bring her back to you."

As Jora'h fixed the Dobro Designate with an implacable gaze, he found that his joy at the prospect of seeing Nira again, of rescuing her from her years of terrible distress and begging her forgiveness, proved to be stronger than his immediate need for vengeance. Keeping his voice flat he said, "Even when Nira is safely returned to me, there is much for which you must atone. After all the pain and strife our Empire has suffered, this news seems as bright to me as the star we lost in the Ildiran sky." He hesitated. "But I am surprised you would reveal such a thing, without asking for anything in return. I always saw you as uncooperative, harsh, and needlessly bitter."

The Dobro Designate was not easily shamed. "Perhaps

you think so, Liege, but I have served the Mage-Imperator and the Ildiran Empire with my every breath. I followed the orders of our father, just as I have obeyed your instructions, whether or not I agreed with them. I stand by every action I have taken." Finally, Udru'h lowered his eyes and backed away to a respectful distance. "I was never your enemy."

130 ☀ ANTON COLICOS

When Anton's escape ship was brought to Mijistra, the Ildirans were astonished to hear of the massacre on Maratha. According to the lithe warrior woman Yazra'h, the Mage-Imperator had long held suspicions about the Klikiss robots. Now his worst fears had been confirmed.

Even under the sunlight and surrounded by people in the Prism Palace, Rememberer Vao'sh remained withdrawn, unresponsive, barely alive. The revered storyteller still could not find his way back to the safety net of *thism*, though it was all around him.

Anton did not give up on his friend.

Treated as a guest, the human historian was fed and given proper care. He recuperated for a day, after which Yazra'h offered to be his assigned escort at Mijistra. But he did not need an escort. "I want to see Vao'sh," he said.

With her exotic face set in a determined expression, the beautiful warrior woman guided Anton through curved corridors saturated with colored light. Her Isix cats prowled along beside them, and Anton uneasily recalled the shadow lions on the dark side of Maratha. But his only real concern was for Vao'sh.

In the Prism Palace's infirmary, the old rememberer lay on a bed bathed in warmth and illumination. Though open, his eyes stared at nothing, blinking only occasionally. The once-expressive lobes on his face were pale. His mind was far gone into madness.

Anton did not ask, so Yazra'h spoke for him and demanded of the medical kithmen who tended Vao'sh, "Has his condition changed?" When the doctors looked anxiously at her Isix cats, she snapped, "Answer my question."

"He is lost and alone, forever wandering at the blind edge of the Lightsource. We can only hope he is happy there."

Anton said, "We fought so hard and endured so much. We battled monsters and robots, and we escaped. We flew our ship without guidance for days." He heaved a long sigh. "I can't believe he would simply surrender now."

Yazra'h glanced at him with respect. With her long hair flowing back from her face like a mane, she looked like a character from legends of fearsome female warriors: Amazon queens, Boudicca, Olga, even Wonder Woman. He thought the Mage-Imperator's daughter would have been pleased by the comparison.

Anton sat for hours at the rememberer's bedside, holding one of the datascreens he had brought along when he'd left Earth. "I'm going to read to you, Vao'sh. Even if you can't hear me, I'll keep you company with more stories. Listen. Try to grasp the thread of my voice and follow it back here."

He called up literature files, cleared his throat, and drew a deep breath. "Homer's epics are the closest thing to the *Saga of Seven Suns* our storytellers have ever created. I'll begin with the *Iliad*." He cleared his throat. "'Sing, O Goddess, of the wrath of Achilles, such a deadly wrath that brought countless woes upon the Achaeans and sent the souls of many mighty heroes down to the house of Death.' "

Anton drew another breath and continued. This was, after all, an epic.

Yazra'h returned often to check on him, making certain that servant kithmen delivered adequate food and drink to him. At first she seemed amused by Anton's devotion, and then touched.

He did not despair. His voice grew rough and cracked, but he continued his best telling of the Trojan War, of the heroes Hector and Achilles, the dangerous love of Paris and Helen, of disgraced Ajax and how he had fallen on his own sword.

Throughout the recitation of the epic, Vao'sh stared blankly at the curved ceiling. At times, Anton would set Homer aside and recount other anecdotes from history, even reminiscences of his lost parents and their archaeological work.

It went on day after day.

When he was halfway through the *Odyssey,* intent on Odysseus's perilous voyage between Scylla and Charybdis, his voice took on a strong, dramatic tone, and the words flowed. At the most exciting point, he glanced down at Vao'sh and paused in mid-stanza.

It seemed to him that the rememberer's skin had flushed with new color. Anton set the datascreen aside. To his astonishment, Vao'sh blinked his normally fixed eyes. Anton leaned forward, eager to see any other movement.

Vao'sh blinked again and turned his face. The remember-er's mouth curved in a smile. "Do not stop there, my friend. Tell me how the story ends."

131 ✴ SULLIVAN GOLD

When the rescued Ildiran miner kithmen, as well as his own crew, were delivered to the Prism Palace, Sullivan Gold felt like a hero. He hadn't planned on that, but saving the Ildirans had been the right thing to do. Lydia would have been proud of him.

Sullivan wasn't the sort of man to travel to exotic places and see the extravagant wonders of the Spiral Arm. He'd never dreamed of finding himself welcomed into the crystal metropolis of Mijistra. Ildiran bureaucrats celebrated their arrival, rewarding the human skyminers for their selfless rescue, pampering them with every possible consideration. He certainly hoped he would receive such a warm welcome when he returned to face the Hansa Chairman.

Kolker, though, remained inconsolable. Here on Ildira, the green priest remained cut off from his telink network, blinded. Sullivan tried to help his glum companion. "I don't think the Ildirans have any worldtrees here, but I'm sure they'll send us home soon. Maybe they can even drop you off at Theroc. You'll just have to wait a little while longer."

Kolker hung his head, weighed down with grief and loneliness. "Every hour seems impossible. Is this how the rest of you live every day? So disconnected. Talking aloud is such a shallow imitation of real communication."

Sullivan squeezed Kolker's shoulder. "Nevertheless, it's all we have, and our civilization has made do. We've muddled along for thousands of years."

Kolker looked at him with a lost expression. "But *have* we muddled along? Truly? Think of all the unnecessary conflicts caused by misunderstandings. Maybe clearer communication would have prevented them."

"You could be right." Sullivan tapped a finger on his lower lip. "Just remember, anytime you really need to talk— in the old-fashioned way—come and see me. I'll be here."

One of the Prism Palace courtiers found the two of them on a sunlit balcony. He wore colorful court robes that looked like a strange theatrical costume. "The Mage-Imperator requests your presence in the skysphere audience hall."

Sullivan grinned at the green priest. "Now that's more like what I was expecting." He felt a spring in his step as they trailed down multicolored halls.

Inside the dazzling royal chamber, Mage-Imperator Jora'h sat in his chrysalis chair. Ildirans of various kiths moved about on the decorated floor. "Sullivan Gold, administrator of the human cloud harvester on Qronha 3," the courtier announced. "And the green priest Kolker."

The Mage-Imperator motioned the two men forward. Though his face already showed age lines, Jora'h looked strong and healthy, in contrast with images Sullivan had seen of his corpulent father. His expression seemed warm and friendly. "We are in your debt, Sullivan Gold. You risked your lives to save many of our miner kithmen from the hydrogues. We thank you for your service to the Ildiran Empire."

"I'm glad I could be of service. It was the right thing to do." Sullivan bowed, hoping to hide his flushed cheeks.

Before the Mage-Imperator could respond, guard kithmen raced into the skysphere audience hall, scattering pilgrims in confusion. Yazra'h bounded along beside them, "Liege, you must see! Up in the sky. Thousands of them!"

Sullivan looked around, seeking answers; Kolker was just as perplexed.

Though attender kithmen rushed toward the chrysalis chair, the Mage-Imperator climbed out and strode down the dais steps. Yazra'h urgently led him onward. "Come with me," he said to his guards.

Since no one had told them to stay back, Sullivan and Kolker followed at a safe distance, curious about the commotion. When they reached the transparent alcove in the side dome, they stared upward to the dazzlingly bright sky. Sullivan's heart sank. He had hoped never to see those terrible things again.

The sky was filled with hydrogue warglobes. Diamond-hulled spheres hovered above the Prism Palace, scores and scores of them. Silence fell like an executioner's axe. The Ildirans stared in disbelief and awe.

"Well, at least they're not attacking." Sullivan's voice, though small, sounded very loud in the hush.

Jora'h turned to him, eyes narrowed. "They will not attack. I must go to the top spire of the Palace and address them."

132 ☀ MAGE-IMPERATOR JORA'H

The myriad enemy battleships hung in the open air like all the stars in the Horizon Cluster. As leader of the Ildiran Empire, Jora'h would face the hydrogues alone.

Because they had not attacked, Jora'h guessed that Osira'h must have communicated with them somehow, accomplished her mission. The girl had succeeded in opening the Ildiran soul to the alien mind-set of the hydrogues. She had brought the hydrogues here, exactly as so many previous Mage-Imperators had hoped. Now it would be up to him.

He suddenly realized that strangers were witnessing this spectacle as well. Sullivan Gold, his green priest, all of the Hansa skyminers, even the human scholar Anton Colicos. Though he despised himself for the thought, Jora'h knew he could never allow them to pass this information along to the Terran Hanseatic League. No one could reveal that hydrogues had come to the Ildiran Empire. Jora'h had to prevent that from happening at all costs.

He stopped at the passage that would take him to the highest platform and spoke quietly to Yazra'h. "Have your guards take custody of all our human guests. They cannot be allowed to return to the Hansa. They have seen too much already."

"Yes, Liege." Yazra'h immediately saw to his instructions.

I am becoming more like my scheming father every day!

He sent his guards away and ascended to the high platform above the Prism Palace's main sphere. No one, not even the entire Solar Navy, could protect him if the deep-core aliens decided to open fire. At the pinnacle of the crystalline structure, Jora'h stood in full view of the hydrogues. His fine robes hung loosely on him, drifting in the breezes. He waited, feeling a sense of impending fate.

All across the city, Ildirans stared into the sky with fear. After the Hyrillka rebellion, their leader had rewoven the strands of *thism* and made them feel whole again. Now, through his command of the soul-threads, he tried to keep his people calm.

Jora'h faced the armada of silent hydrogue ships. A small bubble emerged like a dewdrop from the side of the nearest warglobe. He could sense Osira'h through the *thism* as soon as she drifted free from the high-pressure turmoil within the warglobe.

When the crystalline bubble came to a gentle rest before him on the high platform, he saw his young daughter inside. She appeared tense and exhausted, but unharmed. Her grave expression was far too serious for a little girl.

Jora'h drew another breath to calm himself. Oddly changed, seeming simultaneously strengthened and broken, Osira'h stepped into the bright light and breathed the open air, but she did not smile at her return to freedom.

"The hydrogues have agreed to communicate with you." Each word sounded like a death sentence instead of a cause for celebration. "They may agree to an alliance, but they will impose conditions. If you do not agree, Father, none of us will survive."

Jora'h wanted nothing more than to embrace his daughter, but he did not move as he addressed the hydrogue enemy in the sky. "In exchange for no further aggression against the Ildiran Empire, what do you want?"

When she relayed the answer, Osira'h would not meet her father's eyes. "They require that we help them destroy the humans."

133 ✸ DOBRO DESIGNATE UDRU'H

No longer needing to keep his secret, Designate Udru'h flew with a group of companions down to Dobro's southern continent. The transport pilot quickly found the isolated island where Nira Khali had been hidden for many months.

The Dobro Designate spoke little, but he was glad not to make this journey alone, as he had done on all previous occasions. Daro'h accompanied him; the young Designate-in-waiting had been an apt student and had managed the colony well enough while Udru'h dealt with his brother Rusa'h. Two guards rode along in the transport, as well as a lens kithman, a bureaucrat representative from the Prism Palace, and a medical kithman to ensure that the female green priest received immediate attention if she needed it.

Wrapped in his own thoughts, Udru'h stared out the craft's window as they flew across the terrain approaching the vast lake. Before, he'd had to do everything himself, his thoughts walled off, unable to let anyone else in on the secret. Now the Mage-Imperator knew the truth.

Beside him, Daro'h gazed around with questioning eyes, not sure how to support his uncle. The young man guessed that Udru'h had done something unpleasant, perhaps even unforgivable. He had heard only sketchy details, but soon everything would be explained, once they recovered the green priest.

Though ready to make amends to the Mage-Imperator, Udru'h did not regret what he had done. Even after he delivered Nira to the Mage-Imperator, he knew that *she* would never forgive him. But he didn't want or need her forgiveness. He had done this for his own reasons.

"We are approaching the island, Designate," the pilot said.

Udru'h looked across the expanse of calm water toward the spot of land and its thick vegetation. The green priest had everything she needed there: sunlight, water, and the company of plants. Everything except contact with other people.

Now her exile was over. Udru'h would bring her back. If Osira'h had completed her mission, then the half-breed girl had made all those centuries of experiments worthwhile. Nira would not ever understand that, but she was not required to.

The transport craft landed on the long, tan beach. Udru'h sniffed the air and listened. Daro'h followed his uncle out onto the packed sand, staring into the bright tropical sky and at the dense thickets. He didn't seem to be sure why he was here.

Udru'h waited, but the woman did not appear. Surely Nira had heard the craft arrive. There was no point in her hiding; the island wasn't large. Perhaps she was afraid. She had always hated when Udru'h came to see her, to taunt her with her situation. But she had always shown herself.

"Fan out and search the island. She cannot have gone far."

The other Ildirans forged through the undergrowth, calling Nira's name. Udru'h wandered to where she had made a crude shelter out of branches and fallen foliage. Uneasiness swept through his mind when he saw that the lean-to had collapsed into disrepair. It looked as if no one had been there for a long time.

"Where did she go? Where could she go?"

It took less than an hour for them to cover every patch of land and then search again. Udru'h stood reeling. What would the Mage-Imperator say?

The island was empty, and the green priest woman was gone.

134 ✺ RLINDA KETT

I've been trapped in worse places and with worse people," Rlinda said to BeBob, waving a hand around to indicate the cavern beneath the frozen crust of Plumas. "Even so, I wish we had something to *do*. Maybe we should learn the water-mining business."

"And try some sabotage, you mean?" Clearly suspicious, Caleb Tamblyn looked up from where he was tinkering with a pumping generator. He blew on his cold fingers, scowled at her, then went back to work. "This is a war, not a holiday. Put up with it."

"It's not any kind of war I can understand—and I don't think you do, either." She had never carried any grudge against the Roamers, except when Rand Sorengaard preyed upon her company's ships.

"May I please have another pair of gloves?" BeBob sauntered up, rubbing his hands together. "It's always cold down here."

"We're on an ice moon—it's supposed to be cold." Scowling again, Caleb picked up his tools. When he stood, his knees cracked audibly. "You'll get used to it. Besides, I'm sure you have better conditions than all the Roamer POWs the Eddies took in their raids."

"I'm skeptical of people who describe how good you have it by dredging up something even worse," Rlinda said. BeBob sat beside her on a blocky piece of equipment, but stood up as soon as the metal's chill penetrated his thin trousers.

Seeing the casual way the Tamblyns ran the water mines, Rlinda didn't doubt that she and BeBob could find a way to break free, maybe steal her own *Curiosity* back if Denn Peroni and the Tamblyn brothers hadn't damaged it too much in "fixing" it. For the time being, though, they weren't desperate enough; besides, the EDF would still be after them. They would stay together here and see how things played out.

In the evenings, Rlinda and BeBob had little to do except cuddle in their shared hut, play a few games, and learn some forms of gambling that were popular among the Roamers. During the days, they bundled up and walked along the small ice shelf that butted up against the underground sea.

It was clear that the Tamblyn brothers didn't know what to do with their hostages. Taking prisoners and seizing the damaged *Curiosity* must have seemed like a good idea to them at the time, but now they were stuck with the consequences.

She and BeBob cobbled together enough warm clothes to keep themselves comfortable. Scrawny BeBob was easy to fit. He could borrow old jumpsuits and embroidered shirts from any number of the water miners. Few Roamers were as large as Rlinda, however. She made do with her own captain's clothes, voluminous wraps, and some of her private wardrobe that she had bullied the Tamblyns into letting her remove from the *Curiosity*.

As a businesswoman, she took interest in the large-scale operations on Plumas. The engineering and water distribution followed a reasonable model, and the Roamers had apparently been successful here for several generations, though no one in the Hansa had ever heard of the place.

She and BeBob walked around the complex, crunching over the frozen ground, and looked across the subterranean sea. The two of them stopped in front of a woman who seemed to be carved out of a solid block of ice. She stood upright, locked in place like a statue, but apparently this was a real woman frozen years ago in an accident and now left on display like an ice sculpture. None of the Roamers explained how the frozen woman had gotten here or what they intended to do with her.

As Rlinda watched, lights began to sparkle through the icy coating, as if the woman was gradually melting from the inside out. She and BeBob could see the features of Karla Tamblyn, her skin pale and waxen beneath the glacial placenta. A pool of warmed water began to spread out like a base around her feet.

"Hey!" Rlinda shouted. "Anybody want to take a look at this?"

Some eerie form of internal energy was working through the woman's frozen tissues, a spark that turned the icy cocoon transparent. Slowly, like a snake shedding its skin, the water slid off, one thin layer at a time.

"Maybe she'll want a thermal blanket once she wakes up," BeBob said. "Or some hot tea."

"If you want my bet, she'd rather have a shot of something strong."

The twin brothers Wynn and Torin came out to stand beside Rlinda and BeBob. "She's changed a lot in the past day," Wynn said to his brother, as if inspecting a cargo box. "I just wish Jess had told us what we're supposed to do with her . . . or what to expect."

"Something's happening, that's for sure," Torin said.

BeBob wrapped his arms around his chest. "It's so cold down here I don't see how she can be melting."

Rlinda looked at the dead woman's face, saw delicate features, strong cheekbones, and a noble forehead. Her eyes were strangely open and staring through the frozen sheath.

Wynn saw the two prisoners' curiosity and let out a sigh. "Ah, Karla and Bram had quite a romance, you know. Not that my brother was the easiest man to get along with, but Karla was smart. Bram could complain like no one else, but it never bothered Karla. She simply ignored him when he was being irrational, or she made him feel foolish for pointing out the deficiencies in everyone and everything but himself."

"That's why I never got married," Torin said, standing close to his twin. "Seeing an example like that, I decided I just didn't need all that grief."

Wynn scowled at him. "Then you didn't see all the love

they had too. Better to have a few lows along with the highs
than just live on a flat line, like you do."

"I'll remind you of that the next time you go grumbling—"

The thin ice surrounding Karla's body cracked and splintered. The twins stopped their banter and drew a simultaneous breath. Spiderweb fractures crazed the frozen shell
covering the woman's body. The cracks grew wider with a
sound like twisting bones. Torin shouted.

Behind them, an administrative hut popped open and Andrew, the other brother, stepped out, looking around.

"She's thawing," Wynn called.

Karla's arms were spread, bent at odd angles, and now
one arm slowly straightened. The ice cracked and peeled off,
falling in chunks to the slushy pool that surrounded her on
the ice shelf. The Tamblyn brothers yelped simultaneously
in excitement and fear.

Rlinda took BeBob's arm and pulled him back a step.
"Let's . . . give the lady a little bit of room."

The remainder of the ice fractured and fell like hail onto
the ground. Karla swiveled her head, and small frozen
shards dropped out of her stiff hair. Filmy debris peeled like
scales off her clinging uniform. Her skin had a strange lu-
minous quality, and her hair, though damp, began to twitch
and writhe like Medusa strands. With a sound like glaciers
slamming together, Karla's chest expanded.

Without bothering to throw on a thermal jacket, Andrew
sprinted across the ice shelf, unable to believe what he saw.

Glowing, Karla lifted one foot, broke it free from where
it had been fused to the ground, and took a step forward. Her
movements were clumsy and wooden, but as she moved and
gained balance, the phosphorescent energy within her
swelled, filling her garments, her flesh, and her hair.

"Karla, do you know us?" Wynn stepped tentatively forward. He was searching for something, hoping for a glint of recognition. "Jess brought you here, but he didn't tell us what else to do."

"She's not going to come with an instruction sheet!" Caleb snapped.

The woman turned but did not acknowledge them. She took another step.

Andrew came skidding up next to them. "She's alive! Karla, you've come back."

Crackling with secondhand wental power, she plodded along. With each step, energy shimmered out of her like cold flames, sending tiny cracks and shivers through the solid ice of the ground. Steam began to curl up around her.

Rlinda looked at BeBob. "I don't like this very much. Seems like an awfully chilly reception . . . no pun intended."

"Karla, why won't you say anything? Don't you remember us?" Andrew stepped into her slow but relentless path. He reached out to grab Karla's upper arms to make her look at him.

But as soon as his fingers touched the ice-woman's crackling skin, Andrew screamed, caught in a sudden discharge that flowed from her body into his like a power surge. In a dismissive gesture, Karla swung her hand and knocked him aside, as if he were no more than a lightweight piece of garbage. Spasming in silence, Andrew tumbled in a broken heap on the ice.

Rlinda could tell with a glance that the younger man was dead—either burned or electrocuted.

The reanimated woman stopped and swiveled her head. Her eyes were black, bottomless, empty depths. Steam continued to rise around her like a faint fog. Seeing what she had done, Karla flexed her hand, raised it up so she could stare at her own fingers. Then she looked back at the body of murdered Andrew. Her pale lips curved upward in a satisfied smile.

135 ☀ DD

Once the operation was complete and the compy's internal systems were purged of basic rules and prohibitions, DD did not feel fundamentally different. With or without the programming restrictions, he did not wish to hurt anyone, particularly not his human masters, who had always treated him well.

Sirix would never understand that.

Now that DD had his free will, the Klikiss robots turned him loose and left him unsupervised in the dark and storm-swept ruins. They had other plans afoot, thousands upon thousands of reawakened Klikiss machines and a large assembly of Soldier compies ready to seize the EDF fleet.

For days, robots streamed through the transportals to Szeol, and then moved elsewhere, setting up additional bases, establishing further beachheads from which they could prosecute their genocide against mankind.

When all the robots had gathered, Sirix spoke like a general giving orders to his troops. "We have withdrawn our comrades from inhabited worlds. As we enter this ultimate phase, all Soldier compies distributed throughout the Earth Defense Forces have their ingrained programming. According to the standardized timing sequence, the uprising will occur simultaneously across the entire Hansa military. Soon."

DD was no longer part of their activities. Once Sirix had accomplished what he intended, his interest in the compy waned. After the Klikiss robots and corrupted Soldier compies turned on the Earth Defense Forces and slaughtered the human race, they would get back to liberating the rest of the compies.

Left to explore Szeol as he wished, DD wandered around the dim landscape during the murky days and purplish nights. Monstrous creatures flew past him, composed of sharp wings and trailing tentacles and a far-from-ordinary number of eyes. Though DD cringed, the creatures ignored him as soon as they determined he was indigestible.

Bathed in faint sulfurous fumes, he looked at what had once been a grand Klikiss city. Even if the hatred inspired by the Klikiss race was warranted, the ancient creators were extinct now. And humans were not the same as the Klikiss.

Unfettered and unobserved, the little compy walked to the third trapezoidal framework erected on the canyon's edge. Klikiss symbols surrounded the transportal, each tile indicating a different coordinate for a world that had once been part of the insectoid civilization. Though it balanced on the edge of a precipice, this transportal looked very much like the stone window Margaret and Louis Colicos had discovered inside the cliff city on Rheindic Co.

Standing before this silent trapezoid that had once been used for the interplanetary movements of the ancient race, DD replayed his memories of the last moments on Rheindic Co when he'd been with Margaret and Louis. His mental records were flawless, and he compared the two systems, noting slight differences in the arrangement of coordinate tiles.

In those final moments, when DD had been unable to defend his beloved masters from the murderous Klikiss robots, Louis had managed to activate the transportal. He had sent Margaret through—to somewhere. Although the robots had killed the old man before he could follow her, DD knew that Margaret was out there. Possibly still alive. But where?

The compy stood pondering in front of the ominous stone gate, calculating and assessing. He ran through the entire suite of character analyses from all of his studies. Finally DD reloaded his map of coordinate tiles from Rheindic Co, including records of similar stone windows in other Klikiss ruins. He played and replayed all the subtle character traits he had recorded from his time with Louis Colicos—and he did his best to predict which tile Louis might have selected at random, out of desperation.

Though it was in a different location here, he found the corresponding symbol on the Szeol transportal.

The compy did not hesitate, for he had already decided his best course of action. Soon, surely within the next day, the Klikiss robots would begin their rampage across the Spiral Arm. He had no time to waste.

Sirix had given him free will, and now DD had the opportunity to put it to the test. The compy made this decision based on his own desires and on what would accomplish the most good. The Klikiss robots would never have guessed that he would *want* to leave them, now that they had rewarded him with his freedom.

But what DD wanted most was to get back to where he

felt safe. Therefore, he used his free will, and he *chose* to escape. He selected the right symbol.

When the transportal shimmered and the stone surface became permeable, DD stepped across the gulf of space without looking back.

On the other end, on a particularly alien world, the Friendly compy found himself surrounded by incomprehensible sights and mysteries. The landscape was blasted yet cultivated. Structures had been built, based upon angles not at all associated with human architecture. Lumpy towers rose as if they had been extruded with great effort from a biomechanical ooze that had hardened in a storm, resulting in fantastic shapes.

The air was thick and steamy, so humid that DD suspected human lungs might have found it difficult to breathe. He also detected heavy concentrations of aromatic molecules, organic esters that were so complex and diverse that they seemed a symphony—or language?—of pheromones, odors, musks, and perfumes.

A cacophony of precise musical tones, melodies, and skirling sounds droned through the air. This exotic world presented a complex bedlam of music, chimes, whistles, and chirps.

DD trudged away from the transportal, exploring, looking for someone who might help him.

The color in the sky was wrong, and the mists in the air seemed to come from no natural weather patterns. He didn't know how a human would comprehend such a place. He called out in his synthesized voice. "Hello? Hello?" He broadcast a signal across many bands in the EM spectrum, though he had no wish to contact any Klikiss robots who might be on this planet.

Margaret Colicos had most likely escaped the murderous robots by coming here through the transportal. But what if she had arrived at a place even worse?

He marched along, diligent and curious, exploring his new world and filing away details. If this place was inhabited, some being might have noticed his activation of the trapezoidal stone window. The Friendly compy continued, his optical sensors alert.

After several hours of alien strangeness, he found some-one—*something*—to help him. And shortly thereafter he was reunited at long last with Margaret Colicos.

Facing DD again after so many years, she stared at him with profoundly haunted eyes. She had survived, and changed dramatically—but she did recognize him. Margaret's bleak face showed a flicker of joy.

The woman came to him, her gaze hollow. "DD!" she said. "Oh, the things I have seen."

136 ☀ CELLI

The hydrogues were defeated once again, and the clear skies of Theroc looked wide open. Celli felt that if she extended her arms she could fall upward forever and never reach the clouds. She wanted to celebrate with Solimar.

After the battle, grinning at his unqualified success

against the deep-core aliens, Kotto Okiah had received the thanks and applause of the Theron people with no small measure of embarrassment. He and his fellow Roamers, along with the two technical compies, leaned against their ships, which had landed in the clearing. Kotto couldn't wait to rush back to Osquivel and continue his studies with the small alien derelict.

Thanks to his resonance doorbells, humans now had an effective weapon against the seemingly indestructible warglobes. Even with the clans scattered, the Roamers would pass the word swiftly. Kotto and his companions had then departed without lingering for goodbyes. . . .

The fresh air smelled of mud and rain from the dissipated wental comet. The energy-impregnated water had irrigated the forest ground, inciting a riot of new growth. Doing their own part, Celli and Solimar still went every day to the most grievously wounded sections of the worldforest and danced until their hearts were ready to give out. One leaf at a time, they continued restoring the worldtrees. Theroc seemed to be bursting with life more than ever before.

Out in the forest, Celli ran up to the golem of her brother. "Beneto, just look at all the greenery. I haven't felt so much hope in a long time."

He curled his lips in a smile and took his sister by the arm. "That is only a small part, Celli. The return of the wentals is a cause for joy, and the Roamers have proved to be invaluable allies." His voice sounded like a melody blown through a woodwind instrument. "However, the best is yet to come—and it will be today. I can sense how near they are."

Celli skipped along beside him, eager to see the surprise for herself. When he raised his voice, Beneto could be as loud as a trumpet. In the clearing, he called for all of the green priests to join him and shouted up toward the rebuilt fungus-reef city, asking Father Idriss and Mother Alexa to come down. He sent a signal via telink through the trees so that everyone could share in the event.

Solimar flew overhead on his buzzing gliderbike. As he circled the main clearing, he waved at Celli. Within an hour, all Therons came together, excited and curious. Idriss and Alexa wore colorful clothes, anticipating some kind of celebration. Beneto would not give anyone a clue about what to expect.

The surviving worldtrees seemed to strain against the ground with a restless eagerness. The huge trunks creaked as if the giant trees wanted to uproot themselves and walk along the forest floor. Their fronds brushed together, rustling and whispering even though there was no breeze.

Like the Pied Piper, Beneto led his followers to the temple ring of burned-out tree stumps. As he strode through the forest, branches parted for him. Celli could feel the moist soil pulsing beneath her bare feet, and she wondered what effect the elemental water creatures would have on the living worldtrees. Would they join somehow, double their strength, wentals and verdani? Solimar, Yarrod, and the other green priests felt the growing excitement, though they did not yet understand it.

Beneto raised his bluntly formed hands, and stood in the center of the amphitheater, a synthesis of human and worldtree. He let a faint hum emerge from his mouth, and the trees picked up the sound. It grew to a droning roar, an intense and irresistible shout from the world itself. Beneto took a breath, and the trees fell silent.

Overhead, hundreds—thousands—of huge ships approached from the fringes of space. Each one was shaped like a fantastic tree the size of a small asteroid and powered by a force that made the sentient worldforest on Theroc seem little more than a spark. The treeships had flown in from the beyond, en route ever since the hydrogues had obliterated the first worldtree grove on Corvus Landing. They had crossed incredible distances to where their assistance was desperately needed, back to the heart of the worldforest.

The unbelievably immense structures were grown from a central core of wood, whose branches stretched out and tangled themselves into a structure like a breathtaking thistle, a gigantic organic vessel composed of stems, arcs, and huge unnatural thorns. The burgeoning seeds had extended fronds and thorns, armored with impenetrable wooden coverings and sealed by a protective force that kept them alive in a journey across immeasurable space.

Celli stared, her mouth open. The green priests and Therons shouted and pointed with amazement.

"Now we have sufficient strength to defeat the hydrogues forever. We can prepare for the final war." Beneto looked up at the mammoth organic vessels, and his face held a blissful expression of renewed confidence. "At last, the verdani battleships have arrived."

GLOSSARY OF CHARACTERS
AND TERMINOLOGY

Abel-Wexler—one of the eleven generation ships from Earth, tenth to depart.

Adar—highest military rank in Ildiran Solar Navy.

Aguerra, Raymond—streetwise young man from Earth, former identity of King Peter.

Aguerra, Rita—Raymond's mother.

Alexa, Mother—ruler of Theroc, wife of Father Idriss.

Andez, Shelia—EDF soldier, held captive by Roamers at Osquivel shipyards.

Antero, Haki—Grid 8 admiral.

Aquarius—wental-distribution ship flown by Nikko Chan Tylar.

Archfather—symbolic head of Unison religion on Earth.

attenders—diminutive personal assistants to the Mage-Imperator.

Avi'h—Maratha Designate, youngest son of Mage-Imperator Cyroc'h.

Battleaxe—nickname for former Hansa Chairman Maureen Fitzpatrick.

BeBob—Rlinda Kett's pet name for Branson Roberts.

bekh!—Ildiran curse, "damn!"

Beneto—green priest, second son of Father Idriss and Mother Alexa, killed by hydrogues on Corvus Landing.

Bhali'v—bureaucrat kithman, assistant to Maratha Designate Avi'h.

Big Goose—derogatory Roamer term for Terran Hanseatic League.

blazer—Ildiran illumination source.

Blind Faith—Branson Roberts's ship.

Blue Sky Mine—skymine facility at Golgen, operated by Ross Tamblyn.

Boone's Crossing—Hansa colony world.

Braddox—Roamer outpost.

Brindle, Conrad—Robb Brindle's father, former military officer.

Brindle, Natalie—Robb Brindle's mother, former military officer.

Brindle, Robb—young EDF recruit, comrade of Tasia Tamblyn, captured by hydrogues on Osquivel.

Burton—lost generation ship from Earth, whose descendants are subjects of breeding experiments.

Cain, Eldred—deputy and heir apparent of Basil Wenceslas, pale-skinned and hairless, an art collector.

carbon slammer—new-design EDF weapon, effective at breaking carbon-carbon bonds.

cargo escort—Roamer vessel used to deliver ekti shipments from skymines.

Celli—youngest daughter of Father Idriss and Mother Alexa.

Regan Chalmers—former chairman of the Terran Hanseatic League.

Chan—Roamer clan.

Chan, Marla—Roamer greenhouse expert, mother of Nikko Chan Tylar.

ch'kanh—armored anemone plants that live in the shadowed canyons of Maratha.

Christensen, Tom—"dunsel" commander of EDF rammer ships.

chrysalis chair—reclining throne of the Mage-Imperator.

citysphere—enormous hydrogue habitation complex.

Clarin, Eldon—Roamer inventor, brother of Roberto, killed when hydrogues destroyed Berndt Okiah's new skymine at Erphano.

Clarin, Roberto—administrator of Hurricane Depot, brother of Eldon.

cloud harvester—ekti-gathering facility designed by Hansa; also called a cloud mine.

cohort—battle group of Ildiran Solar Navy consisting of seven maniples, or 343 ships.

Colicos, Anton—son of Margaret and Louis Colicos, translator and student of epic stories, sent to Ildiran Empire to study the *Saga of Seven Suns*.

Colicos, Louis—xeno-archaeologist, husband of Margaret Colicos, specializing in ancient Klikiss artifacts, killed by Klikiss robots at Rheindic Co.

Colicos, Margaret—xeno-archaeologist, wife of Louis Colicos, specializing in ancient Klikiss artifacts, vanished through transportal during Klikiss robot attack on Rheindic Co.

competent computerized companion—intelligent servant robot, called compy, available in Friendly, Teacher, Governess, Listener, and other models.

compy—shortened term for "competent computerized companion."

condorfly—colorful flying insect on Theroc like a giant butterfly, sometimes kept as pets.

Constantine III—Roamer outpost.

Corribus—ancient Klikiss world, where Margaret and Louis Colicos discovered the Klikiss Torch technology, site of one of the first new Hansa colonies.

Corvus Landing—Hansa colony world obliterated by hydrogues.

Covitz, Jan—Dremen mushroom farmer, participant in transportal colonization initiative, father of Orli.

Covitz, Orli—Dremen colonist, joined transportal colonization initiative with her father Jan.

Crenna—former Ildiran splinter colony resettled by humans. Home of Davlin Lotze and Branson Roberts; frozen when hydrogues and faeros destroyed its sun.

cutter—small ship in Ildiran Solar Navy.

Cyroc'h—former Mage-Imperator, father of Jora'h.

Czir'h—Dzelluria Designate-in-waiting.

Daniel—new Prince candidate selected by the Hansa as a potential replacement for Peter.

Daro'h—the Dobro Designate-in-waiting after the death of Mage-Imperator Cyroc'h.

Dasra—gas-giant planet suspected of harboring hydrogues.

Daym—blue supergiant star, one of the Ildiran "seven suns"; also the name of its primary gas-giant planet, site of abandoned Ildiran ekti-harvesting operations.

DD—compy servant assigned to Rheindic Co xeno-archaeology dig, captured by Klikiss robots.

Dekyk—Klikiss robot at Rheindic Co xeno-archaeology dig.

Designate—any purebred noble son of the Mage-Imperator, ruler of an Ildiran world.

diamondfilm—crystalline parchment used for Ildiran documents.

Dobro—Ildiran colony world, site of human-Ildiran breeding camps.

Dremen—Terran colony world, dim and cloudy; chief products are saltpond caviar and genetically enhanced mushrooms.

drogue—deprecatory term for hydrogues.

dunsel—slang term for token human commanders aboard EDF rammer ships.

Durris—trinary star system, close white and orange stars orbited by a red dwarf; three of the Ildiran "seven suns."

EA—Tasia Tamblyn's personal compy; her memory was wiped when she was interrogated by Basil Wenceslas.

Earth Defense Forces—Terran space military, headquartered on Mars but with jurisdiction throughout the Terran Hanseatic League.

Ebbe, Jack—cryoengineering specialist on Jonah 12.

Eddies—slang term for soldiers in EDF.

EDF—Earth Defense Forces.

ekti—exotic allotrope of hydrogen used to fuel Ildiran stardrives.

Eld, Erin—"dunsel" commander of EDF rammer ships.

Eolus, Kostas—Grid 5 admiral.

escort—midsize ship in Ildiran Solar Navy.

Estarra—second daughter, fourth child of Father Idriss and Mother Alexa. Current Queen of Terran Hanseatic League, married to King Peter.

faeros—sentient fire entities dwelling within stars.

Fan'nh—qul in Ildiran Solar Navy, in charge of the maniple facing hydrogues at Hrel-oro.

filterfilm—protective eye covering used by Ildirans.

firefever—ancient Ildiran plague.

Fitzpatrick, Maureen—former Chairman of the Terran Hanseatic League, grandmother of Patrick Fitzpatrick III.

Fitzpatrick, Patrick, III—spoiled cadet in the Earth Defense Forces, General Lanyan's protégé, presumed dead after Osquivel but captured by Roamers in Del Kellum's shipyards.

Forrey's Folly—Roamer outpost.

fracture-pulse drone—new-design EDF weapon, also called a "frak."

frak—slang term for fracture-pulse drone.

Frederick, King—previous figurehead ruler of the Terran Hanseatic League, assassinated by hydrogue emissary.

fungus reef—giant worldtree growth on Theroc, carved into a habitation by the Therons.

furry cricket—innocuous furry rodent found on Corribus.

Gale'nh—experimental half-breed son of Nira Khali and Adar Kori'nh, third oldest of her children.

gliderbikes—flying contraptions assembled from scavenged engines and framework materials, augmented by colorful condorfly wings.

Gold, Sullivan—administrator of the Hansa's new modular cloud harvester installed at Qronha 3.

Golgen—gas giant where Ross Tamblyn's Blue Sky Mine was destroyed, bombarded by comets targeted by Jess Tamblyn.

Gomez, Charles—human prisoner of the hydrogues, seized at Boone's Crossing.

Goose—derogatory Roamer term for Terran Hanseatic League.

Goswell, Bertram—early Chairman of the Terran Hanseatic League who originally tried to force Roamers to sign Hansa Charter.

grappler pod—small work vehicle used in shipyards of Osquivel.

grazer—slow-moving, hemispherical harvester used on Jonah 12.

Great King—figurehead leader of Terran Hanseatic League.

green priest—servant of the worldforest, able to use worldtrees for instantaneous communication.

GU—analytical compy assigned to work with Kotto Okiah.

Guiding Star—Roamer philosophy and religion, a guiding force in a person's life.

Hadden—EDF trainee.

handlers—Ildiran kith, handlers of the dead.

Hansa—Terran Hanseatic League.

Hansa Headquarters—pyramidal building near the Whisper Palace on Earth.

Hhrenni—star system, site of Chan greenhouse asteroids.

Horizon Cluster—large star cluster near Ildira, location of Hyrillka and many other splinter colonies.

Hosaki—Roamer clan.

Hrel-oro—arid Ildiran mining colony, inhabited primarily by scaly kithmen.

Hroa'x—chief skymining engineer of Ildiran skyfactory on Qronha 3.

Huck, Tabitha—engineer aboard Sullivan Gold's cloud harvester at Qronha 3, former EDF weapons designer.

Huff, Jared—Roamer pilot.

Hurricane Depot—Roamer commercial center and fuel-transfer station, located in a gravitationally stable point between two close-orbiting asteroids, destroyed by EDF.

hydrogues—alien race living at cores of gas-giant planets.

Hyrillka—Ildiran colony in Horizon Cluster, original discovery site of Klikiss robots, main source of the drug shiing.

Idriss, Father—ruler of Theroc, husband of Mother Alexa.

Ildira—home planet of the Ildiran Empire, under the light of seven suns.

Ildiran Empire—large alien empire, the only other major civilization in the Spiral Arm.

Ildirans—humanoid alien race with many different breeds, or kiths.

Ildiran Solar Navy—space military fleet of the Ildiran Empire.

Ilure'l—Ildiran lens kithman, part of the skeleton crew remaining in Maratha Prime.

Isix cats—sleek feline predators native to Ildira; Jora'h's daughter Yazra'h keeps three of them.

jazer—energy weapon used by Earth Defense Forces.

Jonah 12—frozen planetoid, site of Roamer mining base.

Jora'h—Mage-Imperator of the Ildiran Empire.

Jorax—Klikiss robot dismantled by Hansa scientists to study its programming and systems.

Juggernaut—large battleship class in Earth Defense Forces.

Kamarov, Raven—Roamer cargo ship captain, destroyed with his cargo ship on secret EDF raid.

Kellum, Del—Roamer clan leader, in charge of Osquivel shipyards.

Kellum, Zhett—daughter of Del Kellum.

Kett, Rlinda—merchant woman, captain of the *Voracious Curiosity*.

Khali, Nira—female green priest, Prime Designate Jora'h's lover and mother of his half-breed daughter Osira'h. Held captive in breeding camps on Dobro.

kith—a breed of Ildiran.

kleeb—derogatory term for an EDF cadet.

Klikiss—ancient insectlike race, long vanished from the Spiral Arm, leaving only their empty cities.

Klikiss robots—intelligent beetlelike robots built by the Klikiss race.

Klikiss Torch—a weapon/mechanism developed by the ancient Klikiss race to implode gas-giant planets and create new stars.

Kolker—green priest, friend of Yarrod, stationed on Sullivan Gold's modular cloud harvester at Qronha 3.

Kori'nh, Adar—leader of the Ildiran Solar Navy, killed in suicidal assault against hydrogues on Qronha 3.

KR—Analytical compy assigned to work with Kotto Okiah.

Lanyan, General Kurt—commander of Earth Defense Forces.

lens kithman—philosopher priests who help to guide troubled Ildirans, interpreting faint guidance from the *thism*.

Lightsource—the Ildiran version of Heaven, a realm on a higher plane composed entirely of light. Ildirans believe that faint trickles of this light break through into our universe and are channeled through the Mage-Imperator and distributed across their race through the *thism*.

Llaro—abandoned Klikiss world.

Logan, Chrysta—last captain of the lost generation ship *Burton,* led colonists to Dobro.

Lotze, Davlin—Hansa exosociologist and spy on Crenna, sent to Rheindic Co where he discovered how to use the Klikiss transportal system.

lowrider—spiderlike predator on Corribus.

Mage-Imperator—the god-emperor of the Ildiran Empire.

maniple—battle group of Ildiran Solar Navy consisting of seven septas, or 49 ships.

Manta—midsize cruiser class in EDF.

Maratha—Ildiran resort world with extremely long day-and-night cycle.

Maratha Prime—first city on Maratha.

Maratha Secda—sister city on opposite side of Maratha from Prime, currently under construction by Klikiss robots.

Mhas'k—Ildiran agricultural kithman, part of the skeleton crew on Maratha, mated to Syl'k.

Mijistra—glorious capital city of the Ildiran Empire.

Muree'n—experimental half-breed daughter of Nira Khali and a guard kithman, youngest of her children.

Nahton—court green priest on Earth, serves King Peter.

New Portugal—Hansa outpost with EDF facilities, colony known for distilleries and wineries.

nialia—plantmoth grown on Hyrillka, source of shiing.

Nur'of—lead engineer, part of the skeleton crew remaining in Maratha Prime.

O'Barr, Hector—"dunsel" commander of EDF rammer ships.

Odenwald, Sabine—"dunsel" commander of EDF rammer ships.

Okiah, Jhy—Roamer woman, very old, former Speaker of the clans.

Okiah, Kotto—Jhy Okiah's youngest son, brash and eccentric inventor.

Oncier—gas-giant planet, original test site of the Klikiss Torch.

O'nh, Tal—second-highest-ranking officer in Ildiran Solar Navy.

Orra'h—Dzelluria Designate.

Osira'h—daughter of Nira Khali and Jora'h, bred to have unusual telepathic abilities.

Osquivel—ringed gas planet, site of secret Roamer shipyards.

Otema—old green priest, former ambassador from Theroc to Earth, sent to Ildira where she was murdered by the Mage-Imperator.

OX—Teacher compy, one of the oldest Earth robots. Served aboard *Peary*, now instructor and adviser to King Peter.

Palace District— governmental zone around Whisper Palace on Earth.

Palawu, Howard—Chief Science Adviser to King Peter, one of the dissectors of the Klikiss robot Jorax.

Pekar, Jane—governor of Relleker.

Pellidor, Franz—assistant to Basil Wenceslas, an "expediter."

pepperflower tea—Roamer beverage.

Peroni, Cesca—Roamer Speaker of the clans, trained by Jhy Okiah. Cesca was betrothed to Ross Tamblyn, then Reynald of Theroc, but has always loved Jess Tamblyn.

Peroni, Denn—Cesca's father, a Roamer merchant.

Pery'h—the Hyrillka Designate-in-waiting, assassinated by Rusa'h.

Peter, King—successor to Old King Frederick.

plantmoth—nialias of Hyrillka, source of drug shiing on Hyrillka, also called a nialia.

Plumas—frozen moon with deep liquid oceans, site of clan Tamblyn's water industry.

poletrees—tall plants growing in plains on Corribus.

Prime Designate—eldest son and heir apparent of Ildiran Mage-Imperator.

Princess—Nira's pet name for her daughter Osira'h.

Prism Palace—dwelling of the Ildiran Mage-Imperator.

Ptoro—gas-giant planet, site of clan Tylar's "boondoggle" skymine.

pulse-racer—extremely fast stunt vehicle.

Qronha—a close binary system, two of the Ildiran "seven suns." Contains two habitable planets and one gas giant, Qronha 3.

qul—Ildiran military rank, commander of a maniple, or 49 ships.

Ramirez, Elly, Commander—acting commander of Tasia Tamblyn's Manta cruiser.

rammer—kamikaze EDF ship designed to be crewed by Soldier compies.

Relleker—Terran colony world, once popular as a resort.

rememberer—member of the Ildiran storyteller kith.

Remora—small attack ship in Earth Defense Forces.

Rendezvous—inhabited asteroid cluster, hidden center of Roamer government, destroyed by EDF.

Reynald—eldest son of Father Idriss and Mother Alexa, killed in hydrogue attack on Theroc.

Rheindic Co—abandoned Klikiss world, site of major excavation by the Colicos team.

Roachers—derogatory term for Roamers.

Roamers—loose confederation of independent humans, primary producers of ekti stardrive fuel.

Roberts, Branson—former husband and business partner of Rlinda Kett, also called BeBob.

Rod'h—experimental half-breed son of Nira Khali and the Dobro Designate, second oldest of her children.

Ruis, Lupe—mayor of Crenna colony settlement.

Rusa'h—Hyrillka Designate, third noble-born son of the Mage-Imperator.

Saga of Seven Suns—historical and legendary epic of the Ildiran civilization.

Sandoval—Roamer clan.

Sarein—eldest daughter of Father Idriss and Mother Alexa, Theron ambassador to Earth, also Basil Wenceslas's lover.

Sarhi, Padme—Grand Governor of Yreka colony.

septa—small battle group of seven ships in the Ildiran Solar Navy.

septar—commander of a septa.

shadow lion—darkside predator on Maratha.

Shana Rei—legendary "creatures of darkness" in *Saga of Seven Suns.*

Shelby—Roamer pilot.

shiing—stimulant drug made from nialia plantmoths on Hyrillka, dulls Ildiran receptivity to the *thism*.

shizz—Roamer expletive.

Shonor—Ildiran splinter colony.

silver berets—sophisticated special forces trained by EDF.

Sirix—Klikiss robot at Rheindic Co xeno-archaeology dig, leader of robotic revolt against humans, captor of DD.

skymine—ekti-harvesting facility in gas-giant clouds, usually operated by Roamers.

skysphere—main dome of the Ildiran Prism Palace. The skysphere holds exotic plants, insects, and birds, all suspended over the Mage-Imperator's throne room.

Solimar—young green priest, treedancer, and mechanic. Rescued Celli from burning tree during hydrogue attack on Theroc.

Sorengaard, Rand—renegade Roamer pirate, executed by General Lanyan.

soul-threads—connections of *thism* that trickle through from the Lightsource. The Mage-Imperator and lens kithmen are able to see them.

Speaker—political leader of the Roamers.

Spiral Arm—the section of the Milky Way Galaxy settled by the Ildiran Empire and Terran colonies.

splinter colony—an Ildiran colony that meets minimum population requirements.

Stanna, Bill—EDF soldier, held captive by Roamers at Osquivel shipyards, died during an escape attempt.

Stannis, Malcolm—former Chairman of the Terran Hanseatic League, served in the reigns of King Ben and King George, during Earth's first contact with the Ildiran Empire.

Steinman, Hud—old transportal explorer, discovered Corribus on transportal network and decided to settle there.

streamer—fast single ship in Ildiran Solar Navy.

Stromo, Admiral Lev—Admiral in Earth Defense Forces, derisively called "Stay-at-Home Stromo" after he was defeated by the hydrogues at Jupiter.

Stubbs, Danvier—vapor miner on Jonah 12.

sub-*thism* sleep—Ildiran coma.

Swendsen, Lars Rurik—Engineering Specialist, adviser to King Peter, one of the dissectors of Klikiss robot Jorax.

swimmer—Ildiran kith, water dwellers.

Syl'k—Ildiran agricultural kithman, part of the skeleton crew on Maratha, mated to Mhas'k.

Tabeguache, Peter—Grid 1 admiral.

tal—military rank in Ildiran Solar Navy, cohort commander.

Tamblyn, Andrew—one of Jess's uncles, brother to Bram.

Tamblyn, Bram—former scion of clan Tamblyn, father of Ross, Jess, and Tasia, died after his son Ross perished on the Blue Sky Mine.

Tamblyn, Caleb—one of Jess's uncles, brother to Bram.

Tamblyn, Jess—Roamer, second son of Bram Tamblyn, in love with Cesca Peroni, infused with wental energy.

Tamblyn, Karla—Jess's mother, frozen to death in ice accident on Plumas.

Tamblyn, Ross—estranged oldest son of Bram Tamblyn, chief of Blue Sky Mine at Golgen, killed in first hydrogue attack.

Tamblyn, Tasia—Jess Tamblyn's sister, currently serving in the EDF.

Tamblyn, Torin—one of Jess's uncles, brother to Bram.

Tamblyn, Wynn—one of Jess's uncles, brother to Bram.

Team Jade—EDF training group.

Team Sapphire—EDF training group.

telink—instantaneous communication used by green priests.

Telton, Anjea—human prisoner of the hydrogues.

Terran Hanseatic League—commerce-based government of Earth and Terran colonies.

Theroc—forested planet, home of the sentient worldtrees.

Theron—a native of Theroc.

thism—faint racial telepathic link from Mage-Imperator to the Ildiran people.

Thor'h—eldest noble-born son of Mage-Imperator Jora'h, the current Prime Designate.

Throne Hall—the King's main receiving room in the Whisper Palace on Earth.

Trade Standard—common language used in Hanseatic League.

transgate—hydrogue point-to-point transportation system.

transportal—Klikiss instantaneous transportation system.

treedancers—acrobatic performers in the Theron forests.

treeling—a small worldtree sapling, often transported in an ornate pot.

troop carrier—personnel transport ship in Ildiran Solar Navy.

twitcher—EDF stun weapon.

Tylar, Crim—Roamer skyminer on Ptoro, father of Nikko.

Tylar, Marla Chan—Roamer greenhouse engineer, mother of Nikko.

Tylar, Nikko Chan—young Roamer pilot, son of Crim and Marla.

Udru'h—Dobro Designate, second-born noble son of the Mage-Imperator.

Unison—standardized government-sponsored religion for official activities on Earth.

UR—Roamer compy, Governess model at Rendezvous.

Vao'sh—Ildiran rememberer, patron and friend of Anton Colicos, part of the skeleton crew remaining in Maratha Prime.

verdani—organic-based sentience, manifested as the Theron worldforest.

Vik'k—Ildiran digger, part of the skeleton crew remaining in Maratha Prime.

Vinh, Darby—"dunsel" commander of EDF rammer ships.

Voracious Curiosity—Rlinda Kett's merchant ship.

Wan, Purcell—administrative engineer left in charge of Jonah 12 mining base.

warglobe—hydrogue spherical attack vessel.

warliner—largest class of Ildiran battleship.

Wenceslas, Basil—Chairman of the Terran Hanseatic League.

wentals—sentient water-based creatures.

Whisper Palace—magnificent seat of the Hansa government.

Willis, Sheila, Admiral—commander of Grid 7 EDF battle group.

worldforest—the interconnected, semisentient forest based on Theroc.

worldtree—a separate tree in the interconnected, semisentient forest based on Theroc.

Yamane, Kiro—cybernetic specialist held captive by Roamers at Osquivel shipyards.

Yarrod—green priest, younger brother of Mother Alexa.

Yazra'h—oldest daughter of Jora'h, keeps three Isix cats.

Yreka—fringe Hansa colony world; the EDF cracked down on the Yreka colonists for hoarding ekti.

Zan'nh—Ildiran military officer, eldest son of Mage-Imperator Jora'h, new Adar of the Ildiran Solar Navy.

ACKNOWLEDGMENTS

By the fourth book in The *Saga of Seven Suns*, the list of people who have helped me begins to rival the epic cast of characters. In particular, I would like to thank the editorial squad of Jaime Levine, Devi Pillai, John Jarrold, Melissa Weatherill, and Ben Ball; expert advisers and just plain hard workers Catherine Sidor and Diane Jones; sharp-eyed reader Geoffrey Girard; agents John Silbersack, Robert Gottlieb, Kate Scherler, and Kim Whalen at Trident Media Group. And, as always, my wife Rebecca Moesta for keeping my writing, and my life, on the best possible path.

extras

orbit

meet the author

KEVIN J. ANDERSON has written 41 national bestsellers and has over 20 million books in print worldwide in 30 languages. He has been nominated for the Nebula Award, the Bram Stoker Award, and the SFX Readers' Choice Award. His Web site is www.wordfire.com.

and so the story grows

My philosophy in telling a big story (which I learned from Frank Herbert) is "never hold anything back." Consequently, I feel that each successive volume of THE SAGA OF SEVEN SUNS needs to get bigger, more epic, and more dramatic. I open new doors, tie up a few mysteries, reveal some answers, and spring even more questions.

In the beginning, I thought of Jess Tamblyn as my main character in the series, but now I don't know anymore. He's definitely the basic hero, the man with an unrequited love, who suffers great tragedy, comes back with greater strength and power but is no longer quite human. And yet, there are so many other "main characters" that the huge overall PLOT seems to have a life of its own. The plot itself may be my main character.

The plotlines themselves became much more complicated as I wrote each successive book. Instead of a handful of people to follow, I ended up with a genuine crowd, each one clamoring for time on the stage. The novels published as #3 HORIZON STORMS and #4 SCATTERED SUNS were originally conceived as a single volume. But when I had completed the first-draft manuscript, and I saw the enormous stack of pages, I called my editor. "I think we might have a problem." With some brainstorming, we determined that it would have to be broken into two separate volumes, and so I restructured the chapters, added a few storylines that I had wanted to explore (but had already set aside because I sensed that length was going to be a problem), and realized that I finally had the breathing room I needed.

Even though I had the main outline for the whole multivolume story sketched out before I started the first chapter of HIDDEN EMPIRE, the plot and characters grew on its own in unexpected ways. While writing the actual manuscripts, some characters took unexpected actions; minor "walk-on parts" became much more important and demanded expanded storylines of their own. Some of my fictional friends refused to die when the predetermined plot required it.

One of the most startling examples was the character of Davlin Lotze. I originally introduced him as a minor part in Book 1; I had offered to name a character as a prize in a charity auction, and the winners were "David and Linda Lotze." I did not have big plans for him . . . but he just became so interesting that I cast him in larger and larger parts. Patrick Fitzpatrick III was originally just a bully who caused headaches for Tasia during her basic training, but he also proved useful as I made him nastier, even murderous, and then turned him around to become one of the main examples of redemption in the series. Poor, downtrodden Nira was really supposed to die at the end of A FOREST OF STARS, but my test readers practically mutineed. As I considered how I could save her, I realized that I could do so much more with her character . . . and so she escaped the author's clutches.

introducing

If you enjoyed **SCATTERED SUNS**,
look out for

OF FIRE AND NIGHT

Book 5 of The Saga of Seven Suns
by Kevin J. Anderson

ADMIRAL LEV STROMO

For six hours the Manta continued to circle and scan, but the pastel gas giant offered no clues to the rammer fleet, no sign of any hydrogue wreckage.

Stromo could sense that the crew expected him to know what to do. As the commanding officer, he had the ability to make swift decisions, but he'd never been fully briefed nor given suggested responses to alternate scenarios. *Just fetch any escape pods you can find and come home. Report on the amount of damage the rammers caused.* It shouldn't have been complicated. Whether or not the rammers trounced the drogues, it should have been a hell of a battle.

But they could find no trace whatsoever. Stromo was in the dark, and he didn't like it.

He turned his command chair to the green priest at the comm station. Clydia stroked her treeling as if it was a pet, still silent. Gruffly, the Admiral prodded, "Any response from the Chairman yet? We've run full scans twice, and we're not going to find anything. Now long does he want us to wait here?"

On his orders, Clydia had sent a message to Nahton, the Whisper Palace's green priest, who had dutifully informed Chairman Wenceslas. Earth was in a flurry of activity following the arrival of the hydrogue derelict and the thirty EDF prisoners of war. The distracted Chairman had promptly sent back a non-helpful response: "Continue searching. I will provide further instructions as soon as possible."

Stromo was uneasy to just be orbiting this gas giant. At the very least, warglobes had recently obliterated a Hansa cloud harvester here and, quite possibly, all sixty EDF rammer vessels. He had one Manta cruiser, and it wouldn't do much good to stand and fight if the drogues came back.

The green priest stared down at the feathery fronds of her potted plant, receiving some new signal. Stromo held his impatience in check, though he thought that watching a green-skinned woman talk to a little tree seemed a bit silly. Puzzled as she withdrew from telink, Clydia took a second to center herself. "Now the Chairman suggests that you tune a receiver to the following frequency and boost the gain." She rattled off numbers. Even though she herself sat at the comm station, she did not know how to use the sophisticated equipment.

"What's that supposed to do?" Stromo asked.

Without suggesting an answer, Elly Ramirez went to configure the receivers. The navigator and both sensor operators waited to see what would happen. Clydia continued to recite, "Add a booster and a descrambler. The Chairman thinks you might receive a message."

Stromo felt even more confused. "Where would a signal come from? It's a gas giant, uninhabited except for hydrogues—"

"Apparently, a Listener compy was planted aboard the rammers to keep watch on Commander Tamblyn. It was an attempt to gather intelligence about the Roamers." The green priest scowled at her own words, and Ramirez looked incensed. "Through this frequency, you should be able to tap into the compy's surveillance software. If they remain in range, this may allow you to see where they have gone."

Ramirez finished her adjustments, added appropriate EDF codes. The bridge viewing screen suddenly filled with static as if an electronic blizzard had just swept over the cruiser. Gradually, images formed as the signal was strengthened and reinforced; the descramblers stripped out noise and extraneous feedback. Then the picture clarified.

Stromo felt as if someone had hit him on the back of his head. Hard.

The viewer showed a group of humans huddled inside a bizarre cell whose walls looked to be made out of jeweled gelatin. Closest to the compy's surveillance imagers was a scuffed and disheveled Tamblyn; next to her sat a dark-skinned young man who looked oddly familiar. *Brindle*. Yes, that was the young man's name—the volunteer who had gone down in a diving bell to contact the drogues just before the Battle of Osquivel. Robb Brindle! When they'd lost contact with him, the EDF assumed the aliens had destroyed him.

Just like we assumed all the missing soldiers at Osquivel

were dead, rather than detained by the Roamers. Not a very good track record, he thought. Perhaps the Earth Defense Forces should not make so many assumptions.

Stromo saw seven downcast and weak-looking humans. Prisoners of war? Who had ever guessed hydrogues would take prisoners at all? Then, into the field stepped a viscerally frightening Klikiss robot. The captives reacted, cringing away. The black beetle-like robot moved its sharp-pointed appendages in what was clearly a threatening manner.

"Where the hell is that signal coming from?" Stromo demanded. "And what is that Klikiss robot doing there?" He already had plenty of suspicions about the devious alien machines.

Ramirez looked up. "This doesn't make sense, Admiral. The signal originates deep within the gas giant, down in levels where the hydrogues live."

"Impossible! Nobody can survive down there."

The pair of sensor operators also checked their readouts. "Confirmed, Admiral. They're deep inside Qronha 3."

The two Soldier compies manning bridge stations suddenly straightened and froze. Stromo glanced at the military robots in disgust. "What the hell is wrong with them?"

The compies remained rigid, as if they were receiving a signal.

"Check their stations, Ensign Mae," Ramirez said. Terene Mae left her nav console and went over to the closet compy.

The Admiral looked around nervously. "Any sign of hydrogue warglobes? Have they detected us yet? Do they know we're eavesdropping?"

"No indication, sir."

"Stay alert. Be ready to move at the first hint of trouble."

Ensign Mae checked the compy's console, ran a quick

diagnostic to see if some kind of feedback might have influenced the military robots. "There's nothing—"

Both Soldier compies moved with astonishing speed. The nearest one spun its flexible torso, reached up, and clamped a viselike metal hand around Mae's throat. As the compy squeezed with implacable force, the young ensign's eyes bulged. Before she could try to claw free, the compy's other hand grabbed her head and twisted it as if unscrewing a lid. Mae's neck shattered in several places, popping like cracked kindling. The compy dropped her to the deck.

In the same instant, the other compy lunged toward the second sensor operator (Stromo still couldn't remember the young man's name). The sensor operator tried to scramble away, but the military robot punched the young man's sternum with a polymer-sheathed metal fist. The blow had the force of a jackhammer, crushing a crater in the middle of his uniform and exploding his heart. He fell to the deck before blood could even seep out of his smashed ribs.

No more than two seconds had passed. While Stromo sat paralyzed, unable to believe what he had just witnessed, the bridge crew went into a panic. The green priest leapt away from her station and almost knocked over her potted tree, but caught it in time; she cradled it against her chest.

The two mad compies turned from their initial victims, then targeted Stromo and Ramirez, as if homing in on their rank insignia. Ramirez dove for the command chair, but not to hide behind Stromo. She shoved the Admiral aside and fumbled with a compartment at the side of the seat.

While the first Soldier compy lunged toward the command chair like an asteroid on a collision course, Sergeant Zizu threw himself like a wrestler against the other. Despite the military robot's greater mass, the security officer applied enough force to knock it off balance.

Ramirez finally succeeded in activating the thumb-lock and withdrew a twitcher weapon, a sidearm that delivered a powerful stun impulse meant to take down unruly humans. She adjusted the output to maximum and fired a disruptor impulse directly into the compy's face. Though it was not meant to affect circuitry, the scrambling pulse was enough to disorient the compy's programming.

By now the tackled compy had recovered its balance. With a single blow, it knocked Zizu aside and plowed forward with Admiral Stromo in its sights. Stromo scrambled away from the chair.

Cool and angry, Ramirez played the twitcher beam over the second compy's body core as it lurched toward them. She let the beam continue until smoke and sparks boiled from the implanted circuits. A meter away from them, the military robot collapsed into a petrified metal-and-polymer statue.

Then the first attacking compy straightened as its systems reset themselves. It reacquired its target and began to move, still reorganizing its circuits from the twitcher disruption.

Sergeant Zizu detached one of the metal chairs from a bridge station. Yelling like a caveman, he brought the chair's shaft down like a club on the compy's neck. The compy's head bent, some of the neck cables snapped. Zizu struck again and again. The compy shuddered, slowed but continued relentlessly forward until Ramirez slipped behind it. She fumbled with the standard controls embedded between its shoulders, found the emergency deactivation trigger, and the compy fell motionless.

Stromo backed to the other side of the bridge until he

bumped against an empty station. Rattled and wheezing, he held himself up, shaking his head. "This is not possible! Simply not possible."

The rest of the bridge crew stared at their two slain comrades. Ramirez recovered first, used the deactivation trigger on the second compy, just to be sure. She straightened. Her face was flushed, her brow furrowed. "Admiral, remember when King Peter warned us all about the Soldier compies and the Klikiss programming?"

Stromo mopped his forehead. "Yes, the King tried to shut down the factory. But that was just a false alarm. Everything is up and running. No problems."

"Admiral, there is definitely a 'problem.'"

"We just saw a Klikiss robot on the screen. What if it sent some sort of signal?" Zizu suggested.

Ramirez gestured to the bodies of the two dead crewmen and the deactivated compies. "Sir, something is very wrong here. At the very least, I suggest we increase security on the bridge."

He made himself sound strong and confident. He knew Ramirez was going to make the suggestion herself, so he decided to say it first. "More than that, Commander. Let's switch off all the Soldier compies until we can figure out what went wrong here. No sense in taking chances."

"That's what I was hoping you'd say, Admiral." Ramirez activated the fullship intercom. "This is an emergency announcement. All Soldier compies must be isolated and deactivated. Approach them with extreme caution."

"Maybe these two were just flukes," Stromo said in a watery voice.

Ramirez gave him a withering glance that came to crossing the line into insubordination. "I hope we have enough time."

MAGE-IMPERATOR JORA'H

Hydrogue warglobes filled the skies of Ildira. Several of the giant enemy spheres loomed over the Prism Palace while others spread out, ready to obliterate Mijistra and all other Ildiran cities if they were provoked. . . . Though the alien ships reflected the six surviving suns, Mage-Imperator Jora'h felt as if a heavy shadow had fallen across his sky-sphere reception chamber.

The girl Osira'h had brought them here. The Mage-Imperator wasn't sure how his half-breed daughter had forced the deep-core aliens, nor did he completely understand her peculiar powers. He doubted the hydrogues had come willingly. And yet they were here, responding to his demand.

Now it was up to him to resolve the conflict, to convince the hydrogues that Ildirans were no threat. It had worked before, when the now-traitorous Klikiss robots had acted as ambassadors. The hydrogues would send their emissary soon, and Jora'h would begin the most important conversation in his reign. Sitting in his chrysalis chair, he felt cold with the knowledge that his empire was about to change. Never had any Mage-Imperator in the ten thousand years chronicled in the *Saga of Seven Suns* faced a more dangerous and frightening crisis or decision. Now, all of the centuries of planning, all of the intricate schemes of his predecessors, seemed weak and insufficient.

Guard kithmen led by his muscular daughter Yazra'h sought to surround the Mage-Imperator, as if their crystal katanas and body armor could offer any protection against the all-powerful hydrogues.

We have called this down upon ourselves, Jora'h thought. He and his predecessors had *wanted* this to happen, had planned for many generations.

A courier raced into the sun-bright palace chamber. "Liege, Adar Zan'nh insists on speaking with you! His maniple of warliners awaits your order. Should he open fire on the hydrogues?"

Jora'h took the communications device from the fleet-footed man. An image formed of his oldest son, the over-burdened commander of the Ildiran Solar Navy. Zan'nh looked haggard, his eyes bright, yet his face remained set with duty and determination. His topknot was drawn back, oiled in place and clipped by an insignia band.

"Father, my maniple has returned from Hyrillka and joined up with those commanded by Tal O'nh. We are pre-pared to defend Ildira to the death. Simply issue the order."

Jora'h looked at the curved crystalline domes above him. "No, Adar. That would only trigger a massacre." He drew a deep breath, feeling the anxiety and tension chewing within him. "I will see how this plays out. The hydrogues brought Osira'h safely back to us. These warglobes have come . . . at my request."

The words sounded impossible as he spoke them. Even if this ended badly, the Ildiran people would still follow his or-ders, for he was their Mage-Imperator. But how could they ever forgive him? If Jora'h failed here, his empire would be destroyed. His glowing bones would never rest among those of his ancestors in the ossuarium beneath the Prism Palace, and his spirit would no doubt journey to the plane of the Lightsource as a blind man.

But he had to be strong.

"Adar, remove your warliners to a safe distance. Remain vigilant and be ready to respond. I expect a representative of the hydrogues to arrive soon."

With obvious reluctance Zan'nh signed off. The courier retrieved the communications device, gave a formal bow, and sprinted back out of the audience chamber, looking very frightened.

Osira'h walked into the reception hall. The colored lights shining through the segmented crystal panes seemed to shift as if the half-breed girl's innate power could bend light as well as thoughts. "The emissary is coming."

"Did you force him?" Jora'h asked. "Can you control them?"

She gave him an odd, mysterious smile. "The hydrogues choose to believe that they have come of their own free will. But I think maybe they are wrong."

Released from the protective chamber that had allowed her to survive the depths of a gas-giant planet, ethereal Osira'h seemed drained, but her footsteps were not shaky. Her eyes were large, her hair feathery, her face open and yearning. After facing, and then coercing, the hydrogues, she had been through an ordeal that could have stripped away her soul, her mind. But the little girl had unparalleled strength.

If only Jora'h could be as strong. "I will be ready for him."

Her star-reflective eyes took on a glazed distance. Her face twisted as if ripples of pain shot through her, then she calmed herself. "I have directed the emissary, telling him an acceptable route through the Palace corridors." A smile curved her flower-petal lips. "Otherwise he might have smashed directly through the skysphere dome. Hydrogues do not have much patience for obstacles."

The Mage-Imperator did not know how he would deal with the impossibly alien ambassador, what he might have to promise before the hydrogues would leave Ildirans in peace. Jora'h decided he might not want his people to know. "Clear the skysphere hall. I meet with the emissary alone." He glanced down at his young half-breed daughter. "Except for Osira'h. I may need her skills."

Yazra'h stood holding her weapons. "You do not require me for protection, Liege?"

"If I require the protection of my bodyguard, then I will have failed, and the consequences for our race are too frightening to contemplate." He glanced at her. "For now, I want you to isolate our human guests. They have already seen too much, and we must prevent them from learning more."

"Yes, Liege." Yazra'h took several guard kithmen to enforce the command.

Though it upset him, Jora'h needed to keep the humans away. They were heroic Hansa skyminers who had rescued Ildiran refugees from a hydrogue attack, and also a human scholar of the *Saga of Seven Suns* who had survived a Klikiss robot attack and saved Rememberer Vao'sh. By the rules of honor, those men and women should have been treated with every consideration. Instead, now that they had seen his secret negotiations with the hydrogues, Jora'h had no choice but to keep them guarded, to watch their movements at all times. He feared he would never be able to let them go.

As the hall cleared, runners came with breathless messages that a small hydrogue environment chamber was drifting through the wide colored corridors. Jora'h climbed out of his chrysalis chair and stood on the dais. He did not wish to appear weak.

Osira'h came up the steps to the foot of his chrysalis chair. She sat down, looking small and innocent, but Jora'h knew what powers simmered within her mind. The centuries-long breeding program at Dobro had resulted in strong new kiths, particularly the slightly telepathic lens kithmen. With the introduction of human bloodlines to the gene pool, hybrid vigor had offered other possibilities. And then Jora'h had fathered this girl with his beloved human green priest, Nira. Osira'h had exceeded expectations—and she hadn't even been part of the experiments.

"By becoming a bridge, I forced myself into the hydrogue minds," she explained. "I became a conduit. I opened myself to them. They came at my bidding, half because I forced them, half because I lured them. But, Liege"—she looked up and captivated him with her eyes—"just because I made them come here does not mean I can force them to listen or agree."

Jora'h nodded. "That is my task." But the long line of Mage-Imperators who had worked to bring about this day, to open an avenue of survival, had not done enough to prepare him for what exactly he should do.

Even before the hydrogue emissary arrived, Jora'h sensed the disturbing presence, ripples in the air and in the light. A glassy chamber drifted in, reminiscent of the protective "diving bell" that Osira'h had taken into the depths of Qronha 3. Enclosed behind a curved wall, swirling mists of a super-dense atmosphere masked the form of the liquid-metal shape that pulled itself into a humanoid form.

It clothed itself in the mocklery of an embroidered jumpsuit bearing many pockets and zippers and clips. The face was human, the hair long, though carved out of flowing quicksilver. Apparently hydrogues thought all "rock dwellers" looked the same; after mastering the image of one, they did not bother to change.

The hydrogue's voice was a throbbing hum in the air, as if manipulating molecules to transmit sound waves rather than using a simple speaker system. "We have come."

Standing tall, Jora'h did not take a step forward, not wanting to appear in any way threatening. "Thank you." This entire scenario reminded him of a similar encounter between Old King Frederick and the hydrogues. In that instance, the emissary had killed the human King.

"Do you wish to be destroyed?" From the tone of the hydrogue's voice, it sounded like a legitimate question rather than a threat. "By compelling us, you have only brought about our anger."

The Mage-Imperator kept his voice calm, though he felt trapped in a flash flood of events, searching for a lifeline. "I called you here to discuss a peace between hydrogues and Ildirans. Through Osira'h's openness, she has made you see and understand us. How may we secure an end to hostilities?"

"Peace with Ildirans gains us nothing."

Jora'h's mind spun. He wondered if he was feeling a backwash of echoes from all the strangely alien thoughts ripping through the air. "That is not true. Ages ago, we had a compact. We proved there was no need for our races to quarrel." He thought of the merciless hydrogue attacks on Ildiran colony worlds—Hrel-Oro, Hyrillka, even uninhabited Dularix. Those violent and unprovoked strikes served no purpose. The hydrogues were nonsensical.

"It is only because of that ancient alliance that we agreed

to this encounter." *So, the hydrogues had come voluntarily . . . or was the emissary lying?* "Such a compact no longer benefits us. The Klikiss robots no longer speak for you."

"Osira'h speaks for us. We have no need of the Klikiss robots."

Sitting on the step, the girl looked up, as if expecting the Mage-Imperator to find an instant and viable solution. She had done her part.

"Hydrogues do not wish to speak with any planet-dwelling species. You are irrelevant to us. Our true enemies are the faeros and the verdani, yet we have been distracted by your squabbles and drawn into your conflicts."

Jora'h struggled to think of a fulcrum with which he could change the emissary's mind. "And I can put an end to that. Humans continue to deploy their Klikiss Torches against your planets. They can destroy your worlds—but I can make them stop."

"They will be exterminated. Their race is harmful." The emissary pressed closer to the wall of his sphere. "Long ago, we helped the Klikiss robots destroy their creator race. That extermination is the proper model for all future conflicts with planet dwellers." The metal face shifted, and the gaze pierced through the swirling currents. The emissary sounded very reasonable. "Since we have come to Ildira, it would be most efficient if we just eliminated you now."